3 1526 05339038 8

W9-DDJ-388

STREET ANGEL

JIM RUGG

MARUCA

EST

WITHDRAWN

ALIVE

STREET ANGEL

DEADLIEST GIRL ALIVE

IMAGE COMICS, INC. • **Robert Kirkman**: Chief Operating Officer • **Erik Larsen**: Chief Financial Officer • **Todd McFarlane**: President • **Marc Silvestri**: Chief Executive Officer • **Jim Valentino**: Vice President • **Eric Stephenson**: Publisher / Chief Creative Officer • **Jeff Boison**: Director of Publishing Planning & Book Trade Sales • **Chris Ross**: Director of Digital Sales • **Jeff Stang**: Director of Direct Market Sales • **Kat Salazar**: Director of PR & Marketing • **Drew Gill**: Cover Editor • **Heather Doornink**: Production Director • **Nicole Lapalme**: Controller • IMAGECOMICS.COM

STREET ANGEL: DEADLIEST GIRL ALIVE. First printing. October 2019. Published by Image Comics, Inc. Office of publication: 2701 NW Vaughn St., Suite 780, Portland, OR 97210. Copyright © 2019 Jim Rugg and Brian Maruca. All rights reserved. Contains material originally published as Street Angel's Dog, Street Angel: After School Kung Fu Special, The Street Angel Gang, Street Angel: Superhero for a Day, Street Angel vs Ninjatech, and Street Angel Goes to Juvie. "Street Angel," its logos, and the likenesses of all characters herein are trademarks of Jim Rugg and Brian Maruca, unless otherwise noted. "Image" and the Image Comics logos are registered trademarks of Image Comics, Inc. No part of this publication may be reproduced or transmitted, in any form or by any means (except for short excerpts for journalistic or review purposes), without the express written permission of Jim Rugg, Brian Maruca, or Image Comics, Inc. All names, characters, events, and locales in this publication are entirely fictional. Any resemblance to actual persons (living or dead), events, or places, without satirical intent, is coincidental. Printed in the USA. For information regarding the CPSIA on this printed material call: 203-595-3636. For international rights, contact: foreignlicensing@imagecomics.com. ISBN: 978-1-5343-1350-7.

image

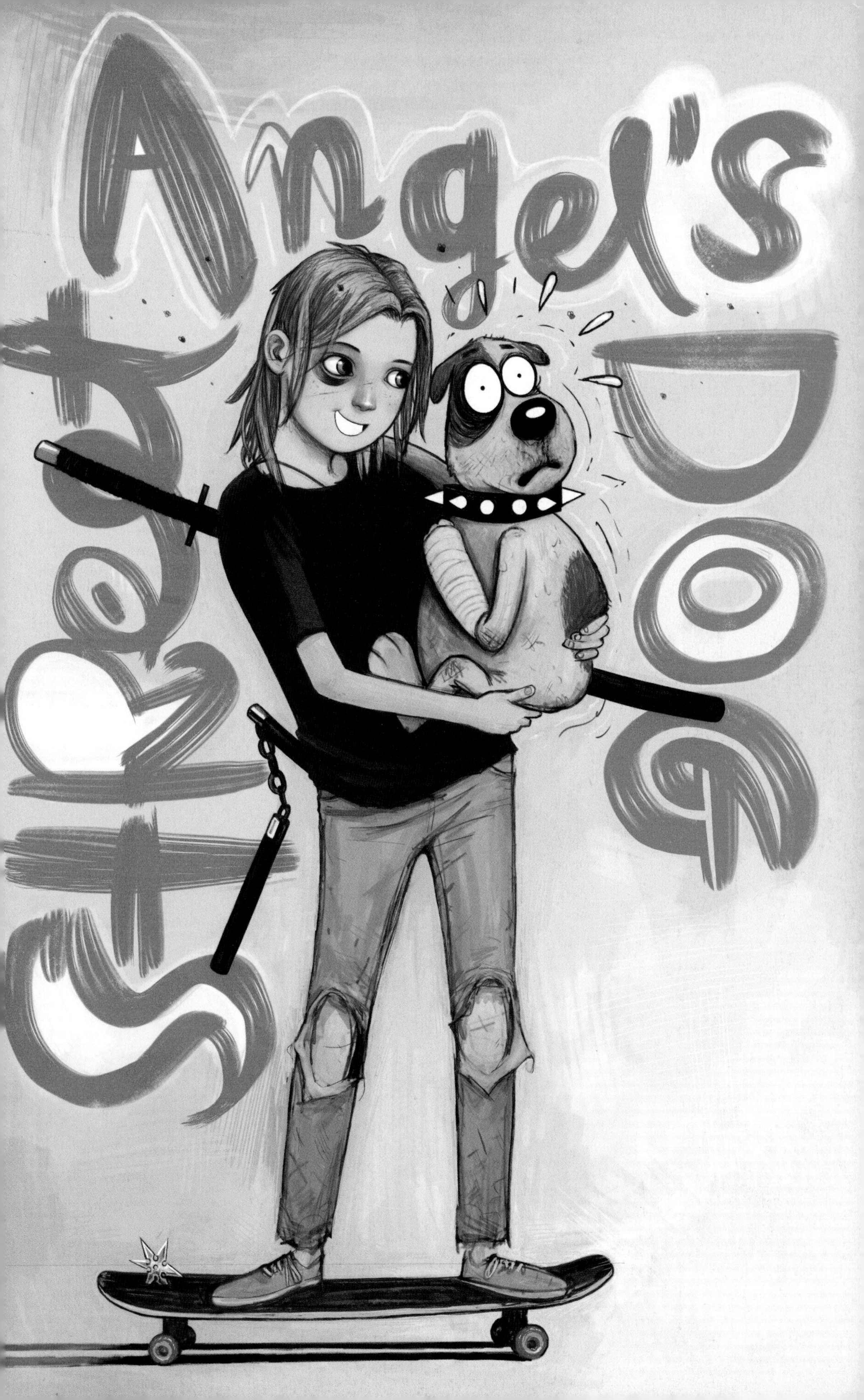
Angel's
Dog

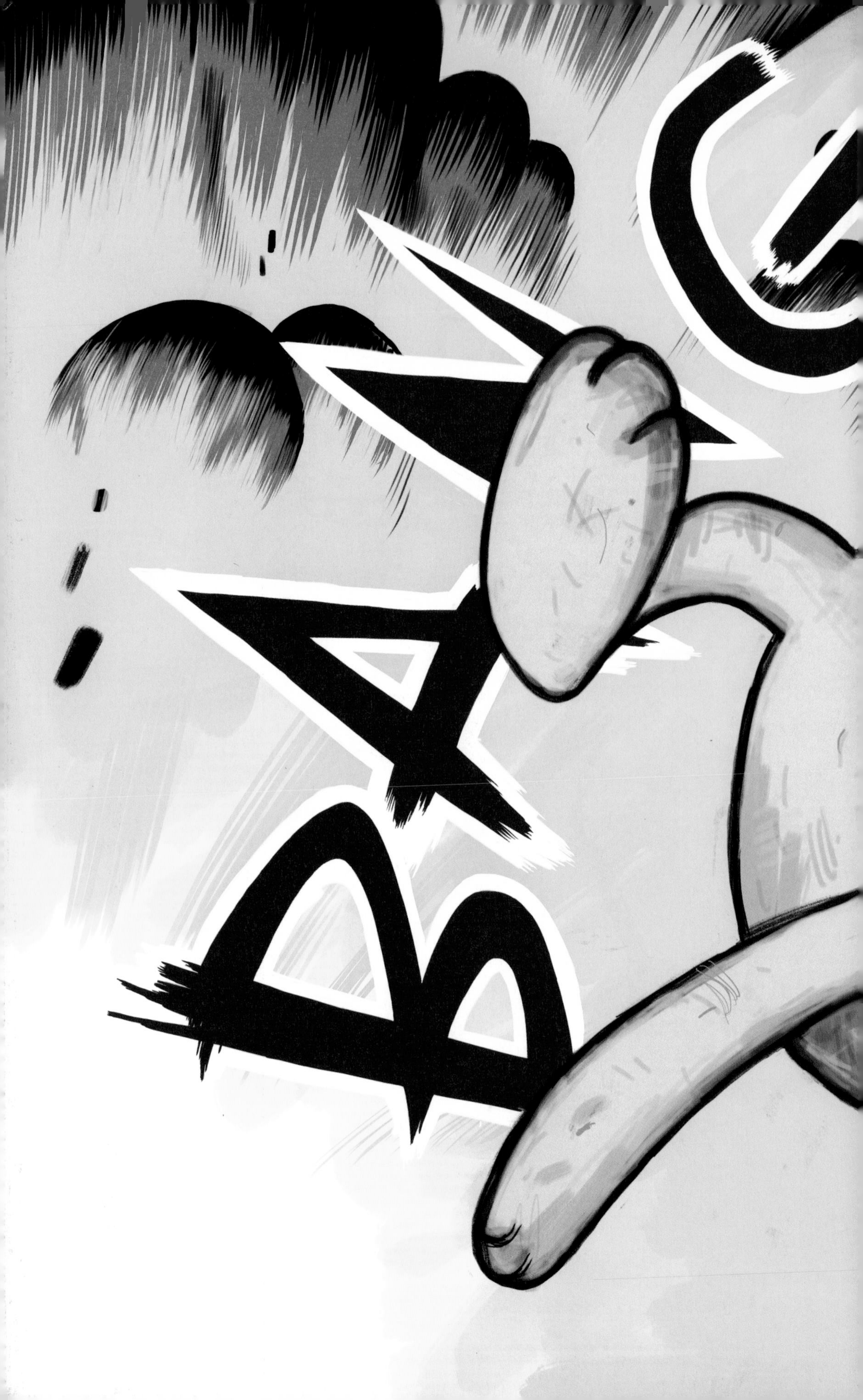
BANG

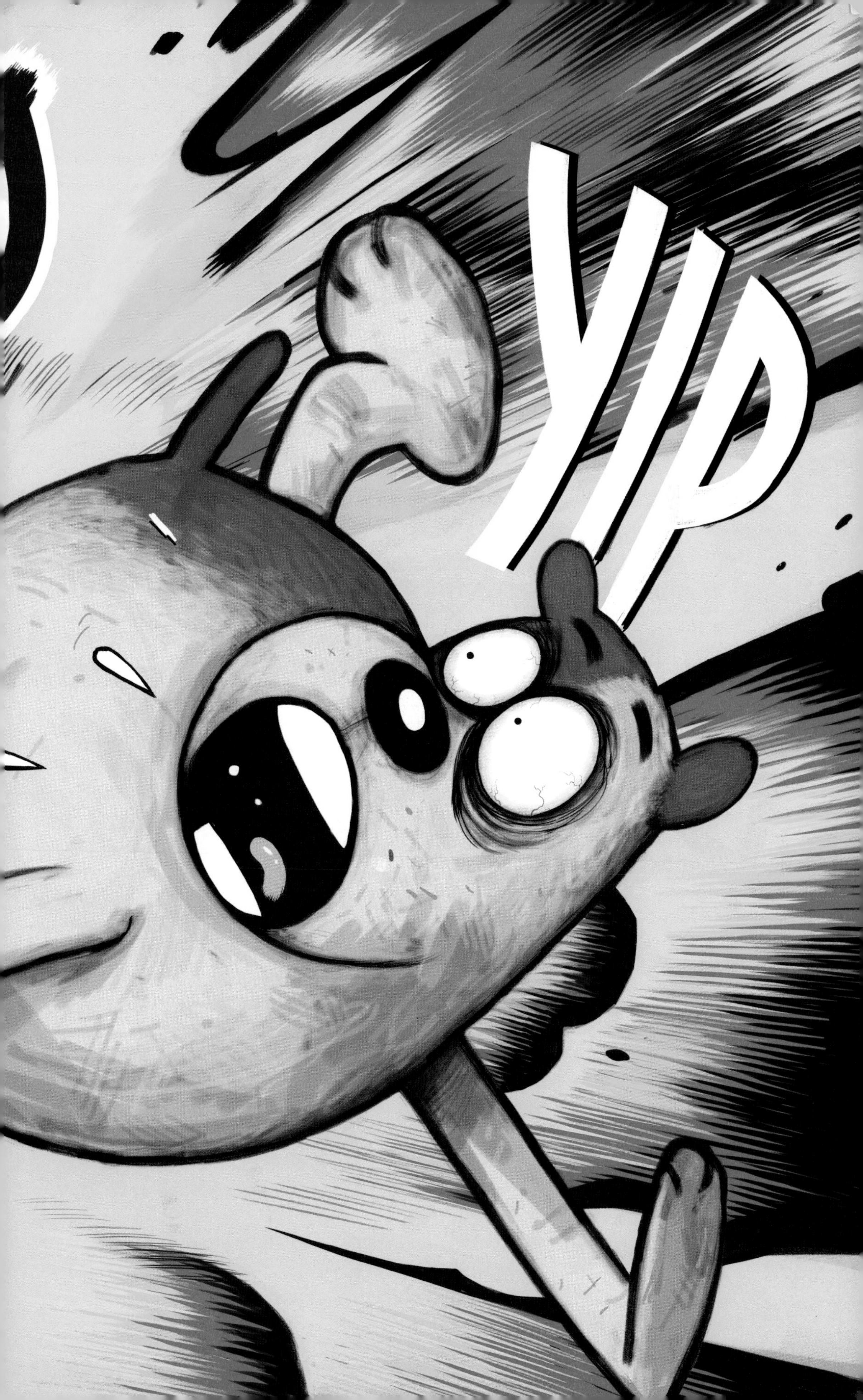
YIP

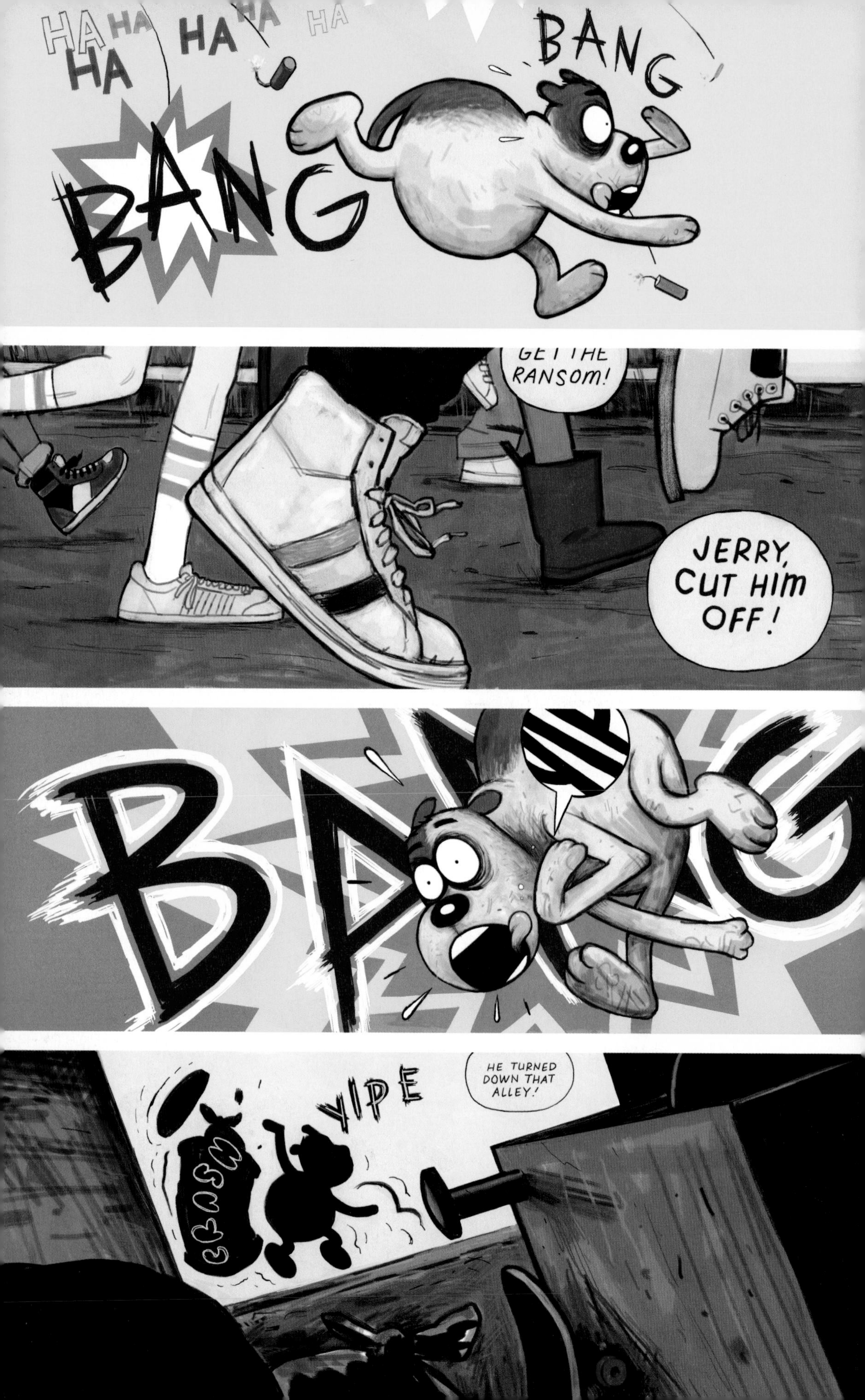
HA HA HA HA HA HA
BANG
BANG
GET THE RANSOM!
JERRY, CUT HIM OFF!
CRASH
YIPE
HE TURNED DOWN THAT ALLEY!

JESSE SANCHEZ is the Deadliest GIRL alive, a homeless NINJA on a Skateboard.

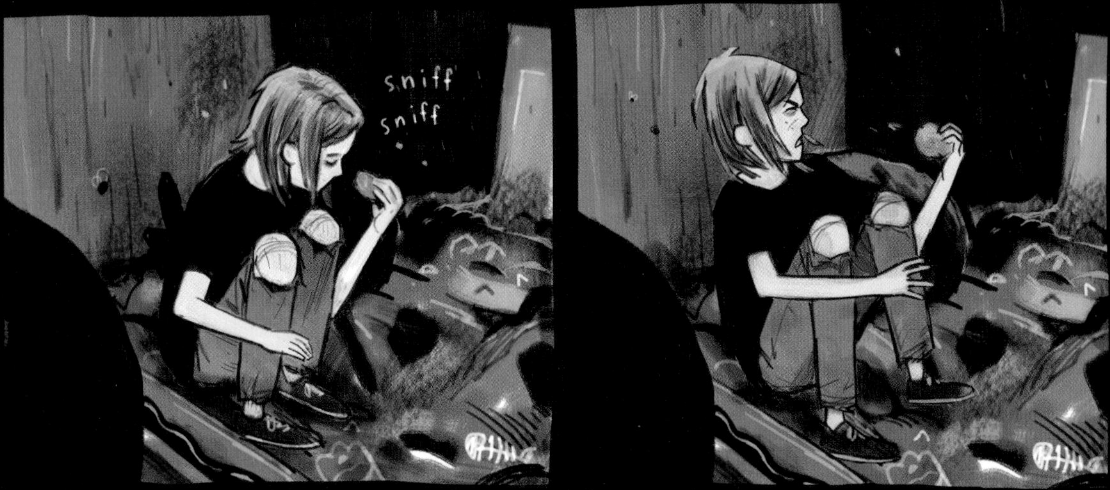
sniff
sniff

In Wilksboro, Angel City's toughest neighborhood...

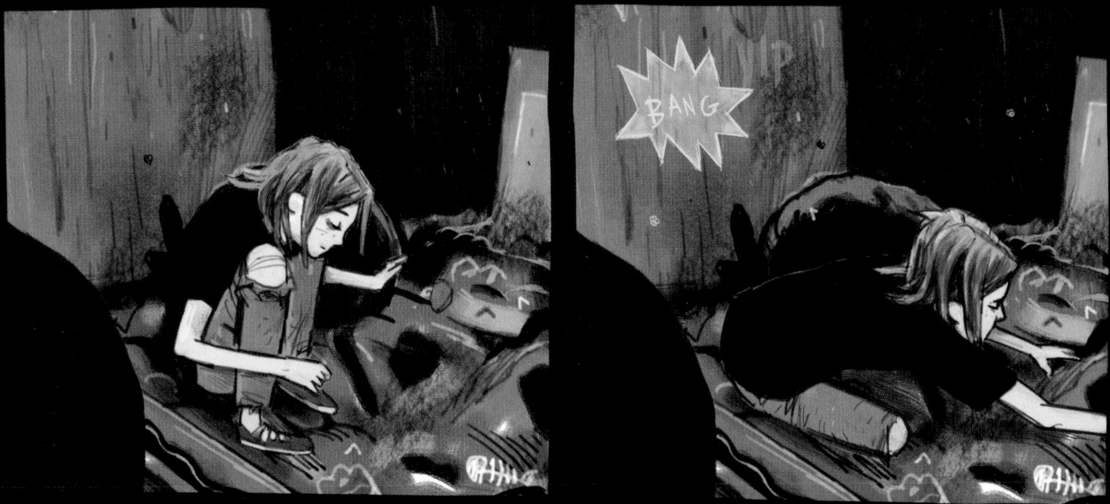
BANG
YIP

...she FIGHTS ninjas, drugs, nepotism, and pre-algebra as--

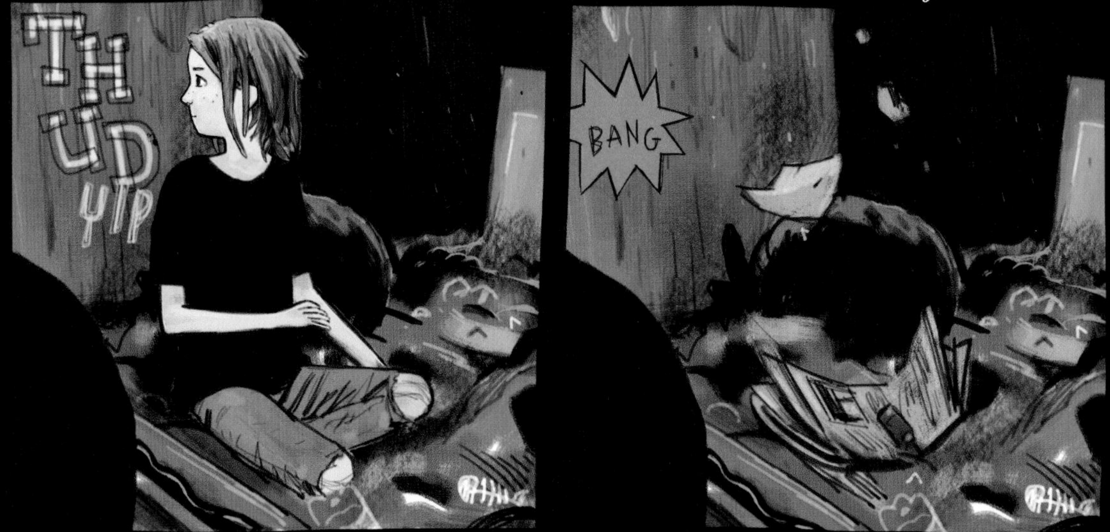
THUD
YIP
BANG

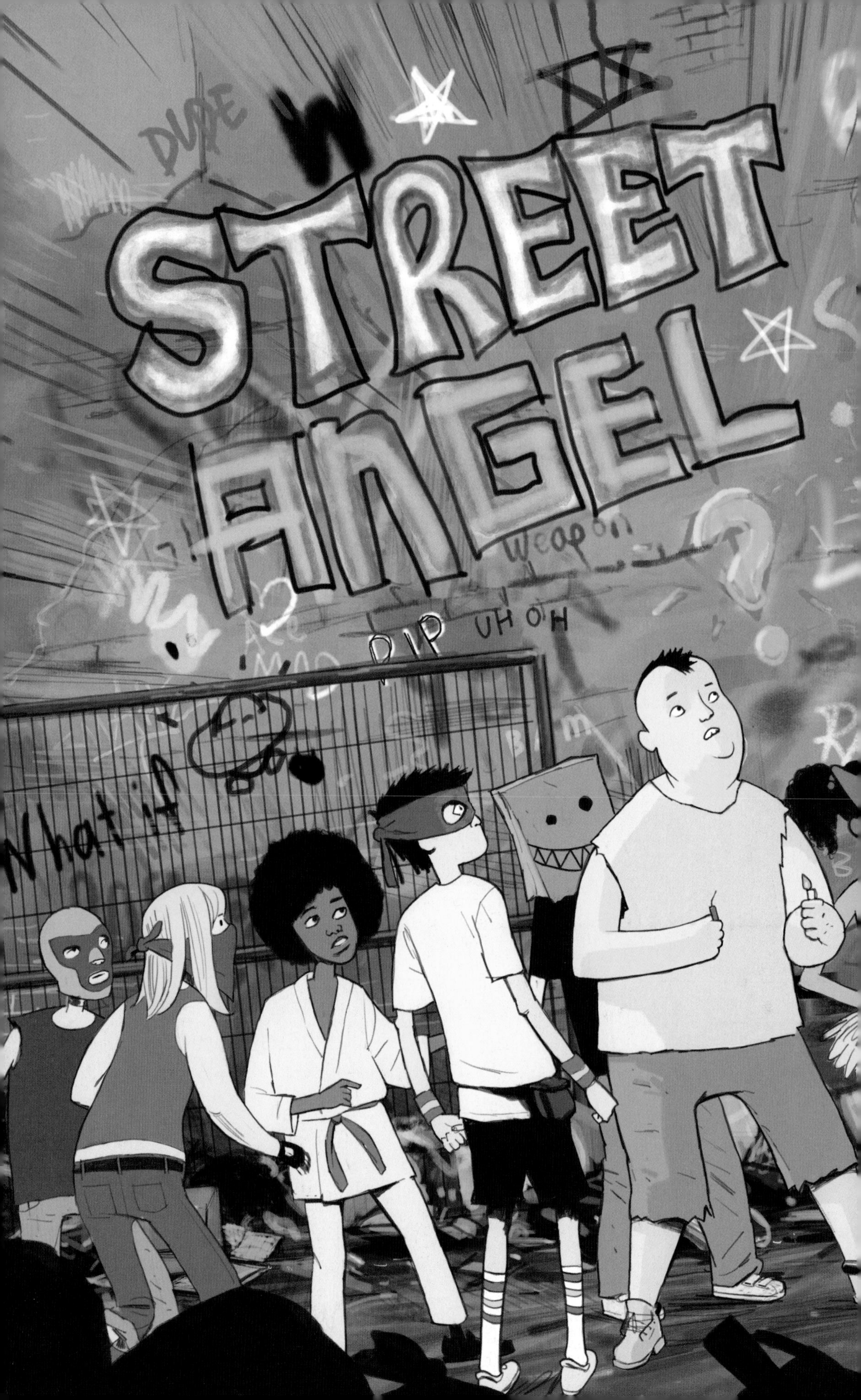
DUDE
STREET ANGEL
weapon
RIP
UH OH
What if

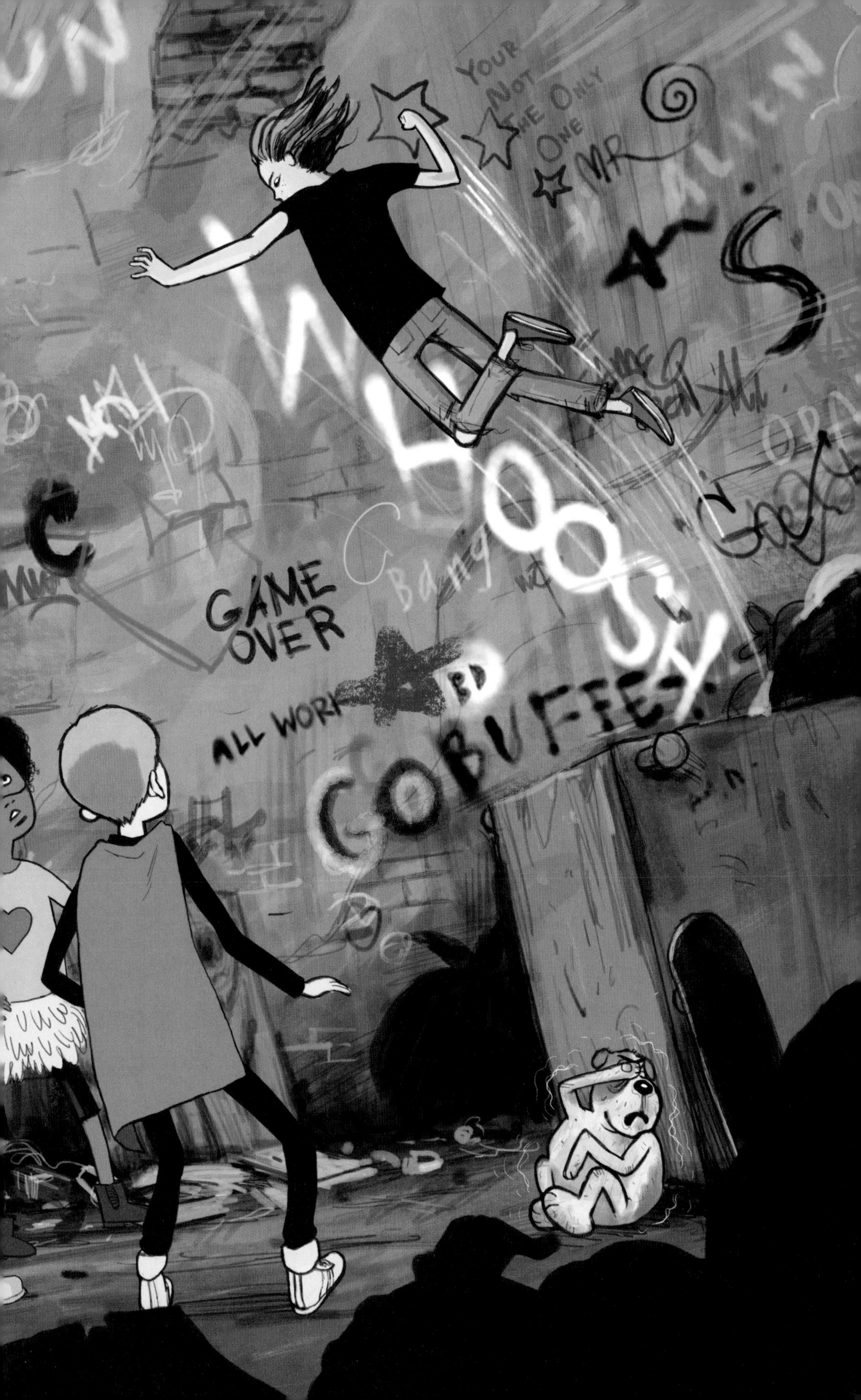

WHOOSH!
GAME OVER
ALL WORK
GOBUFFEE
YOUR NOT THE ONLY ONE
Bang

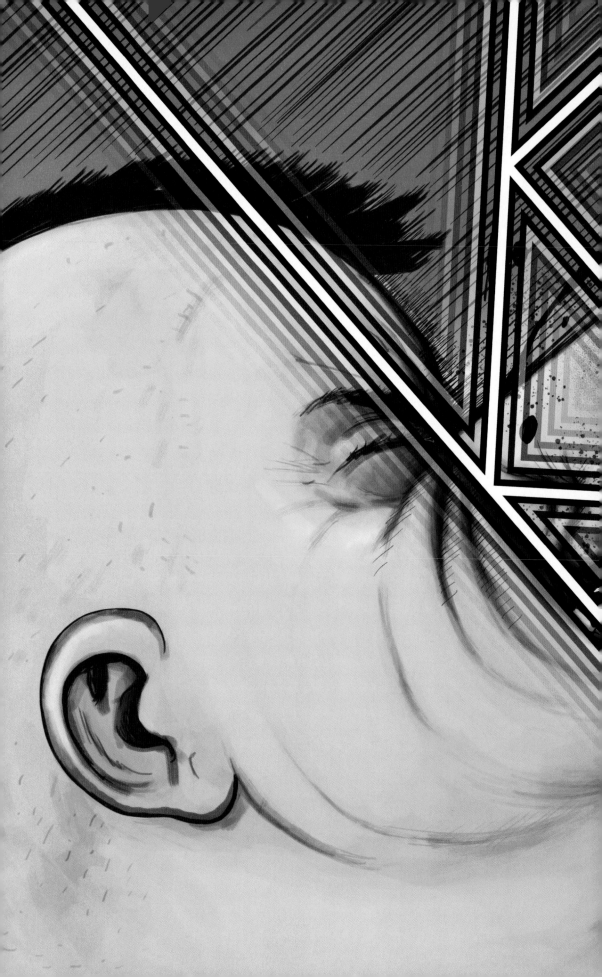

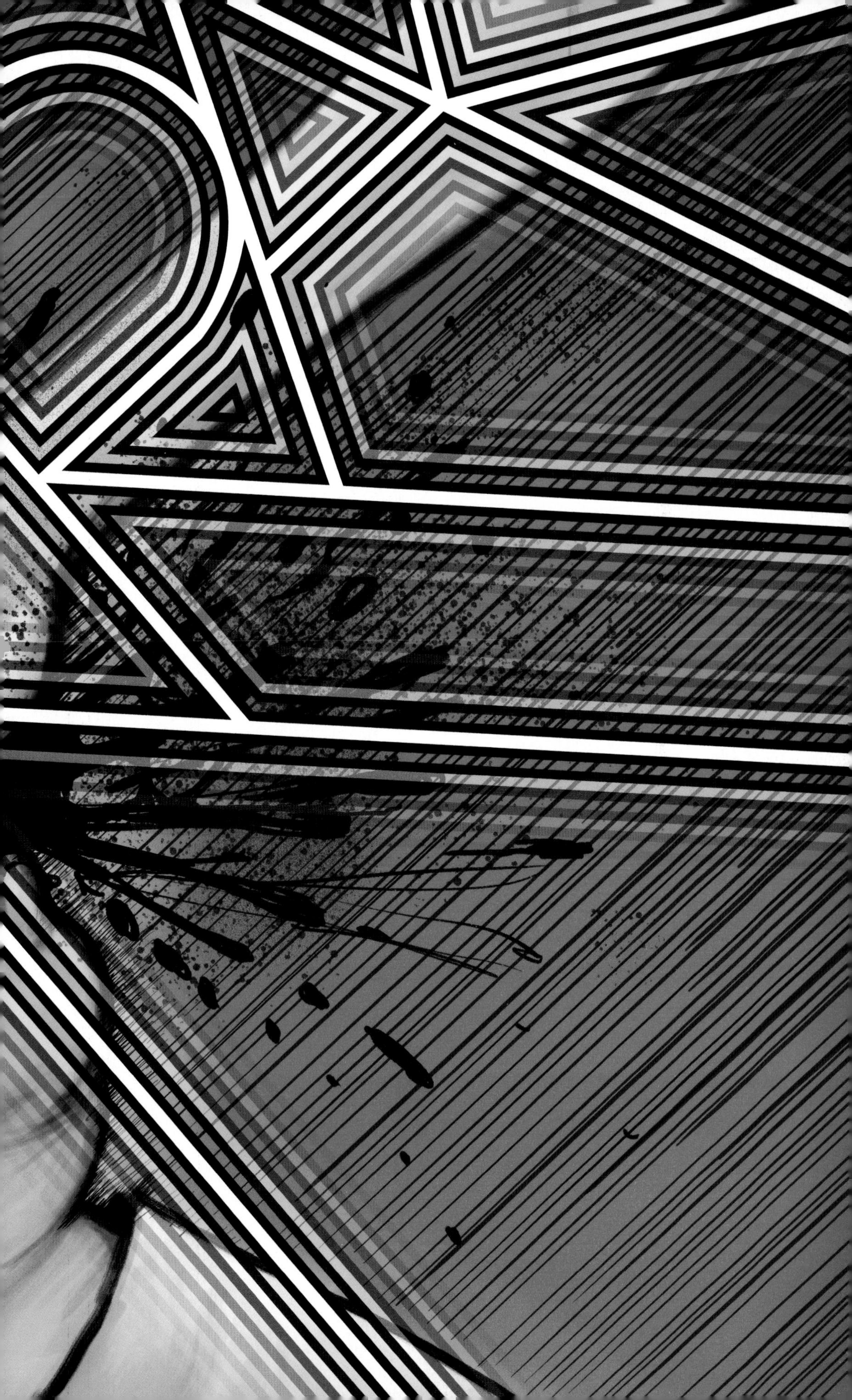

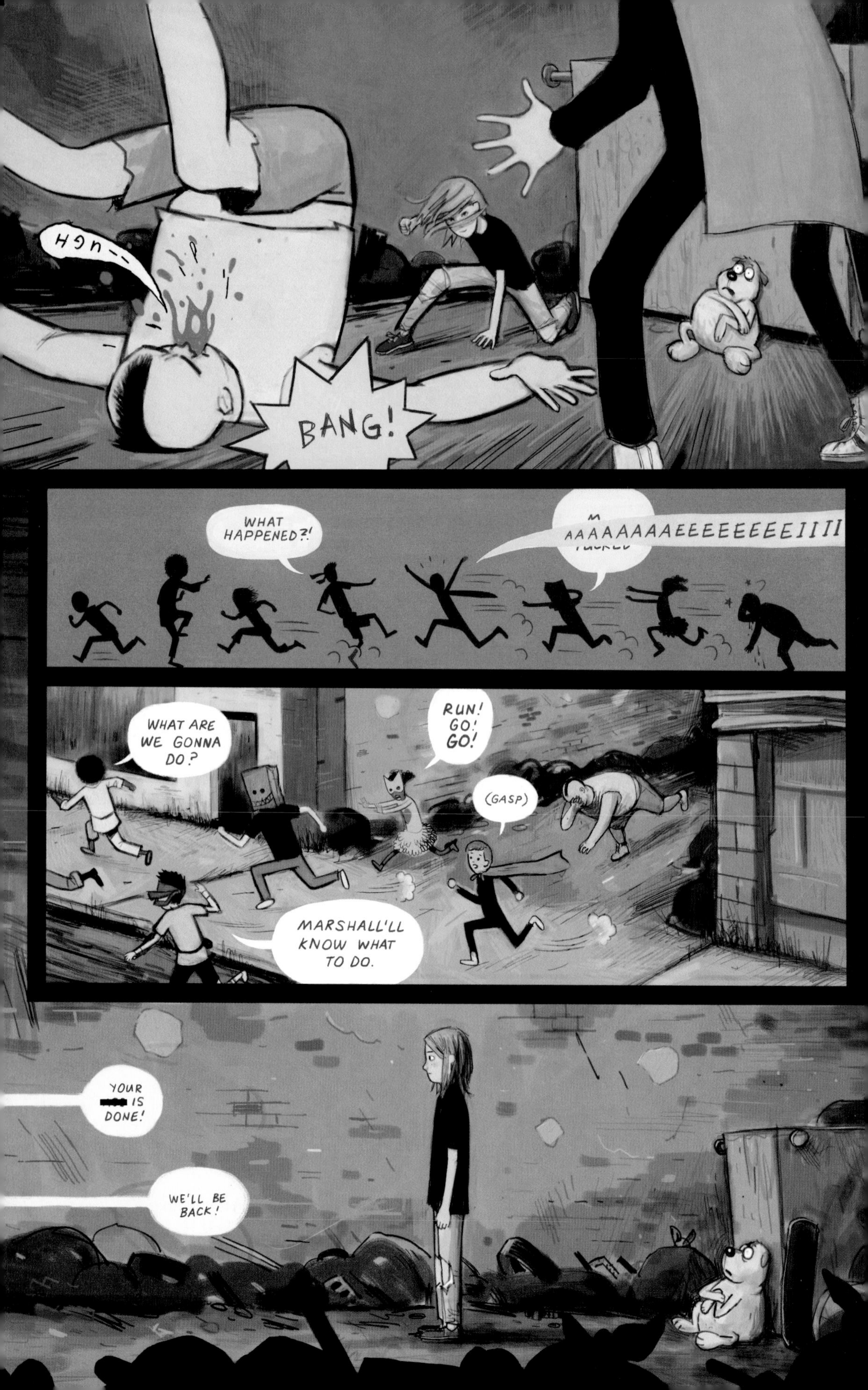
UGH--
BANG!
WHAT HAPPENED?!
AAAAAAAAEEEEEEEEIIII
WHAT ARE WE GONNA DO?
RUN! GO! GO!
(GASP)
MARSHALL'LL KNOW WHAT TO DO.
YOUR [redacted] IS DONE!
WE'LL BE BACK!

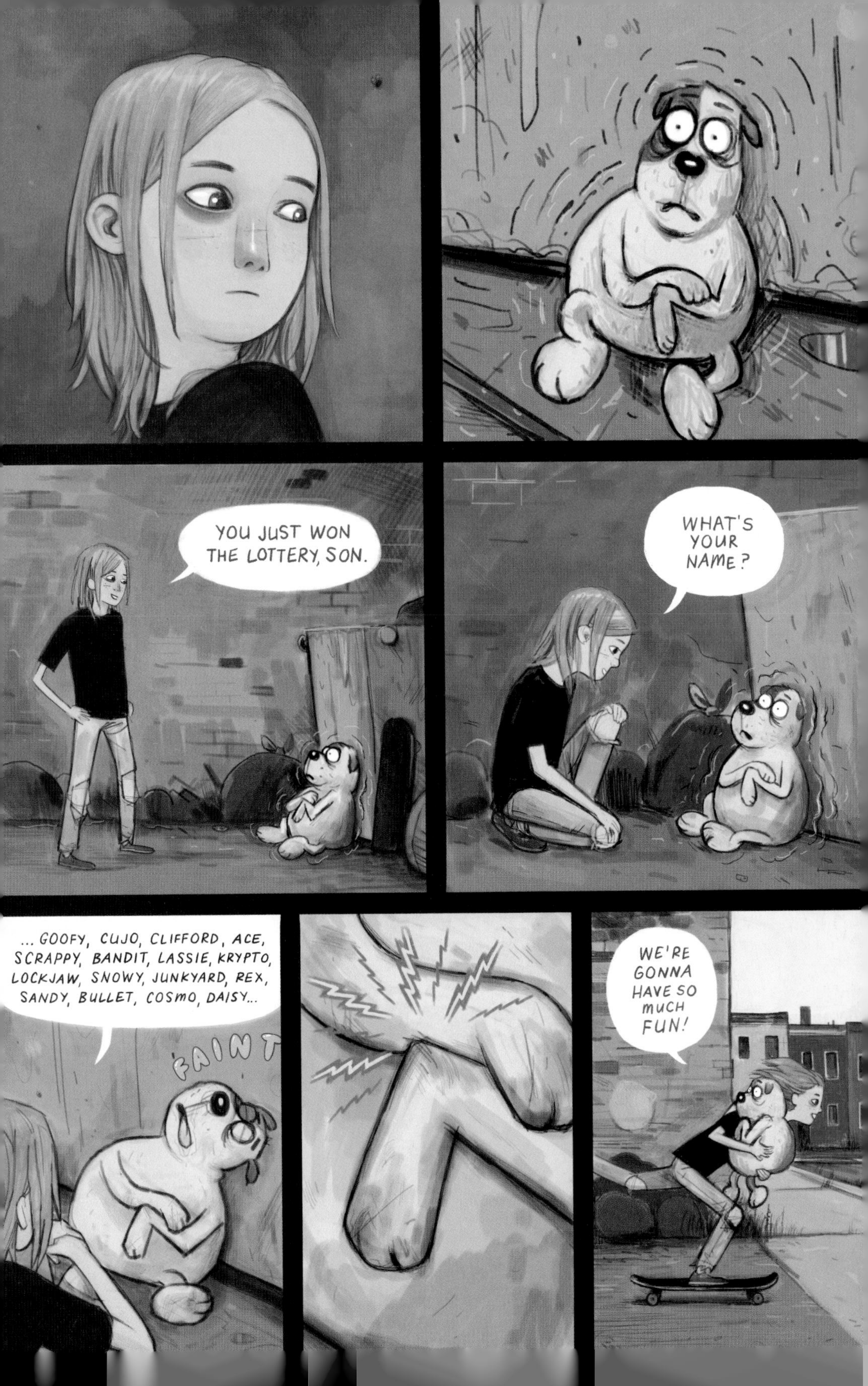
YOU JUST WON THE LOTTERY, SON.
WHAT'S YOUR NAME?
...GOOFY, CUJO, CLIFFORD, ACE, SCRAPPY, BANDIT, LASSIE, KRYPTO, LOCKJAW, SNOWY, JUNKYARD, REX, SANDY, BULLET, COSMO, DAISY...
FAINT
WE'RE GONNA HAVE SO MUCH FUN!

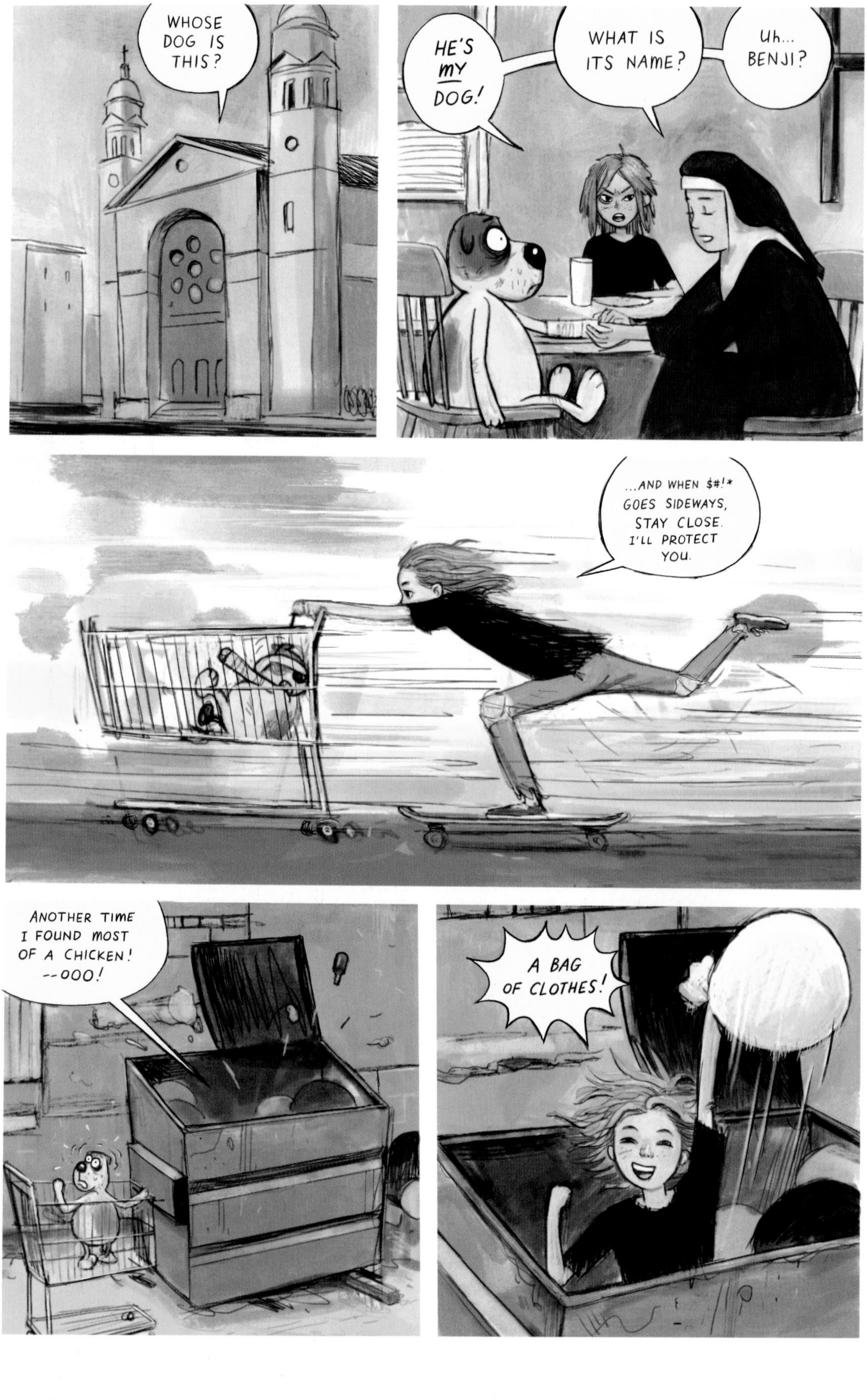
WHOSE DOG IS THIS?
HE'S my DOG!
WHAT IS ITS NAME?
Uh... BENJI?
...AND WHEN $#!* GOES SIDEWAYS, STAY CLOSE. I'LL PROTECT YOU.
ANOTHER TIME I FOUND MOST OF A CHICKEN! --OOO!
A BAG OF CLOTHES!

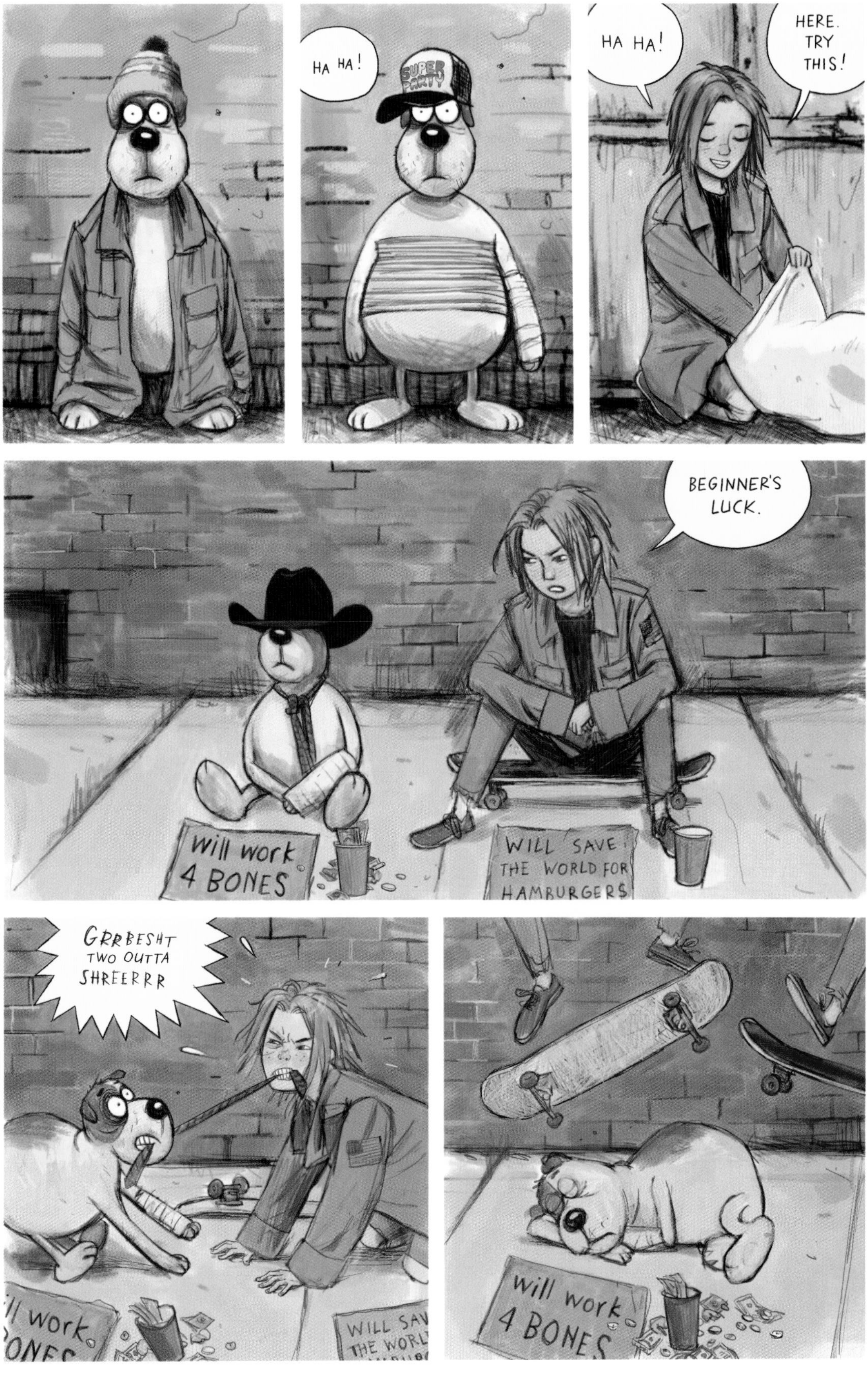
HA HA!
SUPER PARTY
HA HA!
HERE. TRY THIS!
BEGINNER'S LUCK.
will work 4 BONES
WILL SAVE THE WORLD FOR HAMBURGERS
GRRBESHT TWO OUTTA SHREERRR
will work 4 BONES

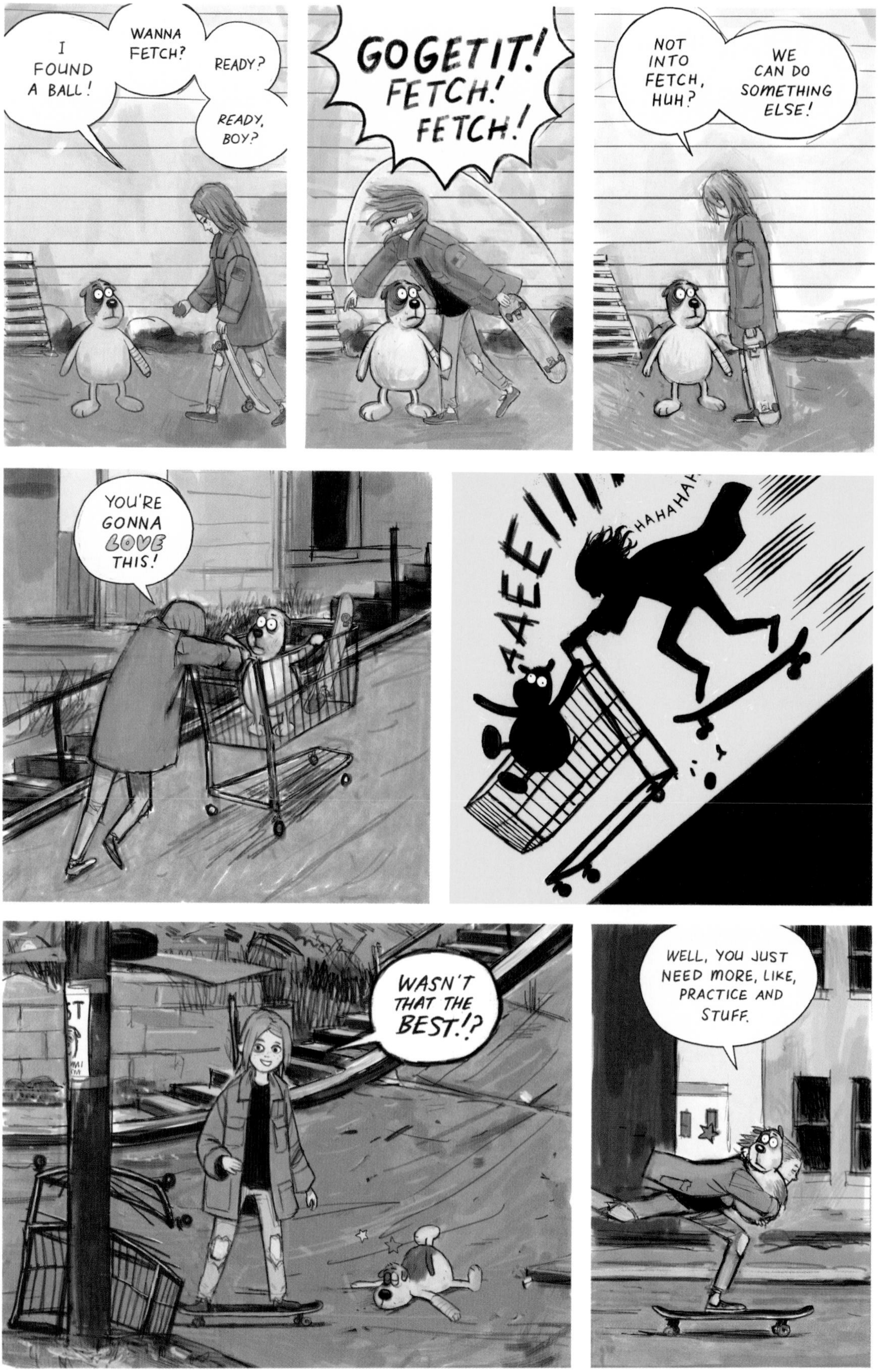
I FOUND A BALL!
WANNA FETCH?
READY?
READY, BOY?
GOGETIT! FETCH! FETCH!
NOT INTO FETCH, HUH?
WE CAN DO SOMETHING ELSE!
YOU'RE GONNA LOVE THIS!
AAAEEE!!!!
HAHAHA
WASN'T THAT THE BEST!?
WELL, YOU JUST NEED MORE, LIKE, PRACTICE AND STUFF.

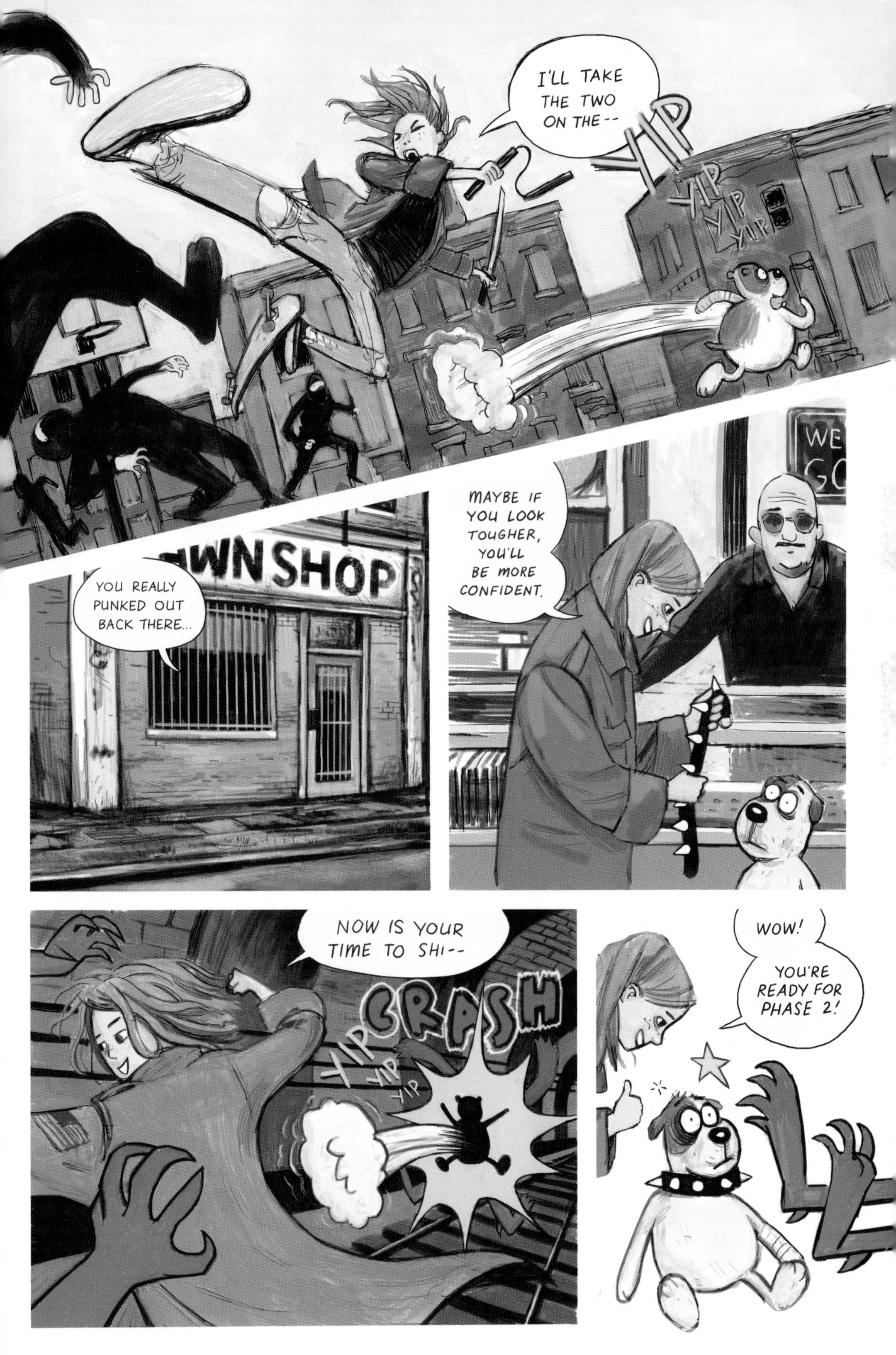
I'LL TAKE THE TWO ON THE--
YIP
YIP YIP YIP YIP
YOU REALLY PUNKED OUT BACK THERE...
WNSHOP
MAYBE IF YOU LOOK TOUGHER, YOU'LL BE MORE CONFIDENT.
NOW IS YOUR TIME TO SHI--
CRASH
YIP YIP YIP
WOW!
YOU'RE READY FOR PHASE 2!

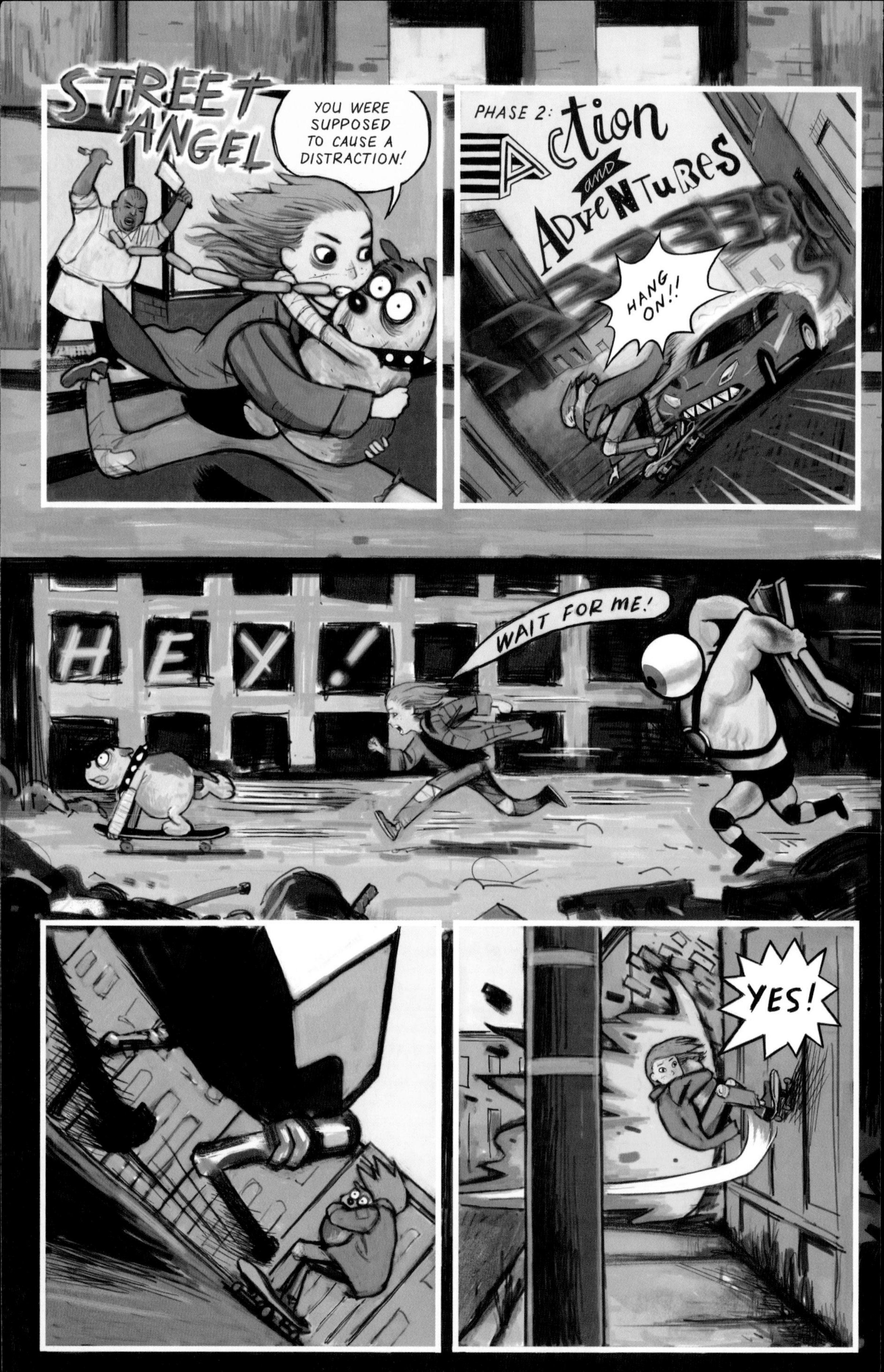
STREET ANGEL
YOU WERE SUPPOSED TO CAUSE A DISTRACTION!
PHASE 2: Action and Adventures
HANG ON!!
HEY!
WAIT FOR ME!
YES!

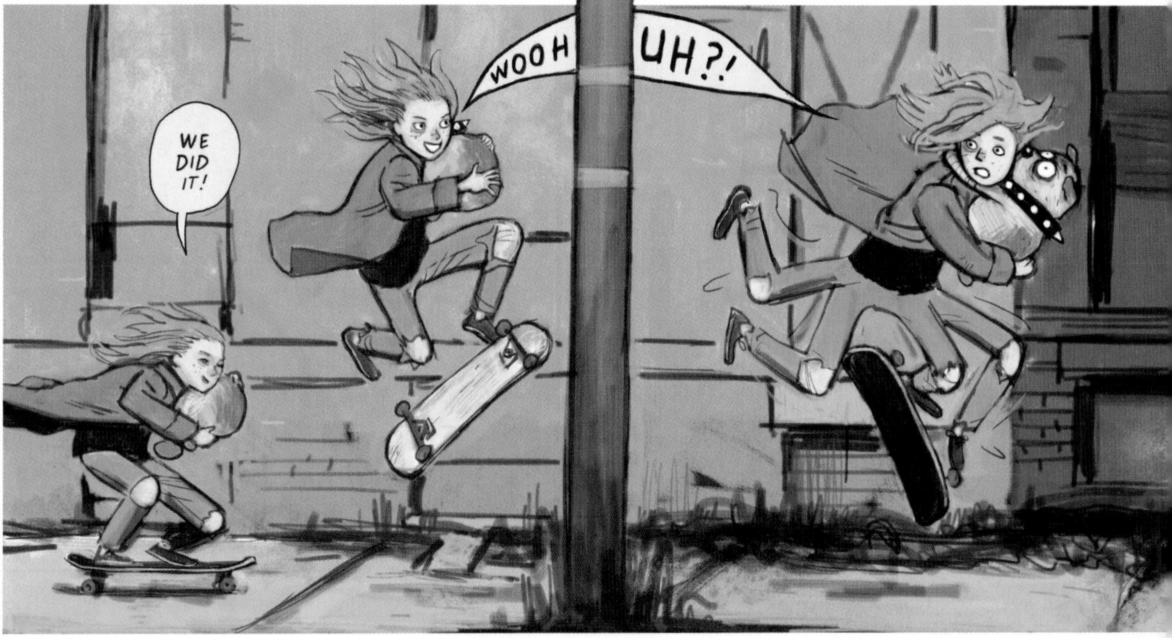
WE DID IT!
WOOH
UH?!

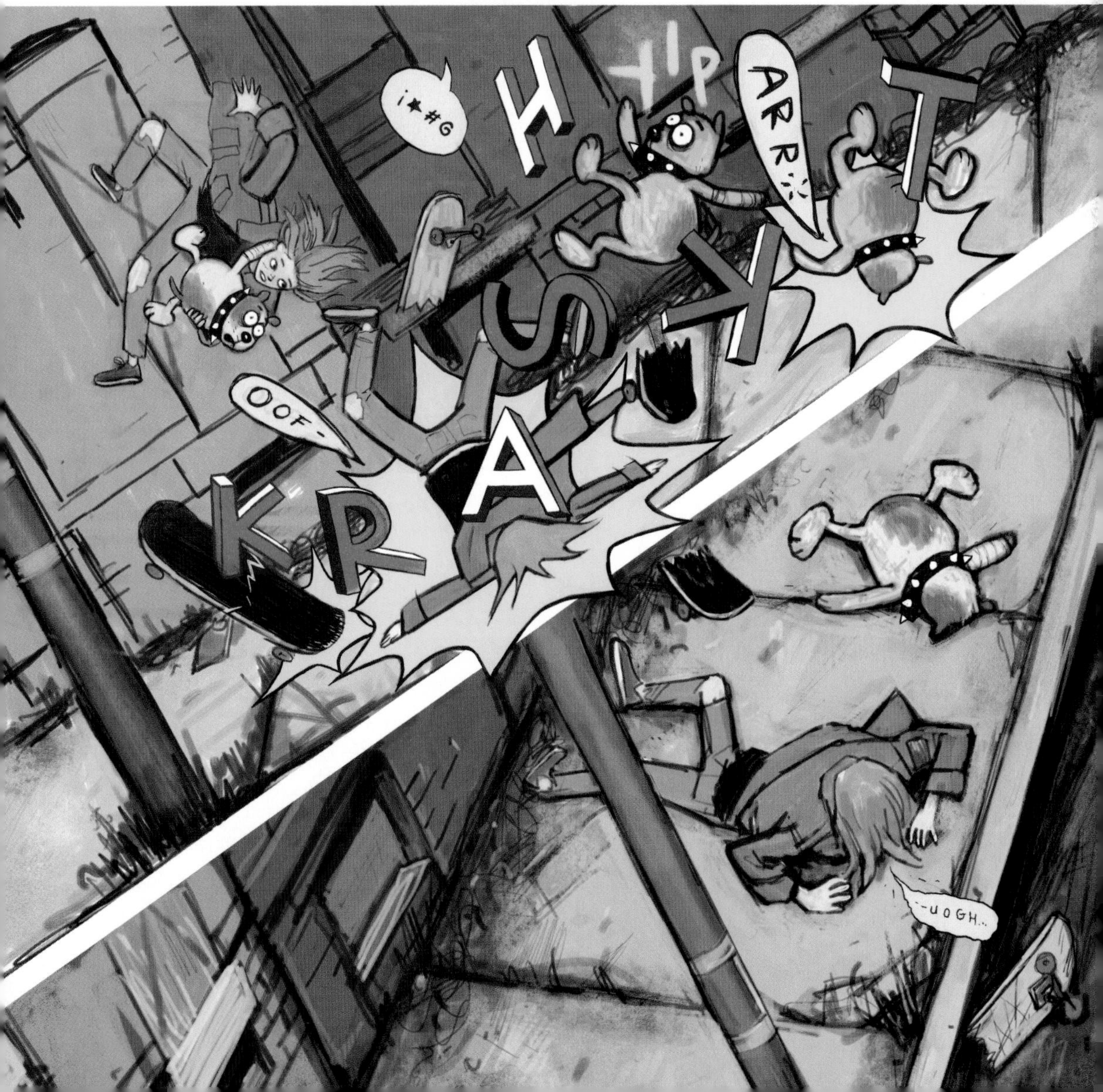
ARR
OOF-
--UOGH..

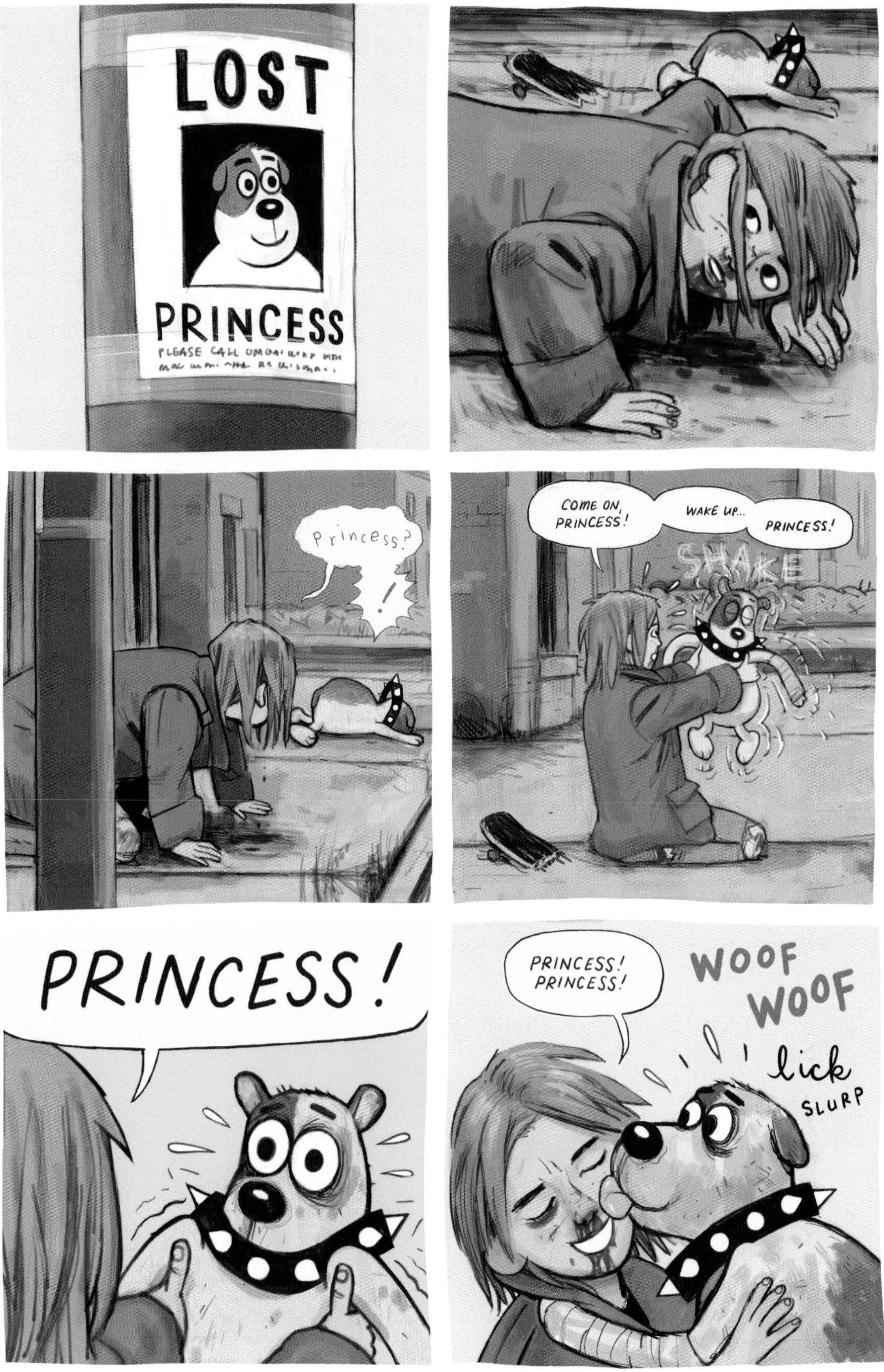

LOST
PRINCESS
PLEASE CALL
Princess?
!
COME ON, PRINCESS!
WAKE UP...
PRINCESS!
SHAKE
PRINCESS!
PRINCESS! PRINCESS!
WOOF
WOOF
lick
SLURP

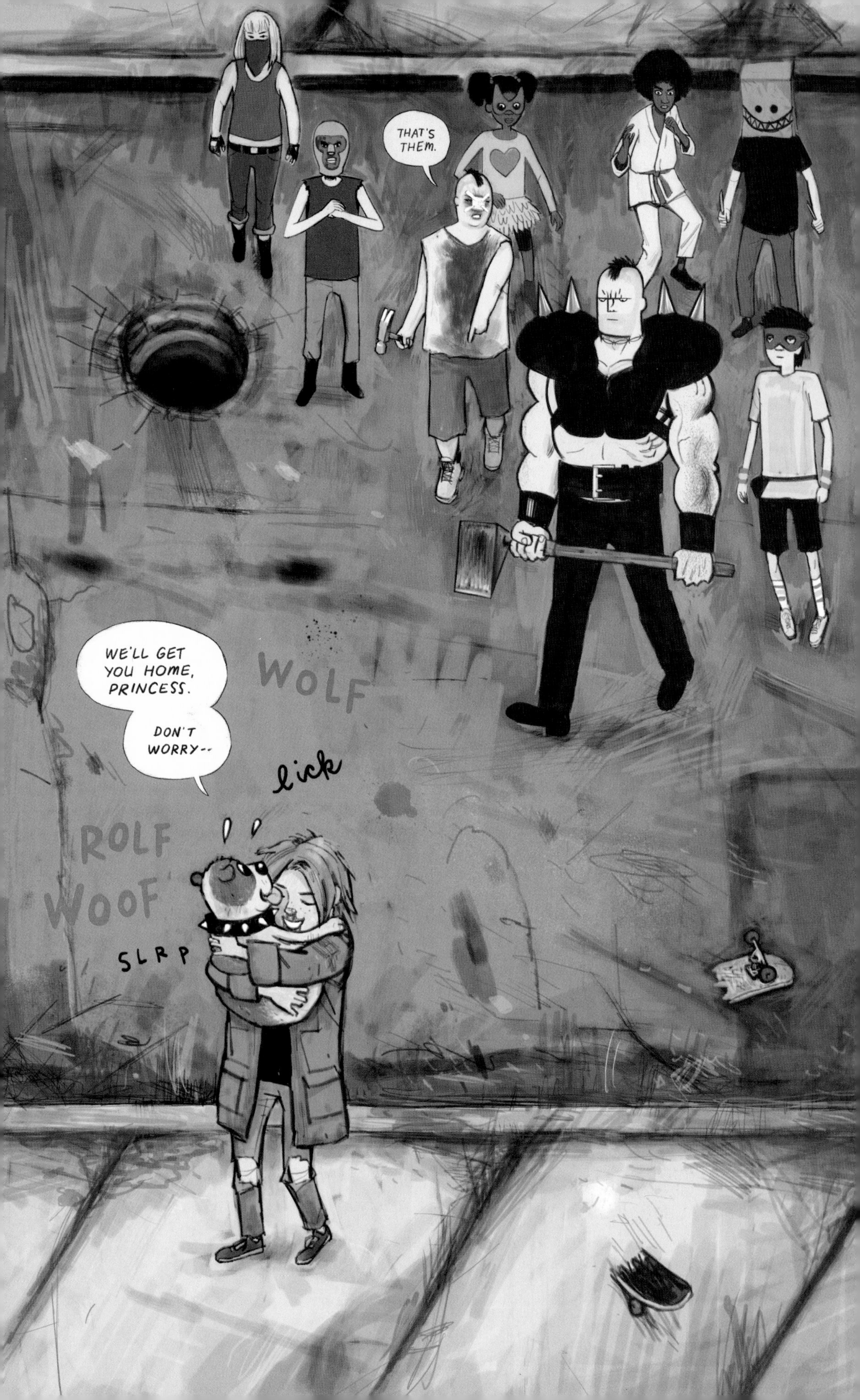
THAT'S THEM.
WE'LL GET YOU HOME, PRINCESS.
DON'T WORRY--
WOLF
lick
ROLF
WOOF
SLRP

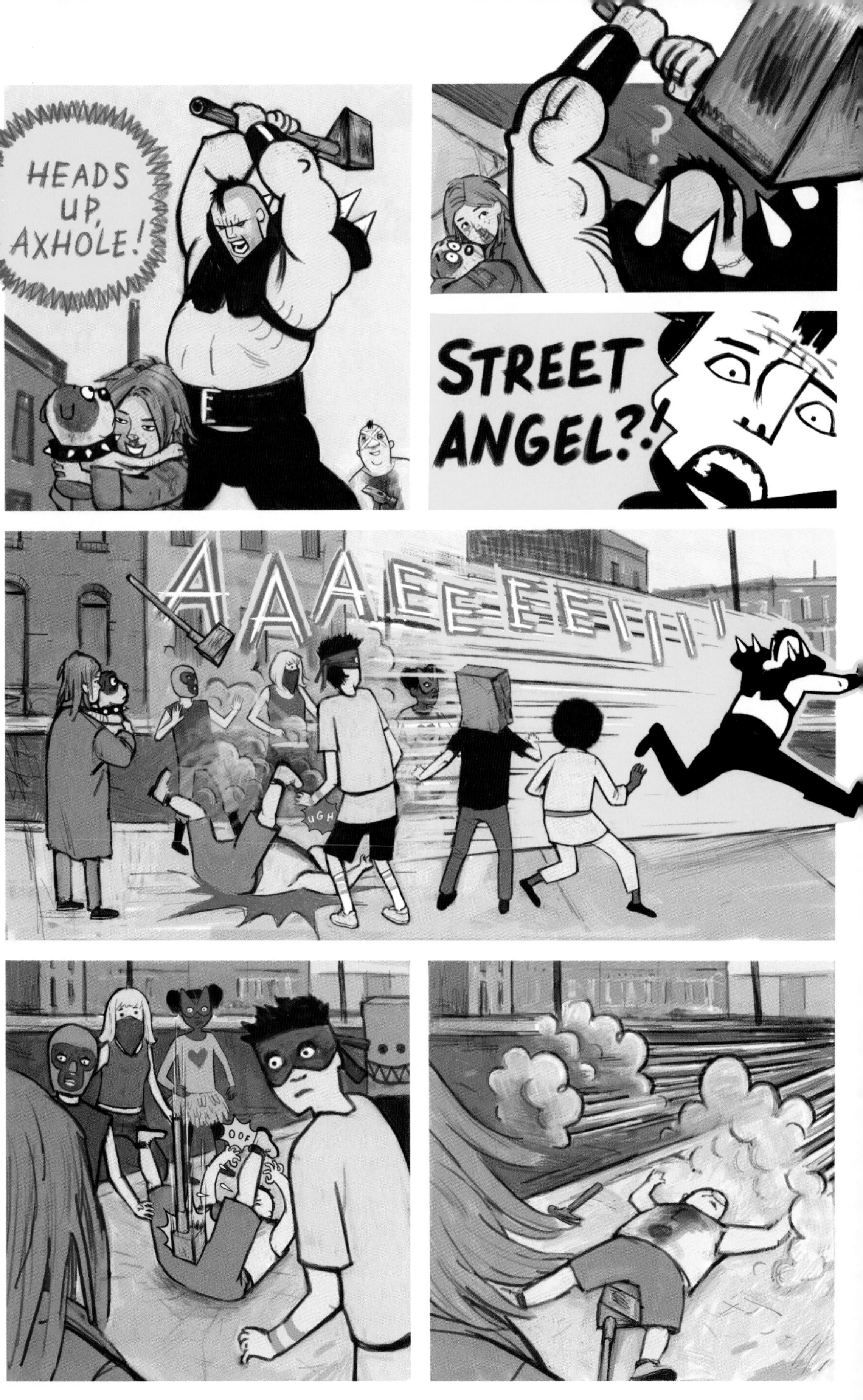
HEADS UP, AXHOLE!
?
STREET ANGEL?!
AAAEEEEIIII
UGH
OOF

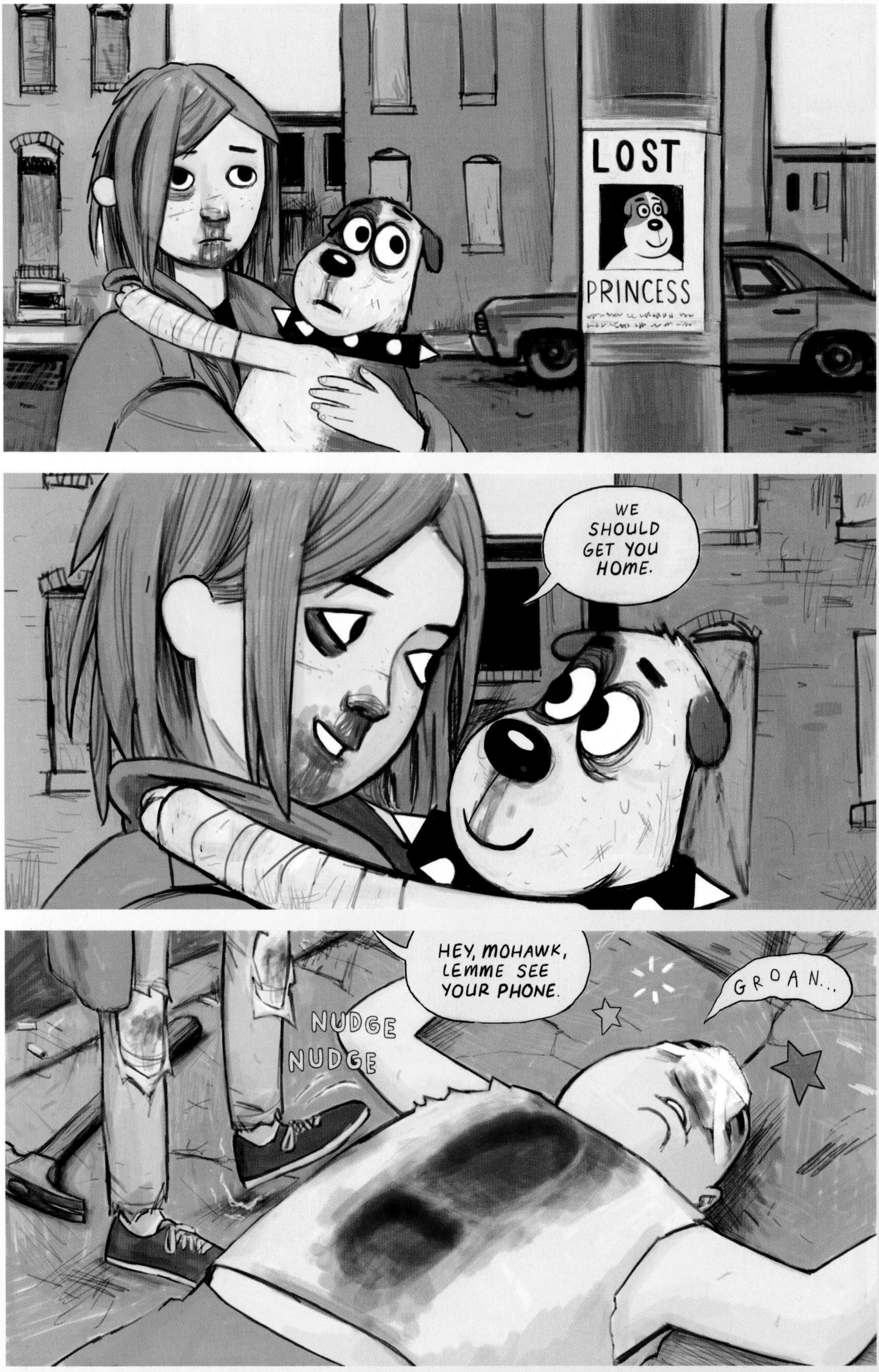
LOST
PRINCESS
WE SHOULD GET YOU HOME.
HEY, MOHAWK, LEMME SEE YOUR PHONE.
NUDGE
NUDGE
GROAN...

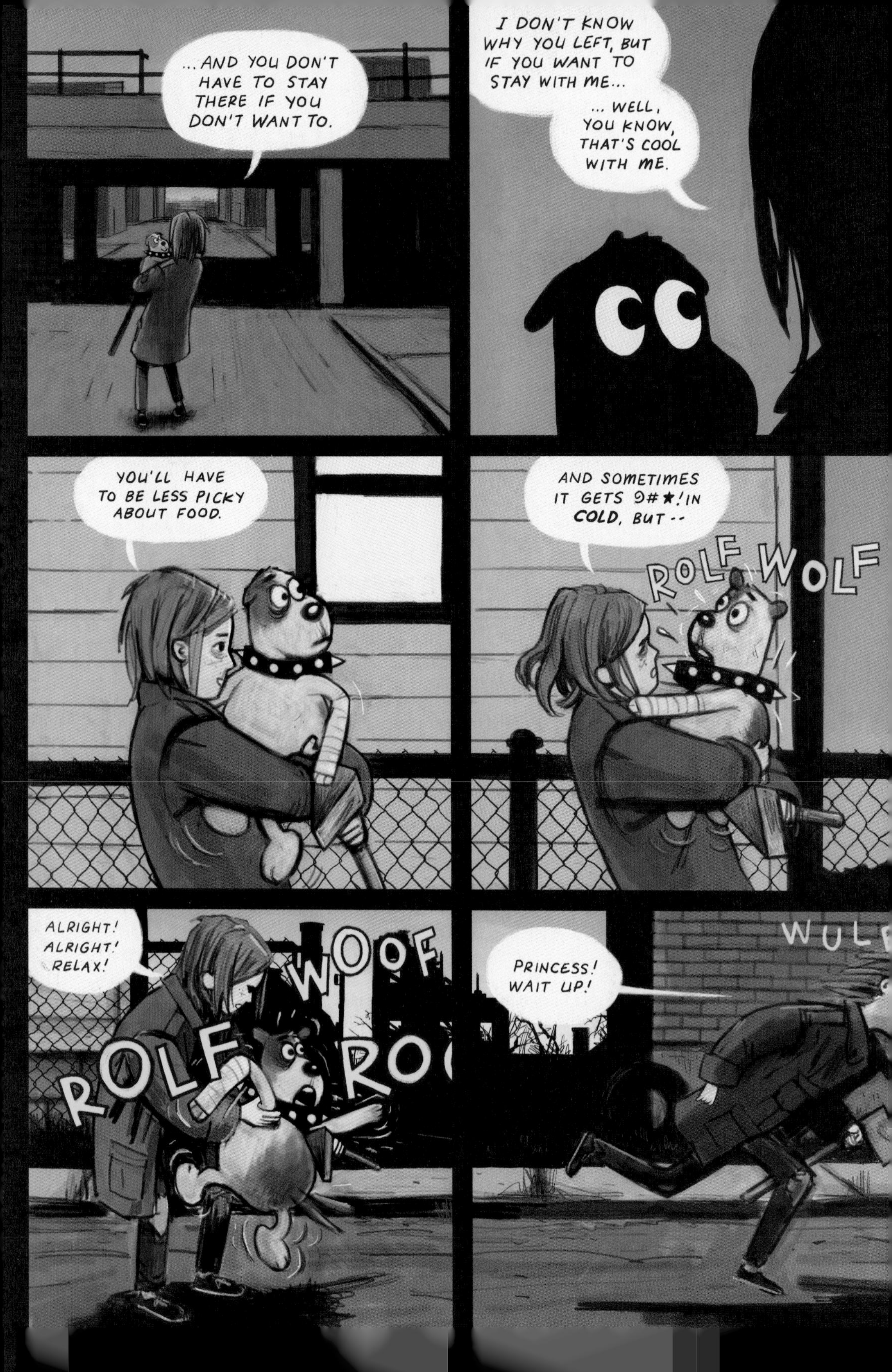
...AND YOU DON'T HAVE TO STAY THERE IF YOU DON'T WANT TO.
I DON'T KNOW WHY YOU LEFT, BUT IF YOU WANT TO STAY WITH ME...
... WELL, YOU KNOW, THAT'S COOL WITH ME.
YOU'LL HAVE TO BE LESS PICKY ABOUT FOOD.
AND SOMETIMES IT GETS 9#★! IN COLD, BUT --
ROLF WOLF
ALRIGHT! ALRIGHT! RELAX!
WOOF
ROLF
ROO
PRINCESS! WAIT UP!
WULF

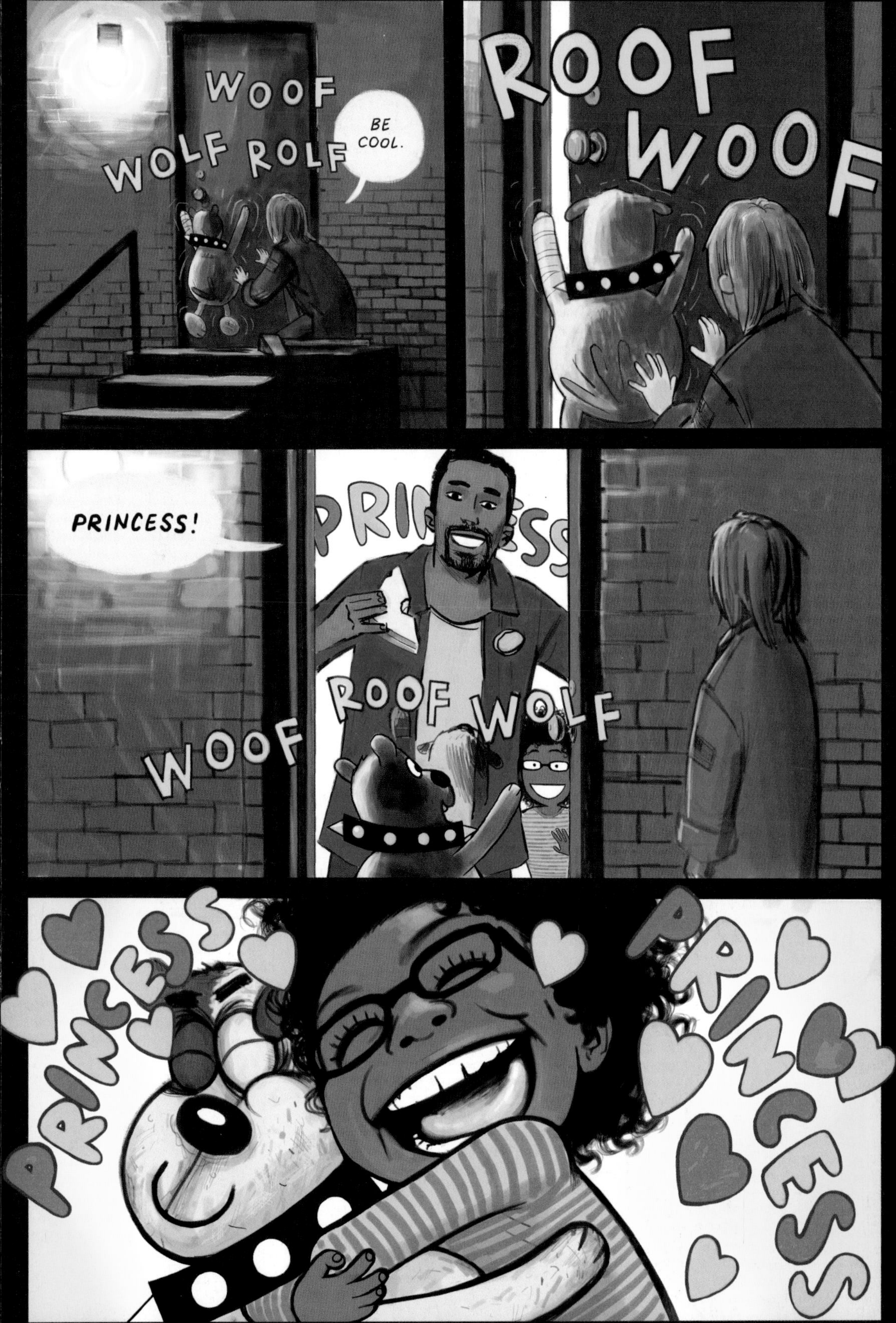
WOOF
WOLF ROLF
BE COOL.
ROOF
WOOF
PRINCESS!
PRINCESS
ROOF
WOOF WOLF
PRINCESS
PRINCESS
PRINCESS
PRINCESS

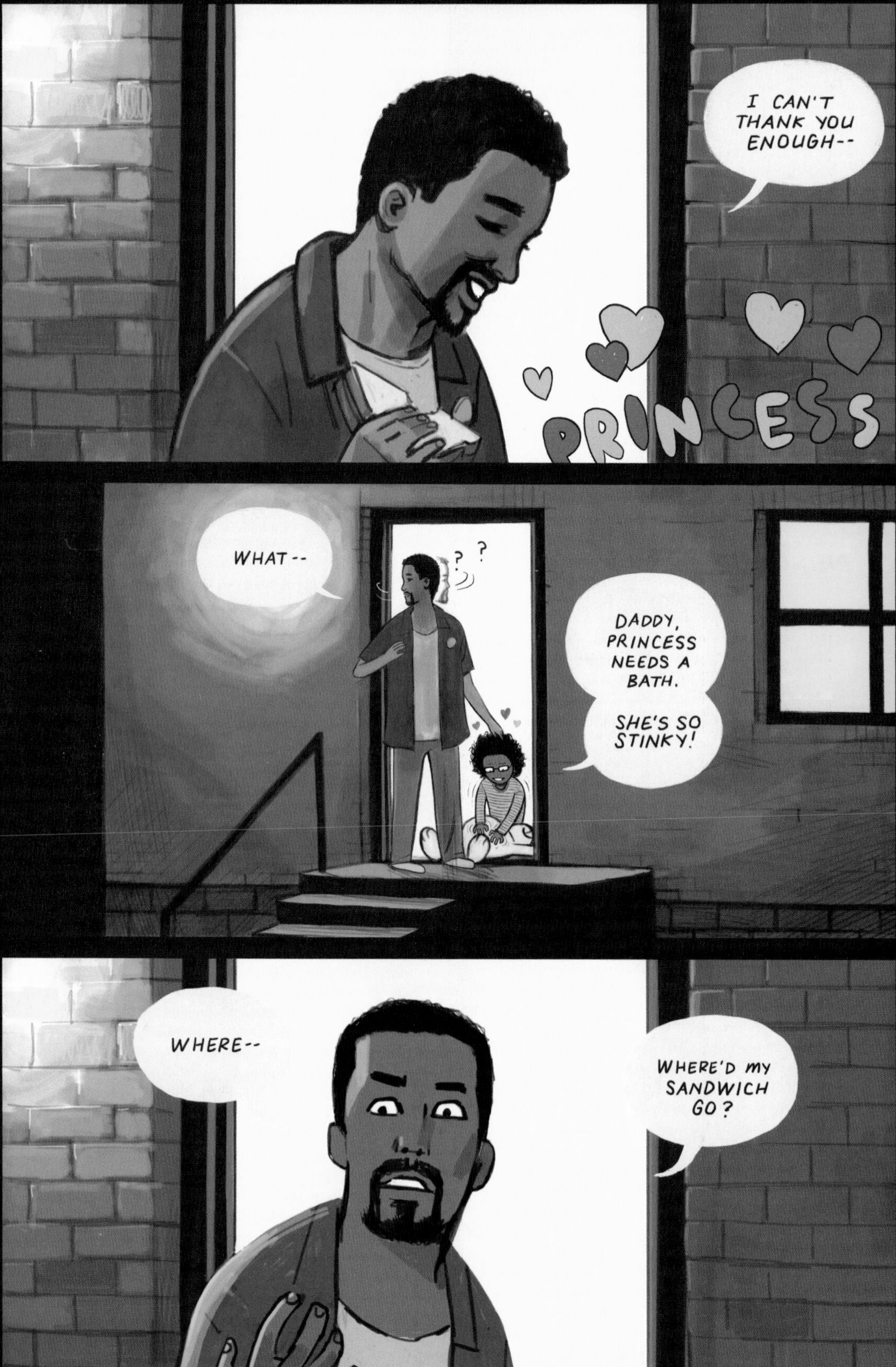
I CAN'T THANK YOU ENOUGH--
PRINCESS
WHAT--
? ?
DADDY, PRINCESS NEEDS A BATH.
SHE'S SO STINKY!
WHERE--
WHERE'D MY SANDWICH GO?

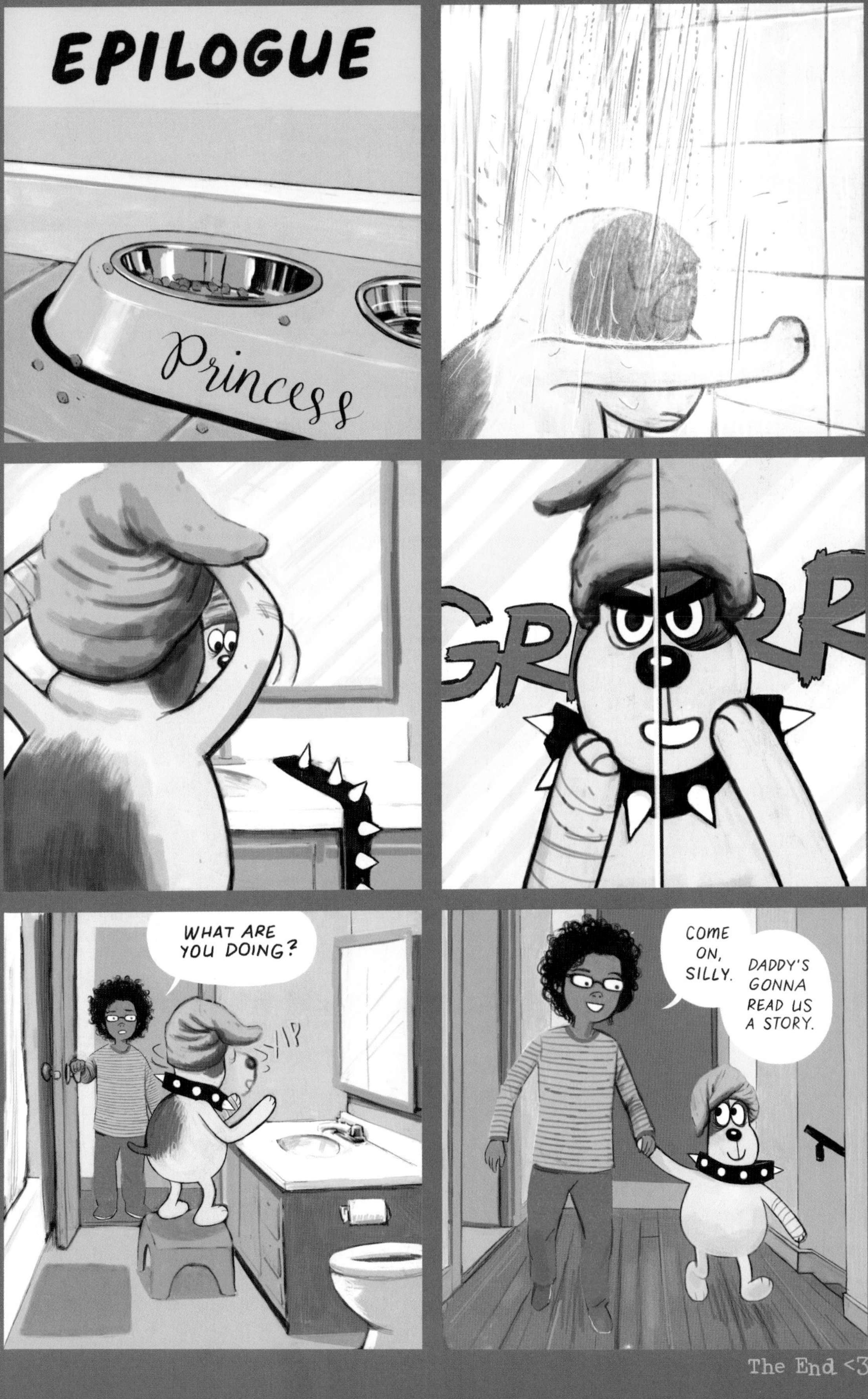
EPILOGUE
Princess
GRRR
WHAT ARE YOU DOING?
YIP
COME ON, SILLY.
DADDY'S GONNA READ US A STORY.

The End <3

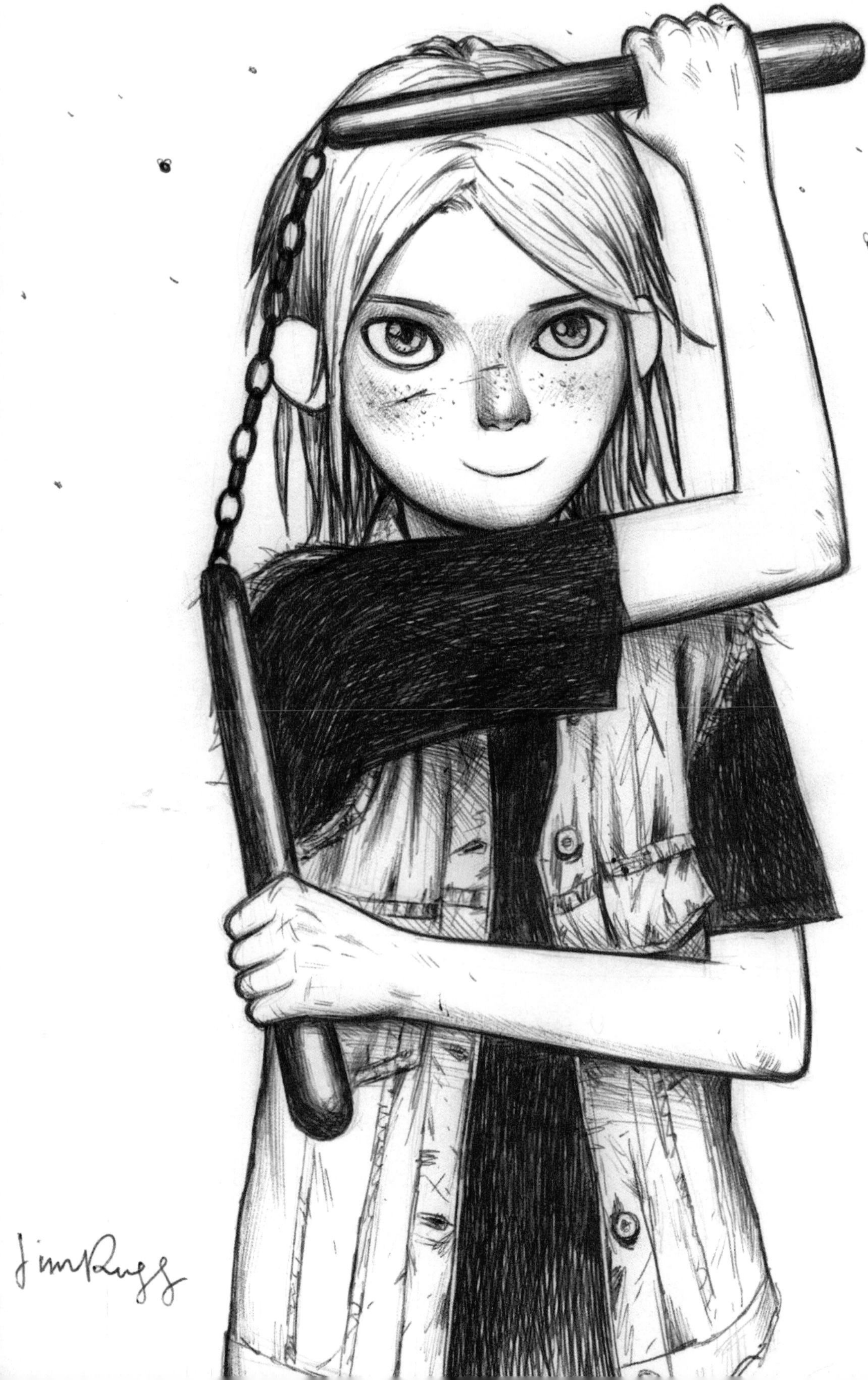
Jim Rugg

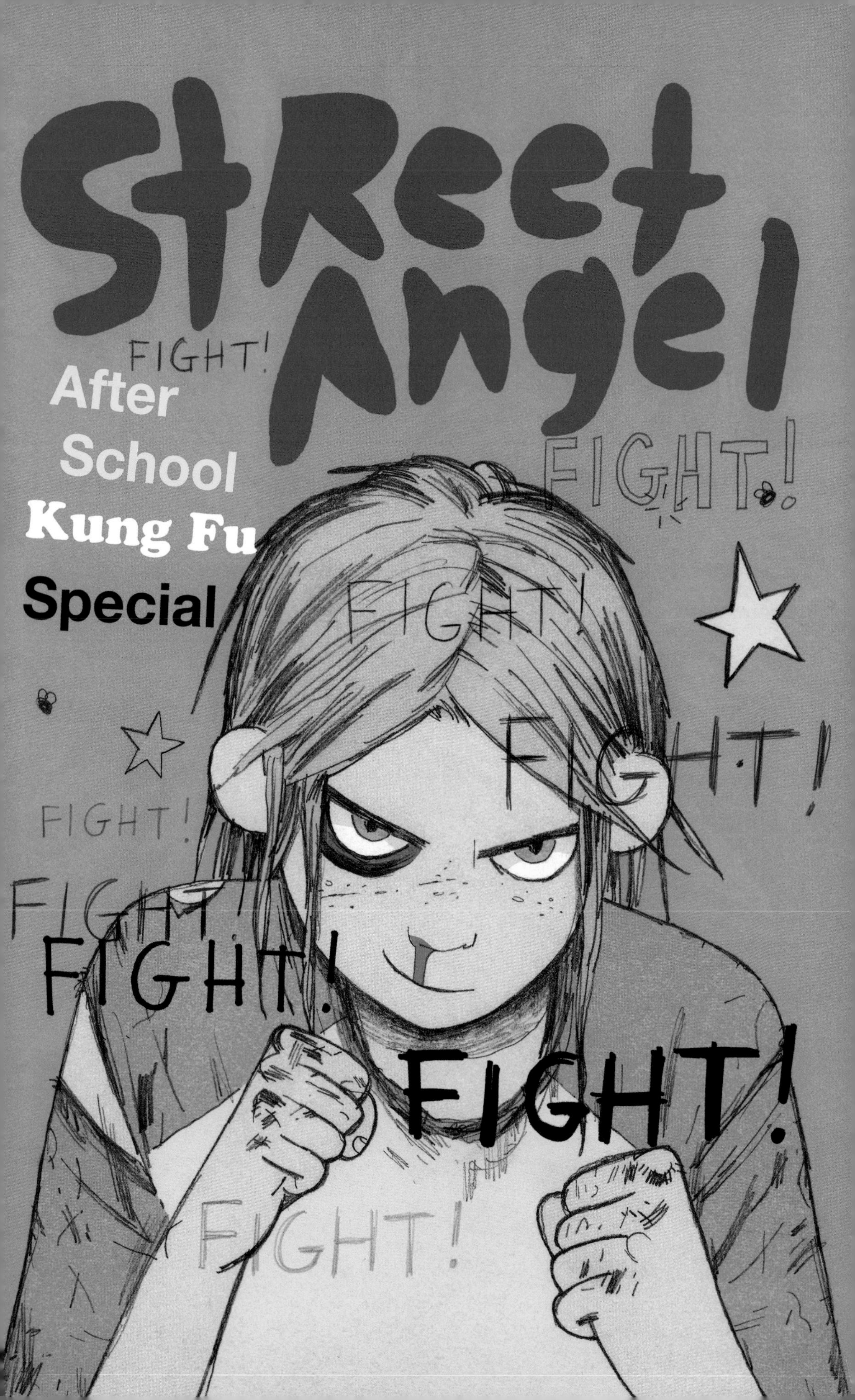
Street Angel
FIGHT!
After School
Kung Fu
Special
FIGHT!
FIGHT!
FIGHT!
FIGHT!
FIGHT!
FIGHT!
FIGHT!

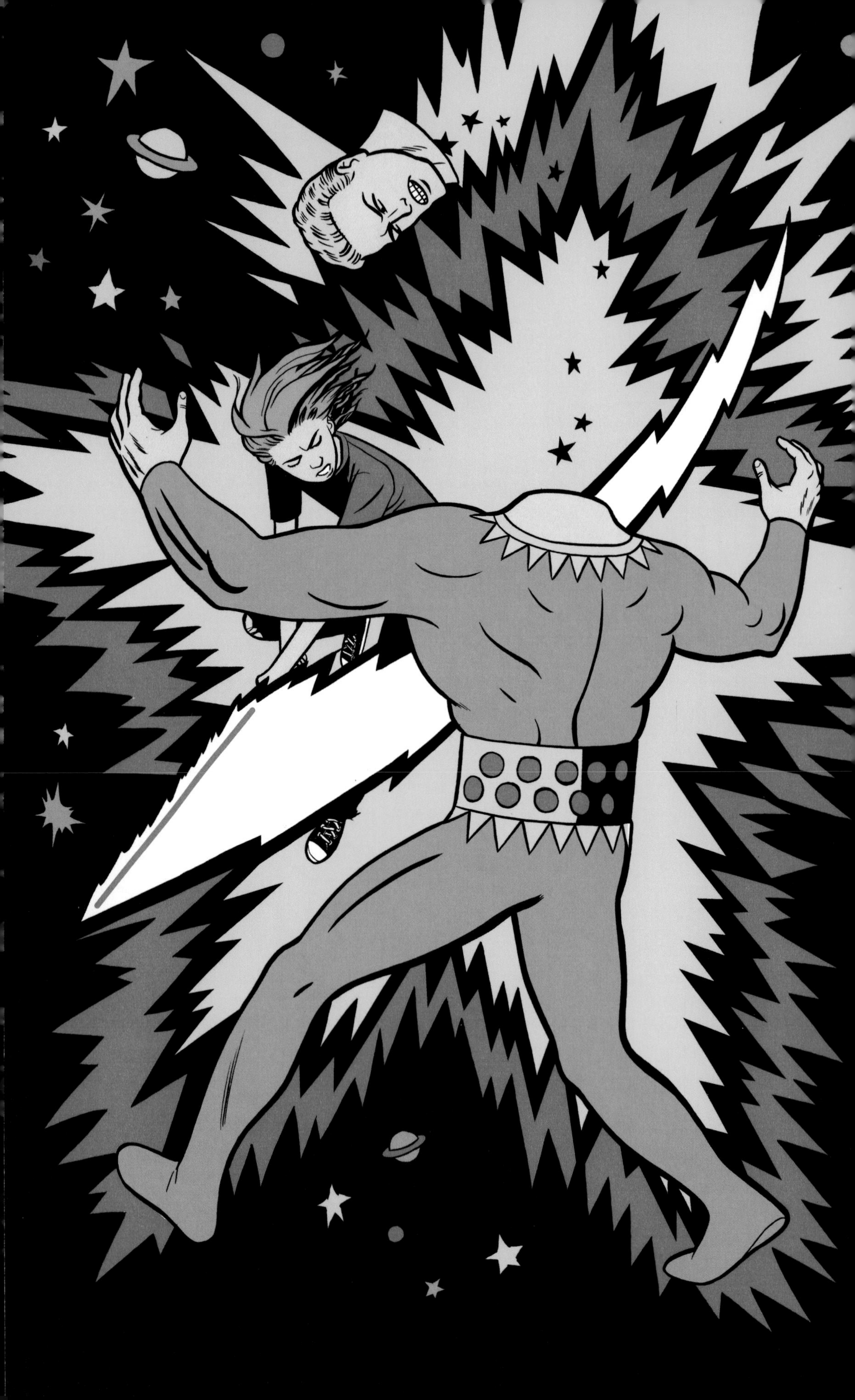

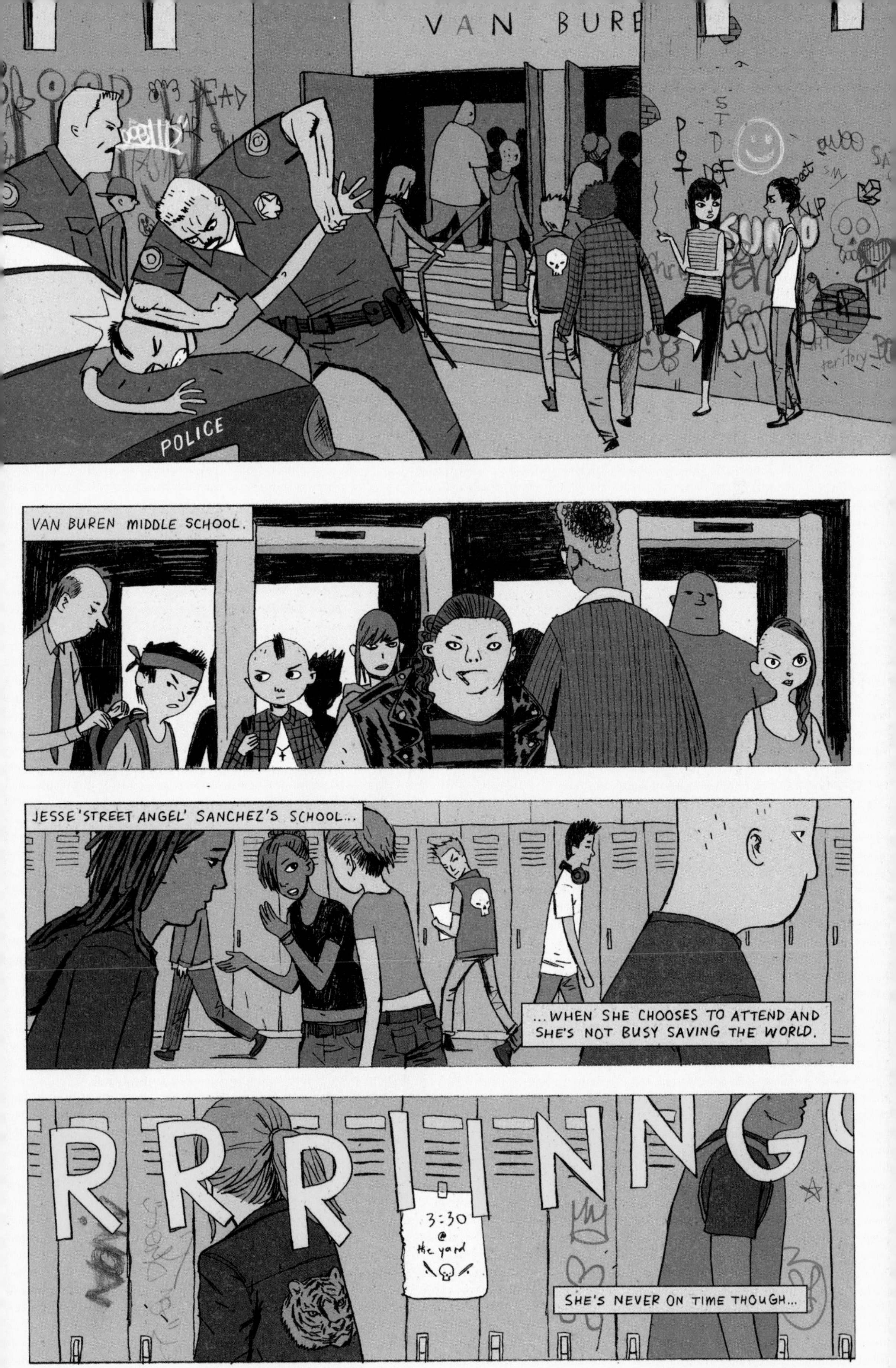
VAN BURE
POLICE
VAN BUREN MIDDLE SCHOOL.
JESSE 'STREET ANGEL' SANCHEZ'S SCHOOL...
...WHEN SHE CHOOSES TO ATTEND AND SHE'S NOT BUSY SAVING THE WORLD.
RRRIINNG
3:30 @ the yard
SHE'S NEVER ON TIME THOUGH...

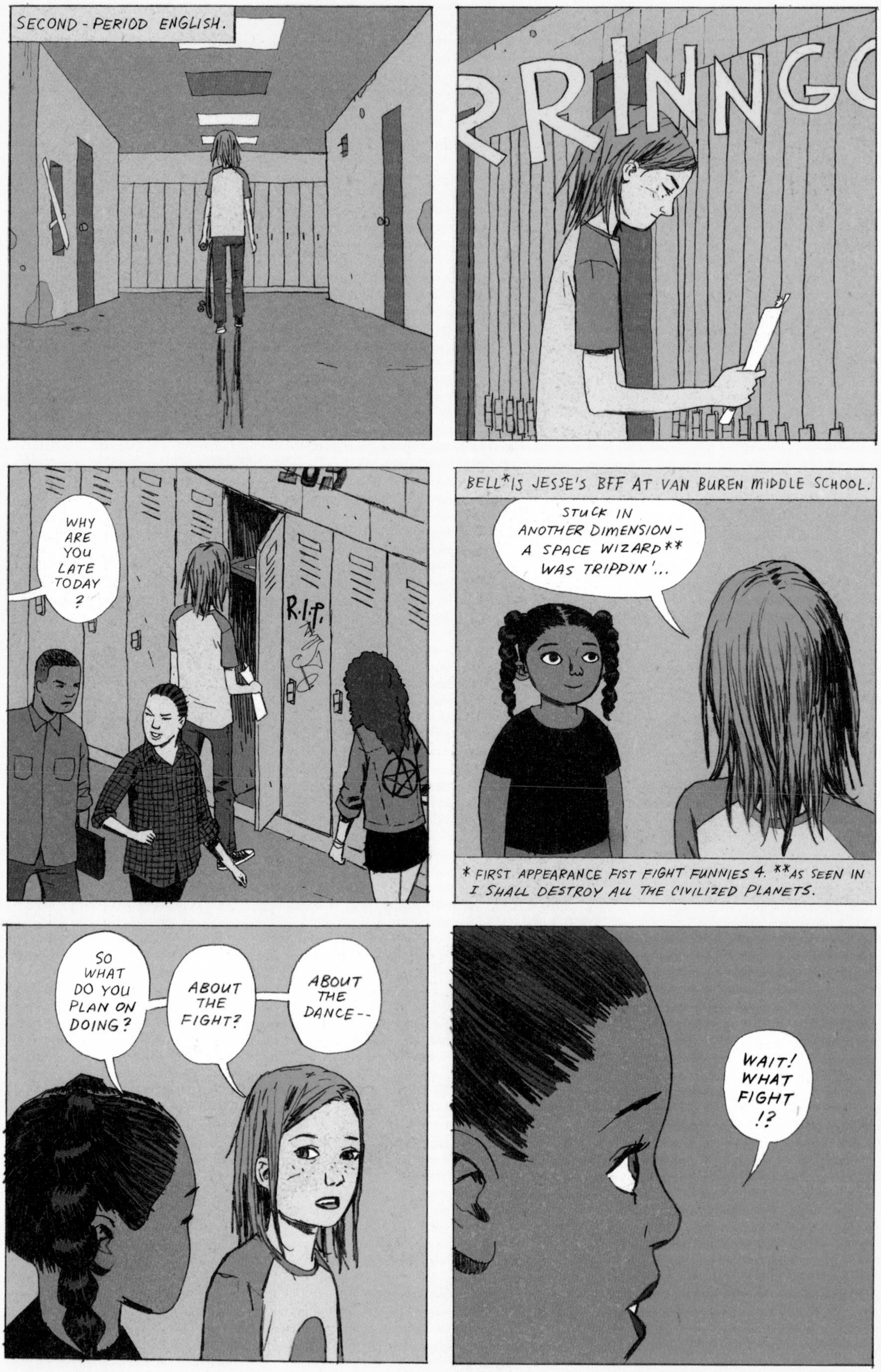
SECOND-PERIOD ENGLISH.
RRINNG
WHY ARE YOU LATE TODAY?
R.I.P.
BELL* IS JESSE'S BFF AT VAN BUREN MIDDLE SCHOOL.
STUCK IN ANOTHER DIMENSION— A SPACE WIZARD** WAS TRIPPIN'...
* FIRST APPEARANCE FIST FIGHT FUNNIES 4. **AS SEEN IN I SHALL DESTROY ALL THE CIVILIZED PLANETS.
SO WHAT DO YOU PLAN ON DOING?
ABOUT THE FIGHT?
ABOUT THE DANCE--
WAIT! WHAT FIGHT !?

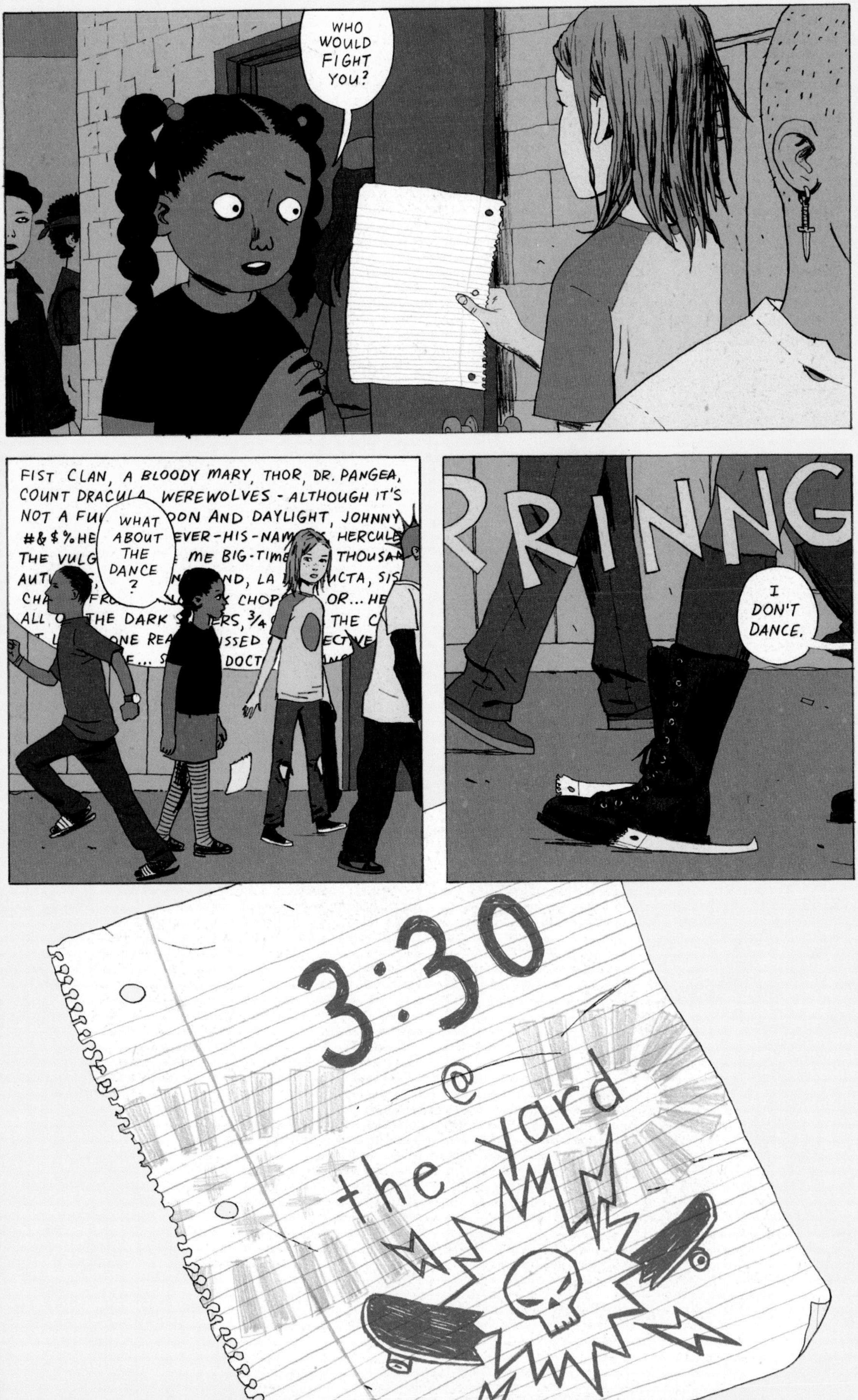
WHO WOULD FIGHT YOU?
FIST CLAN, A BLOODY MARY, THOR, DR. PANGEA,
COUNT DRACULA, WEREWOLVES - ALTHOUGH IT'S
WHAT ABOUT THE DANCE?
RRINNG
I DON'T DANCE.
3:30 @ the yard

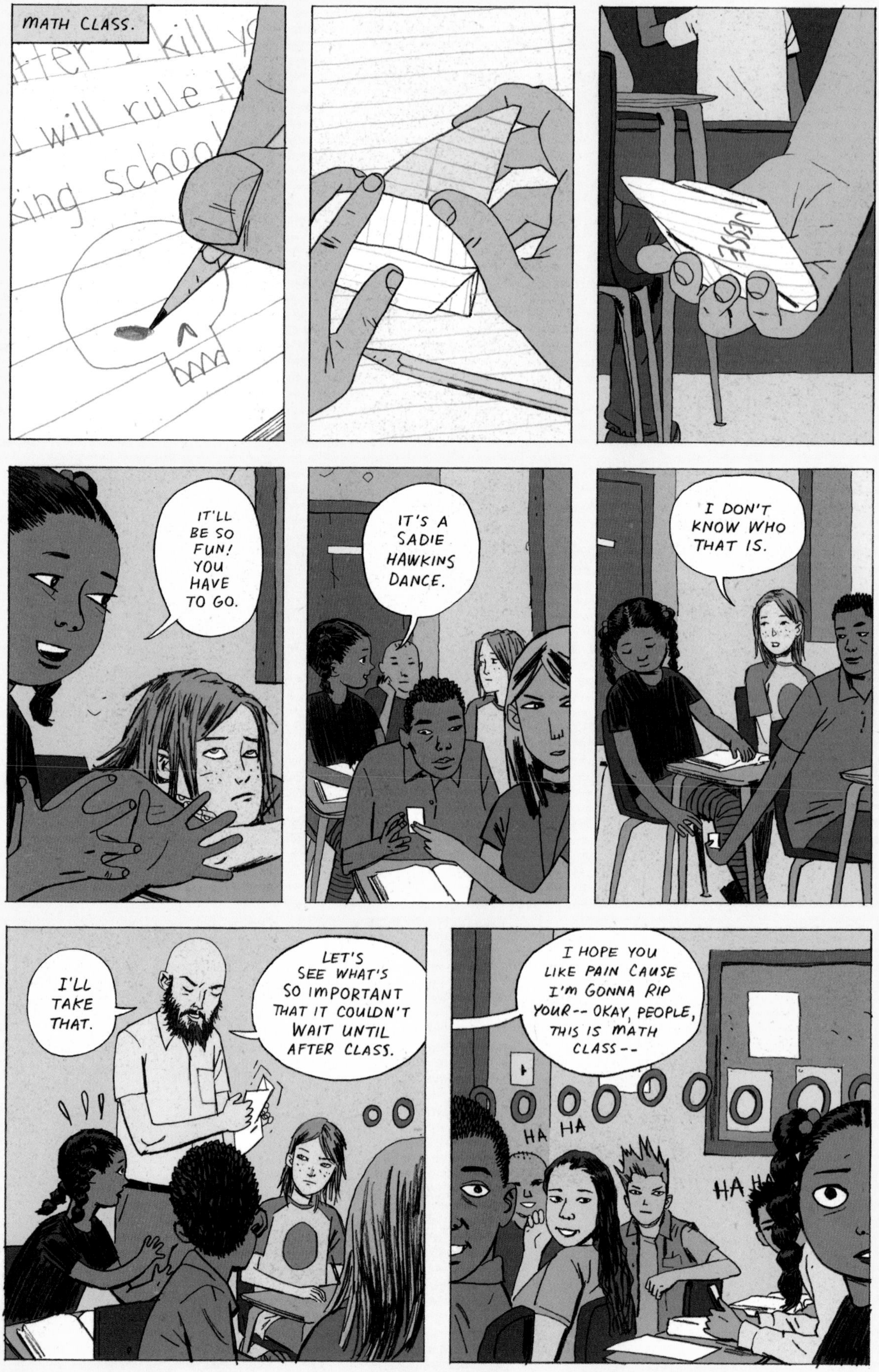
MATH CLASS.
After I kill y
I will rule t
king schoo
JESSE
IT'LL BE SO FUN! YOU HAVE TO GO.
IT'S A SADIE HAWKINS DANCE.
I DON'T KNOW WHO THAT IS.
I'LL TAKE THAT.
LET'S SEE WHAT'S SO IMPORTANT THAT IT COULDN'T WAIT UNTIL AFTER CLASS.
I HOPE YOU LIKE PAIN CAUSE I'M GONNA RIP YOUR-- OKAY, PEOPLE, THIS IS MATH CLASS--
HA HA
HA

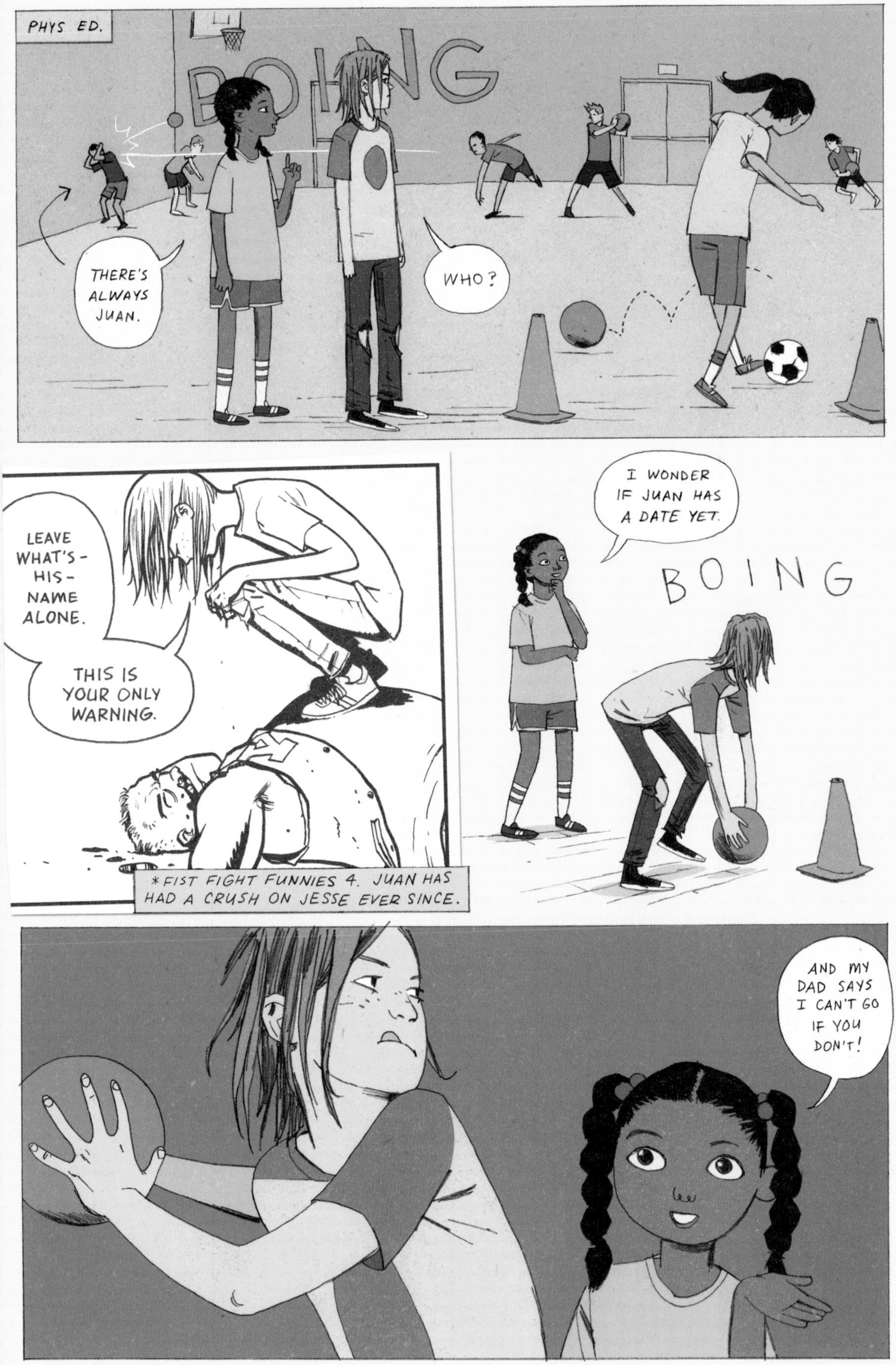
PHYS ED.
BOING
THERE'S ALWAYS JUAN.
WHO?
LEAVE WHAT'S-HIS-NAME ALONE.
THIS IS YOUR ONLY WARNING.
*FIST FIGHT FUNNIES 4. JUAN HAS HAD A CRUSH ON JESSE EVER SINCE.
I WONDER IF JUAN HAS A DATE YET.
BOING
AND MY DAD SAYS I CAN'T GO IF YOU DON'T!

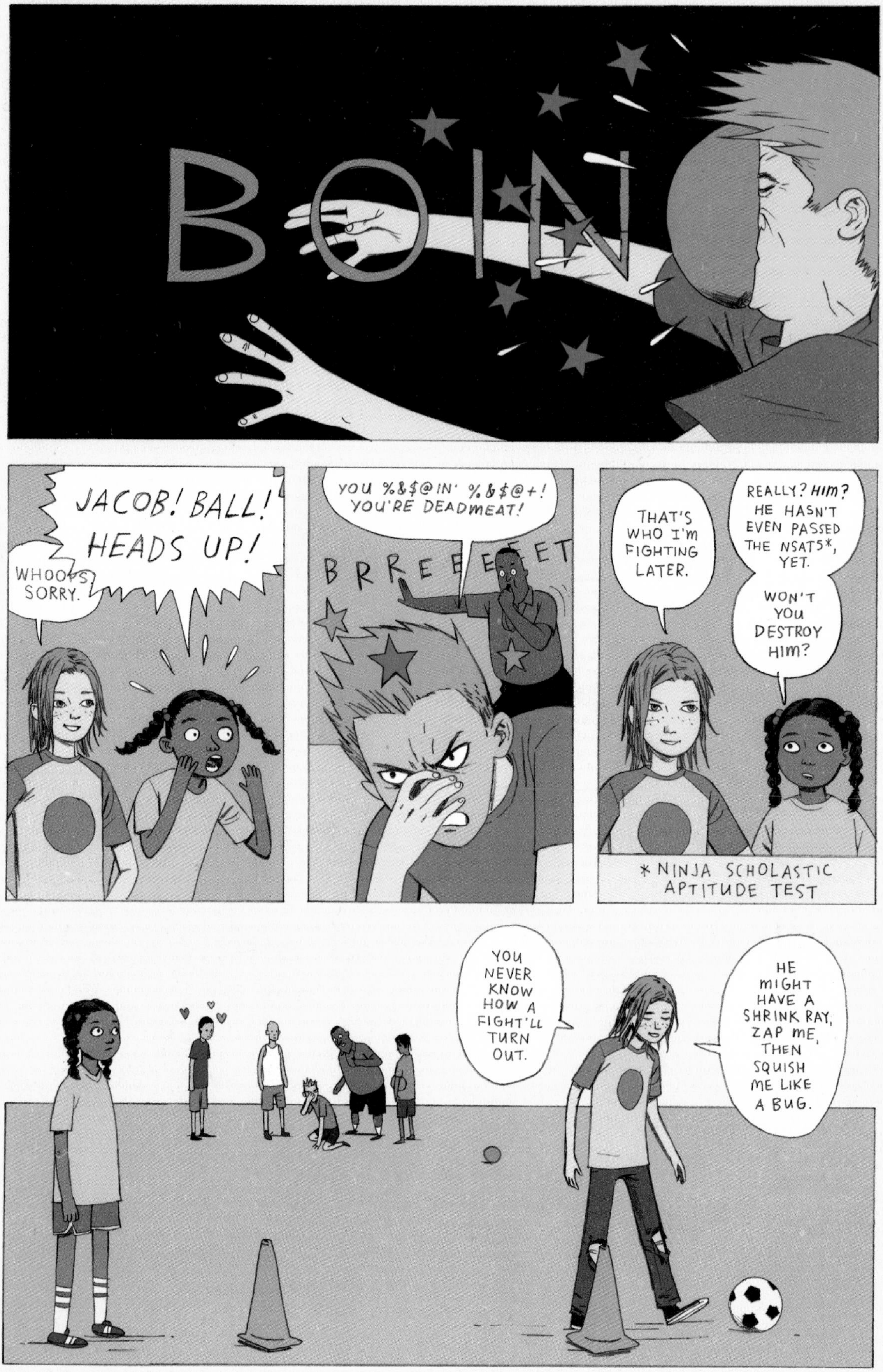
BOING
JACOB! BALL! HEADS UP!
WHOOPS SORRY.
YOU %&$@IN' %&$@+! YOU'RE DEADMEAT!
BRREEEEET
THAT'S WHO I'M FIGHTING LATER.
REALLY? HIM? HE HASN'T EVEN PASSED THE NSATS*, YET.
WON'T YOU DESTROY HIM?
* NINJA SCHOLASTIC APTITUDE TEST
YOU NEVER KNOW HOW A FIGHT'LL TURN OUT.
HE MIGHT HAVE A SHRINK RAY, ZAP ME, THEN SQUISH ME LIKE A BUG.

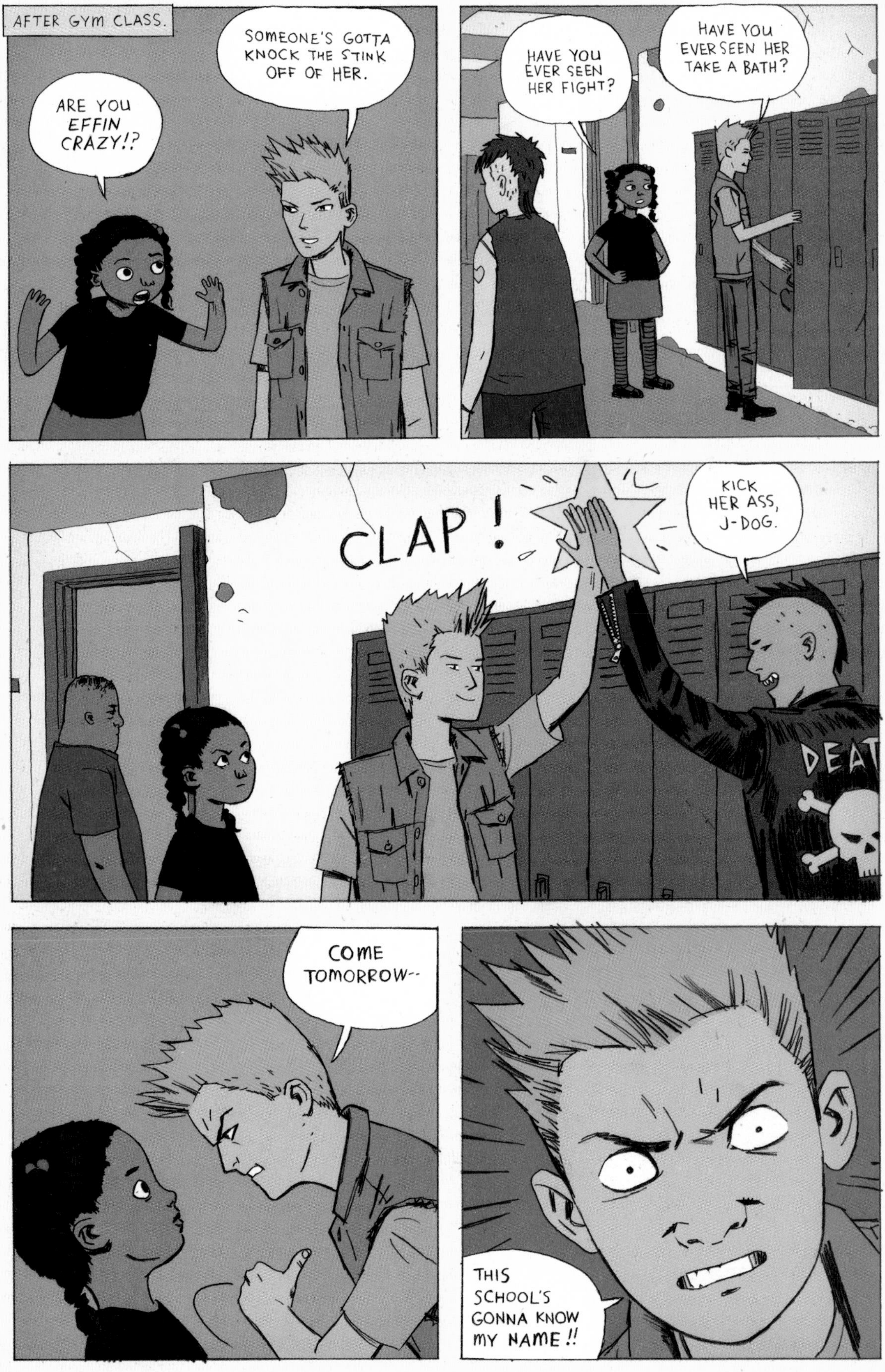

AFTER GYM CLASS.
ARE YOU EFFIN CRAZY!?
SOMEONE'S GOTTA KNOCK THE STINK OFF OF HER.
HAVE YOU EVER SEEN HER FIGHT?
HAVE YOU EVER SEEN HER TAKE A BATH?
CLAP!
KICK HER ASS, J-DOG.
DEAT
COME TOMORROW--
THIS SCHOOL'S GONNA KNOW MY NAME!!

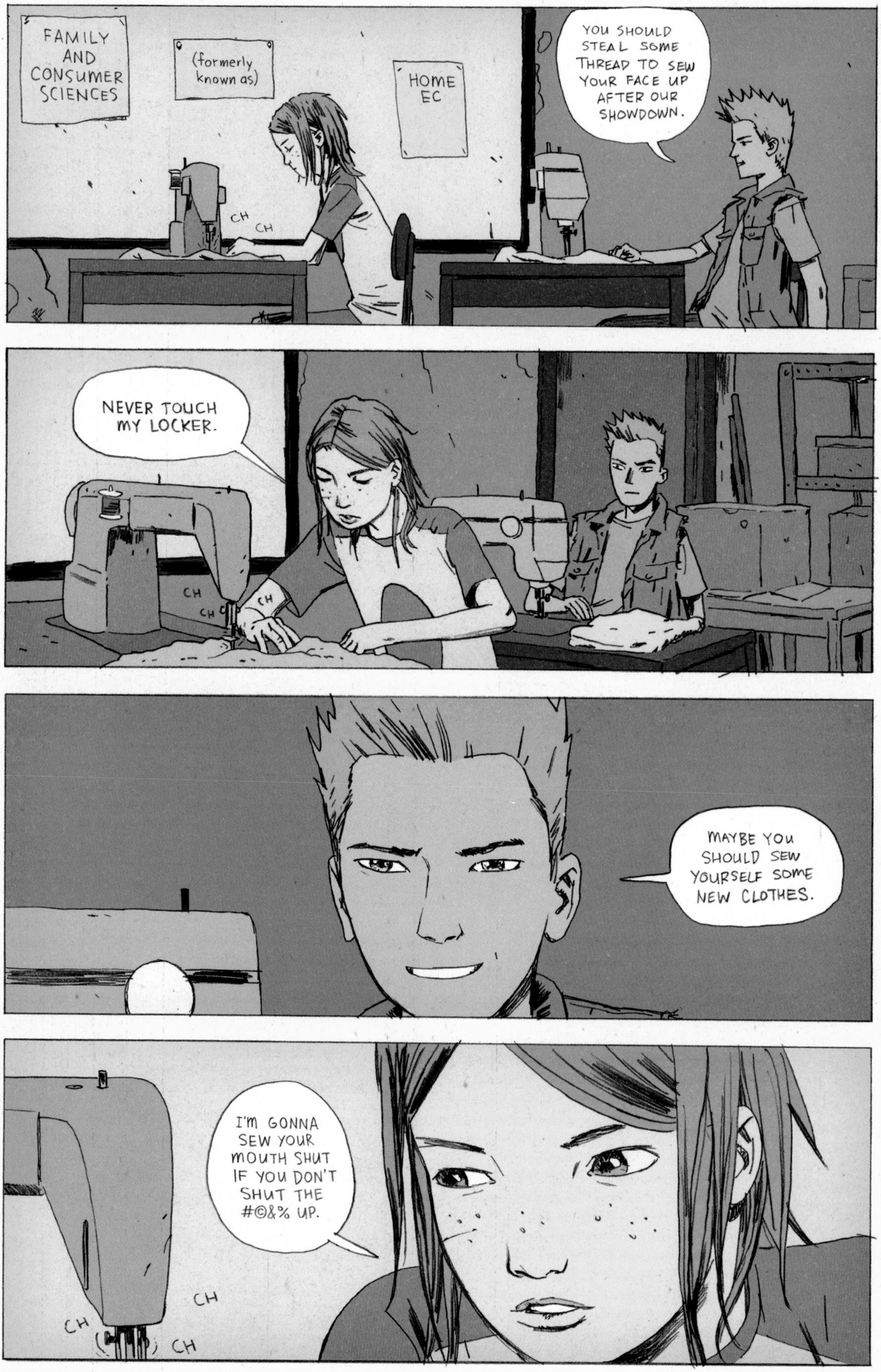
FAMILY AND CONSUMER SCIENCES
(formerly known as)
HOME EC
CH CH
YOU SHOULD STEAL SOME THREAD TO SEW YOUR FACE UP AFTER OUR SHOWDOWN.
NEVER TOUCH MY LOCKER.
CH CH CH
MAYBE YOU SHOULD SEW YOURSELF SOME NEW CLOTHES.
I'M GONNA SEW YOUR MOUTH SHUT IF YOU DON'T SHUT THE #©&% UP.
CH CH CH

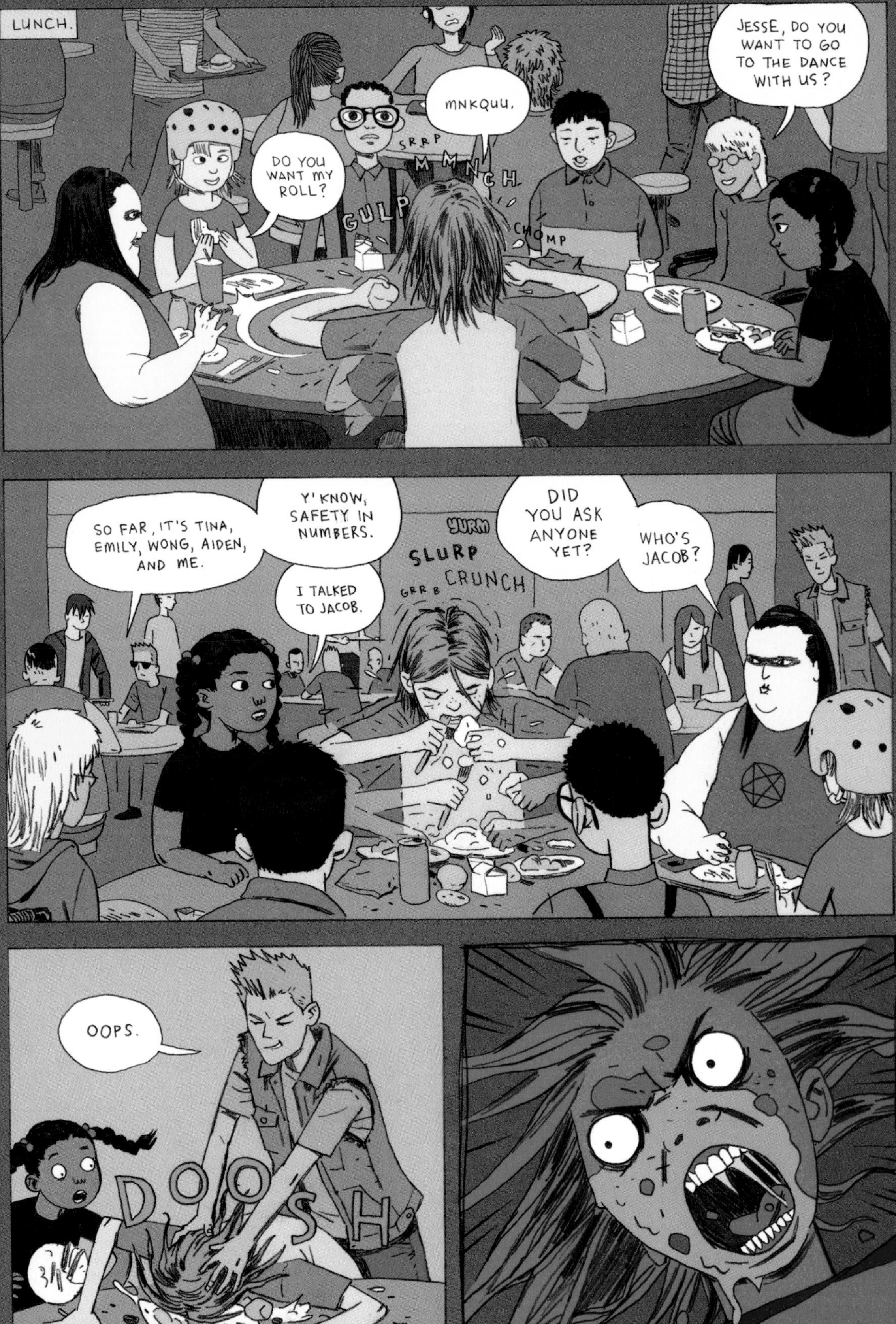
LUNCH.
DO YOU WANT MY ROLL?
MNKQUU.
SRRP
MMNCH
GULP
CHOMP
JESSE, DO YOU WANT TO GO TO THE DANCE WITH US?
SO FAR, IT'S TINA, EMILY, WONG, AIDEN, AND ME.
Y'KNOW, SAFETY IN NUMBERS.
I TALKED TO JACOB.
YURM
SLURP
GRRB
CRUNCH
DID YOU ASK ANYONE YET?
WHO'S JACOB?
OOPS.
DOOSH

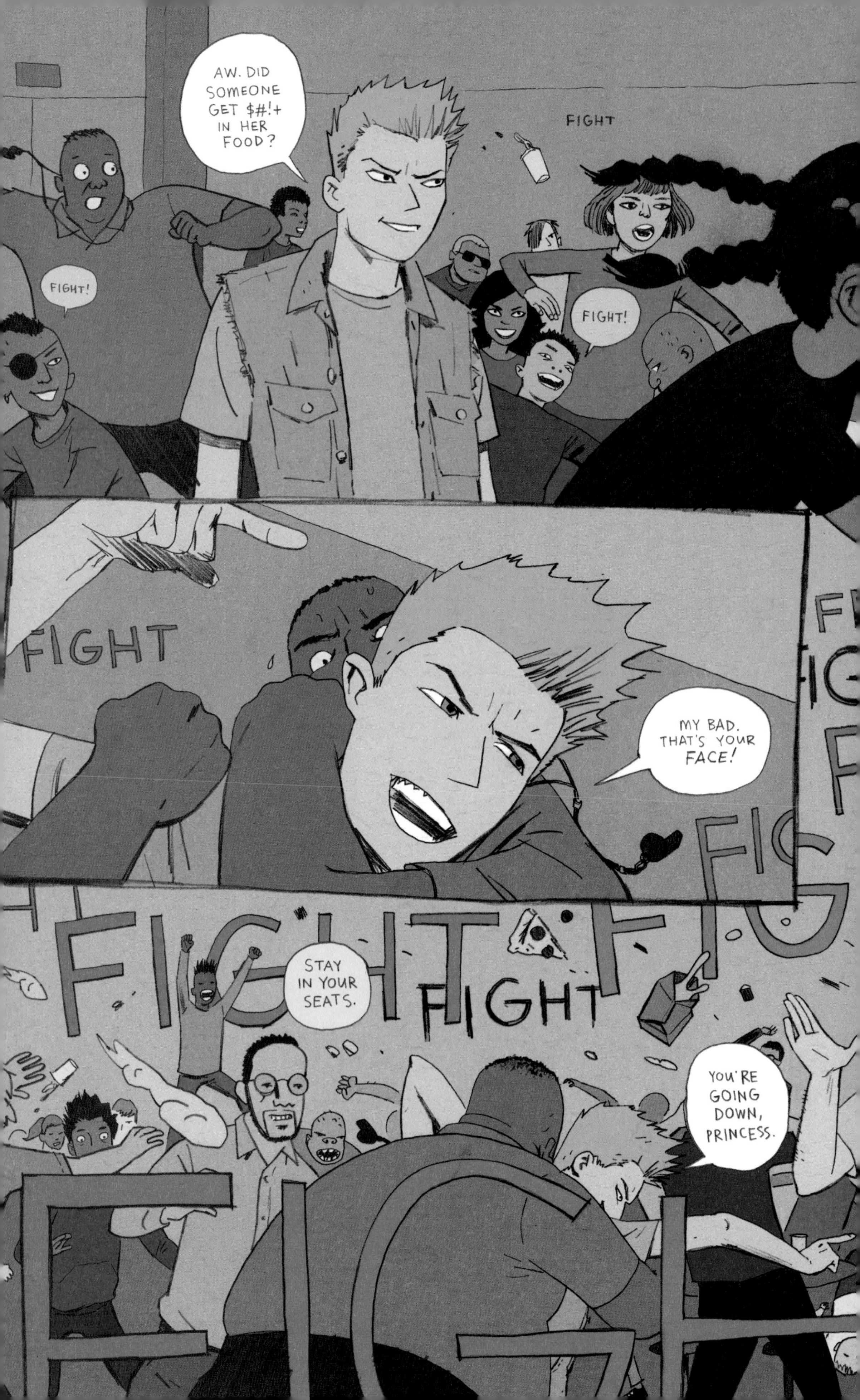
AW. DID SOMEONE GET $#!+ IN HER FOOD?
FIGHT
FIGHT!
FIGHT!
FIGHT
MY BAD. THAT'S YOUR FACE!
STAY IN YOUR SEATS.
FIGHT
YOU'RE GOING DOWN, PRINCESS.

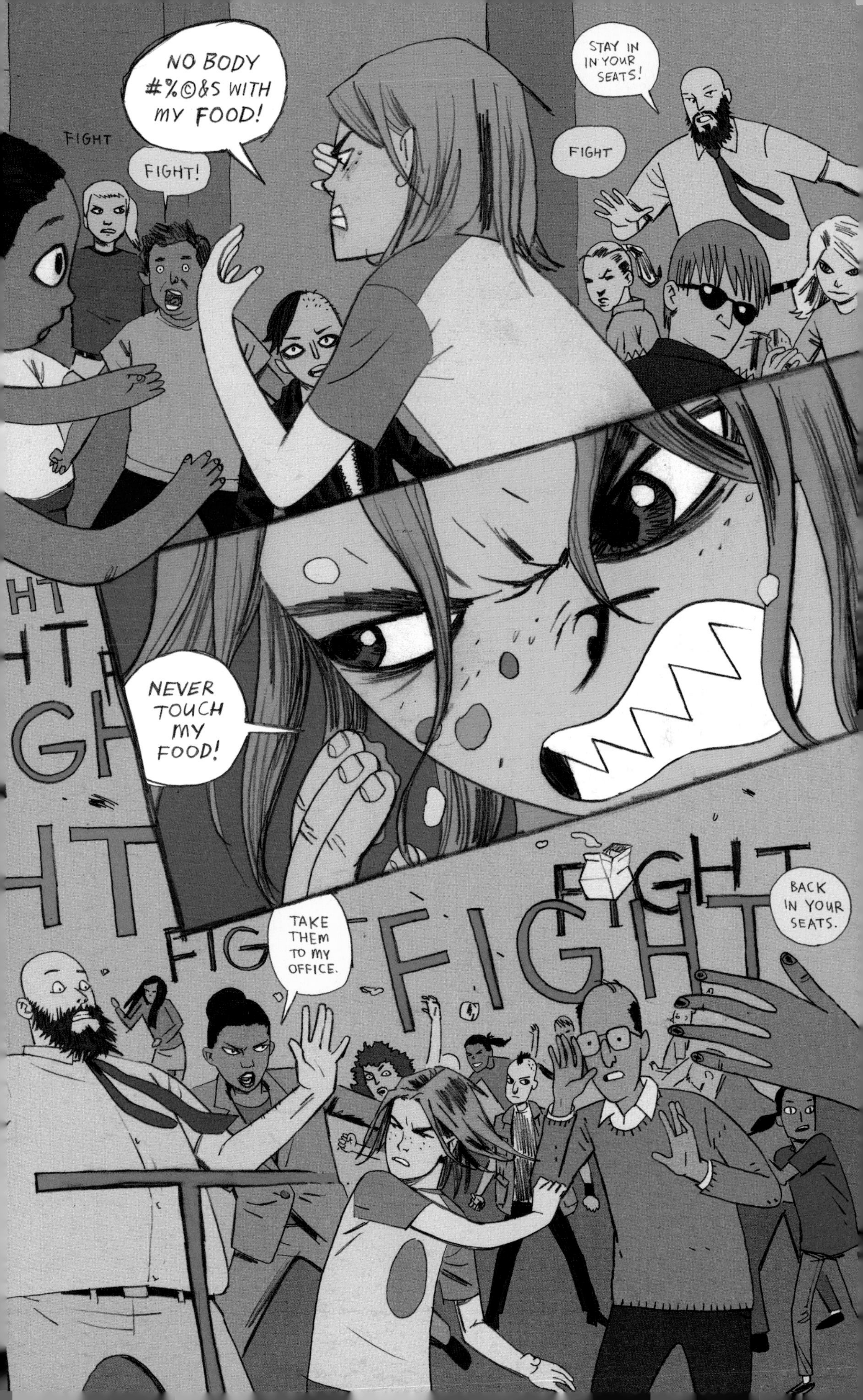
FIGHT
NO BODY #%©&S WITH MY FOOD!
FIGHT!
STAY IN IN YOUR SEATS!
FIGHT
NEVER TOUCH MY FOOD!
TAKE THEM TO MY OFFICE.
FIGHT
FIGHT
BACK IN YOUR SEATS.

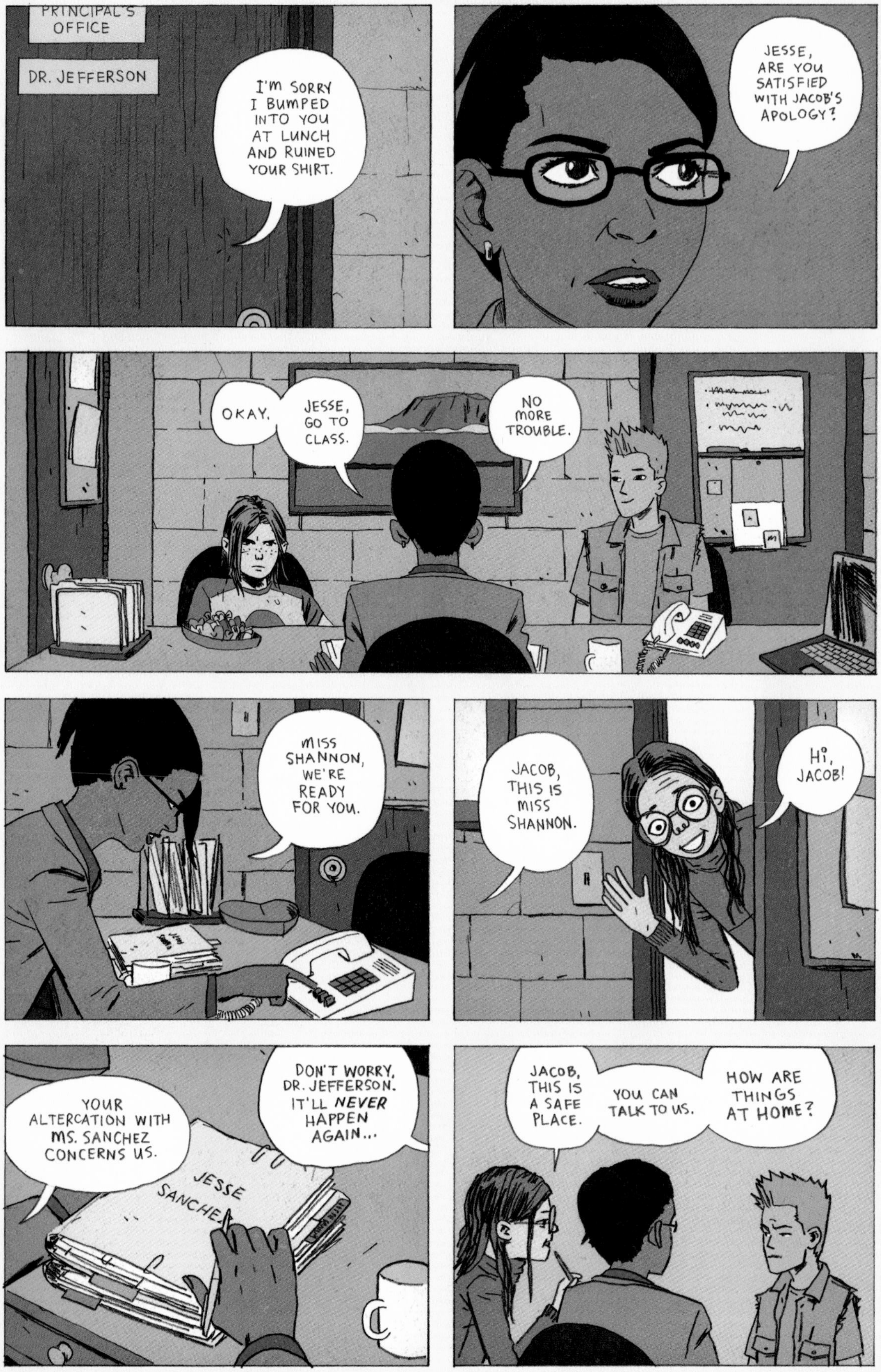
PRINCIPAL'S OFFICE
DR. JEFFERSON
I'M SORRY I BUMPED INTO YOU AT LUNCH AND RUINED YOUR SHIRT.
JESSE, ARE YOU SATISFIED WITH JACOB'S APOLOGY?
OKAY.
JESSE, GO TO CLASS.
NO MORE TROUBLE.
MISS SHANNON, WE'RE READY FOR YOU.
JACOB, THIS IS MISS SHANNON.
HI, JACOB!
YOUR ALTERCATION WITH MS. SANCHEZ CONCERNS US.
JESSE SANCHE
DON'T WORRY, DR. JEFFERSON. IT'LL *NEVER* HAPPEN AGAIN...
JACOB, THIS IS A SAFE PLACE.
YOU CAN TALK TO US.
HOW ARE THINGS AT HOME?

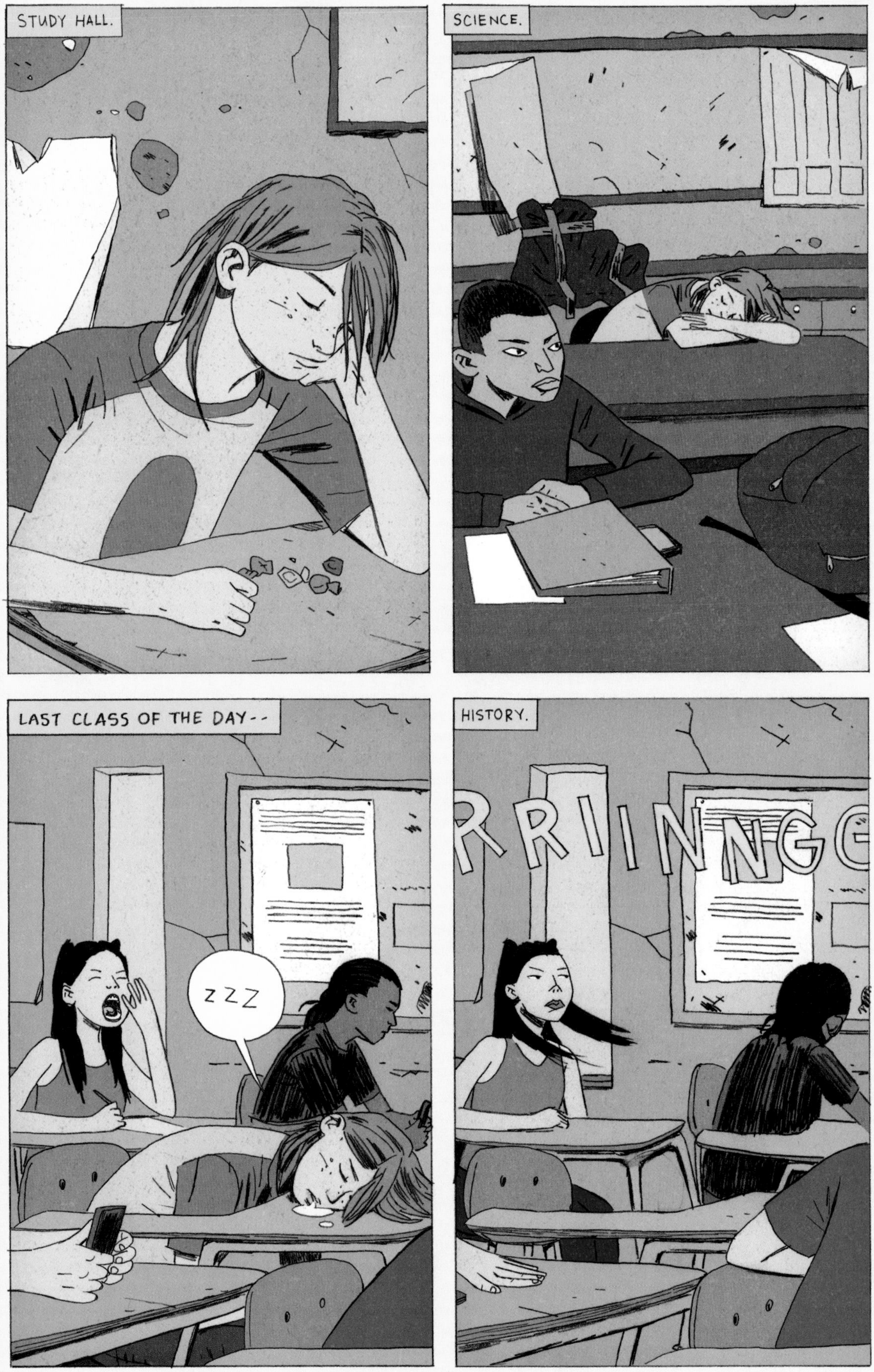
STUDY HALL.
SCIENCE.
LAST CLASS OF THE DAY--
ZZZ
HISTORY.
RRIINNGG

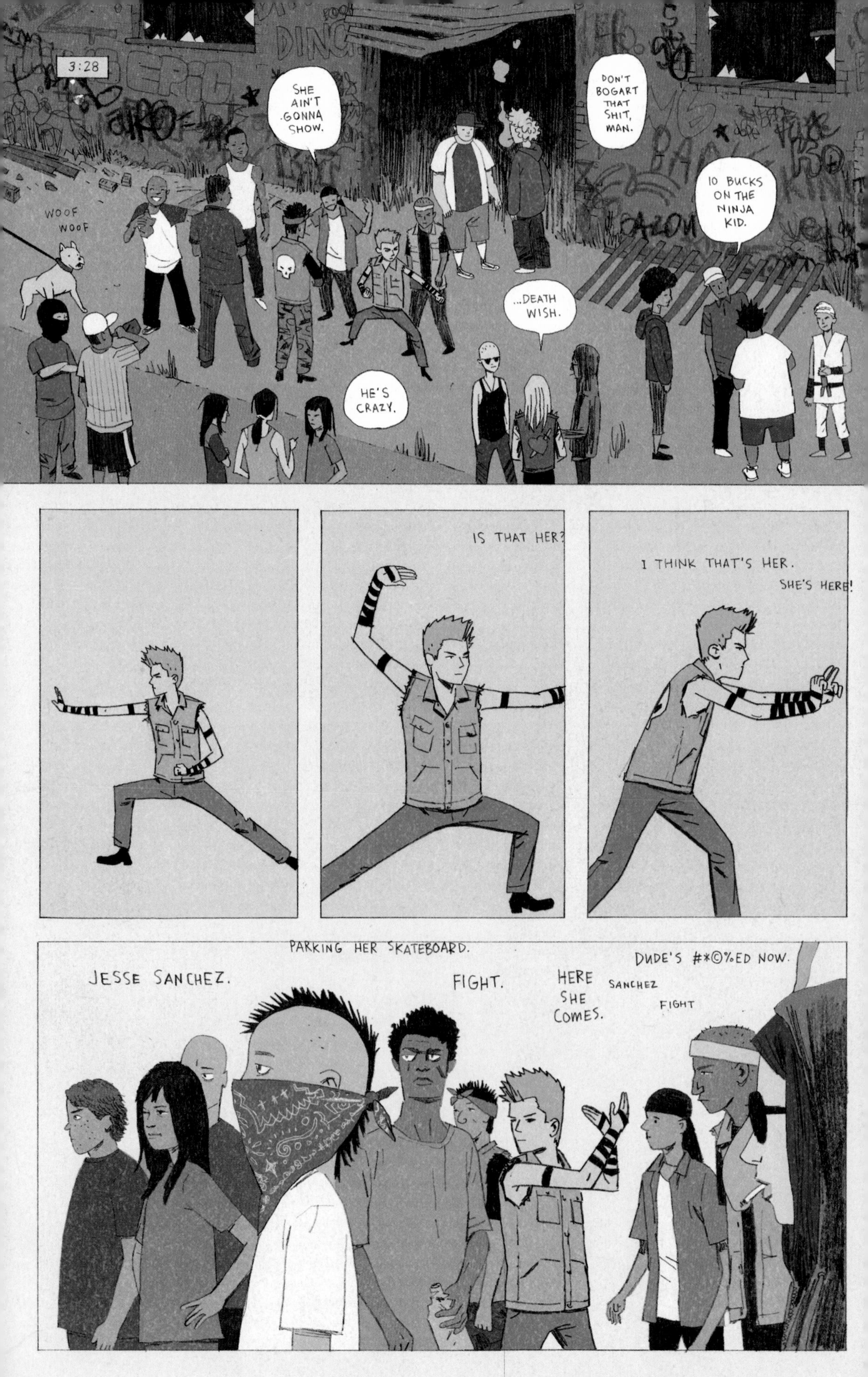
3:28
SHE AIN'T GONNA SHOW.
DON'T BOGART THAT SHIT, MAN.
10 BUCKS ON THE NINJA KID.
WOOF WOOF
...DEATH WISH.
HE'S CRAZY.
IS THAT HER?
I THINK THAT'S HER.
SHE'S HERE!
JESSE SANCHEZ.
PARKING HER SKATEBOARD.
FIGHT.
HERE SHE COMES.
SANCHEZ
FIGHT
DUDE'S #*©%ED NOW.

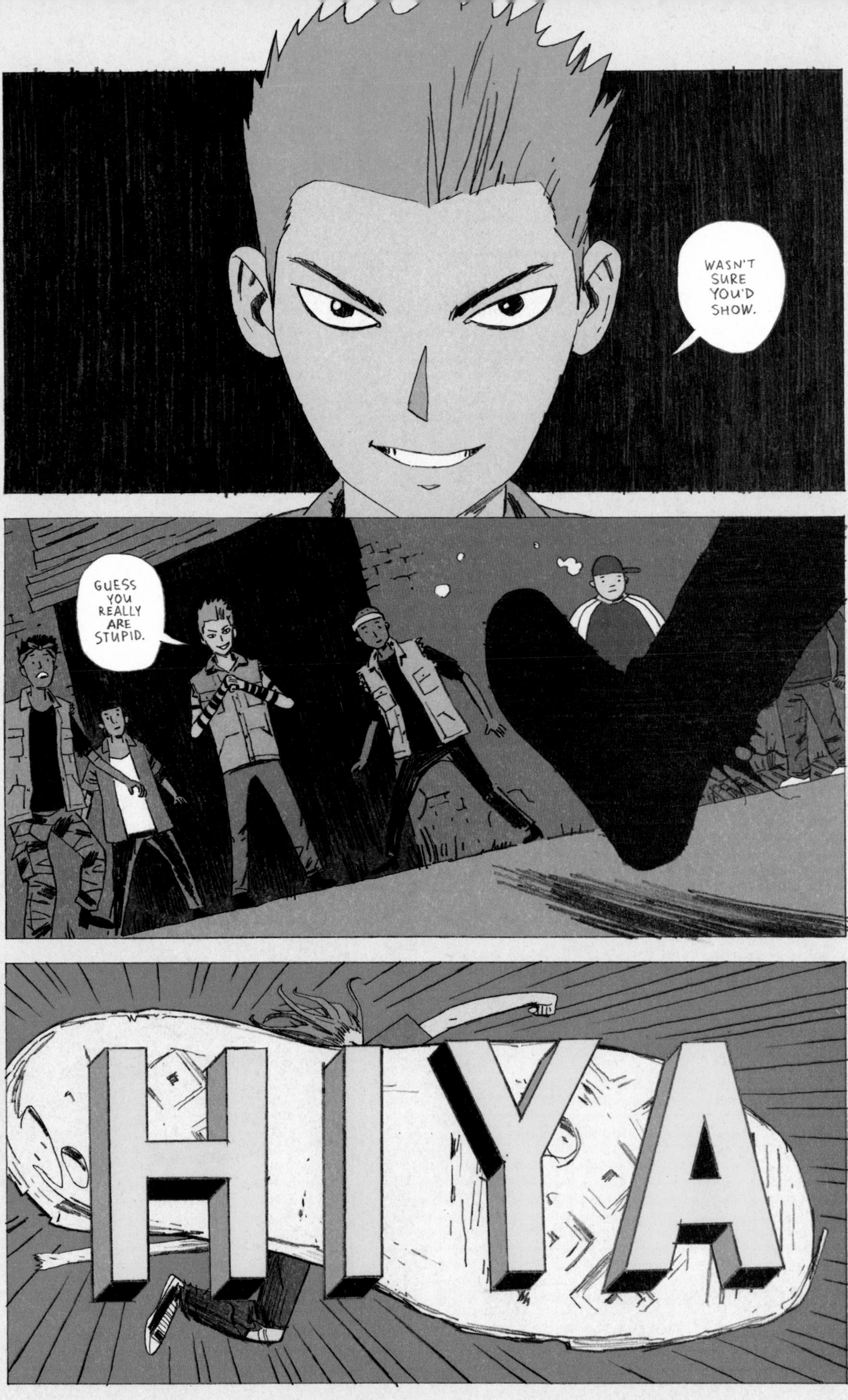
WASN'T SURE YOU'D SHOW.
GUESS YOU REALLY ARE STUPID.
HIYA

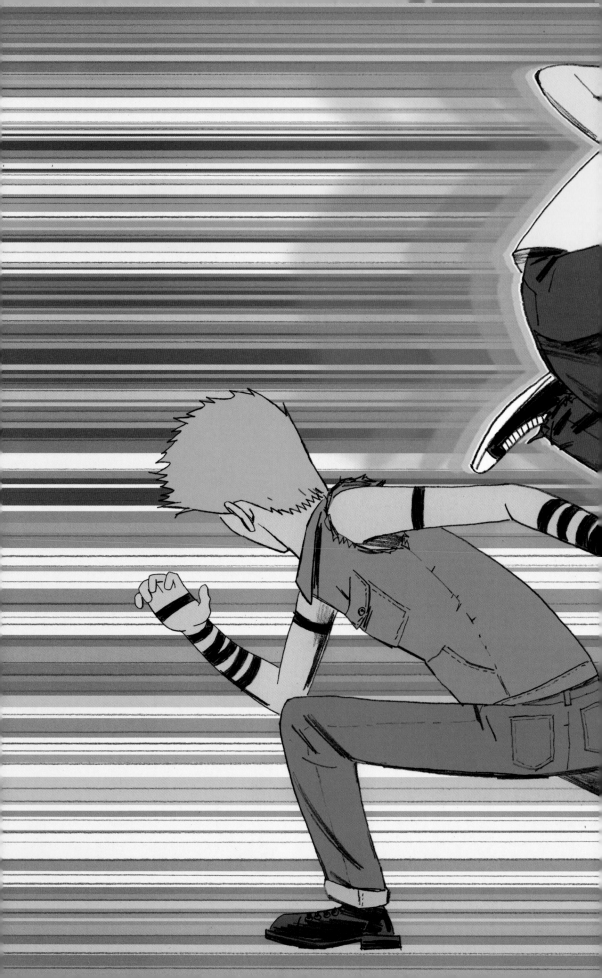

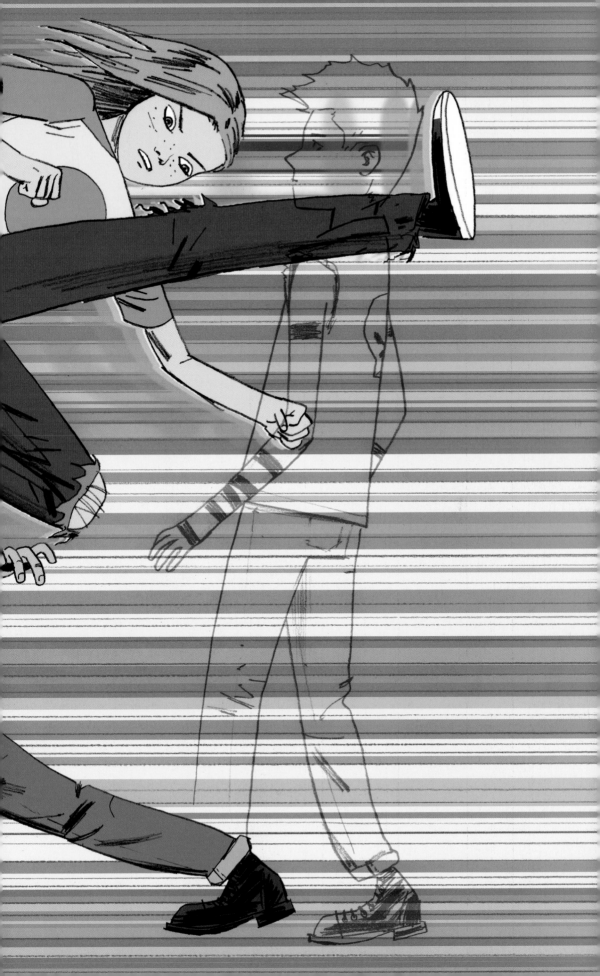

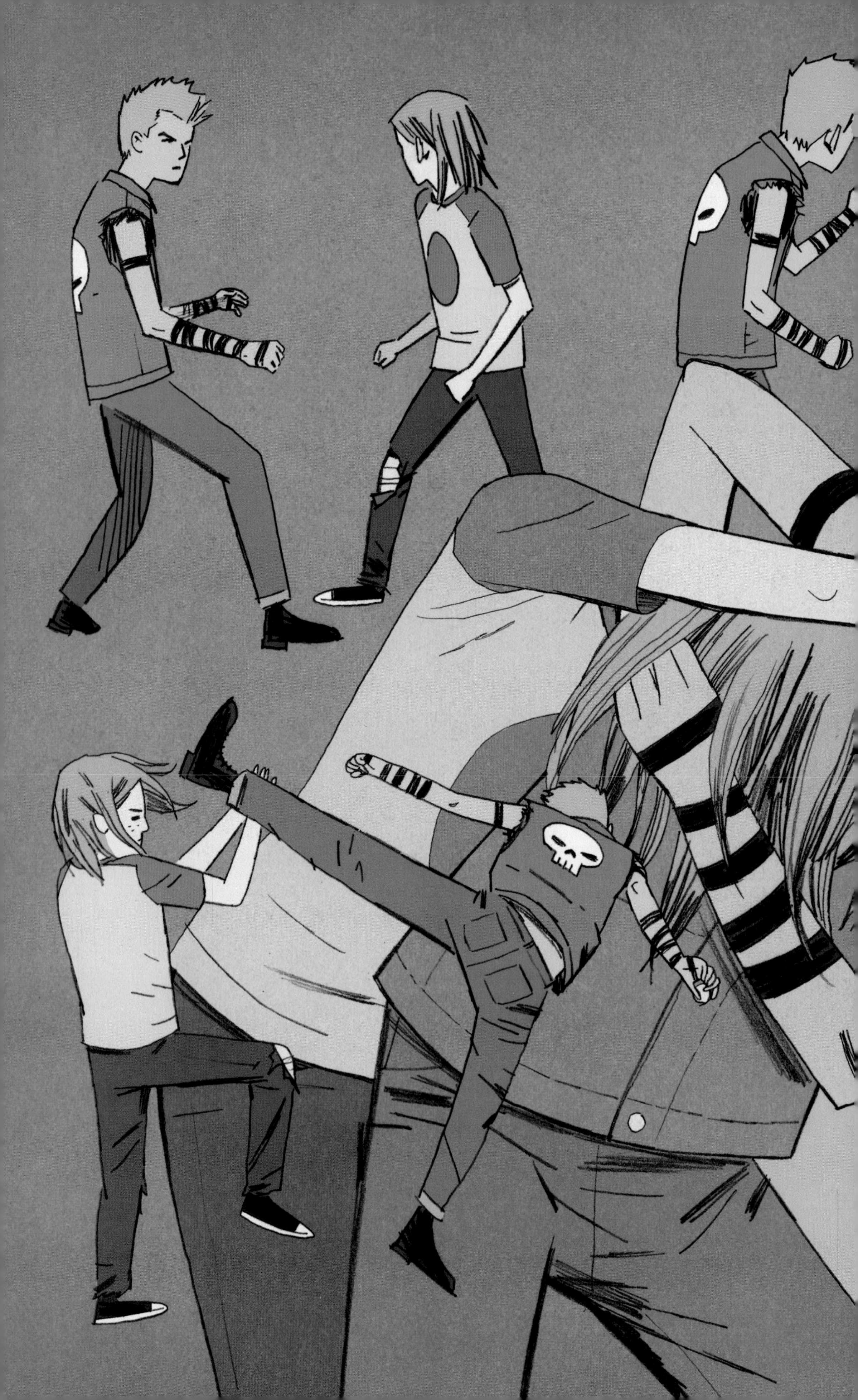

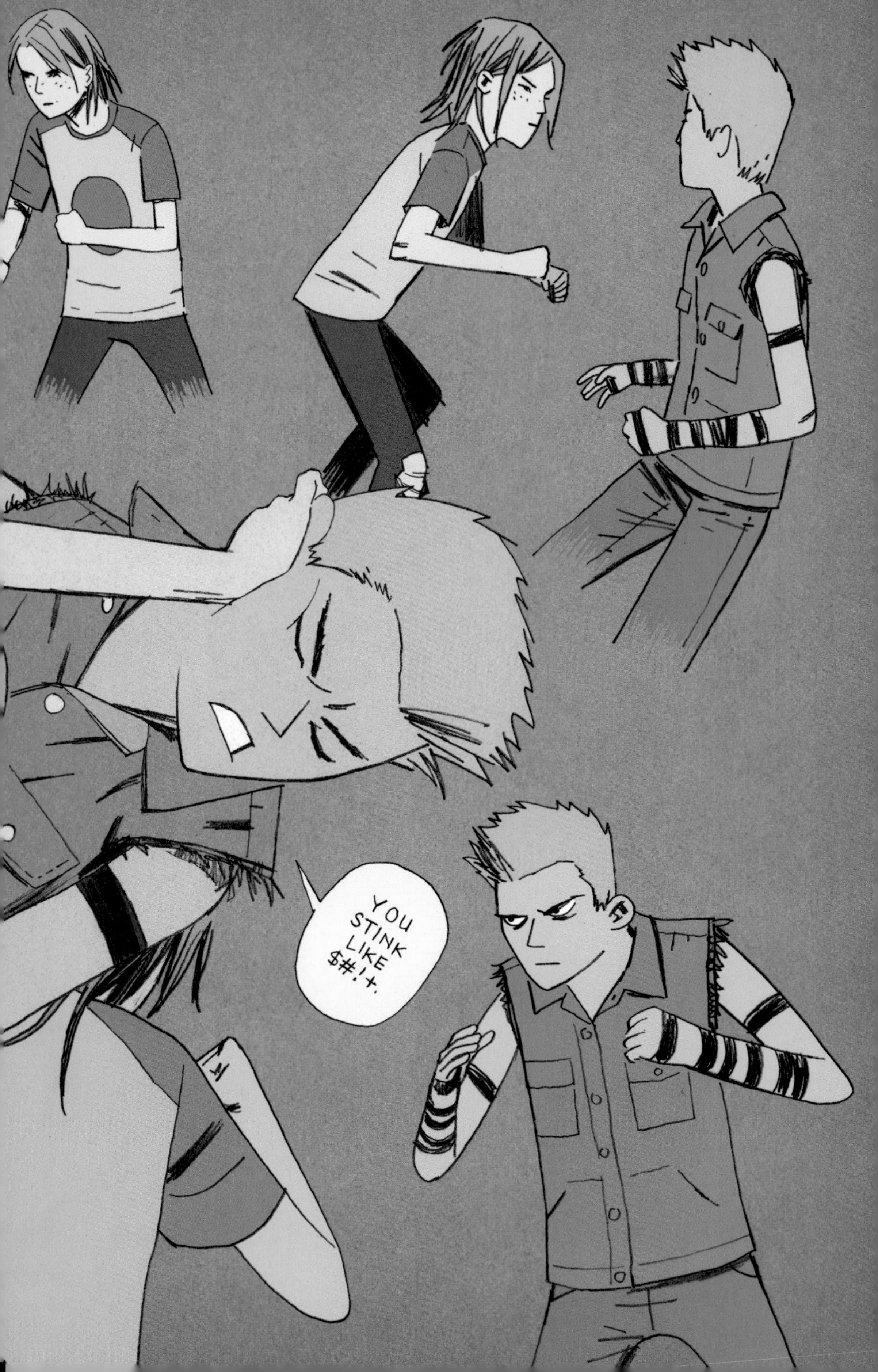
YOU STINK LIKE $#!+.

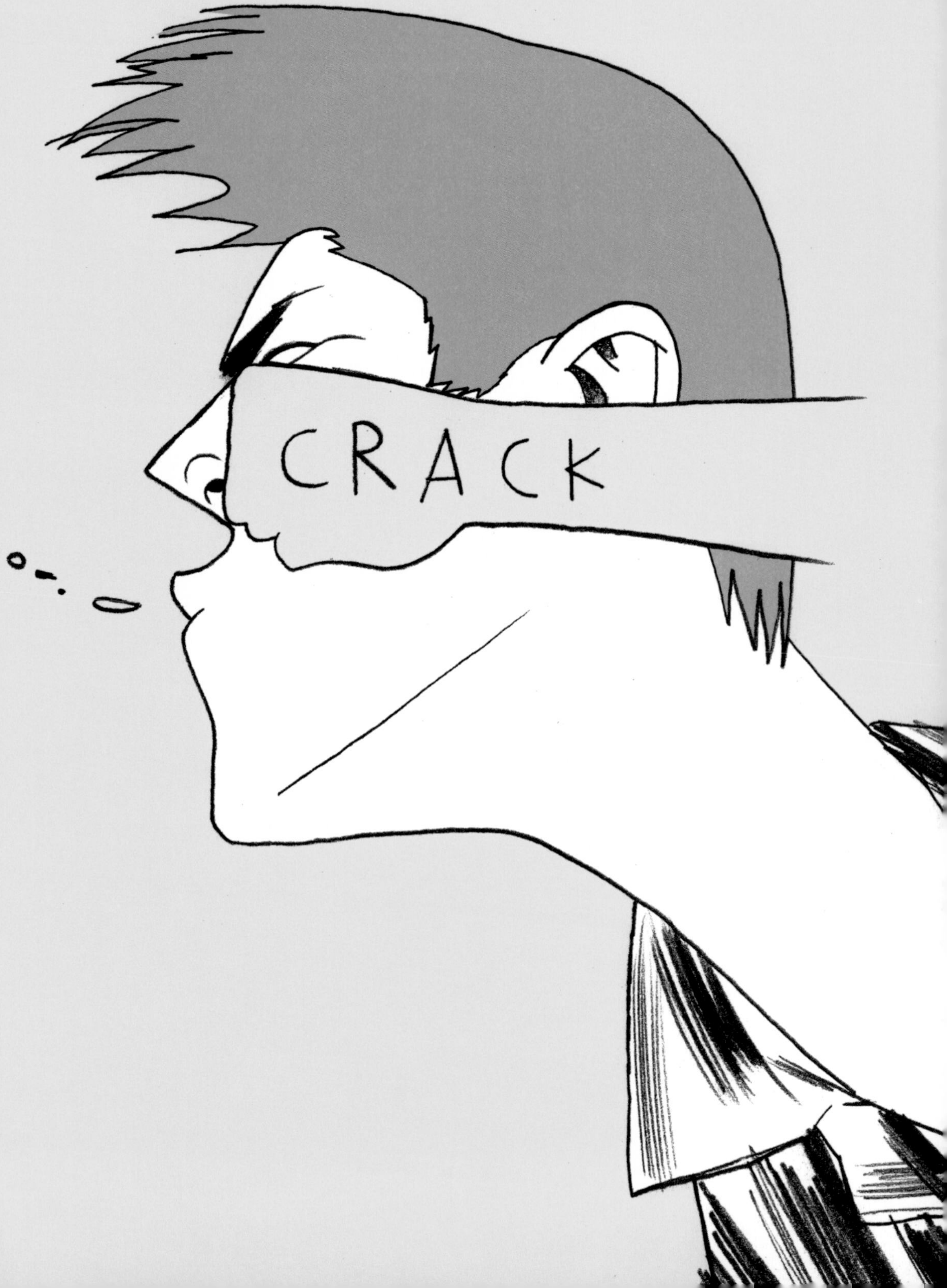
CRACK

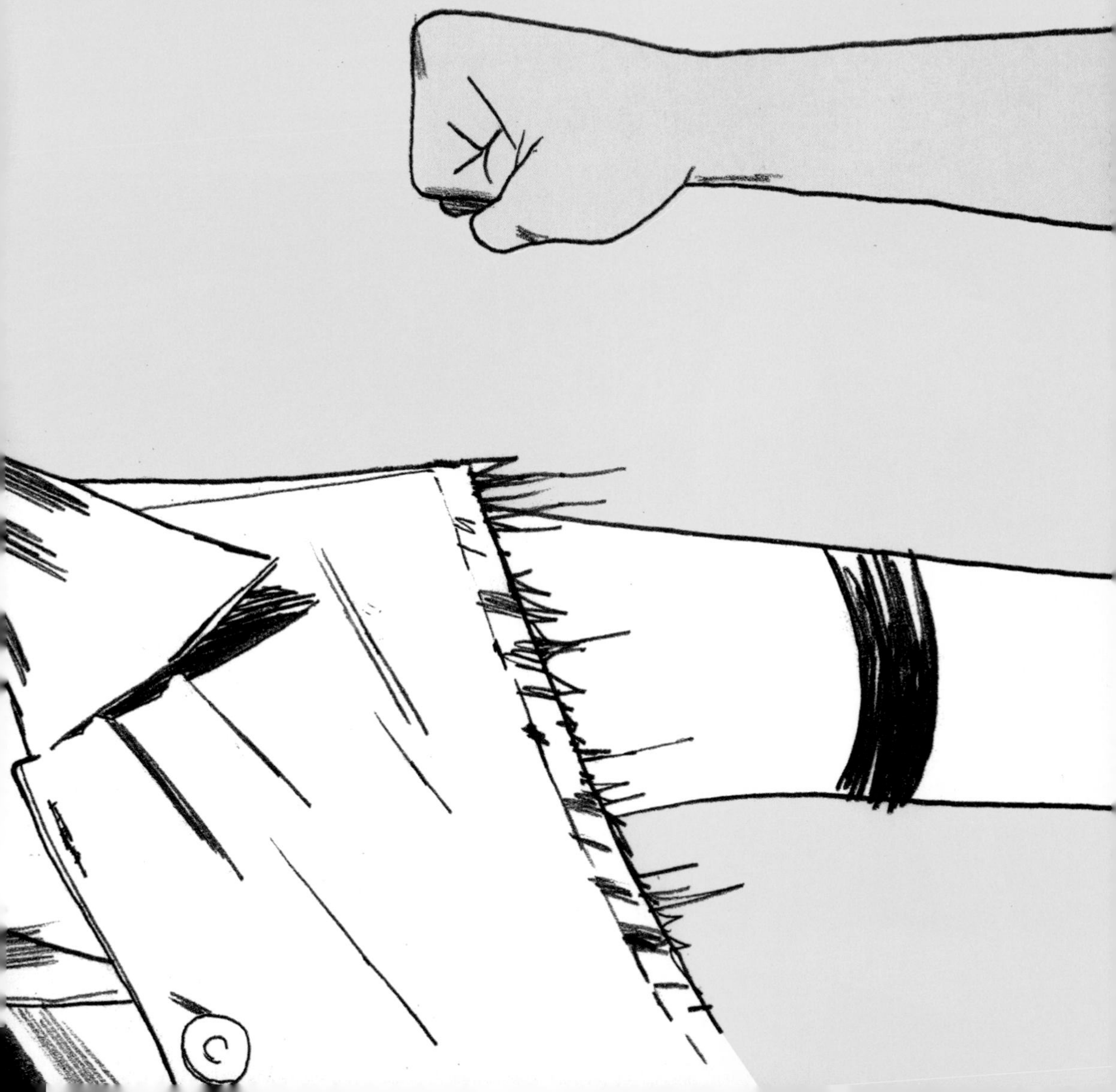

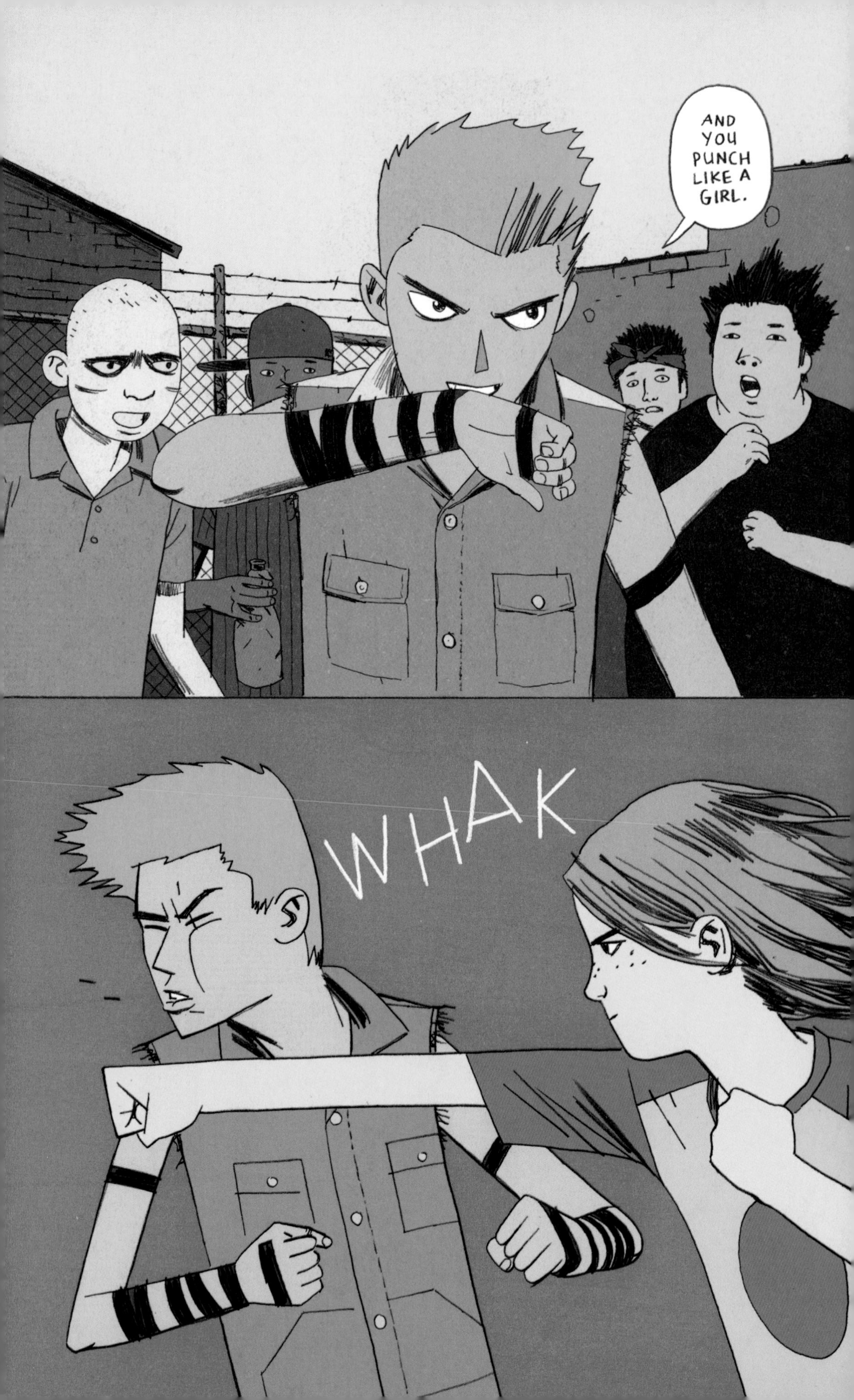
AND YOU PUNCH LIKE A GIRL.
WHAK

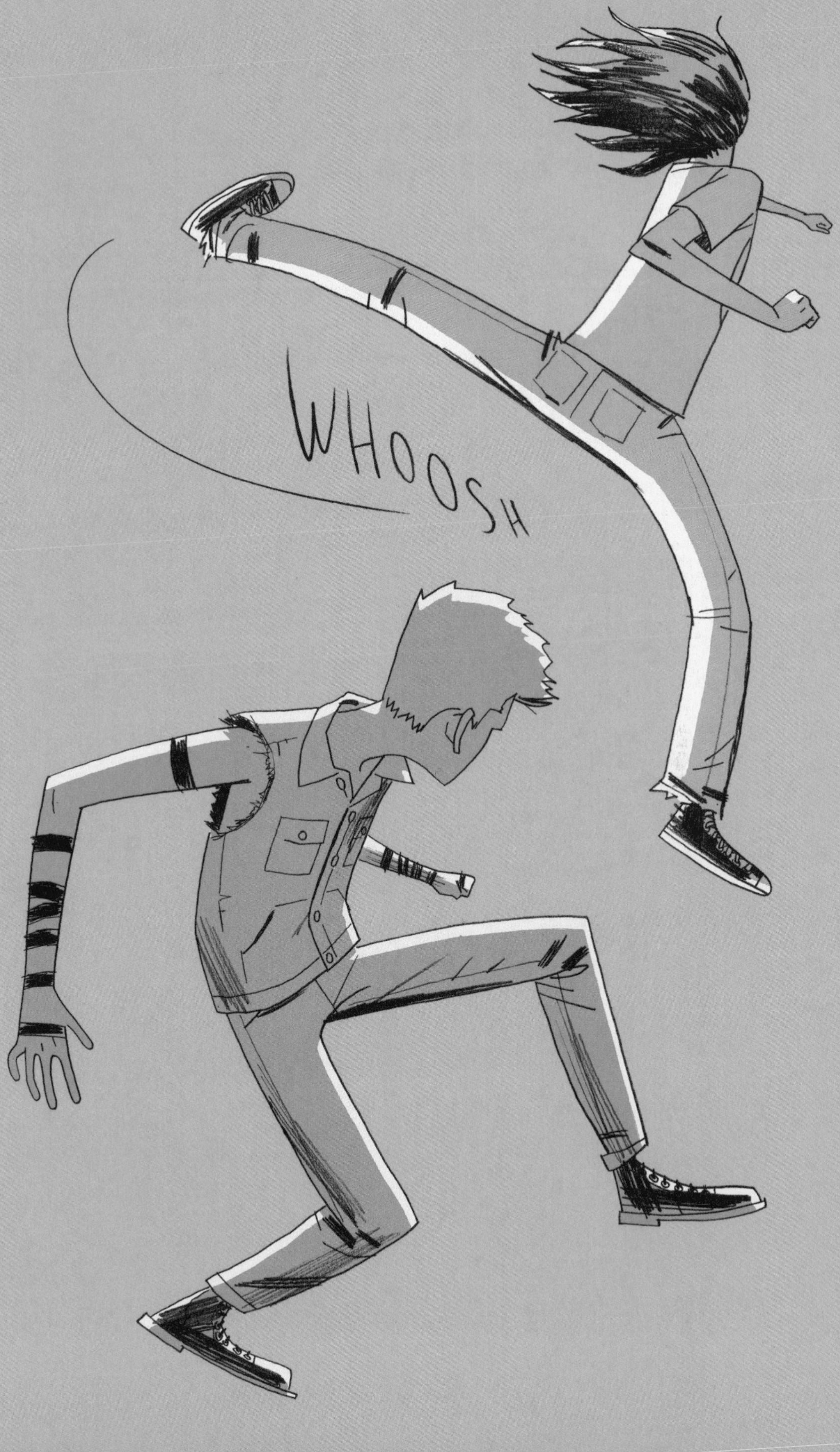
WHOOSH

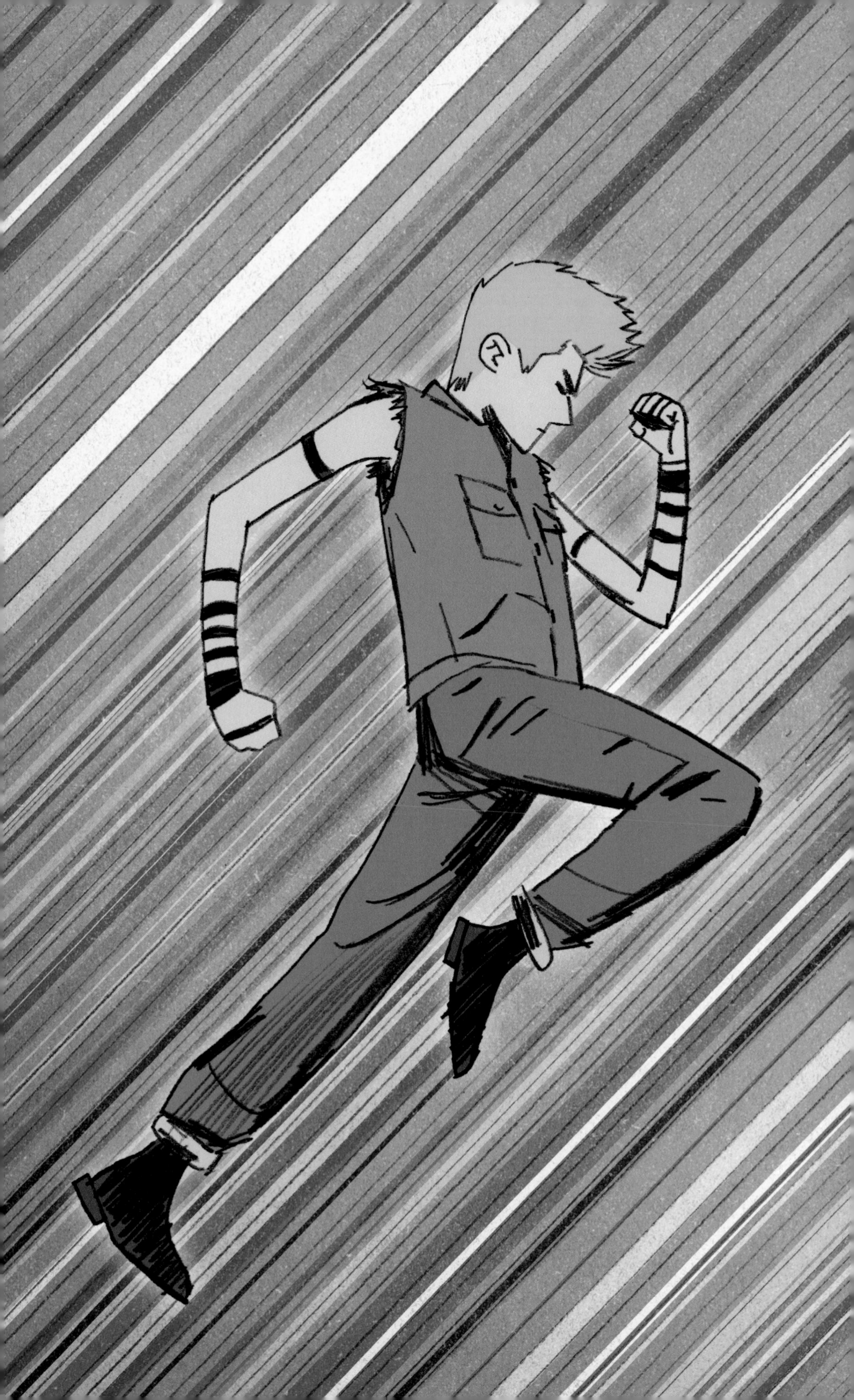

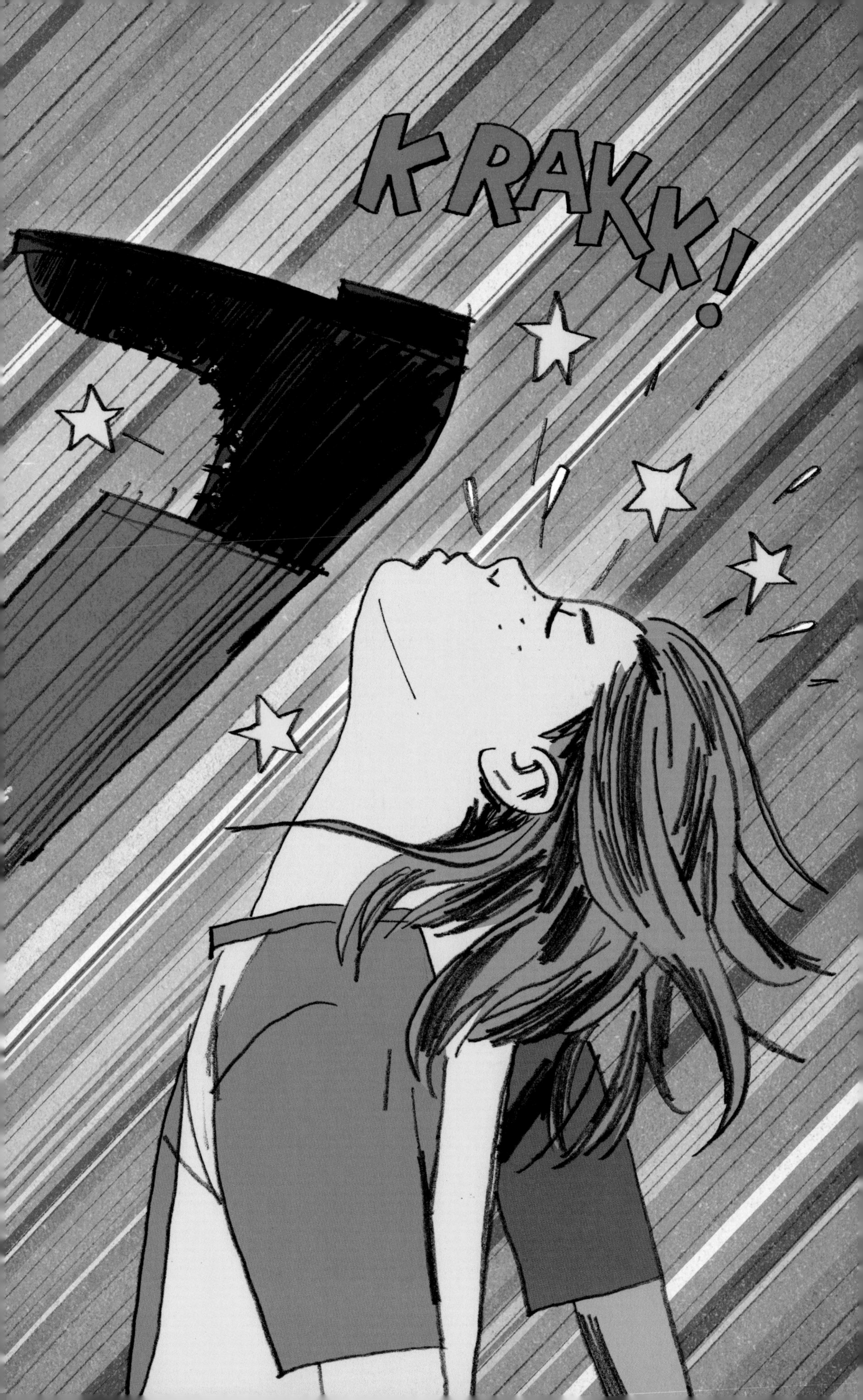
KRAKK!

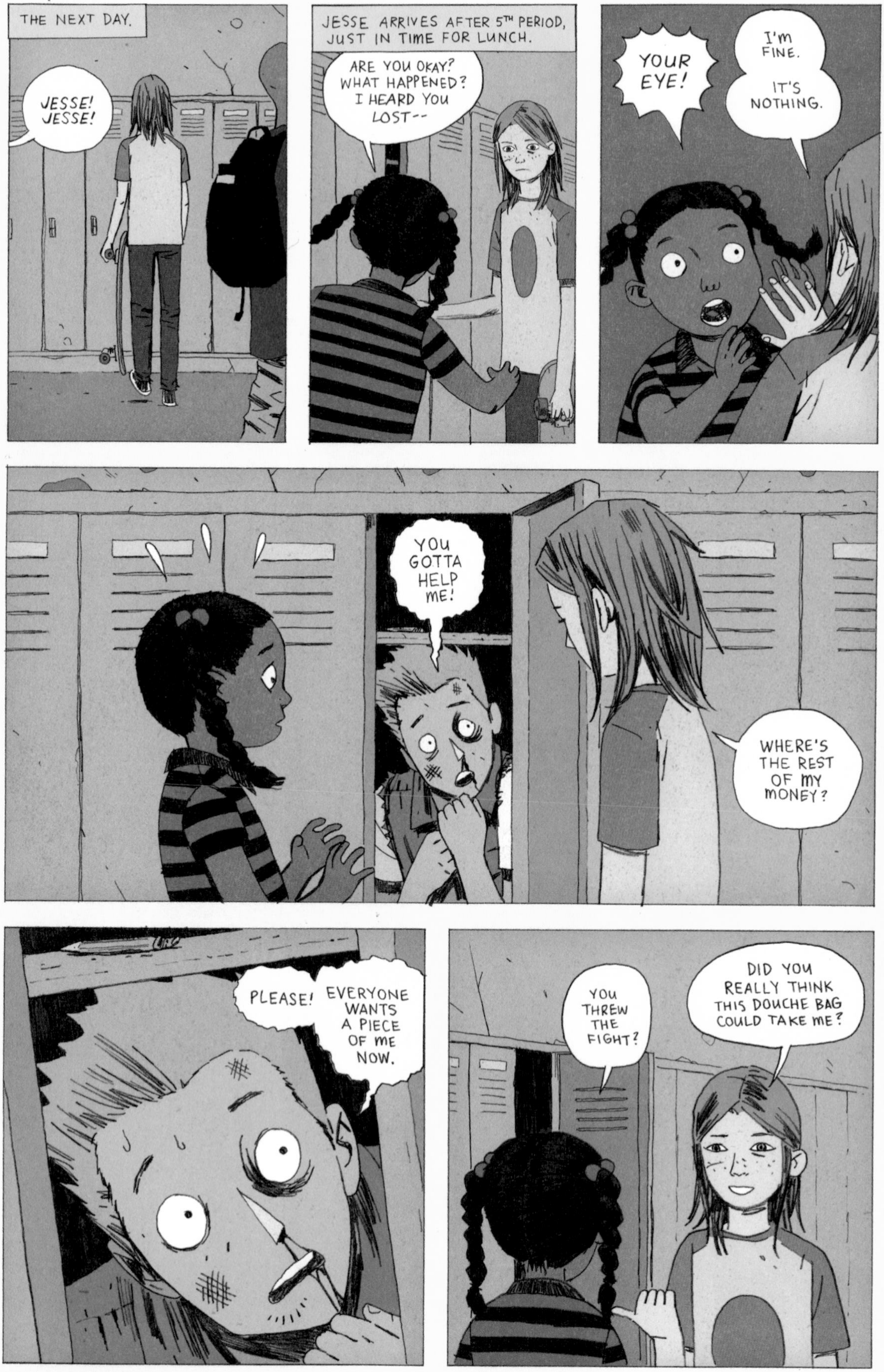
THE NEXT DAY.
JESSE! JESSE!
JESSE ARRIVES AFTER 5TH PERIOD, JUST IN TIME FOR LUNCH.
ARE YOU OKAY? WHAT HAPPENED? I HEARD YOU LOST--
YOUR EYE!
I'm FINE.
IT'S NOTHING.
YOU GOTTA HELP ME!
WHERE'S THE REST OF MY MONEY?
PLEASE!
EVERYONE WANTS A PIECE OF ME NOW.
YOU THREW THE FIGHT?
DID YOU REALLY THINK THIS DOUCHE BAG COULD TAKE ME?

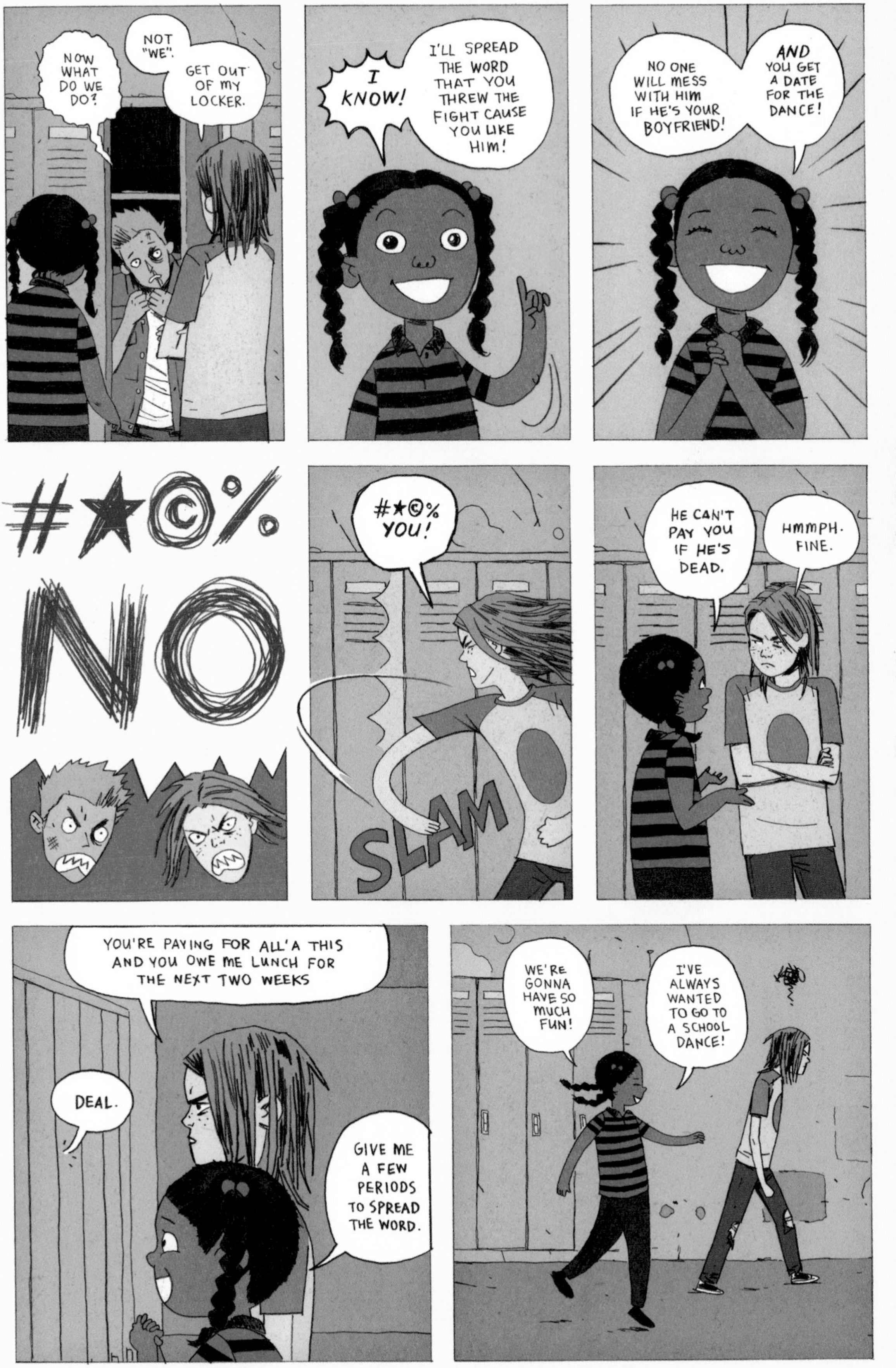
NOW WHAT DO WE DO?
NOT "WE".
GET OUT OF MY LOCKER.
I KNOW!
I'LL SPREAD THE WORD THAT YOU THREW THE FIGHT CAUSE YOU LIKE HIM!
NO ONE WILL MESS WITH HIM IF HE'S YOUR BOYFRIEND!
AND YOU GET A DATE FOR THE DANCE!
#★©% NO
#★©% YOU!
SLAM
HE CAN'T PAY YOU IF HE'S DEAD.
HMMPH. FINE.
YOU'RE PAYING FOR ALL'A THIS AND YOU OWE ME LUNCH FOR THE NEXT TWO WEEKS
DEAL.
GIVE ME A FEW PERIODS TO SPREAD THE WORD.
WE'RE GONNA HAVE SO MUCH FUN!
I'VE ALWAYS WANTED TO GO TO A SCHOOL DANCE!

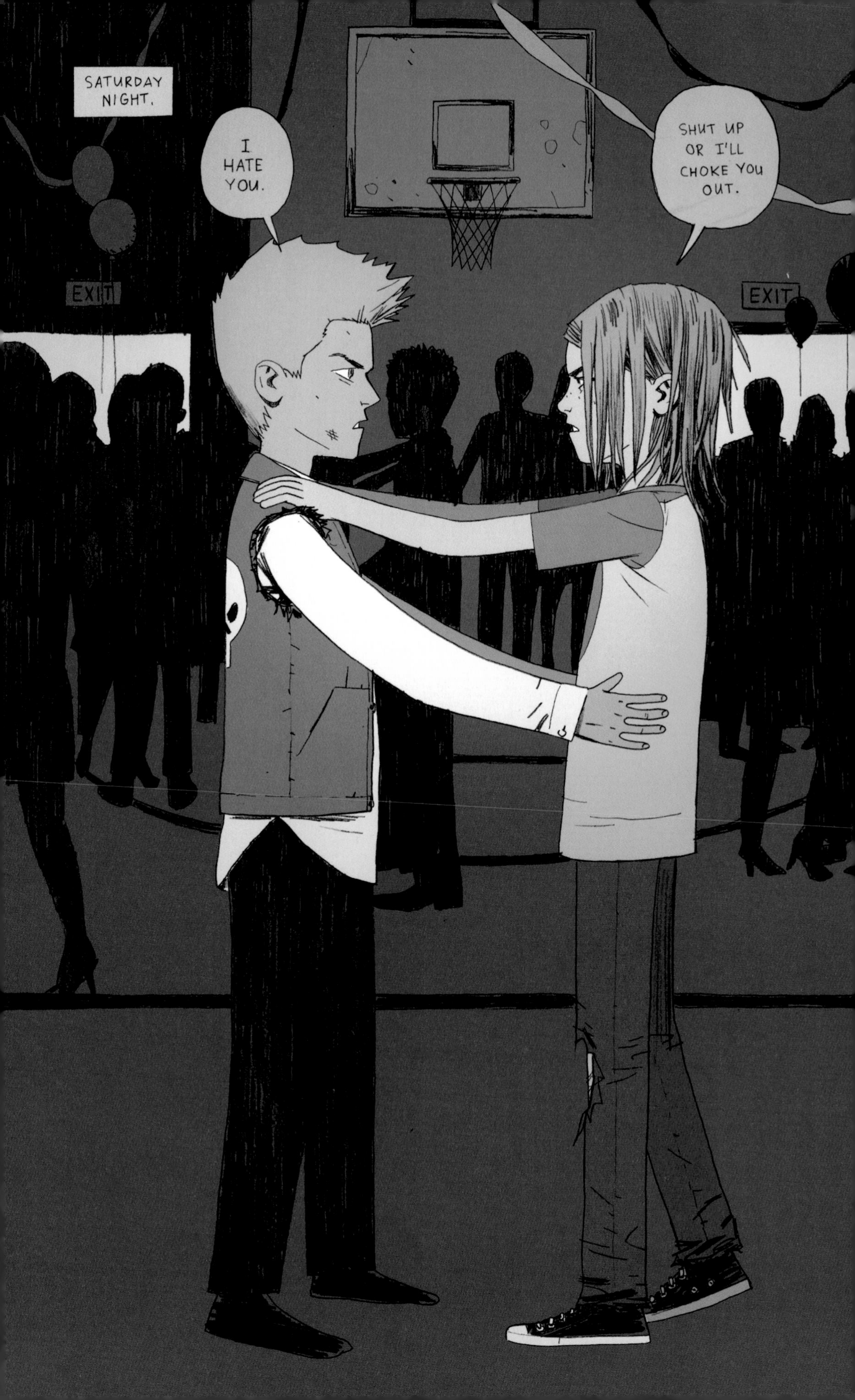
SATURDAY NIGHT.
I HATE YOU.
SHUT UP OR I'LL CHOKE YOU OUT.
EXIT
EXIT

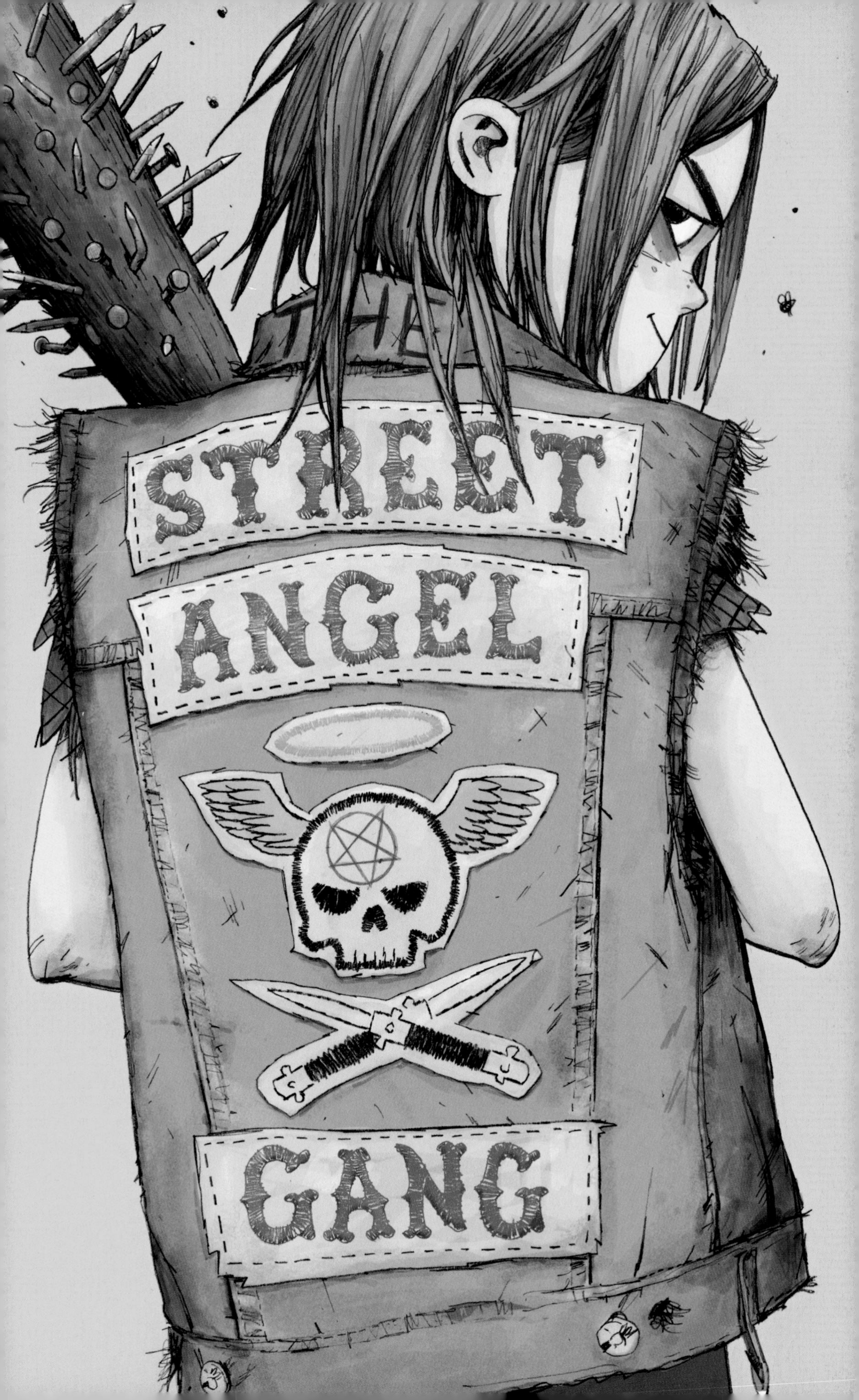
THE
STREET
ANGEL
GANG

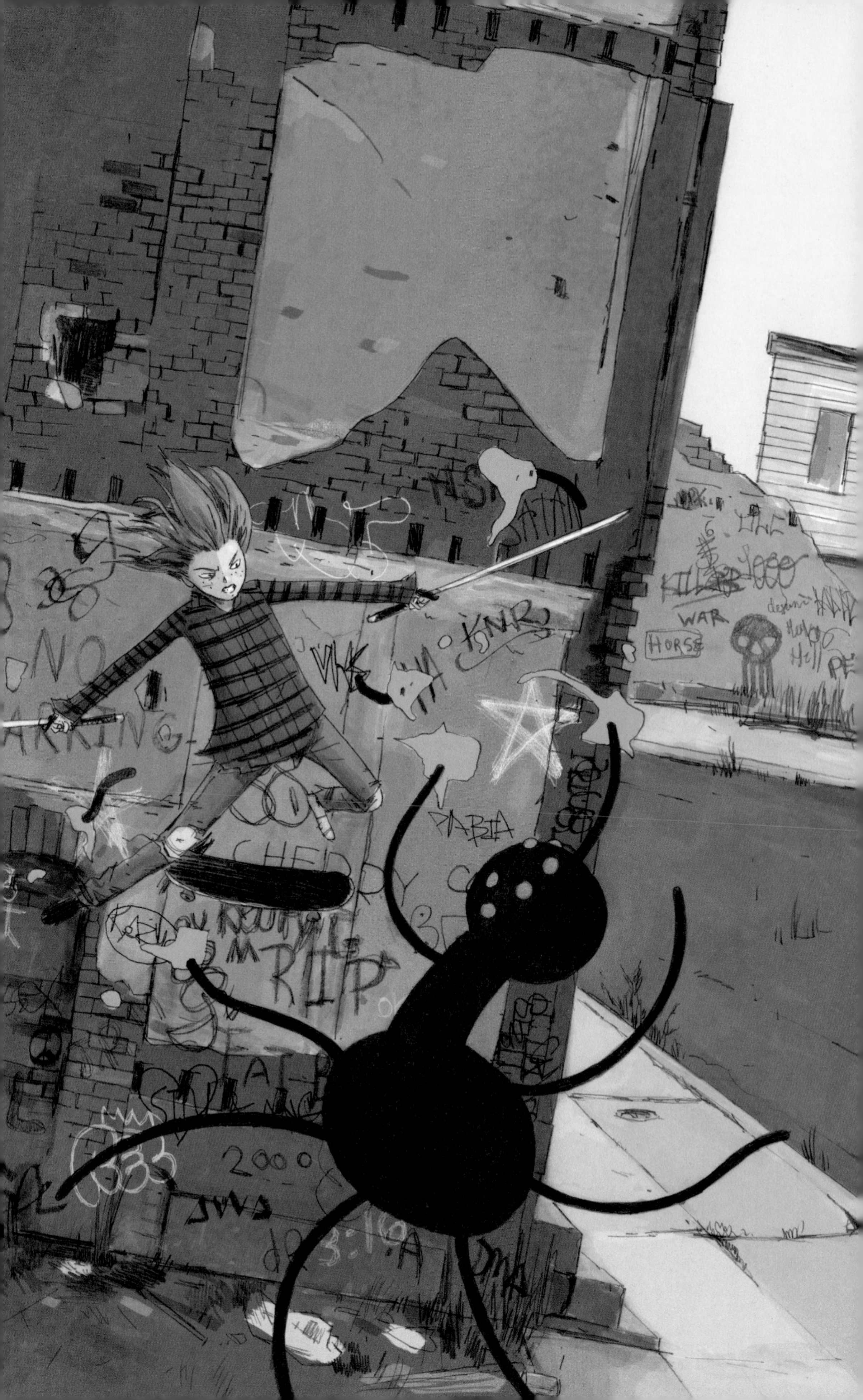
NO
ARKING
WAR
HORSE
RIP
2000

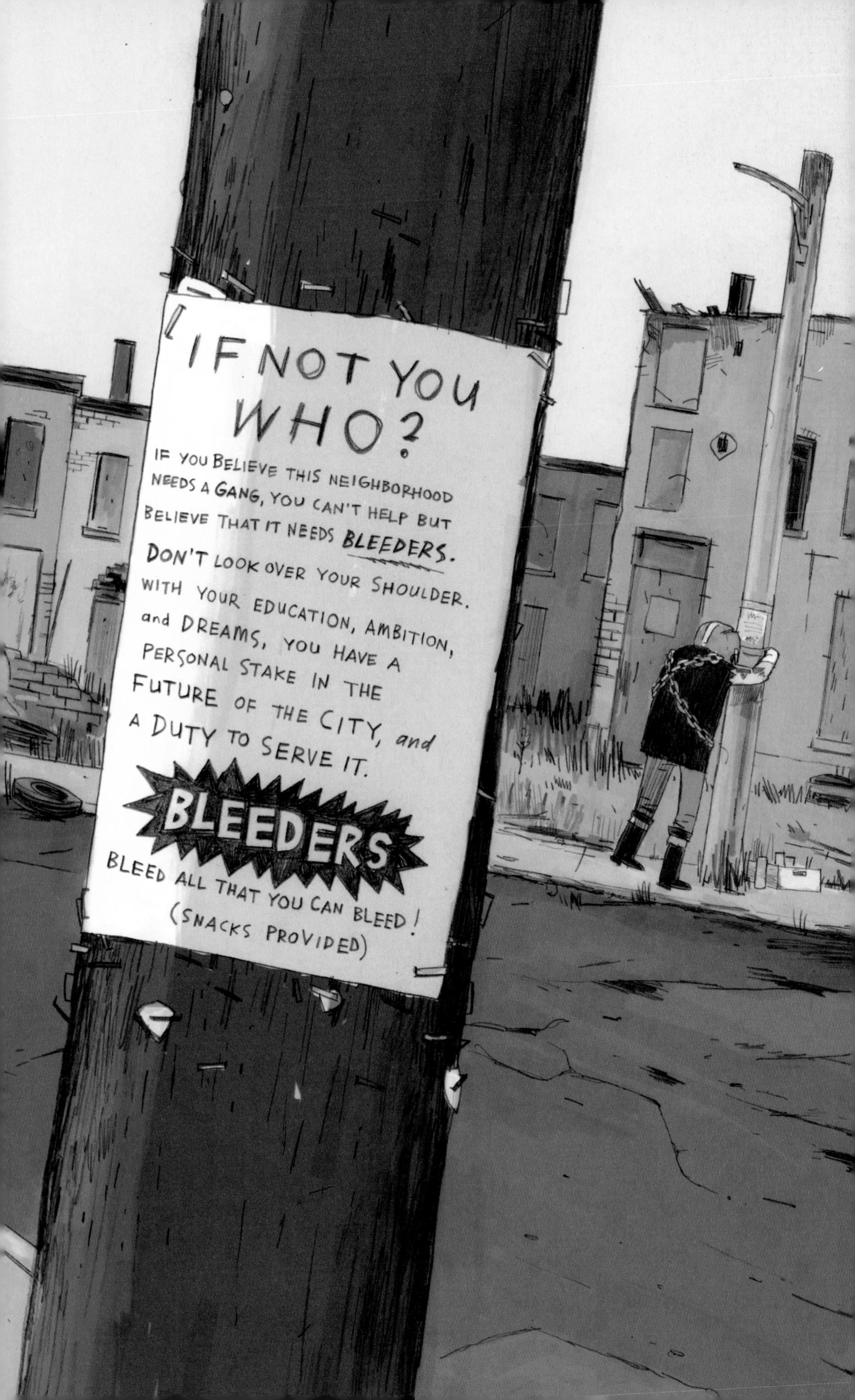
IF NOT YOU WHO?
IF YOU BELIEVE THIS NEIGHBORHOOD NEEDS A GANG, YOU CAN'T HELP BUT BELIEVE THAT IT NEEDS BLEEDERS.
DON'T LOOK OVER YOUR SHOULDER. WITH YOUR EDUCATION, AMBITION, and DREAMS, YOU HAVE A PERSONAL STAKE IN THE FUTURE OF THE CITY, and A DUTY TO SERVE IT.
BLEEDERS
BLEED ALL THAT YOU CAN BLEED!
(SNACKS PROVIDED)

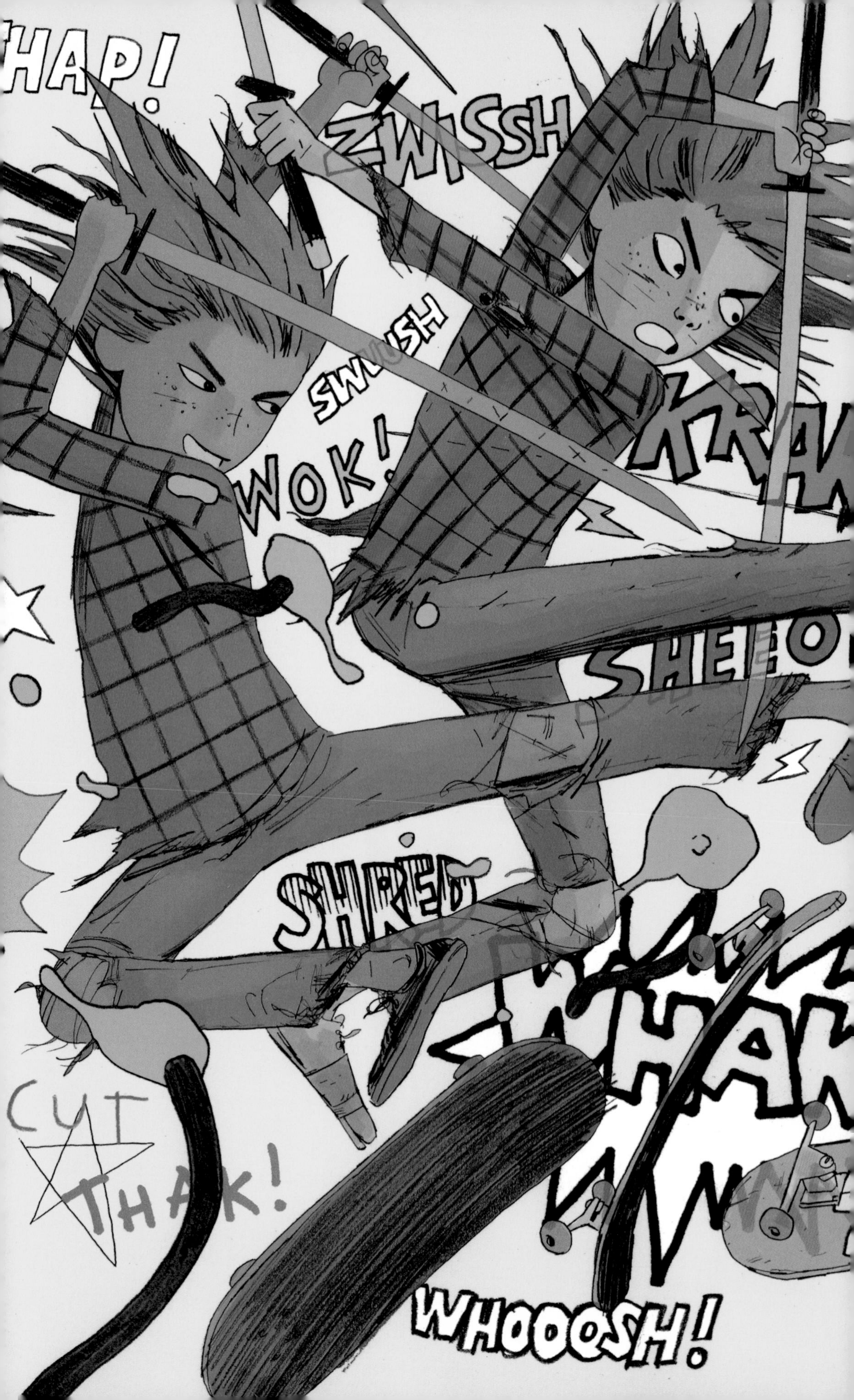
HAP!
ZWISSH
SWUSH
WOK!
SHRED
CUT
THAK!
WHOOOSH!

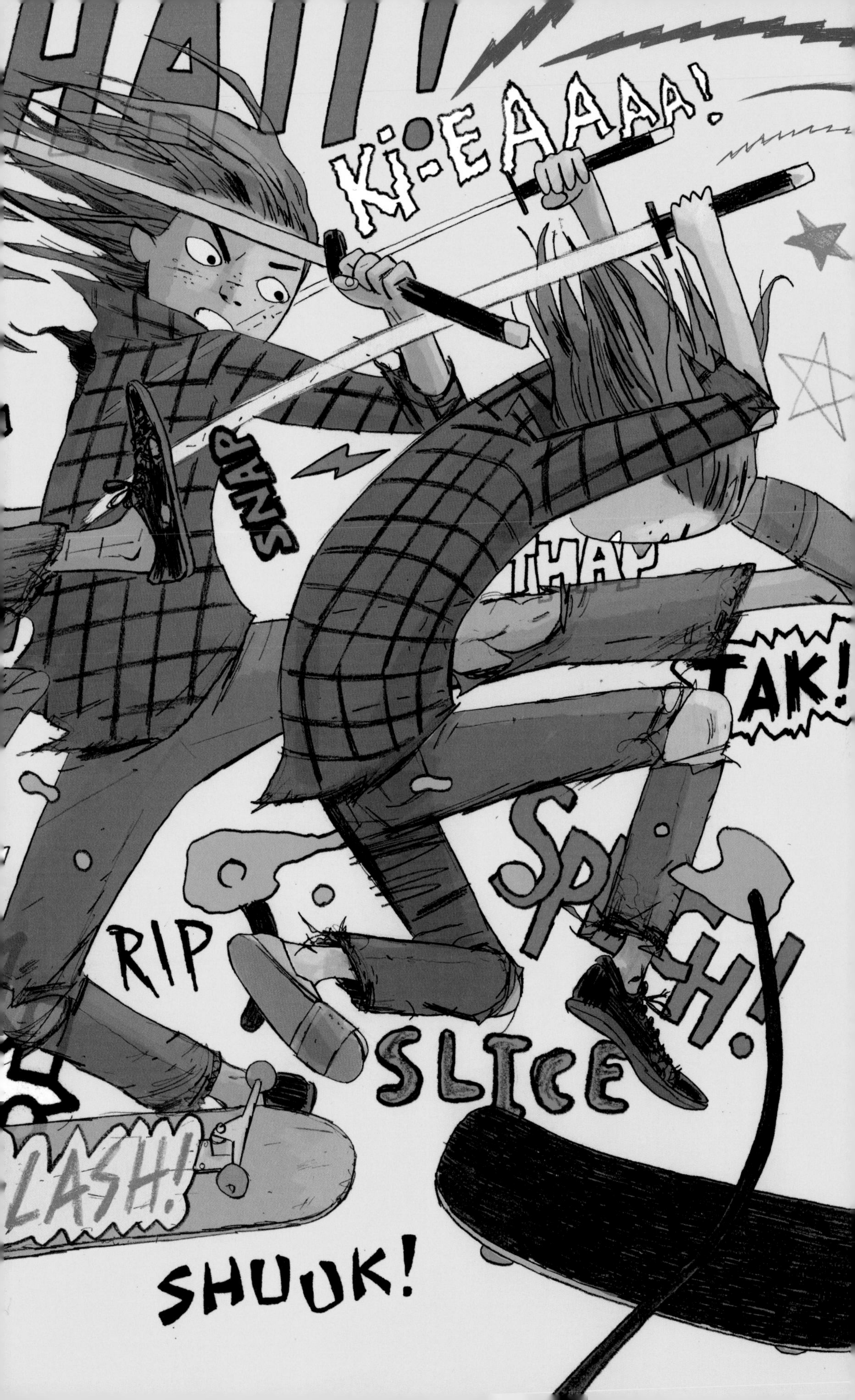
KI-EAAAA!
SNAP
TAK!
RIP
SLICE
SHUUK!

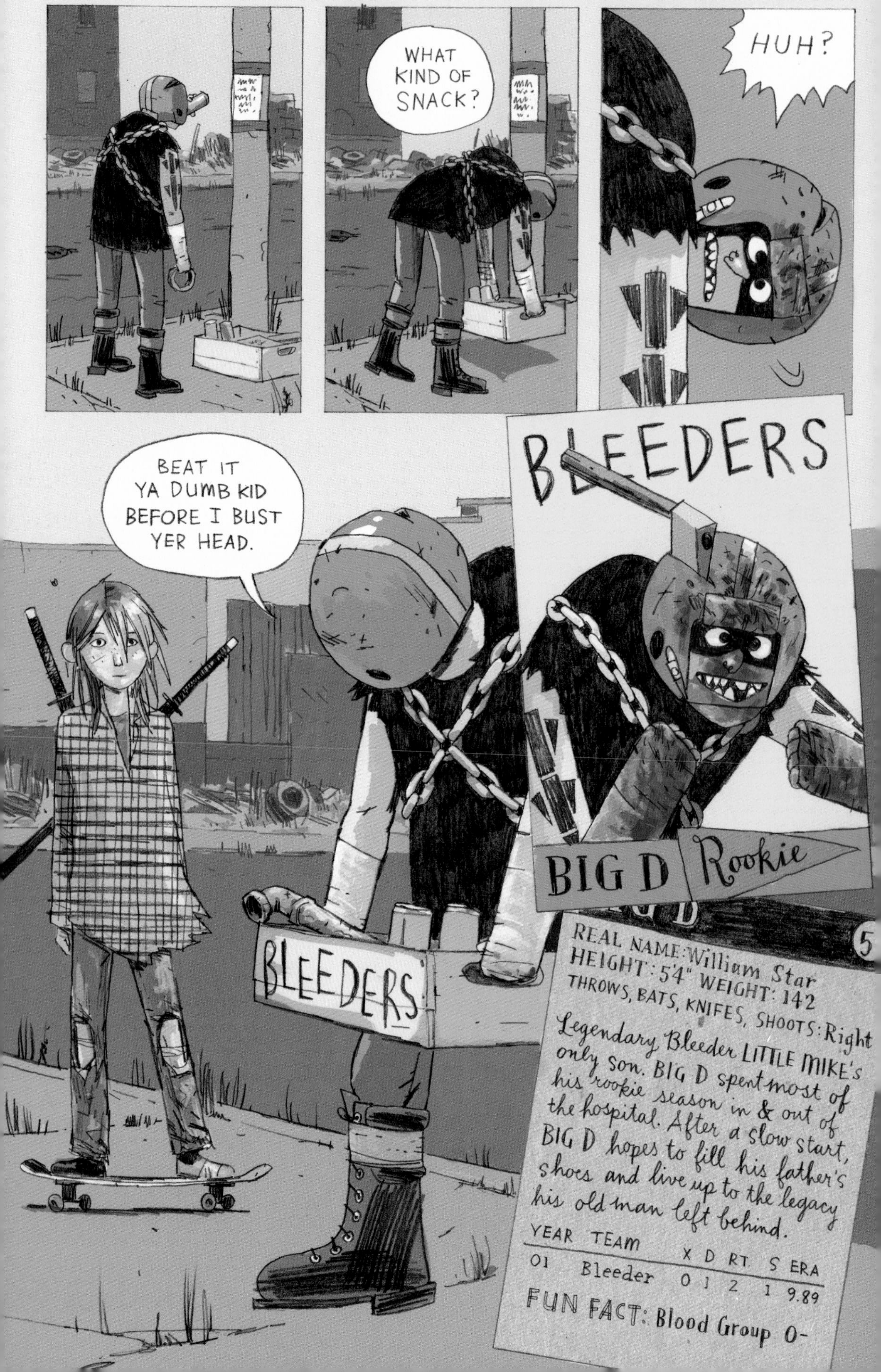
WHAT KIND OF SNACK?
HUH?
BEAT IT YA DUMB KID BEFORE I BUST YER HEAD.
BLEEDERS
BLEEDERS
BIG D
Rookie
5
REAL NAME: William Star
HEIGHT: 5'4" WEIGHT: 142
THROWS, BATS, KNIFES, SHOOTS: Right
Legendary Bleeder LITTLE MIKE's only son. BIG D spent most of his rookie season in & out of the hospital. After a slow start, BIG D hopes to fill his father's shoes and live up to the legacy his old man left behind.
YEAR TEAM X D RT. S ERA
01 Bleeder 0 1 2 1 9.89
FUN FACT: Blood Group O-

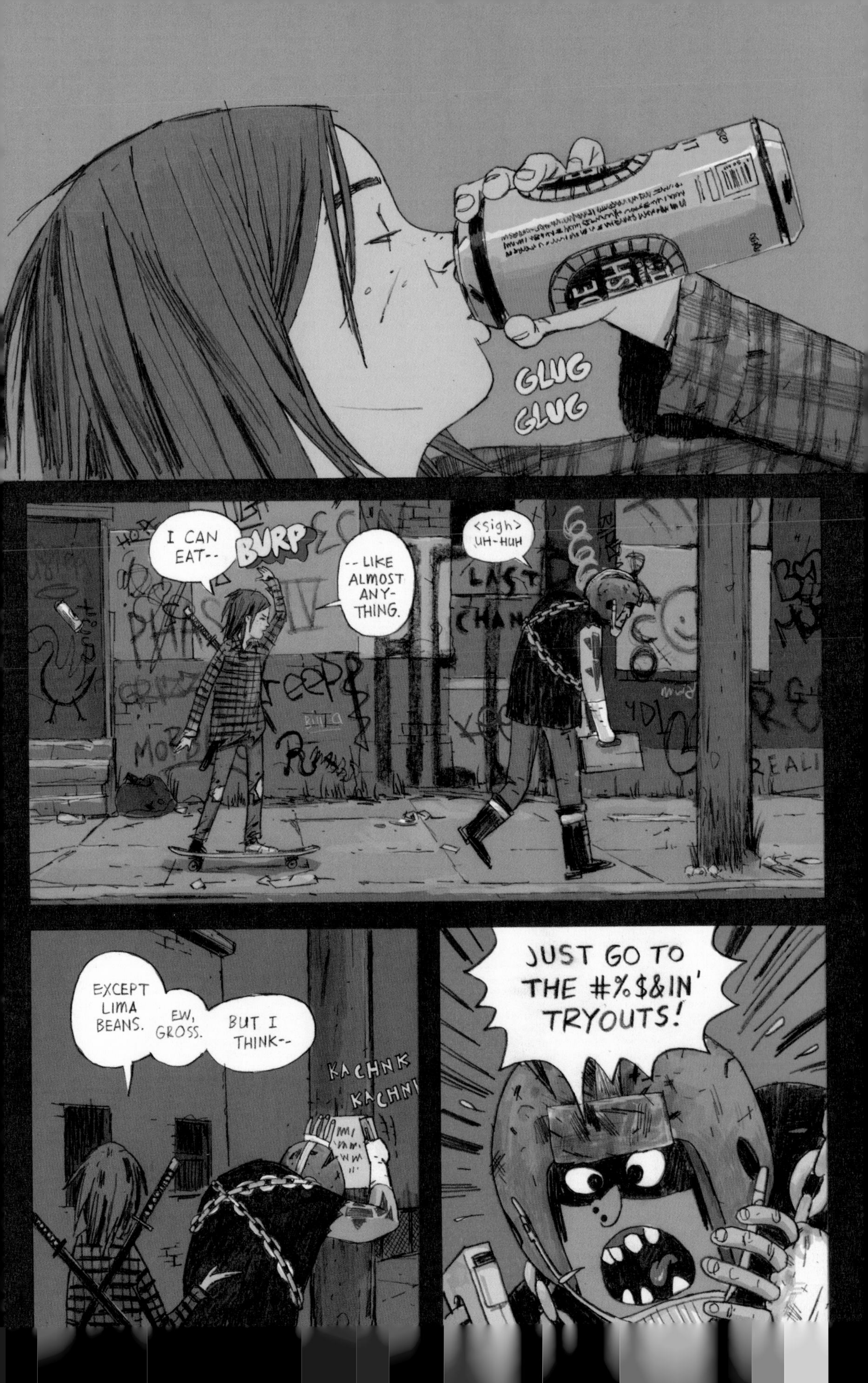
GLUG
GLUG
I CAN EAT--
BURP
--LIKE ALMOST ANY-THING.
<sigh> UH-HUH
LAST CHAN
EXCEPT LIMA BEANS.
EW, GROSS.
BUT I THINK--
KACHNK
KACHNK
JUST GO TO THE #%$&IN' TRYOUTS!

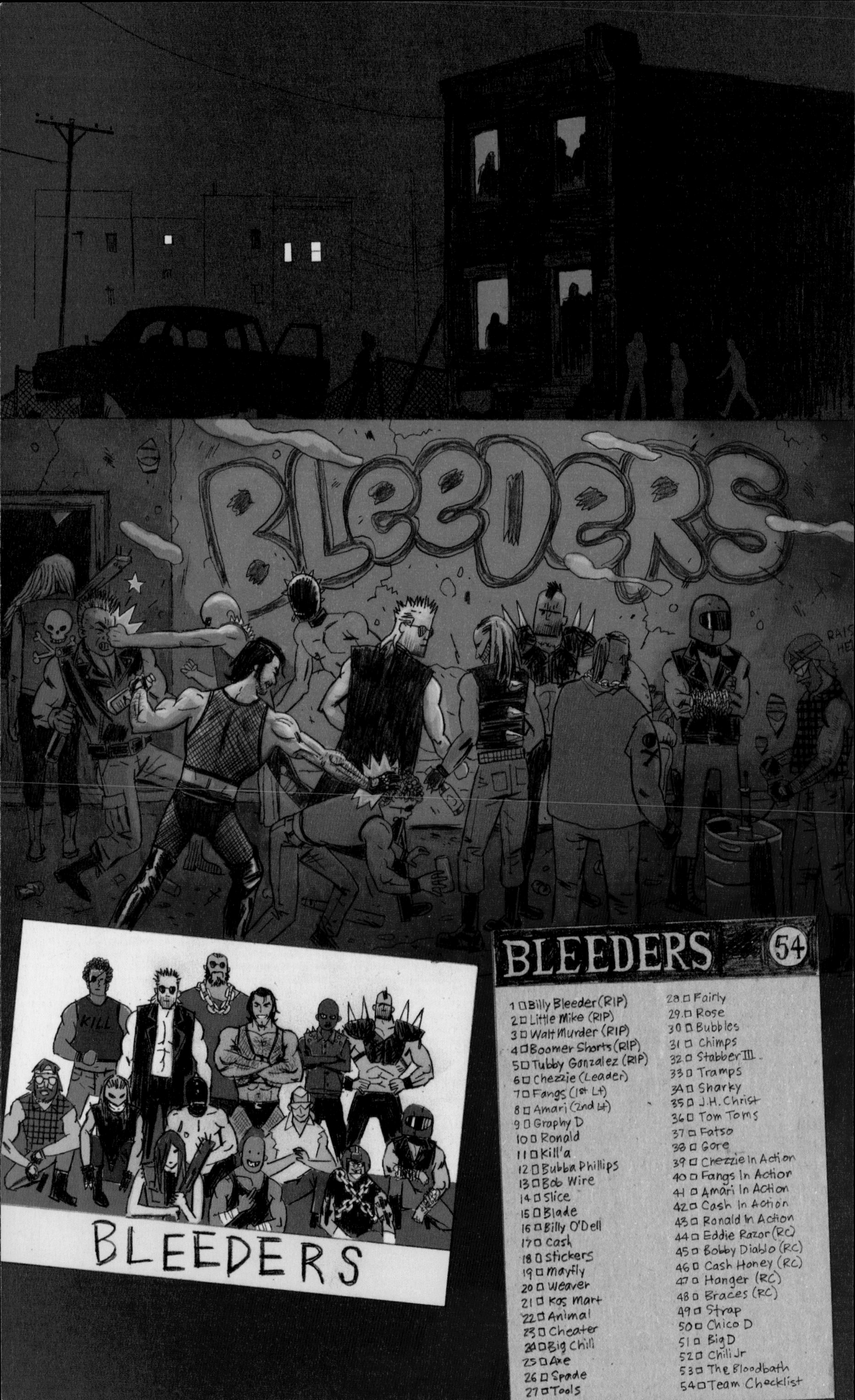
BLEEDERS
KILL
BLEEDERS
BLEEDERS 54
1 □ Billy Bleeder (RIP)
2 □ Little Mike (RIP)
3 □ Walt Murder (RIP)
4 □ Boomer Shorts (RIP)
5 □ Tubby Gonzalez (RIP)
6 □ Chezzie (Leader)
7 □ Fangs (1st Lt)
8 □ Amari (2nd Lt)
9 □ Graphy D
10 □ Ronald
11 □ Kill'a
12 □ Bubba Phillips
13 □ Bob Wire
14 □ Slice
15 □ Blade
16 □ Billy O'Dell
17 □ Cash
18 □ Stickers
19 □ Mayfly
20 □ Weaver
21 □ Kos Mart
22 □ Animal
23 □ Cheater
24 □ Big Chill
25 □ Axe
26 □ Spade
27 □ Tools
28. □ Fairly
29. □ Rose
30 □ Bubbles
31 □ Chimps
32 □ Stabber III
33 □ Tramps
34 □ Sharky
35 □ J.H. Christ
36 □ Tom Toms
37 □ Fatso
38 □ Gore
39 □ Chezzie In Action
40 □ Fangs In Action
41 □ Amari In Action
42 □ Cash In Action
43 □ Ronald In Action
44 □ Eddie Razor (RC)
45 □ Bobby Diablo (RC)
46 □ Cash Honey (RC)
47 □ Hanger (RC)
48 □ Braces (RC)
49 □ Strap
50 □ Chico D
51 □ Big D
52 □ Chili Jr
53 □ The Bloodbath
54 □ Team Checklist

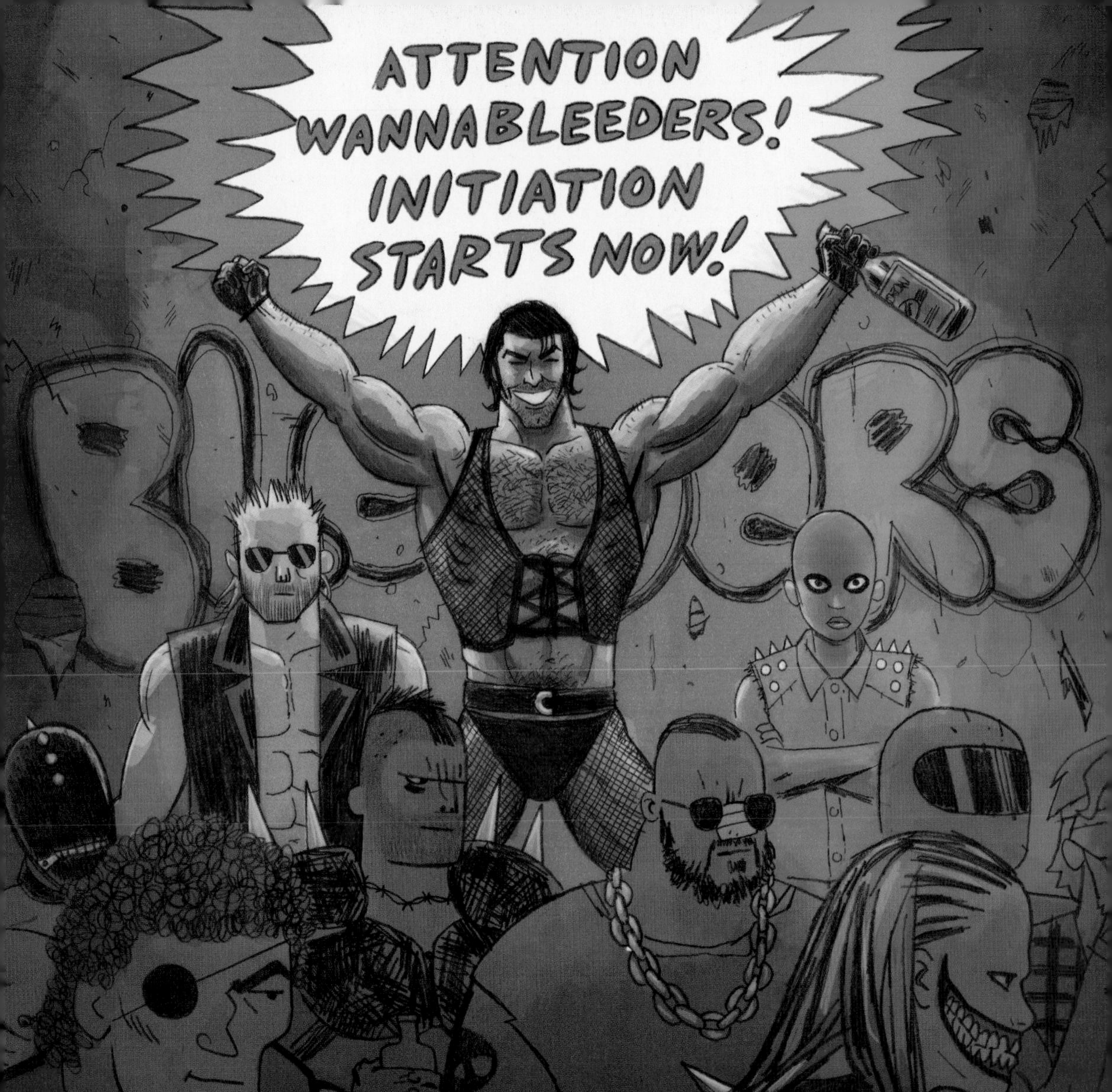
ATTENTION WANNABLEEDERS! INITIATION STARTS NOW!

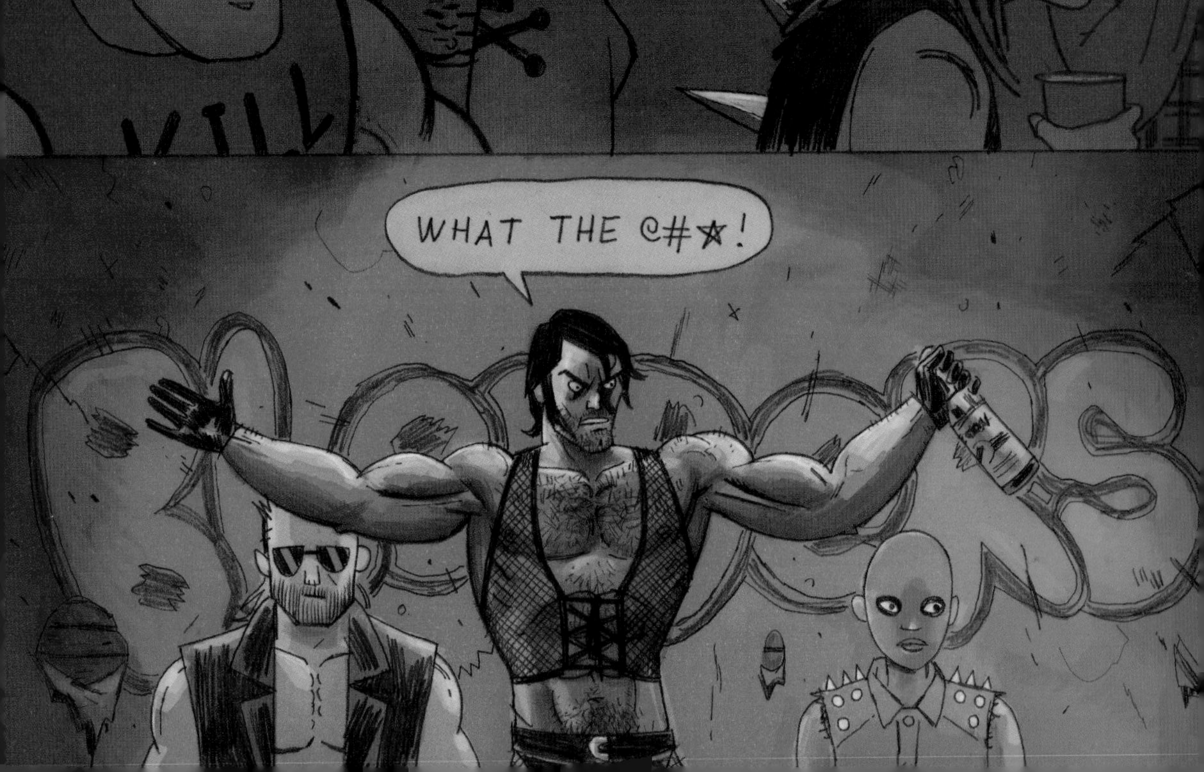
WHAT THE @#☆!

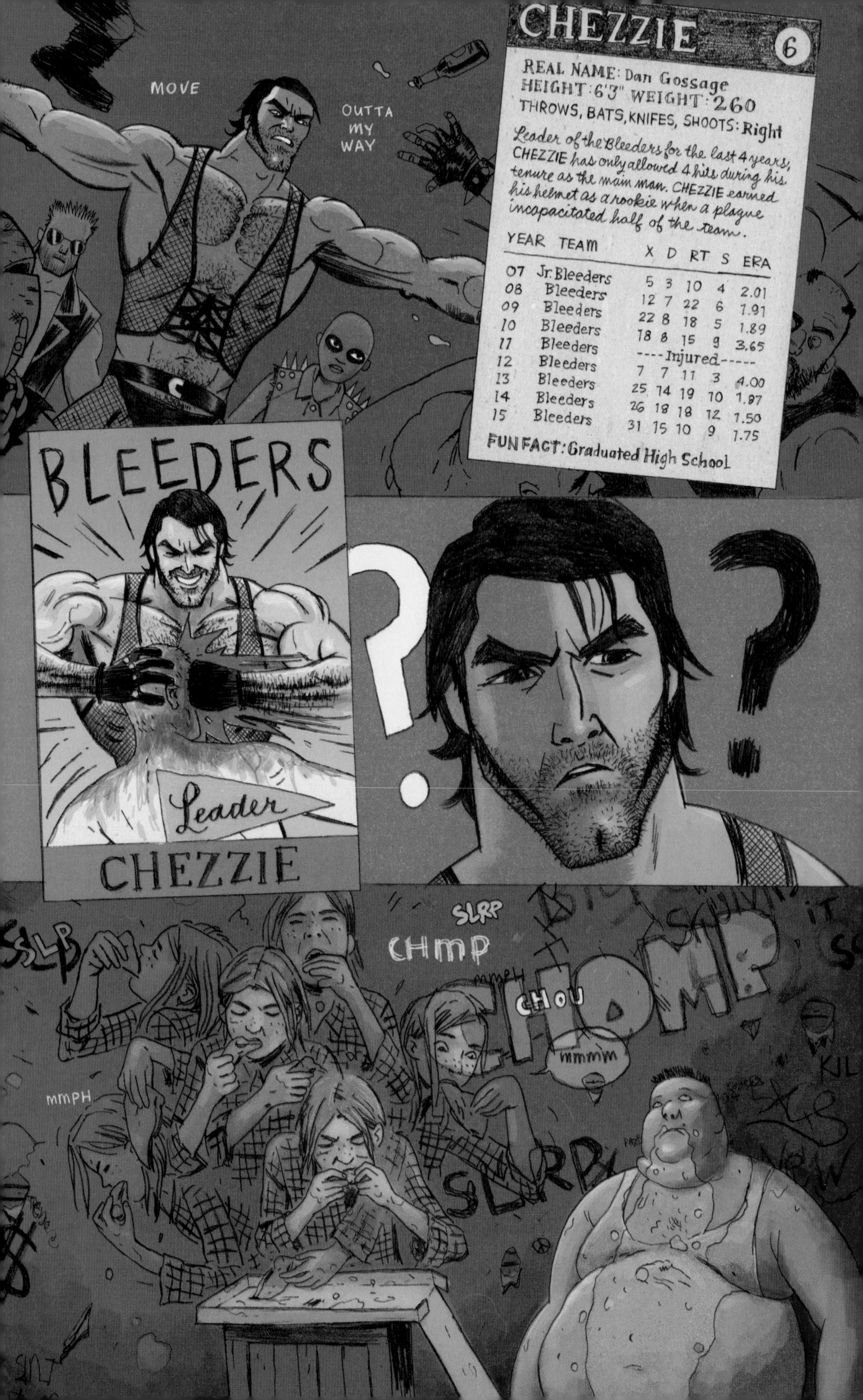
MOVE
OUTTA MY WAY
CHEZZIE 6
REAL NAME: Dan Gossage
HEIGHT: 6'3" WEIGHT: 260
THROWS, BATS, KNIFES, SHOOTS: Right
Leader of the Bleeders for the last 4 years, CHEZZIE has only allowed 4 hits during his tenure as the main man. CHEZZIE earned his helmet as a rookie when a plague incapacitated half of the team.
YEAR TEAM X D RT S ERA
07 Jr. Bleeders 5 3 10 4 2.01
08 Bleeders 12 7 22 6 1.91
09 Bleeders 22 8 18 5 1.89
10 Bleeders 18 8 15 9 3.65
11 Bleeders ----Injured-----
12 Bleeders 7 7 11 3 4.00
13 Bleeders 25 14 19 10 1.87
14 Bleeders 26 18 18 12 1.50
15 Bleeders 31 15 10 9 1.75
FUN FACT: Graduated High School
BLEEDERS
Leader
CHEZZIE
?
?
SSLB
SLRP
CHMP
mmph
CHOU
CHOMP
mmmm
mmPH
SLRP

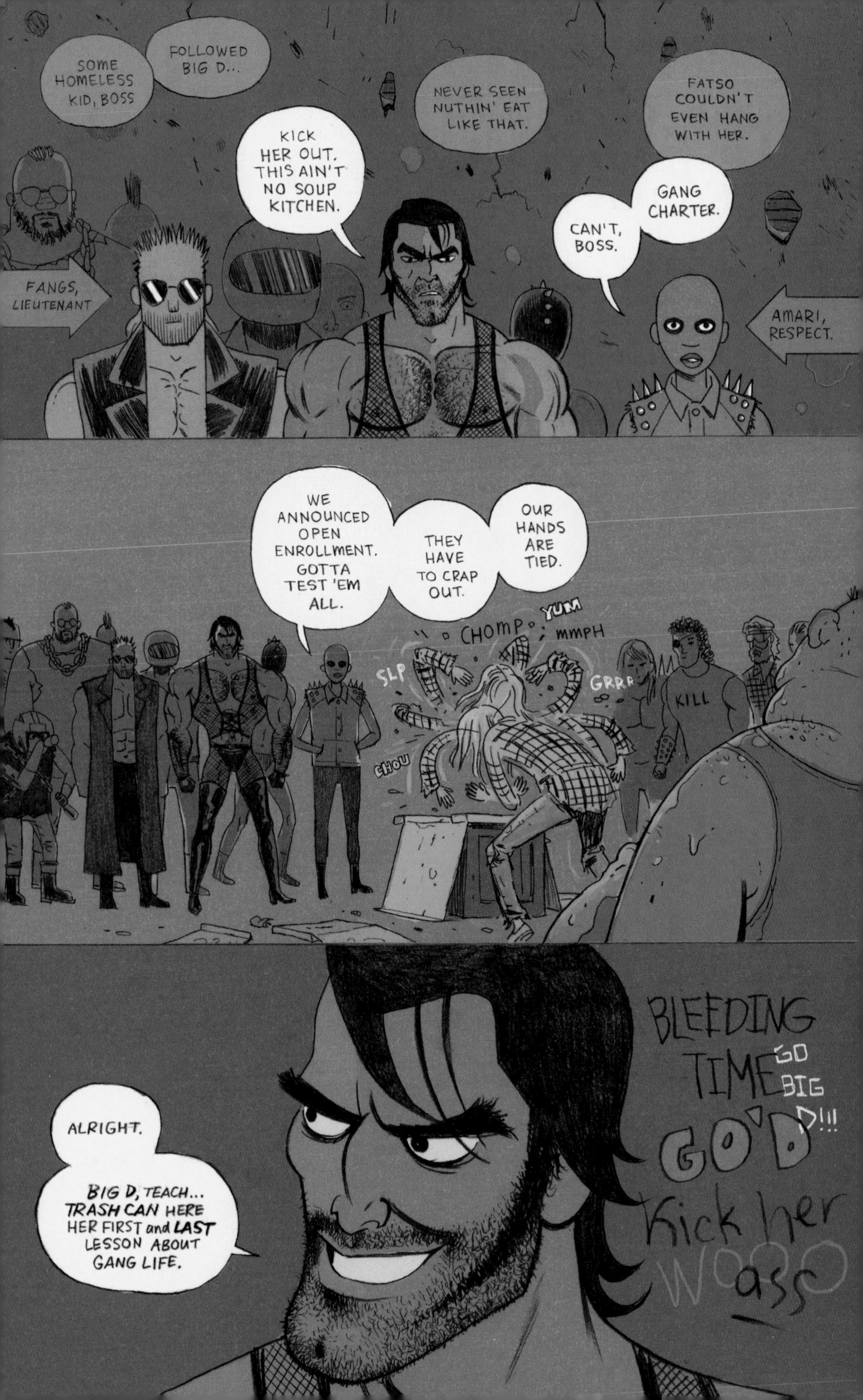
SOME HOMELESS KID, BOSS
FOLLOWED BIG D...
KICK HER OUT. THIS AIN'T NO SOUP KITCHEN.
NEVER SEEN NUTHIN' EAT LIKE THAT.
FATSO COULDN'T EVEN HANG WITH HER.
CAN'T, BOSS.
GANG CHARTER.
FANGS, LIEUTENANT
AMARI, RESPECT.
WE ANNOUNCED OPEN ENROLLMENT. GOTTA TEST 'EM ALL.
THEY HAVE TO CRAP OUT.
OUR HANDS ARE TIED.
CHOMP
YUM
mmpH
SLP
GRRR
CHOU
KILL
ALRIGHT.
BIG D, TEACH... TRASH CAN HERE HER FIRST and LAST LESSON ABOUT GANG LIFE.
BLEEDING TIME
GO BIG D!!!
GO D
Kick her ass
WOOO

GANG RULE #1: @#★! ROLLS DOWN HILL.

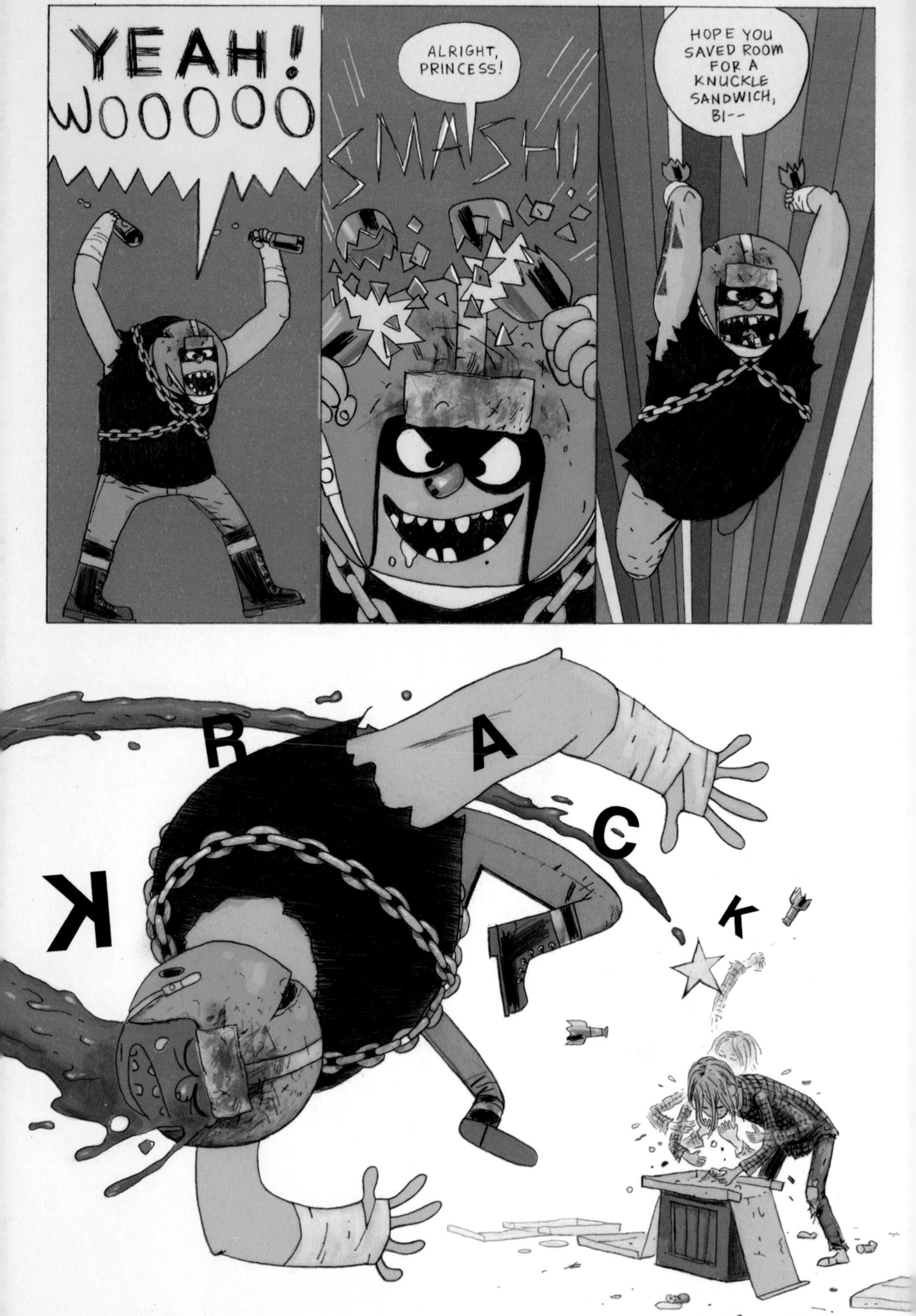
YEAH! WOOOOO
ALRIGHT, PRINCESS!
SMASH!
HOPE YOU SAVED ROOM FOR A KNUCKLE SANDWICH, BI--
KRACK

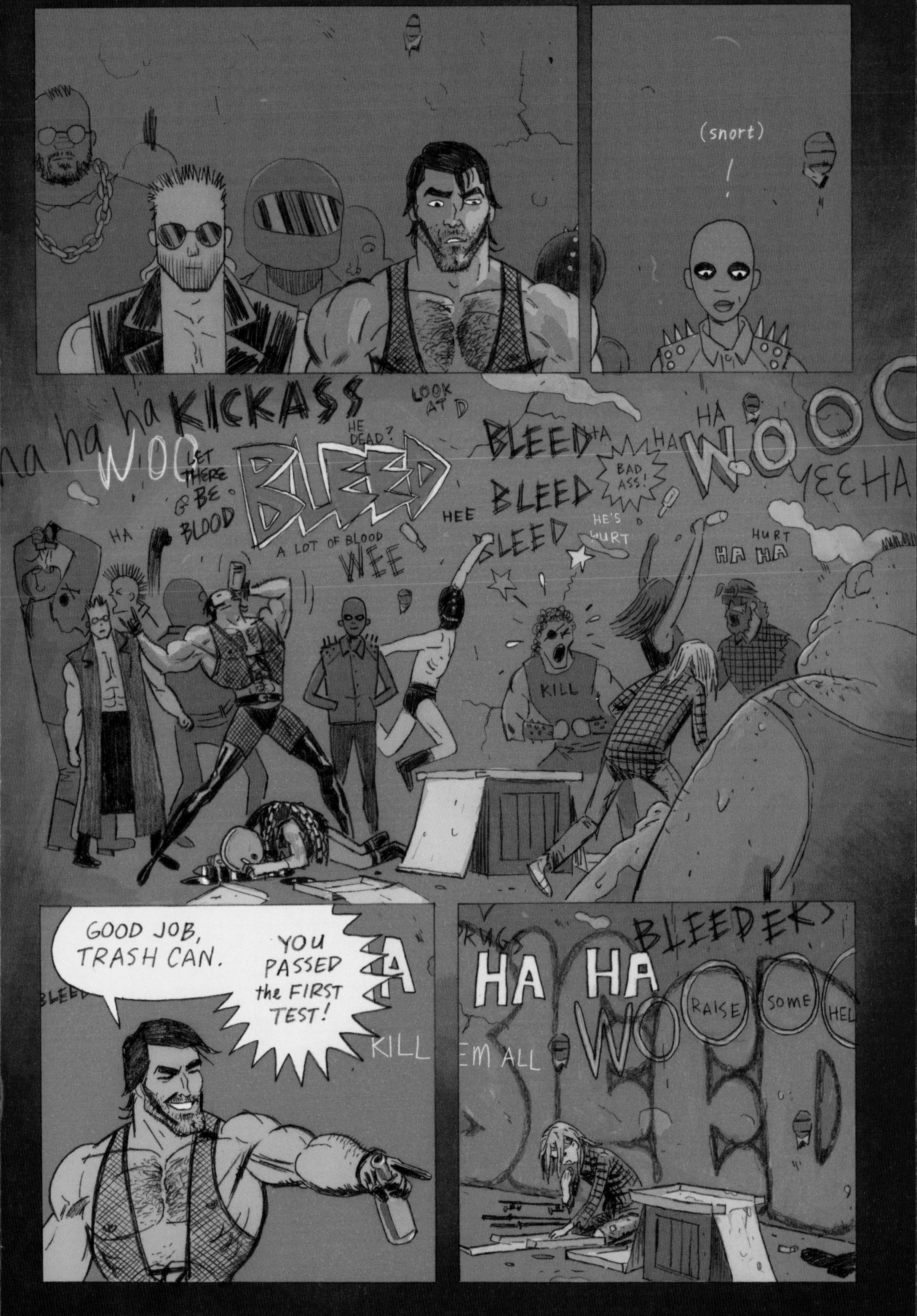

(snort)
ha ha ha
KICKASS
LOOK AT D
HE DEAD?
WOO
LET THERE BE BLOOD
BLEED
A LOT OF BLOOD
WEE
HEE
BLEED
BLEED
BLEED
HA
BAD ASS!
HE'S HURT
HA
WOO
YEEHA
HURT
HA HA
KILL
GOOD JOB, TRASH CAN.
YOU PASSED the FIRST TEST!
HA HA HA
BLEEDERS
KILL EM ALL
WOO
RAISE SOME HELL

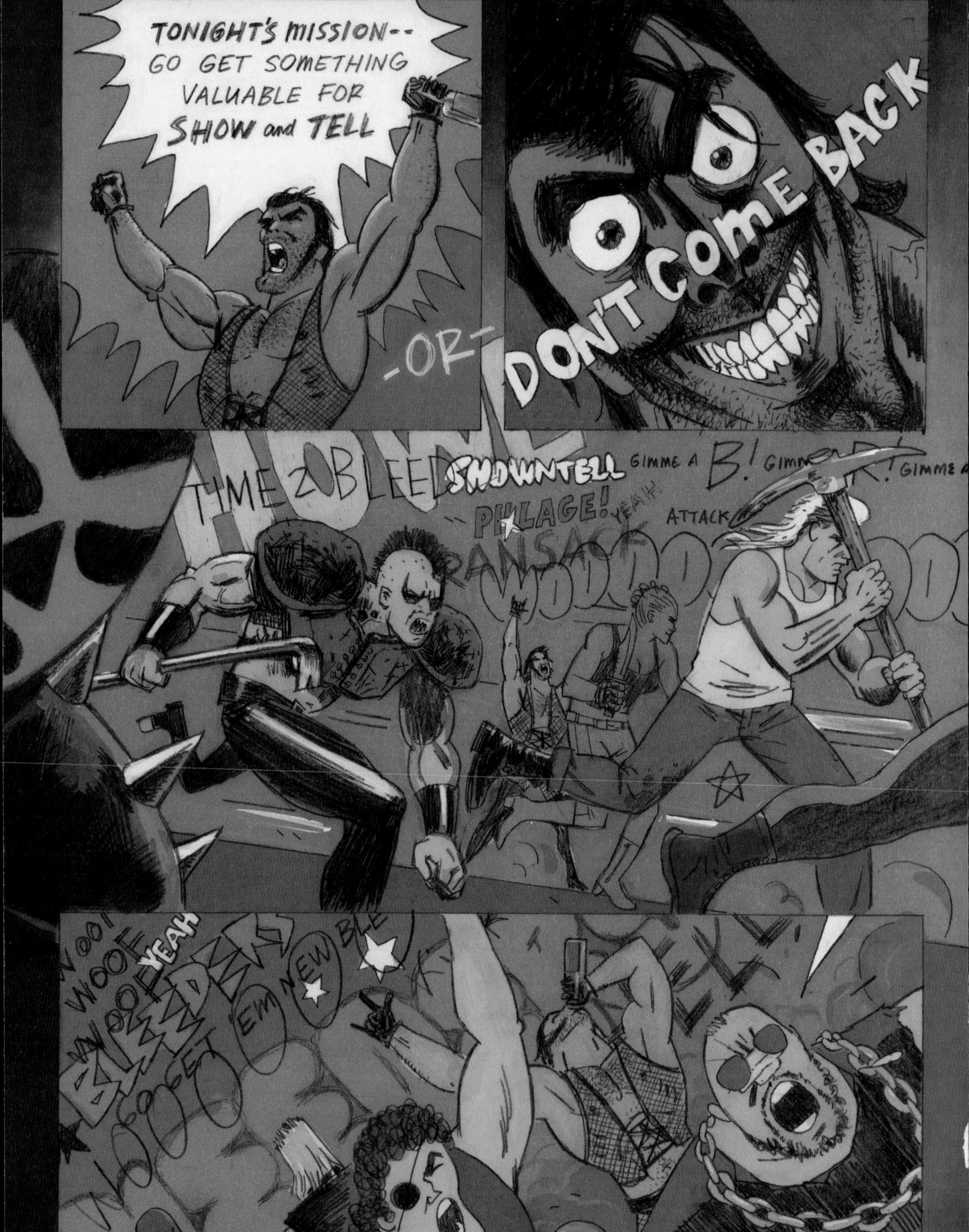
TONIGHT'S MISSION-- GO GET SOMETHING VALUABLE FOR SHOW and TELL
-OR-
DON'T COME BACK
TIME 2 BLEED
SHOWNTELL
GIMME A B!
GIMME A
PILLAGE!
YEAH!
ATTACK
RANSACK
WOOF
YEAH
BLEED
KILL

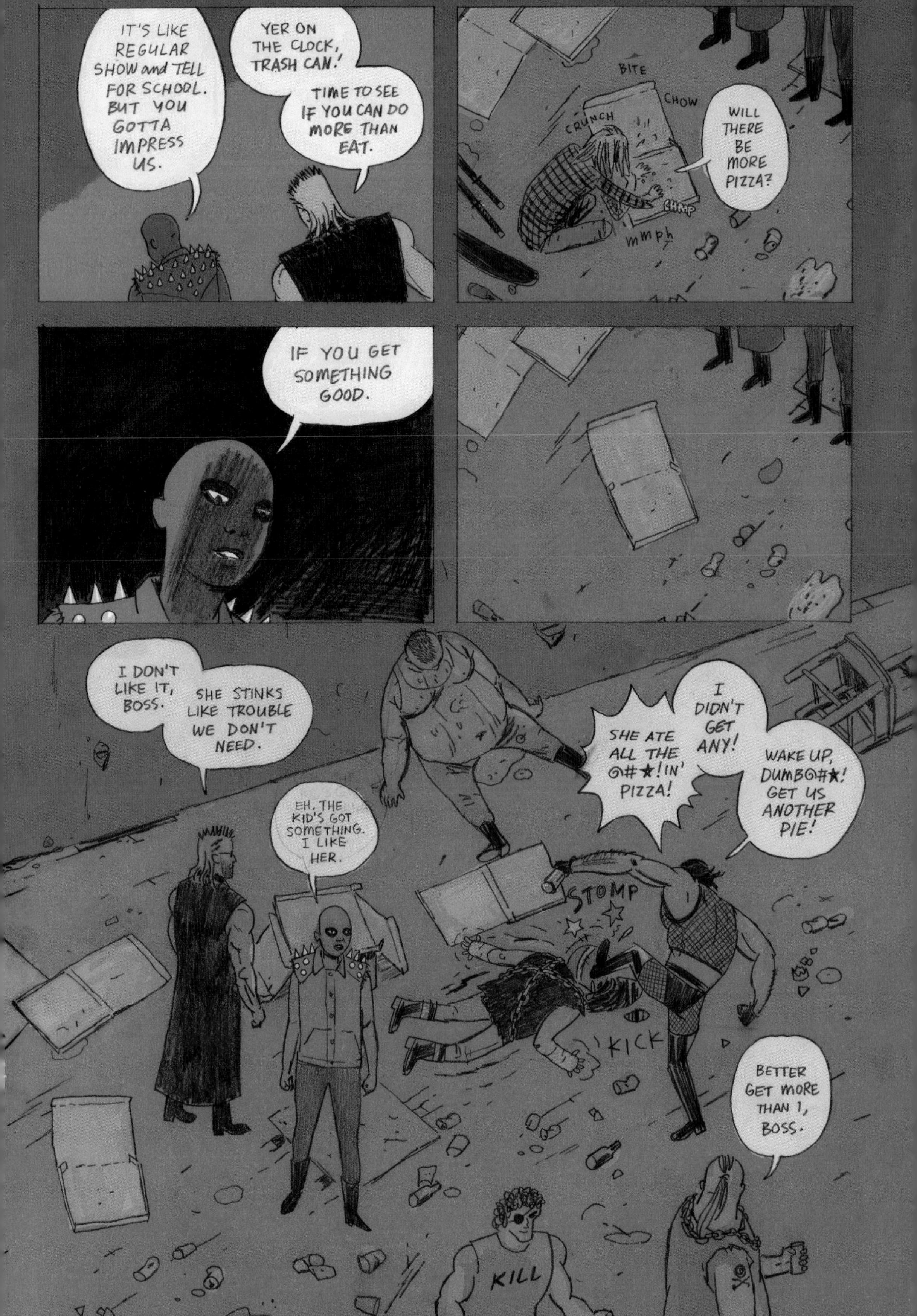
IT'S LIKE REGULAR SHOW and TELL FOR SCHOOL. BUT YOU GOTTA IMPRESS US.
YER ON THE CLOCK, TRASH CAN.'
TIME TO SEE IF YOU CAN DO MORE THAN EAT.
BITE
CHOW
CRUNCH
WILL THERE BE MORE PIZZA?
CHMP
mmph
IF YOU GET SOMETHING GOOD.
I DON'T LIKE IT, BOSS.
SHE STINKS LIKE TROUBLE WE DON'T NEED.
SHE ATE ALL THE @#★!IN' PIZZA!
I DIDN'T GET ANY!
WAKE UP, DUMB@#★! GET US ANOTHER PIE!
EH, THE KID'S GOT SOMETHING. I LIKE HER.
STOMP
KICK
BETTER GET MORE THAN 1, BOSS.
KILL

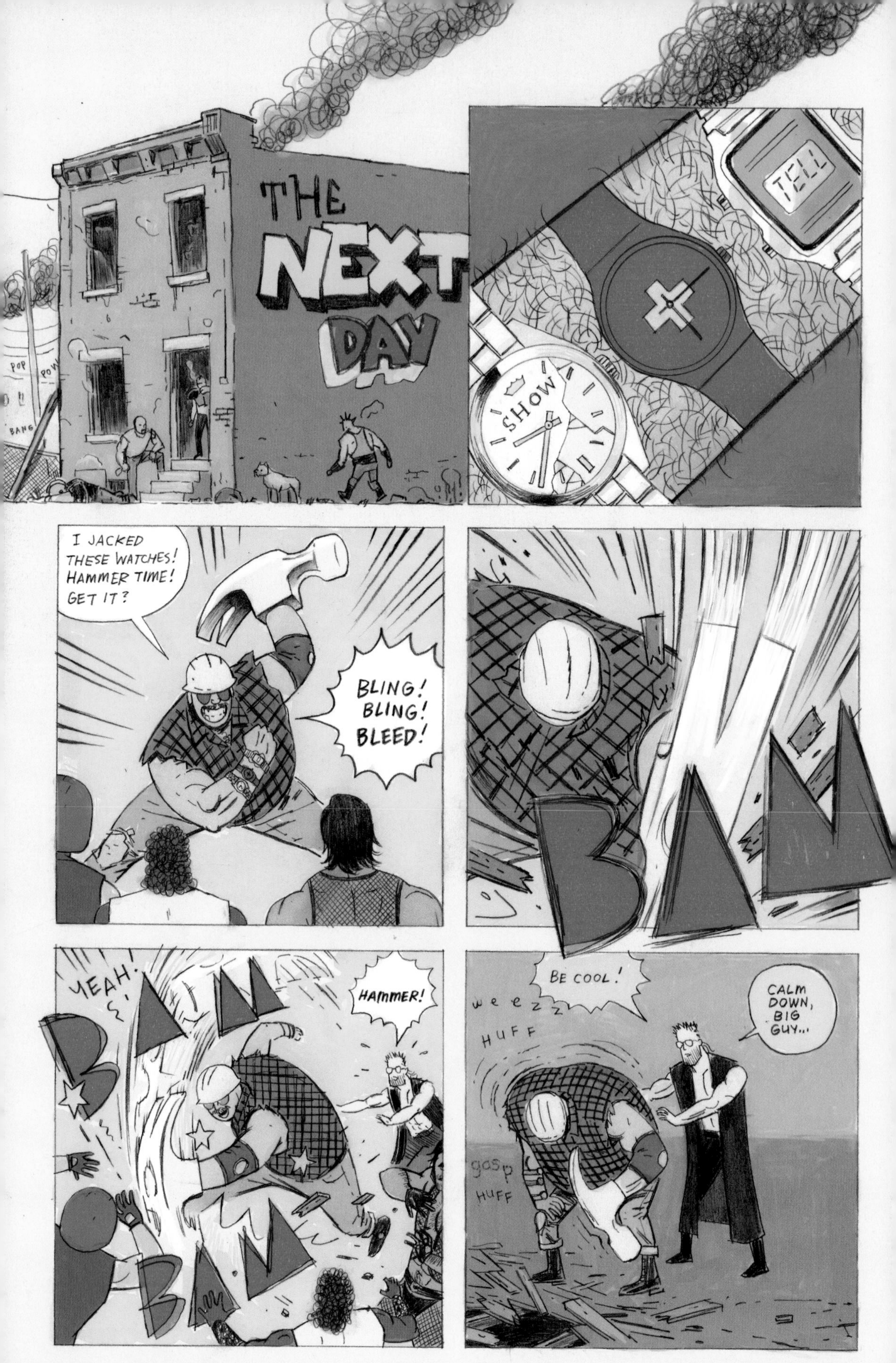
POP
POW
BANG
THE NEXT DAY
TELL
SHOW
I JACKED THESE WATCHES! HAMMER TIME! GET IT?
BLING! BLING! BLEED!
BAM
YEAH!
BAM
HAMMER!
BAM
BE COOL!
weezz
HUFF
CALM DOWN, BIG GUY...
gasp
HUFF

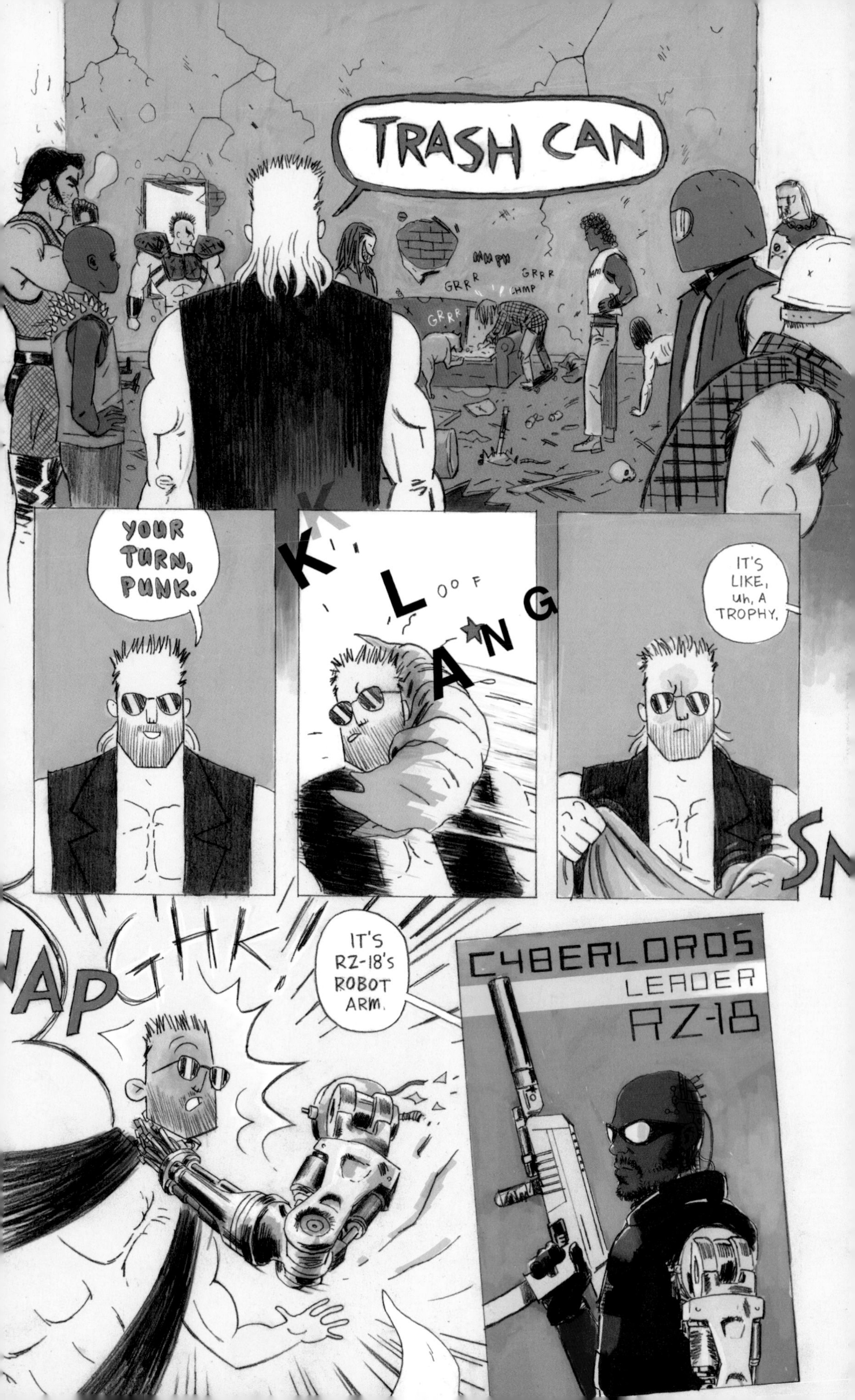
TRASH CAN
MMPH
GRRR
GRRR
CHMP
GRRR
YOUR TURN, PUNK.
KLANG
OOF
IT'S LIKE, uh, A TROPHY.
SNAP
GHK
IT'S RZ-18's ROBOT ARM.
CYBERLORDS
LEADER
RZ-18

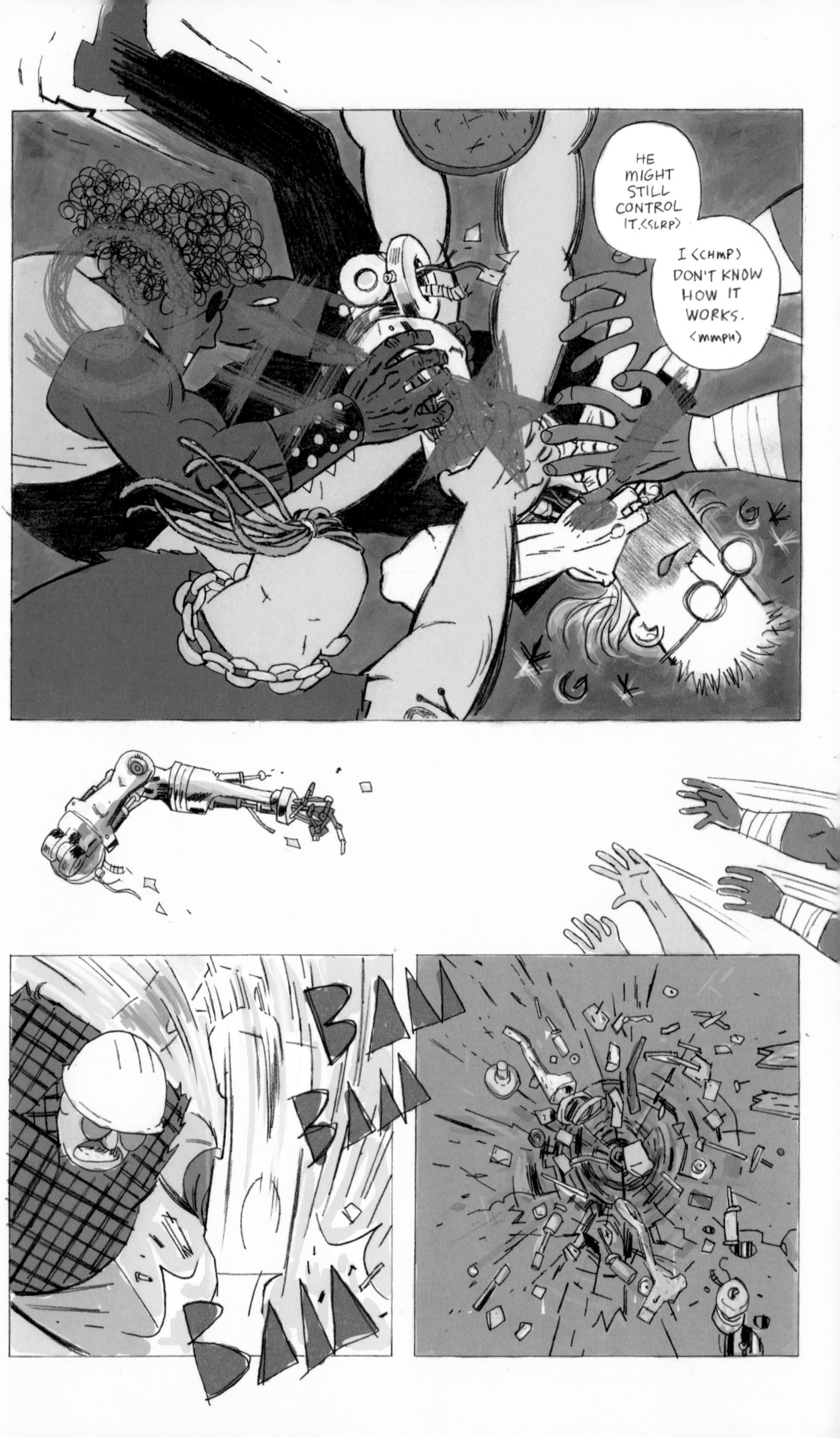
HE MIGHT STILL CONTROL IT. <SLRP>
I <CHMP> DON'T KNOW HOW IT WORKS. <MMPH>

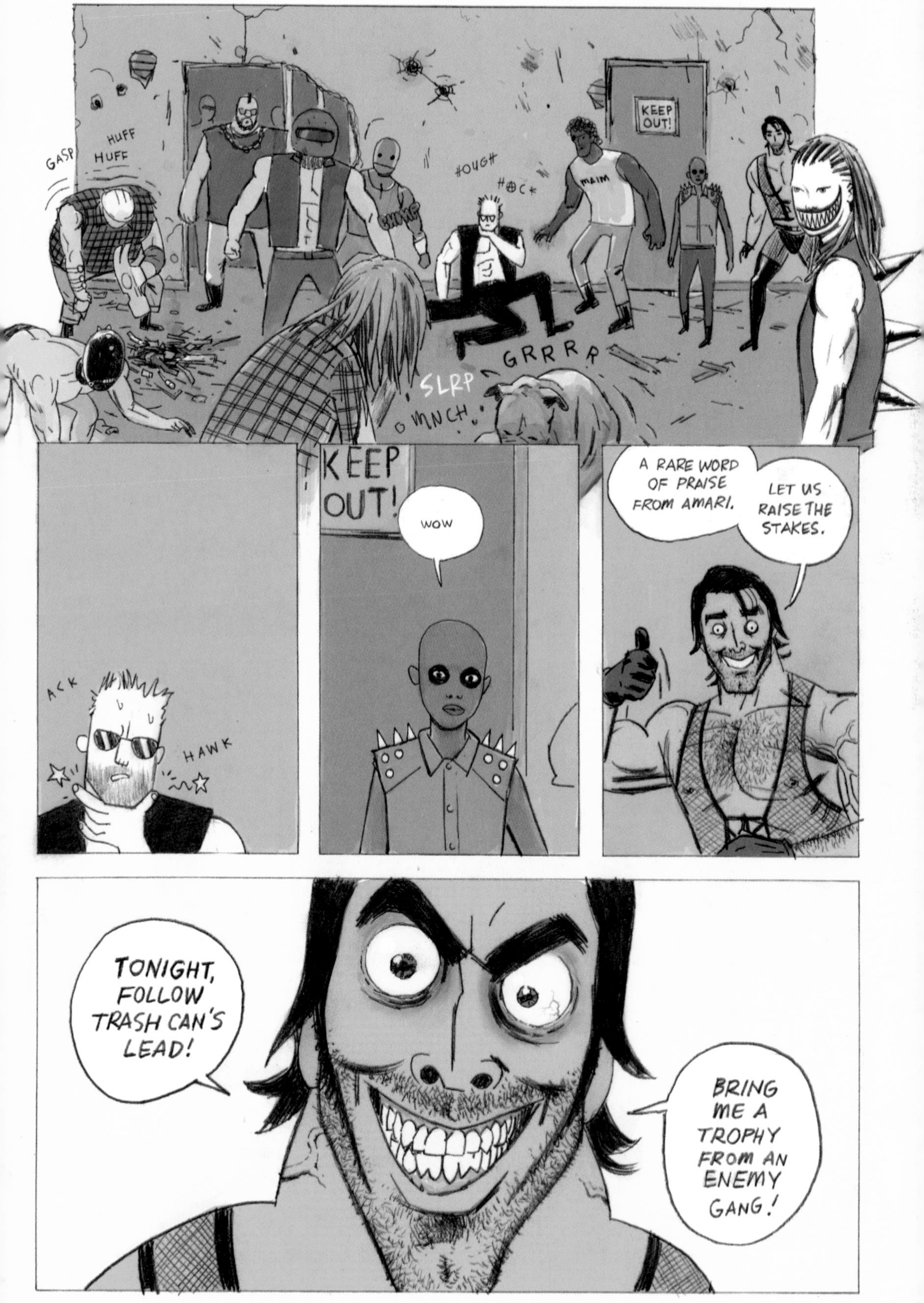
GASP
HUFF HUFF
KEEP OUT!
MAIM
GRRRR
SLRP
ACK
HAWK
KEEP OUT!
WOW
A RARE WORD OF PRAISE FROM AMARI.
LET US RAISE THE STAKES.
TONIGHT, FOLLOW TRASH CAN'S LEAD!
BRING ME A TROPHY FROM AN ENEMY GANG!

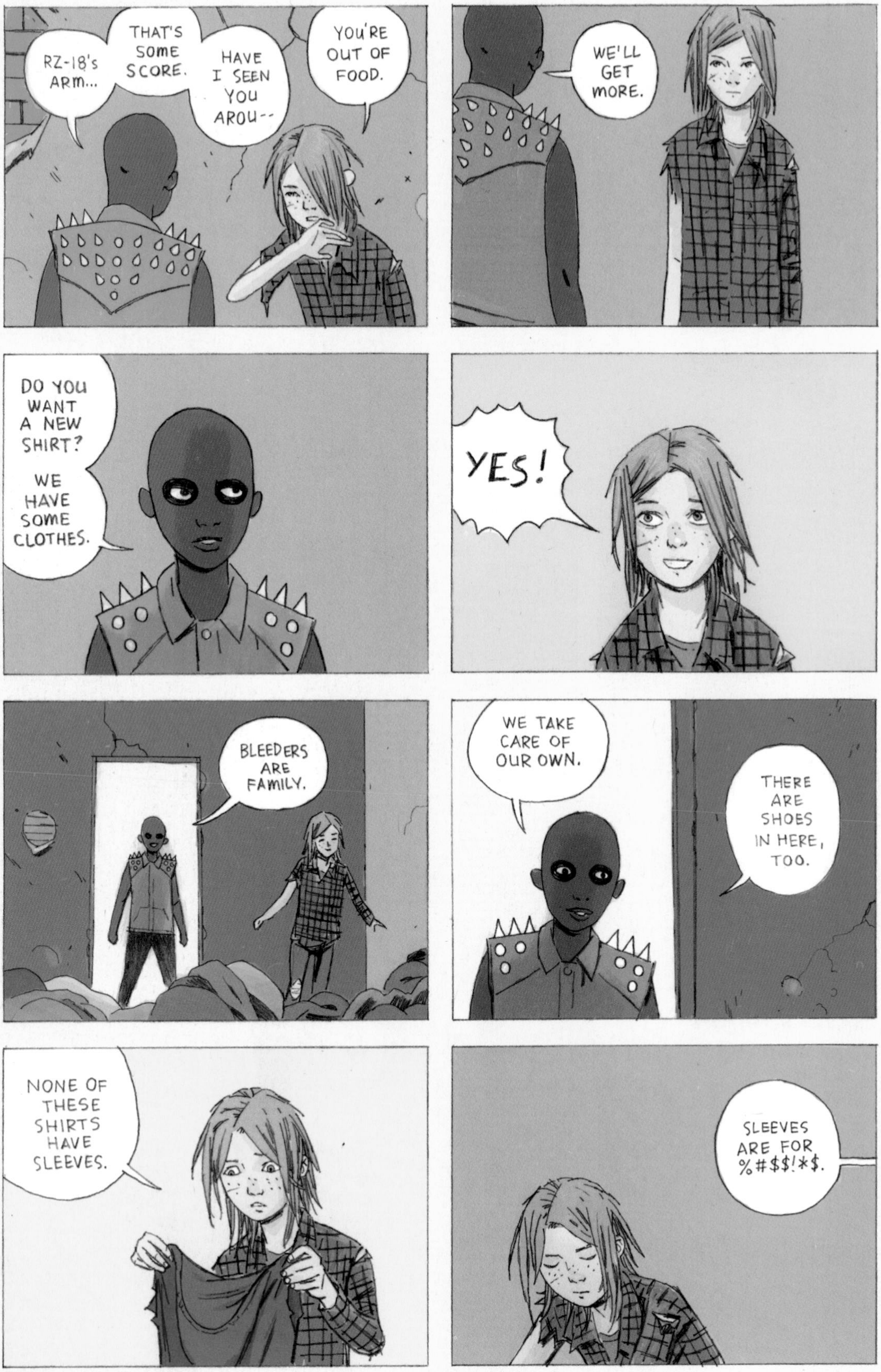
RZ-18's ARM...
THAT'S SOME SCORE.
HAVE I SEEN YOU AROU--
YOU'RE OUT OF FOOD.
WE'LL GET MORE.
DO YOU WANT A NEW SHIRT?
WE HAVE SOME CLOTHES.
YES!
BLEEDERS ARE FAMILY.
WE TAKE CARE OF OUR OWN.
THERE ARE SHOES IN HERE, TOO.
NONE OF THESE SHIRTS HAVE SLEEVES.
SLEEVES ARE FOR %#$$!*$.

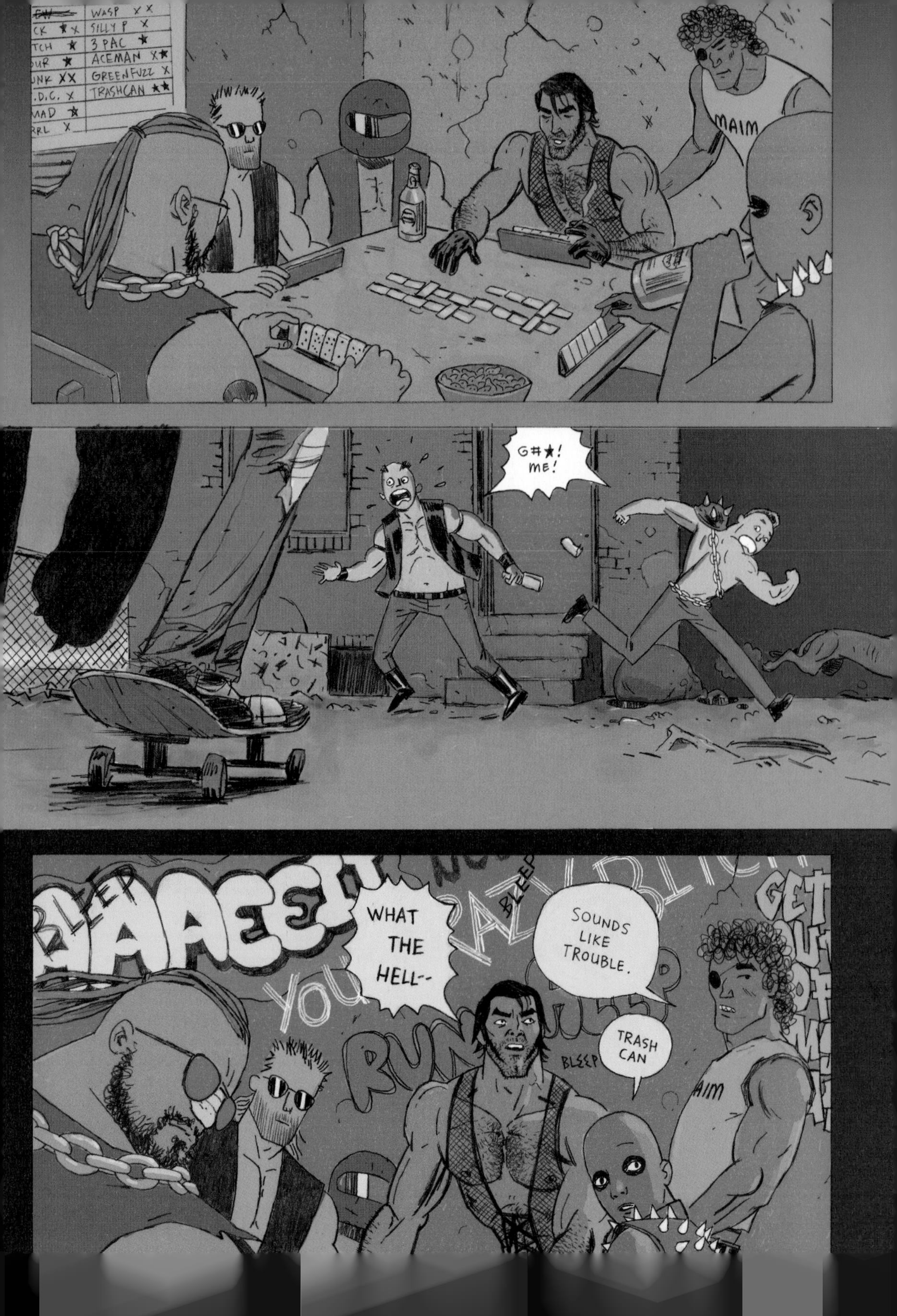
WASP X X
SILLY P X
3 PAC ★
ACEMAN X★
GREENFUZZ X
TRASHCAN ★★
MAIM
G#★! me!
BLEEP
WHAT THE HELL--
YOU
BLEEP
SOUNDS LIKE TROUBLE.
RUN
TRASH CAN
BLEEP
MAIM

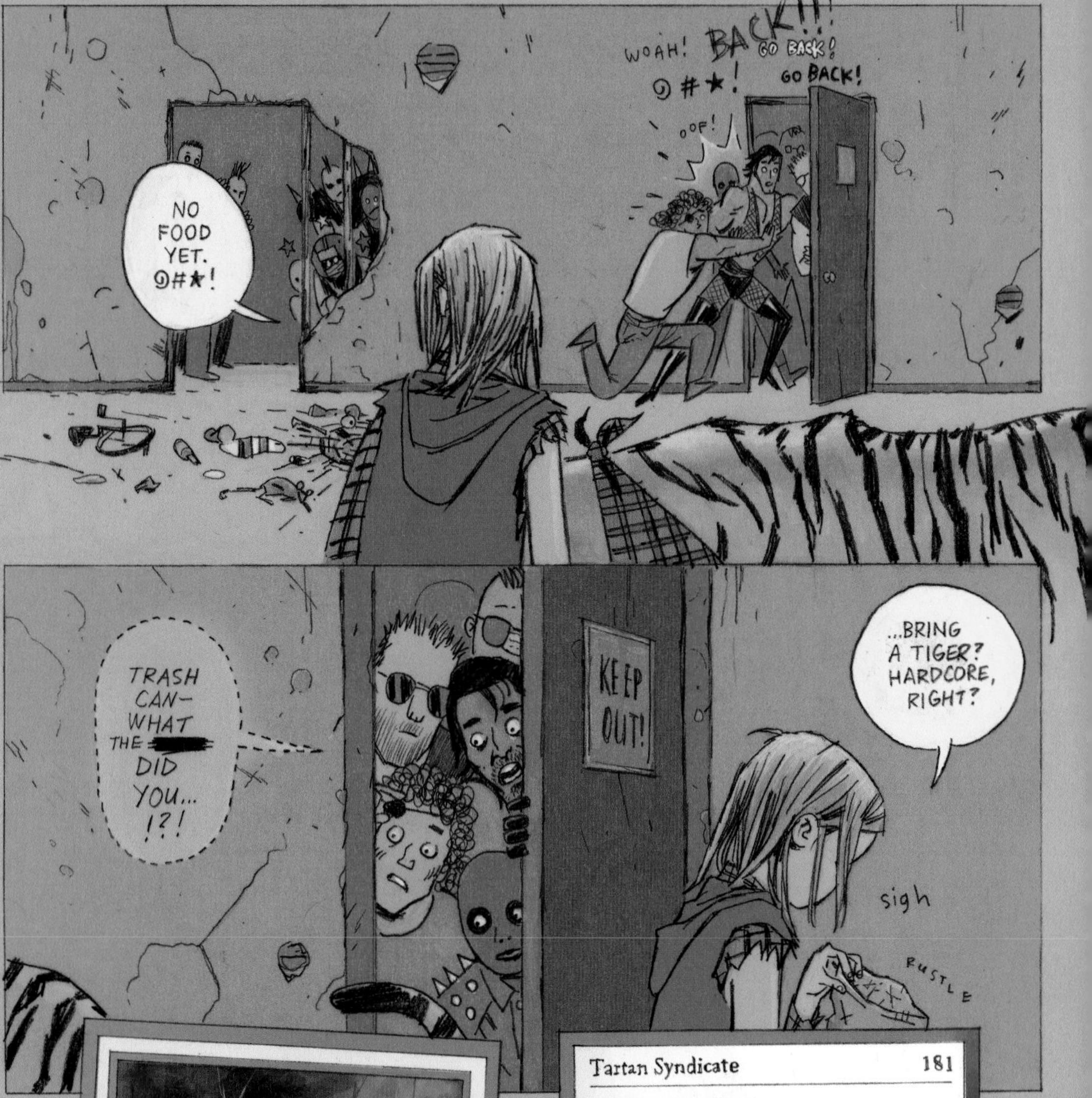
NO FOOD YET. 9#★!
WOAH! 9#★!
BACK!!!
GO BACK!
GO BACK!
OOF!
TRASH CAN— WHAT THE [redacted] DID YOU... !?!
...BRING A TIGER? HARDCORE, RIGHT?
KEEP OUT!
sigh
RUSTLE

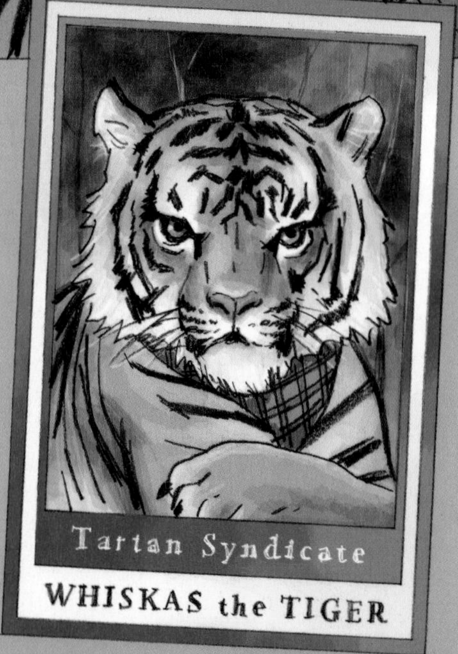
Tartan Syndicate
WHISKAS the TIGER

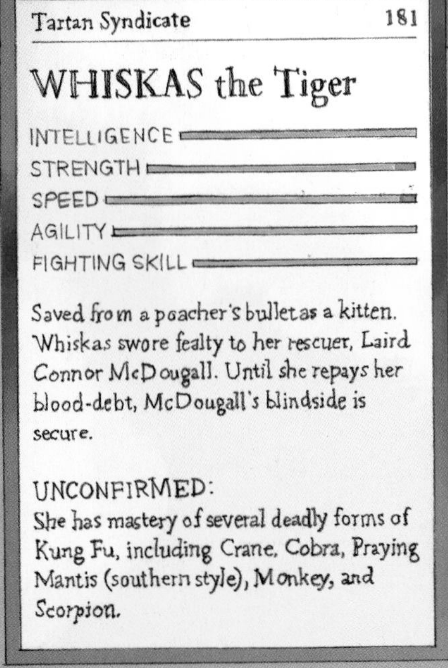
Tartan Syndicate
181
WHISKAS the Tiger
INTELLIGENCE
STRENGTH
SPEED
AGILITY
FIGHTING SKILL
Saved from a poacher's bullet as a kitten. Whiskas swore fealty to her rescuer, Laird Connor McDougall. Until she repays her blood-debt, McDougall's blindside is secure.
UNCONFIRMED:
She has mastery of several deadly forms of Kung Fu, including Crane, Cobra, Praying Mantis (southern style), Monkey, and Scorpion.

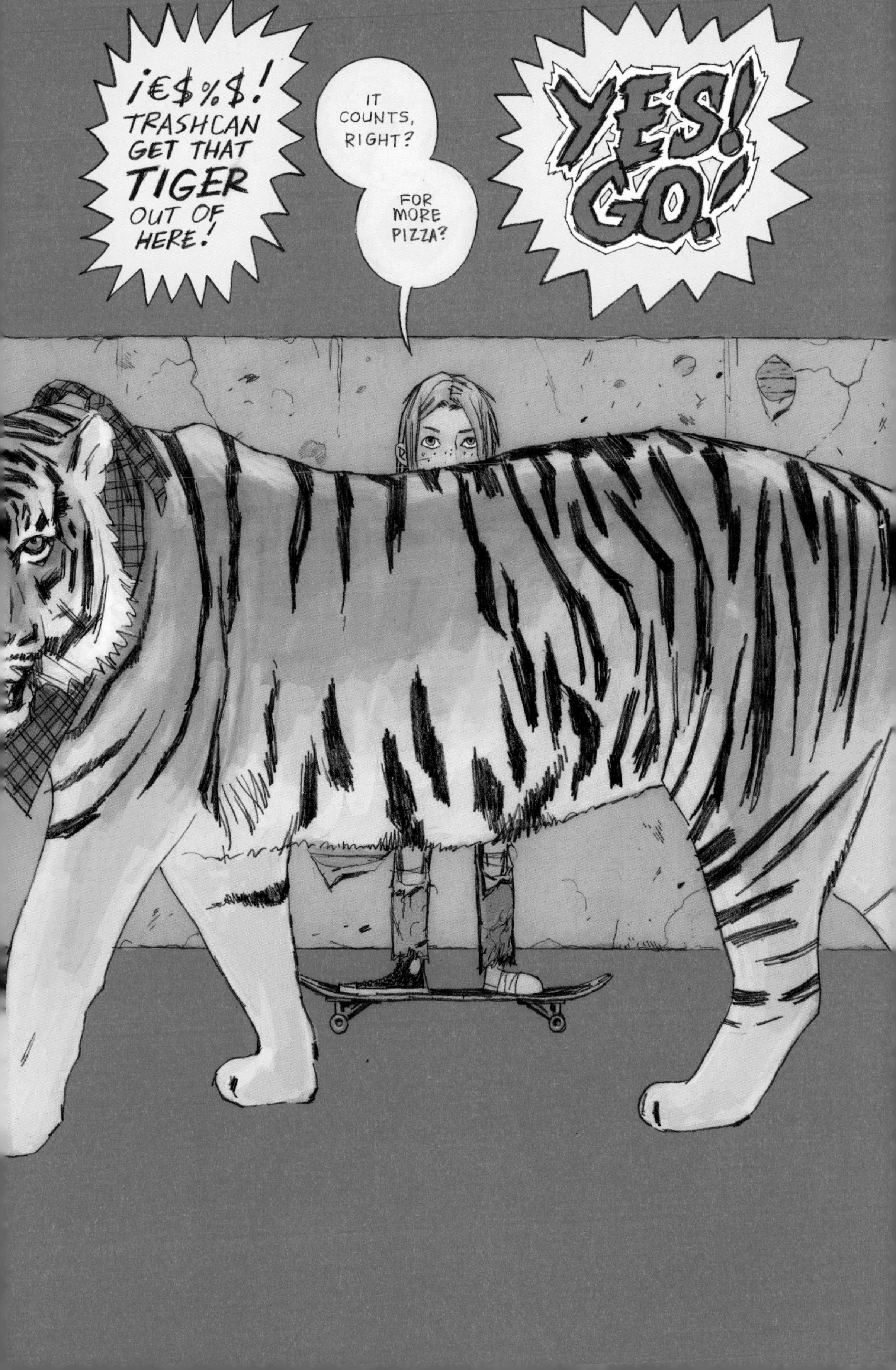
¡€$%$! TRASHCAN GET THAT TIGER OUT OF HERE!
IT COUNTS, RIGHT?
FOR MORE PIZZA?
YES! GO!

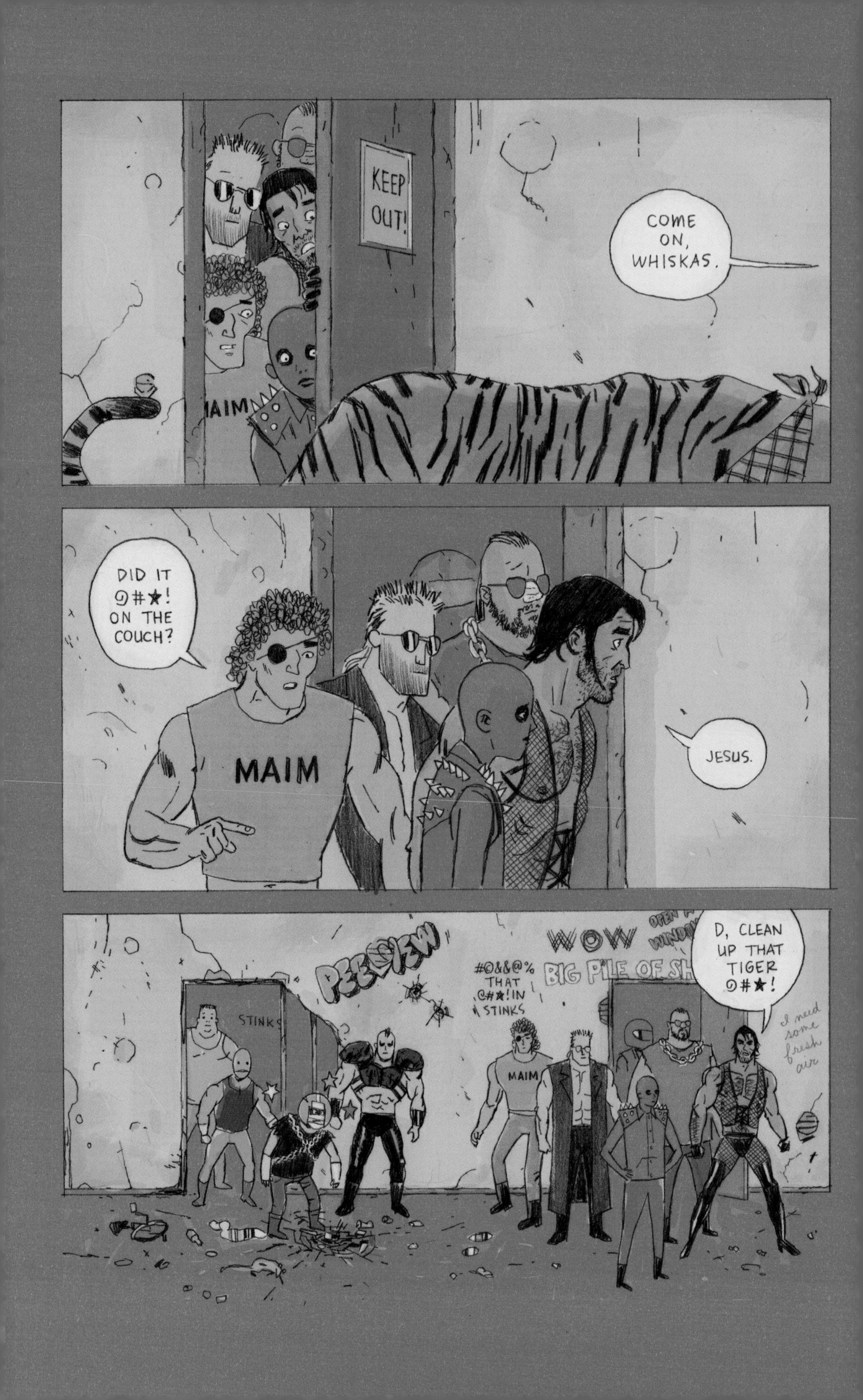
KEEP OUT!
MAIM
COME ON, WHISKAS.
DID IT @#★! ON THE COUCH?
MAIM
JESUS.
WOW
BIG PILE OF SH
#@&@% THAT @#★!IN STINKS
STINKS
MAIM
D, CLEAN UP THAT TIGER @#★!
I need some fresh air

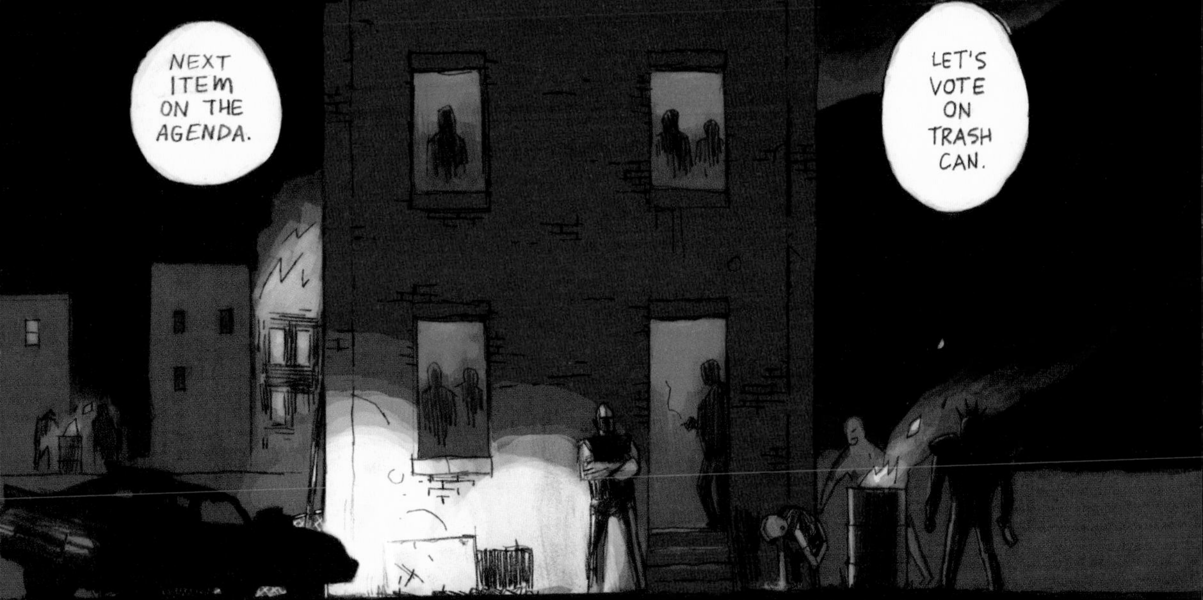

NEXT ITEM ON THE AGENDA.
LET'S VOTE ON TRASH CAN.

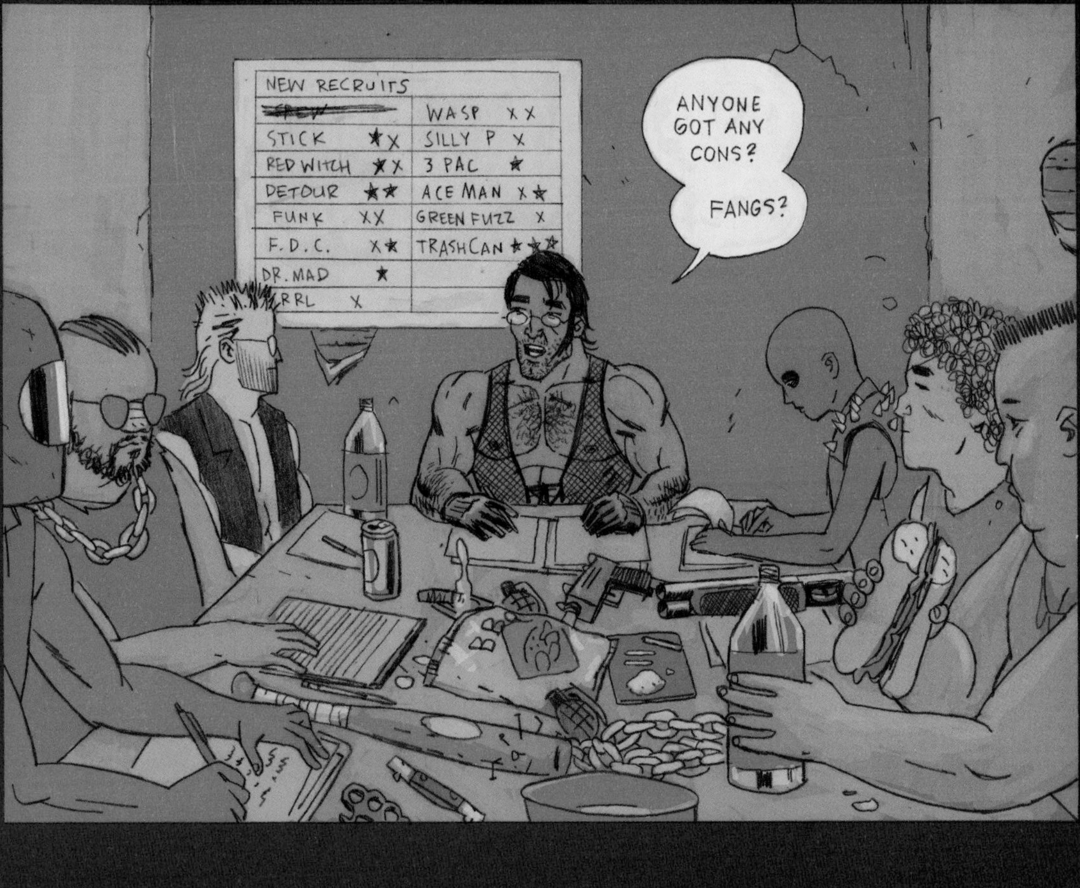

NEW RECRUITS
STICK
RED WITCH
DETOUR
FUNK
F.D.C.
DR. MAD
RRL
WASP
SILLY P
3 PAC
ACE MAN
GREEN FUZZ
TRASHCAN
ANYONE GOT ANY CONS?
FANGS?

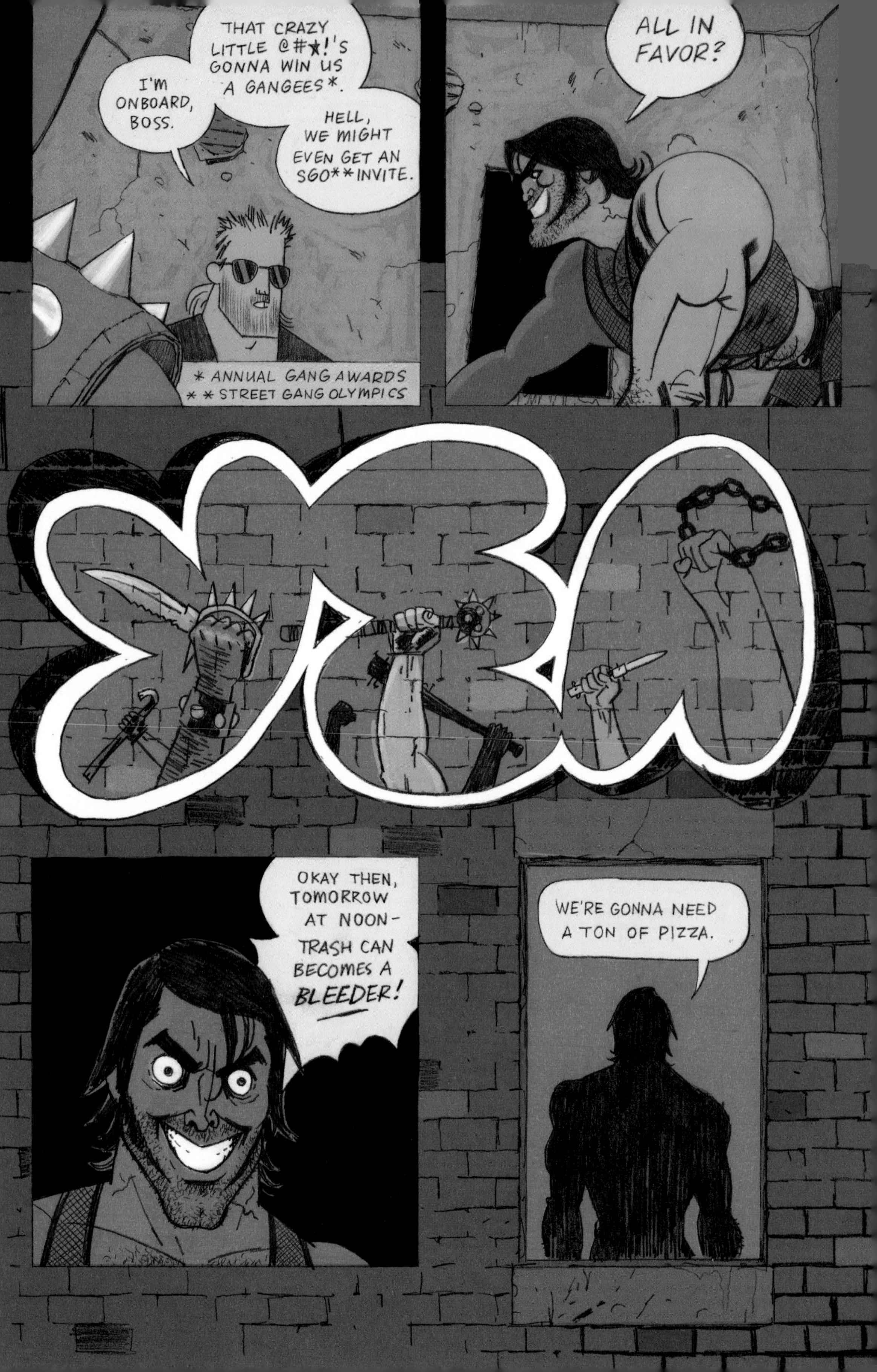
I'M ONBOARD, BOSS.
THAT CRAZY LITTLE @#*!'S GONNA WIN US A GANGEES*.
HELL, WE MIGHT EVEN GET AN SGO** INVITE.
* ANNUAL GANG AWARDS
** STREET GANG OLYMPICS
ALL IN FAVOR?
OKAY THEN, TOMORROW AT NOON- TRASH CAN BECOMES A BLEEDER!
WE'RE GONNA NEED A TON OF PIZZA.

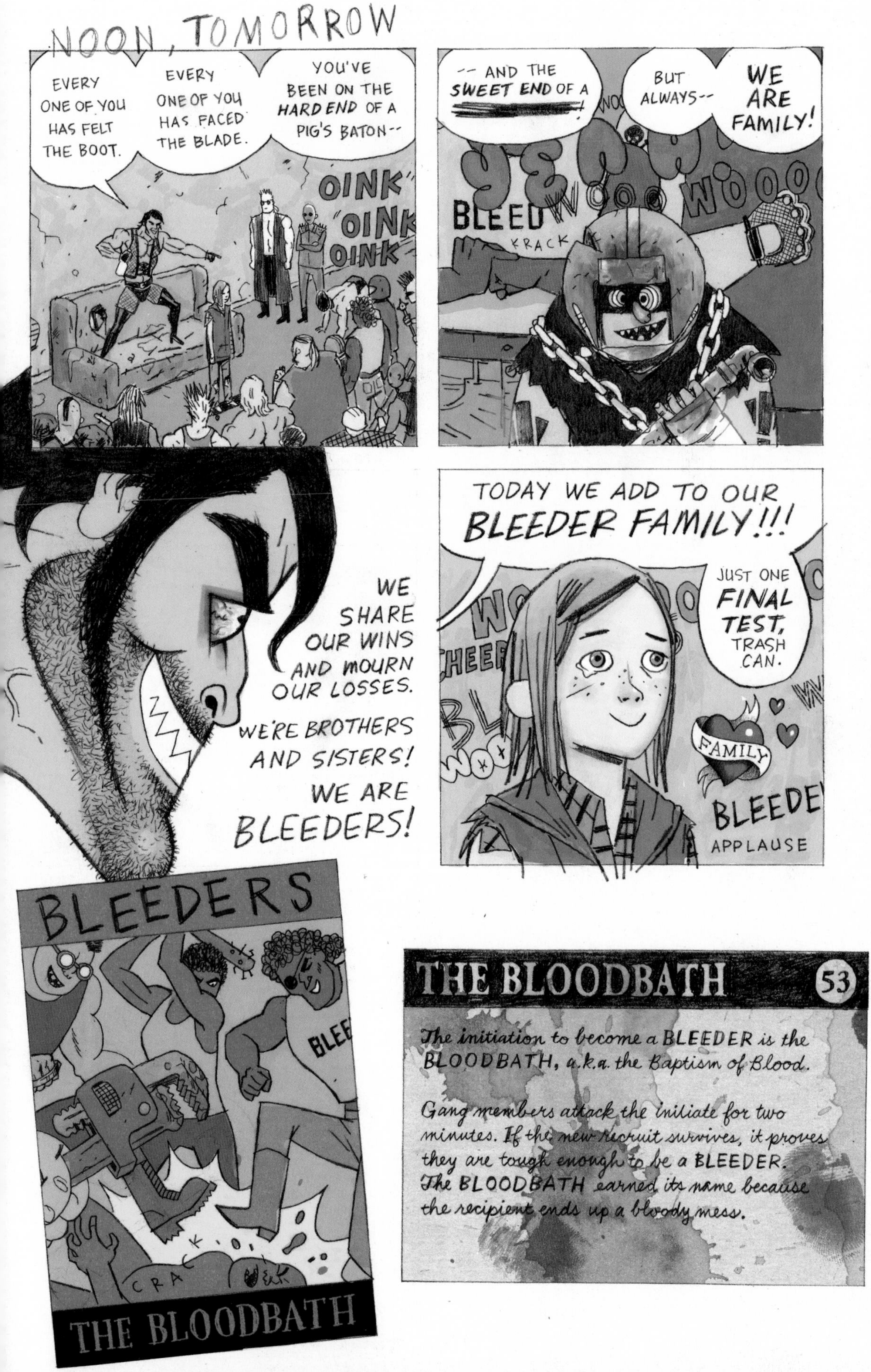
NOON, TOMORROW
EVERY ONE OF YOU HAS FELT THE BOOT.
EVERY ONE OF YOU HAS FACED THE BLADE.
YOU'VE BEEN ON THE HARD END OF A PIG'S BATON--
OINK "OINK OINK
-- AND THE SWEET END OF A [redacted]!
BUT ALWAYS--
WE ARE FAMILY!
BLEED
KRACK
WOOO
WE SHARE OUR WINS AND MOURN OUR LOSSES.
WE'RE BROTHERS AND SISTERS!
WE ARE BLEEDERS!
TODAY WE ADD TO OUR BLEEDER FAMILY!!!
JUST ONE FINAL TEST, TRASH CAN.
CHEER
FAMILY
BLEEDE
APPLAUSE
BLEEDERS
BLEE
CRA
THE BLOODBATH
THE BLOODBATH 53
The initiation to become a BLEEDER is the BLOODBATH, a.k.a. the Baptism of Blood.
Gang members attack the initiate for two minutes. If the new recruit survives, it proves they are tough enough to be a BLEEDER. The BLOODBATH earned its name because the recipient ends up a bloody mess.

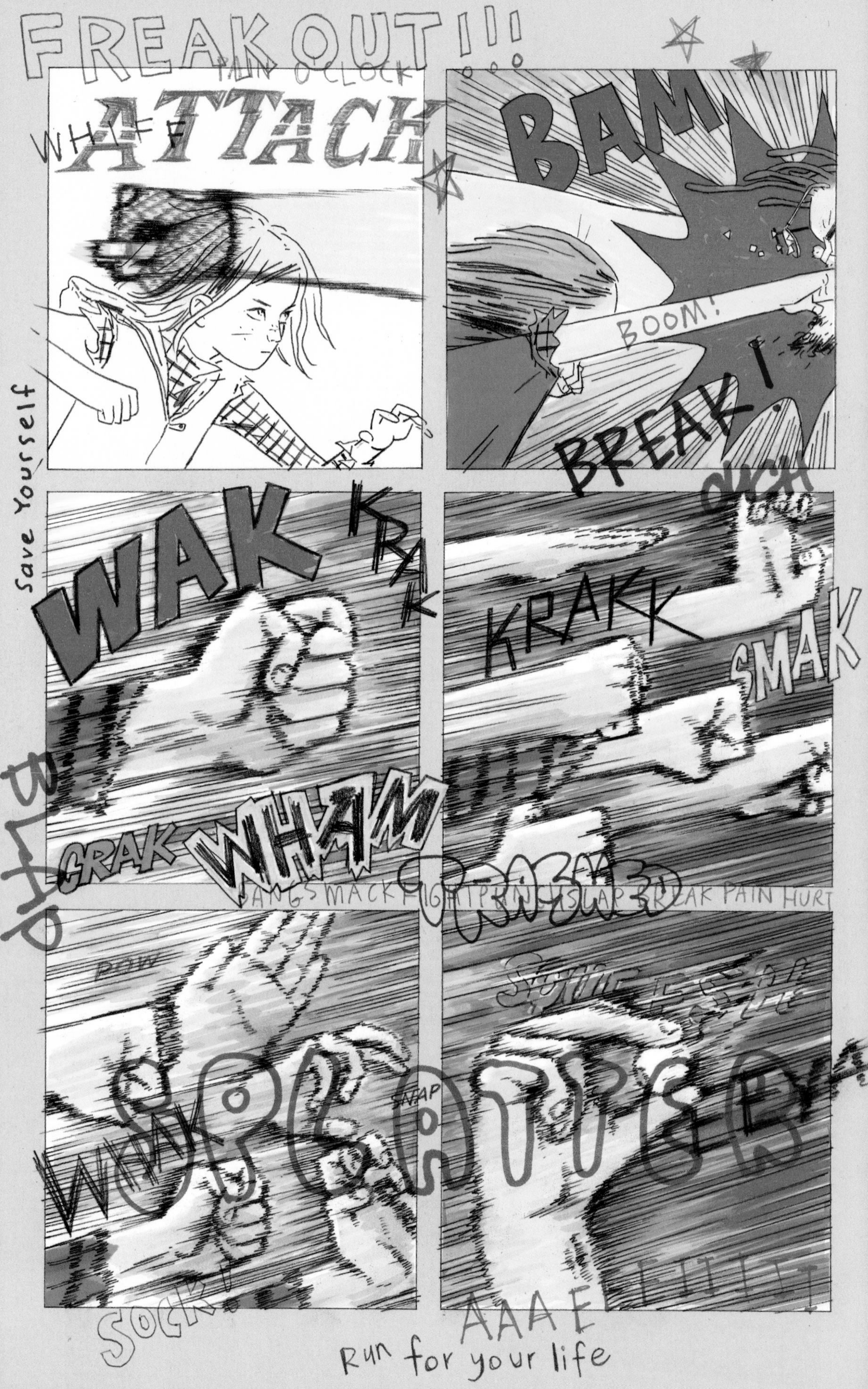
FREAKOUT!!!
WHIFF
ATTACK
BAM
BOOM!
BREAK!
Save Yourself
WAK
KRAK
OUCH
KRAKK
SMAK
CRAK
WHAM
BANG SMACK FIGHT PUNCH SLAP BREAK PAIN HURT
POW
SNAP
SOCK!
AAAEIIIIII
Run for your life

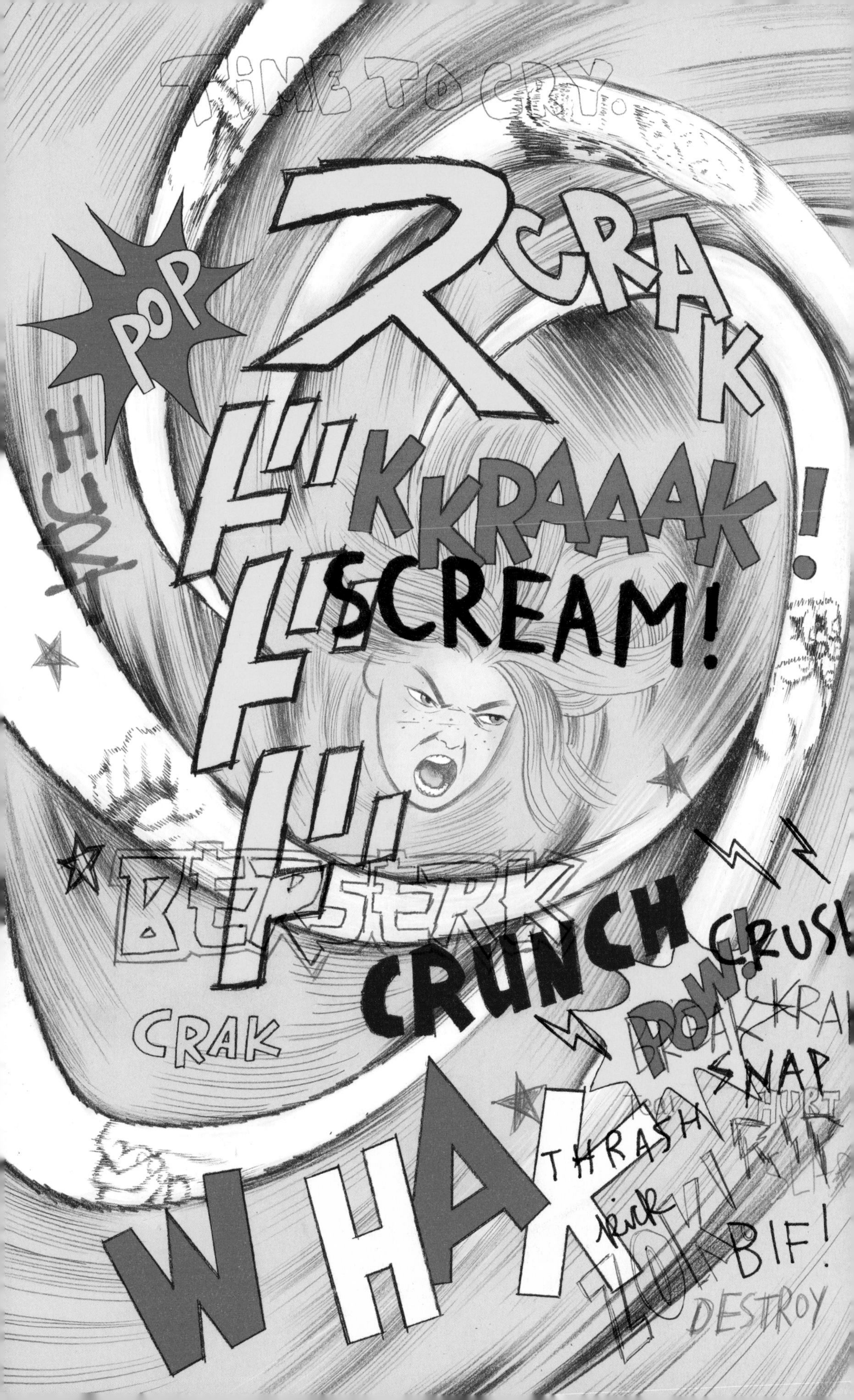

TIME TO CRY.
POP
CRAK
HURT
KKRAAAK!
SCREAM!
BERSERK
CRUNCH
POW!
CRAK
SNAP
THRASH
HURT
BIF!
DESTROY

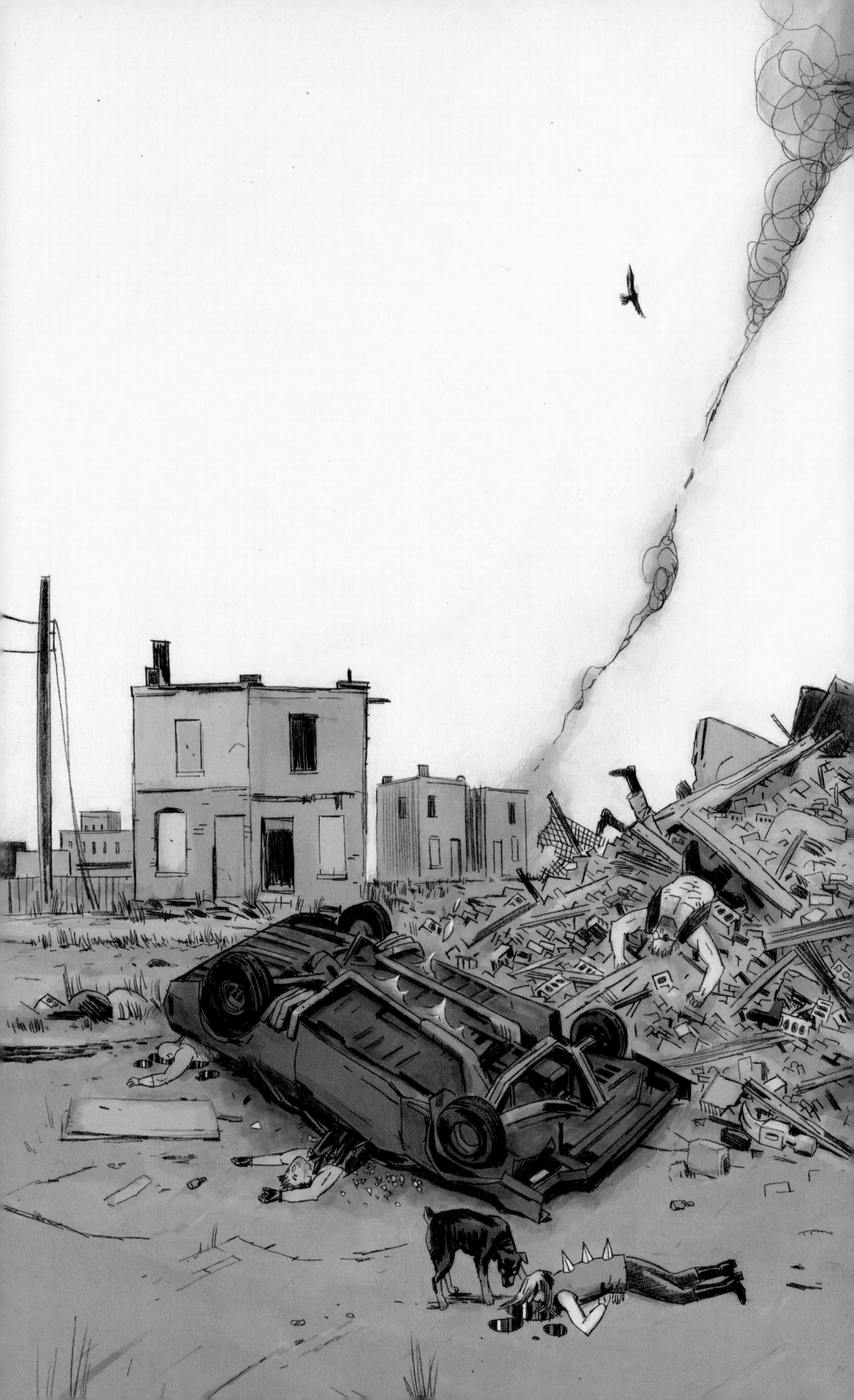

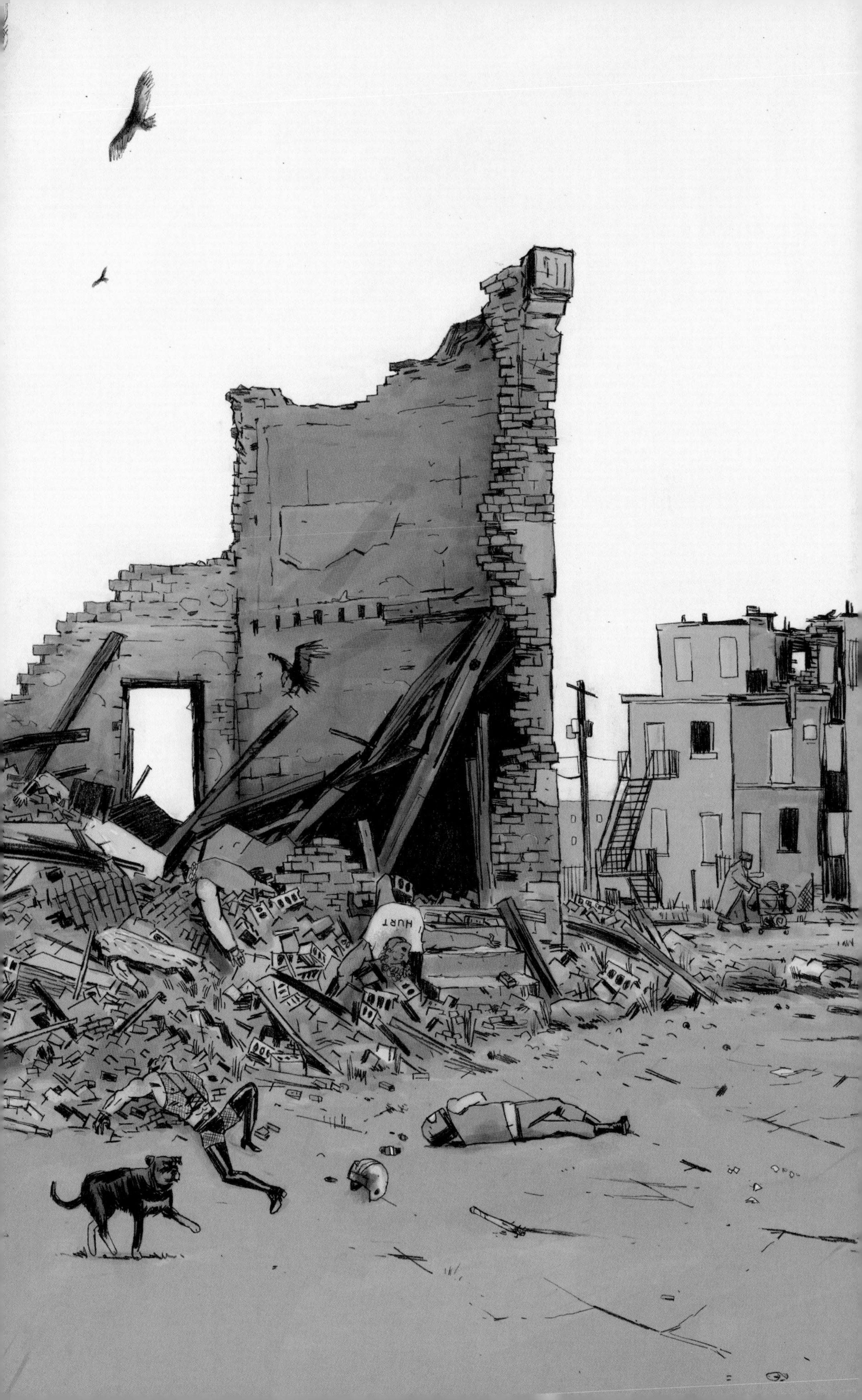
HURT

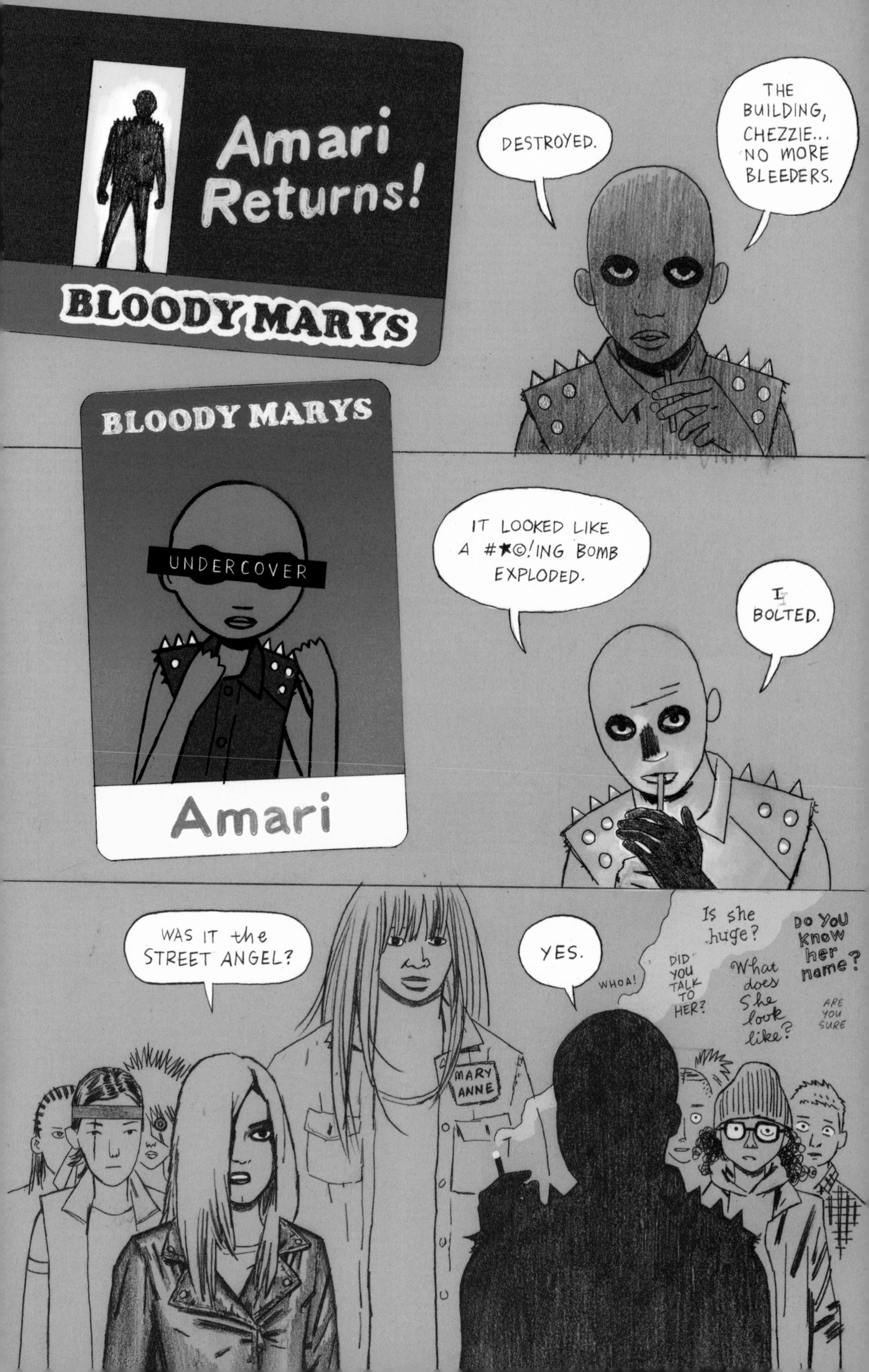
Amari Returns!
BLOODY MARYS
DESTROYED.
THE BUILDING, CHEZZIE... NO MORE BLEEDERS.
BLOODY MARYS
UNDERCOVER
Amari
IT LOOKED LIKE A #★©!ING BOMB EXPLODED.
I BOLTED.
WAS IT the STREET ANGEL?
YES.
MARY ANNE
WHOA!
DID YOU TALK TO HER?
Is she huge?
What does She look like?
Do YoU know her name?
ARE YOU SURE

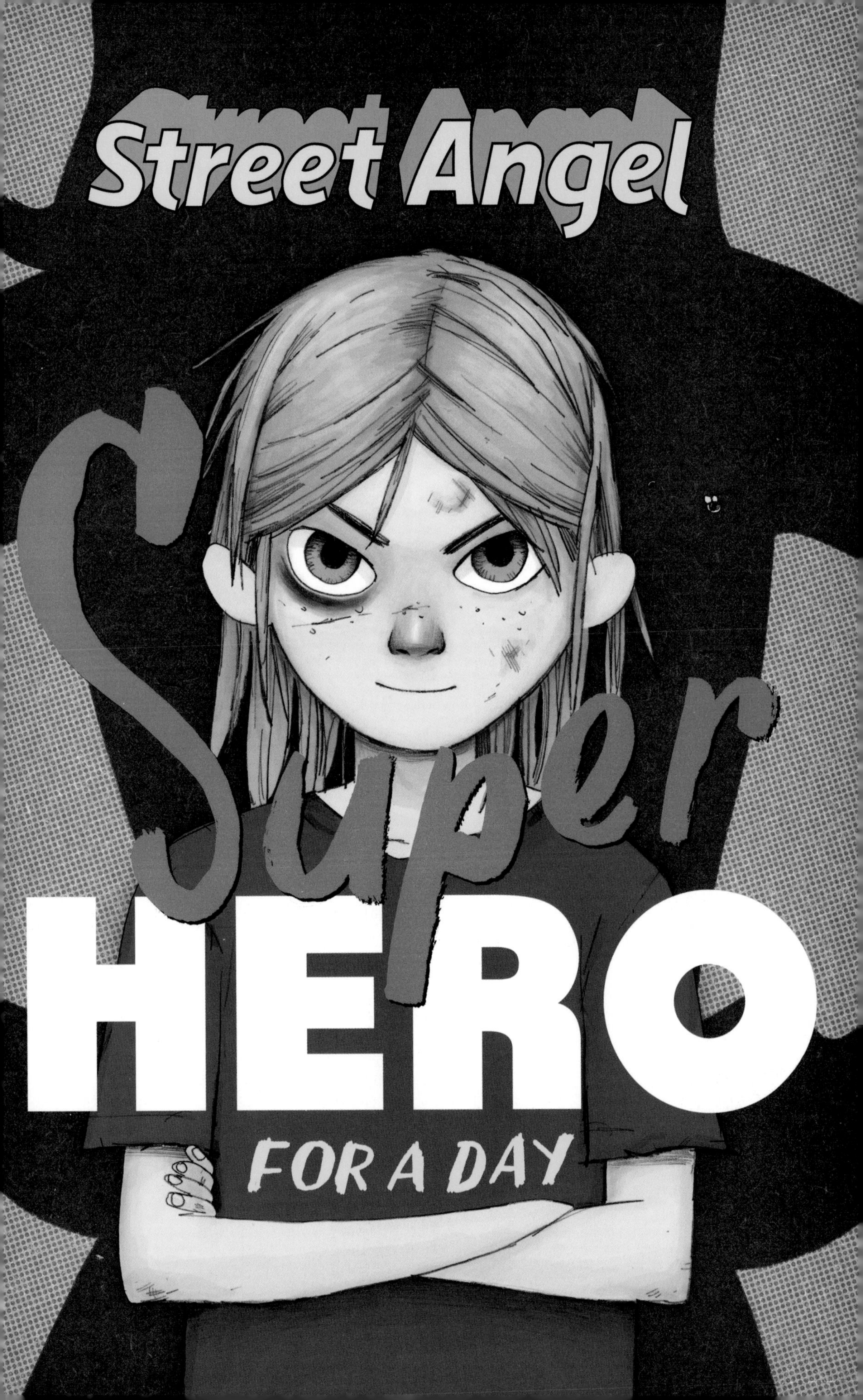
Street Angel
Super
HERO
FOR A DAY

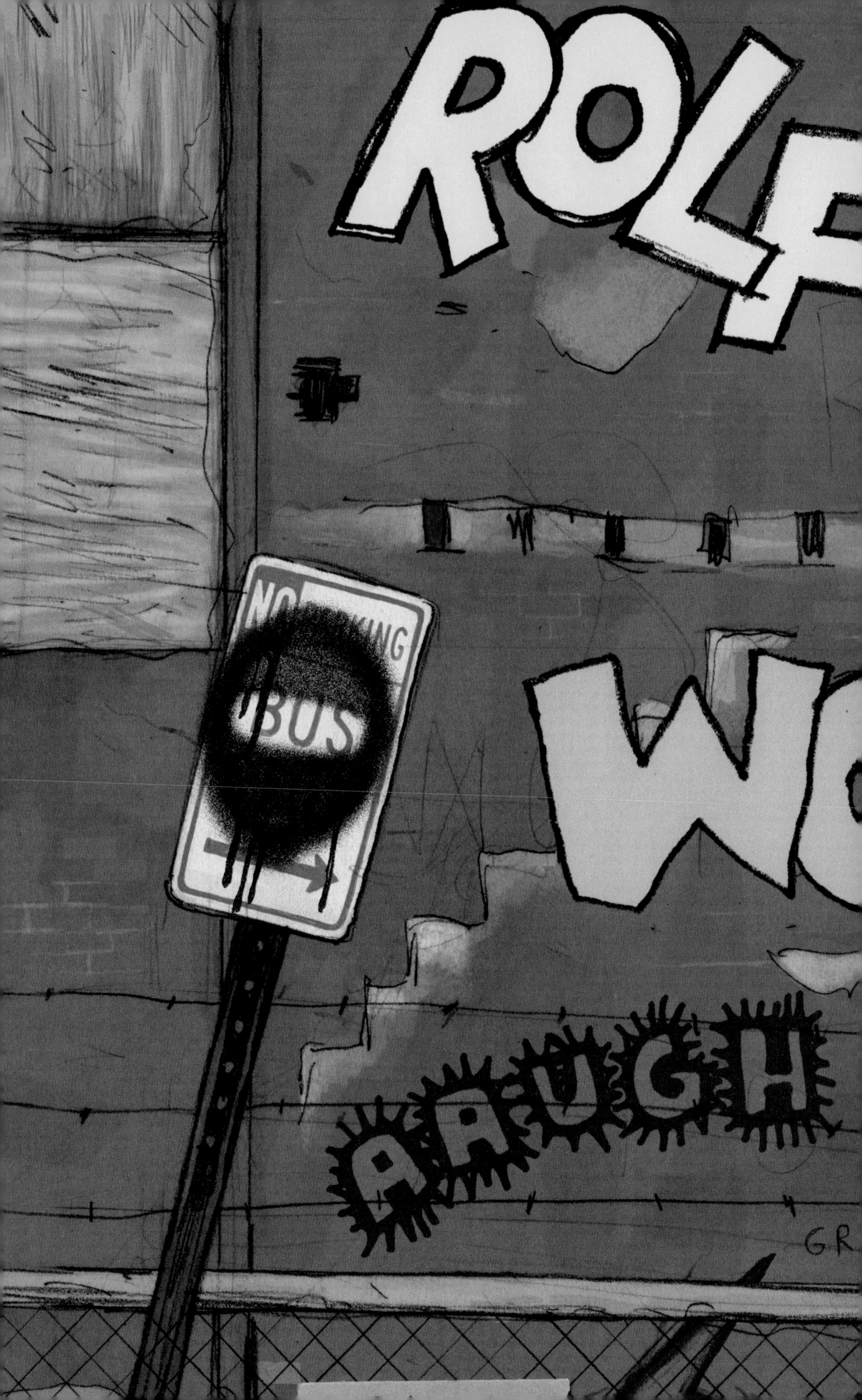
ROLF
NO KING
BUS
AAUGH

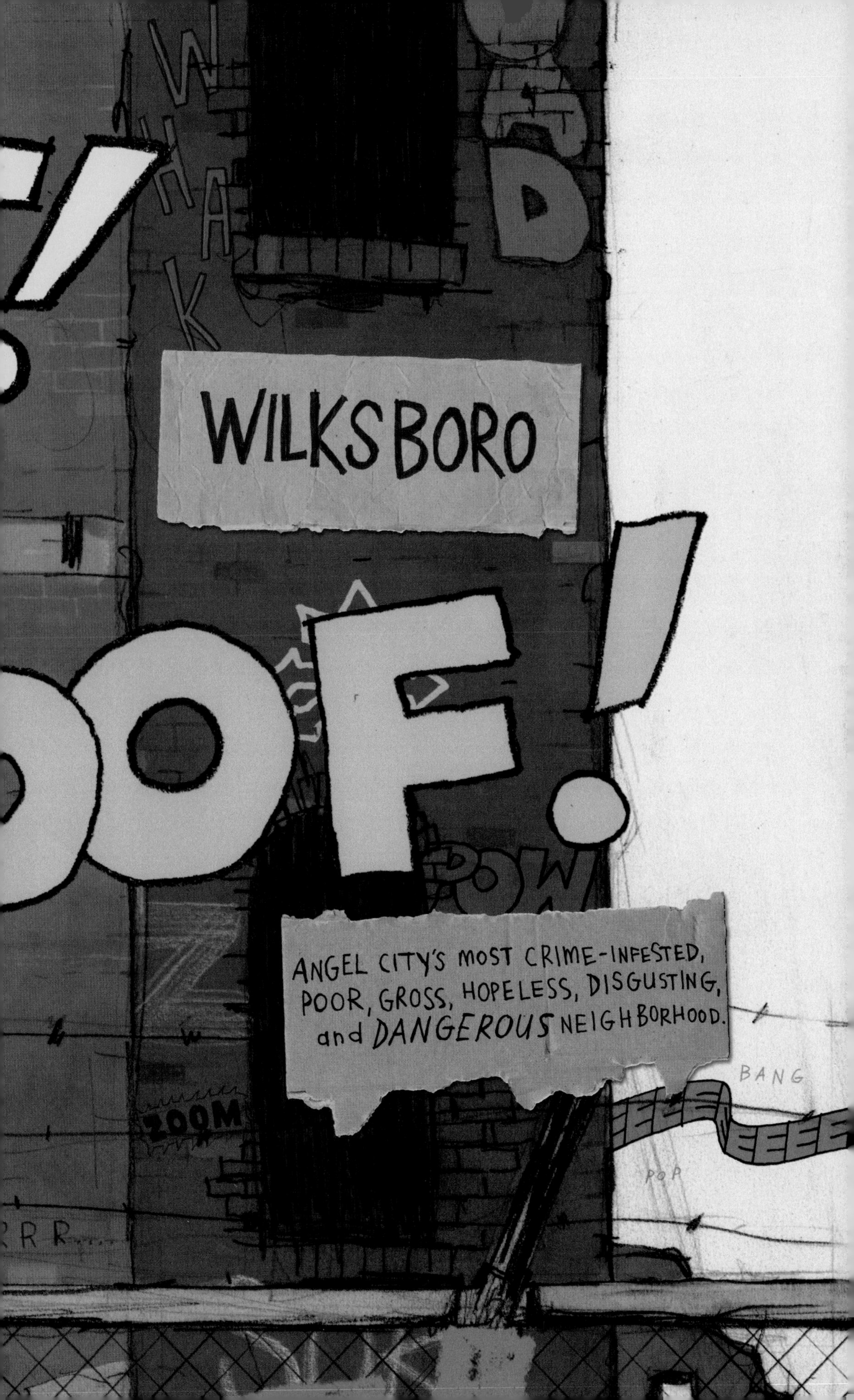
WILKSBORO
OOF!
POW
ANGEL CITY'S MOST CRIME-INFESTED, POOR, GROSS, HOPELESS, DISGUSTING, and DANGEROUS NEIGHBORHOOD.
BANG
ZOOM
POP

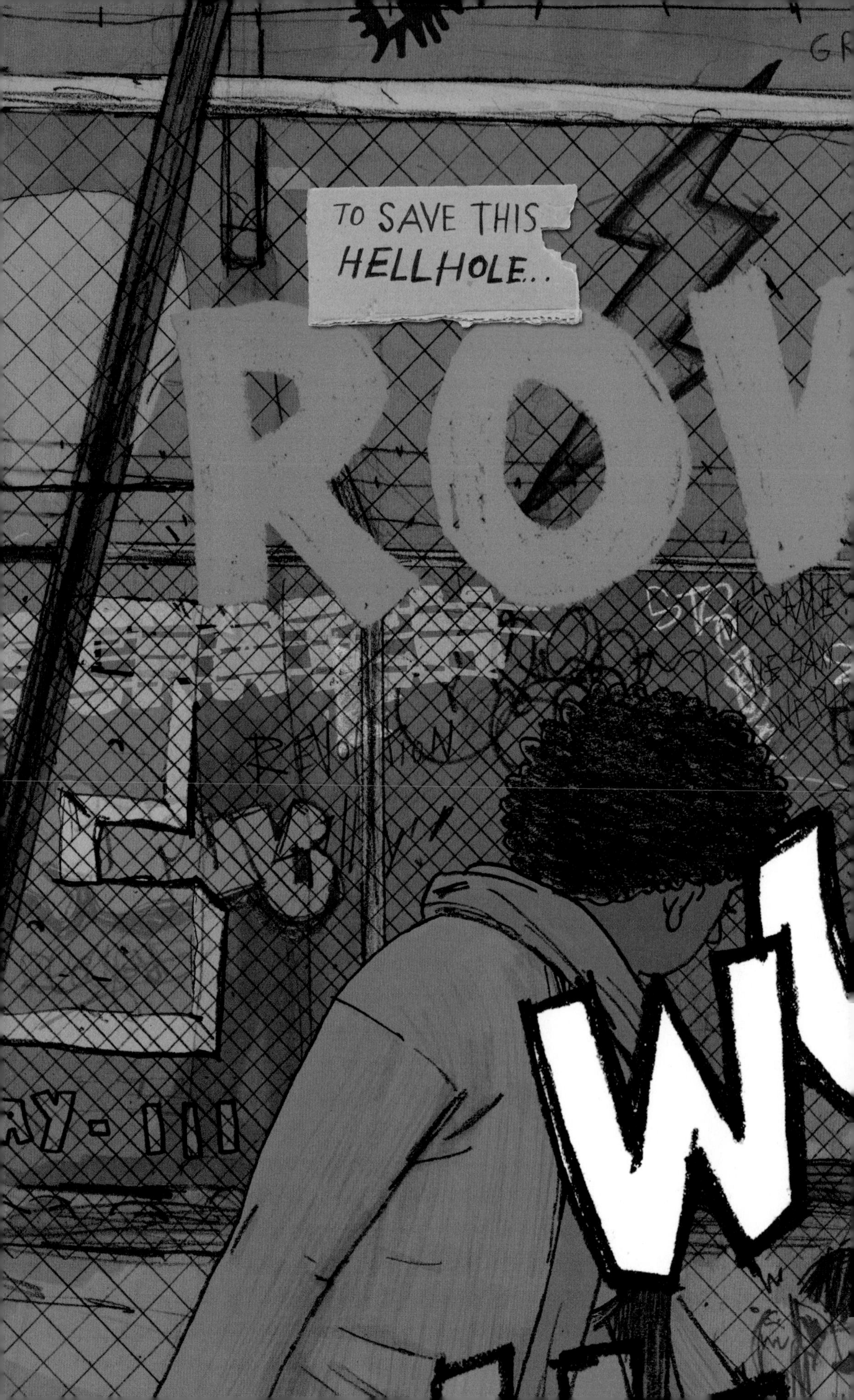
TO SAVE THIS HELLHOLE...

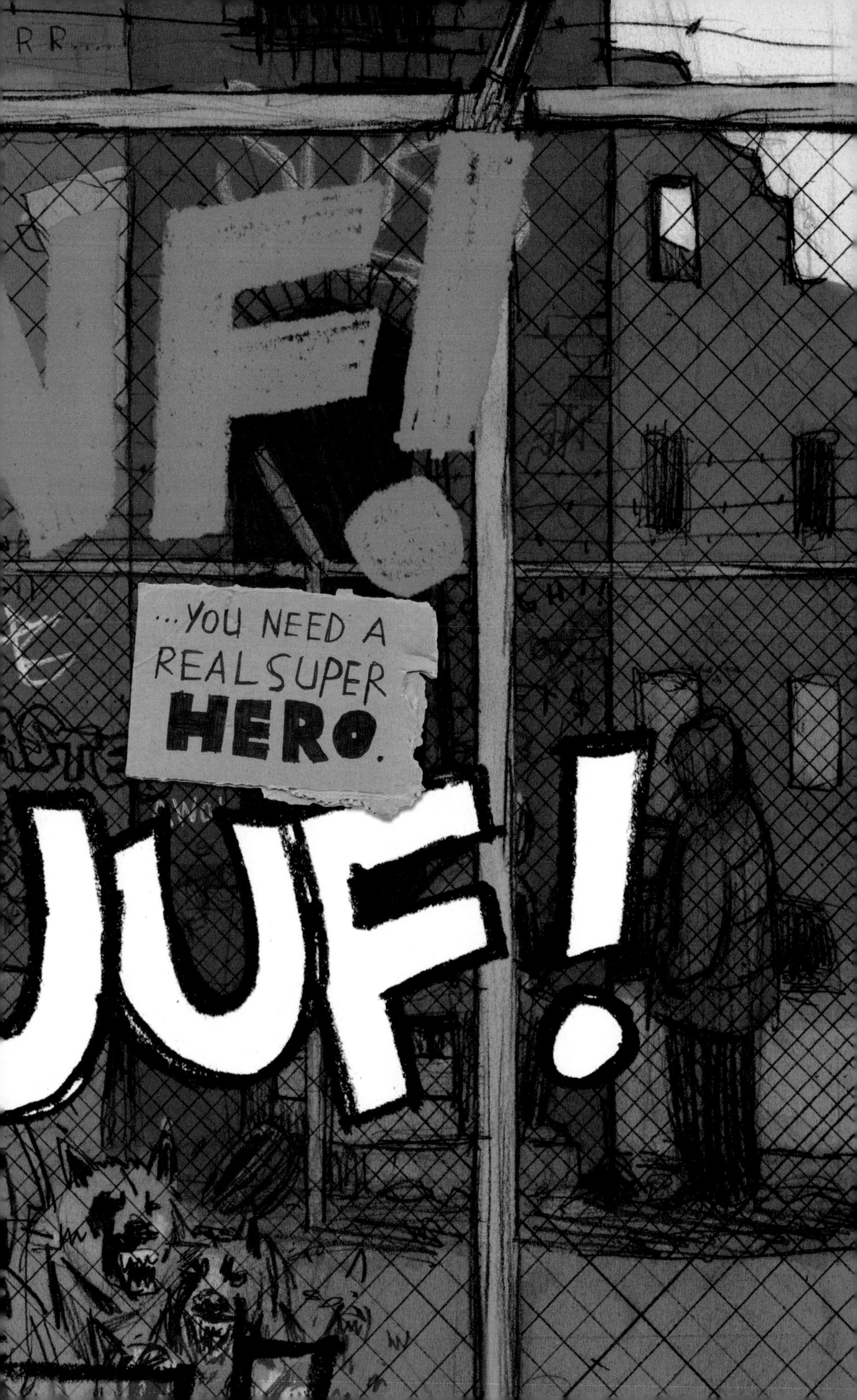
RR.....
UF!
...YOU NEED A REAL SUPER HERO.
UF!

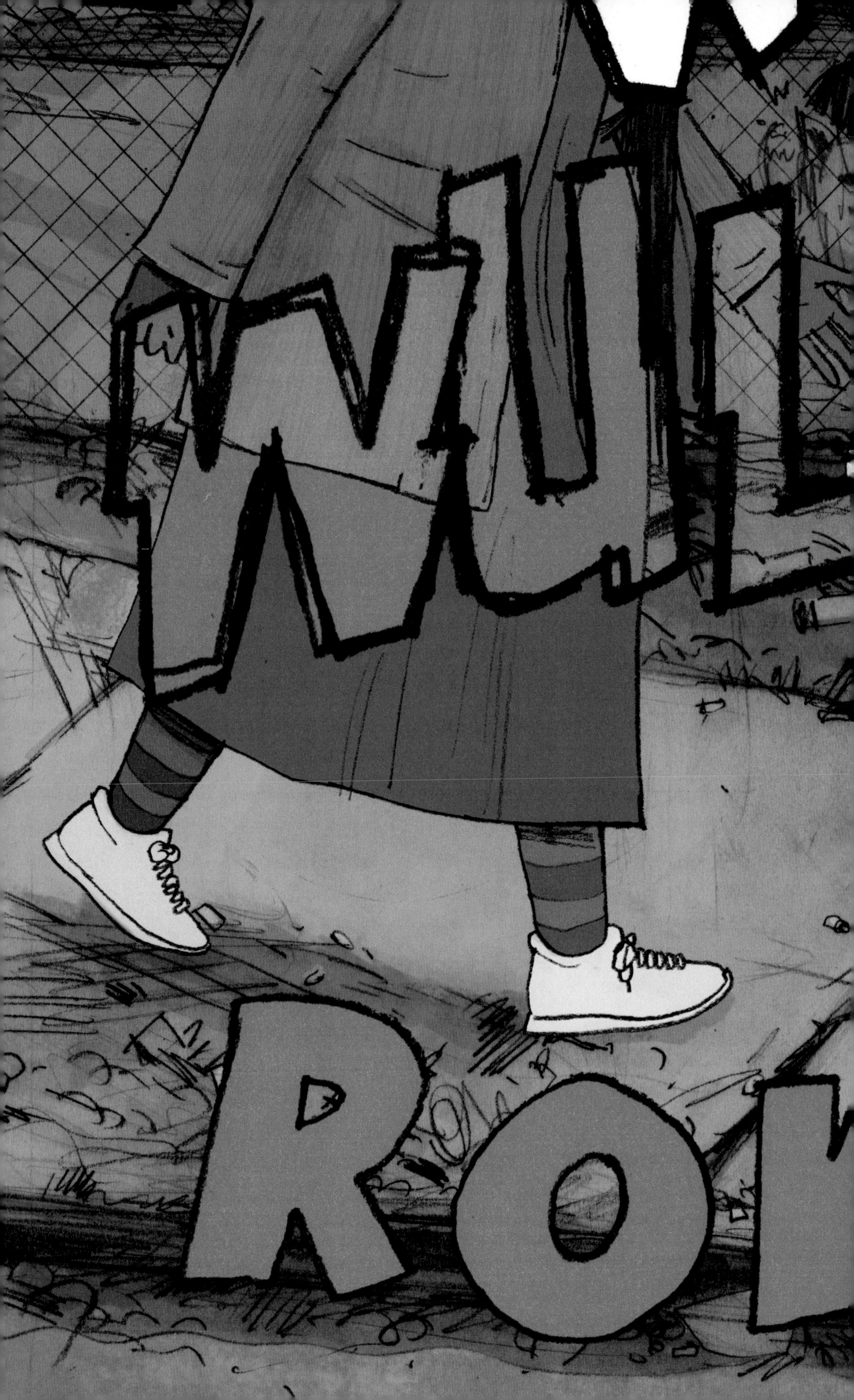

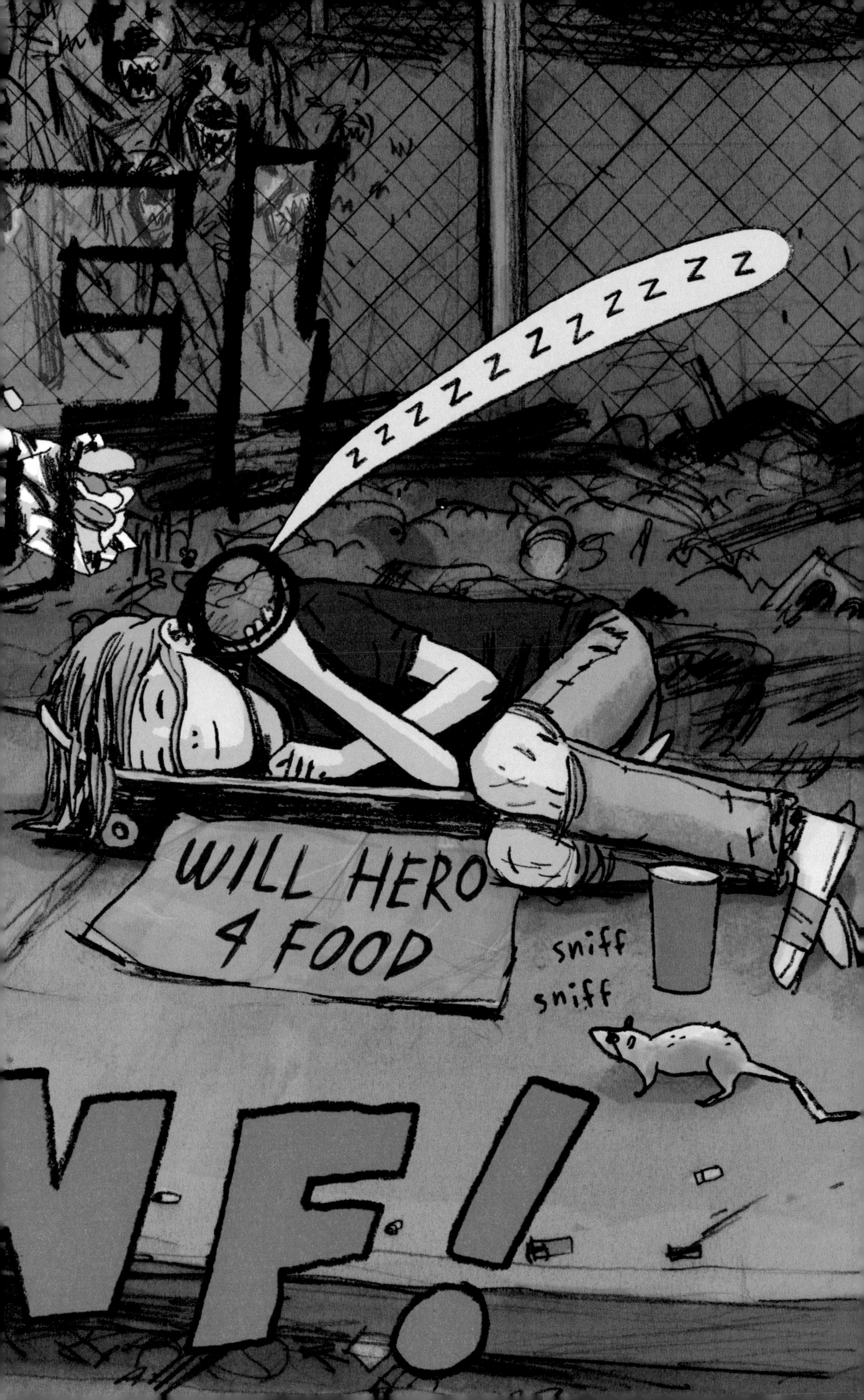
zzzzzzzzzzzz
WILL HERO 4 FOOD
sniff
sniff

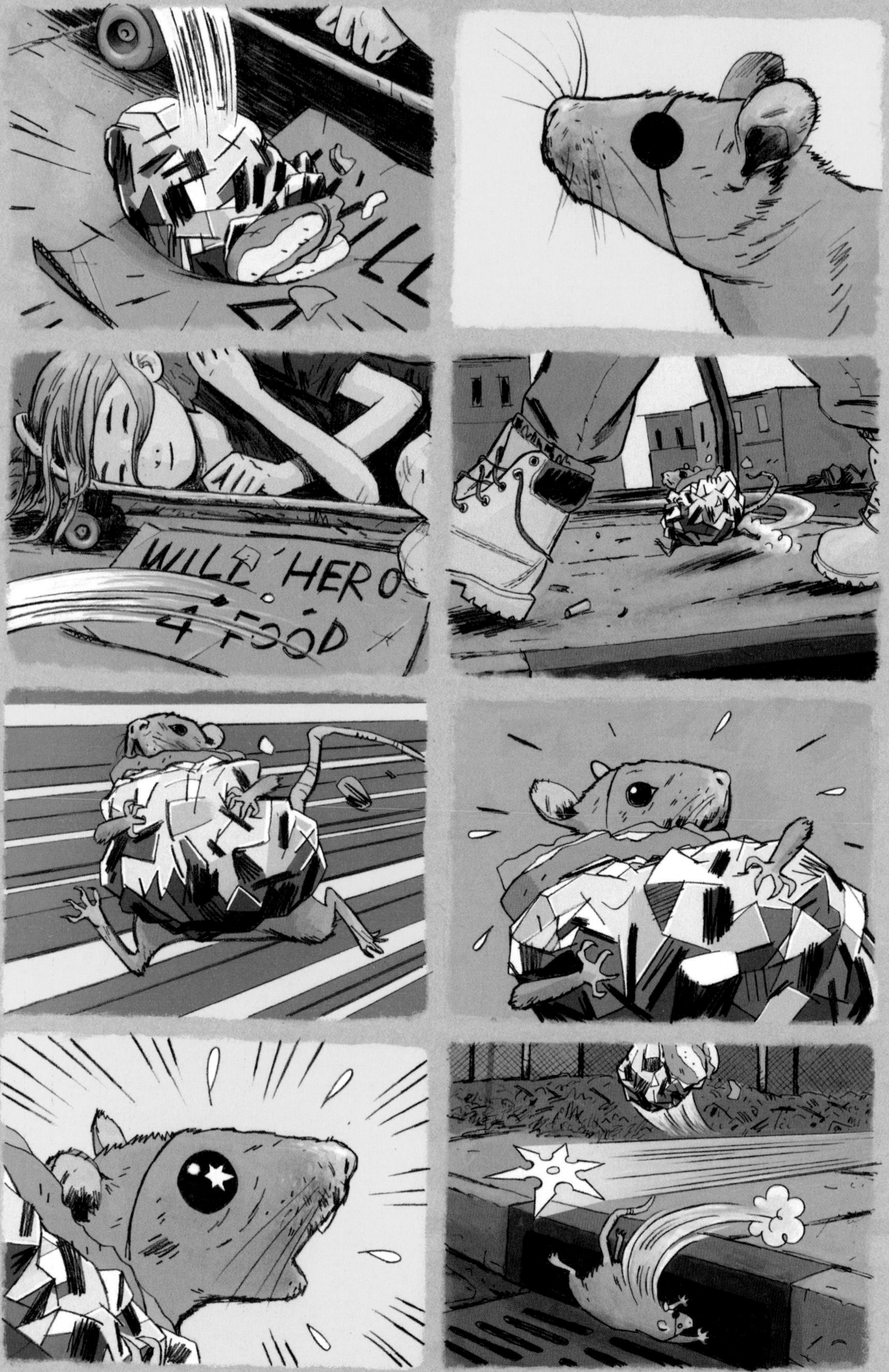
WILL HERO
4 FOOD

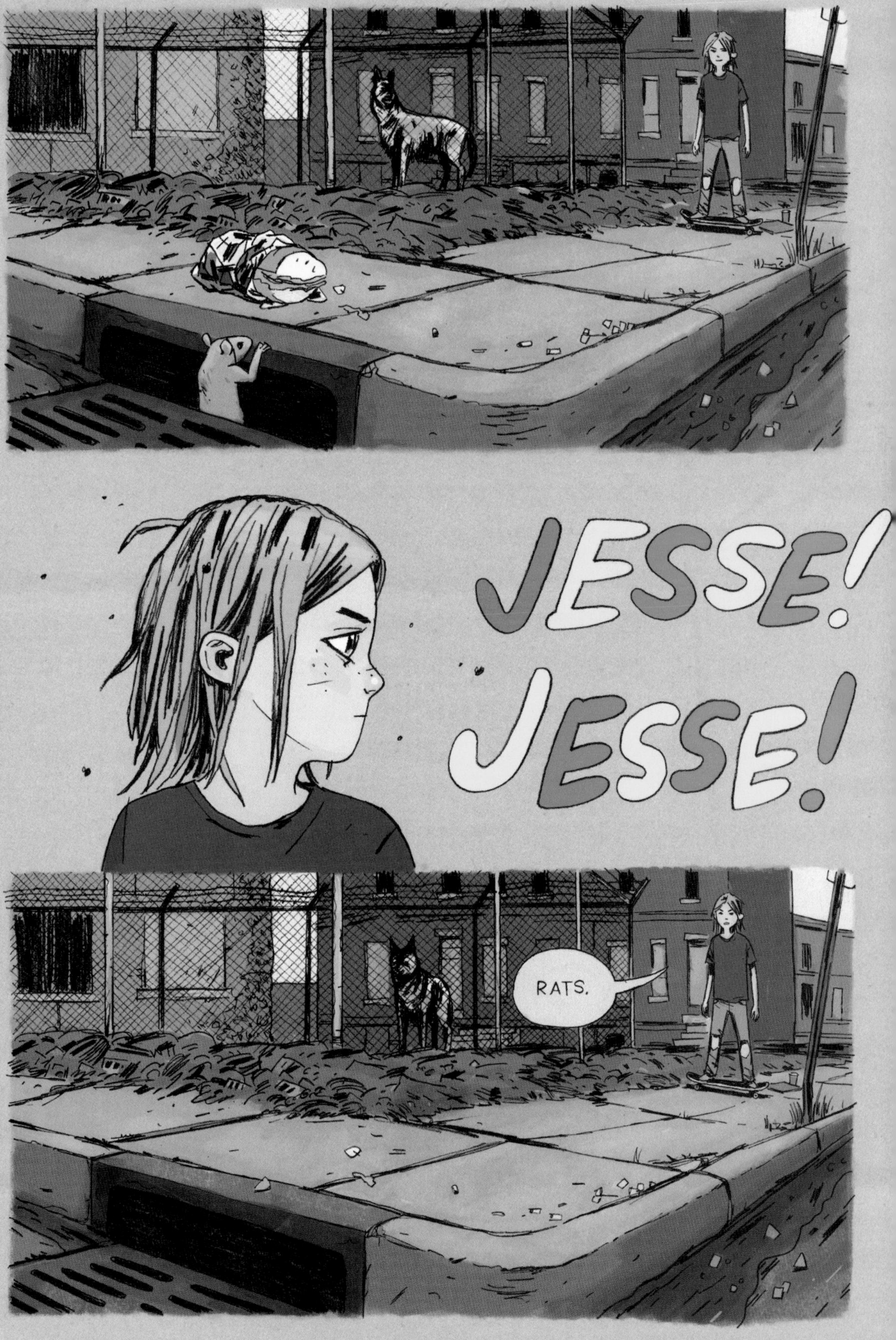
JESSE! JESSE!
RATS.

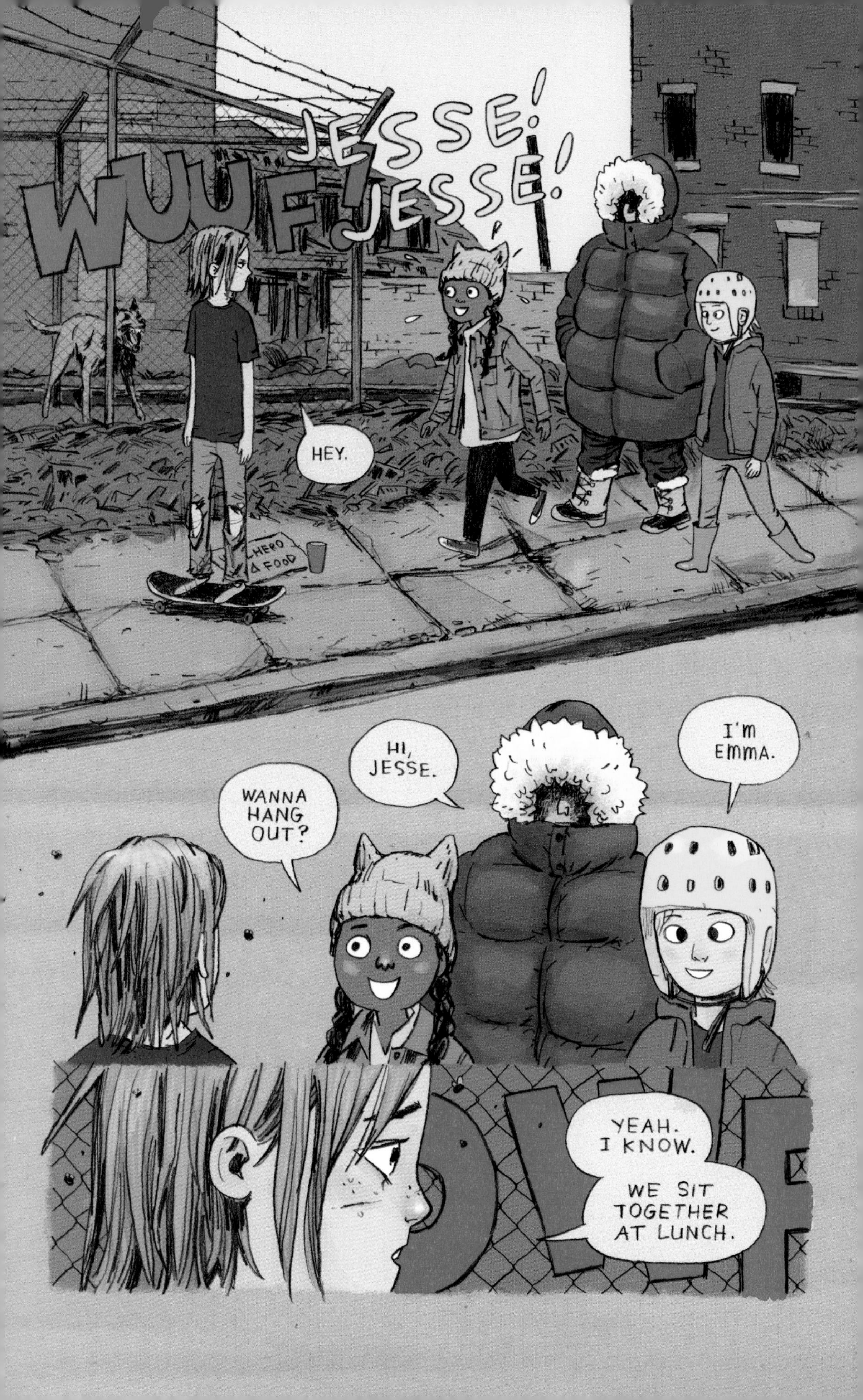

WUUF!
JESSE!
JESSE!
HEY.
HI, JESSE.
I'm EMMA.
WANNA HANG OUT?
YEAH. I KNOW.
WE SIT TOGETHER AT LUNCH.

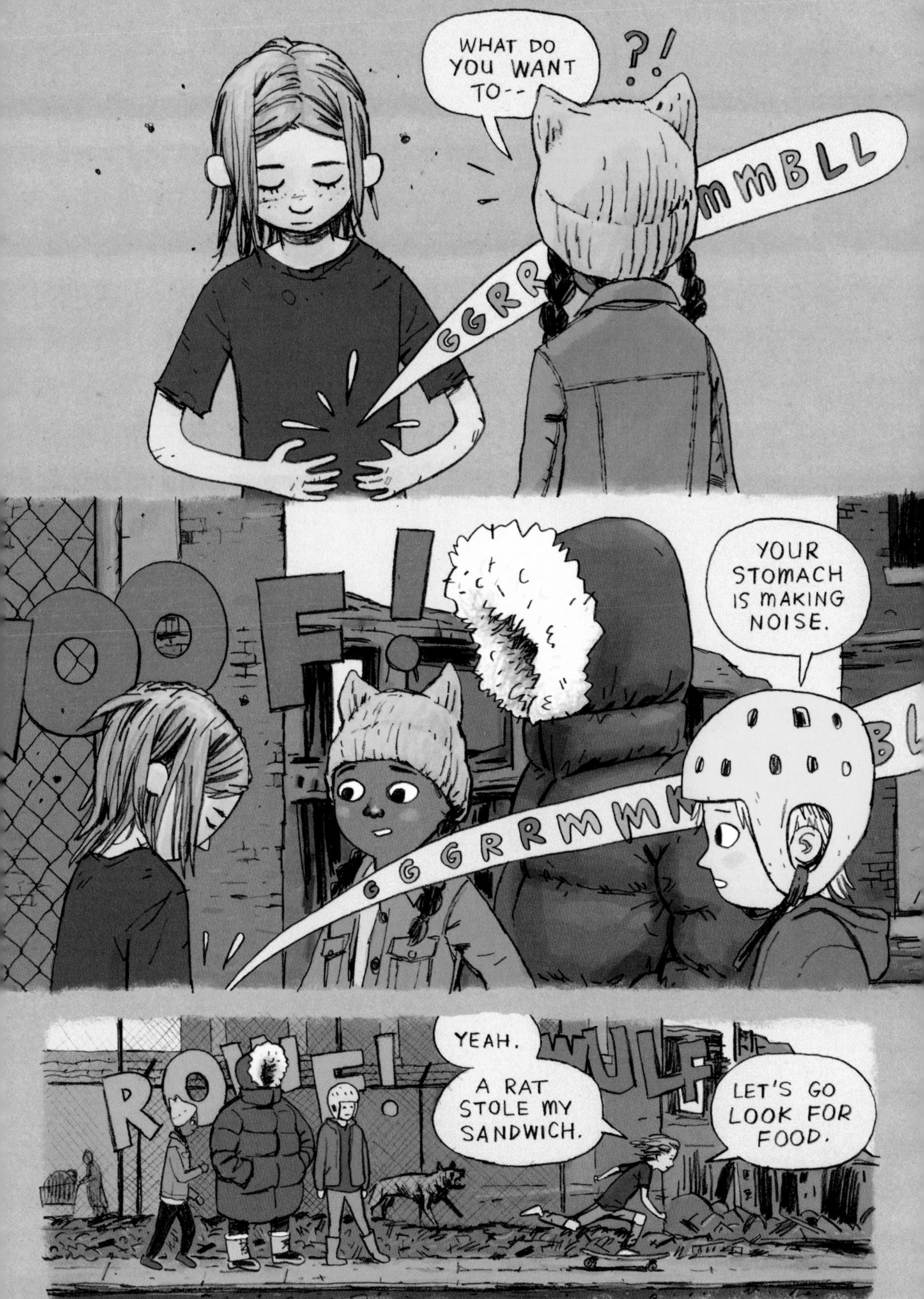

WHAT DO YOU WANT TO--
?!
GGRR
mmBLL
YOUR STOMACH IS MAKING NOISE.
YEAH.
A RAT STOLE MY SANDWICH.
LET'S GO LOOK FOR FOOD.

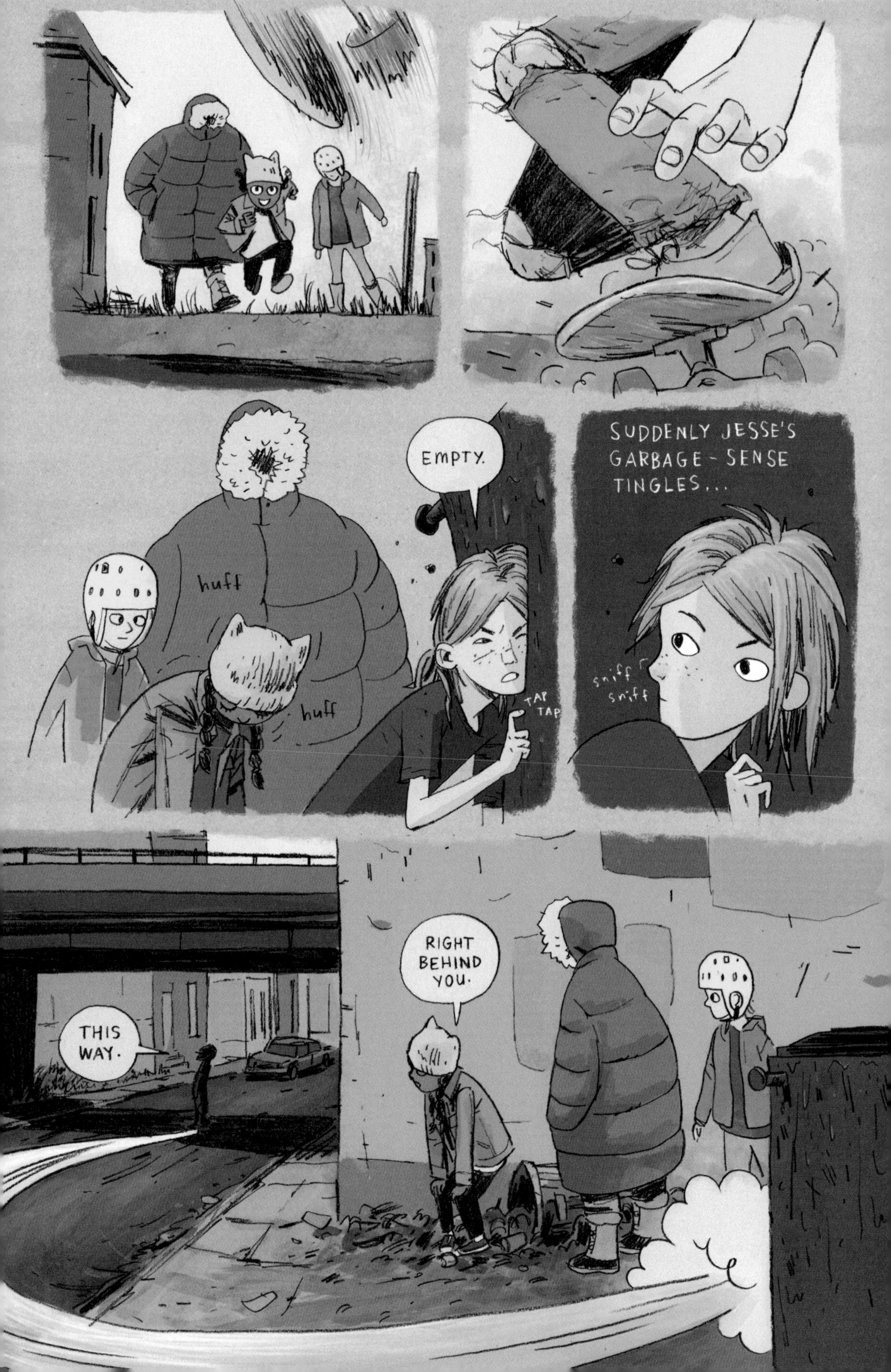
huff
huff
EMPTY.
TAP
TAP
SUDDENLY JESSE'S GARBAGE-SENSE TINGLES...
sniff
sniff
THIS WAY.
RIGHT BEHIND YOU.

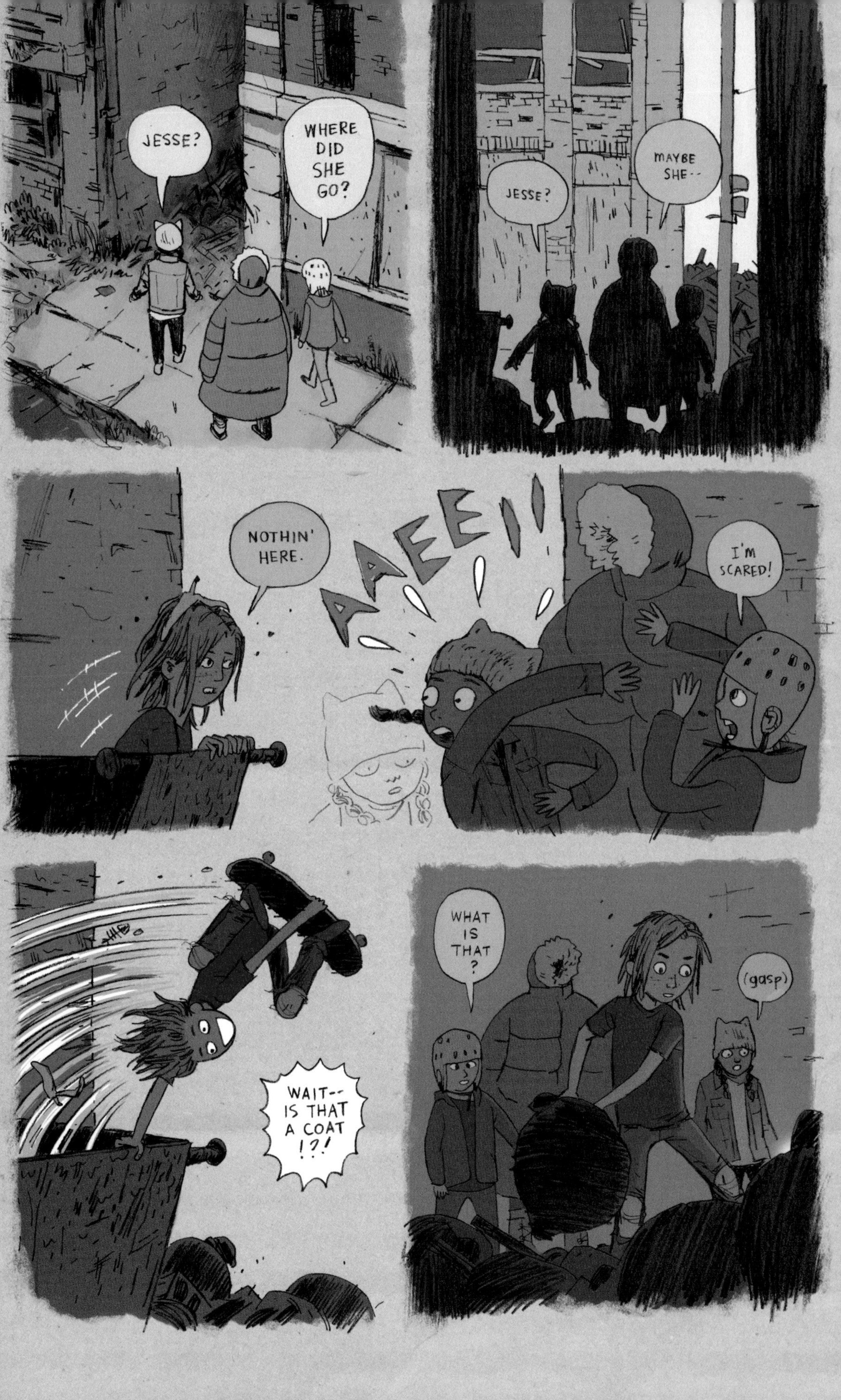
JESSE?
WHERE DID SHE GO?
JESSE?
MAYBE SHE--
NOTHIN' HERE.
AAEE!!
I'M SCARED!
WAIT-- IS THAT A COAT !?!
WHAT IS THAT ?
(gasp)

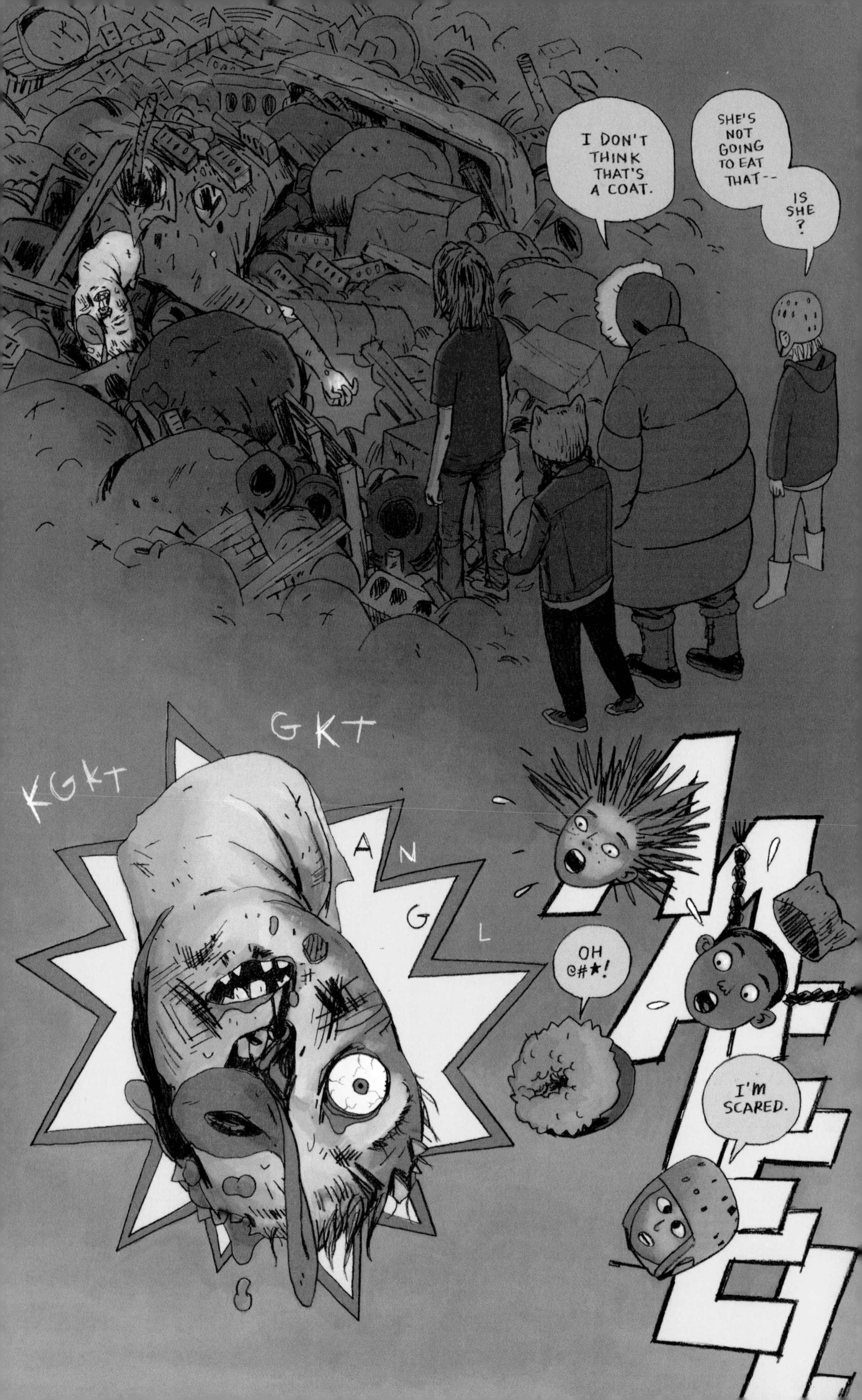
I DON'T THINK THAT'S A COAT.
SHE'S NOT GOING TO EAT THAT--
IS SHE?
GKT
KGKT
ANGL
OH @#★!
I'M SCARED.

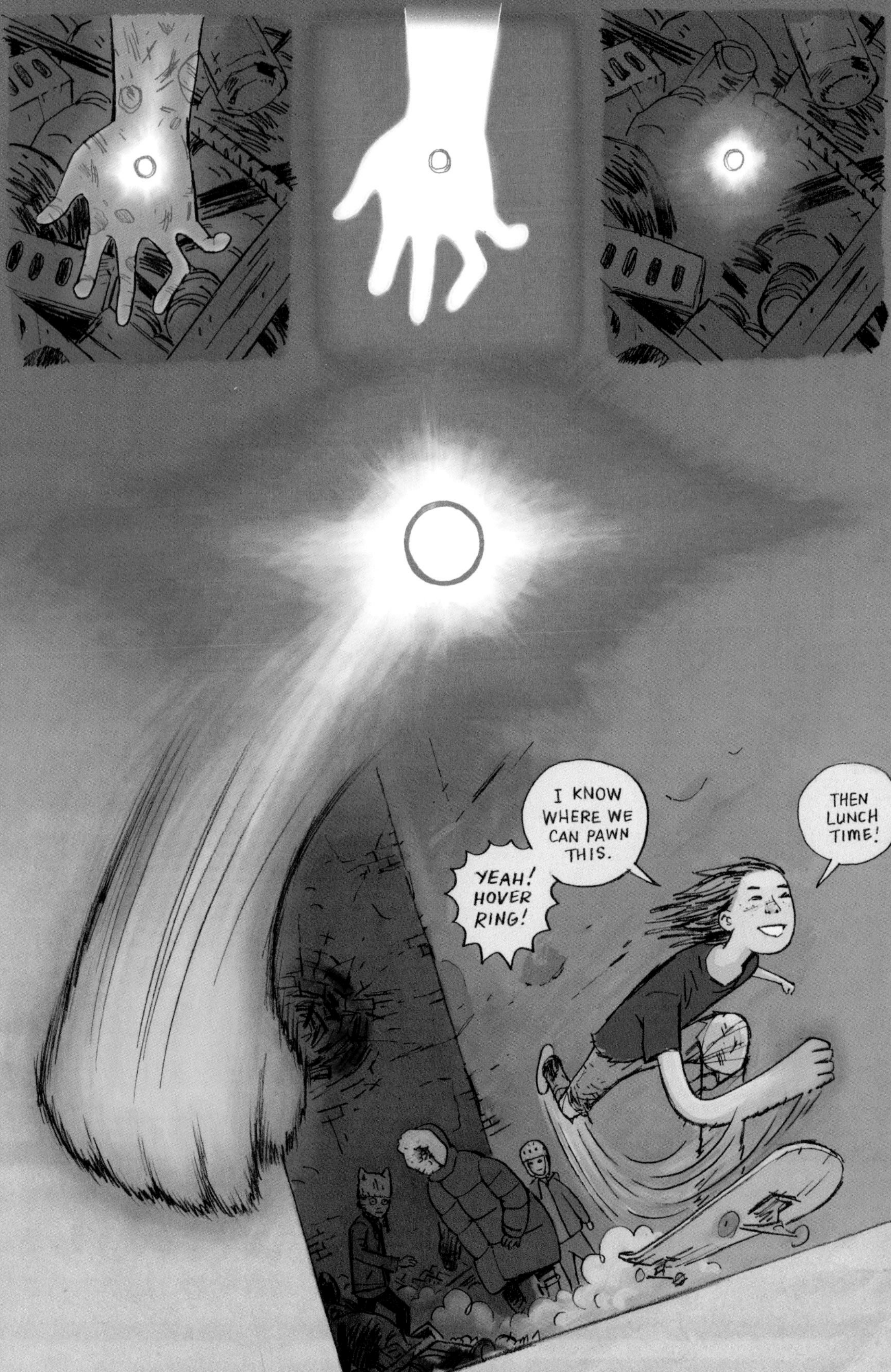
I KNOW WHERE WE CAN PAWN THIS.
YEAH! HOVER RING!
THEN LUNCH TIME!

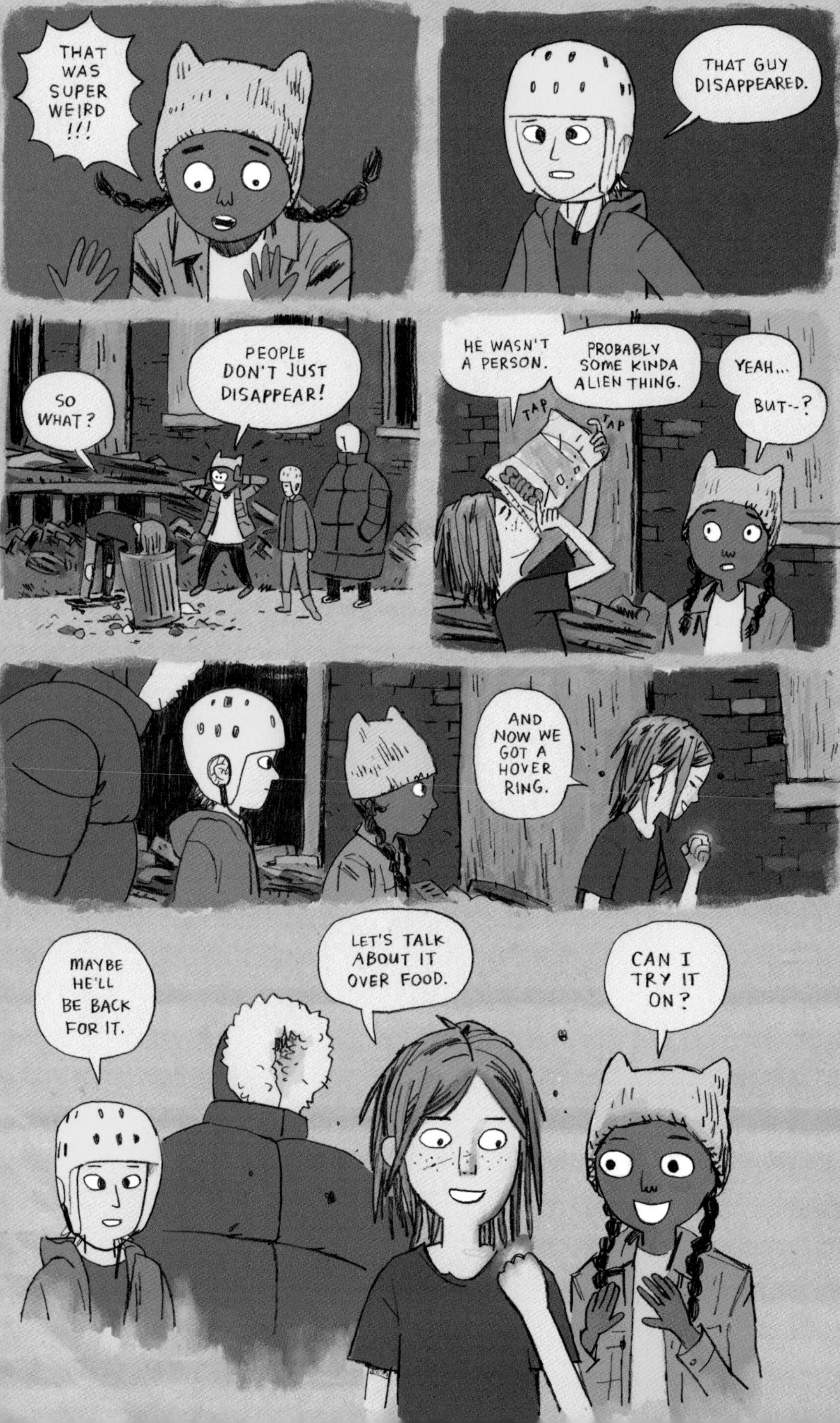
THAT WAS SUPER WEIRD !!!
THAT GUY DISAPPEARED.
SO WHAT?
PEOPLE DON'T JUST DISAPPEAR!
HE WASN'T A PERSON.
PROBABLY SOME KINDA ALIEN THING.
TAP
TAP
YEAH...
BUT--?
AND NOW WE GOT A HOVER RING.
MAYBE HE'LL BE BACK FOR IT.
LET'S TALK ABOUT IT OVER FOOD.
CAN I TRY IT ON?

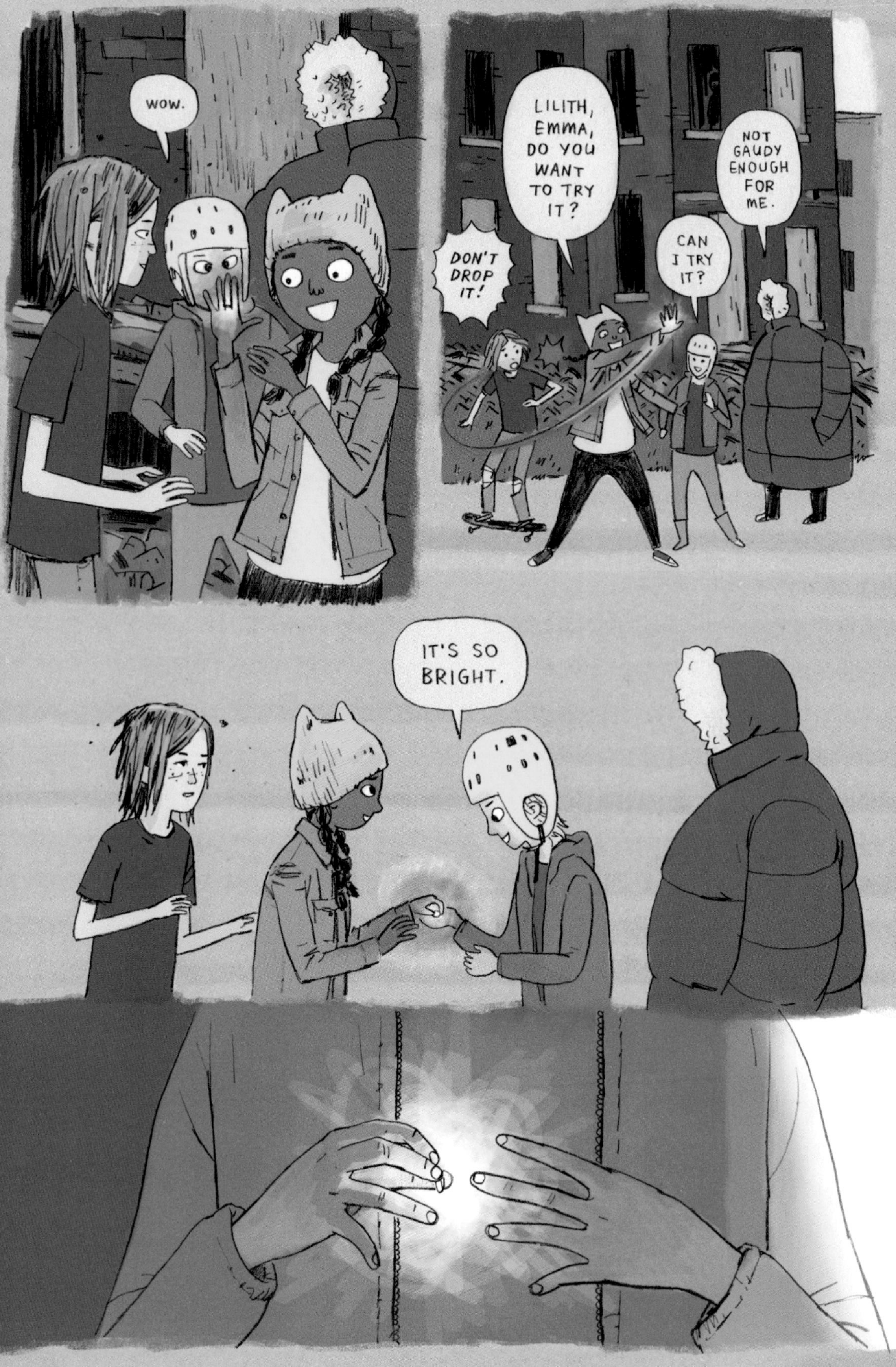
WOW.
LILITH, EMMA, DO YOU WANT TO TRY IT?
DON'T DROP IT!
NOT GAUDY ENOUGH FOR ME.
CAN I TRY IT?
IT'S SO BRIGHT.

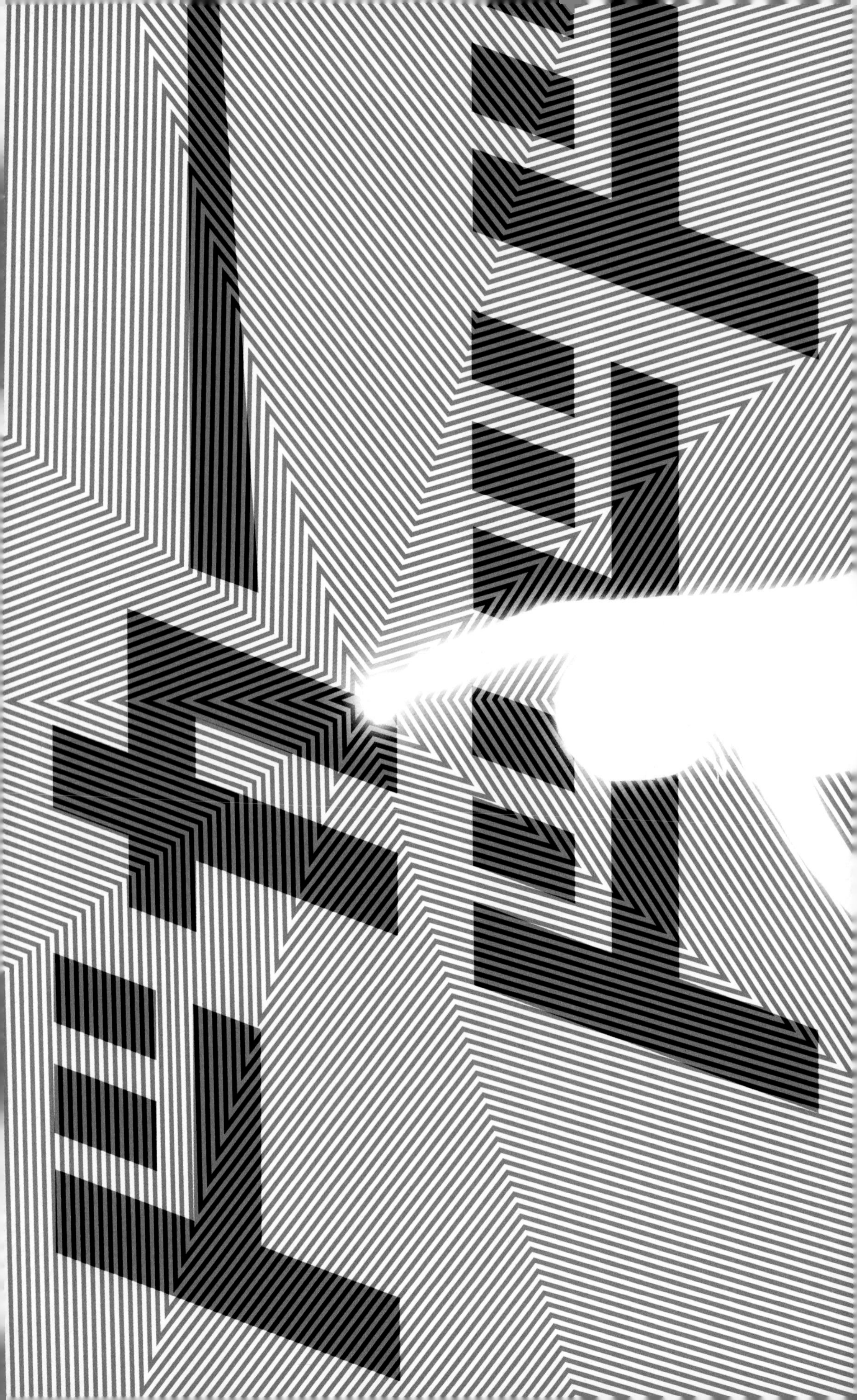
ドカー
ドッド

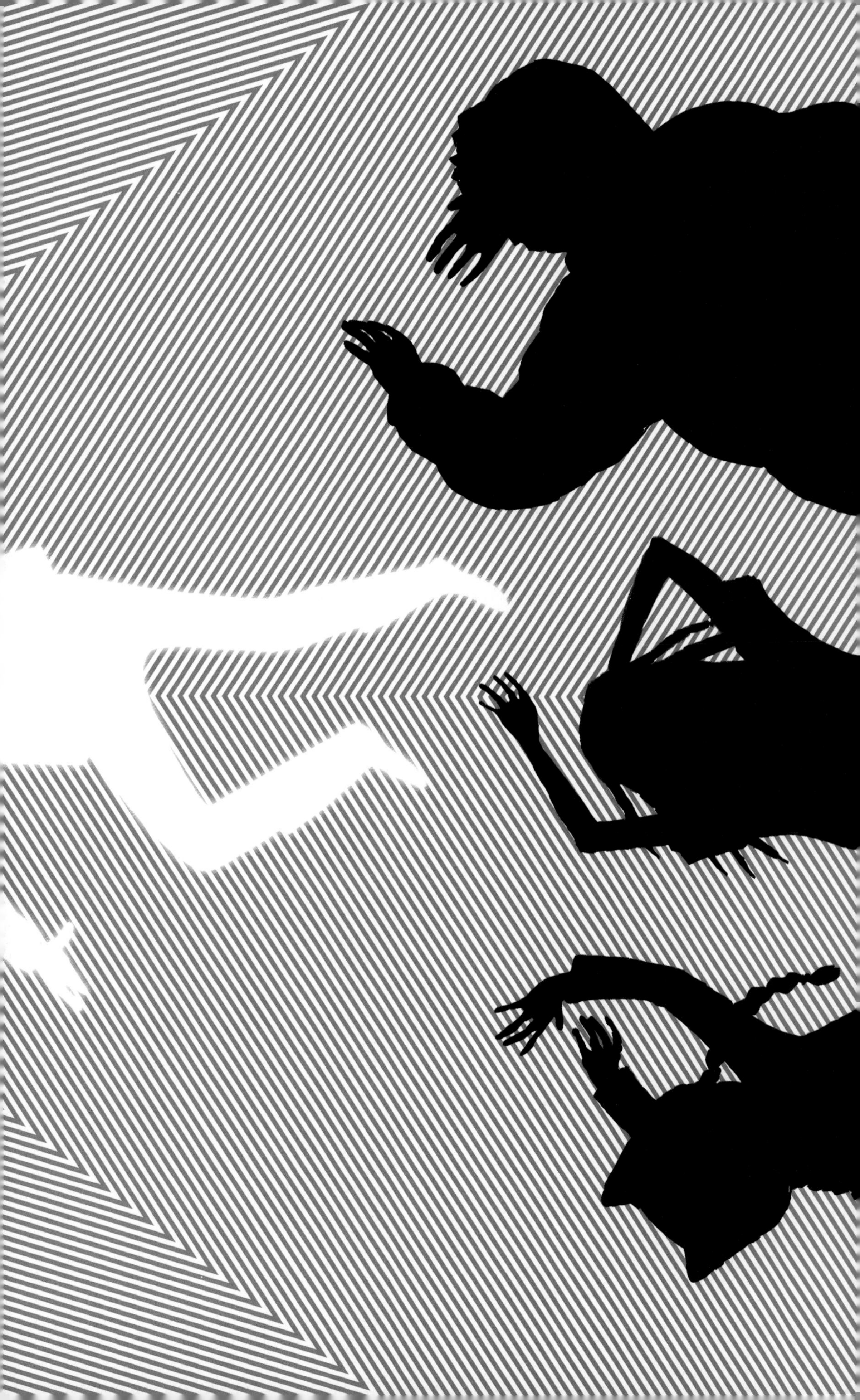

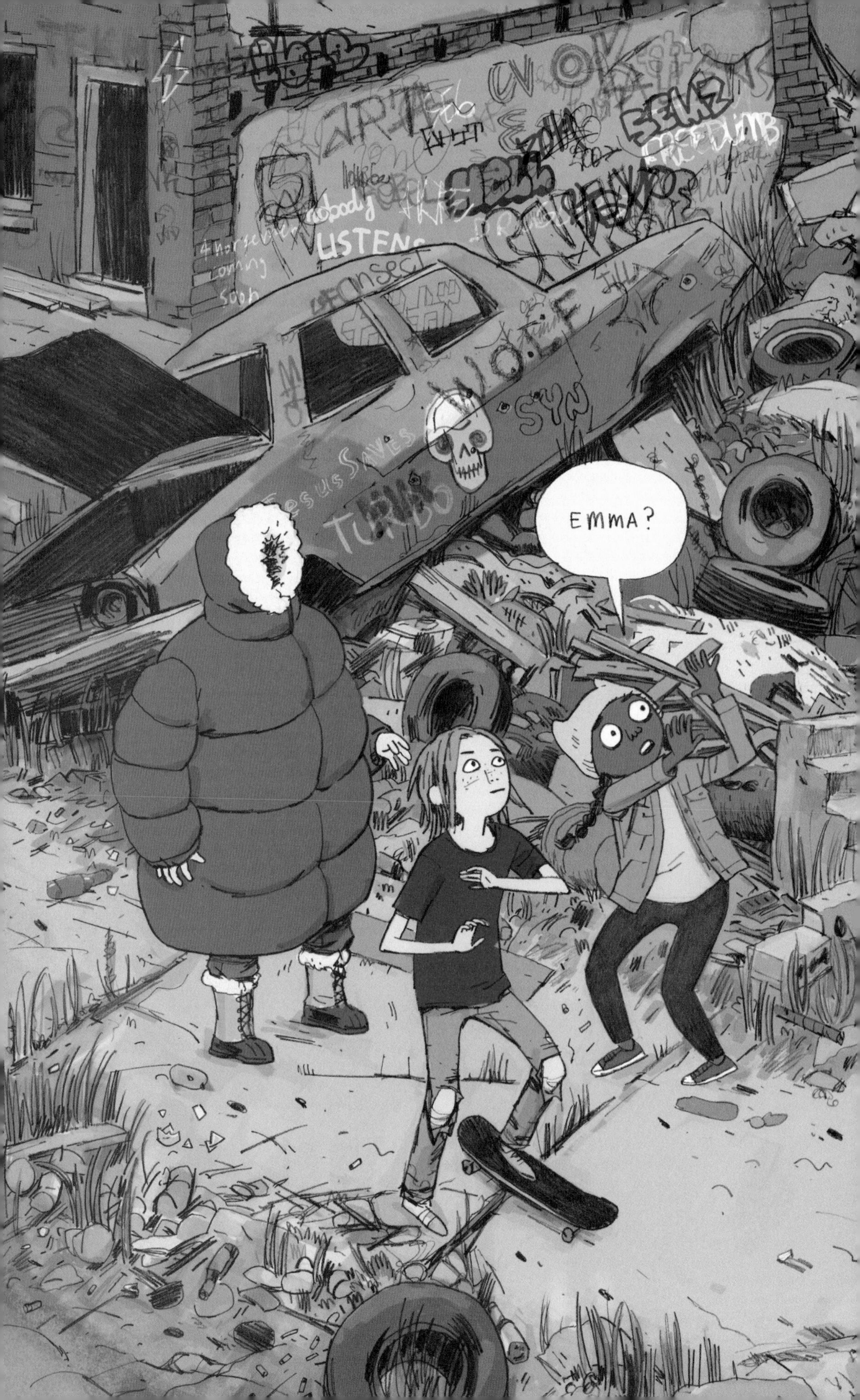
EMMA?
Jesus Saves
TURBO
SYN

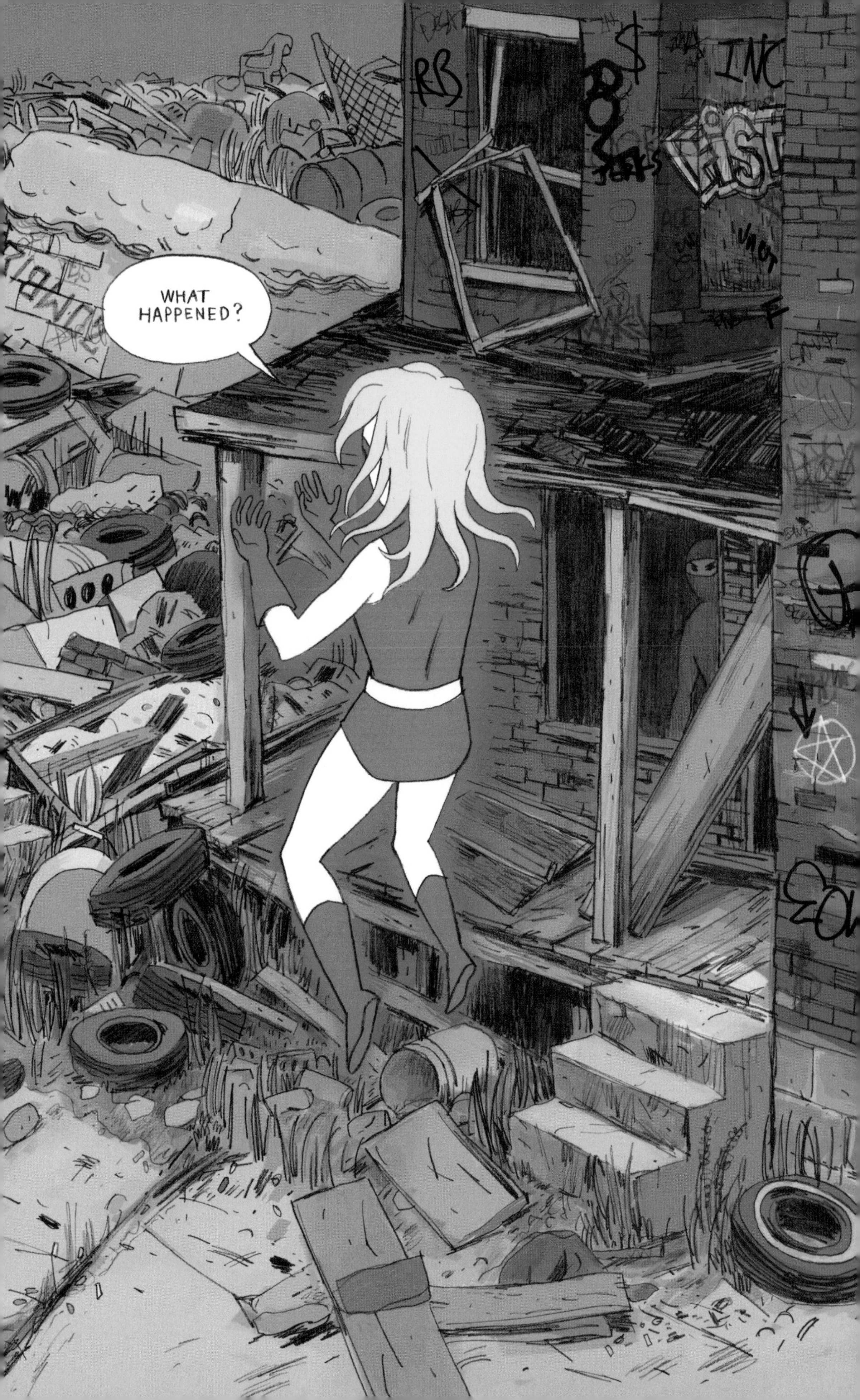
WHAT HAPPENED?

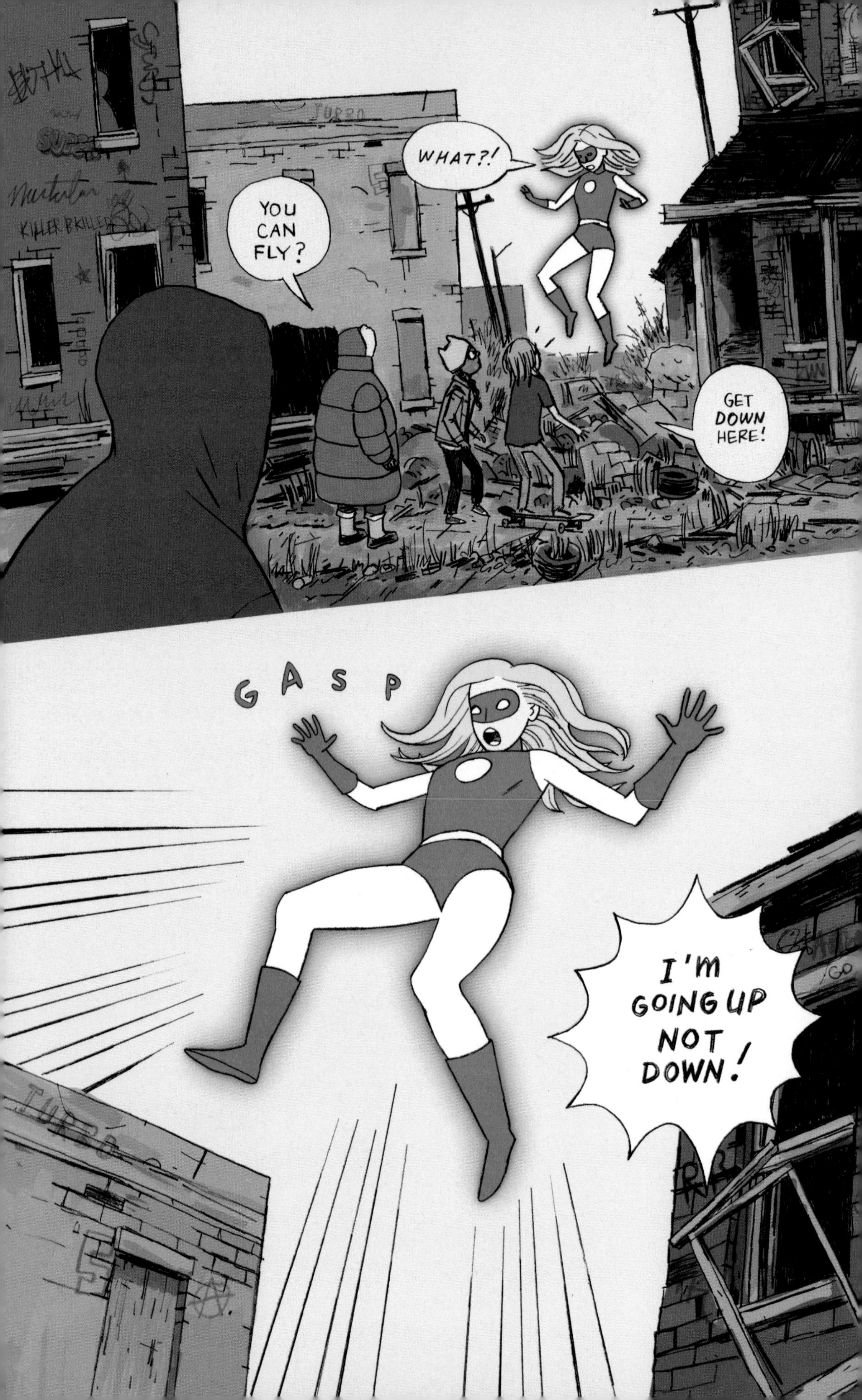
WHAT?!
YOU CAN FLY?
GET DOWN HERE!
GASP
I'M GOING UP NOT DOWN!

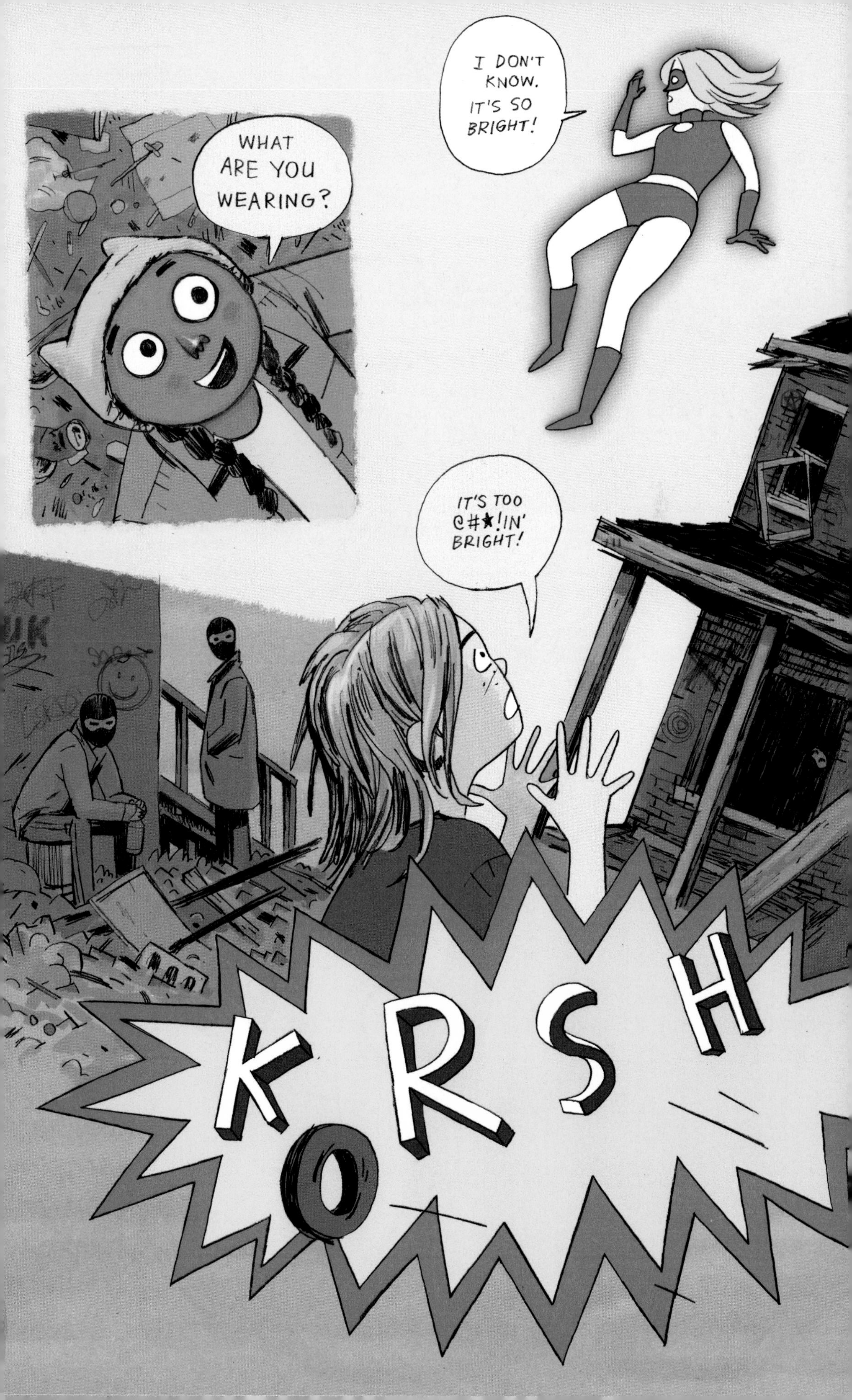

WHAT ARE YOU WEARING?
I DON'T KNOW. IT'S SO BRIGHT!
IT'S TOO @#★!IN' BRIGHT!
KRSHOH

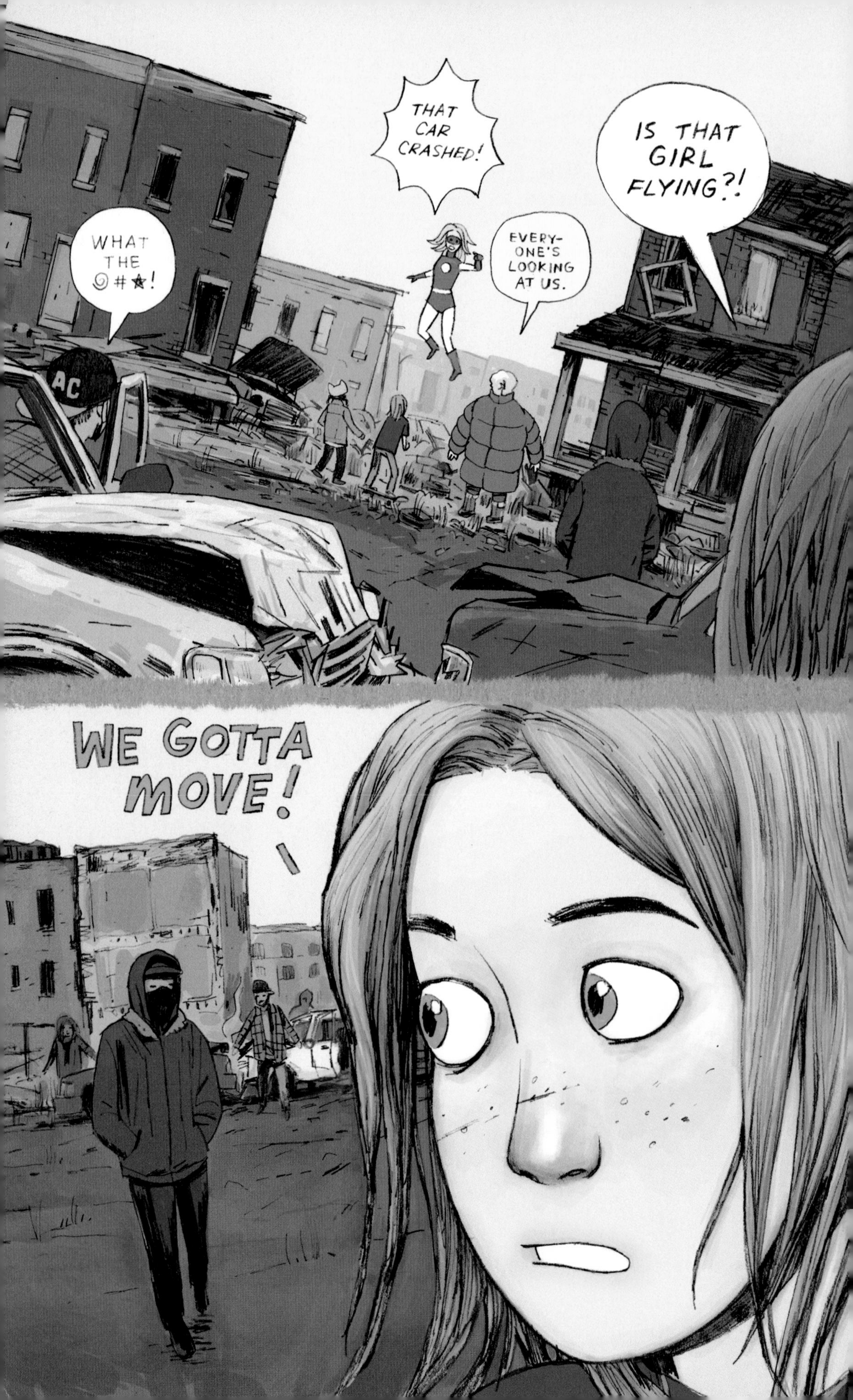
WHAT THE @#★!
THAT CAR CRASHED!
EVERY-ONE'S LOOKING AT US.
IS THAT GIRL FLYING?!
AC
WE GOTTA MOVE!

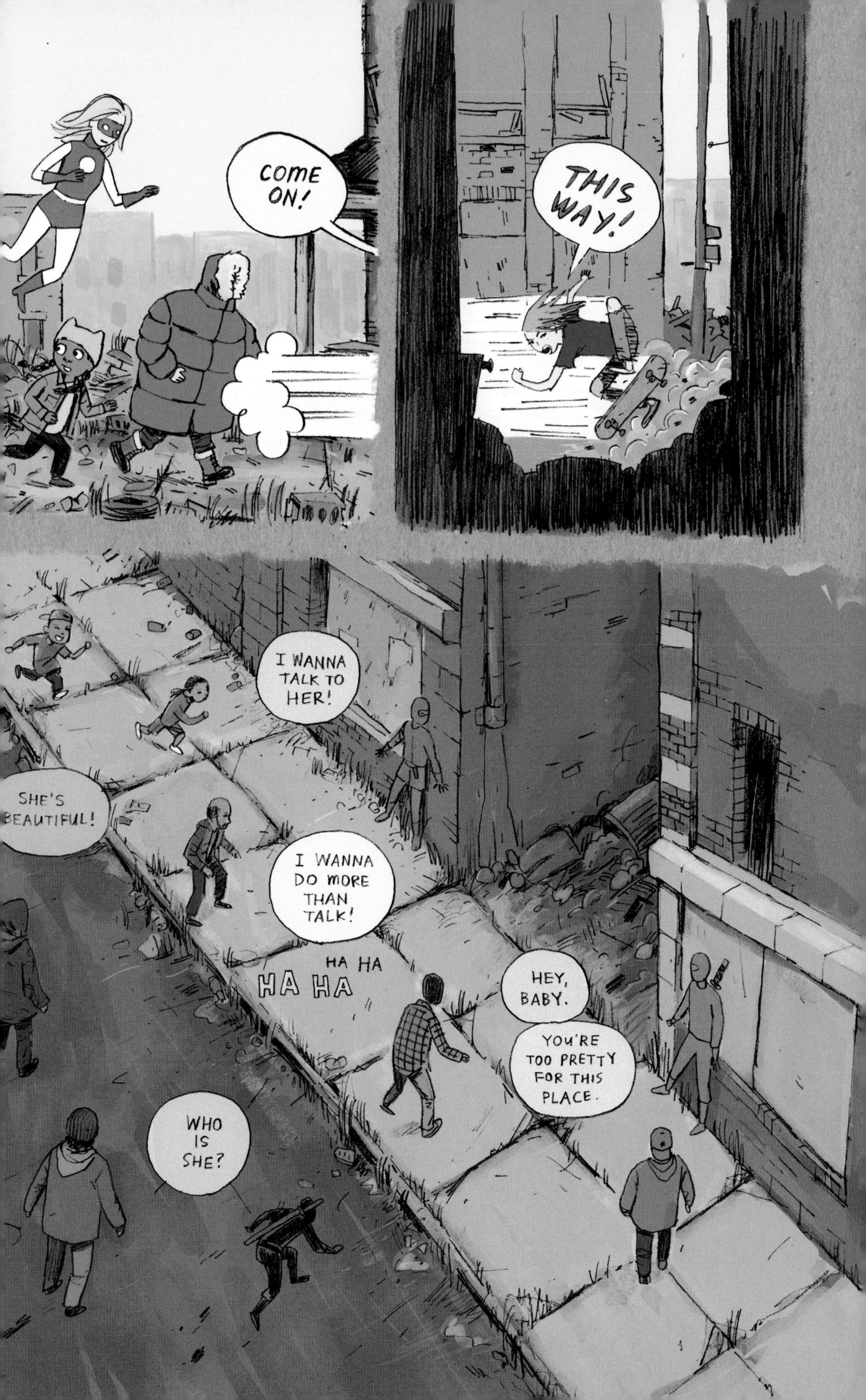
COME ON!
THIS WAY!
I WANNA TALK TO HER!
SHE'S BEAUTIFUL!
I WANNA DO MORE THAN TALK!
HA HA
HA HA
HEY, BABY.
YOU'RE TOO PRETTY FOR THIS PLACE.
WHO IS SHE?

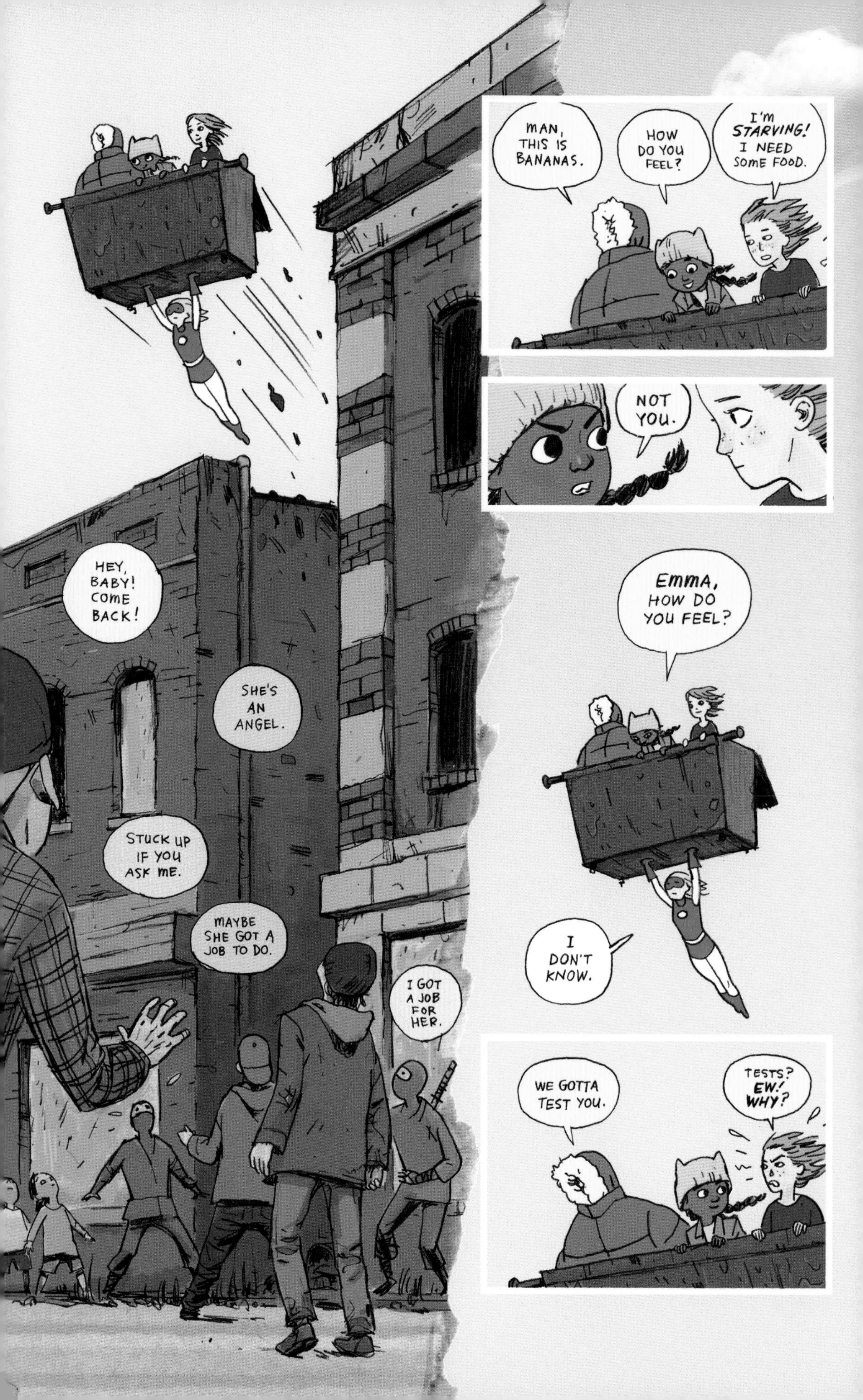
MAN, THIS IS BANANAS.
HOW DO YOU FEEL?
I'M STARVING! I NEED SOME FOOD.
NOT YOU.
EMMA, HOW DO YOU FEEL?
I DON'T KNOW.
WE GOTTA TEST YOU.
TESTS? EW! WHY?
HEY, BABY! COME BACK!
SHE'S AN ANGEL.
STUCK UP IF YOU ASK ME.
MAYBE SHE GOT A JOB TO DO.
I GOT A JOB FOR HER.

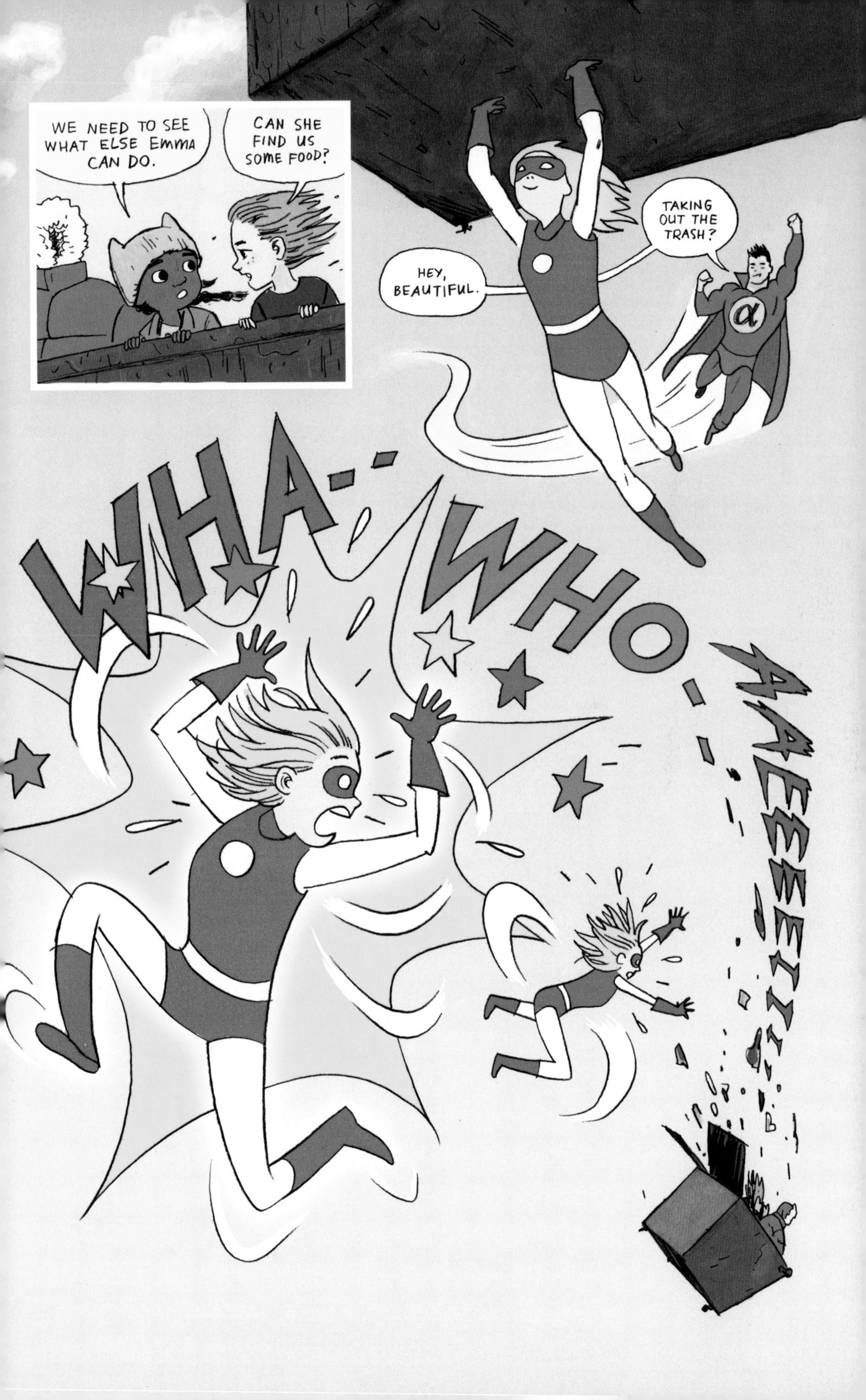

WE NEED TO SEE WHAT ELSE Emma CAN DO.
CAN SHE FIND US SOME FOOD?
TAKING OUT THE TRASH?
HEY, BEAUTIFUL.
WHA--
WHO--
AAEEEEIII

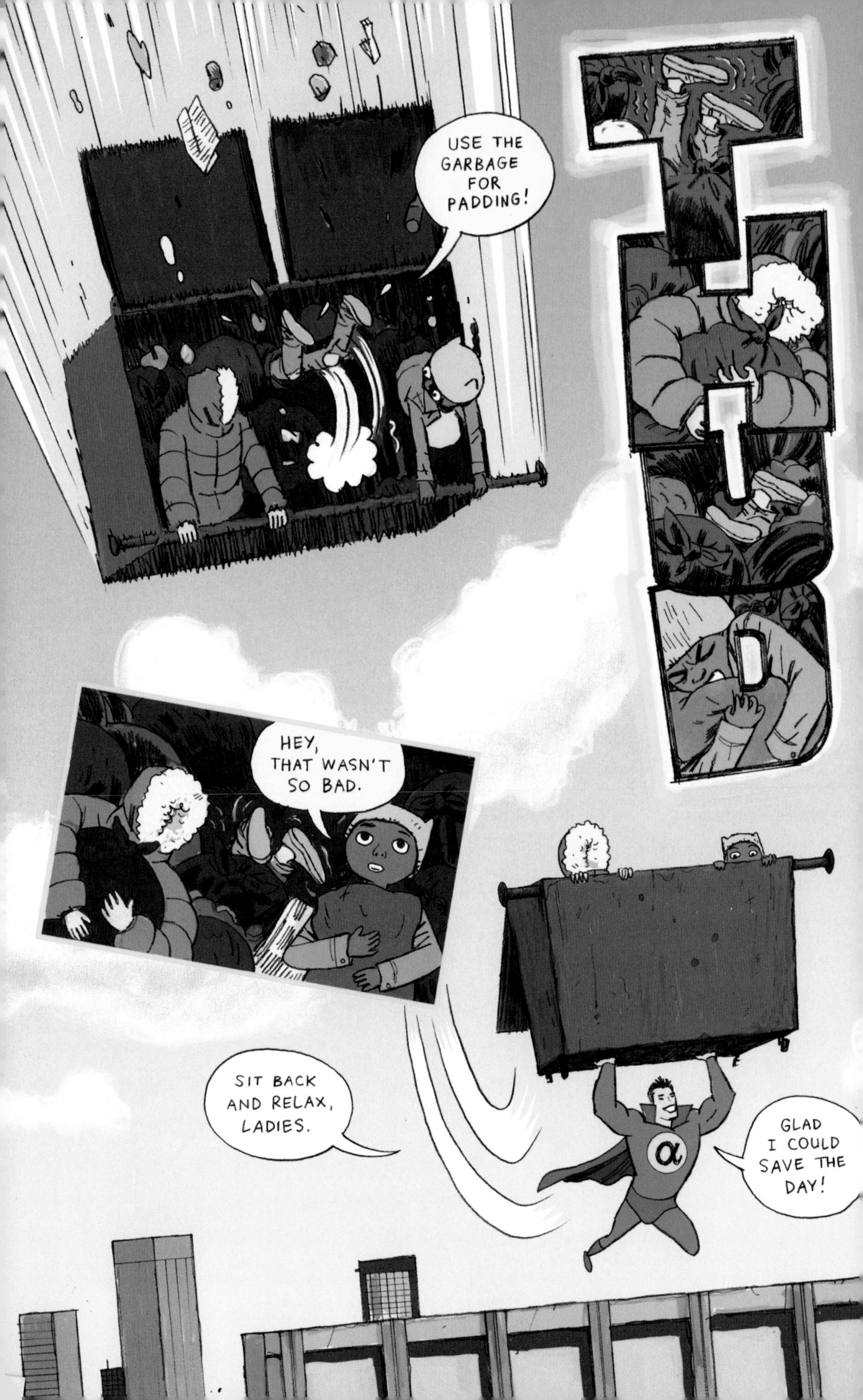
USE THE GARBAGE FOR PADDING!
HEY, THAT WASN'T SO BAD.
SIT BACK AND RELAX, LADIES.
GLAD I COULD SAVE THE DAY!

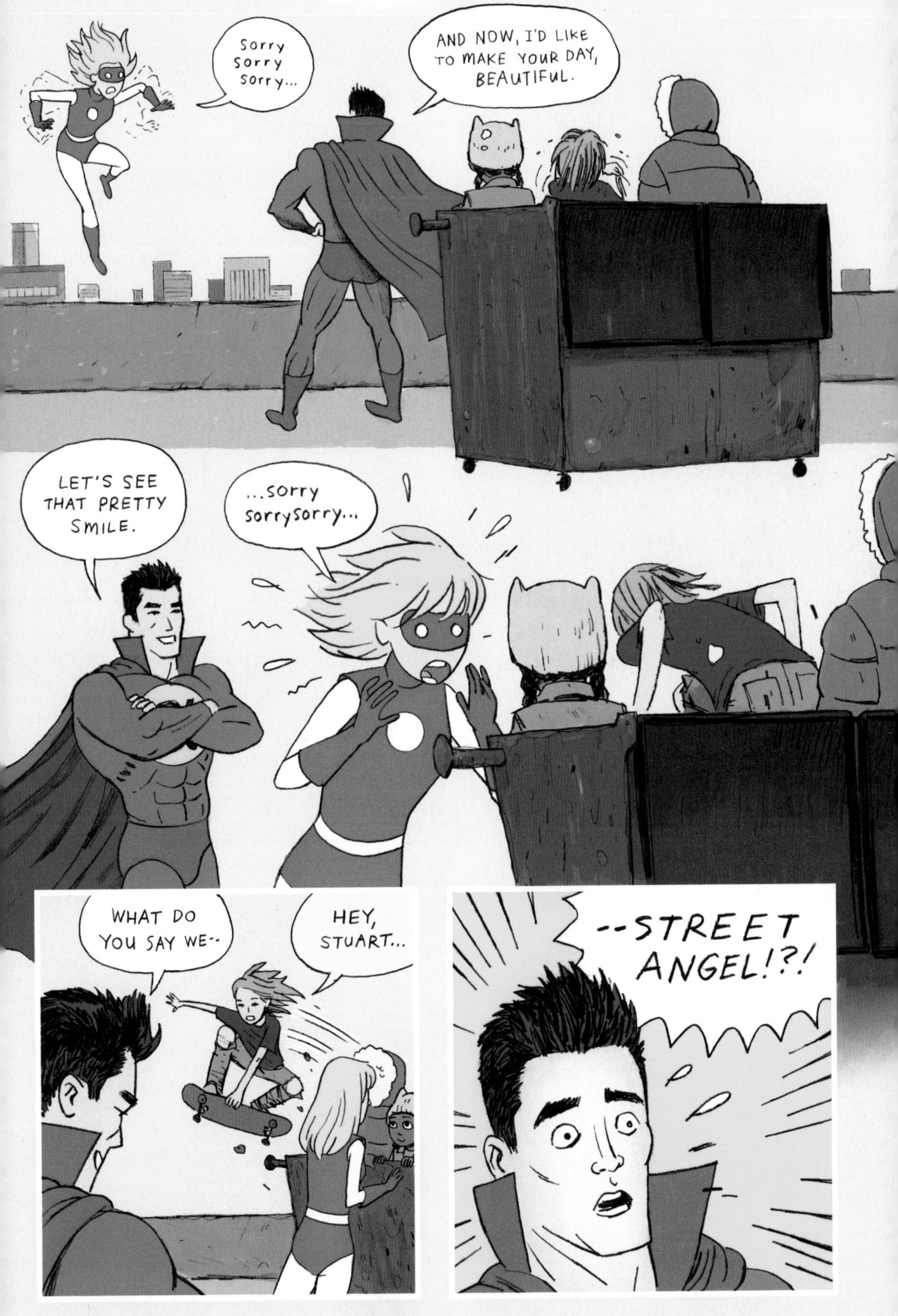
Sorry sorry sorry...
AND NOW, I'D LIKE TO MAKE YOUR DAY, BEAUTIFUL.
LET'S SEE THAT PRETTY SMILE.
...sorry sorrysorry...
WHAT DO YOU SAY WE--
HEY, STUART...
--STREET ANGEL!?!

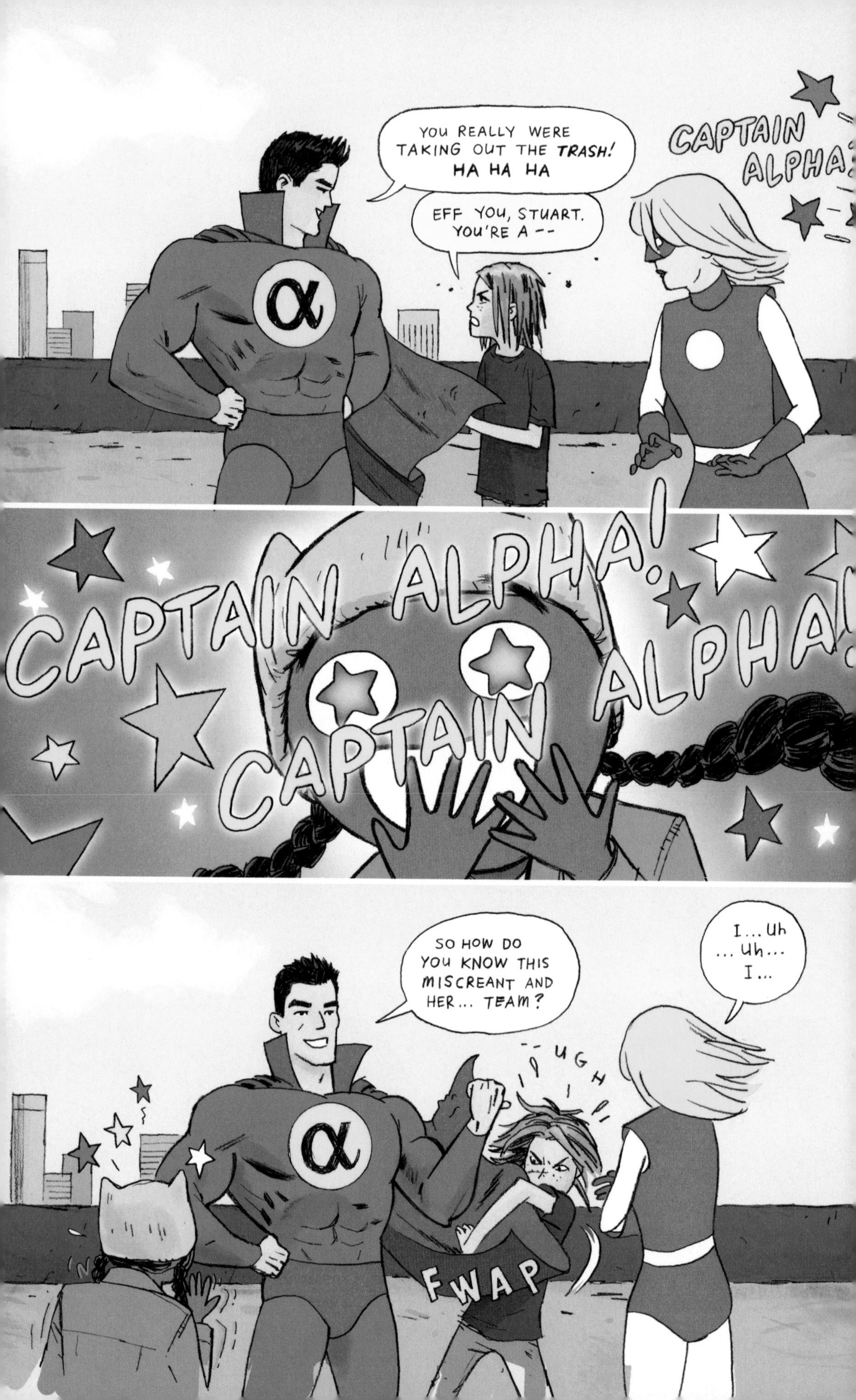
YOU REALLY WERE TAKING OUT THE TRASH! HA HA HA
EFF YOU, STUART. YOU'RE A --
CAPTAIN ALPHA!
CAPTAIN ALPHA!
CAPTAIN ALPHA!
CAPTAIN ALPHA!
SO HOW DO YOU KNOW THIS MISCREANT AND HER... TEAM?
I... uh ... uh... I...
UGH
FWAP

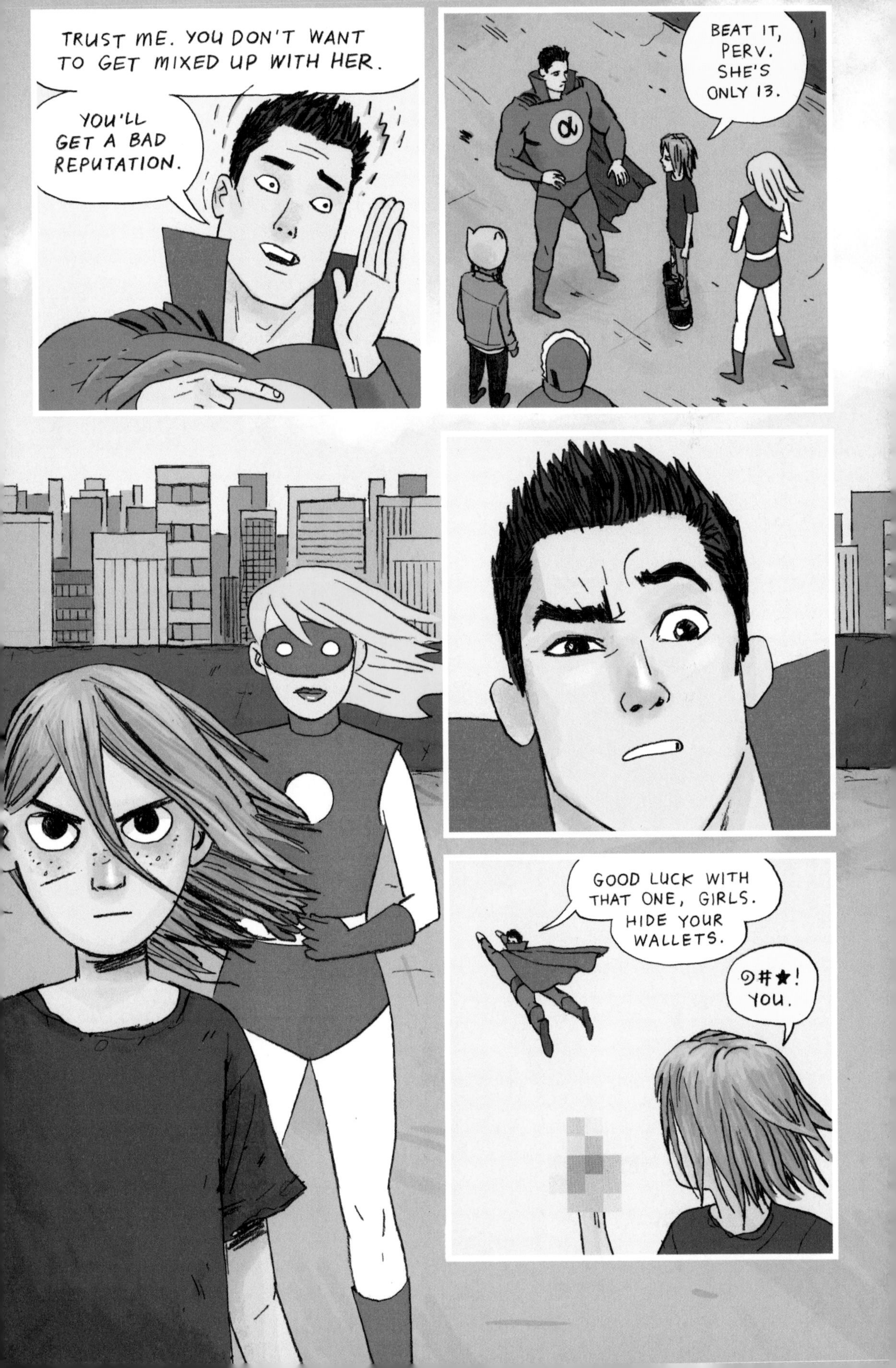
TRUST ME. YOU DON'T WANT TO GET MIXED UP WITH HER.
YOU'LL GET A BAD REPUTATION.
BEAT IT, PERV. SHE'S ONLY 13.
GOOD LUCK WITH THAT ONE, GIRLS. HIDE YOUR WALLETS.
@#★! YOU.

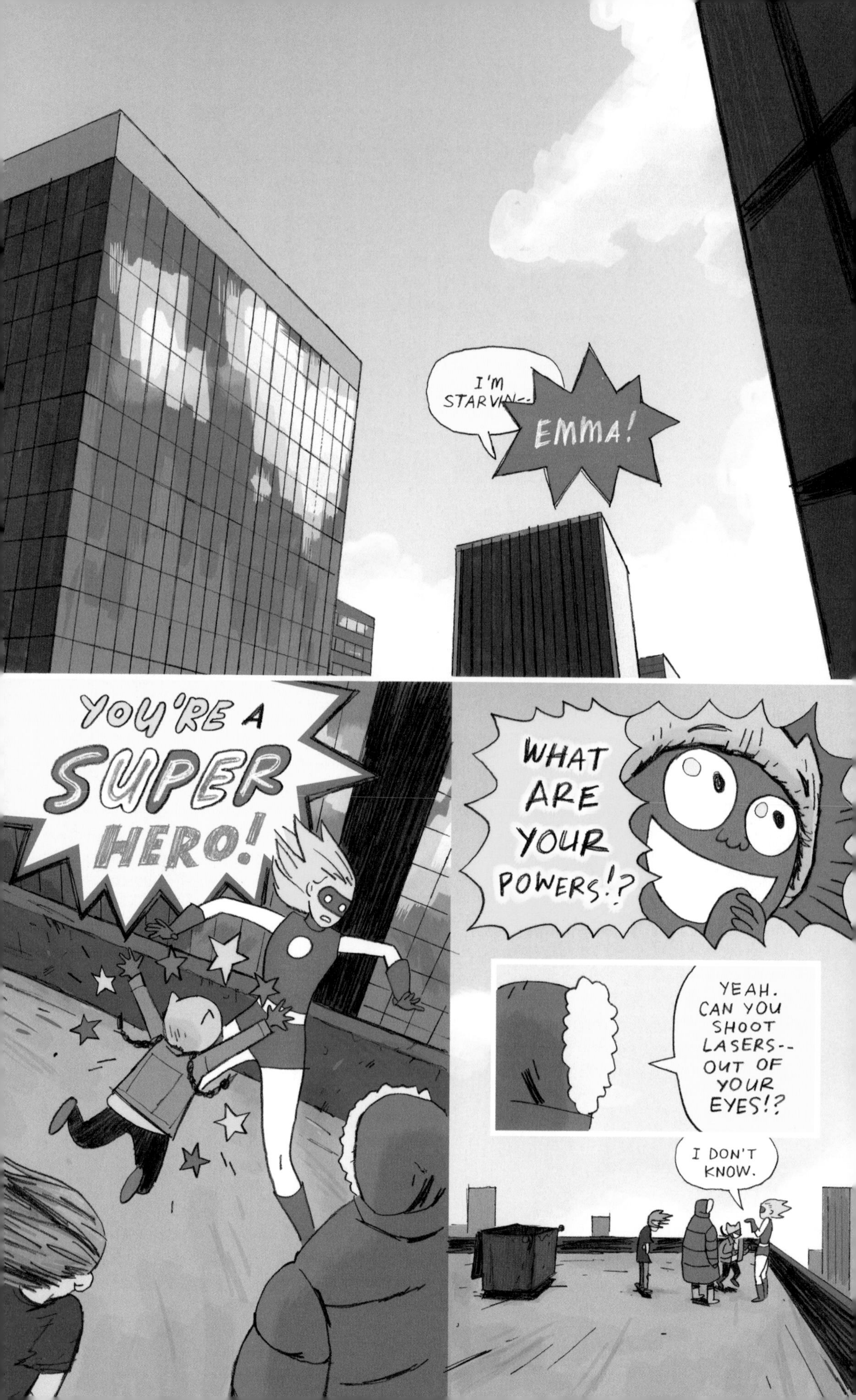
I'M STARVIN--
EMMA!
YOU'RE A SUPER HERO!
WHAT ARE YOUR POWERS!?
YEAH. CAN YOU SHOOT LASERS-- OUT OF YOUR EYES!?
I DON'T KNOW.

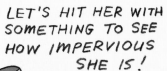

LET'S HIT HER WITH SOMETHING TO SEE HOW IMPERVIOUS SHE IS!

NO! WAIT! START WITH SOMETHING EASY

CAN YOU LIFT, uh...

...Hmm...

THERE ISN'T MUCH TO LIFT ON THIS ROOF.

WHAT ABOUT INVISIBILITY?

OR ENERGY BEAMS?

OR-

OR FINDING ME A G.D. SANDWICH?

C'MON! JESSE, THIS IS AMAZING!

HAVE YOU EVER SEEN ANYTHING LIKE THIS? EVER?!?

YES.

TWICE.

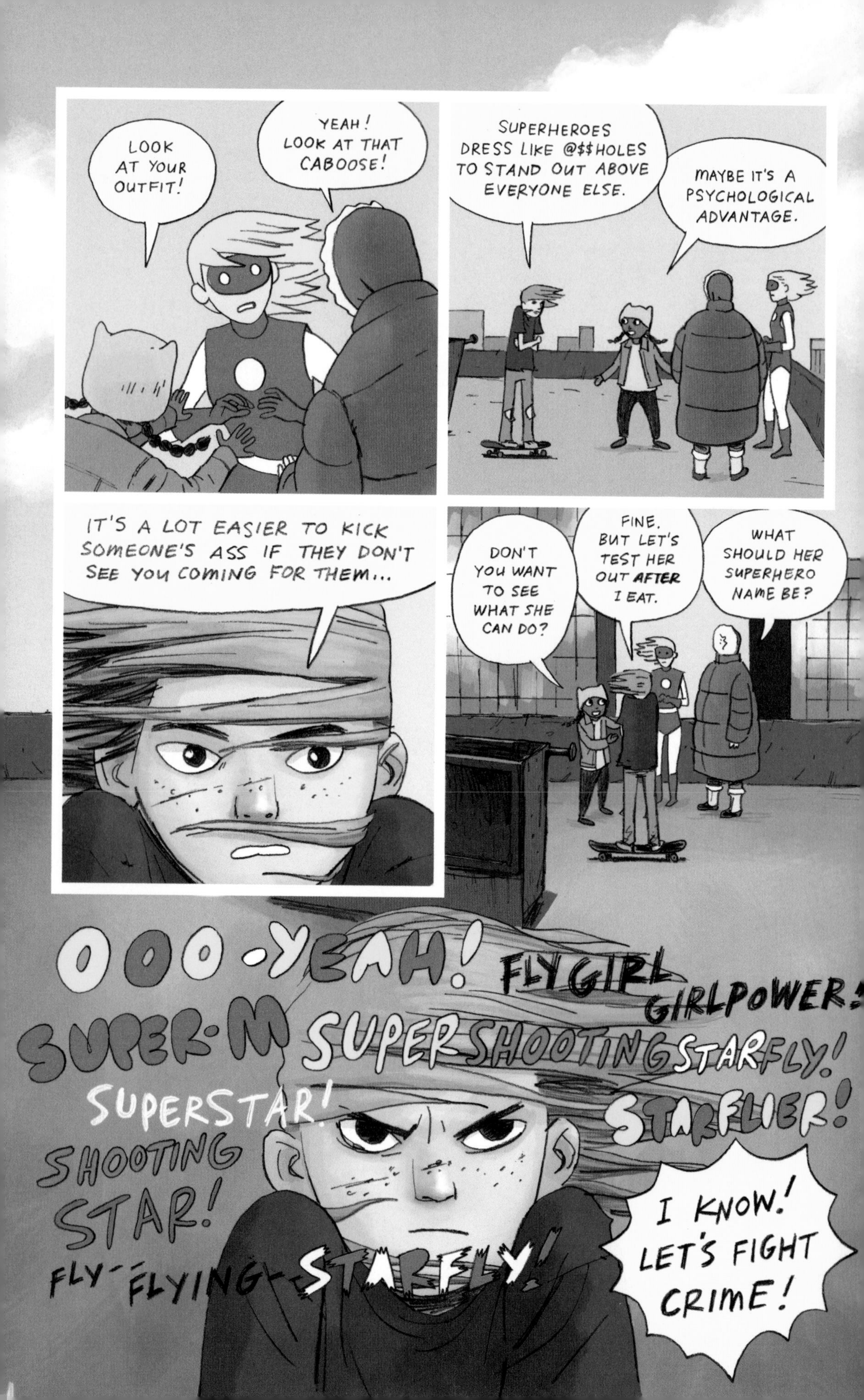
LOOK AT YOUR OUTFIT!
YEAH! LOOK AT THAT CABOOSE!
SUPERHEROES DRESS LIKE @$$HOLES TO STAND OUT ABOVE EVERYONE ELSE.
MAYBE IT'S A PSYCHOLOGICAL ADVANTAGE.
IT'S A LOT EASIER TO KICK SOMEONE'S ASS IF THEY DON'T SEE YOU COMING FOR THEM...
DON'T YOU WANT TO SEE WHAT SHE CAN DO?
FINE. BUT LET'S TEST HER OUT AFTER I EAT.
WHAT SHOULD HER SUPERHERO NAME BE?
OOO-YEAH!
FLY GIRL
GIRLPOWER!
SUPER-M
SUPER SHOOTING STARFLY!
SUPERSTAR!
STARFLIER!
SHOOTING STAR!
FLY--FLYING-STARFLY!
I KNOW! LET'S FIGHT CRIME!

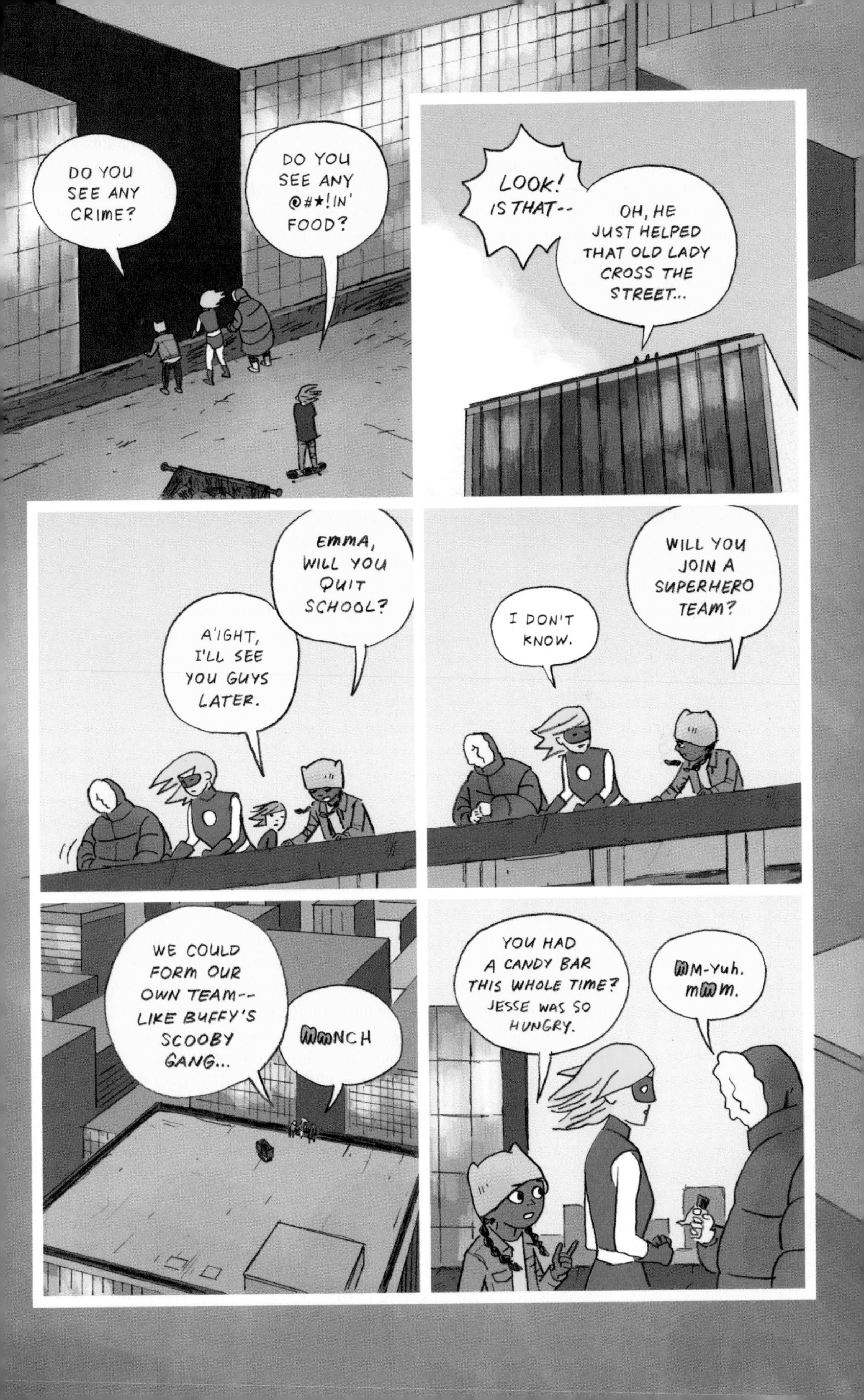
DO YOU SEE ANY CRIME?
DO YOU SEE ANY @#★!IN' FOOD?
LOOK! IS THAT--
OH, HE JUST HELPED THAT OLD LADY CROSS THE STREET...
EMMA, WILL YOU QUIT SCHOOL?
A'IGHT, I'LL SEE YOU GUYS LATER.
WILL YOU JOIN A SUPERHERO TEAM?
I DON'T KNOW.
WE COULD FORM OUR OWN TEAM-- LIKE BUFFY'S SCOOBY GANG...
MMNCH
YOU HAD A CANDY BAR THIS WHOLE TIME? JESSE WAS SO HUNGRY.
MM-YUH. MMM.

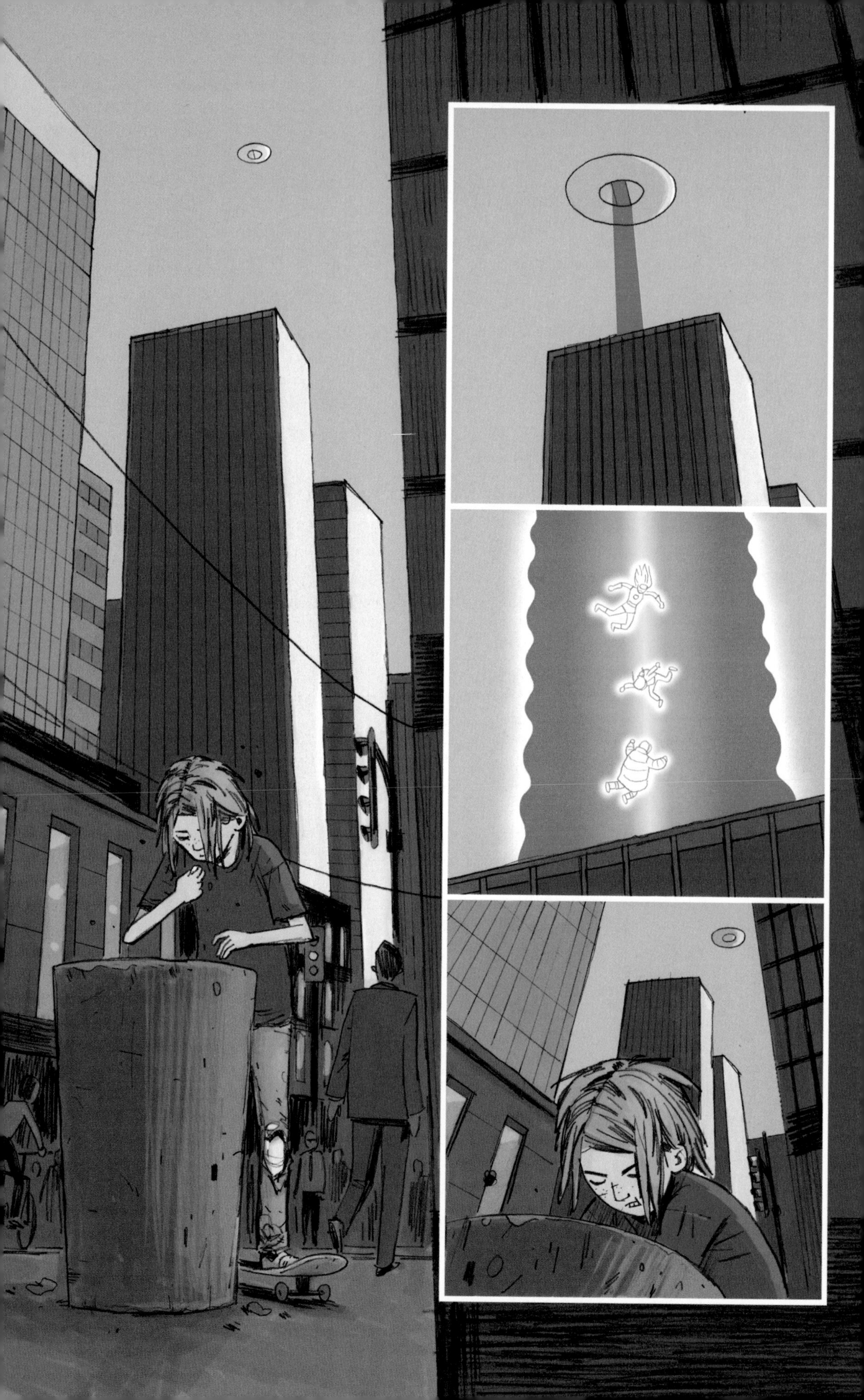

The Next Day

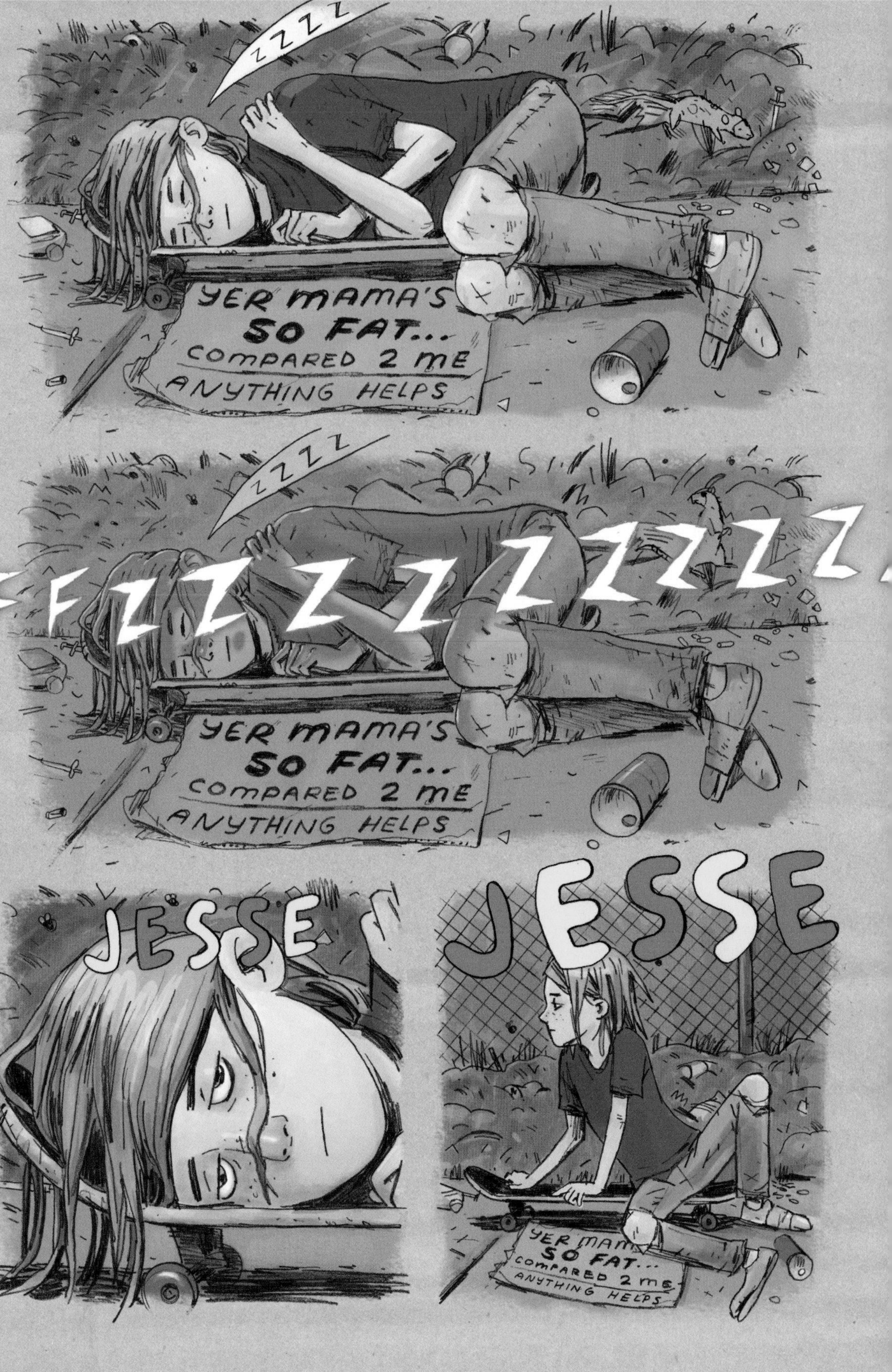
ZZZZ
YER MAMA'S SO FAT... COMPARED 2 ME
ANYTHING HELPS
ZZZZ
FFZZZZZZZZZ
YER MAMA'S SO FAT... COMPARED 2 ME
ANYTHING HELPS
JESSE
JESSE
YER MAMA'S SO FAT... COMPARED 2 ME
ANYTHING HELPS

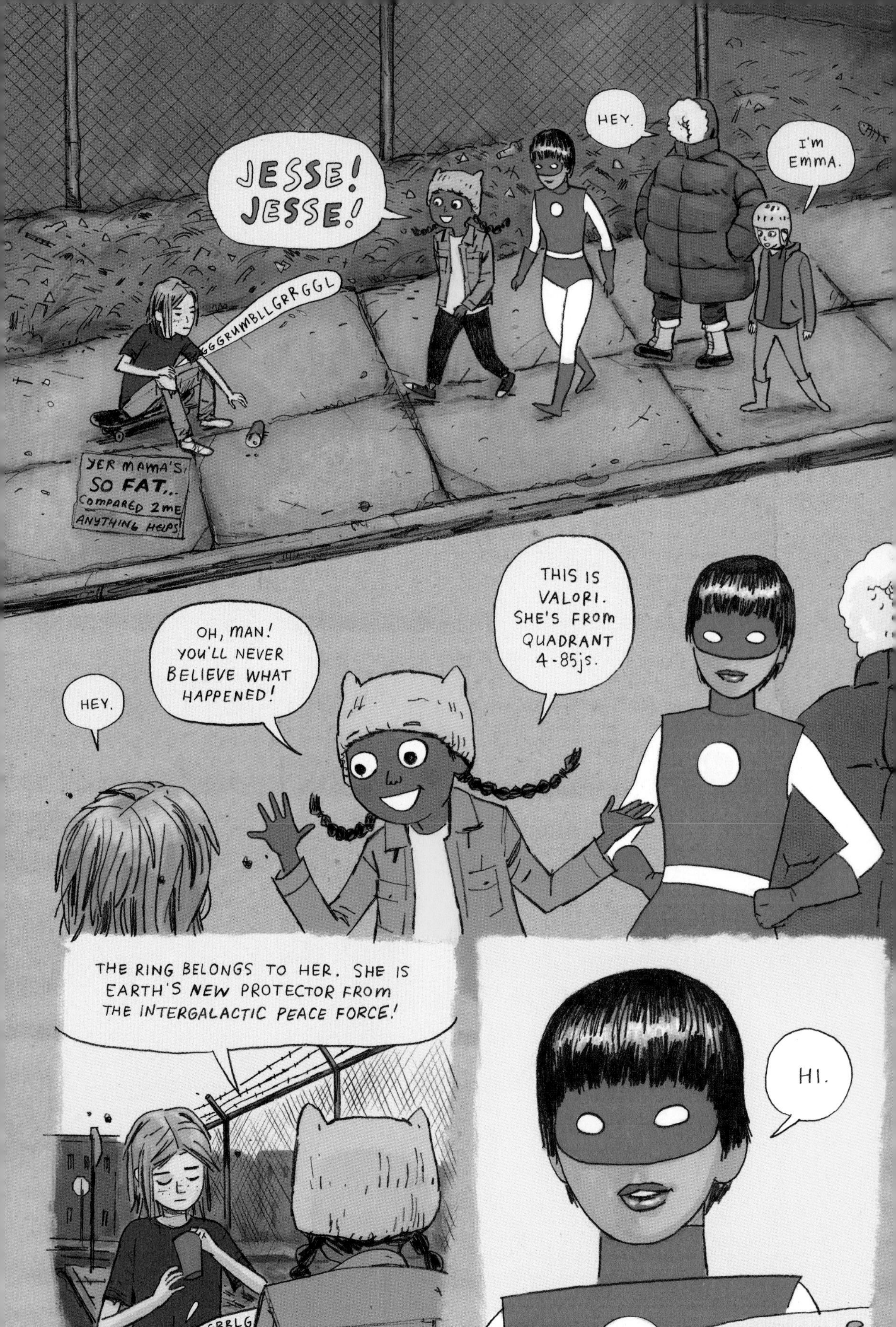

JESSE! JESSE!
GGGRUMBLLGRRGGL
HEY.
I'm EMMA.
YER MAMA'S SO FAT... COMPARED 2 ME
ANYTHING HELPS
HEY.
OH, MAN! YOU'LL NEVER BELIEVE WHAT HAPPENED!
THIS IS VALORI. SHE'S FROM QUADRANT 4-85js.
THE RING BELONGS TO HER. SHE IS EARTH'S NEW PROTECTOR FROM THE INTERGALACTIC PEACE FORCE!
GRRLG
HI.

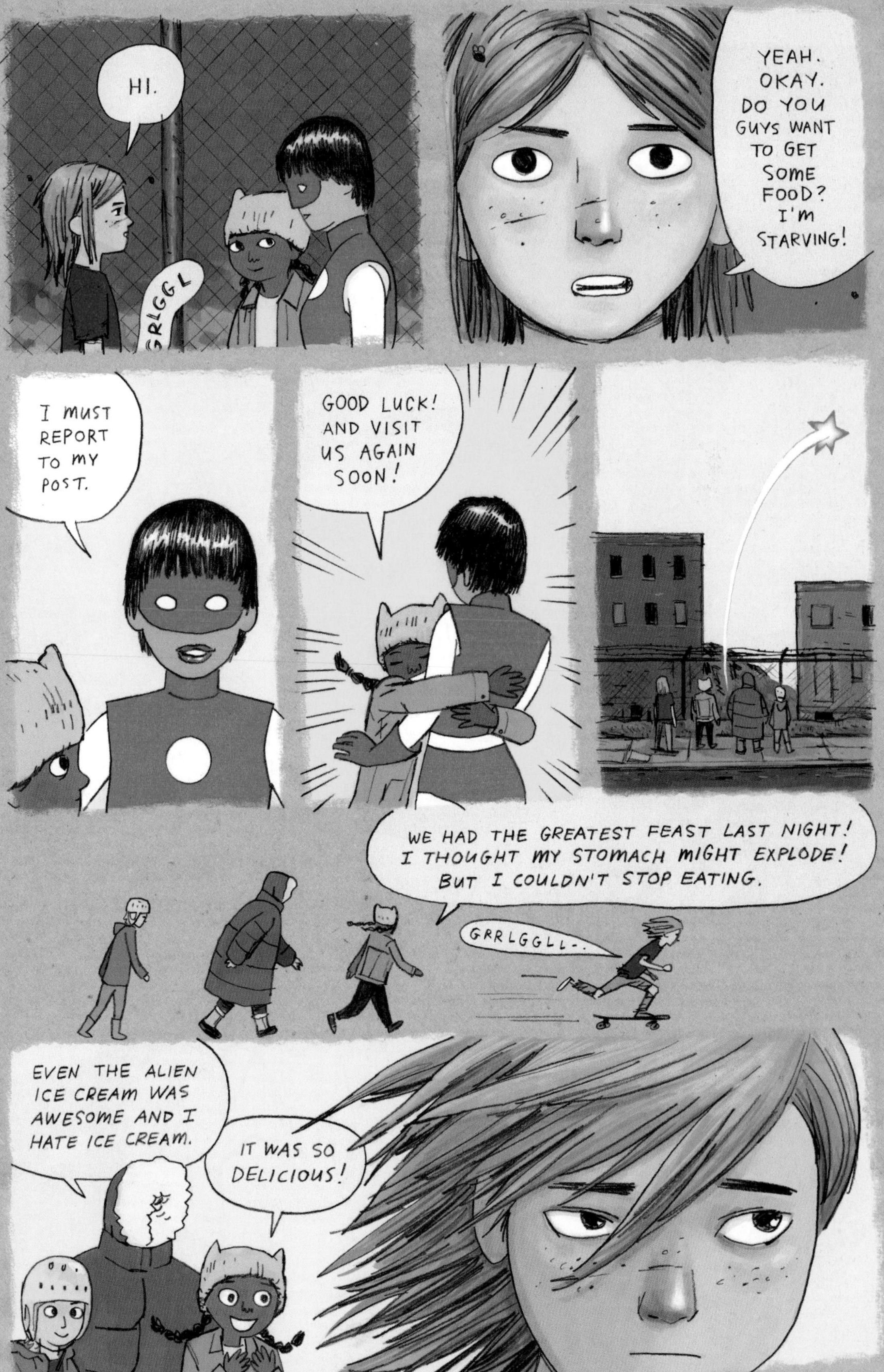
HI.
GRLGGL
YEAH. OKAY. DO YOU GUYS WANT TO GET SOME FOOD? I'M STARVING!
I MUST REPORT TO MY POST.
GOOD LUCK! AND VISIT US AGAIN SOON!
WE HAD THE GREATEST FEAST LAST NIGHT! I THOUGHT MY STOMACH MIGHT EXPLODE! BUT I COULDN'T STOP EATING.
GRRLGGLL..
EVEN THE ALIEN ICE CREAM WAS AWESOME AND I HATE ICE CREAM.
IT WAS SO DELICIOUS!

The End

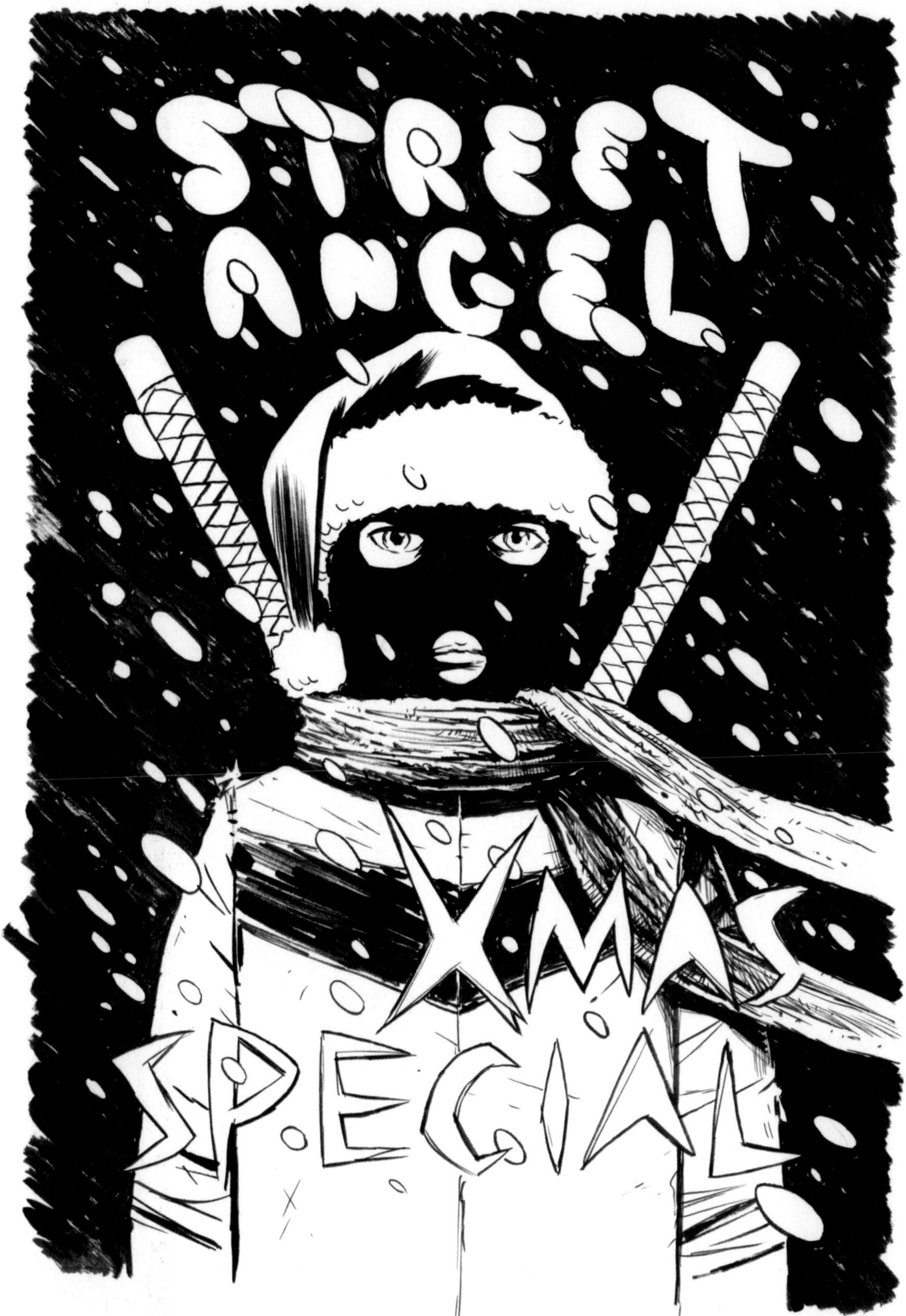
STREET ANGEL
XMAS SPECIAL

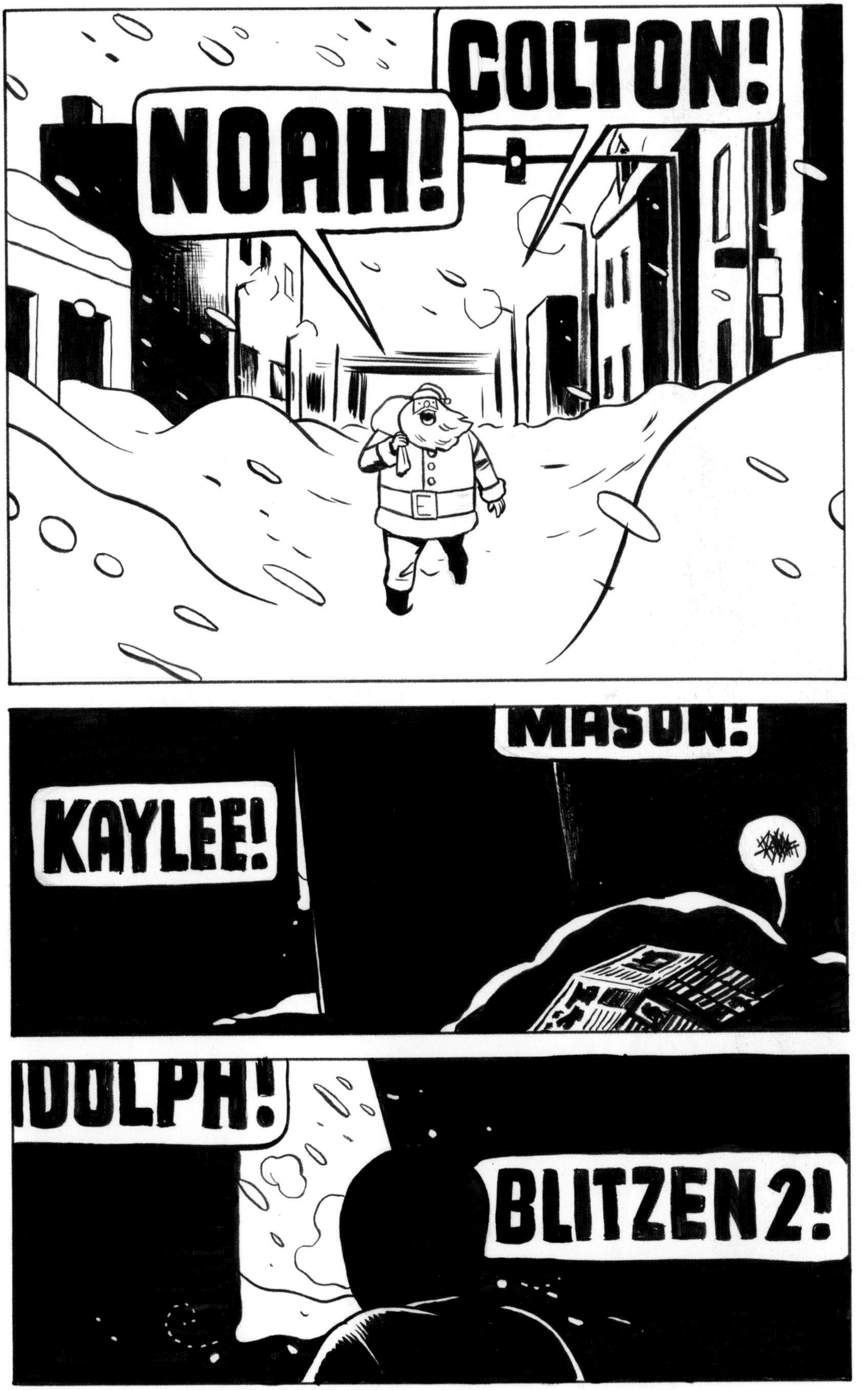
NOAH!
COLTON!
KAYLEE!
MASON!
DOLPH!
BLITZEN 2!

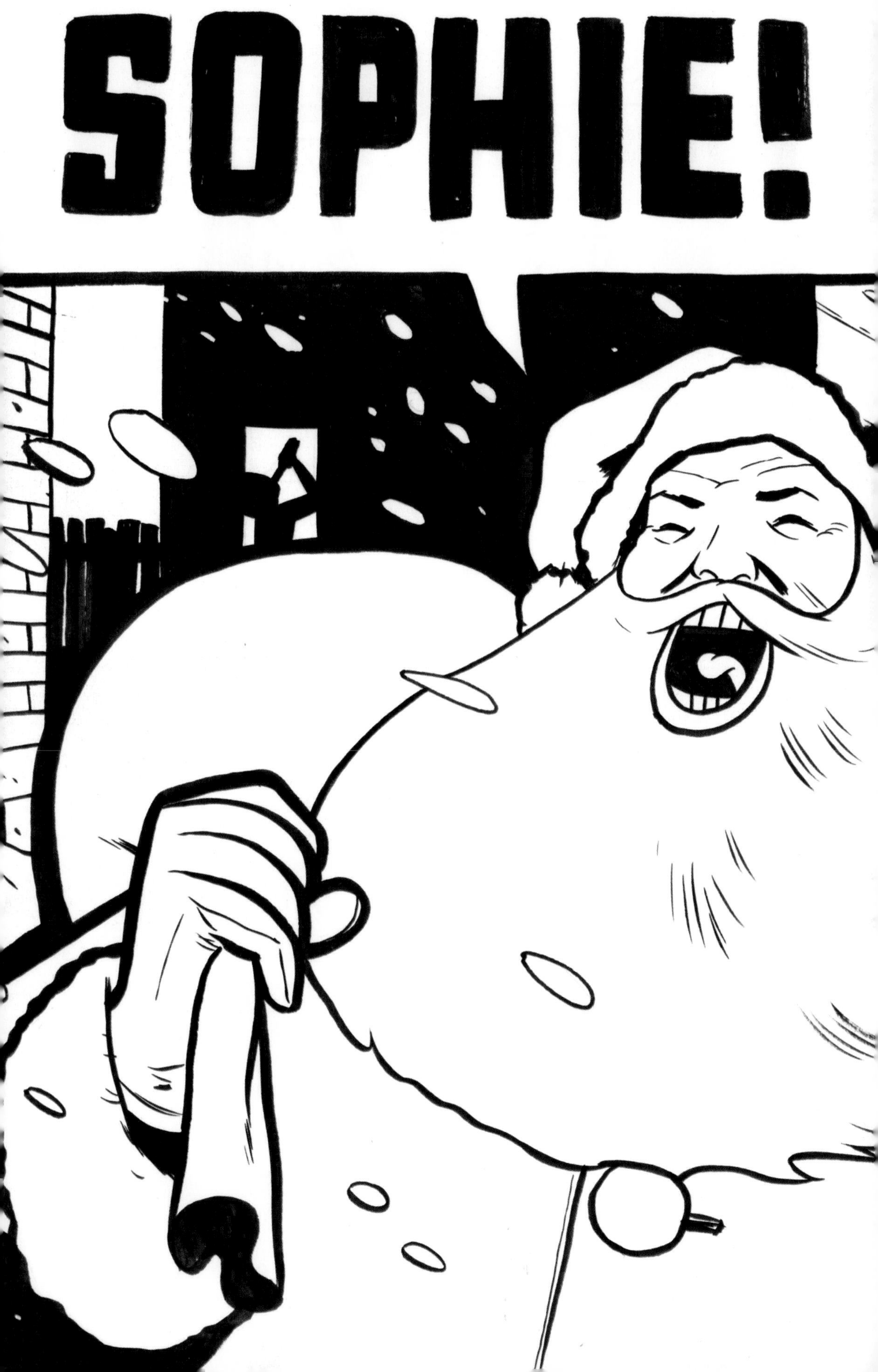
SOPHIE!

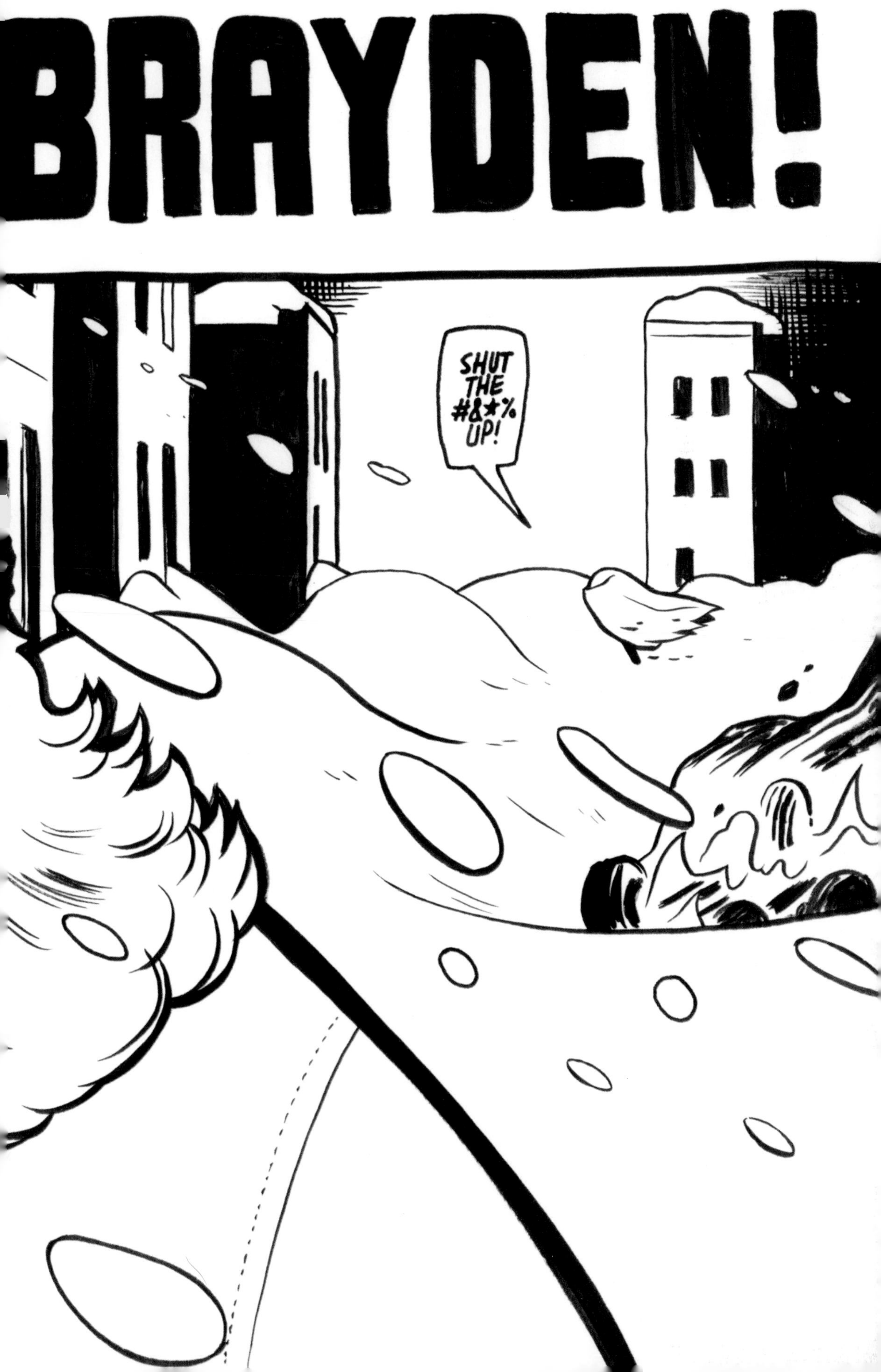
BRAYDEN!
SHUT THE #&★% UP!

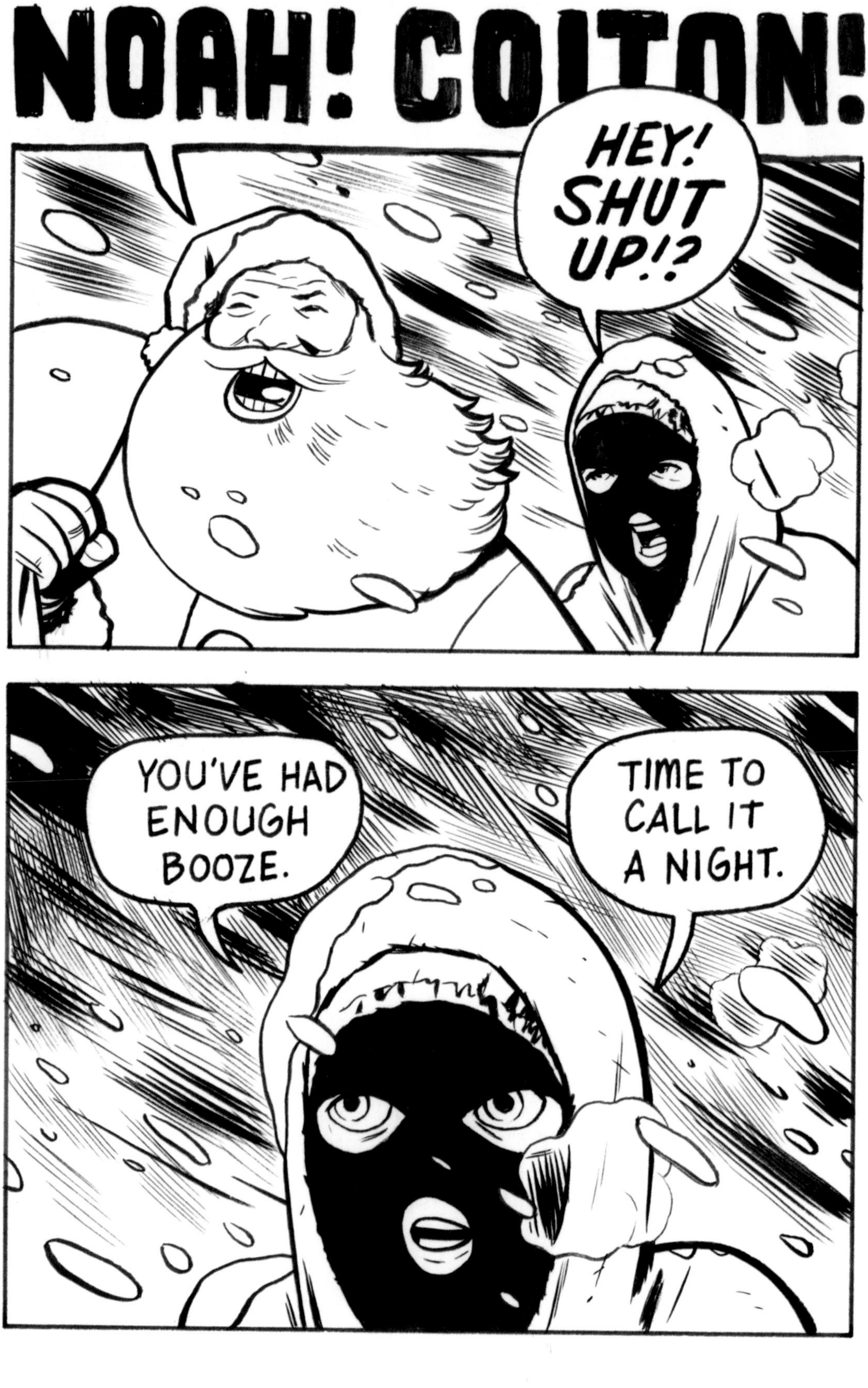
NOAH! COLTON!
HEY! SHUT UP!?
YOU'VE HAD ENOUGH BOOZE.
TIME TO CALL IT A NIGHT.

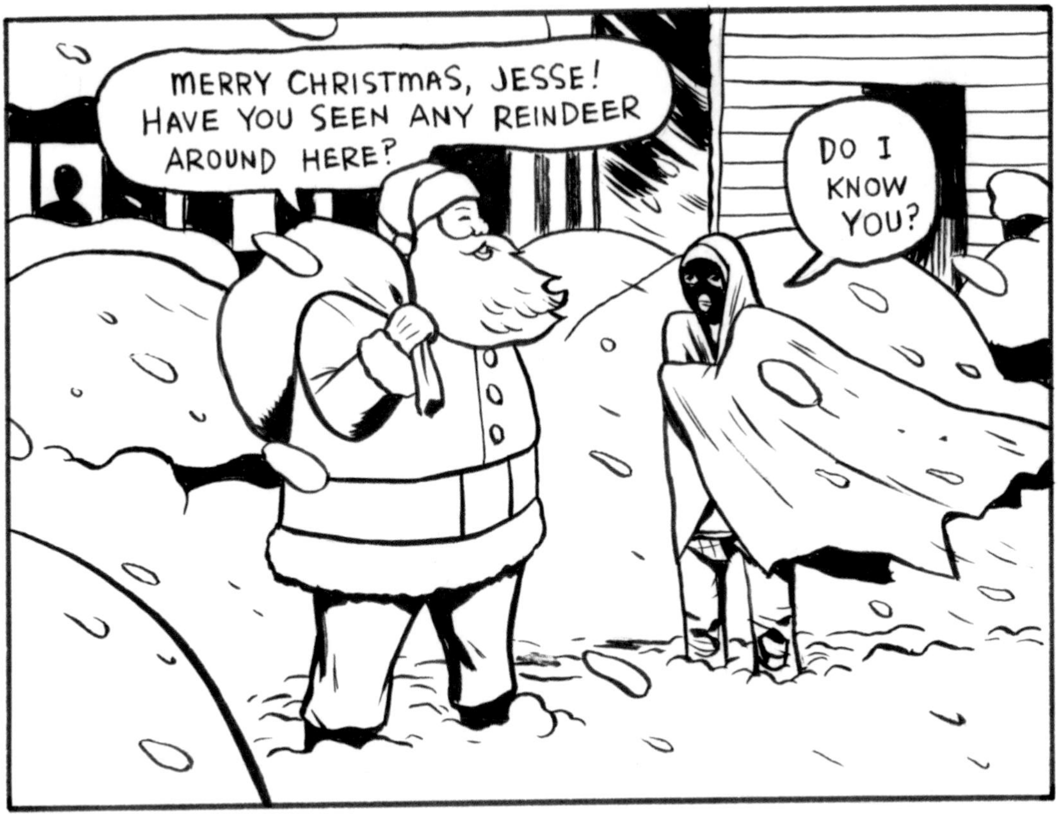
MERRY CHRISTMAS, JESSE! HAVE YOU SEEN ANY REINDEER AROUND HERE?
DO I KNOW YOU?

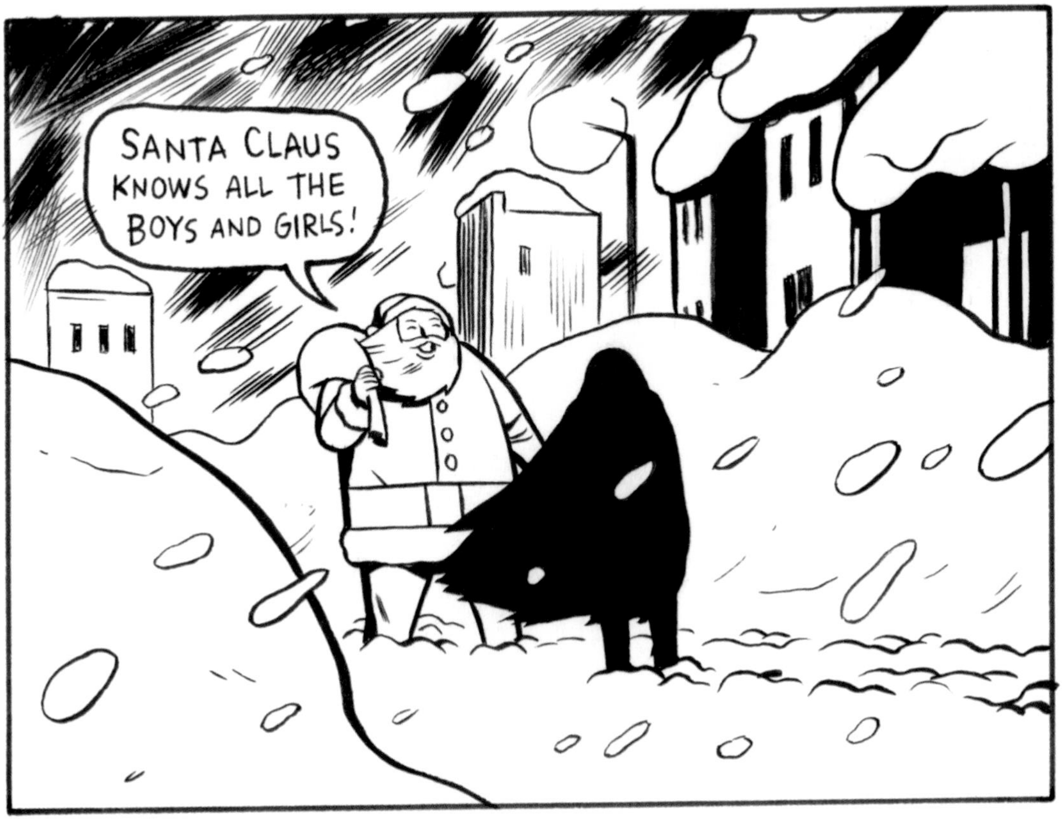
SANTA CLAUS KNOWS ALL THE BOYS AND GIRLS!

KAYLEE! MASON!

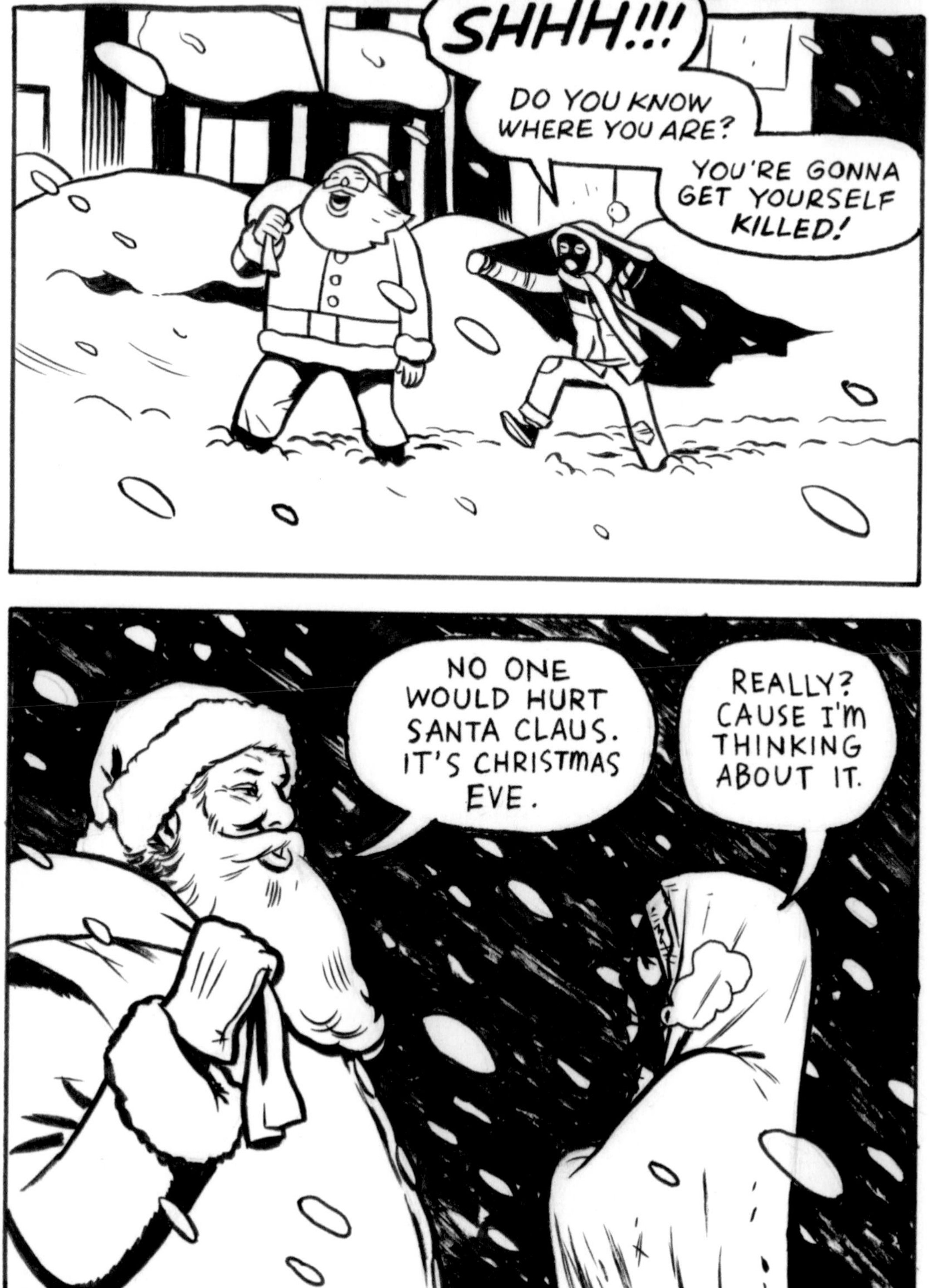
SHHH!!!
DO YOU KNOW WHERE YOU ARE?
YOU'RE GONNA GET YOURSELF KILLED!
NO ONE WOULD HURT SANTA CLAUS. IT'S CHRISTMAS EVE.
REALLY? CAUSE I'M THINKING ABOUT IT.

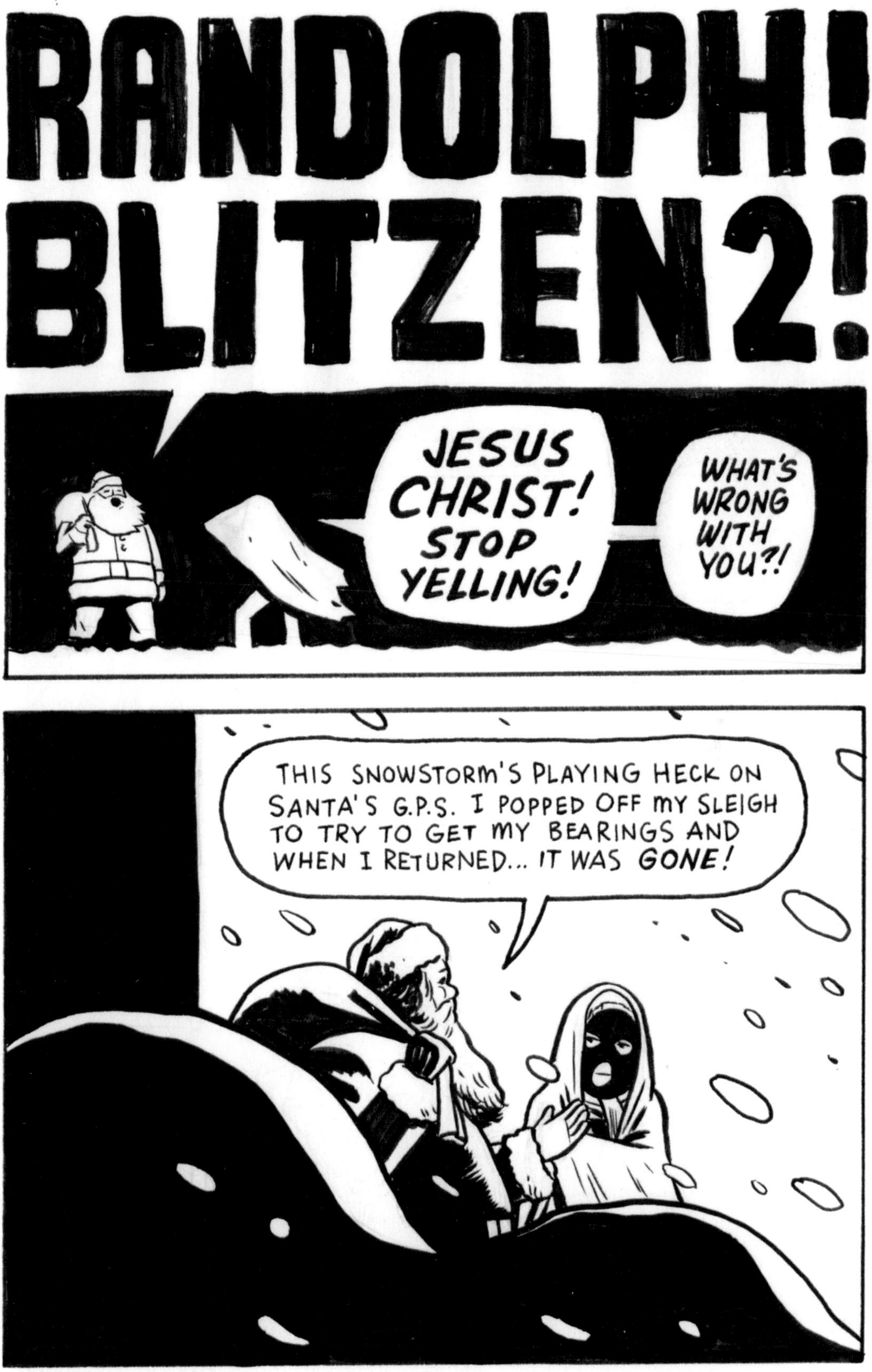
RANDOLPH! BLITZEN2!
JESUS CHRIST! STOP YELLING!
WHAT'S WRONG WITH YOU?!
THIS SNOWSTORM'S PLAYING HECK ON SANTA'S G.P.S. I POPPED OFF MY SLEIGH TO TRY TO GET MY BEARINGS AND WHEN I RETURNED... IT WAS GONE!

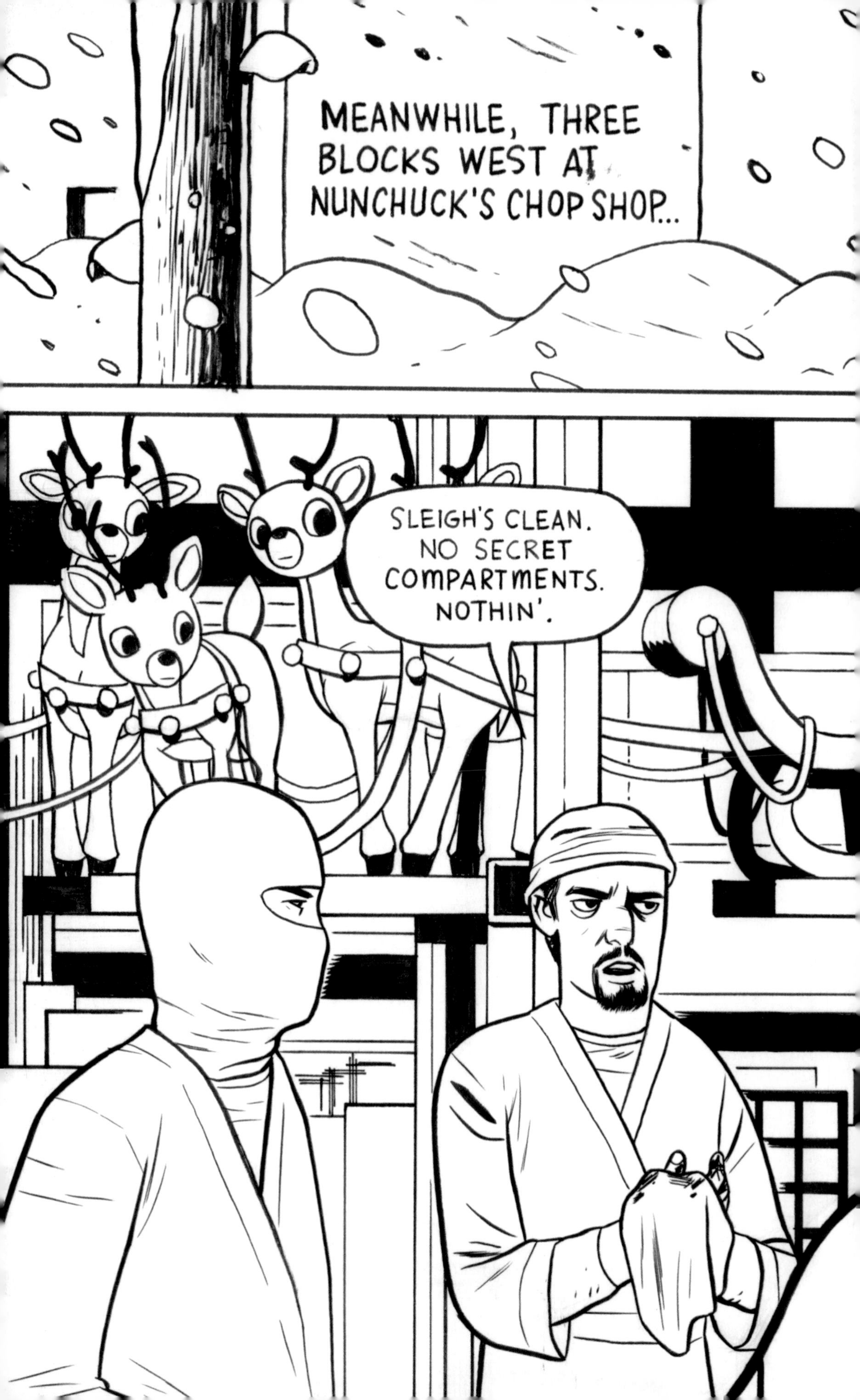
MEANWHILE, THREE BLOCKS WEST AT NUNCHUCK'S CHOP SHOP...
SLEIGH'S CLEAN. NO SECRET COMPARTMENTS. NOTHIN'.

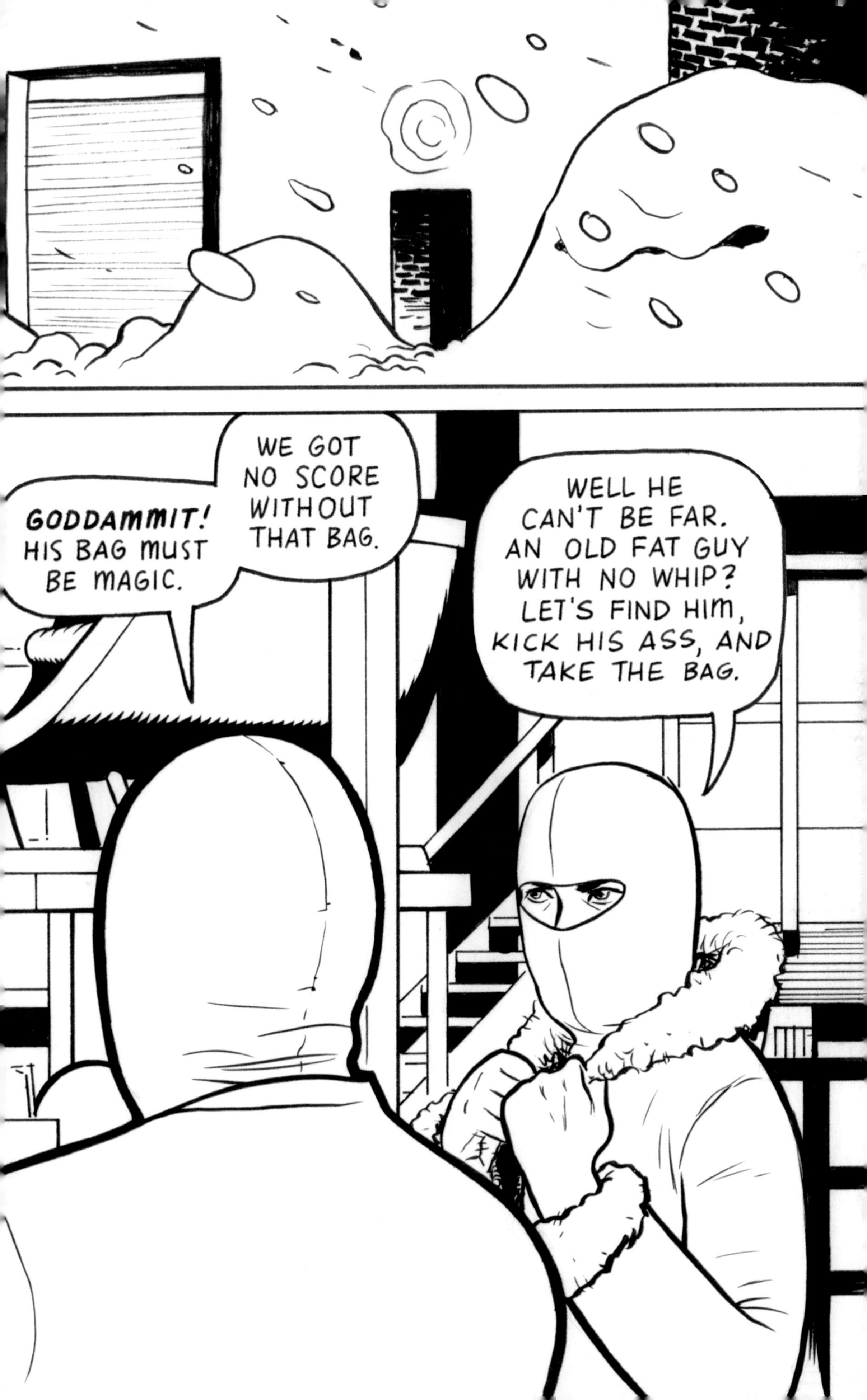

GODDAMMIT! HIS BAG MUST BE MAGIC.
WE GOT NO SCORE WITHOUT THAT BAG.
WELL HE CAN'T BE FAR. AN OLD FAT GUY WITH NO WHIP? LET'S FIND HIM, KICK HIS ASS, AND TAKE THE BAG.

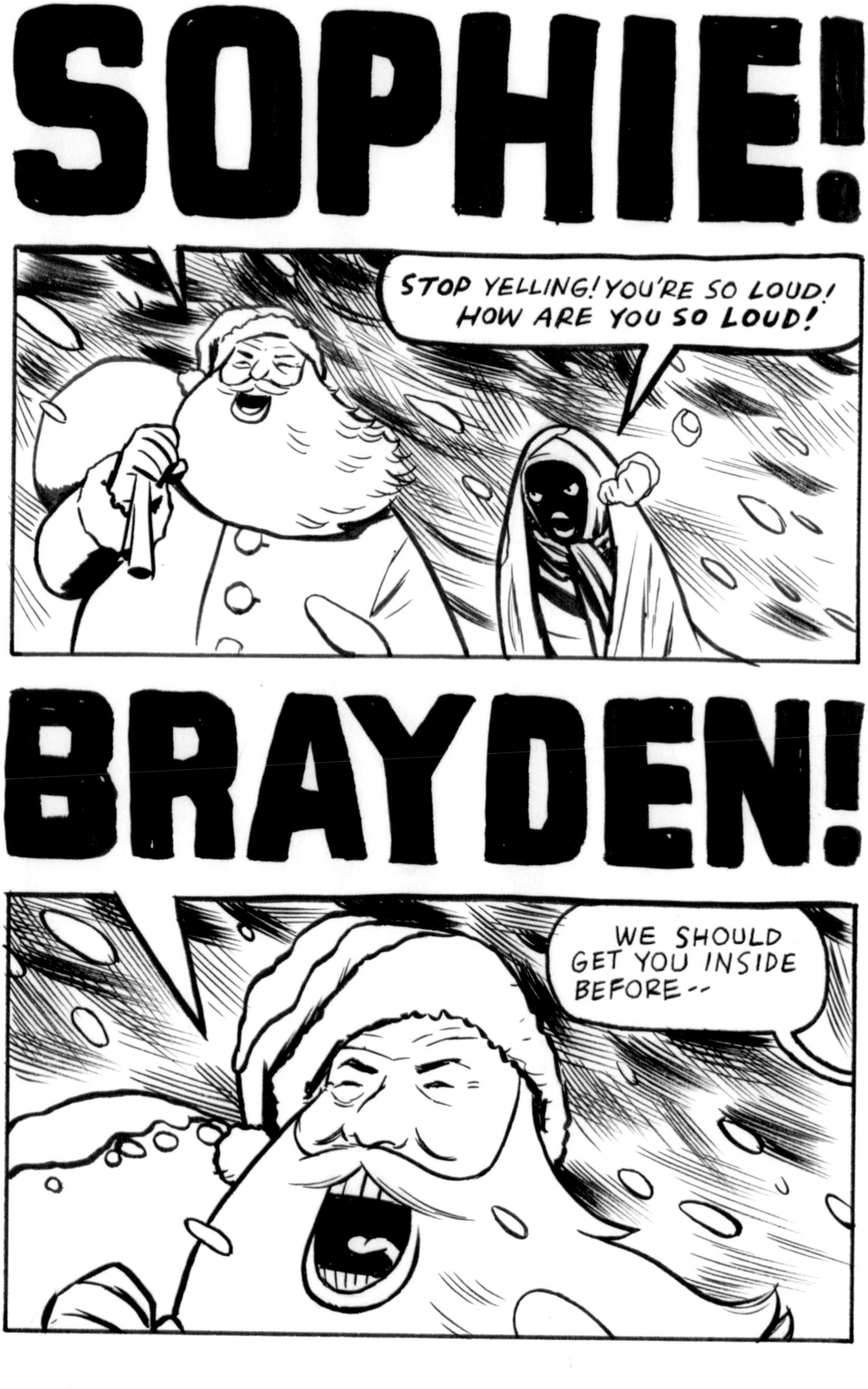
SOPHIE!
STOP YELLING! YOU'RE SO LOUD! HOW ARE YOU SO LOUD!
BRAYDEN!
WE SHOULD GET YOU INSIDE BEFORE--

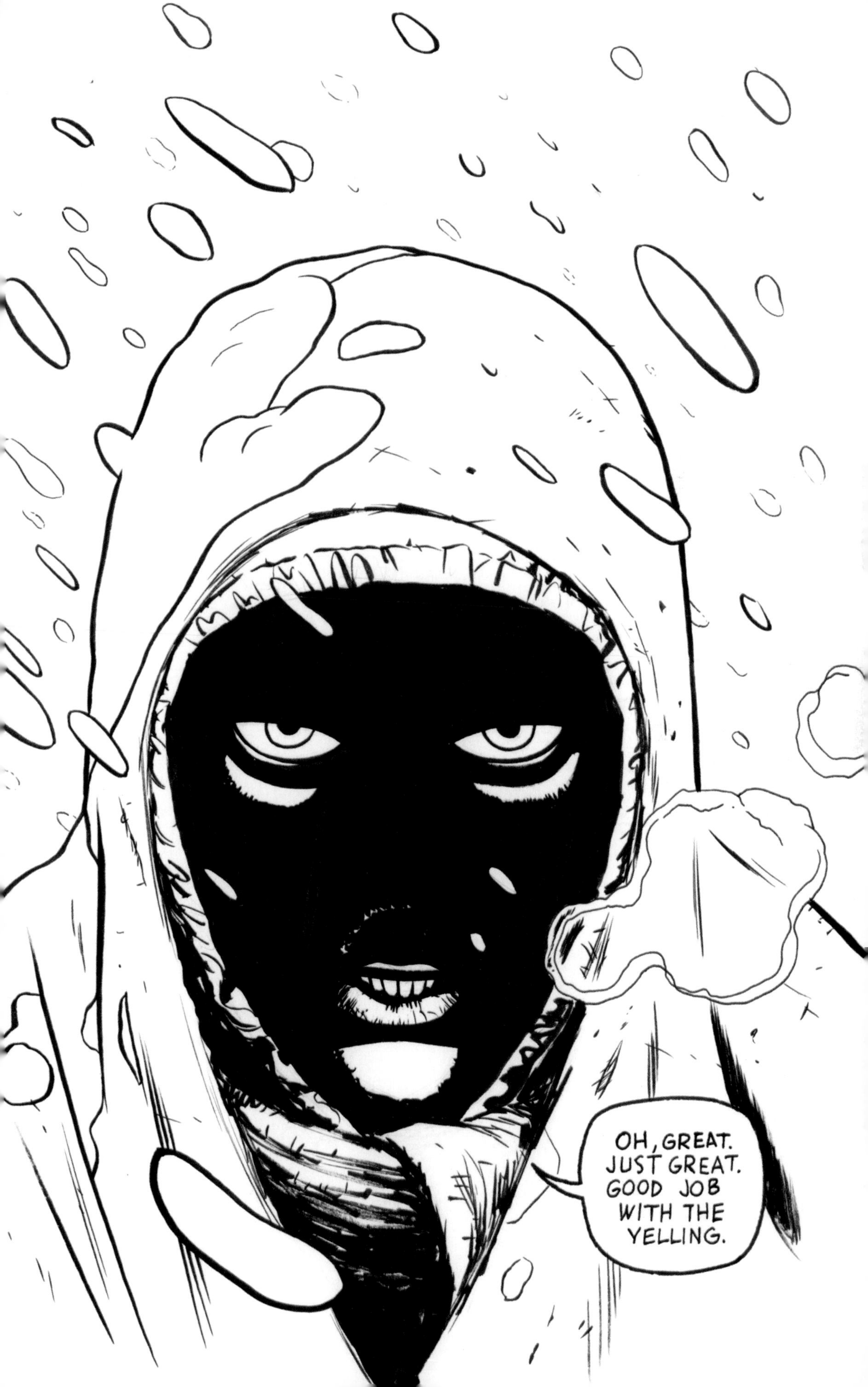
OH, GREAT. JUST GREAT. GOOD JOB WITH THE YELLING.

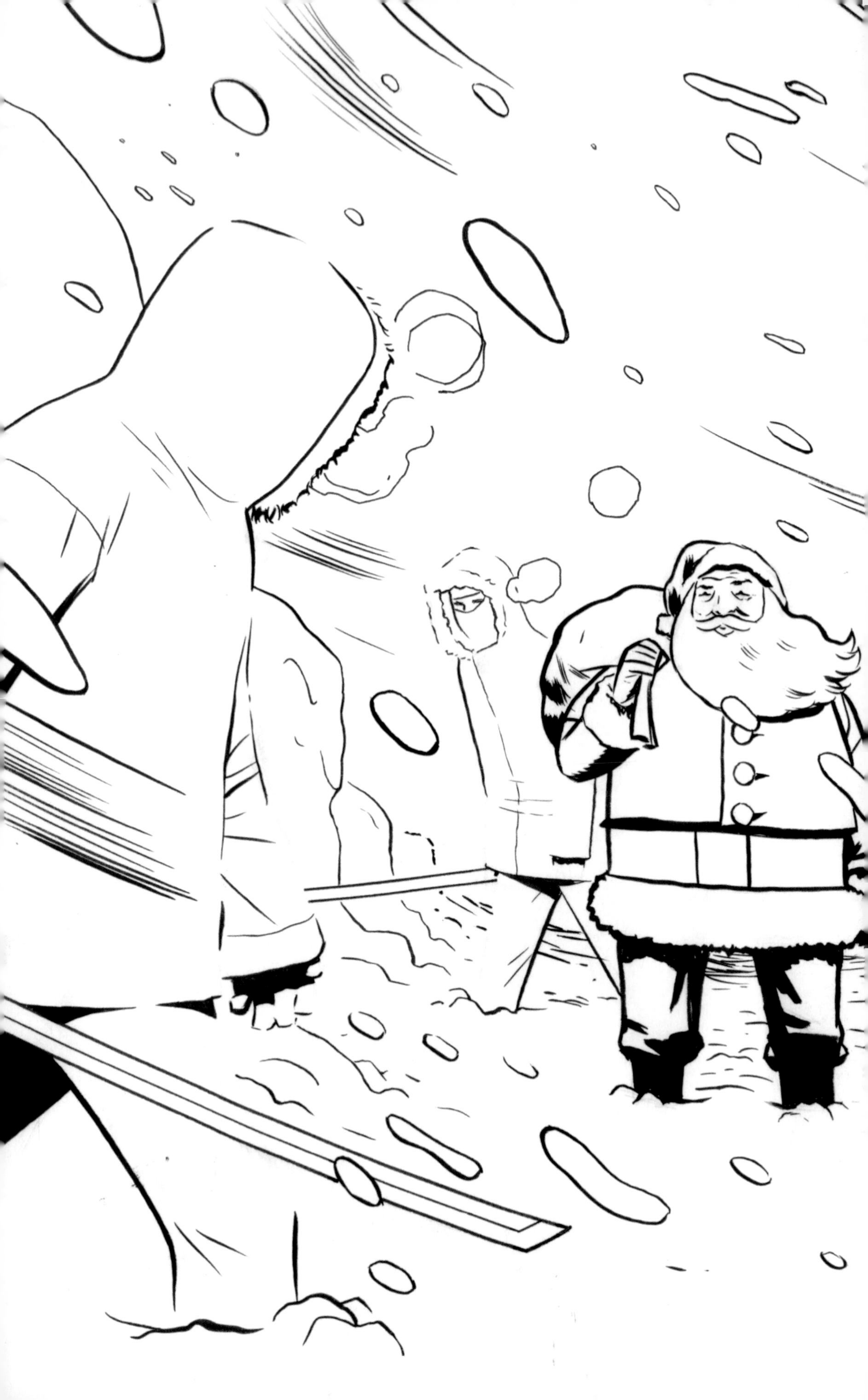

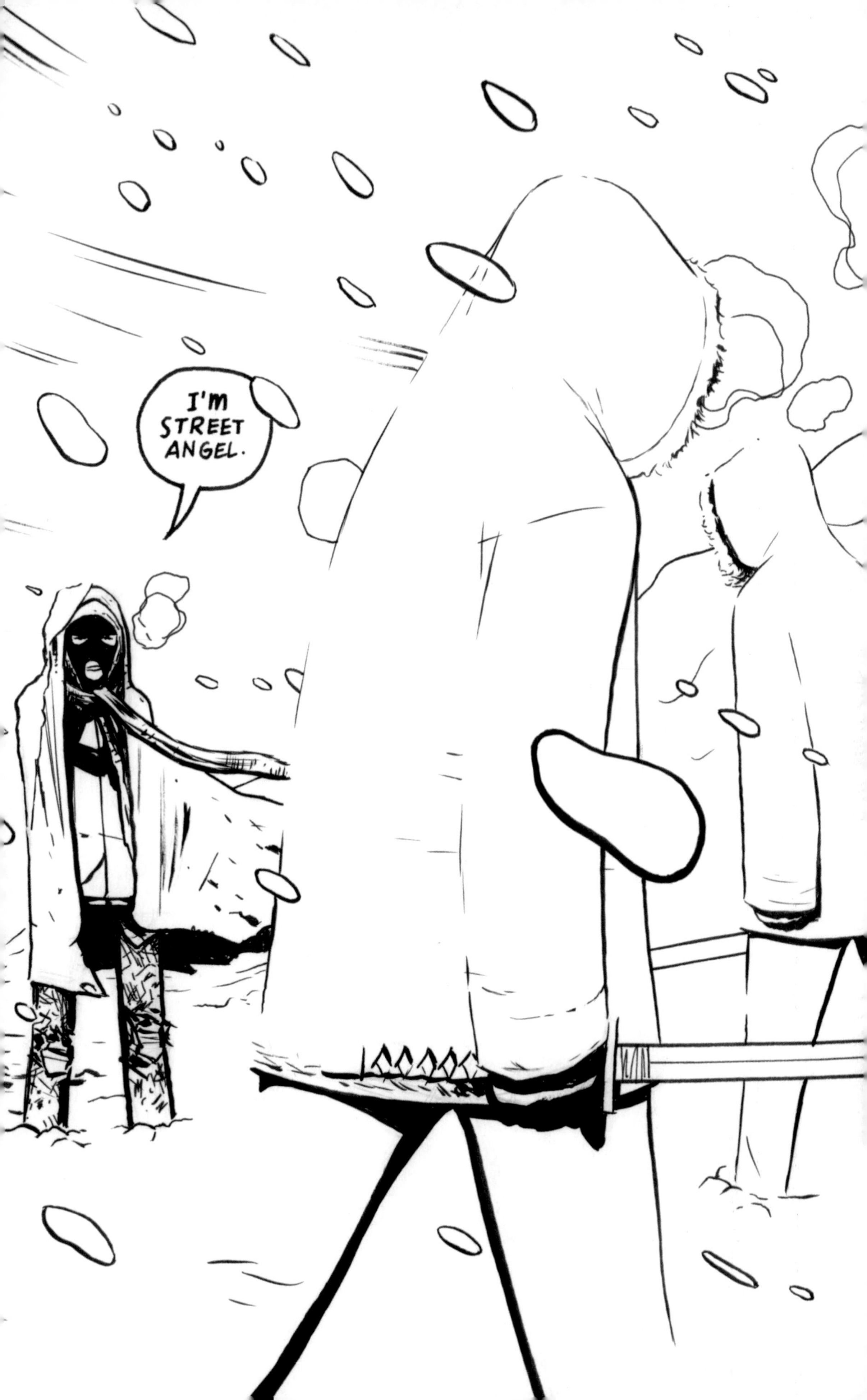
I'M STREET ANGEL.

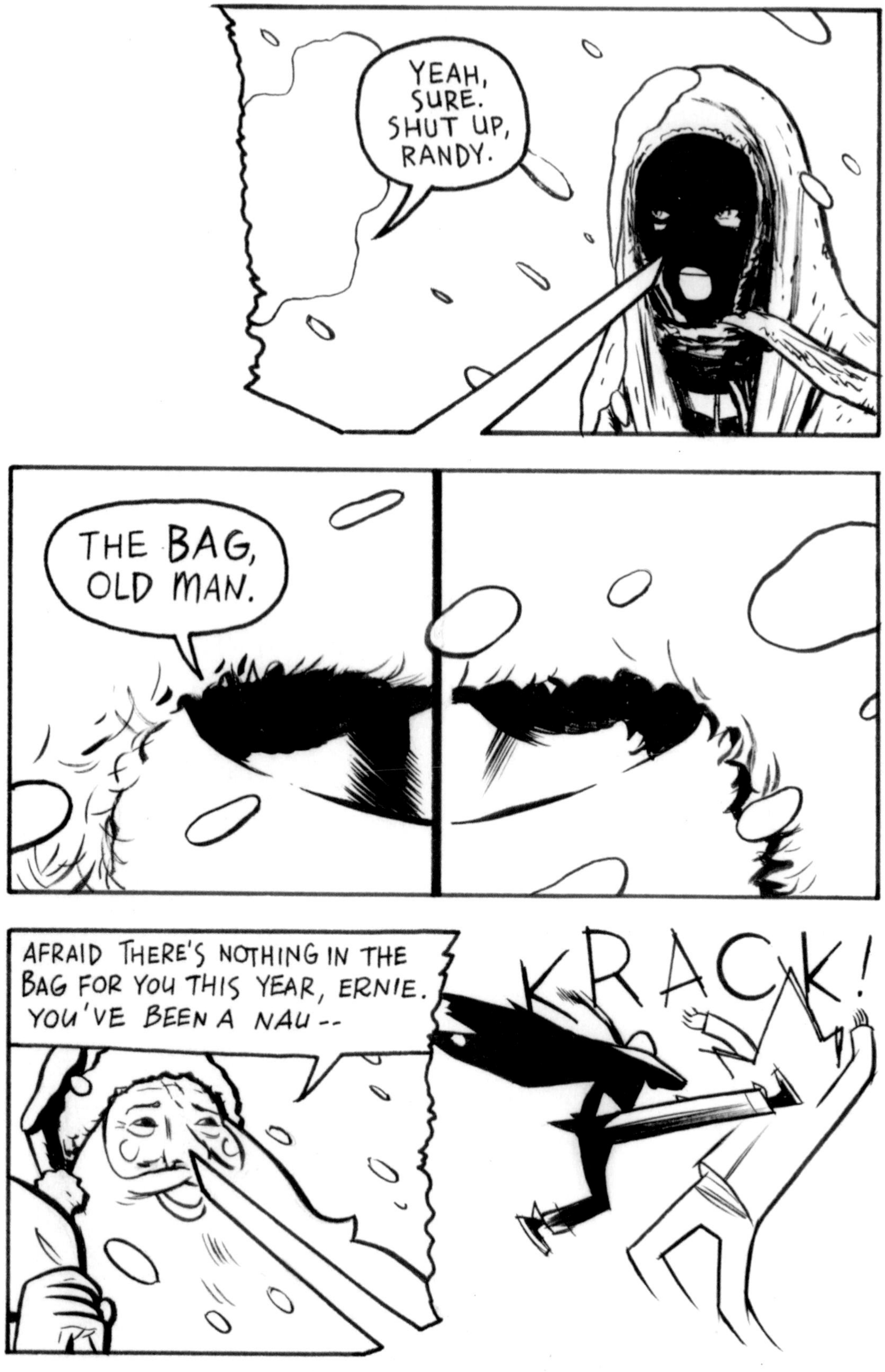
YEAH, SURE. SHUT UP, RANDY.
THE BAG, OLD MAN.
AFRAID THERE'S NOTHING IN THE BAG FOR YOU THIS YEAR, ERNIE. YOU'VE BEEN A NAU--
KRACK!

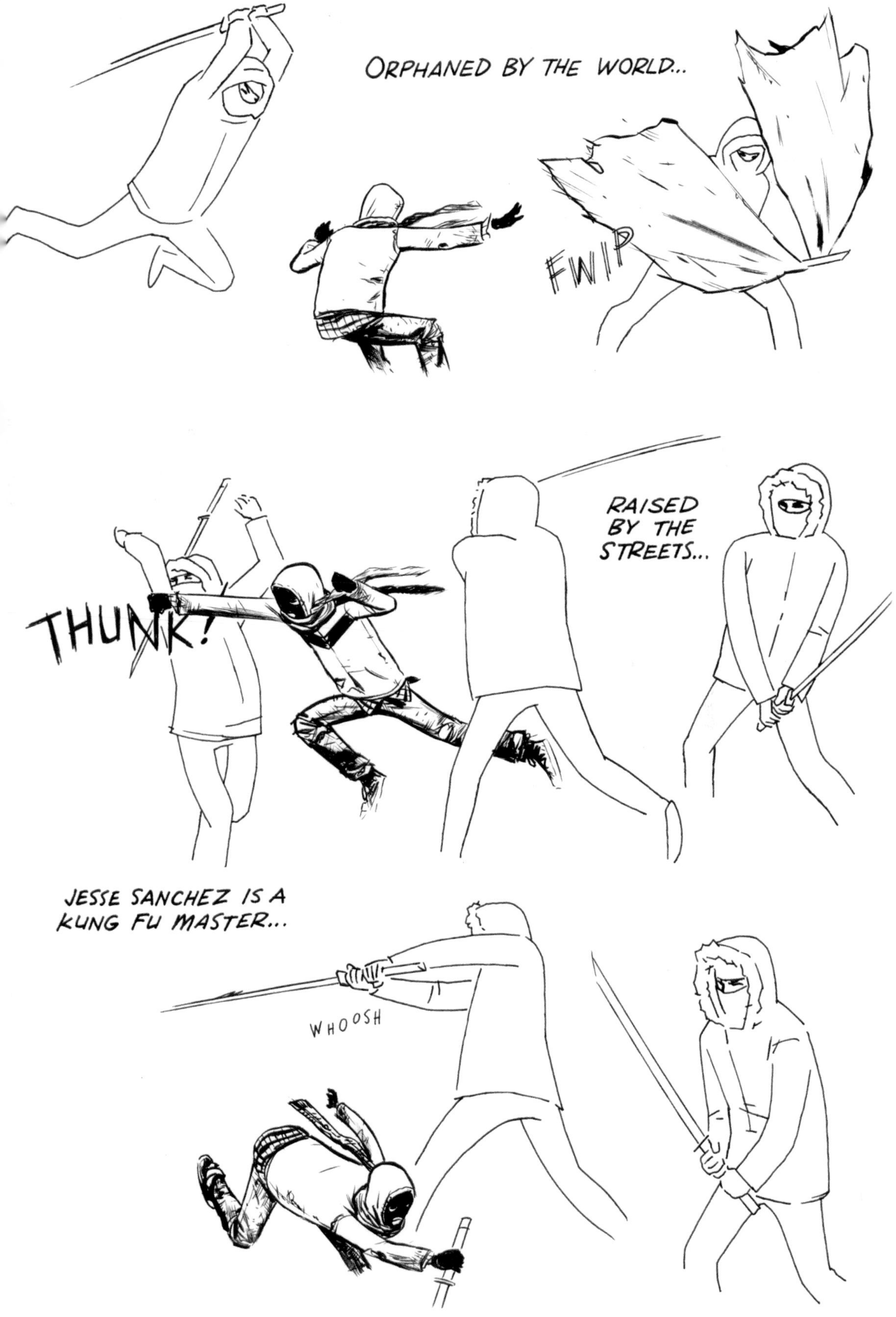
ORPHANED BY THE WORLD...
FWIP
THUNK!
RAISED BY THE STREETS...
JESSE SANCHEZ IS A KUNG FU MASTER...
WHOOSH

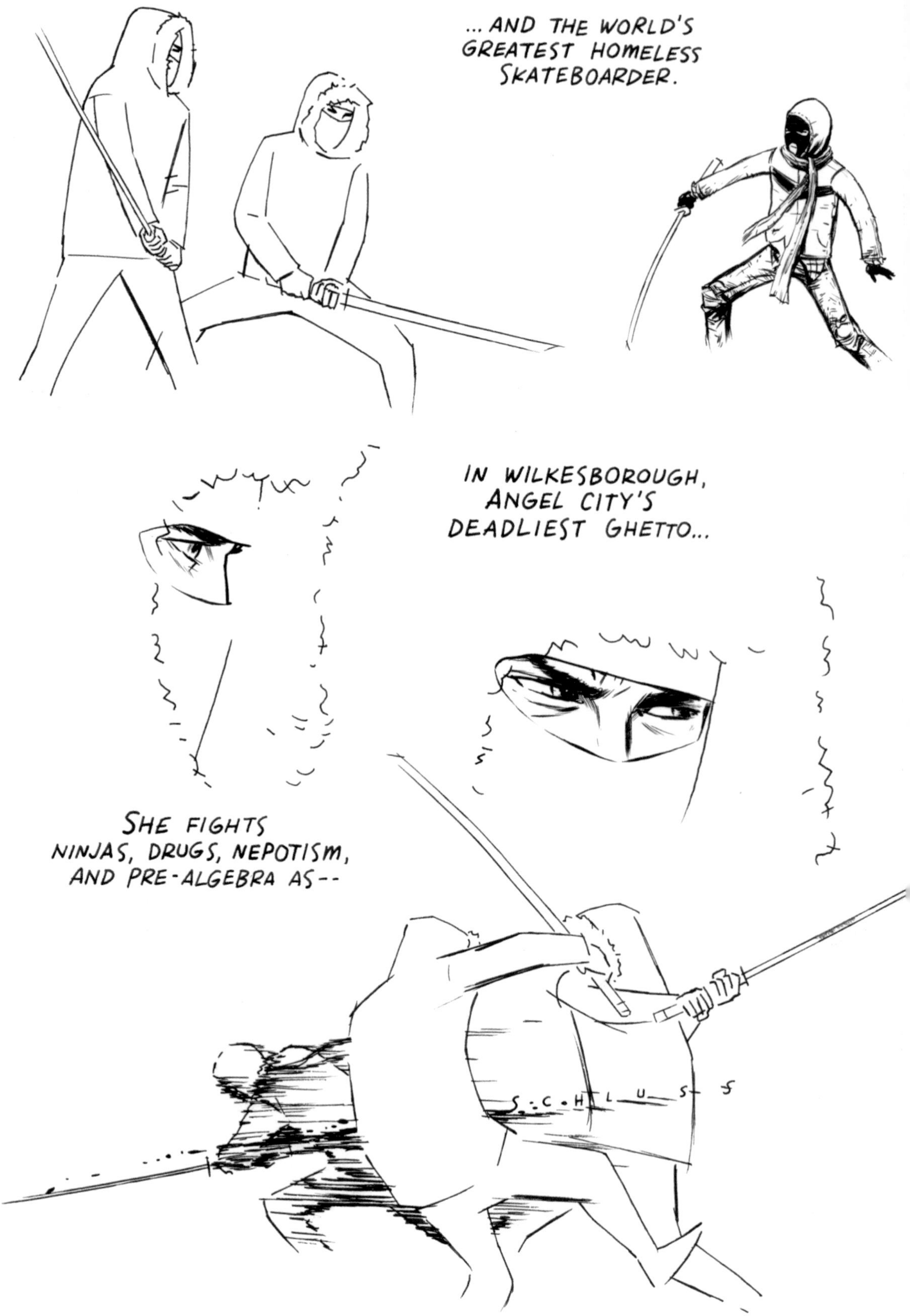
...AND THE WORLD'S GREATEST HOMELESS SKATEBOARDER.
IN WILKESBOROUGH, ANGEL CITY'S DEADLIEST GHETTO...
SHE FIGHTS NINJAS, DRUGS, NEPOTISM, AND PRE-ALGEBRA AS--
S-C-H-L-U-S-S

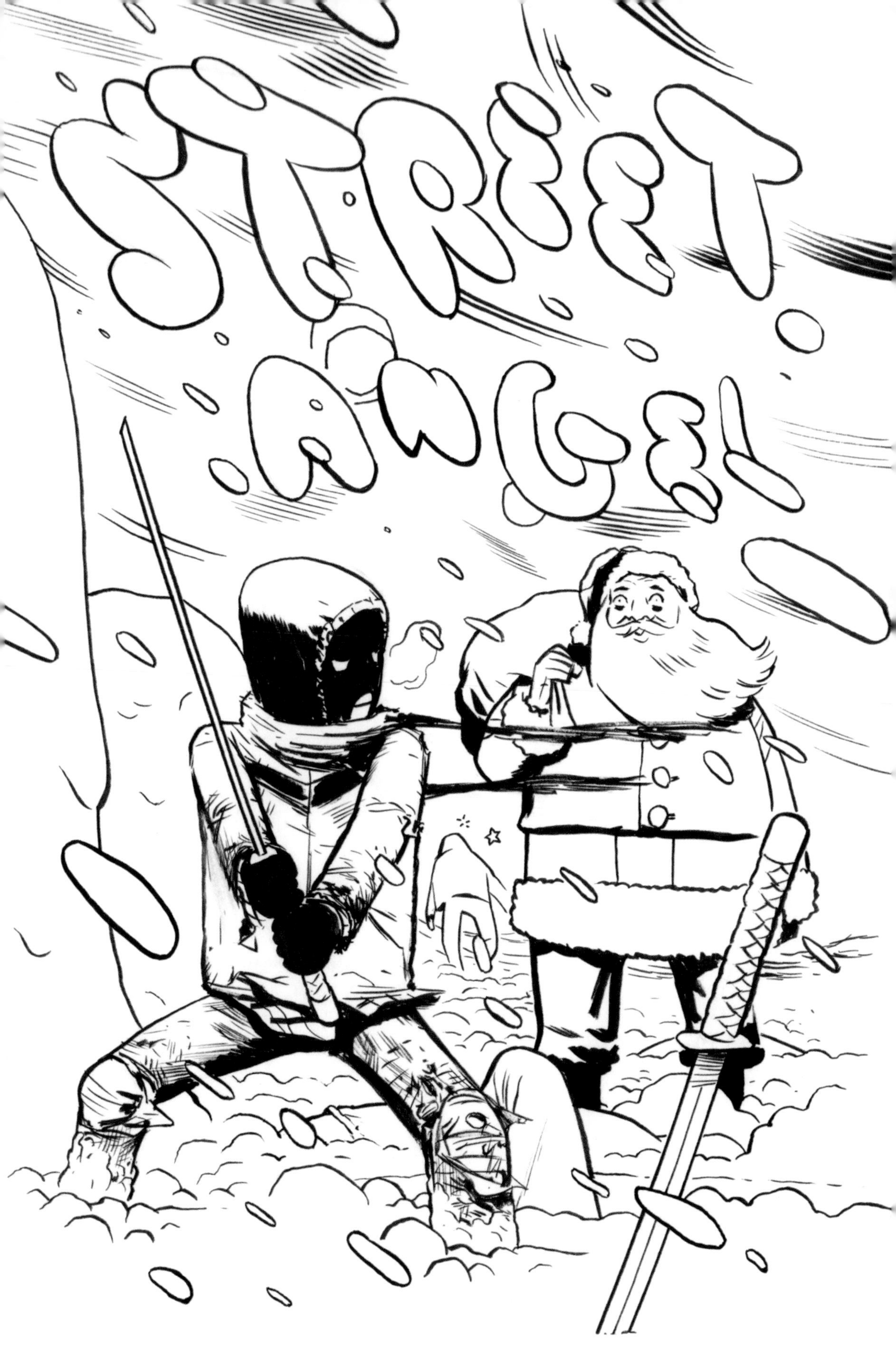
STREET ANGEL

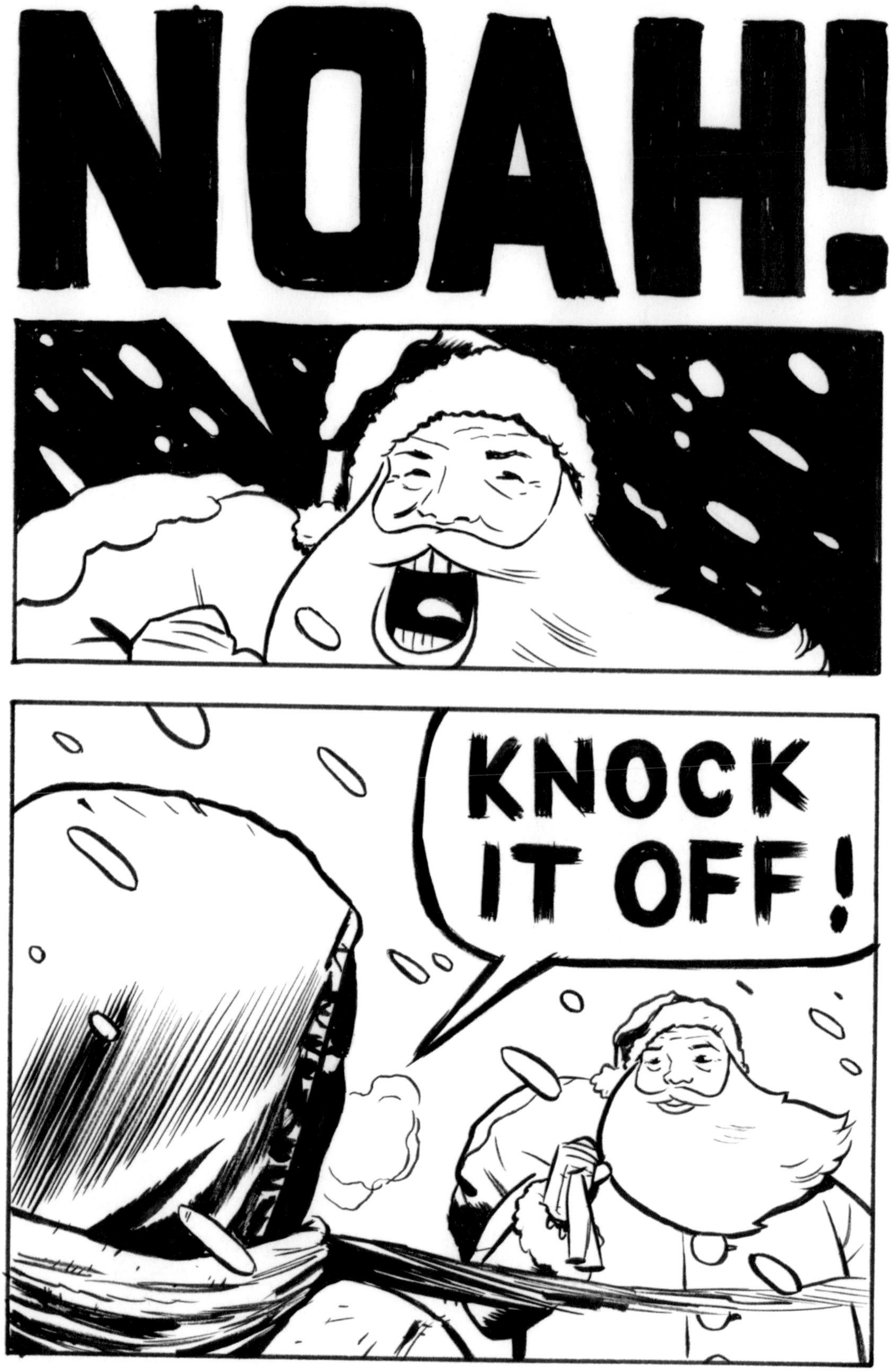
NOAH!
KNOCK IT OFF!

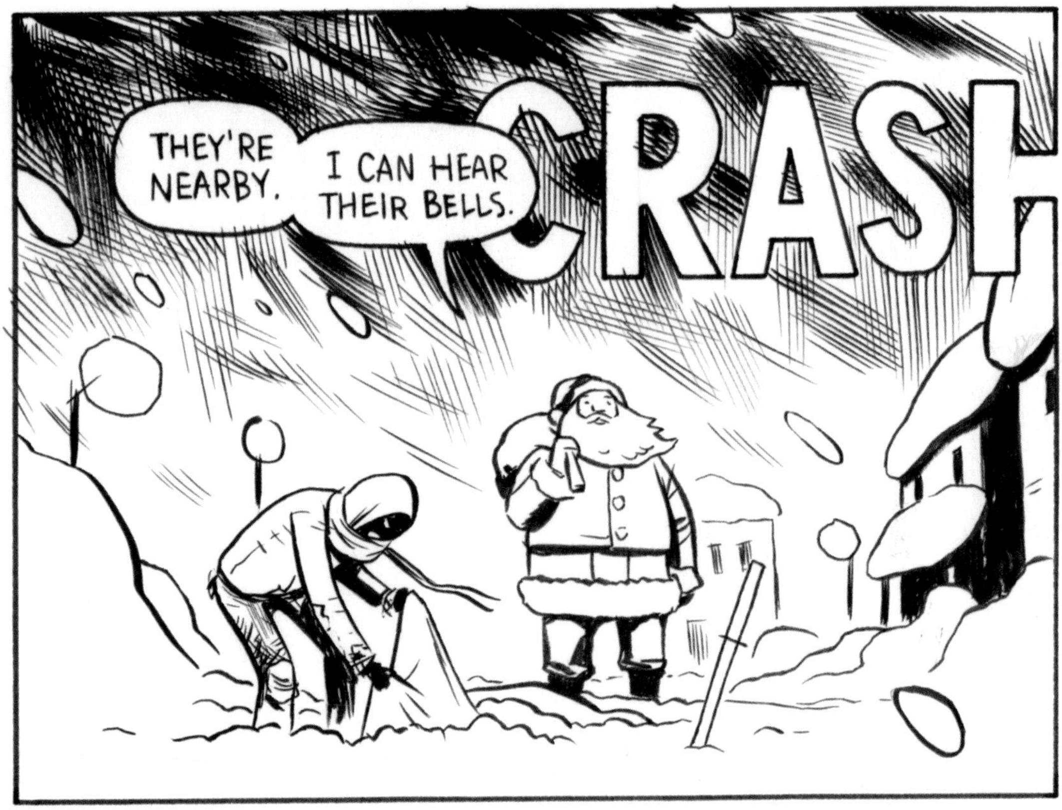
THEY'RE NEARBY.
I CAN HEAR THEIR BELLS.
CRASH

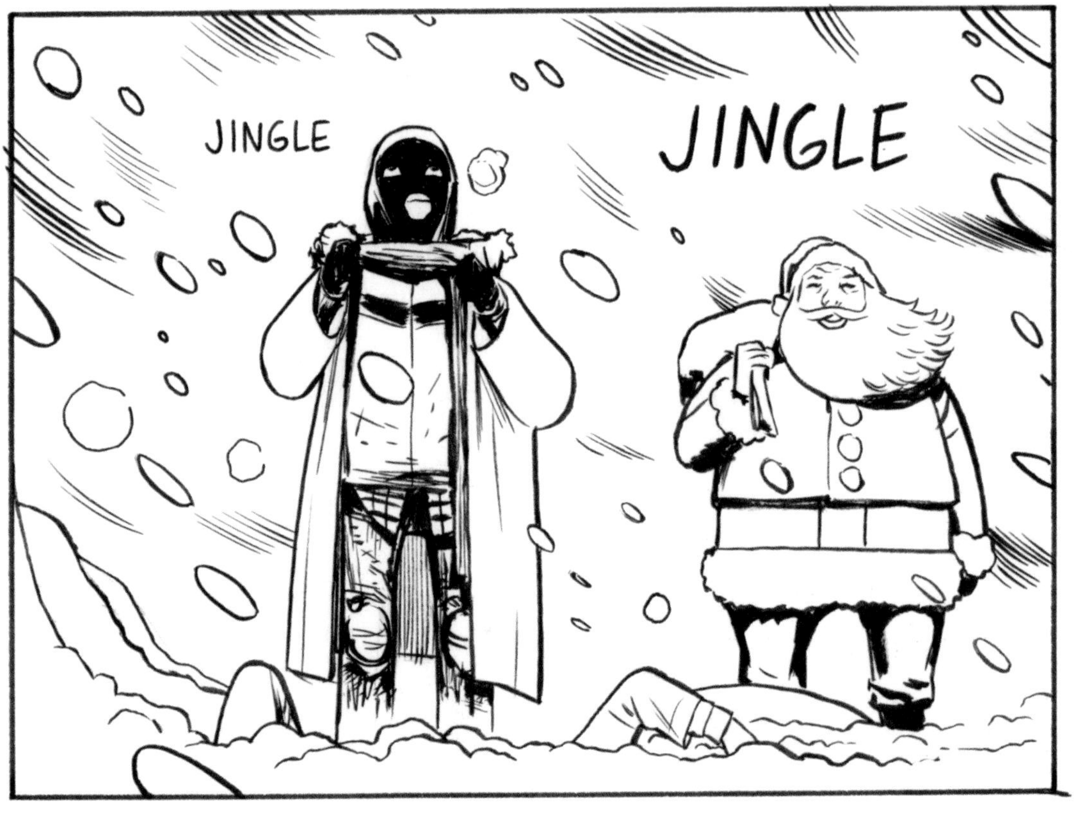
JINGLE
JINGLE

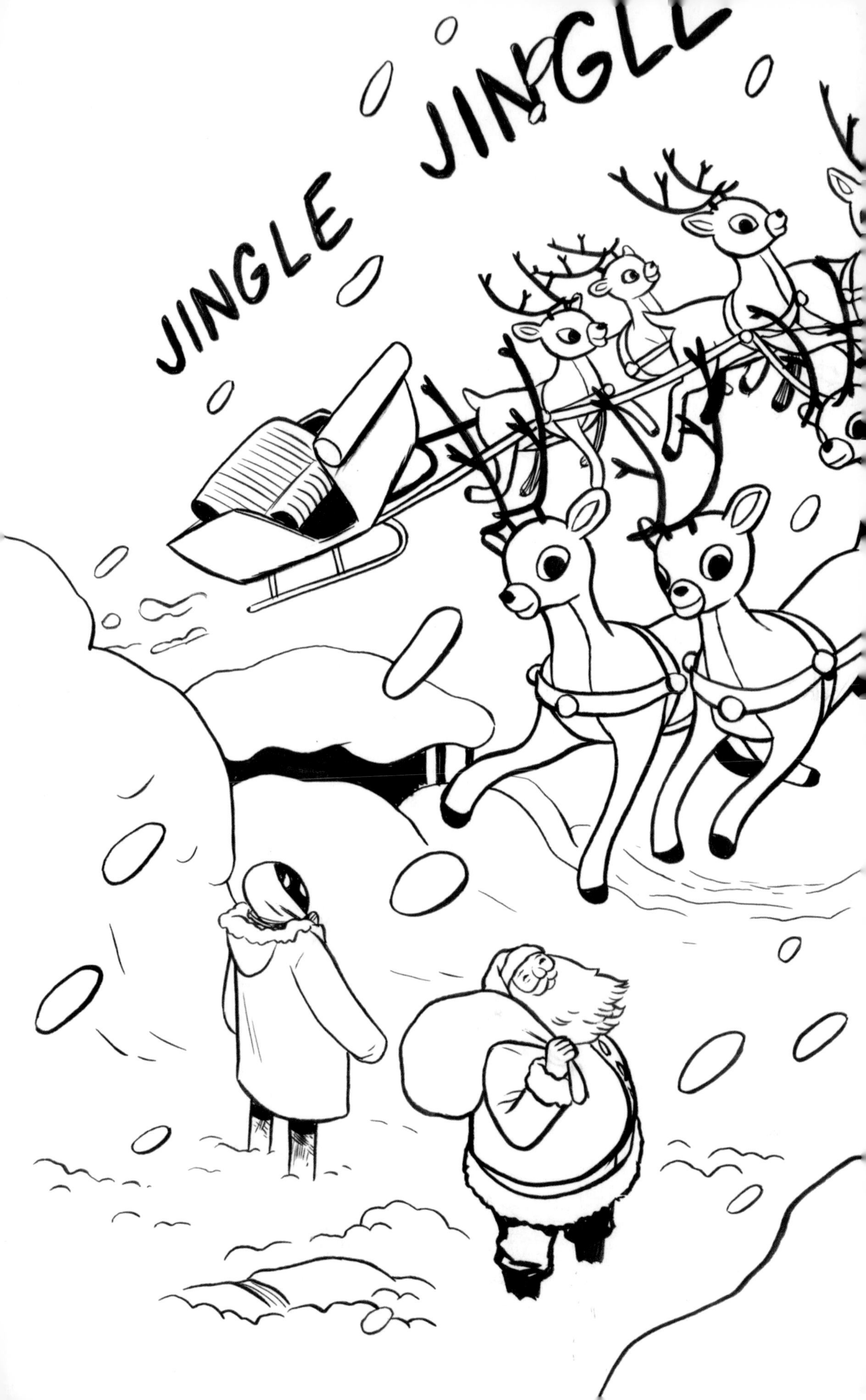

JINGLE
JINGLE

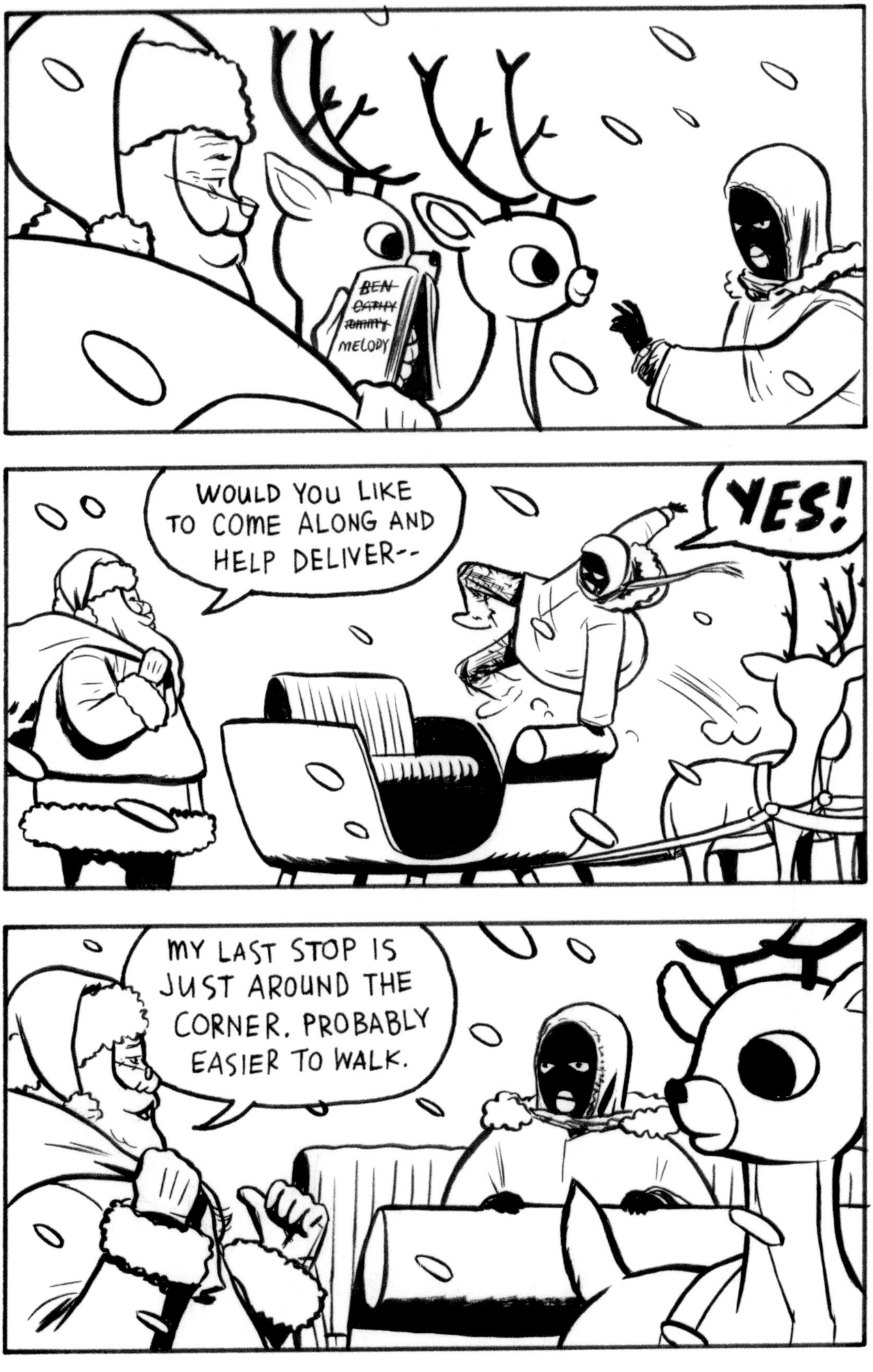
BEN
CATHY
MELODY
WOULD YOU LIKE TO COME ALONG AND HELP DELIVER--
YES!
MY LAST STOP IS JUST AROUND THE CORNER. PROBABLY EASIER TO WALK.

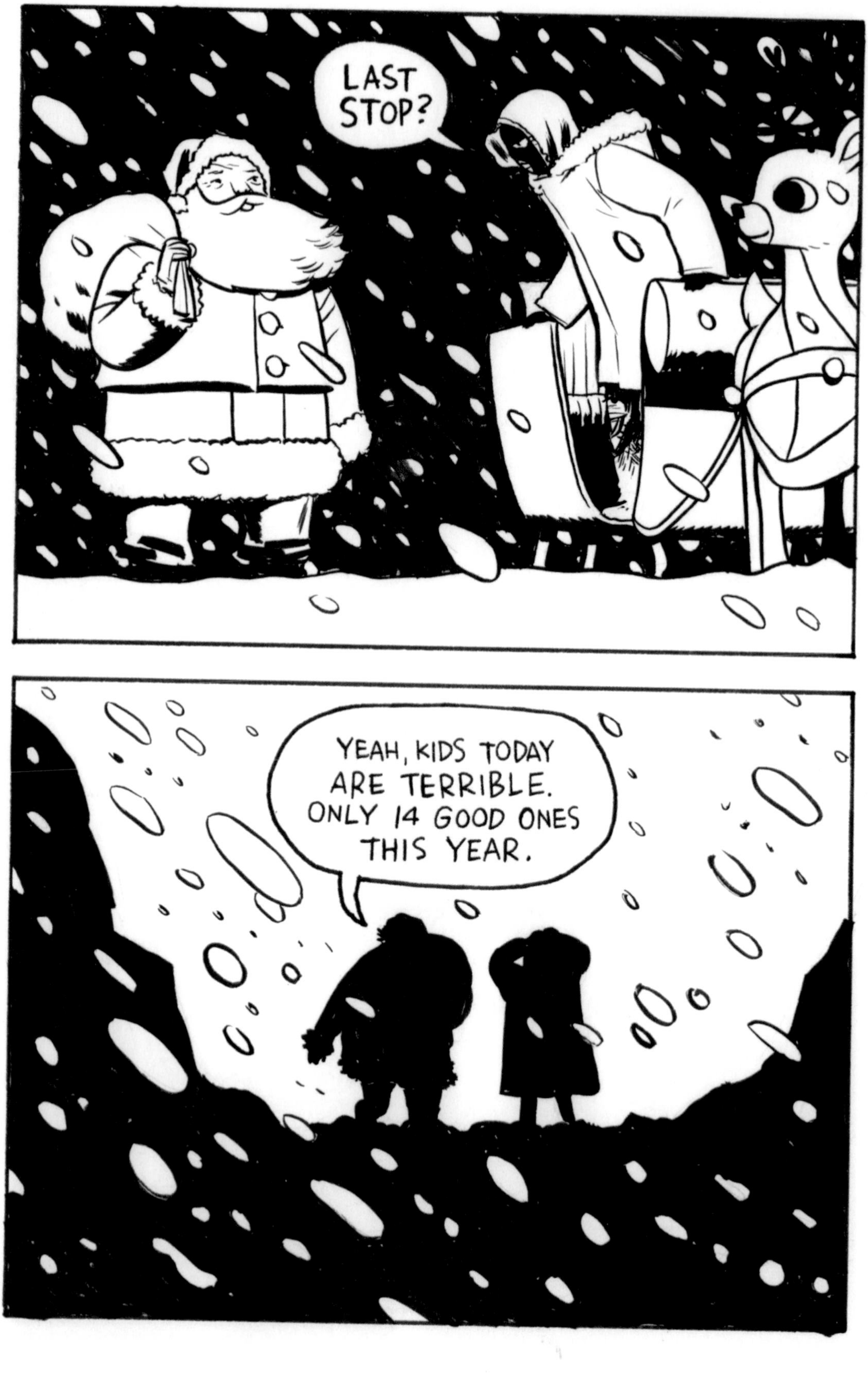
LAST STOP?
YEAH, KIDS TODAY ARE TERRIBLE. ONLY 14 GOOD ONES THIS YEAR.

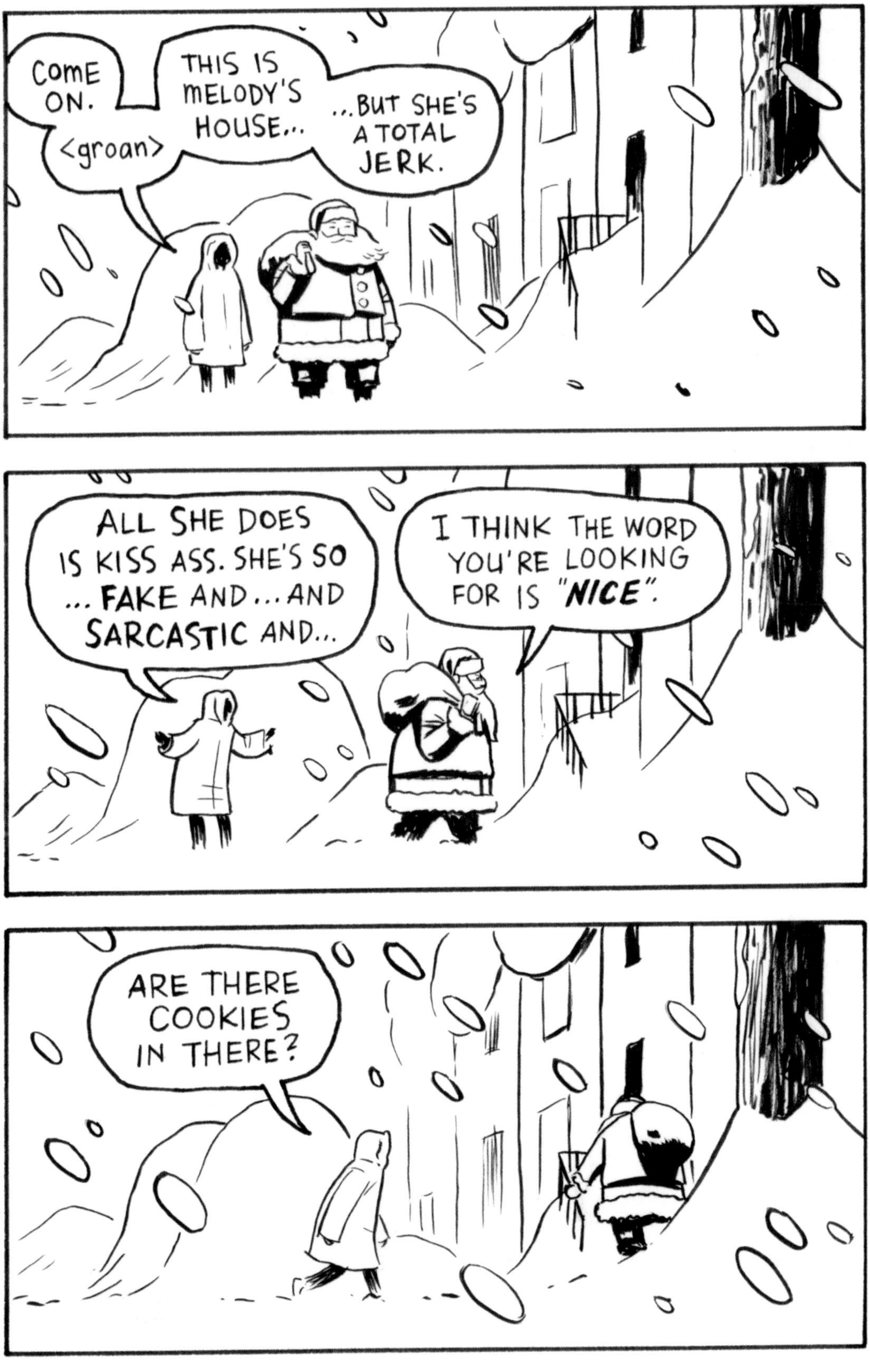
COME ON.
<groan>
THIS IS MELODY'S HOUSE...
...BUT SHE'S A TOTAL JERK.
ALL SHE DOES IS KISS ASS. SHE'S SO ... **FAKE** AND ... AND **SARCASTIC** AND...
I THINK THE WORD YOU'RE LOOKING FOR IS "***NICE***".
ARE THERE COOKIES IN THERE?

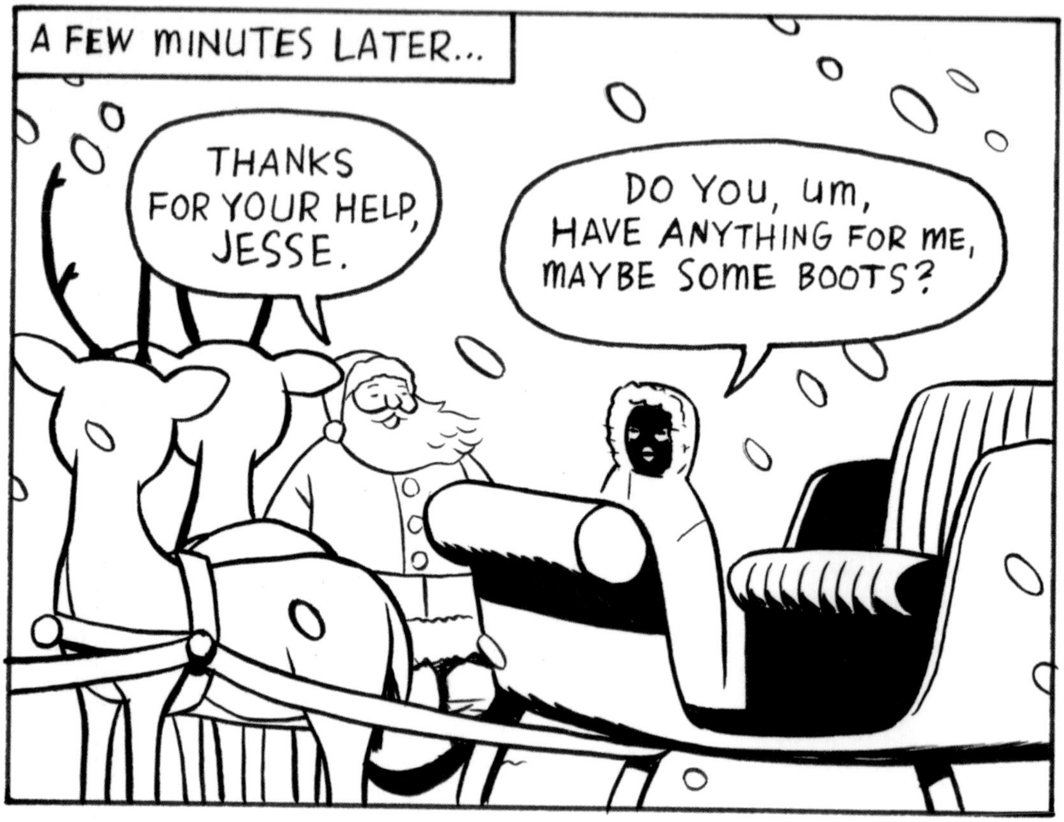
A FEW MINUTES LATER...
THANKS FOR YOUR HELP, JESSE.
DO YOU, UM, HAVE ANYTHING FOR ME, MAYBE SOME BOOTS?

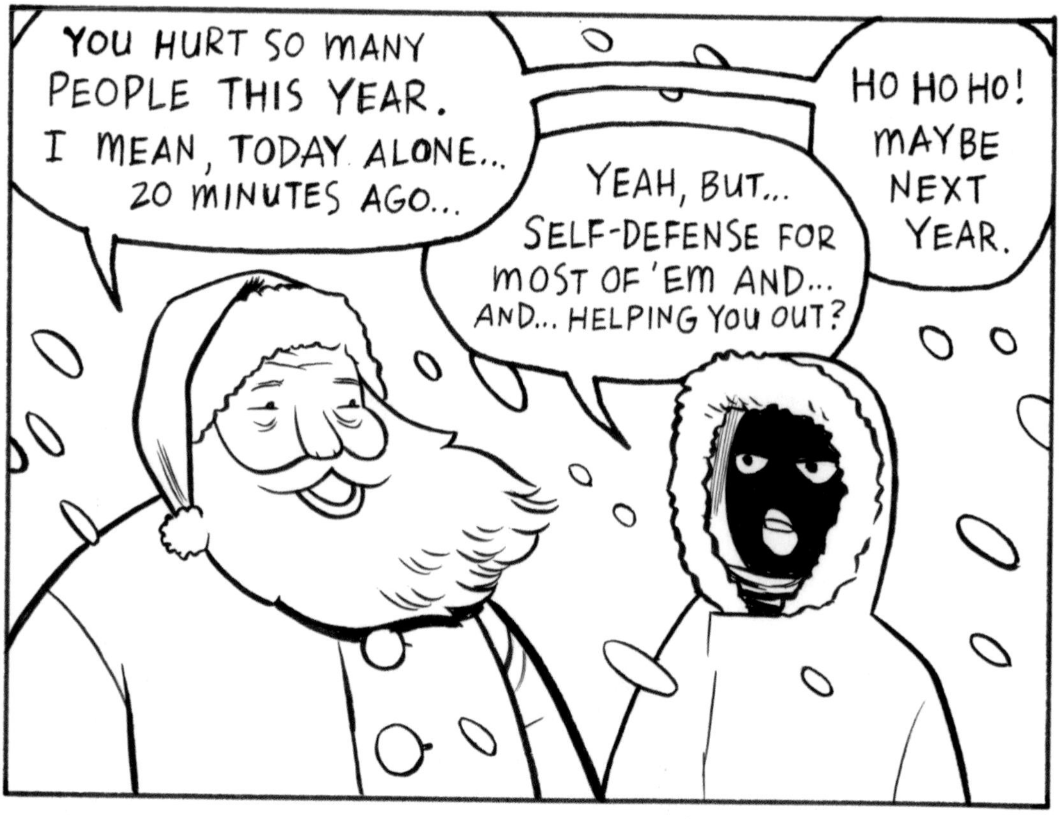
YOU HURT SO MANY PEOPLE THIS YEAR. I MEAN, TODAY ALONE... 20 MINUTES AGO...
YEAH, BUT... SELF-DEFENSE FOR MOST OF 'EM AND... AND... HELPING YOU OUT?
HO HO HO! MAYBE NEXT YEAR.

NOW, NOAH! NOW, COLTON! NOW KAYLEE AND MASON!
ON, RANDOLPH! ON, BLITZEN 2! ON, LEXI AND BRAYDEN!

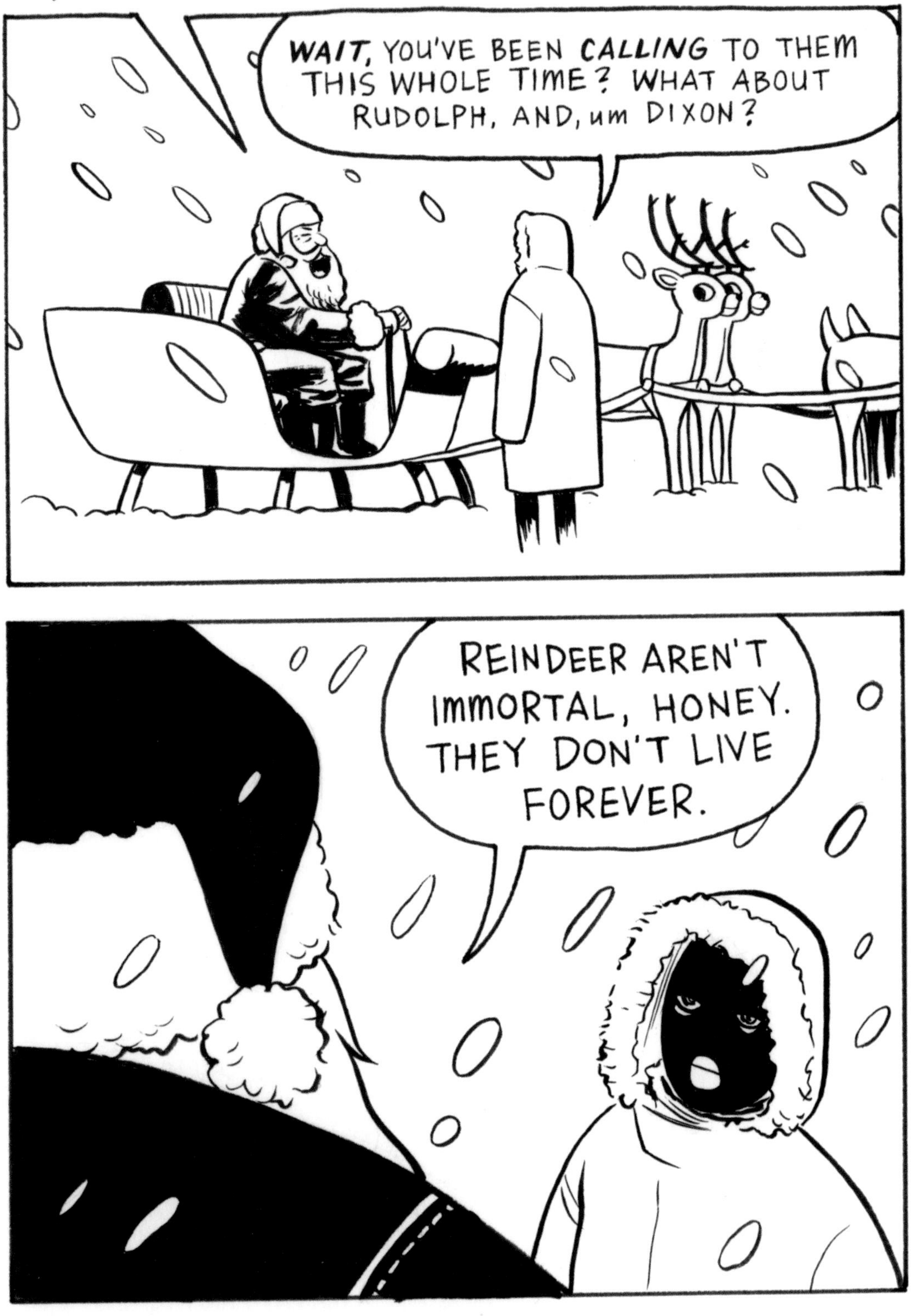
WAIT, YOU'VE BEEN CALLING TO THEM THIS WHOLE TIME? WHAT ABOUT RUDOLPH, AND, um DIXON?
REINDEER AREN'T IMMORTAL, HONEY. THEY DON'T LIVE FOREVER.

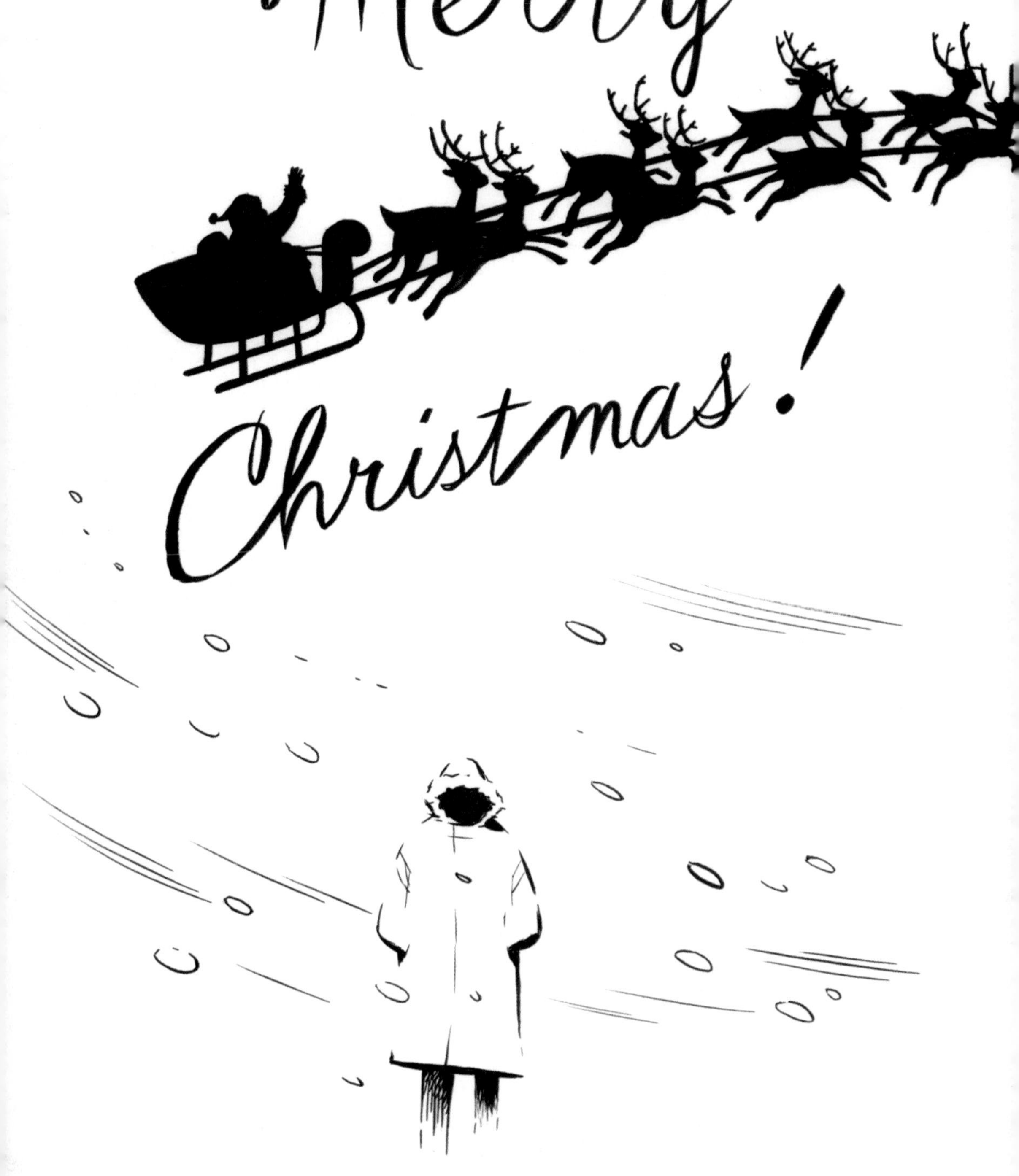
Merry
Christmas!

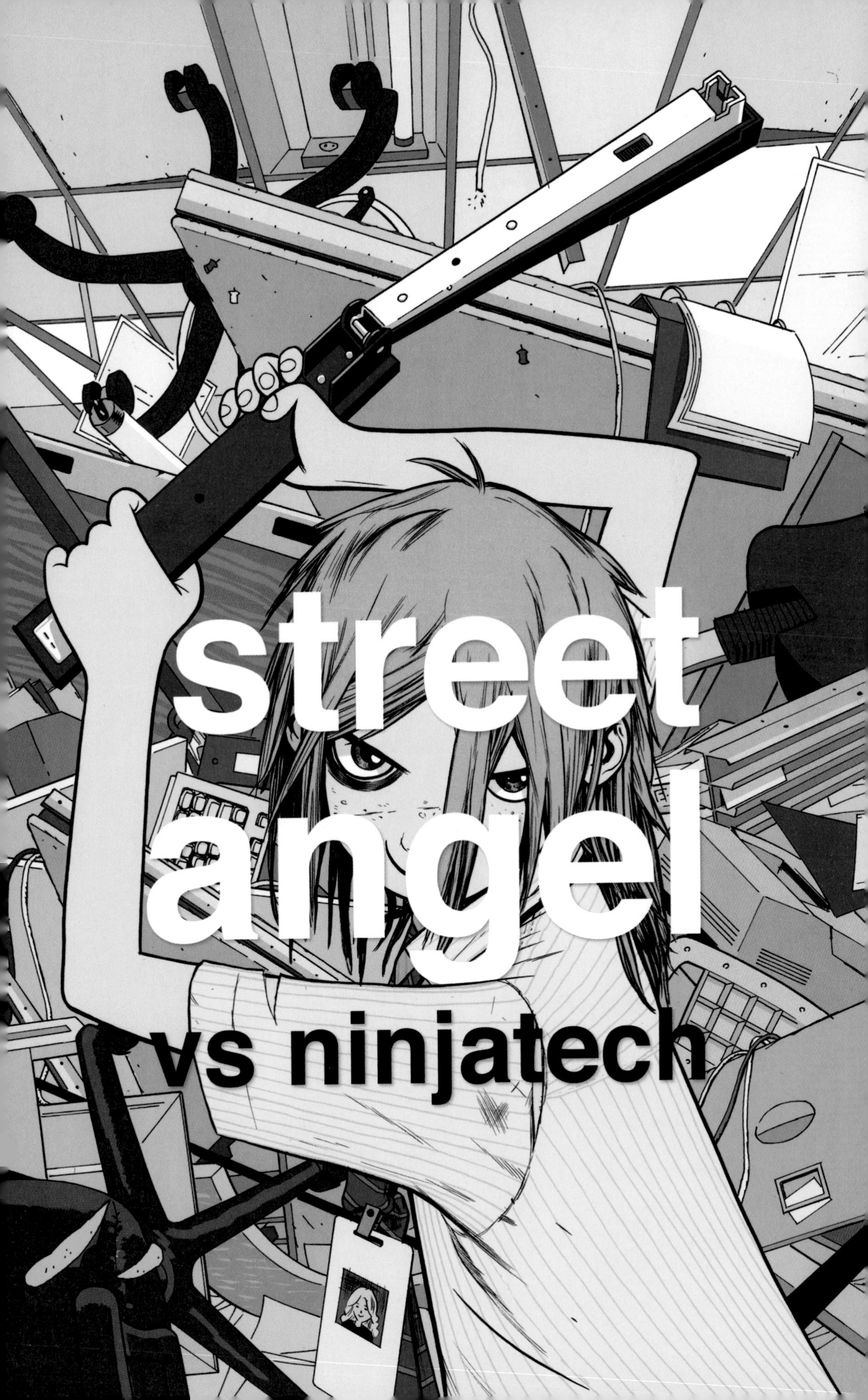
street
angel
vs ninjatech

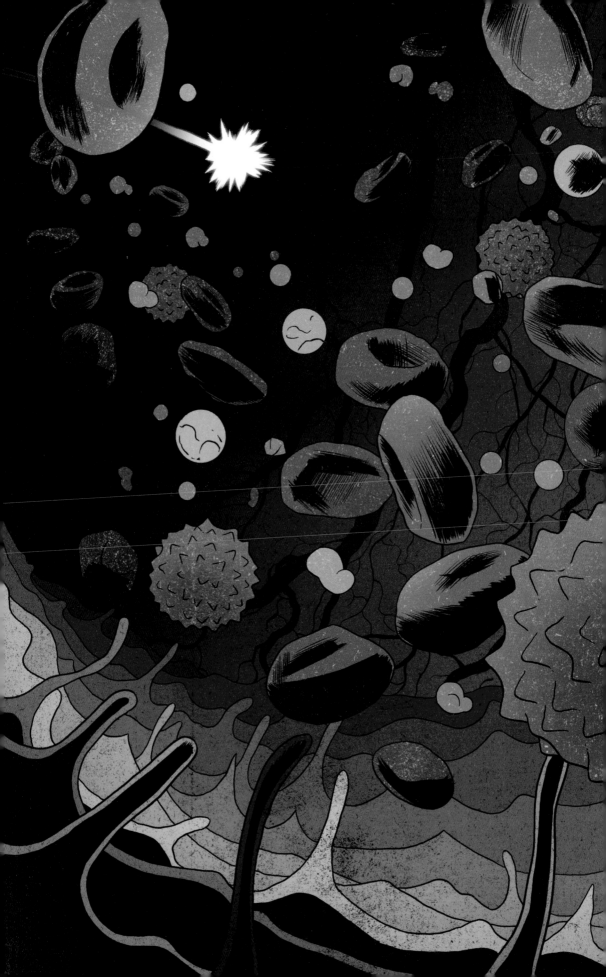

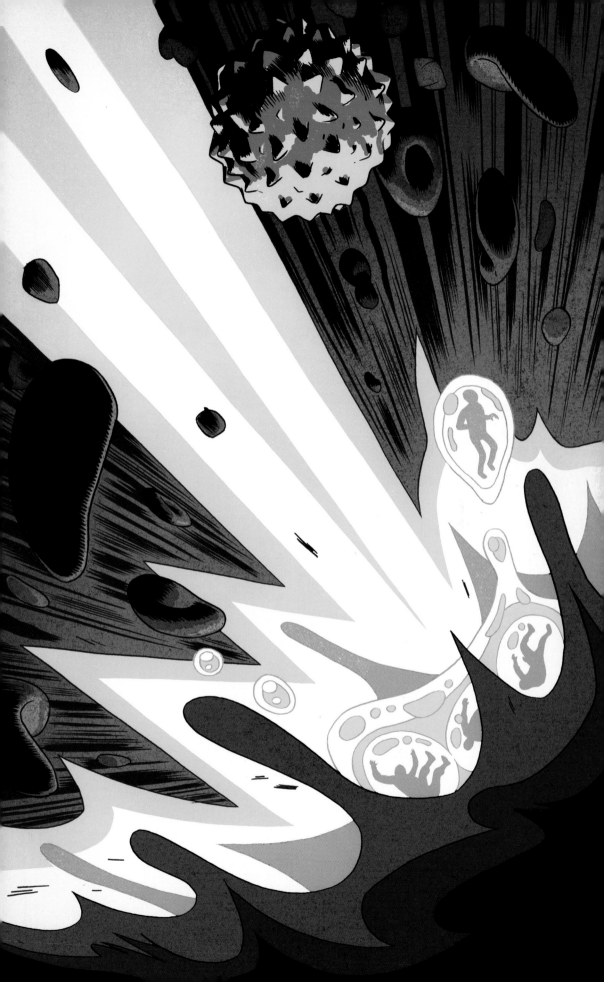

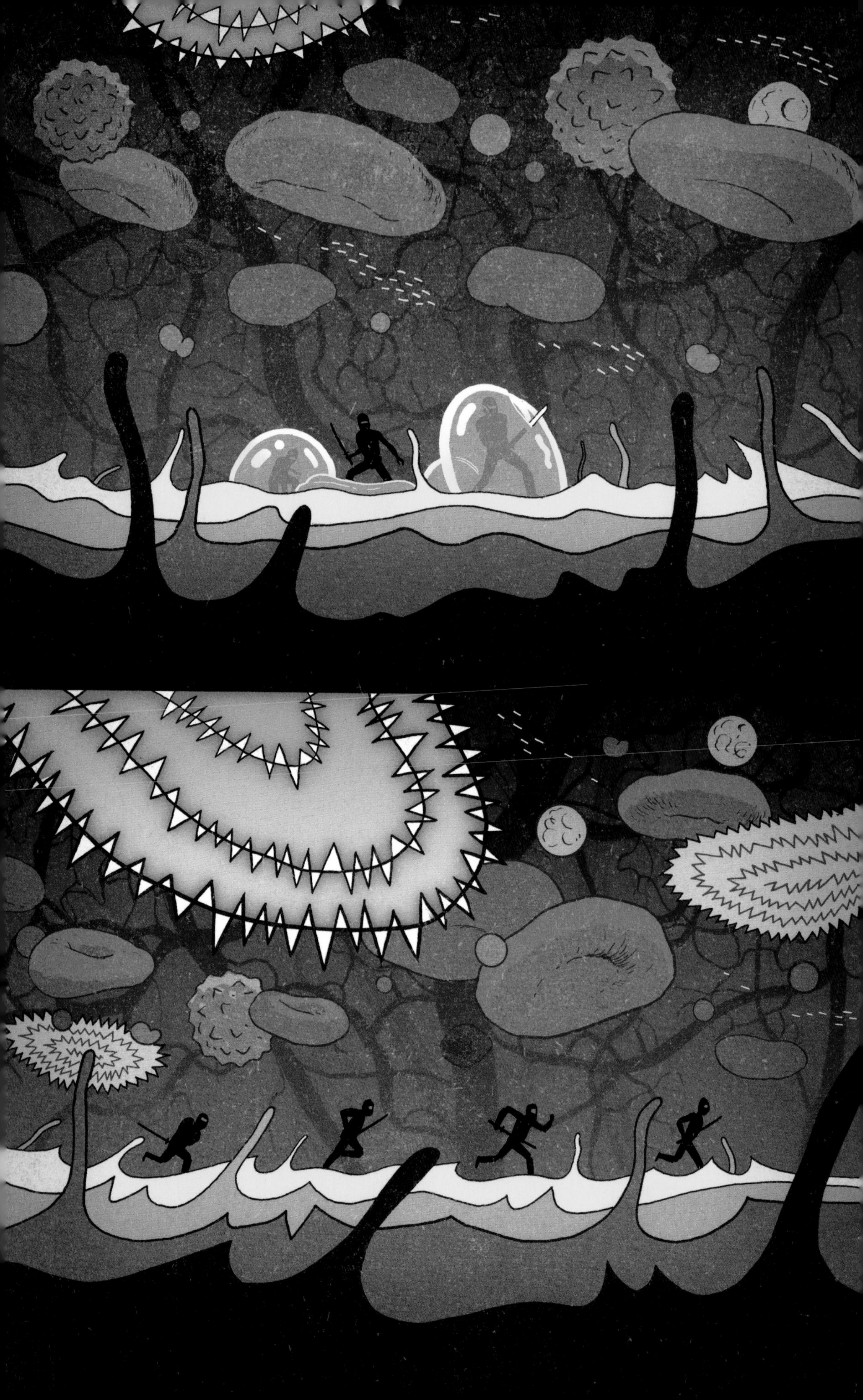

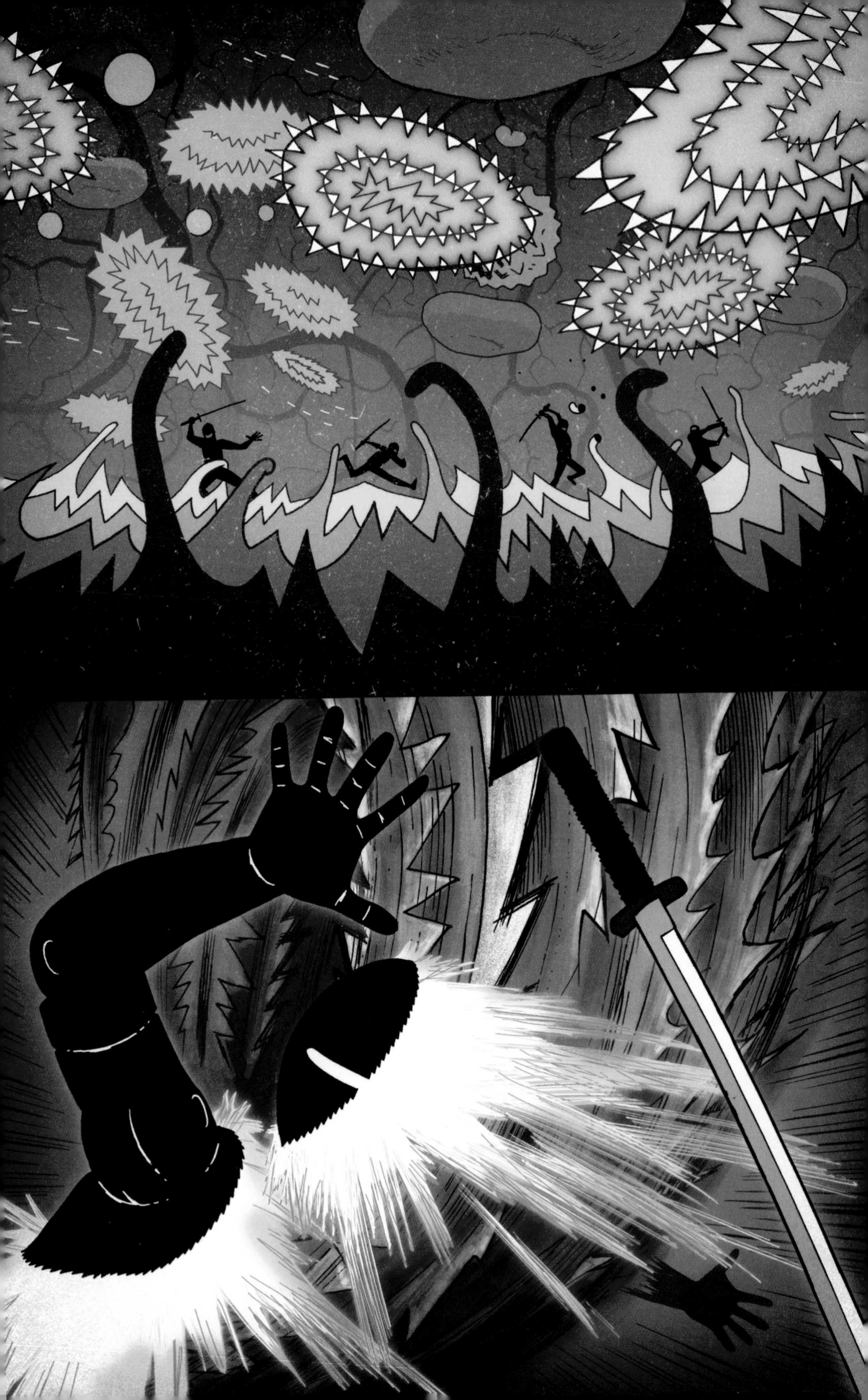

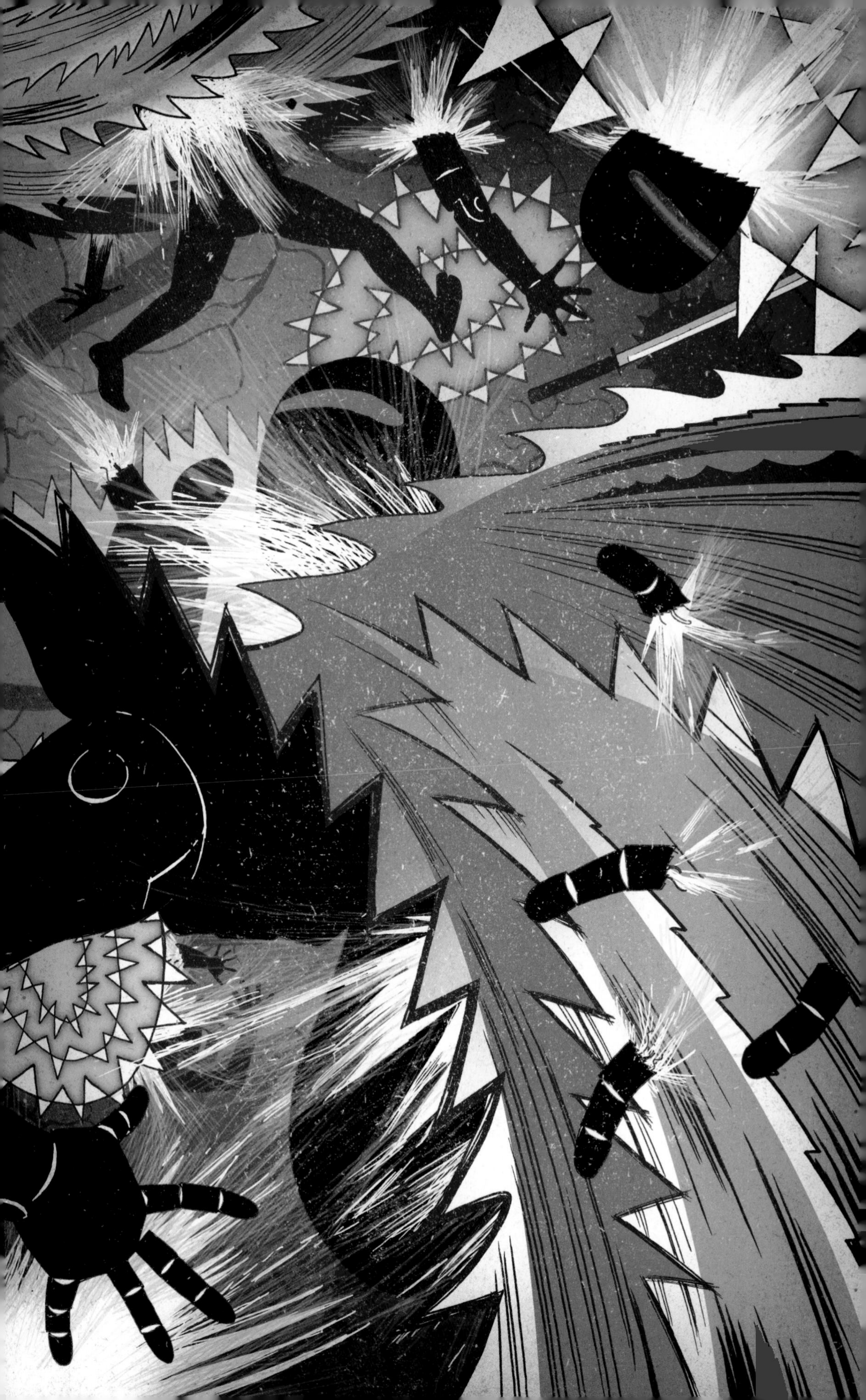

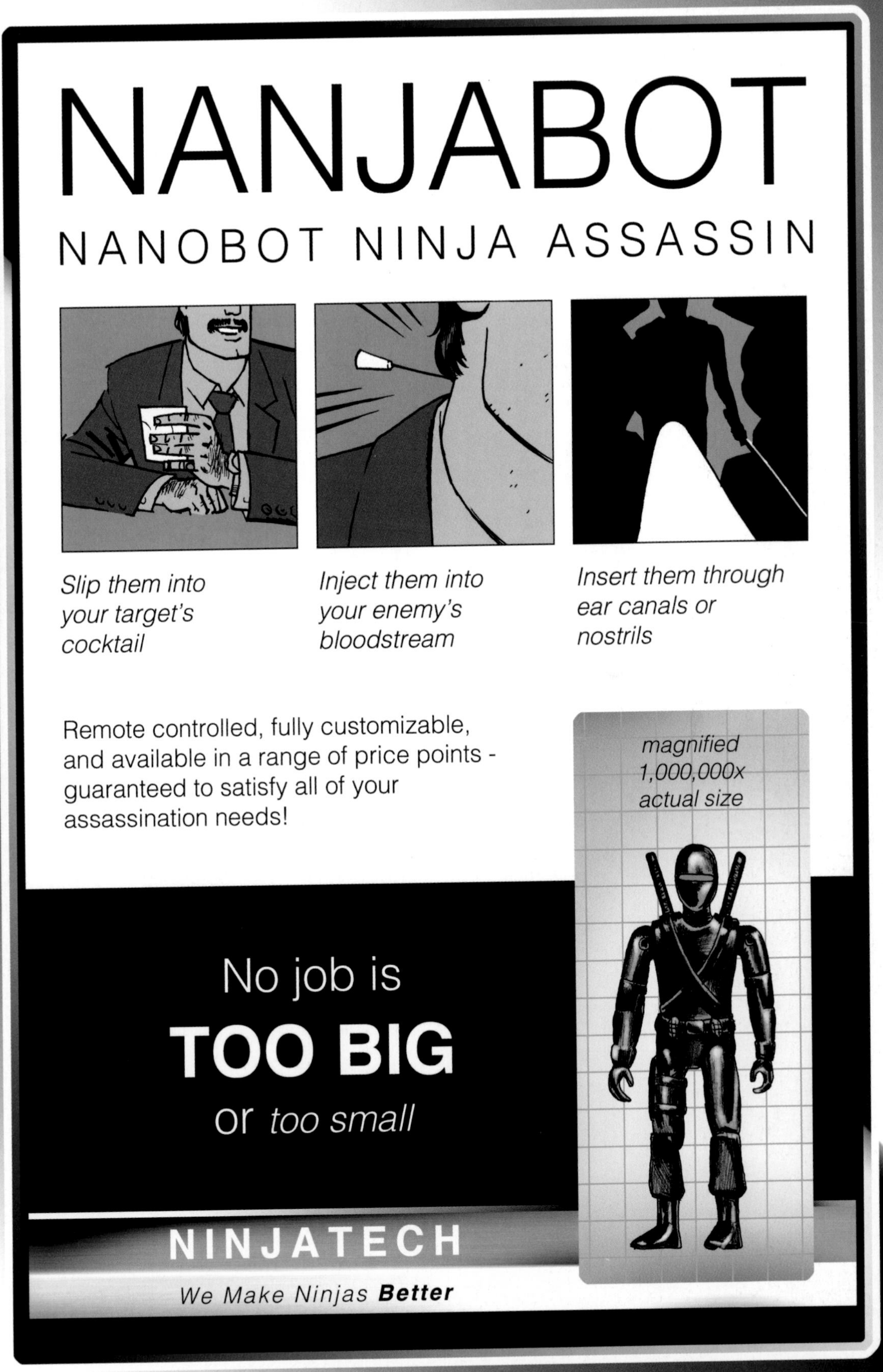
NANJABOT
NANOBOT NINJA ASSASSIN
Slip them into your target's cocktail
Inject them into your enemy's bloodstream
Insert them through ear canals or nostrils
Remote controlled, fully customizable, and available in a range of price points - guaranteed to satisfy all of your assassination needs!
magnified 1,000,000x actual size
No job is
TOO BIG
or too small
NINJATECH
We Make Ninjas Better

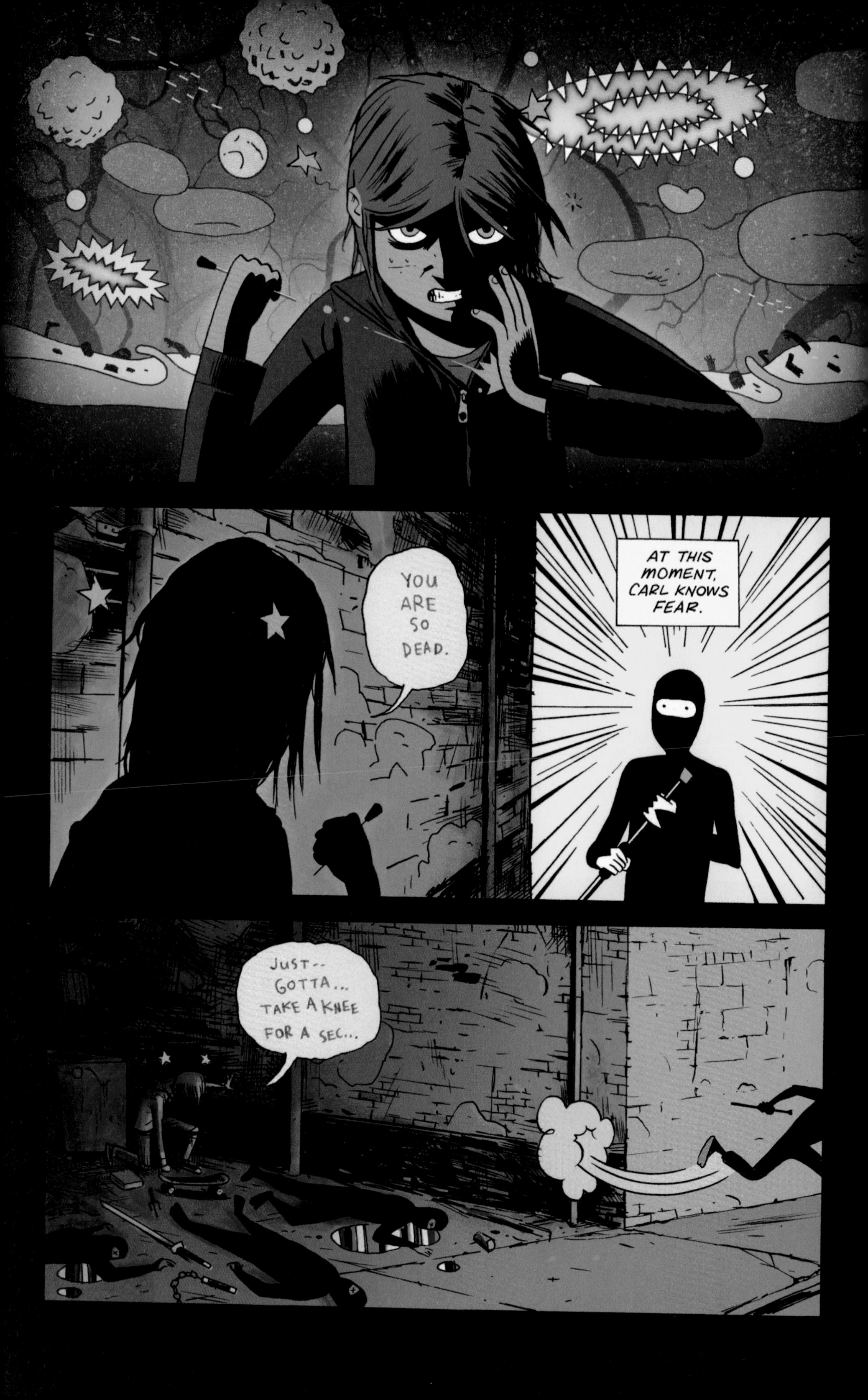
YOU ARE SO DEAD.
AT THIS MOMENT, CARL KNOWS FEAR.
JUST-- GOTTA... TAKE A KNEE FOR A SEC...

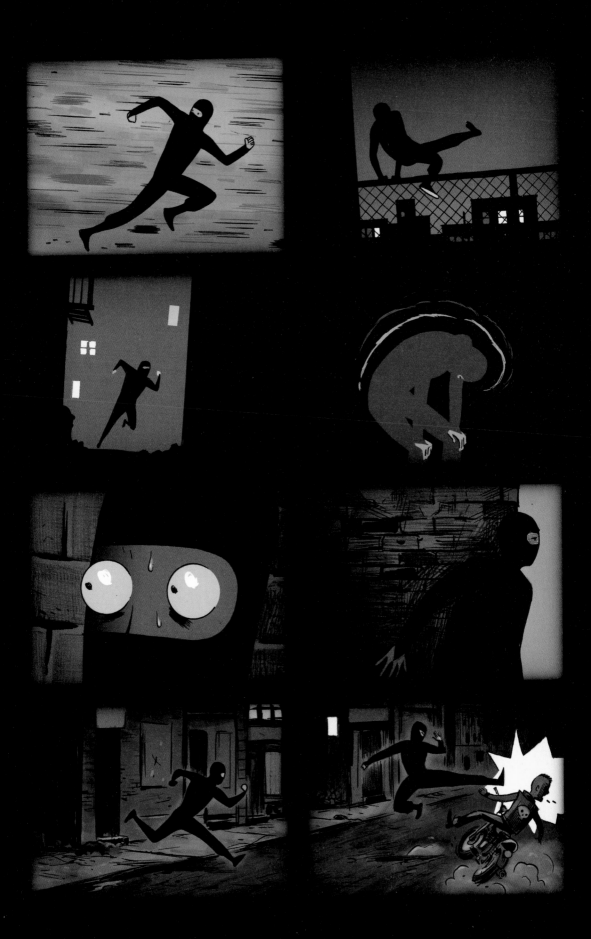

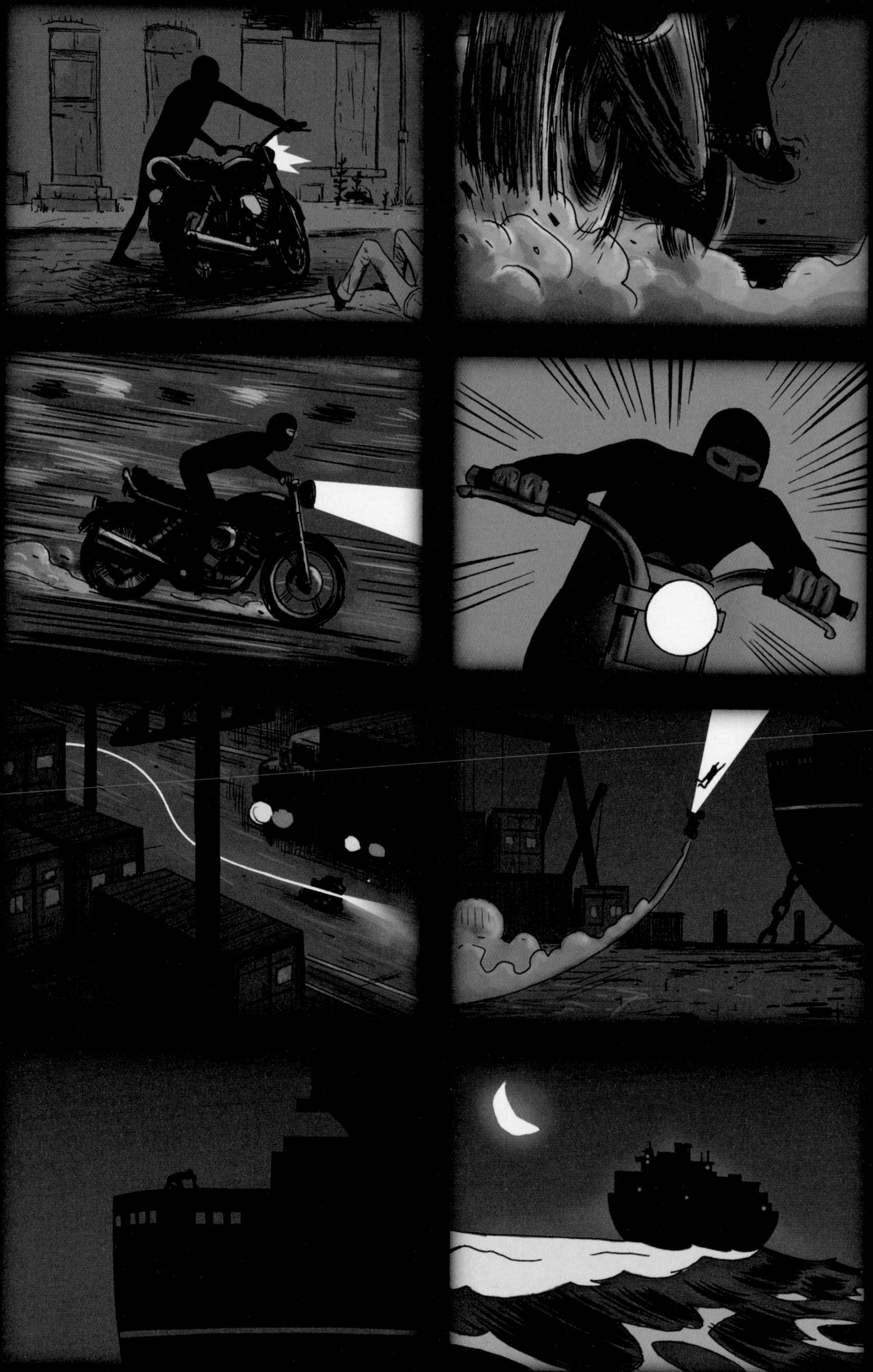

LATER THAT NIGHT...

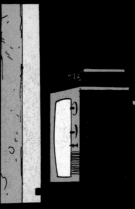

BALD EAGLE- THE CRAZIEST SOB YOU'LL EVER MEET and STREET ANGEL'S SELF-PROCLAIMED MENTOR.*

GROUND: DEAD AS A DOORNAIL--

YOUR BOOK

MY BOOK!

* HIS "STICK" to HER "BATMAN."

WHATSA MATTER WITH YOU?

NOTHIN

THANK YOU, STREET ANGEL! THANK YOU!

YOU HAVE SAVED THE MRKUASI WORLD TONIGHT!

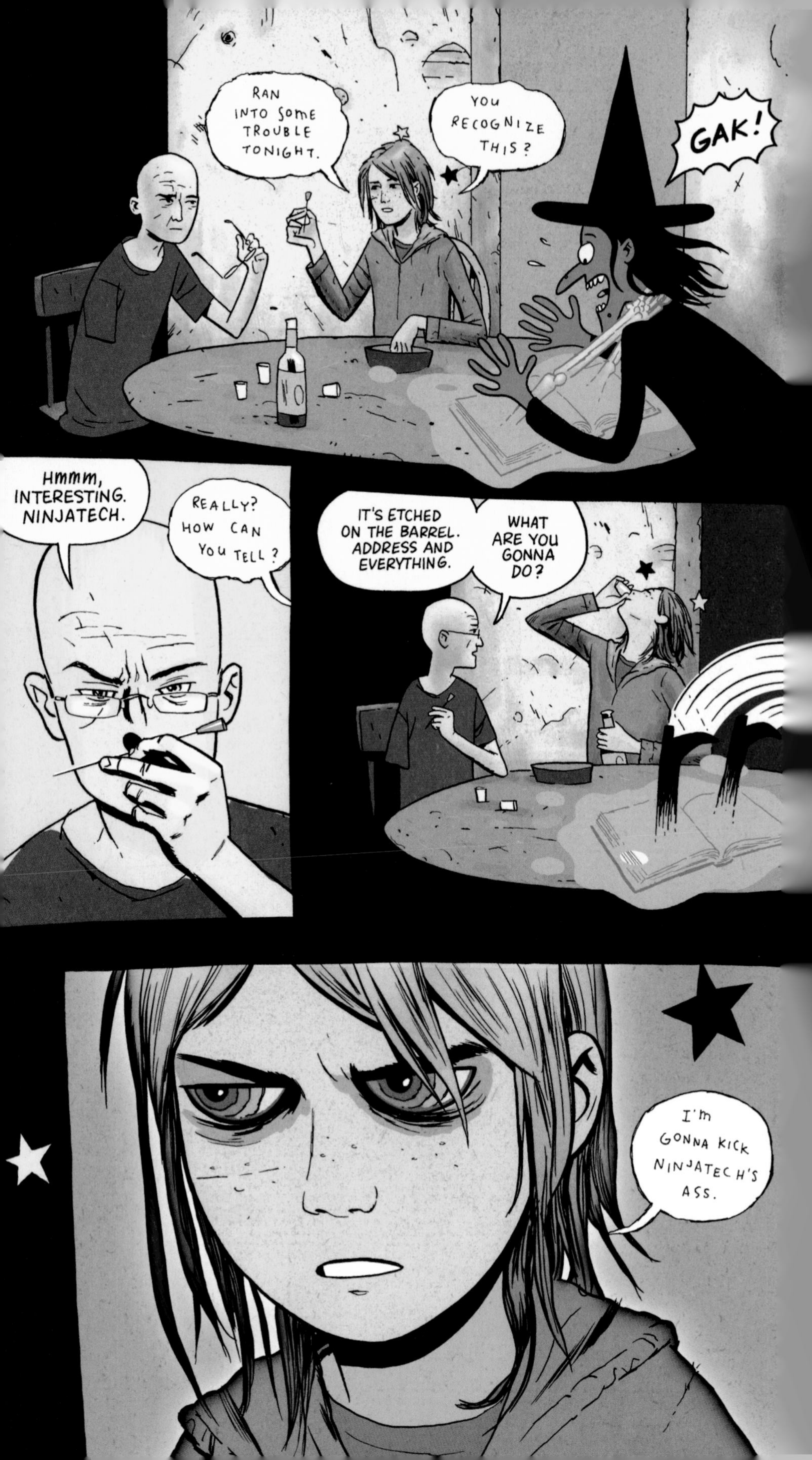
RAN INTO SOME TROUBLE TONIGHT.
YOU RECOGNIZE THIS?
GAK!
Hmmm, INTERESTING. NINJATECH.
REALLY? HOW CAN YOU TELL?
IT'S ETCHED ON THE BARREL. ADDRESS AND EVERYTHING.
WHAT ARE YOU GONNA DO?
I'm GONNA KICK NINJATECH'S ASS.

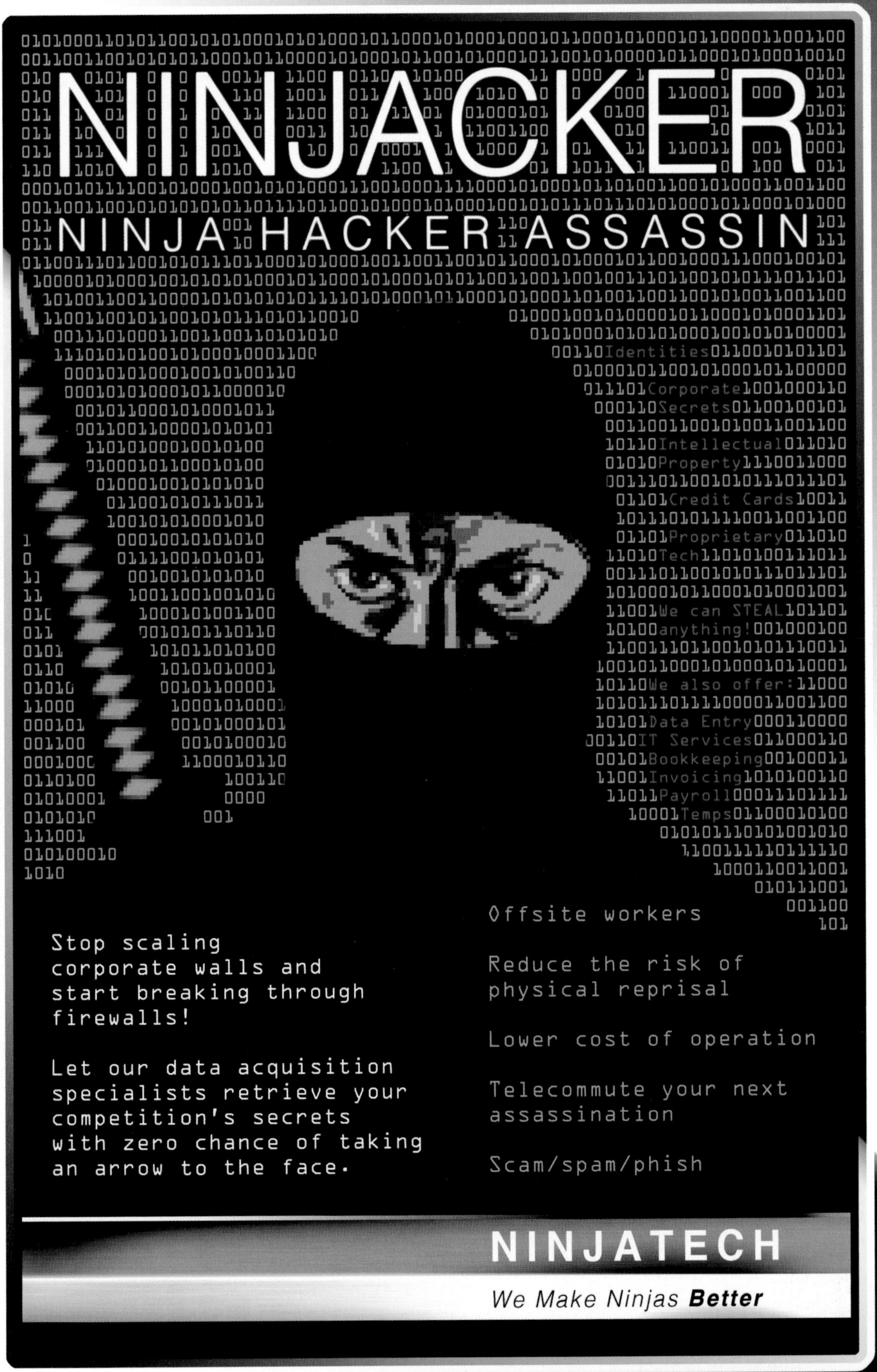

NINJACKER
NINJA HACKER ASSASSIN
Identities
Corporate Secrets
Intellectual Property
Credit Cards
Proprietary Tech
We can STEAL anything!
We also offer:
Data Entry
IT Services
Bookkeeping
Invoicing
Payroll
Temps
Stop scaling corporate walls and start breaking through firewalls!
Let our data acquisition specialists retrieve your competition's secrets with zero chance of taking an arrow to the face.
Offsite workers
Reduce the risk of physical reprisal
Lower cost of operation
Telecommute your next assassination
Scam/spam/phish
NINJATECH
We Make Ninjas Better

THE NEXT MORNING...

WHAT COULD #*$&ING WAN FOR 2 GODD

NINJATECH EMPLOYEE PARKING LOT.

W A# P

CONVENIENTLY, IT'S BRING-YOUR-DAUGHTER-TO-WORK DAY AT NINJATECH.

HEY!

SWIP

GIMME YOUR BADGE AND MASK.

NO ONE'S GONNA GET HURT.

?

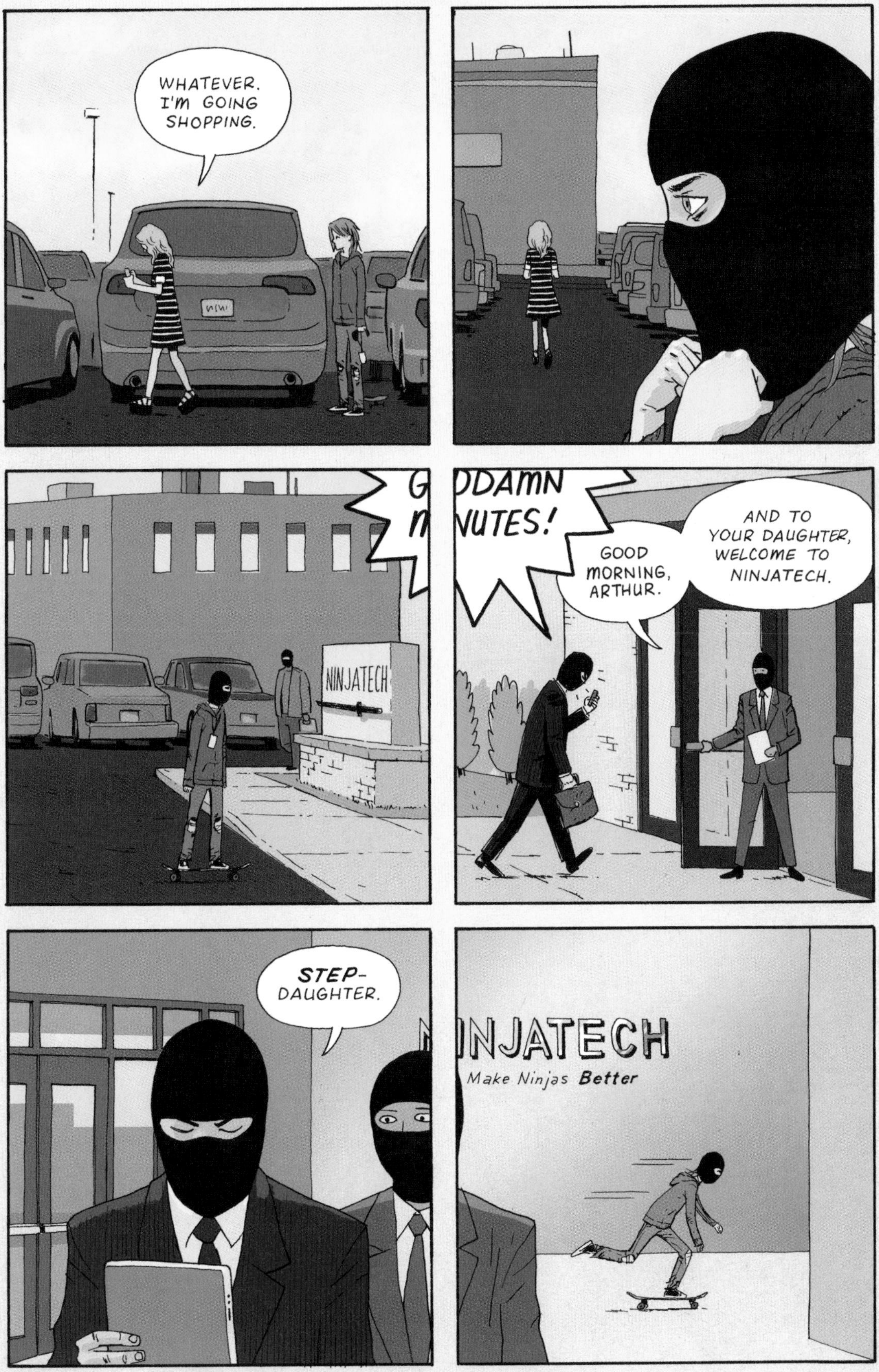
WHATEVER. I'M GOING SHOPPING.
NINJATECH
G DDAMN
M NUTES!
GOOD MORNING, ARTHUR.
AND TO YOUR DAUGHTER, WELCOME TO NINJATECH.
STEP-DAUGHTER.
N NJATECH
Make Ninjas Better

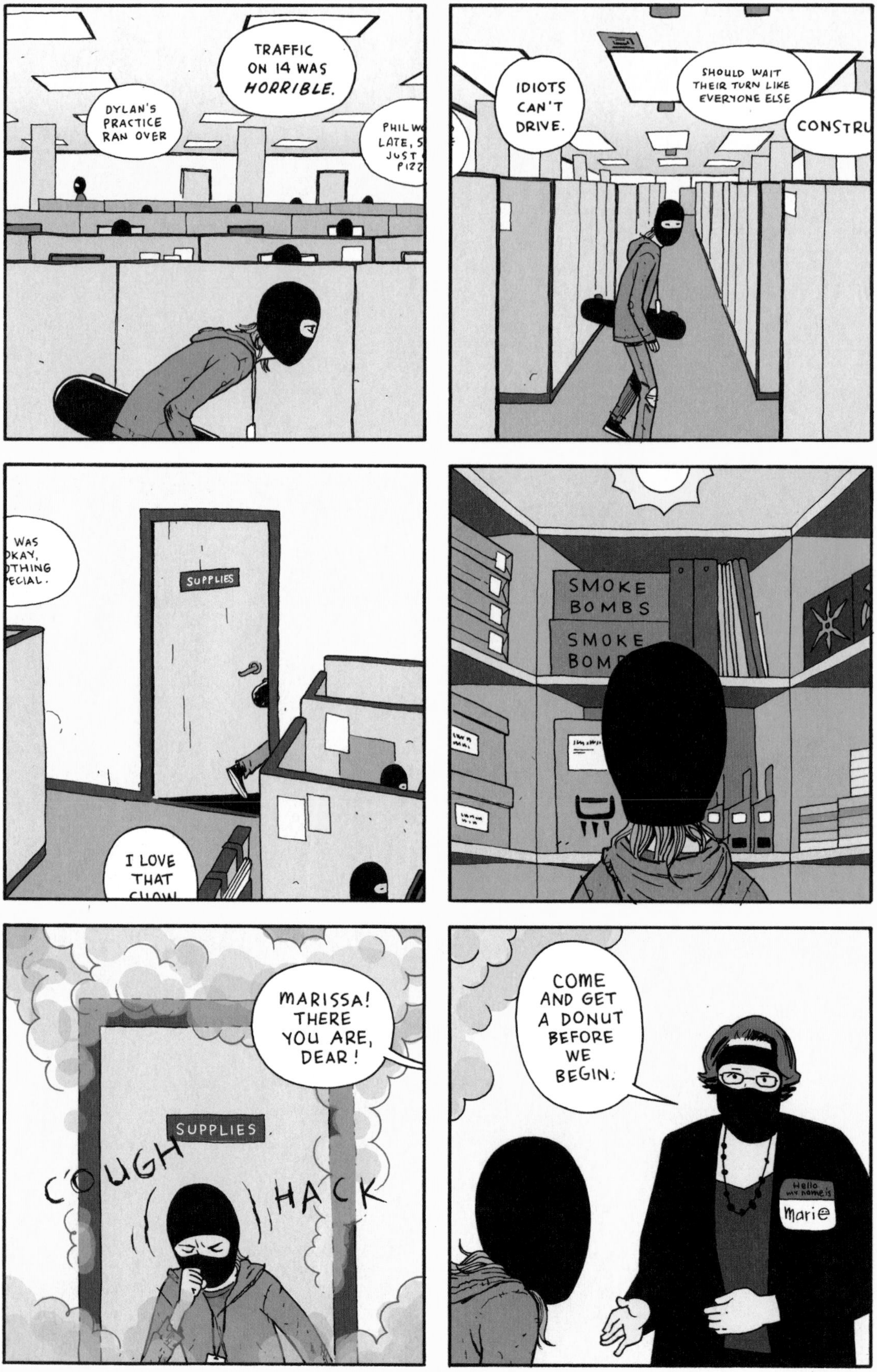

DYLAN'S PRACTICE RAN OVER
TRAFFIC ON 14 WAS HORRIBLE.
IDIOTS CAN'T DRIVE.
SHOULD WAIT THEIR TURN LIKE EVERYONE ELSE
SUPPLIES
I LOVE THAT
SMOKE BOMBS
SMOKE
MARISSA! THERE YOU ARE, DEAR!
SUPPLIES
COUGH
HACK
COME AND GET A DONUT BEFORE WE BEGIN.
Hello my name is
Marie

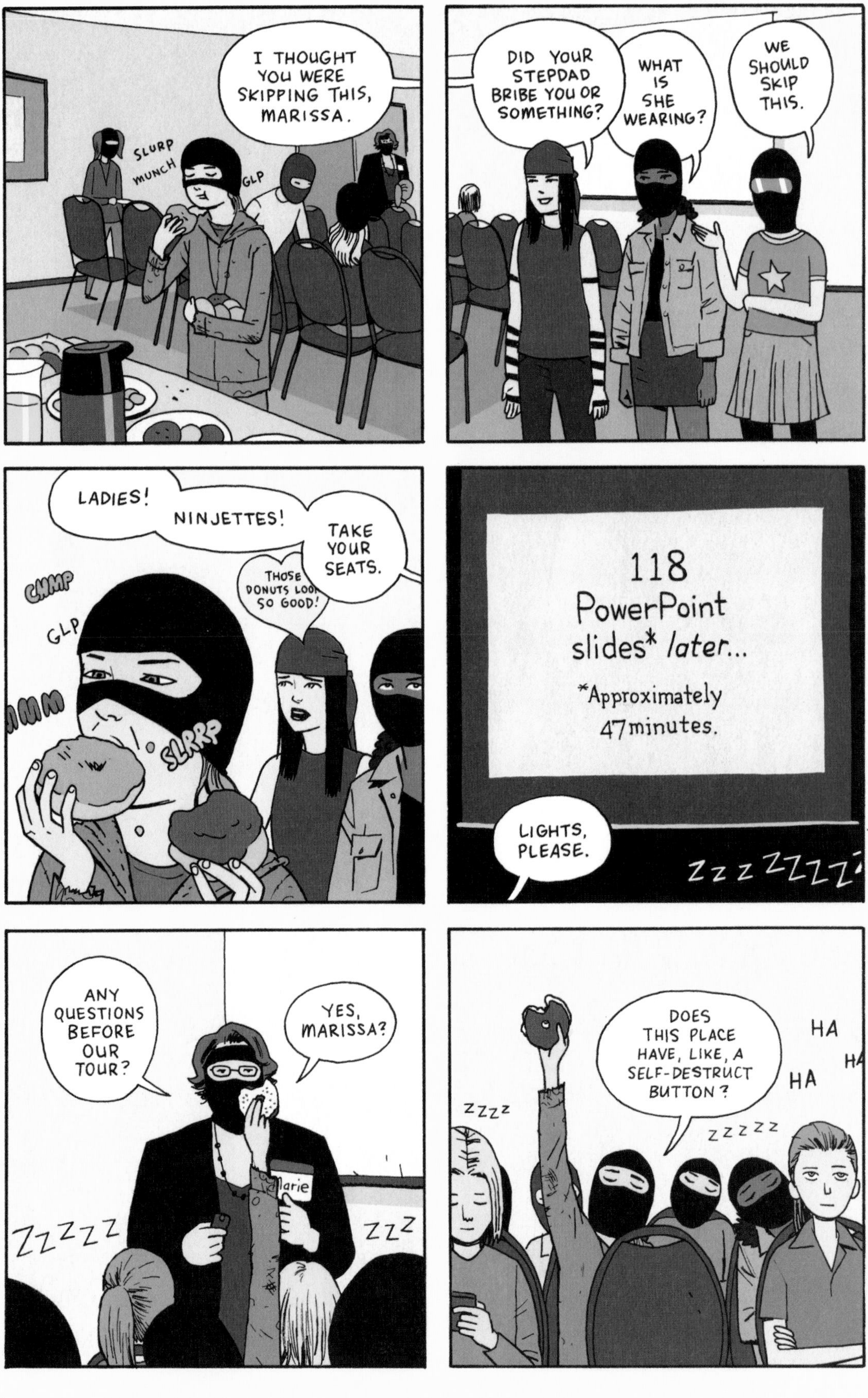
I THOUGHT YOU WERE SKIPPING THIS, MARISSA.
SLURP
MUNCH
GLP
DID YOUR STEPDAD BRIBE YOU OR SOMETHING?
WHAT IS SHE WEARING?
WE SHOULD SKIP THIS.
LADIES!
NINJETTES!
TAKE YOUR SEATS.
CHMP
GLP
SLRRP
118 PowerPoint slides* *later*...
*Approximately 47 minutes.
LIGHTS, PLEASE.
Z z z ZZZZ
ANY QUESTIONS BEFORE OUR TOUR?
YES, MARISSA?
Marie
ZZZZZ
ZZZ
DOES THIS PLACE HAVE, LIKE, A SELF-DESTRUCT BUTTON?
HA
HA
ZZZZ
ZZZZZ

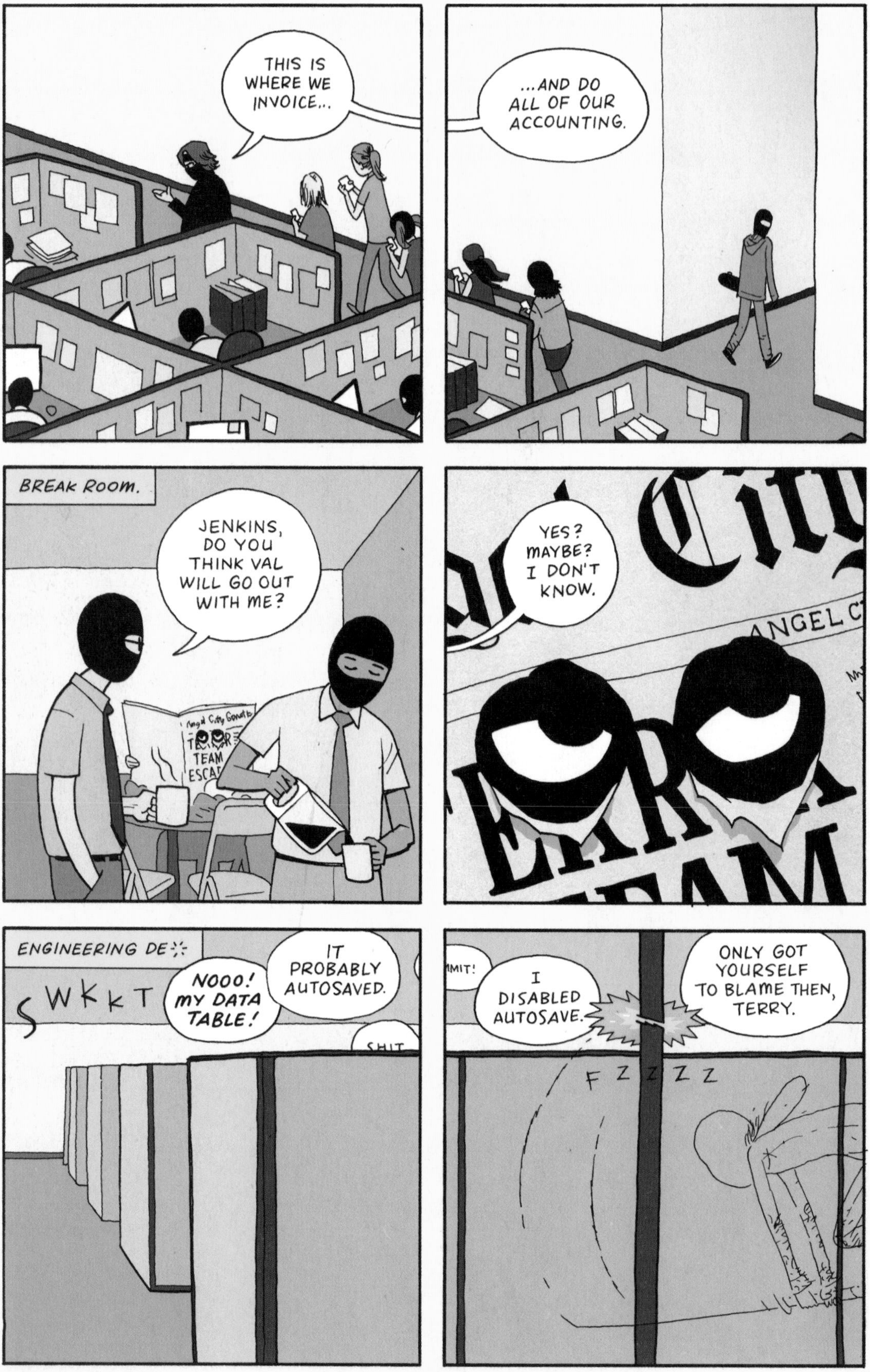
THIS IS WHERE WE INVOICE...
...AND DO ALL OF OUR ACCOUNTING.
BREAK ROOM.
JENKINS, DO YOU THINK VAL WILL GO OUT WITH ME?
TEAM
YES? MAYBE? I DON'T KNOW.
ENGINEERING DE
SWKKT
NOOO! MY DATA TABLE!
IT PROBABLY AUTOSAVED.
I DISABLED AUTOSAVE.
ONLY GOT YOURSELF TO BLAME THEN, TERRY.
FZZZZ

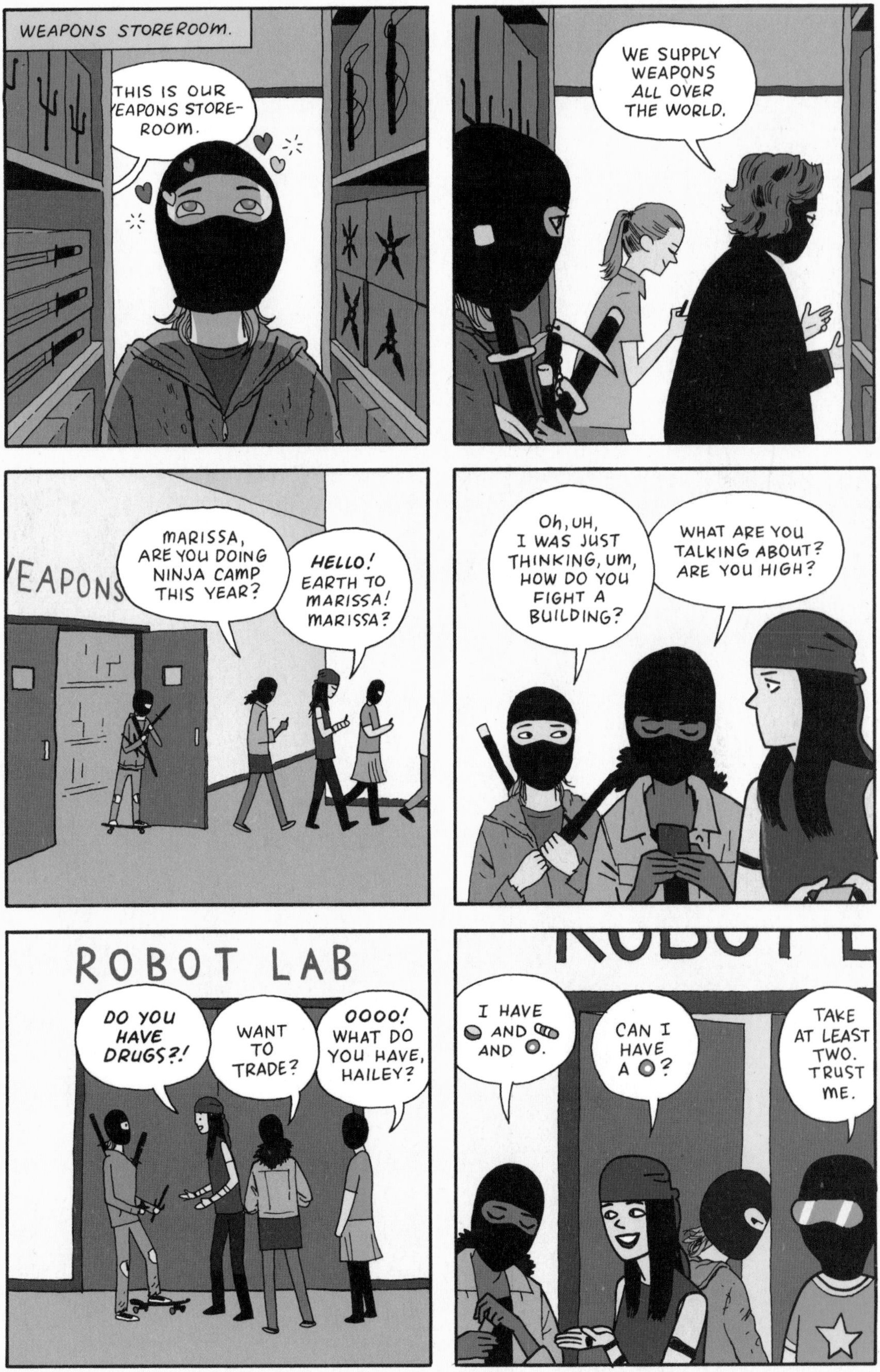
WEAPONS STOREROOM.
THIS IS OUR WEAPONS STORE-ROOM.
WE SUPPLY WEAPONS ALL OVER THE WORLD.
EAPONS
MARISSA, ARE YOU DOING NINJA CAMP THIS YEAR?
HELLO! EARTH TO MARISSA! MARISSA?
Oh, UH, I WAS JUST THINKING, UM, HOW DO YOU FIGHT A BUILDING?
WHAT ARE YOU TALKING ABOUT? ARE YOU HIGH?
ROBOT LAB
DO YOU HAVE DRUGS?!
WANT TO TRADE?
OOOO! WHAT DO YOU HAVE, HAILEY?
I HAVE AND AND .
CAN I HAVE A ?
TAKE AT LEAST TWO. TRUST ME.

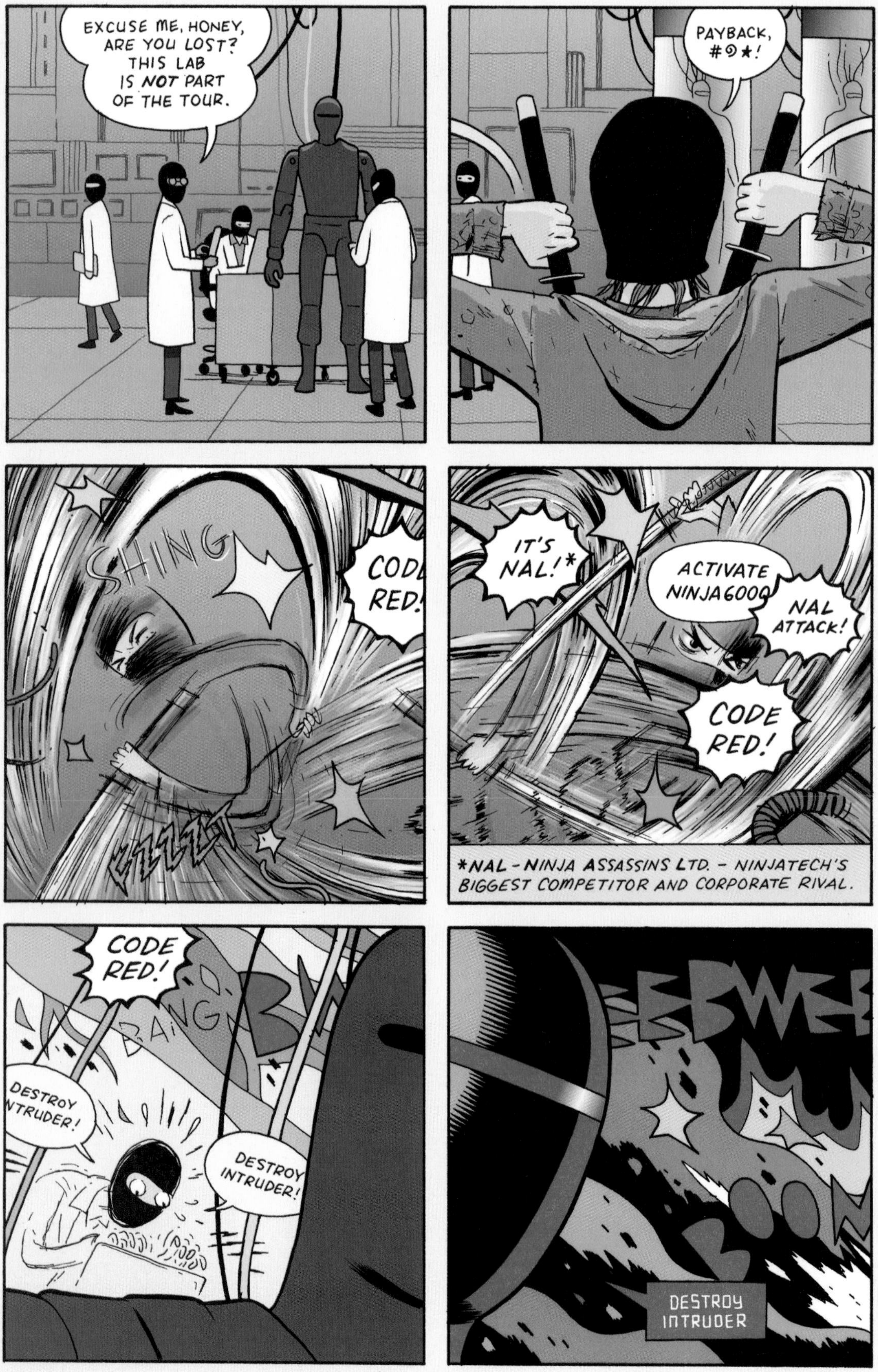

EXCUSE ME, HONEY, ARE YOU LOST? THIS LAB IS **NOT** PART OF THE TOUR.
PAYBACK, #୨★!
SHING
COD RED!
IT'S NAL!*
ACTIVATE NINJA6000
NAL ATTACK!
CODE RED!
*NAL - NINJA ASSASSINS LTD. - NINJATECH'S BIGGEST COMPETITOR AND CORPORATE RIVAL.
CODE RED!
BANG
DESTROY INTRUDER!
DESTROY INTRUDER!
DESTROY INTRUDER

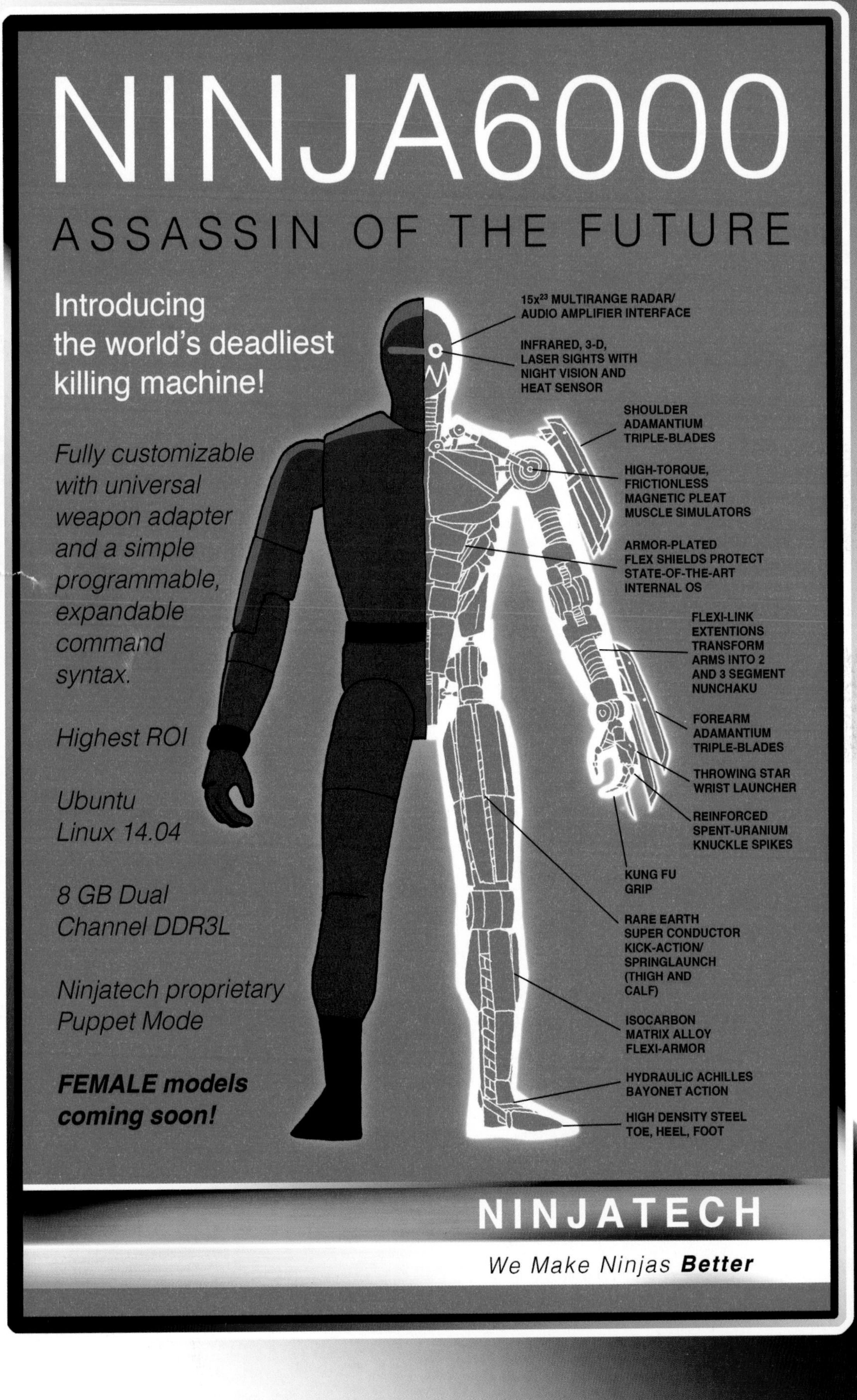

NINJA6000
ASSASSIN OF THE FUTURE
Introducing the world's deadliest killing machine!
Fully customizable with universal weapon adapter and a simple programmable, expandable command syntax.
Highest ROI
Ubuntu Linux 14.04
8 GB Dual Channel DDR3L
Ninjatech proprietary Puppet Mode
FEMALE models coming soon!
15x23 MULTIRANGE RADAR/ AUDIO AMPLIFIER INTERFACE
INFRARED, 3-D, LASER SIGHTS WITH NIGHT VISION AND HEAT SENSOR
SHOULDER ADAMANTIUM TRIPLE-BLADES
HIGH-TORQUE, FRICTIONLESS MAGNETIC PLEAT MUSCLE SIMULATORS
ARMOR-PLATED FLEX SHIELDS PROTECT STATE-OF-THE-ART INTERNAL OS
FLEXI-LINK EXTENTIONS TRANSFORM ARMS INTO 2 AND 3 SEGMENT NUNCHAKU
FOREARM ADAMANTIUM TRIPLE-BLADES
THROWING STAR WRIST LAUNCHER
REINFORCED SPENT-URANIUM KNUCKLE SPIKES
KUNG FU GRIP
RARE EARTH SUPER CONDUCTOR KICK-ACTION/ SPRINGLAUNCH (THIGH AND CALF)
ISOCARBON MATRIX ALLOY FLEXI-ARMOR
HYDRAULIC ACHILLES BAYONET ACTION
HIGH DENSITY STEEL TOE, HEEL, FOOT
NINJATECH
We Make Ninjas Better

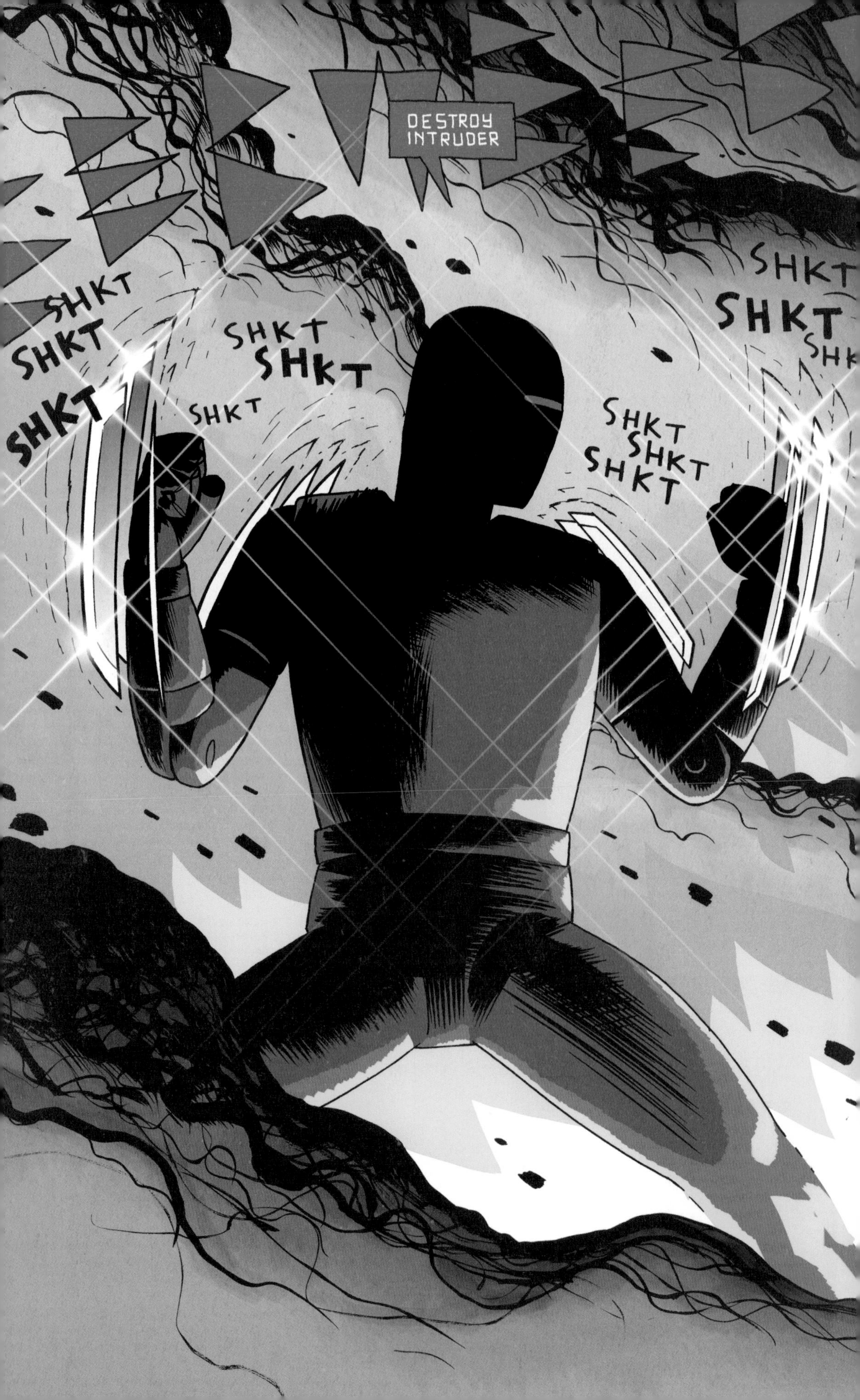
DESTROY INTRUDER
SHKT
SHKT
SHKT
SHKT
SHKT
SHKT
SHKT
SHKT
SHKT
SHKT
SHKT
SHKT

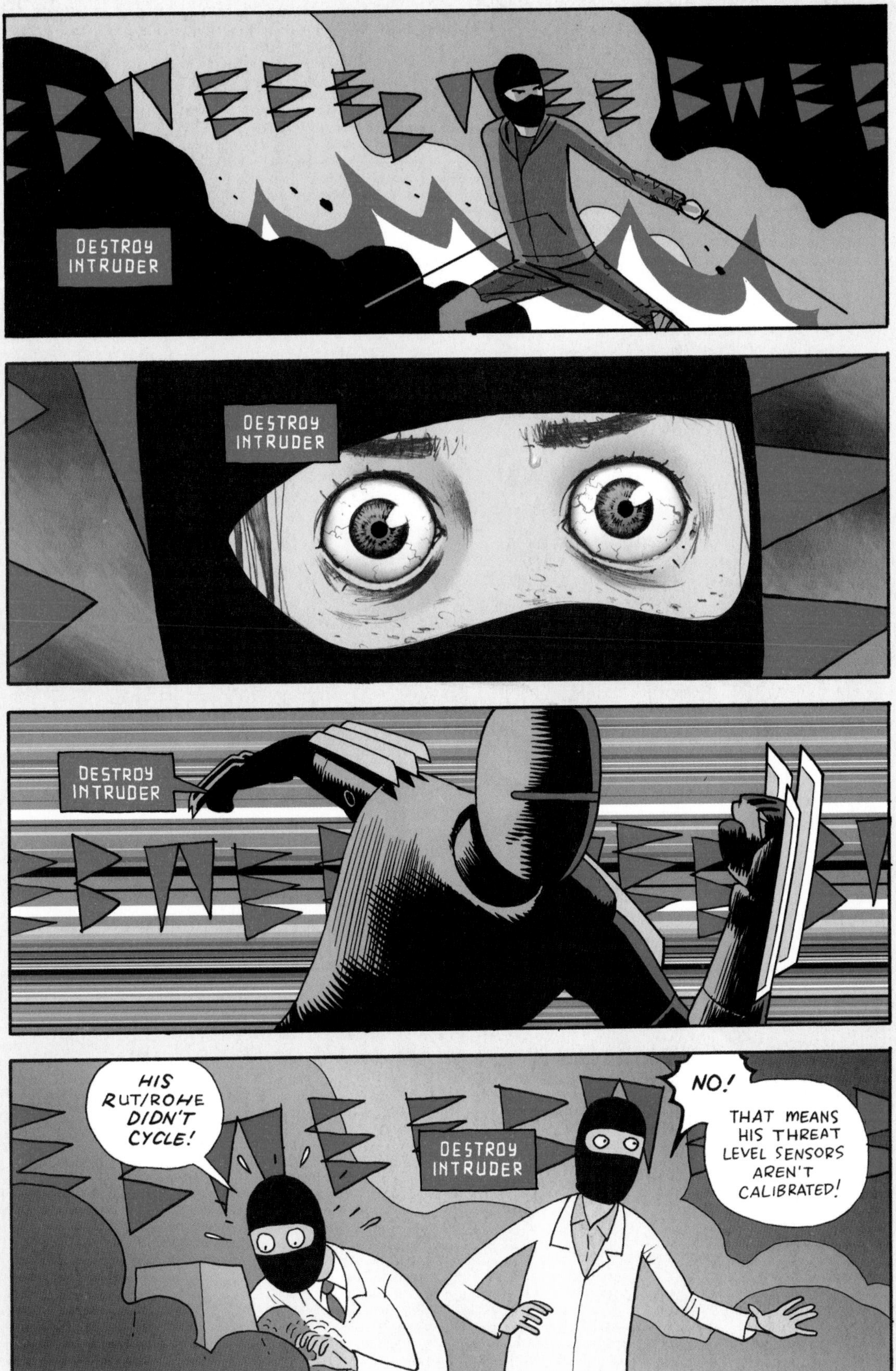
DESTROY INTRUDER
DESTROY INTRUDER
DESTROY INTRUDER
HIS RUT/ROHE DIDN'T CYCLE!
DESTROY INTRUDER
NO!
THAT MEANS HIS THREAT LEVEL SENSORS AREN'T CALIBRATED!

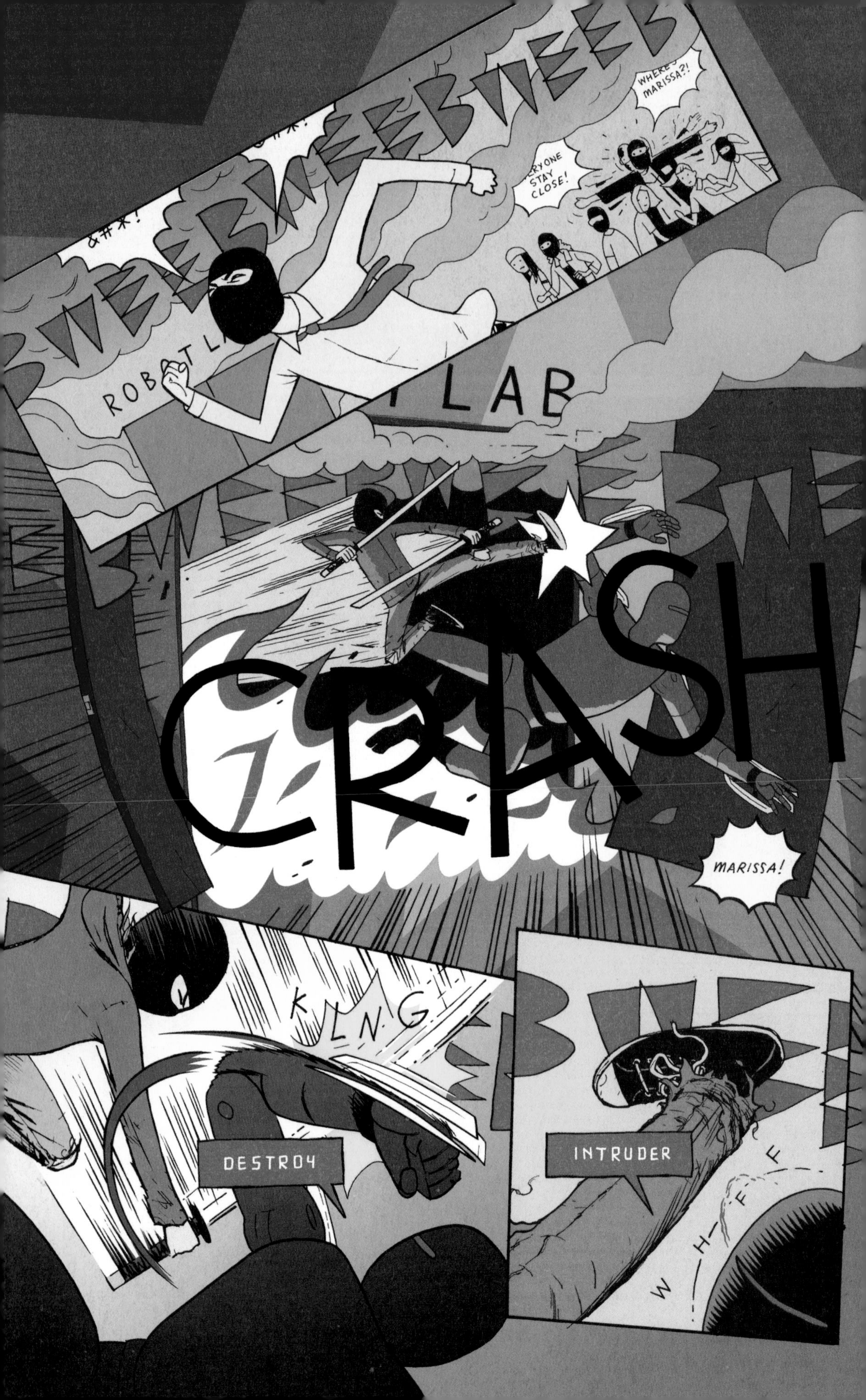
&#*!
ERYONE STAY CLOSE!
WHERE'S MARISSA?!
LAB
CRASH
MARISSA!
KLNG
DESTROY
INTRUDER
W-H-F-F

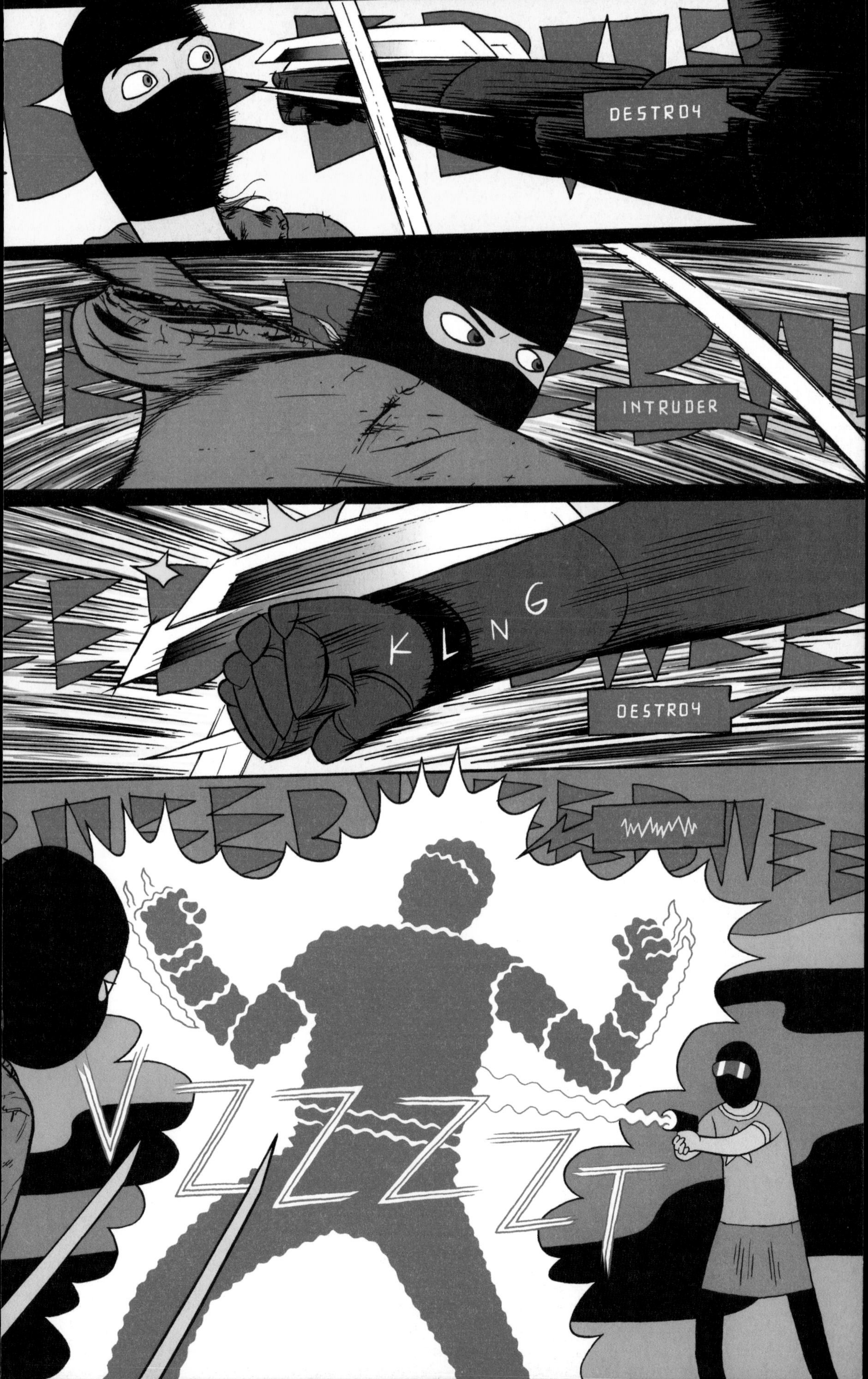
DESTROY
INTRUDER
KLNG
DESTROY
VZZZZZT

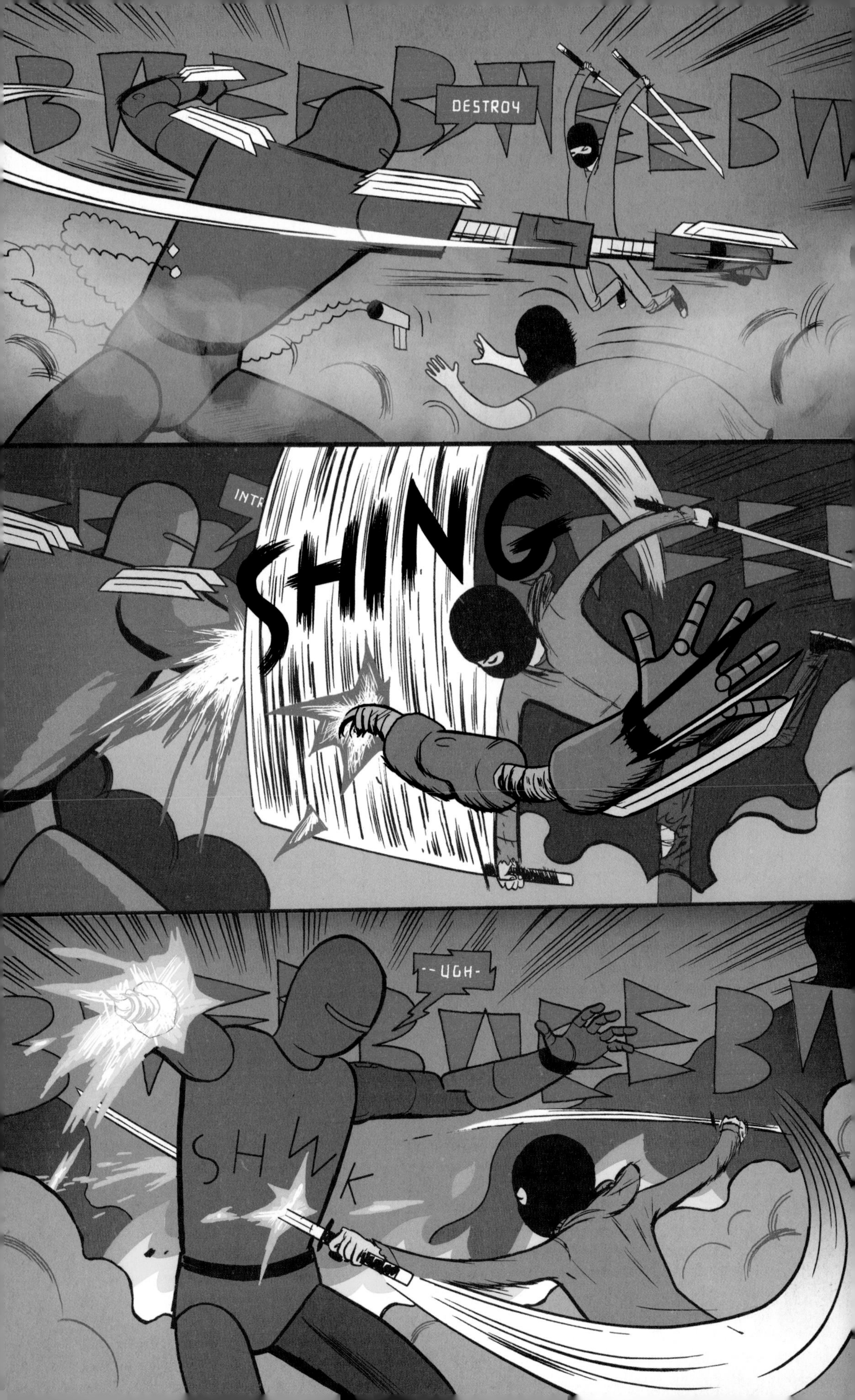
DESTROY
INTR
SHING
--UGH-
SHWK

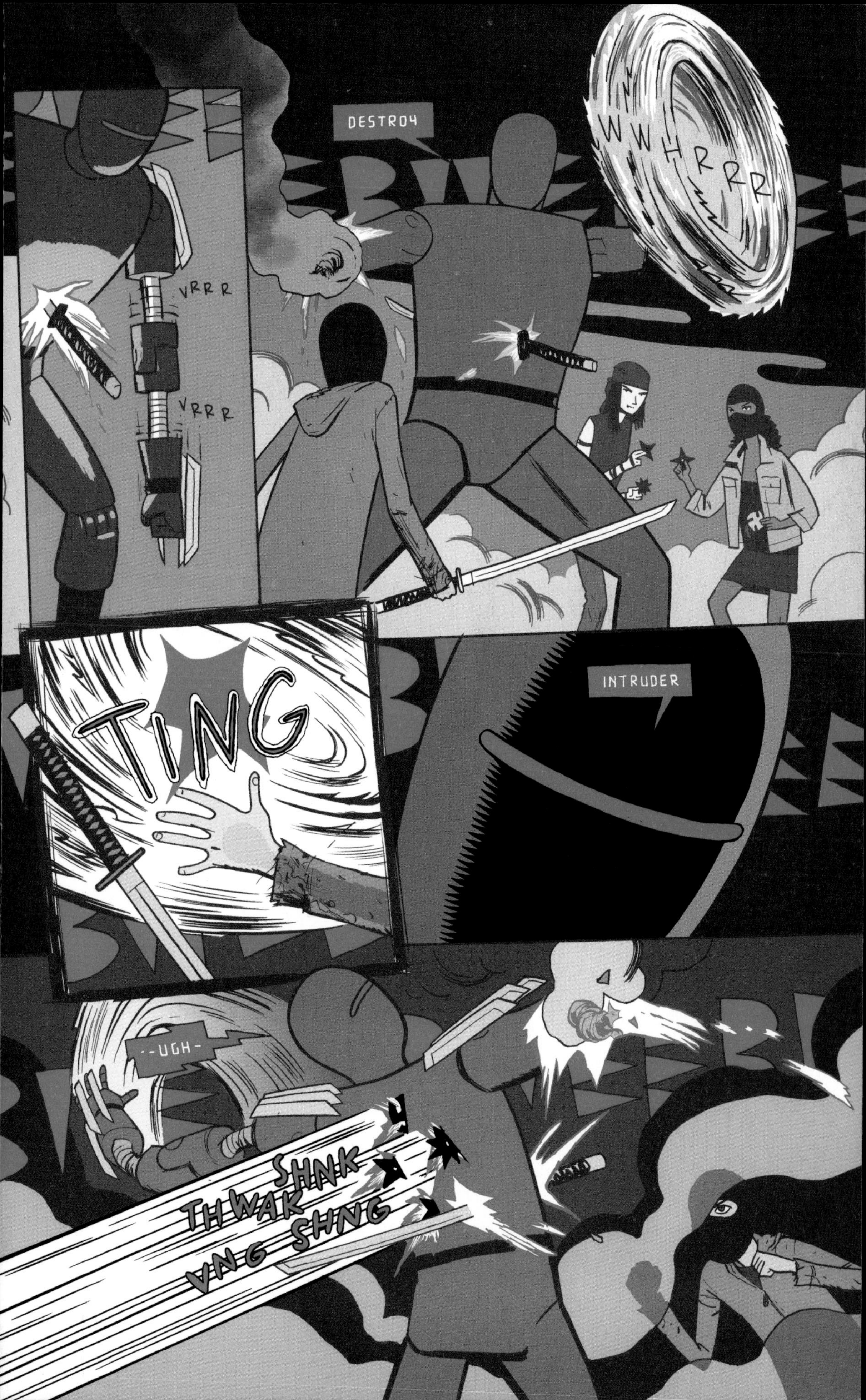
DESTROY
WWHRRRR
VRRR
VRRR
TING
INTRUDER
--UGH-
SHNK
THWAK
VNG SHNG

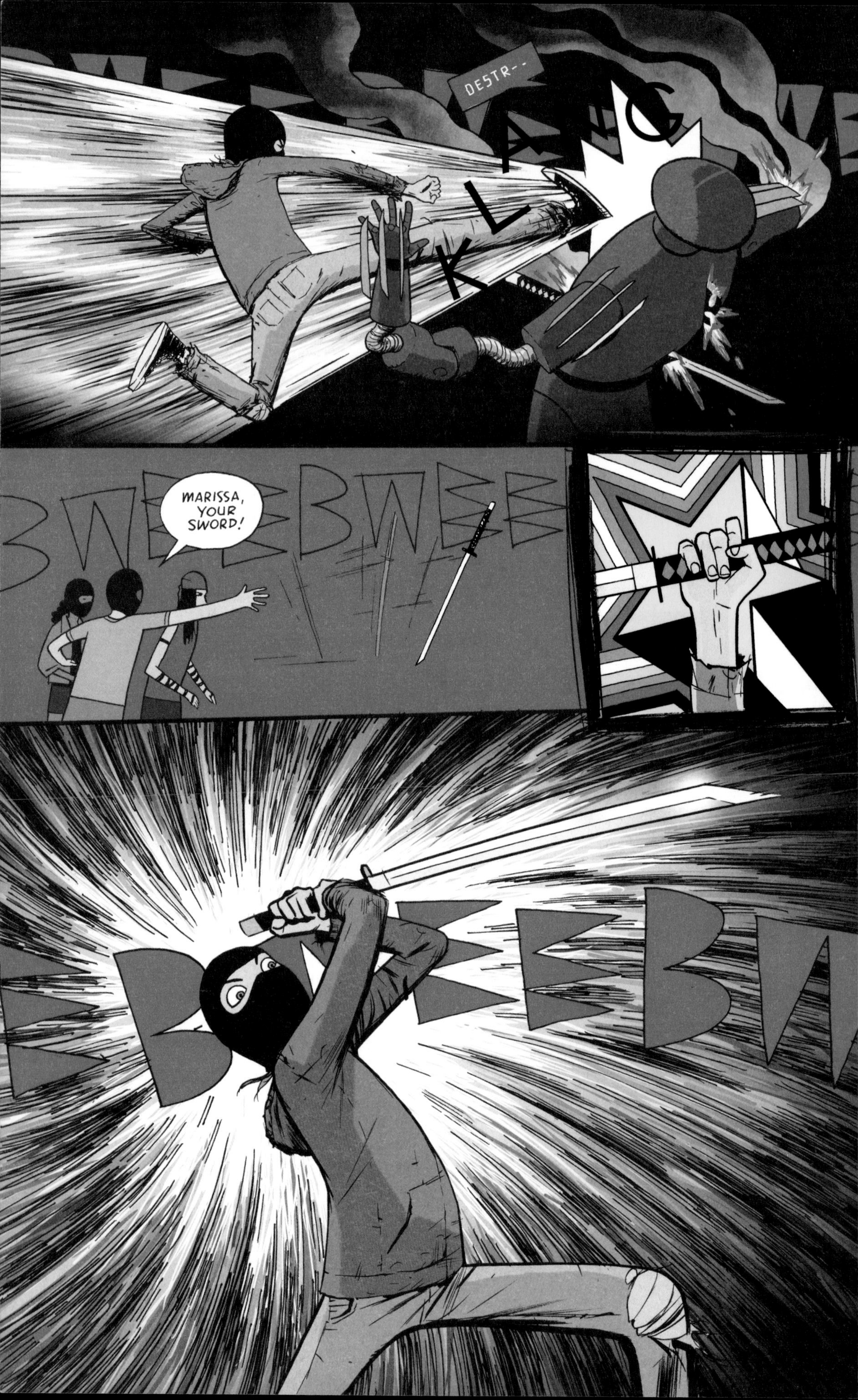
DESTR--
KLANG
MARISSA, YOUR SWORD!

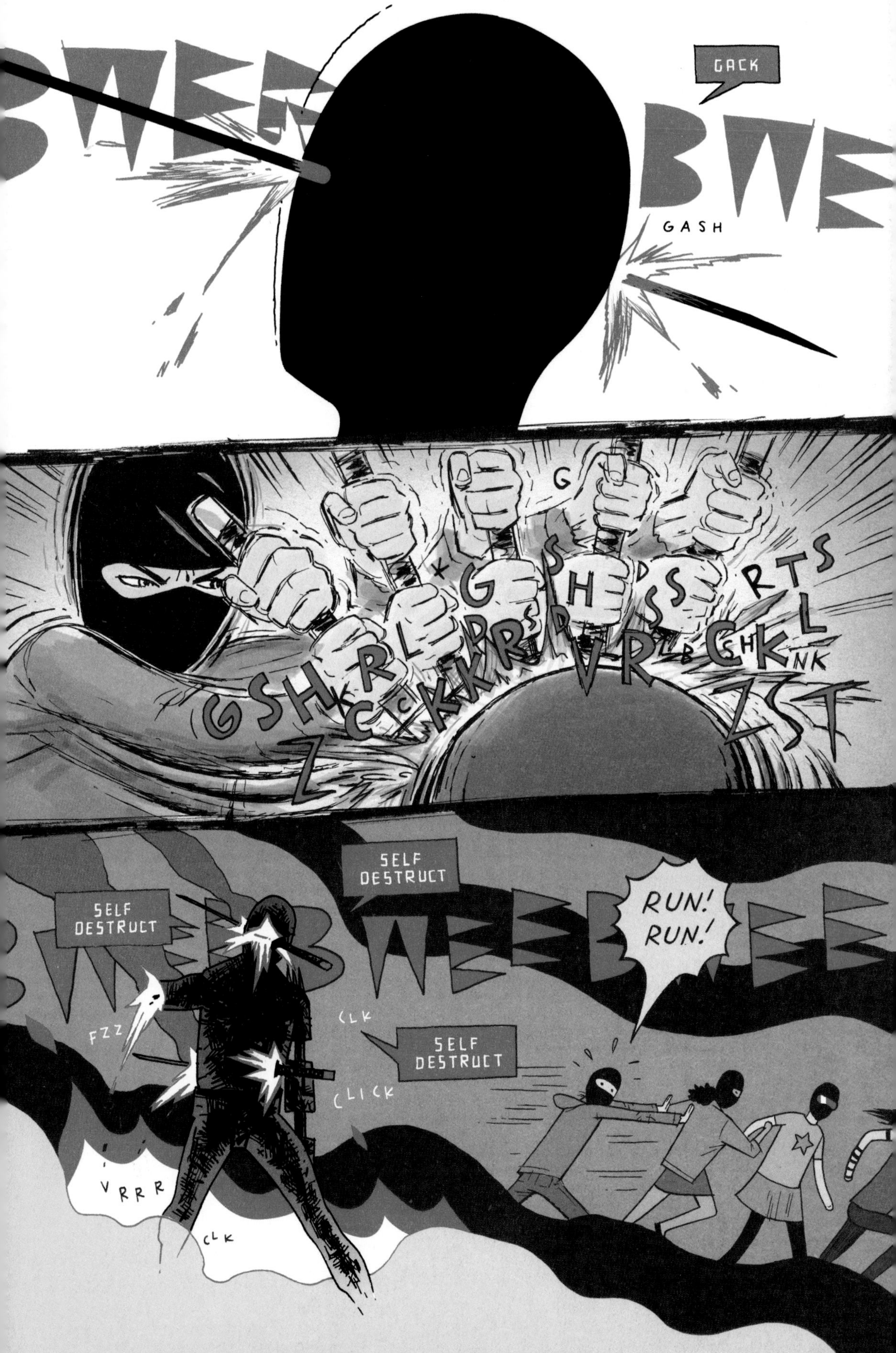
GACK
GASH
SELF DESTRUCT
SELF DESTRUCT
RUN! RUN!
FZZ
CLK
SELF DESTRUCT
CLICK
VRRR
CLK

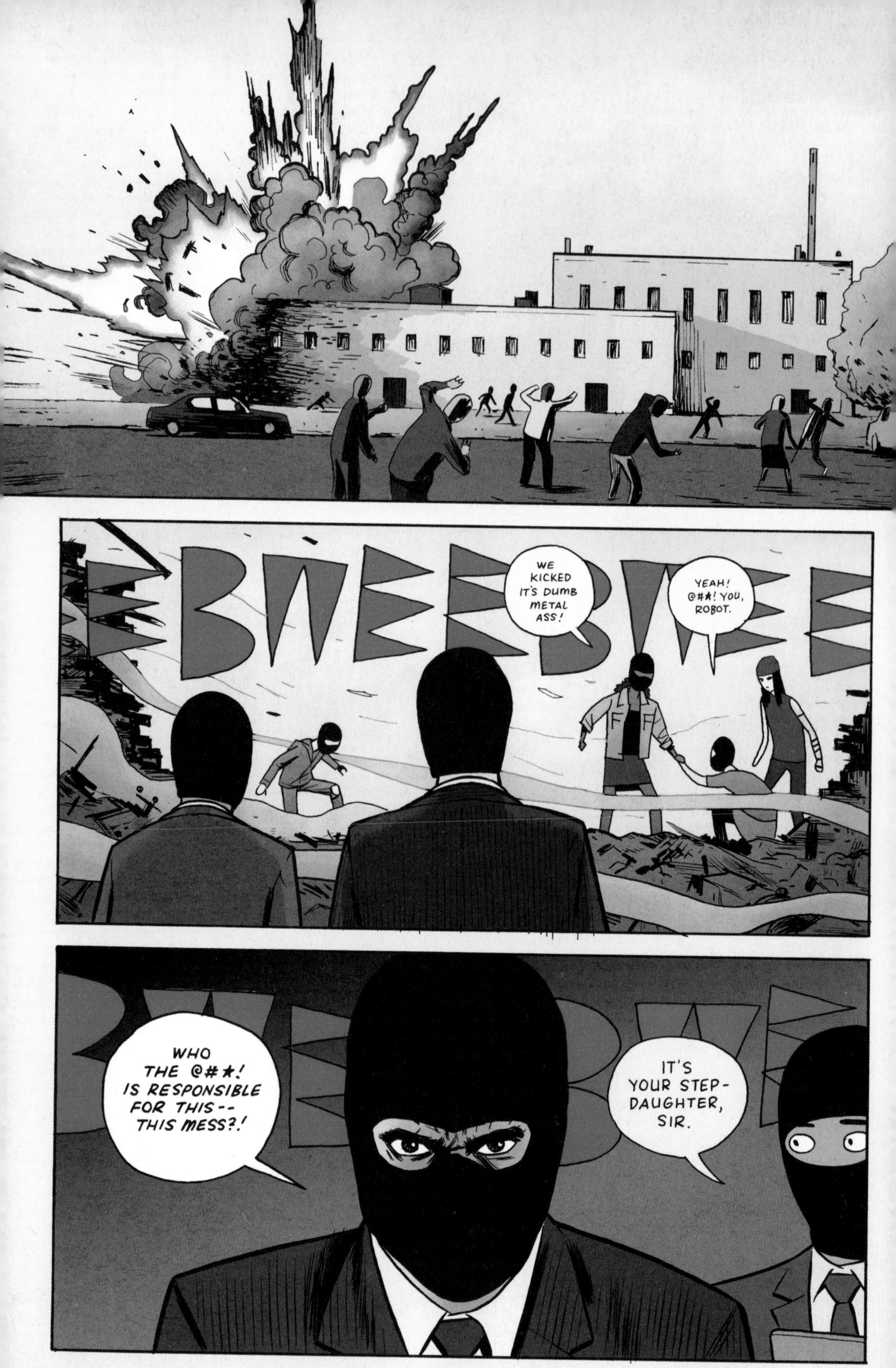
BWEEBWEE
WE KICKED IT'S DUMB METAL ASS!
YEAH! @#★! YOU, ROBOT.
WHO THE @#★! IS RESPONSIBLE FOR THIS-- THIS MESS?!
IT'S YOUR STEP-DAUGHTER, SIR.

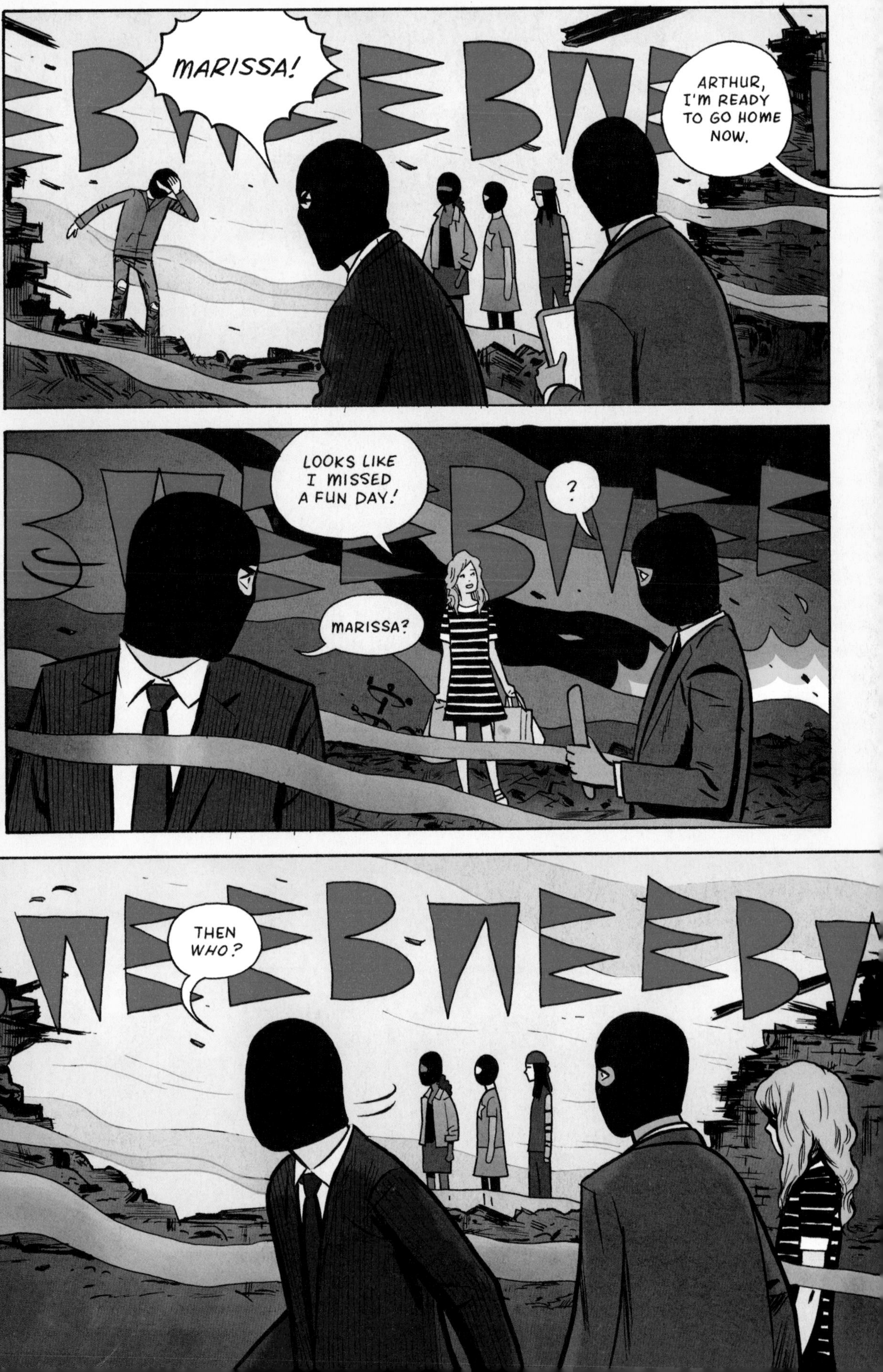
MARISSA!
ARTHUR, I'M READY TO GO HOME NOW.
LOOKS LIKE I MISSED A FUN DAY!
?
MARISSA?
THEN WHO?

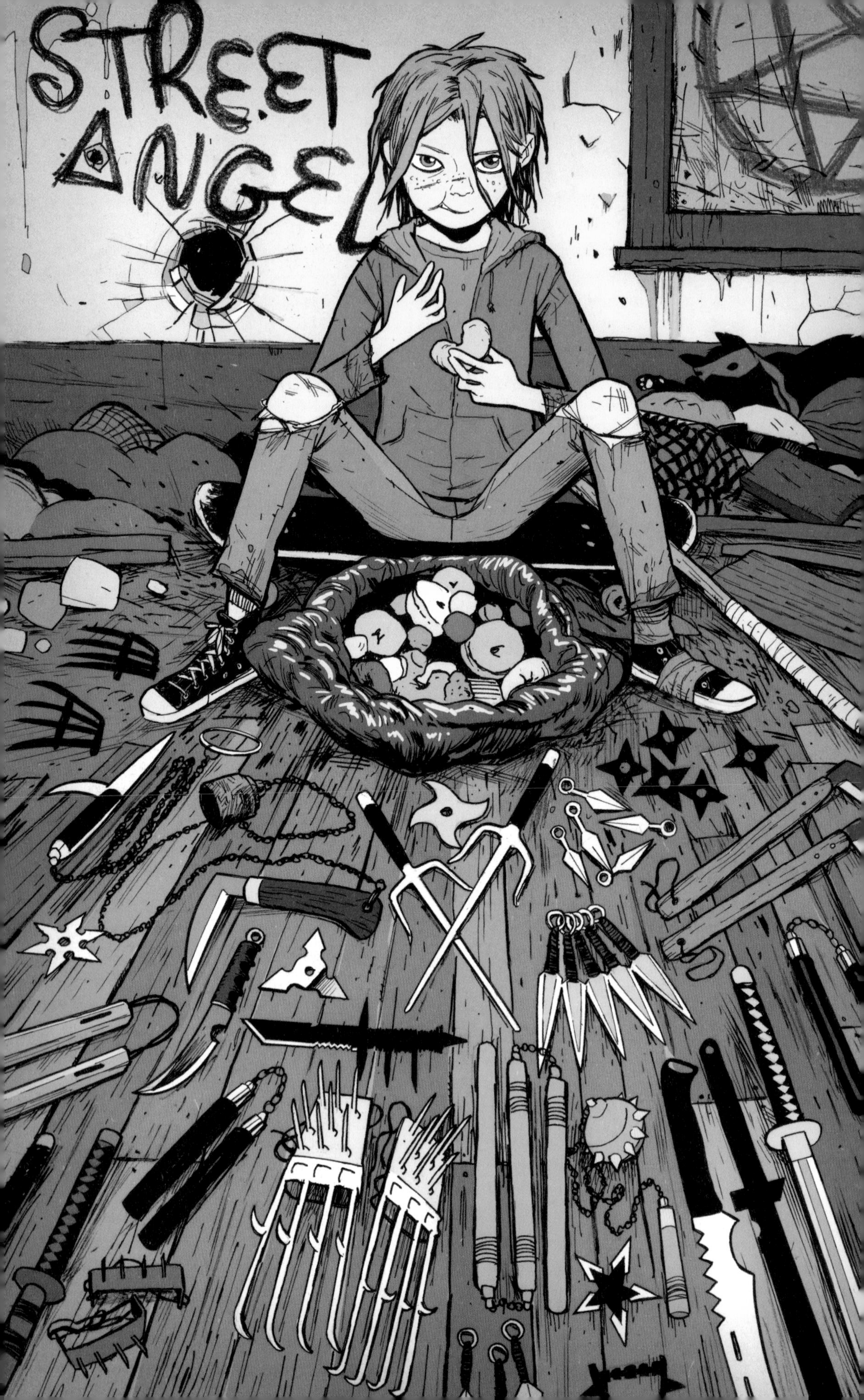
STREET ANGEL

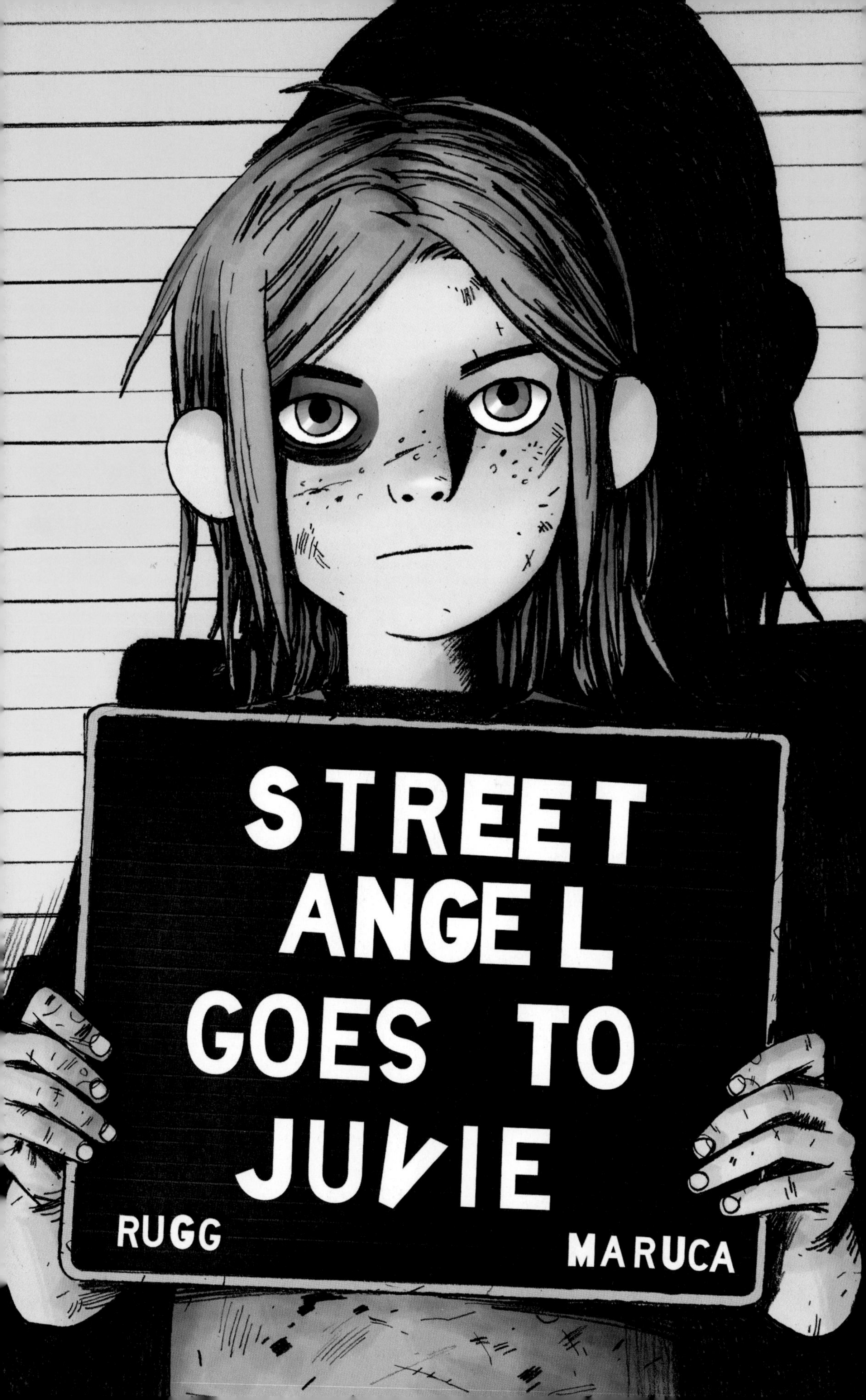
STREET
ANGEL
GOES TO
JUVIE
RUGG
MARUCA

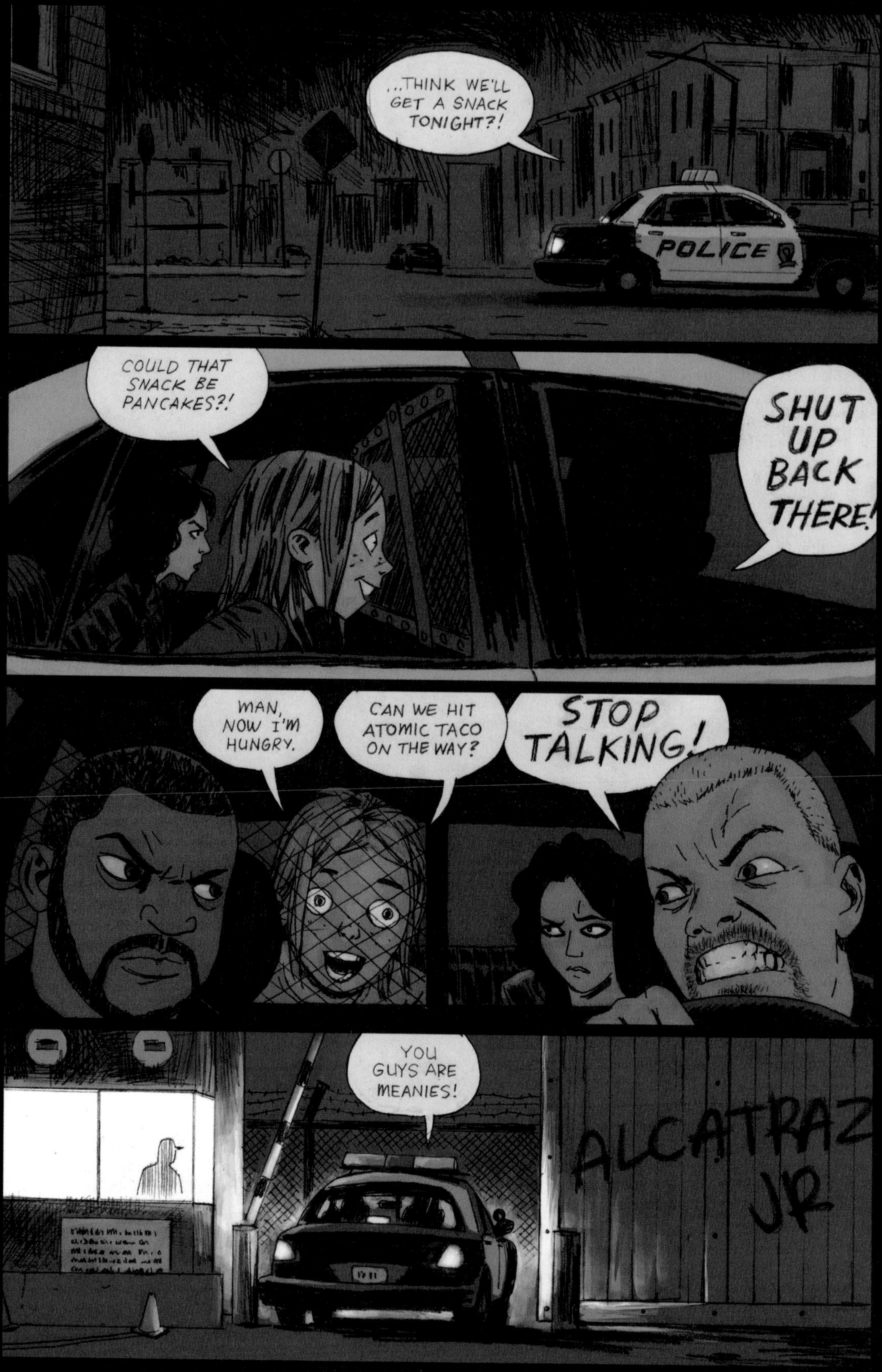
...THINK WE'LL GET A SNACK TONIGHT?!
POLICE
COULD THAT SNACK BE PANCAKES?!
SHUT UP BACK THERE!
MAN, NOW I'M HUNGRY.
CAN WE HIT ATOMIC TACO ON THE WAY?
STOP TALKING!
YOU GUYS ARE MEANIES!
ALCATRAZ JR

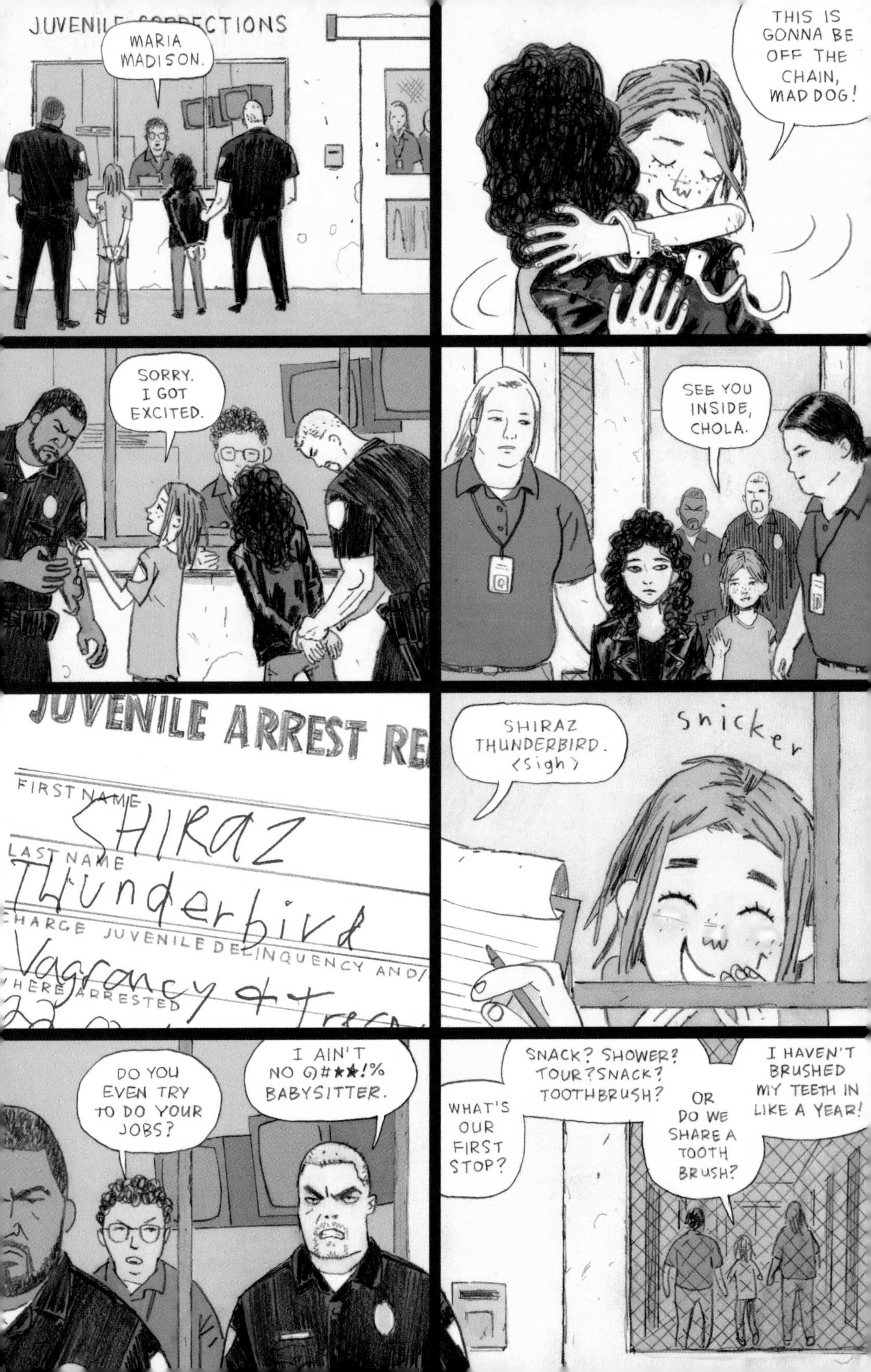
JUVENILE CORRECTIONS
MARIA MADISON.
THIS IS GONNA BE OFF THE CHAIN, MAD DOG!
SORRY. I GOT EXCITED.
SEE YOU INSIDE, CHOLA.
JUVENILE ARREST RE
FIRST NAME Shiraz
LAST NAME Thunderbird
CHARGE JUVENILE DELINQUENCY AND/
Vagrancy & Tres
HERE ARRESTED
SHIRAZ THUNDERBIRD. <sigh>
snicker
DO YOU EVEN TRY TO DO YOUR JOBS?
I AIN'T NO @#★★!% BABYSITTER.
WHAT'S OUR FIRST STOP?
SNACK? SHOWER? TOUR? SNACK? TOOTHBRUSH?
OR DO WE SHARE A TOOTH BRUSH?
I HAVEN'T BRUSHED MY TEETH IN LIKE A YEAR!

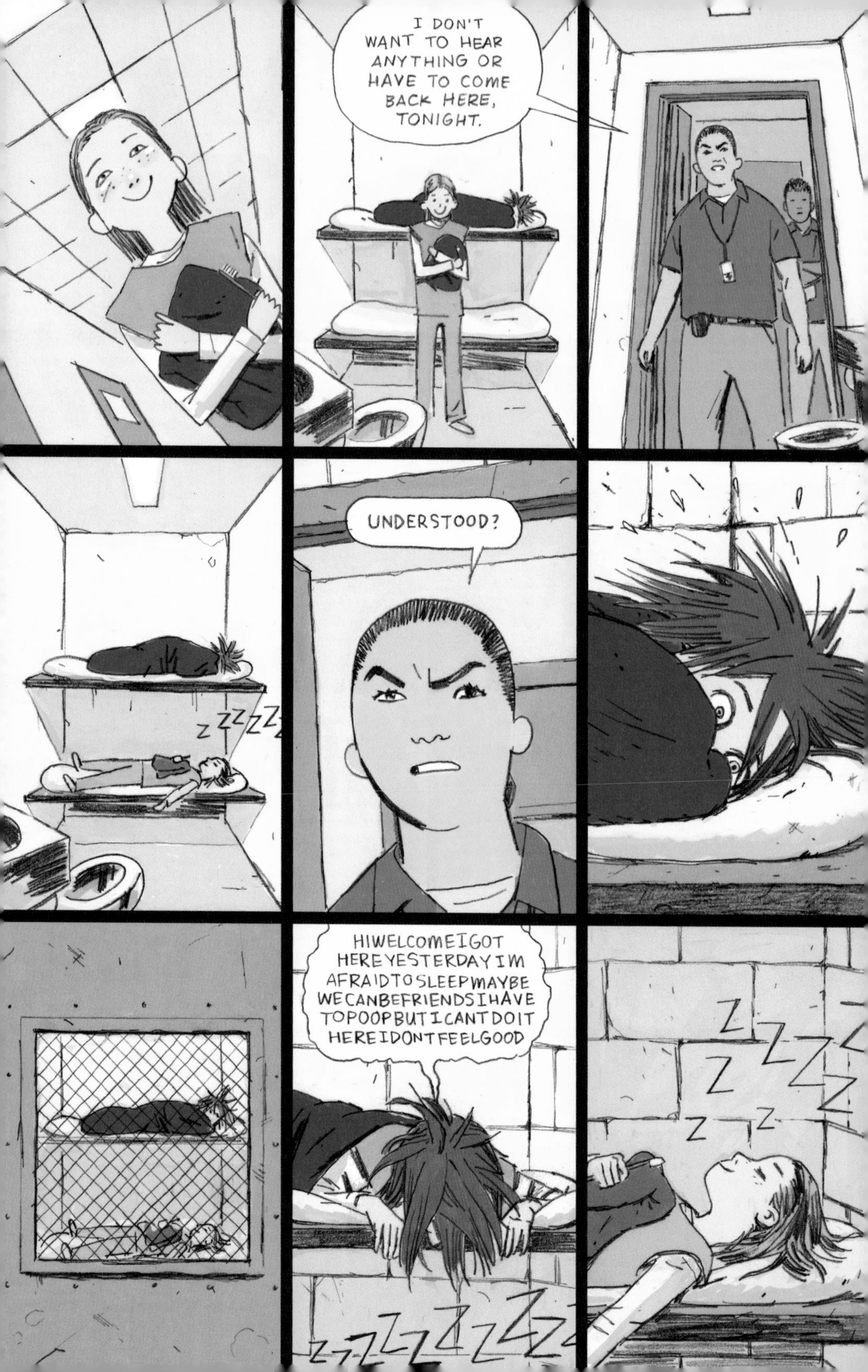
I DON'T WANT TO HEAR ANYTHING OR HAVE TO COME BACK HERE, TONIGHT.
UNDERSTOOD?
HIWELCOMEIGOT HEREYESTERDAYIM AFRAIDTOSLEEPMAYBE WECANBEFRIENDSIHAVE TOPOOPBUTICANTDOIT HEREIDONTFEELGOOD

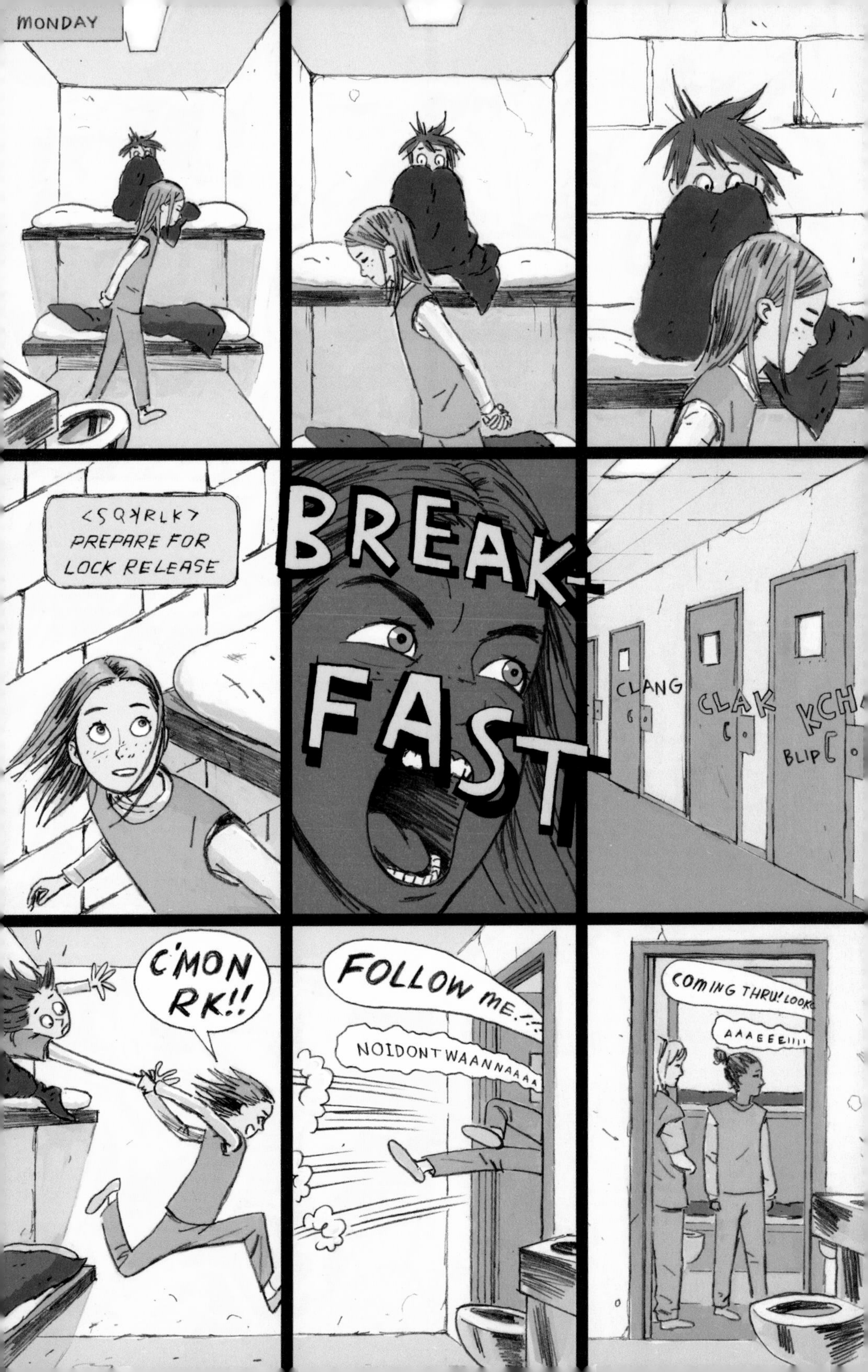
MONDAY
<SQKRLK> PREPARE FOR LOCK RELEASE
BREAK-FAST
CLANG
CLAK
KCH
BLIP
C'MON RK!!
FOLLOW ME.!.!
NOIDONTWAANNAAAA
COMING THRU! LOOK
AAAEEEE!!!!

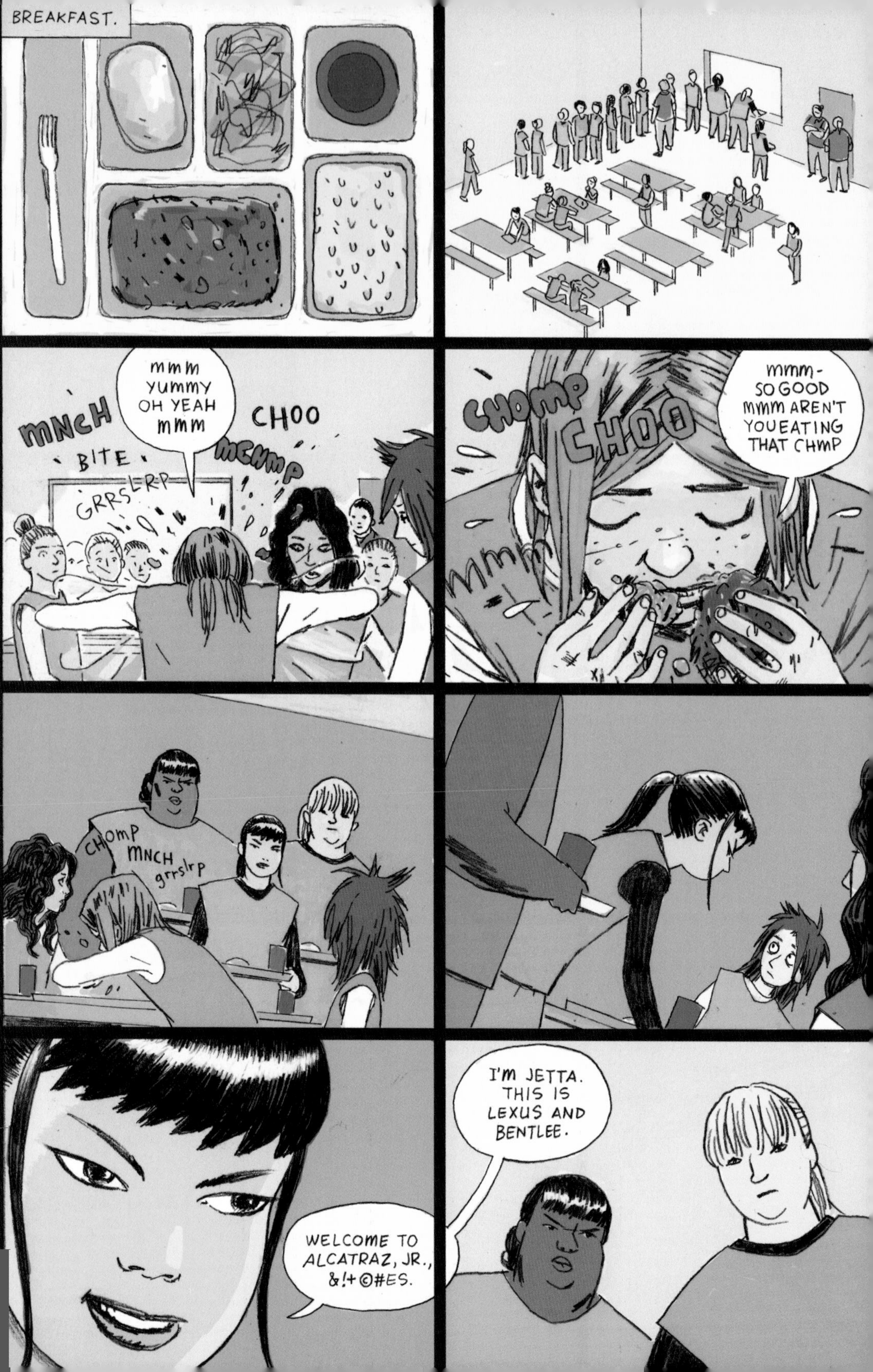
BREAKFAST.
mmm YUMMY OH YEAH mmm
MNCH
BITE
GRRSLRP
CHOO
MCHMP
mmm- SO GOOD mmm AREN'T YOU EATING THAT CHMP
CHOMP
CHOO
mmm
CHOMP
MNCH
grrslrp
WELCOME TO ALCATRAZ, JR., &!+©#ES.
I'M JETTA. THIS IS LEXUS AND BENTLEE.

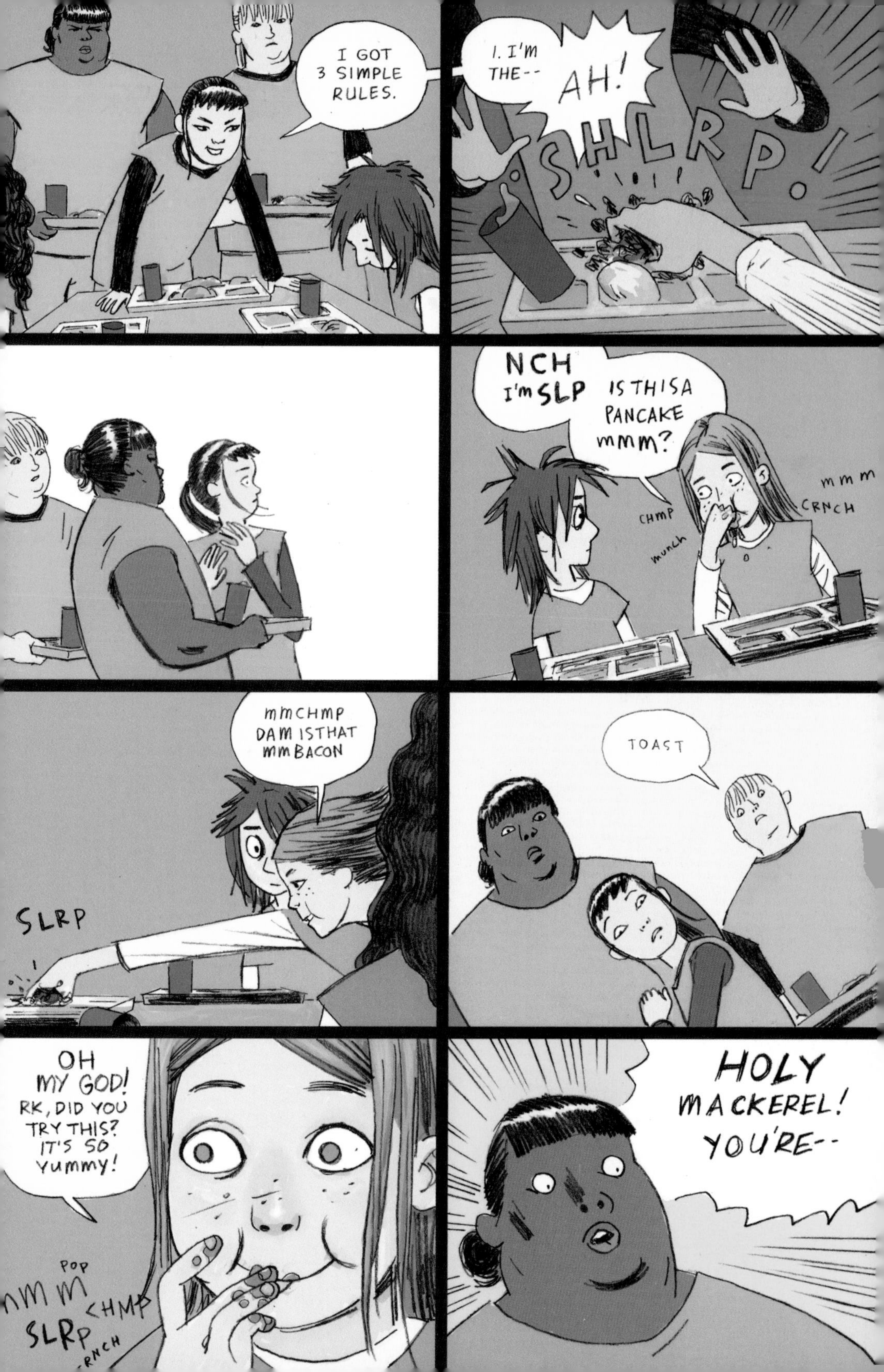
I GOT 3 SIMPLE RULES.
1. I'M THE--
AH!
SHLRP!
NCH I'm SLP IS THIS A PANCAKE mmm?
CHMP
munch
mmm
CRNCH
mmCHMP DAM IS THAT mm BACON
SLRP
TOAST
OH MY GOD! RK, DID YOU TRY THIS? IT'S SO YUMMY!
POP
mmm
CHMP
SLRP
-RNCH
HOLY MACKEREL! YOU'RE--

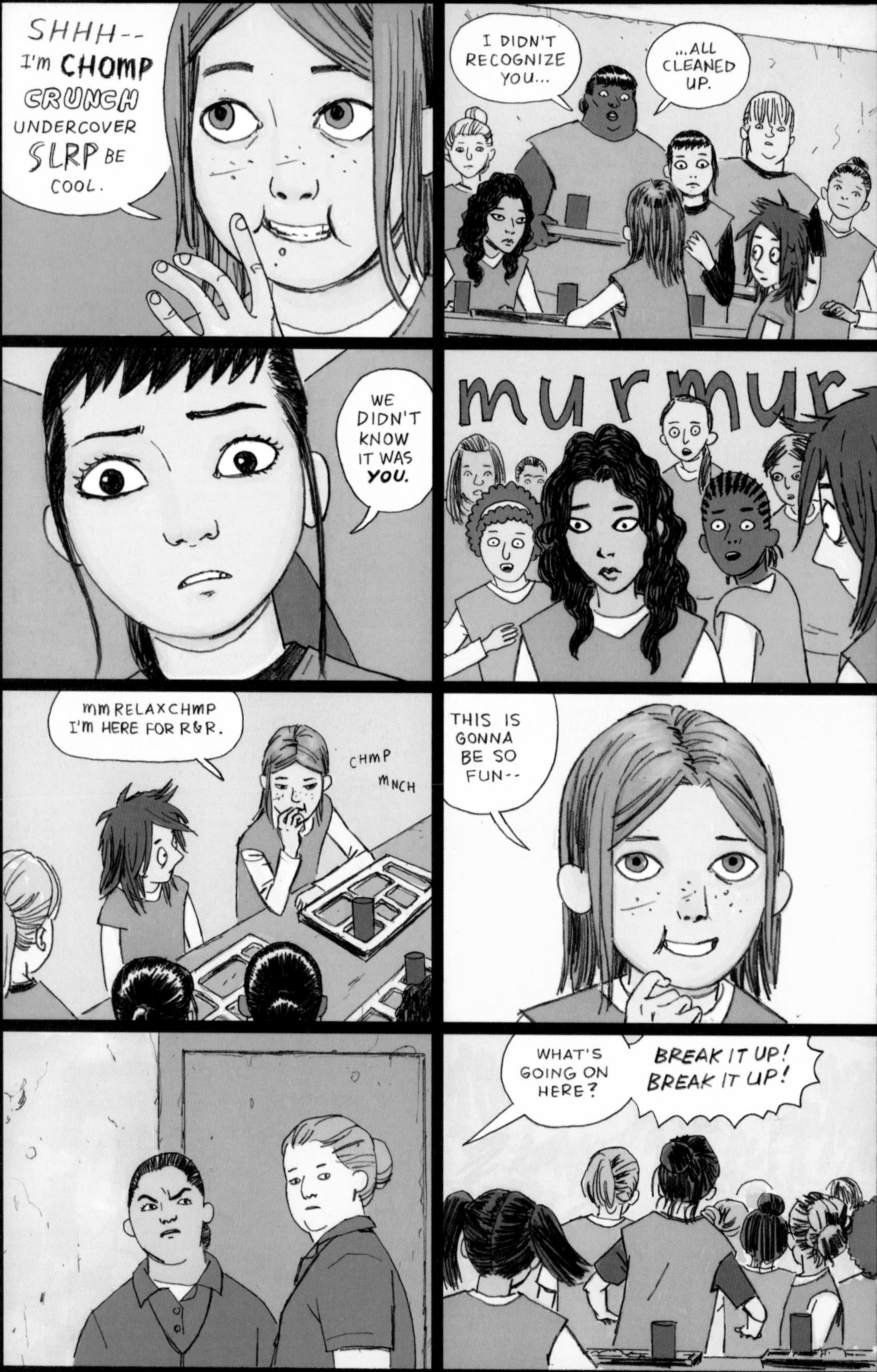
SHHH-- I'm CHOMP CRUNCH UNDERCOVER SLRP BE COOL.
I DIDN'T RECOGNIZE YOU...
...ALL CLEANED UP.
WE DIDN'T KNOW IT WAS YOU.
murmur
mm RELAXCHMP I'M HERE FOR R&R.
CHMP
MNCH
THIS IS GONNA BE SO FUN--
WHAT'S GOING ON HERE?
BREAK IT UP! BREAK IT UP!

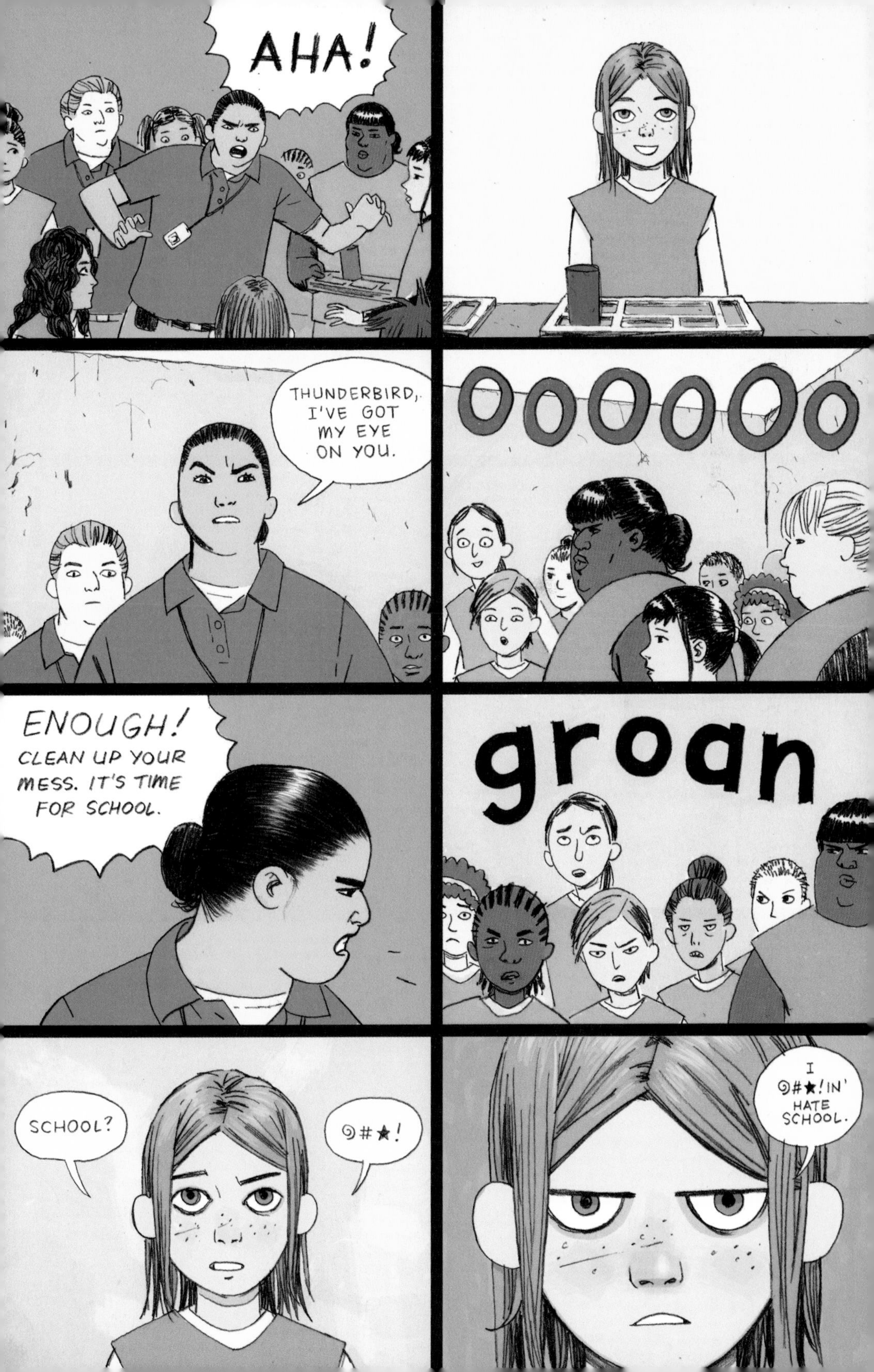
AHA!
THUNDERBIRD, I'VE GOT MY EYE ON YOU.
OOOOOO
ENOUGH! CLEAN UP YOUR MESS. IT'S TIME FOR SCHOOL.
groan
SCHOOL?
୨#★!
I ୨#★!IN' HATE SCHOOL.

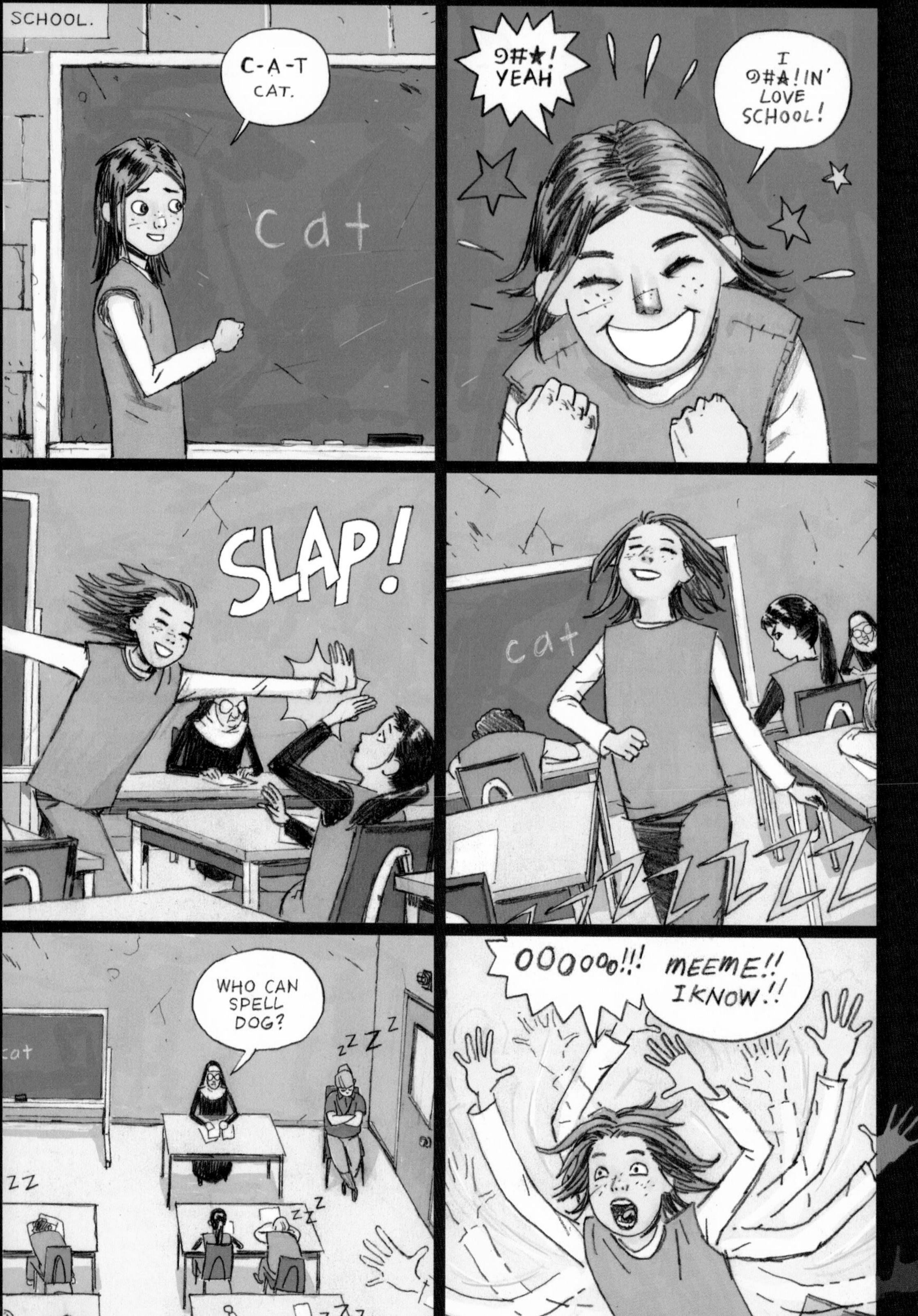
SCHOOL.
C-A-T CAT.
cat
9#★! YEAH
I 9#A!IN' LOVE SCHOOL!
SLAP!
cat
WHO CAN SPELL DOG?
cat
OOOOoo!!! MEEME!! IKNOW!!

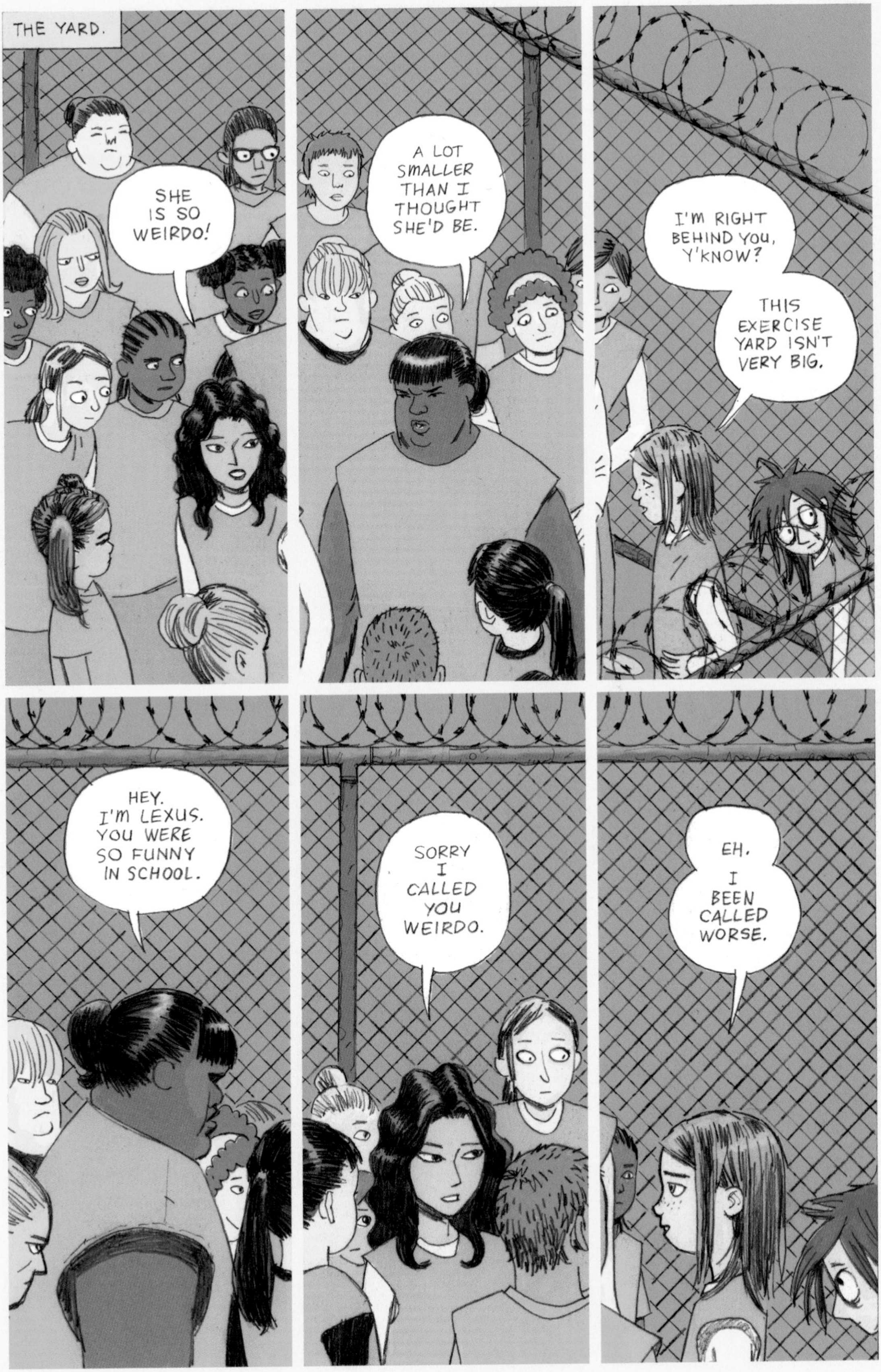
THE YARD.
SHE IS SO WEIRDO!
A LOT SMALLER THAN I THOUGHT SHE'D BE.
I'M RIGHT BEHIND YOU, Y'KNOW?
THIS EXERCISE YARD ISN'T VERY BIG.
HEY. I'M LEXUS. YOU WERE SO FUNNY IN SCHOOL.
SORRY I CALLED YOU WEIRDO.
EH.
I BEEN CALLED WORSE.

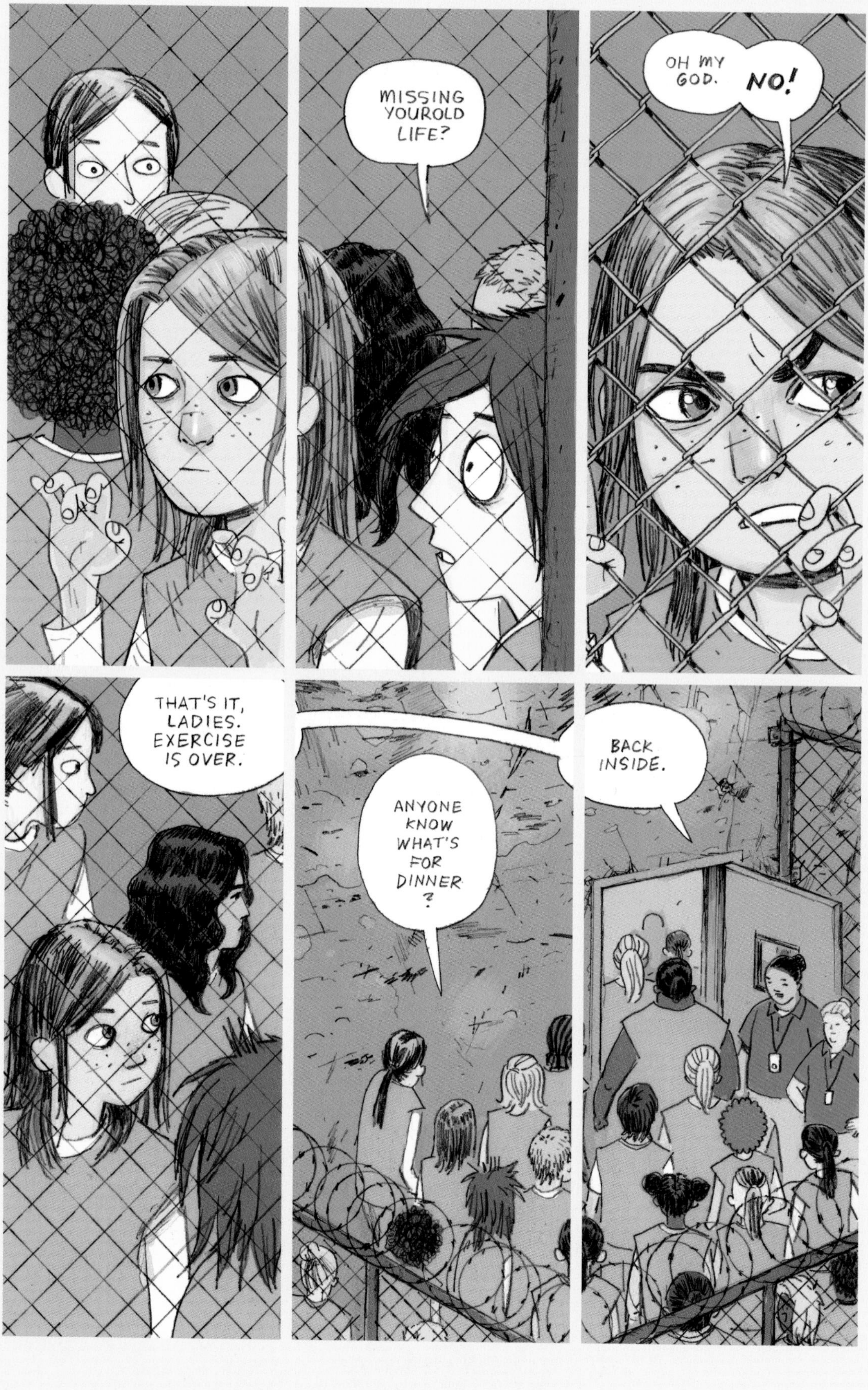
MISSING YOUROLD LIFE?
OH MY GOD.
NO!
THAT'S IT, LADIES. EXERCISE IS OVER.
BACK INSIDE.
ANYONE KNOW WHAT'S FOR DINNER?

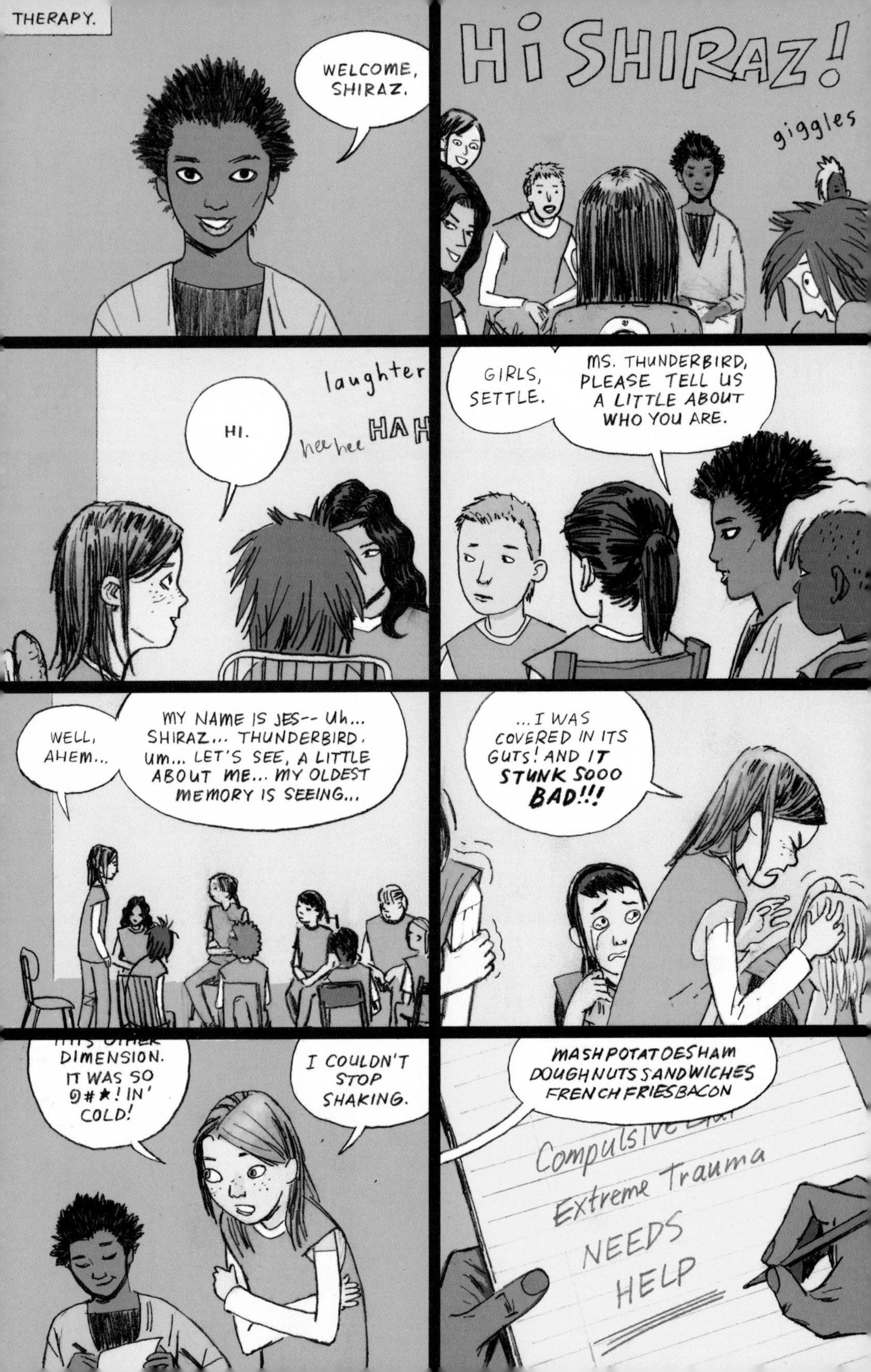
THERAPY.
WELCOME, SHIRAZ.
Hi SHIRAZ!
giggles
laughter
HI.
hee hee HAH
GIRLS, SETTLE.
MS. THUNDERBIRD, PLEASE TELL US A LITTLE ABOUT WHO YOU ARE.
WELL, AHEM...
MY NAME IS JES-- Uh... SHIRAZ... THUNDERBIRD. Um... LET'S SEE, A LITTLE ABOUT ME... MY OLDEST MEMORY IS SEEING...
...I WAS COVERED IN ITS GUTS! AND IT STUNK SOOO BAD!!!
DIMENSION. IT WAS SO @#*! IN' COLD!
I COULDN'T STOP SHAKING.
MASHPOTATOESHAM DOUGHNUTSSANDWICHES FRENCHFRIESBACON
Extreme Trauma
NEEDS HELP

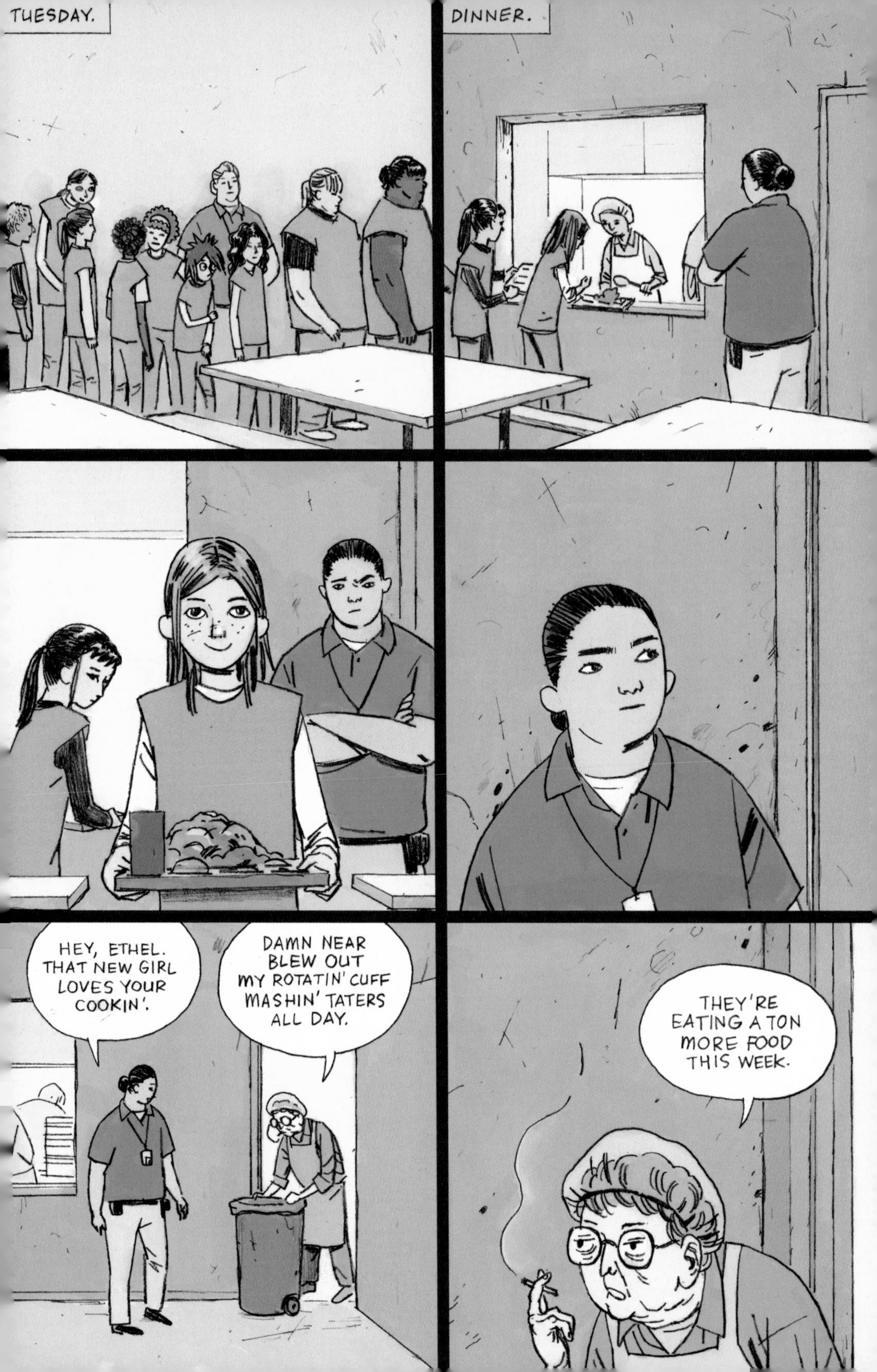
TUESDAY.
DINNER.
HEY, ETHEL. THAT NEW GIRL LOVES YOUR COOKIN'.
DAMN NEAR BLEW OUT MY ROTATIN' CUFF MASHIN' TATERS ALL DAY.
THEY'RE EATING A TON MORE FOOD THIS WEEK.

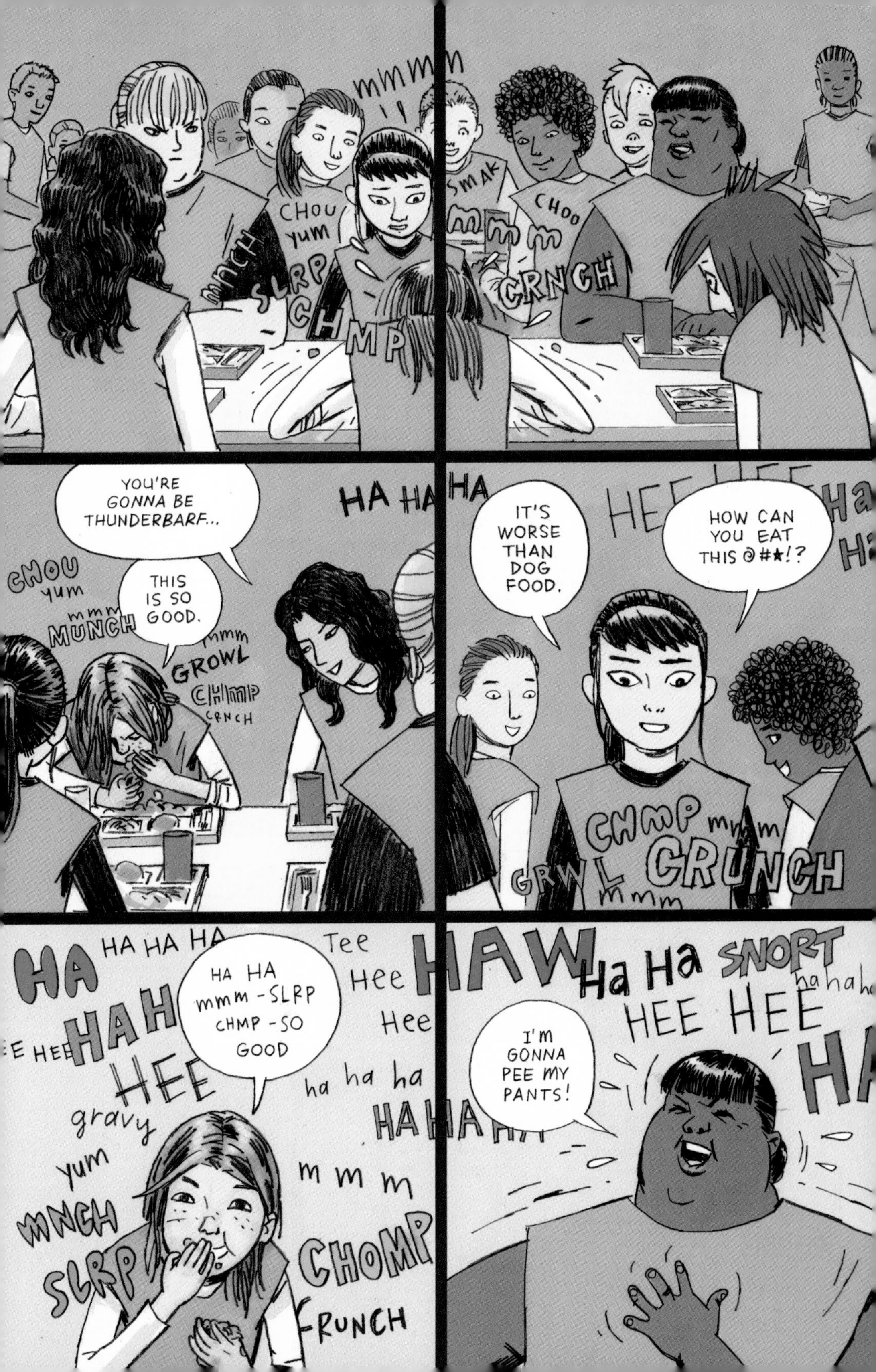
mmmm
CHOU
yum
MUNCH
SLRP
CHMP
SMAK
CHOO
mmm
GRNCH
YOU'RE GONNA BE THUNDERBARF...
HA HA HA
CHOU
yum
mmm
MUNCH
THIS IS SO GOOD.
mmm
GROWL
CHMP
CRNCH
IT'S WORSE THAN DOG FOOD.
HOW CAN YOU EAT THIS @#★!?
CHMP
mmm
GRWL
GRUNCH
mmm
HA
HA HA HA
HAH
HEE
Tee
Hee
Hee
HA HA mmm -SLRP CHMP -SO GOOD
ha ha ha
gravy
yum
MNCH
SLRP
mmm
CHOMP
CRUNCH
HAW
Ha Ha
SNORT
HEE HEE
I'M GONNA PEE MY PANTS!

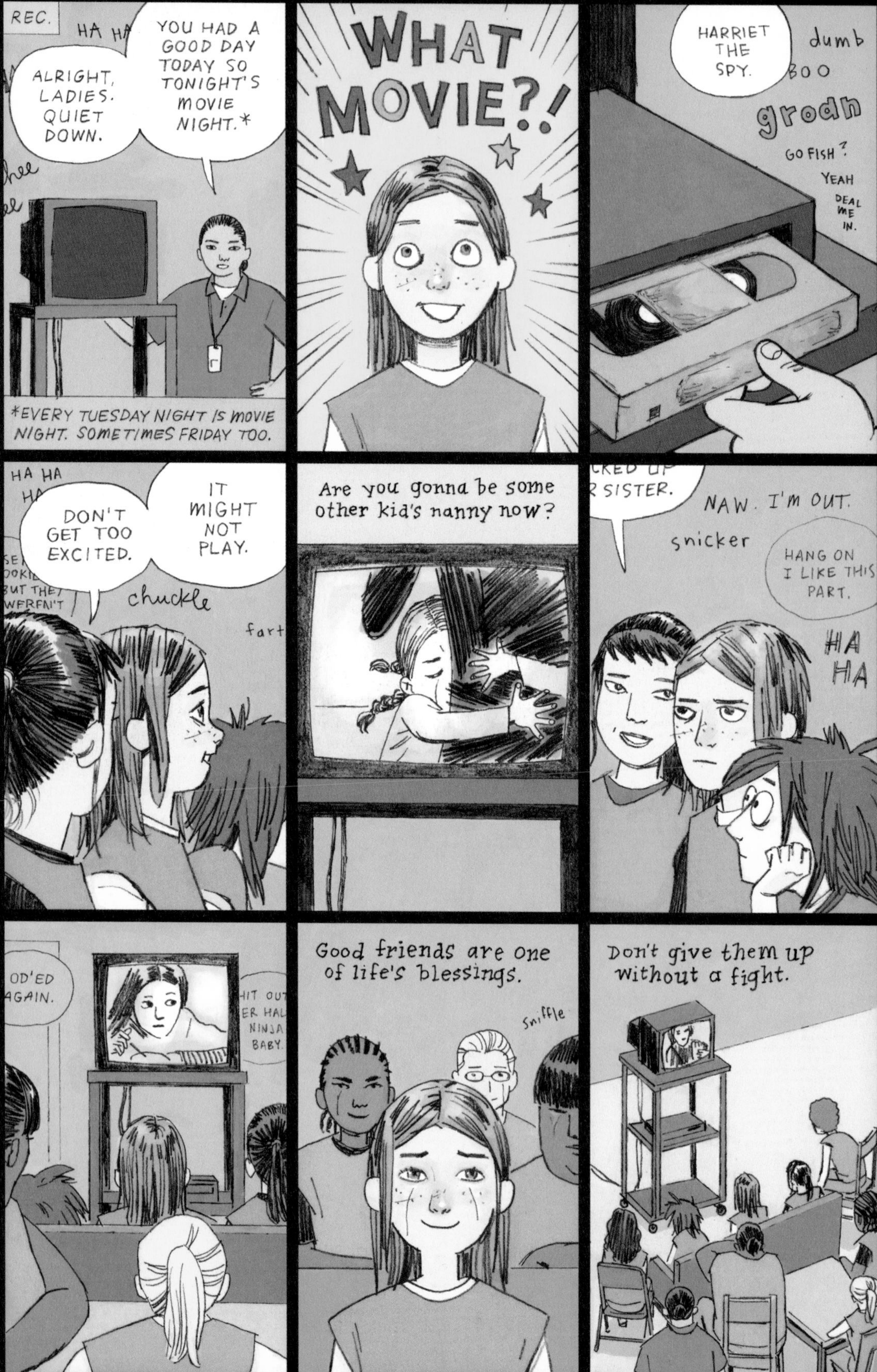
REC.
HA HA
ALRIGHT, LADIES. QUIET DOWN.
YOU HAD A GOOD DAY TODAY SO TONIGHT'S MOVIE NIGHT.*
*EVERY TUESDAY NIGHT IS MOVIE NIGHT. SOMETIMES FRIDAY TOO.
WHAT MOVIE?!
HARRIET THE SPY.
dumb
BOO
groan
GO FISH?
YEAH
DEAL ME IN.
HA HA
DON'T GET TOO EXCITED.
IT MIGHT NOT PLAY.
chuckle
fart
Are you gonna be some other kid's nanny now?
R SISTER.
NAW. I'M OUT.
snicker
HANG ON I LIKE THIS PART.
HA HA
OD'ED AGAIN.
Good friends are one of life's blessings.
sniffle
Don't give them up without a fight.

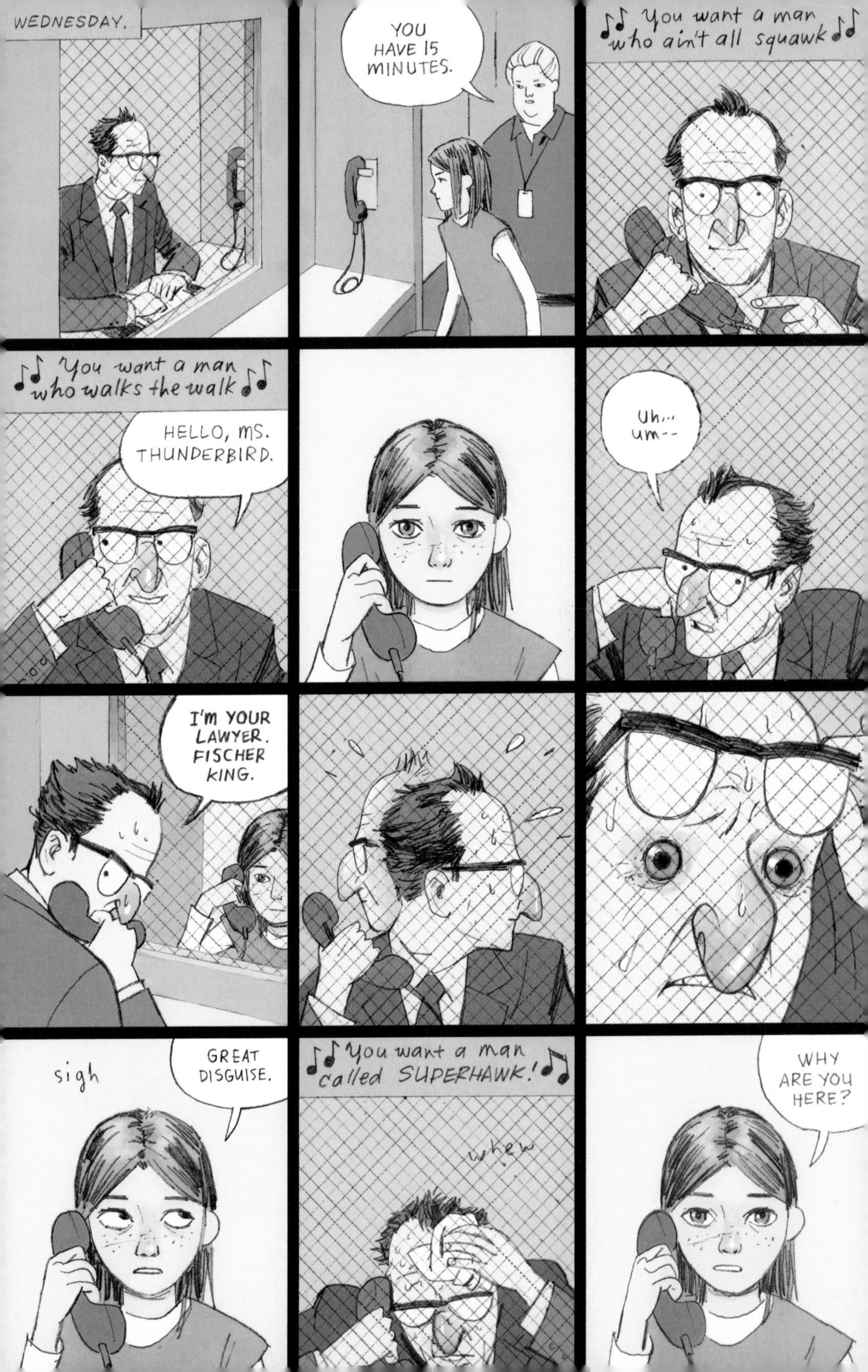

WEDNESDAY.
YOU HAVE 15 MINUTES.
♪♪ You want a man who ain't all squawk ♪♪
♪♪ You want a man who walks the walk ♪♪
HELLO, MS. THUNDERBIRD.
Uh... um--
I'M YOUR LAWYER. FISCHER KING.
sigh
GREAT DISGUISE.
♪♪ You want a man called SUPERHAWK! ♪♪
whew
WHY ARE YOU HERE?

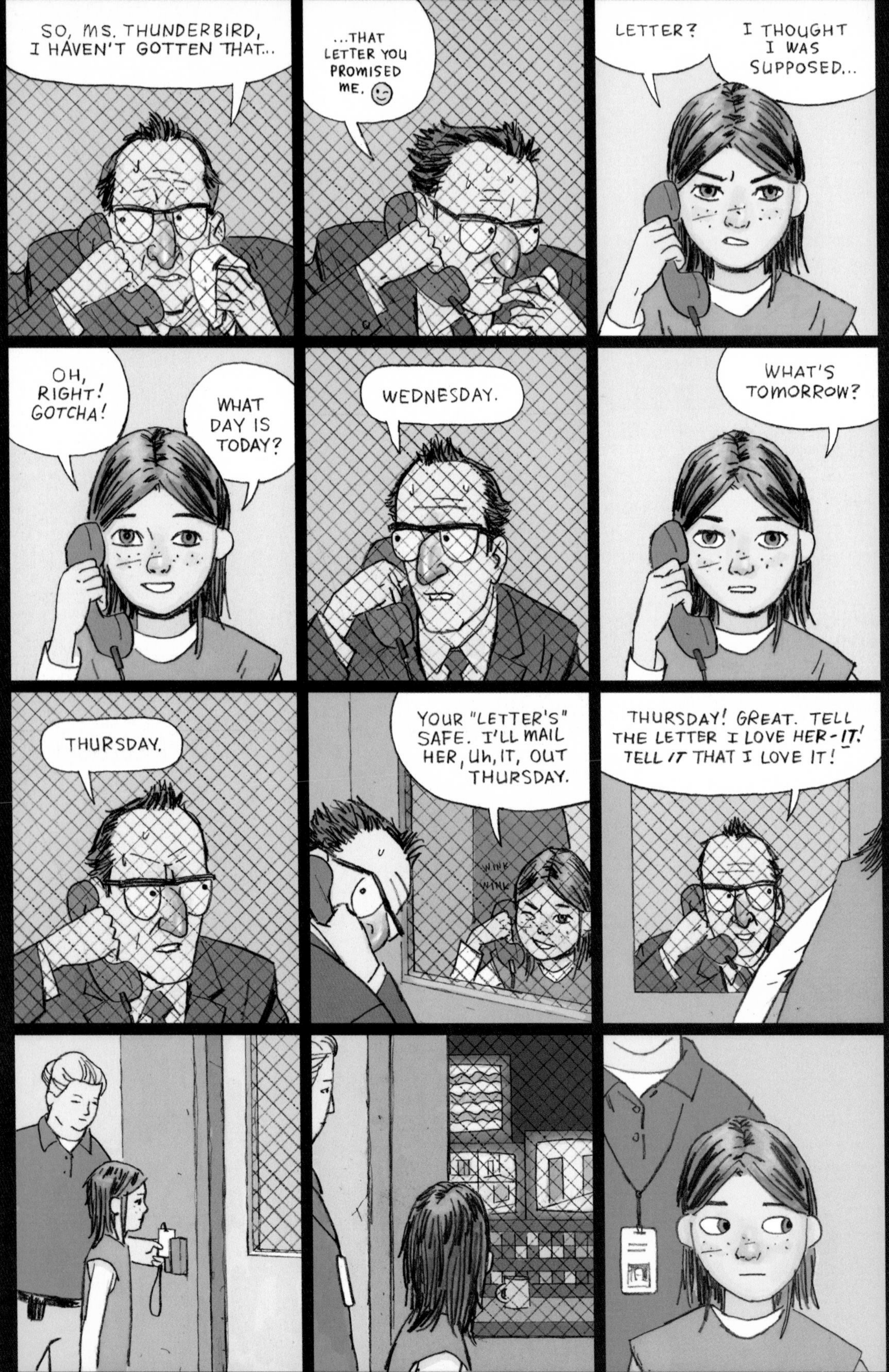

SO, MS. THUNDERBIRD, I HAVEN'T GOTTEN THAT...
...THAT LETTER YOU PROMISED ME.
LETTER?
I THOUGHT I WAS SUPPOSED...
OH, RIGHT! GOTCHA!
WHAT DAY IS TODAY?
WEDNESDAY.
WHAT'S TOMORROW?
THURSDAY.
YOUR "LETTER'S" SAFE. I'LL MAIL HER, Uh, IT, OUT THURSDAY.
WINK
WINK
THURSDAY! GREAT. TELL THE LETTER I LOVE HER-IT! TELL IT THAT I LOVE IT!

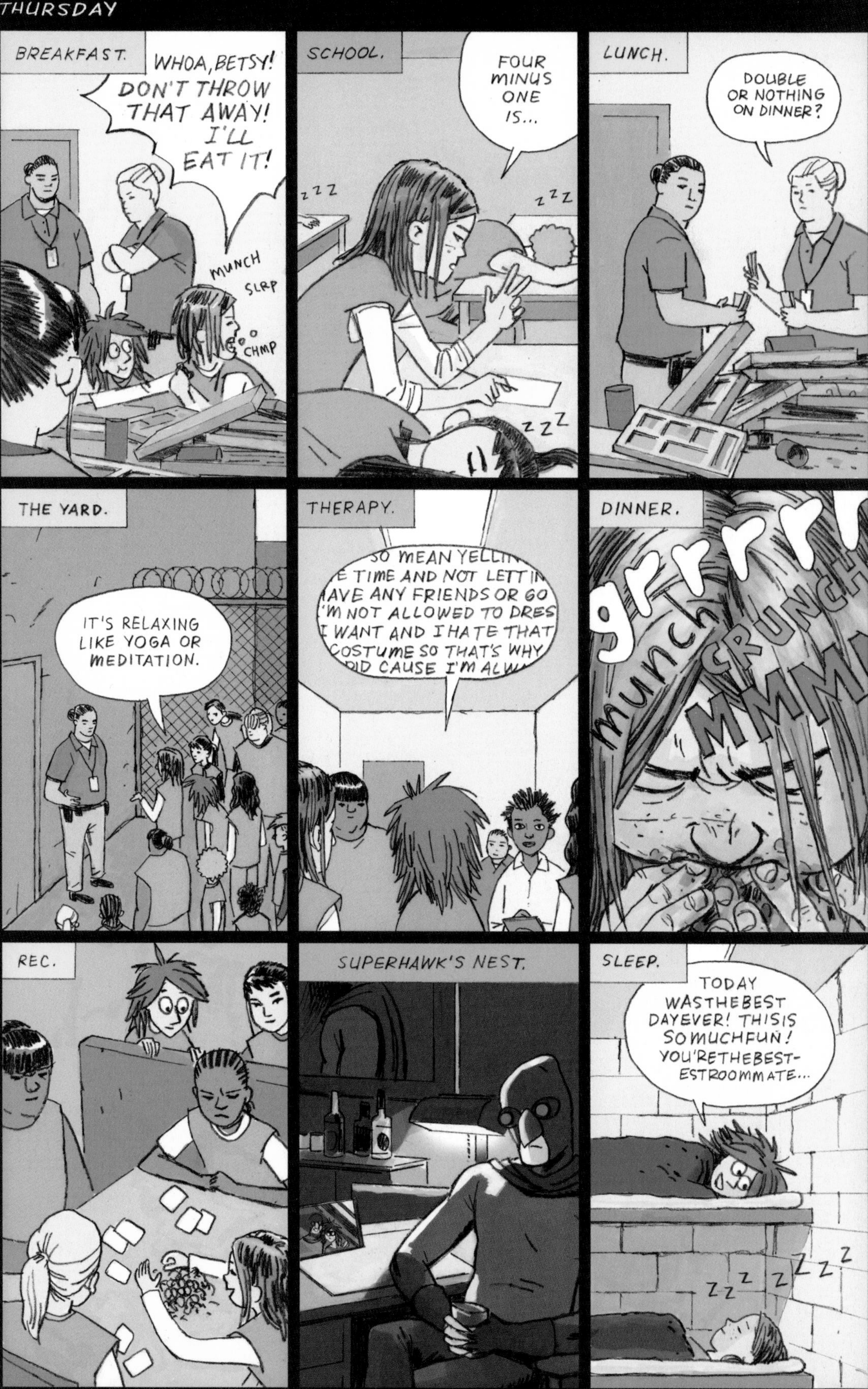
THURSDAY
BREAKFAST.
WHOA, BETSY! DON'T THROW THAT AWAY! I'LL EAT IT!
MUNCH
SLRP
CHMP
SCHOOL.
FOUR MINUS ONE IS...
Z Z Z
Z Z Z
Z Z Z
LUNCH.
DOUBLE OR NOTHING ON DINNER?
THE YARD.
IT'S RELAXING LIKE YOGA OR MEDITATION.
THERAPY.
SO MEAN YELLIN
E TIME AND NOT LETT IN
AVE ANY FRIENDS OR GO
I'M NOT ALLOWED TO DRES
I WANT AND I HATE THAT
COSTUME SO THAT'S WHY
DID CAUSE I'M ALW
DINNER.
grrrr
munch
CRUNCH
MMMM
REC.
SUPERHAWK'S NEST.
SLEEP.
TODAY WASTHEBEST DAYEVER! THISIS SOMUCHFUN! YOU'RETHEBEST-ESTROOMMATE...
Z Z Z Z Z Z

FRIDAY

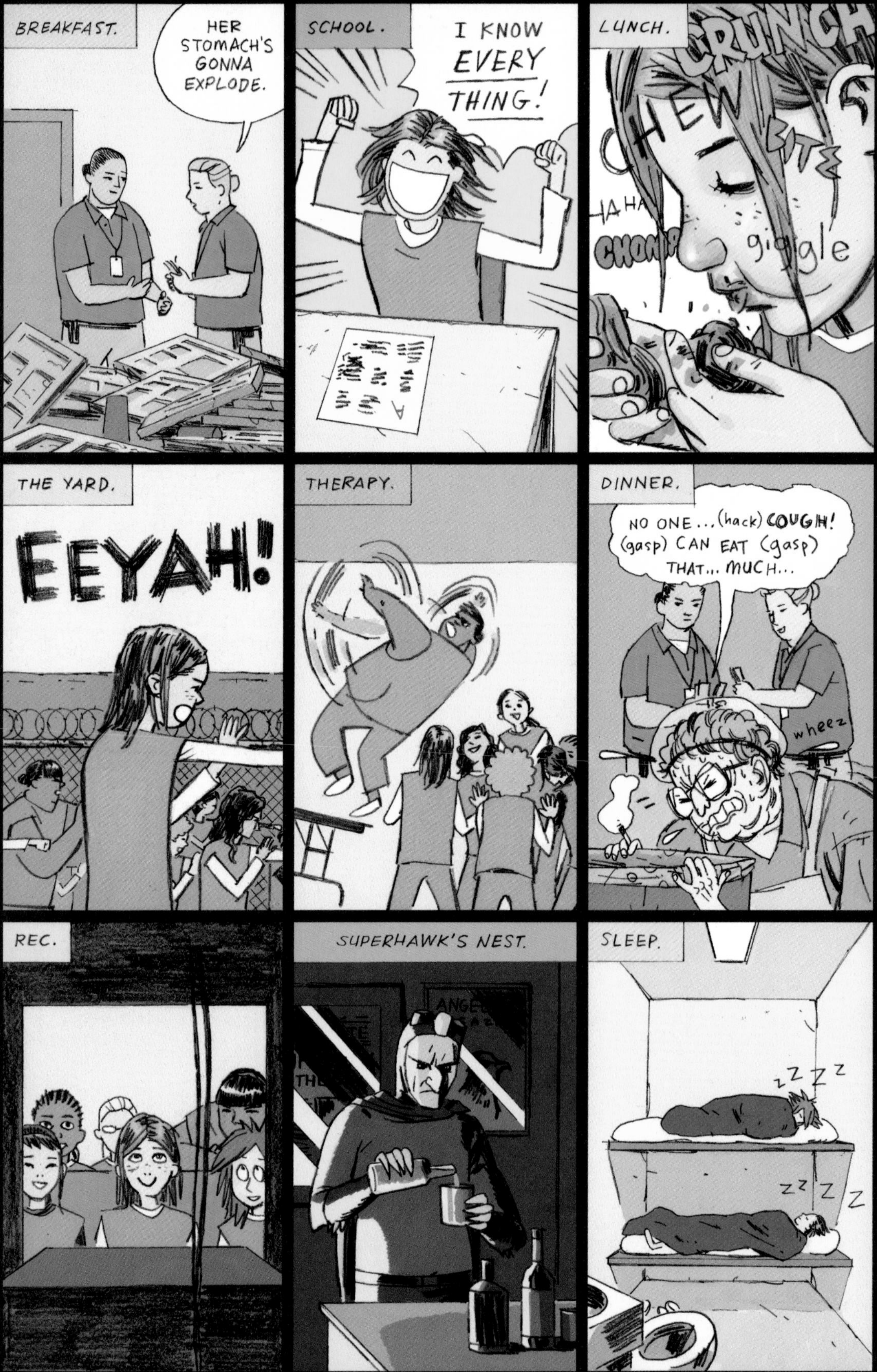

BREAKFAST.
HER STOMACH'S GONNA EXPLODE.
SCHOOL.
I KNOW EVERY THING!
LUNCH.
CRUNCH
CHEW
BITE
giggle
THE YARD.
EEYAH!
THERAPY.
DINNER.
NO ONE... (hack) COUGH! (gasp) CAN EAT (gasp) THAT... MUCH...
wheez
REC.
SUPERHAWK'S NEST.
SLEEP.
Z Z Z Z
Z Z Z Z

SATURDAY

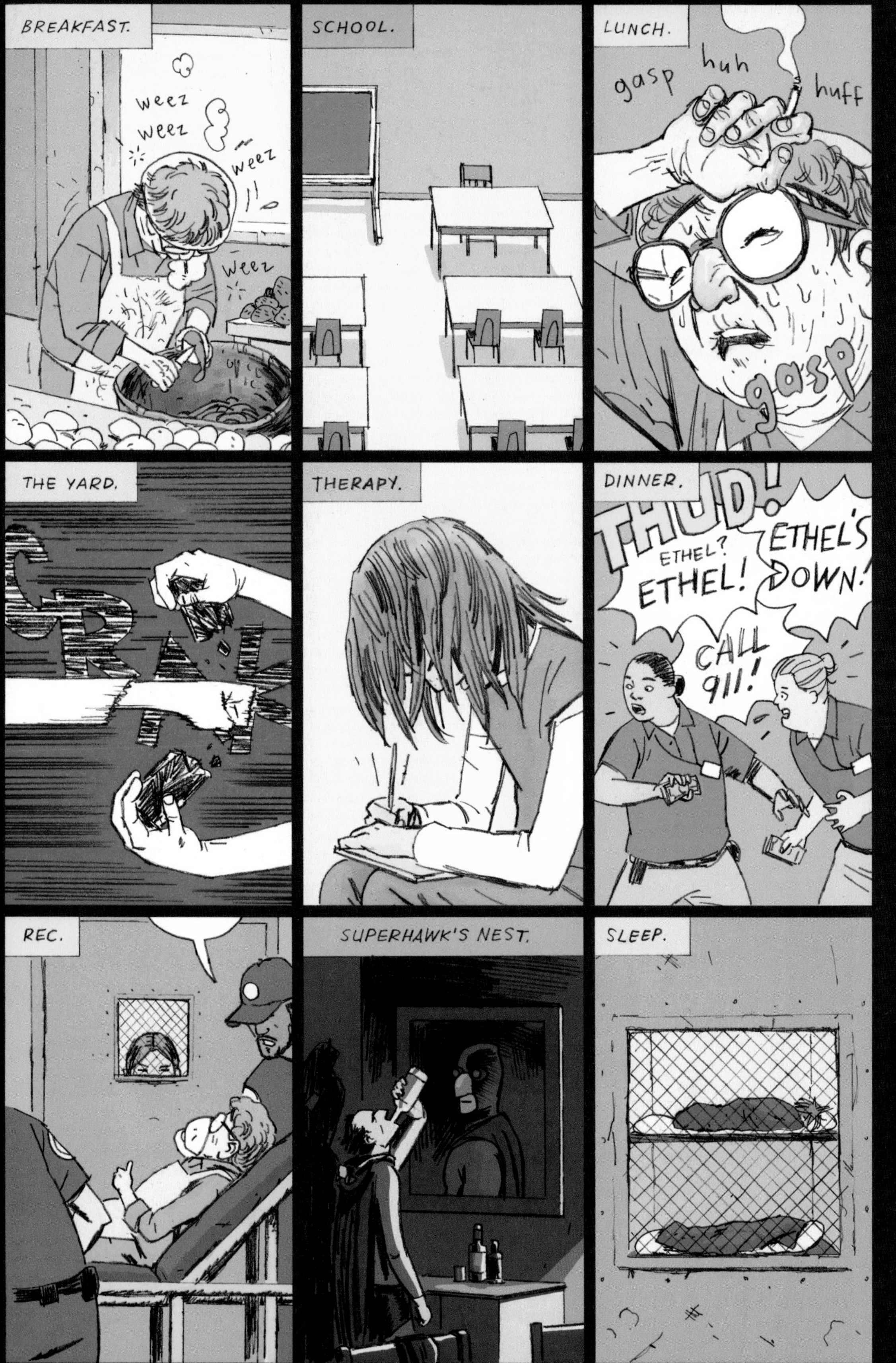
BREAKFAST.
weez
weez
weez
weez
SCHOOL.
LUNCH.
gasp
huh
huff
gasp
THE YARD.
THERAPY.
DINNER.
THUD!
ETHEL? ETHEL!
ETHEL'S DOWN!
CALL 911!
REC.
SUPERHAWK'S NEST.
SLEEP.

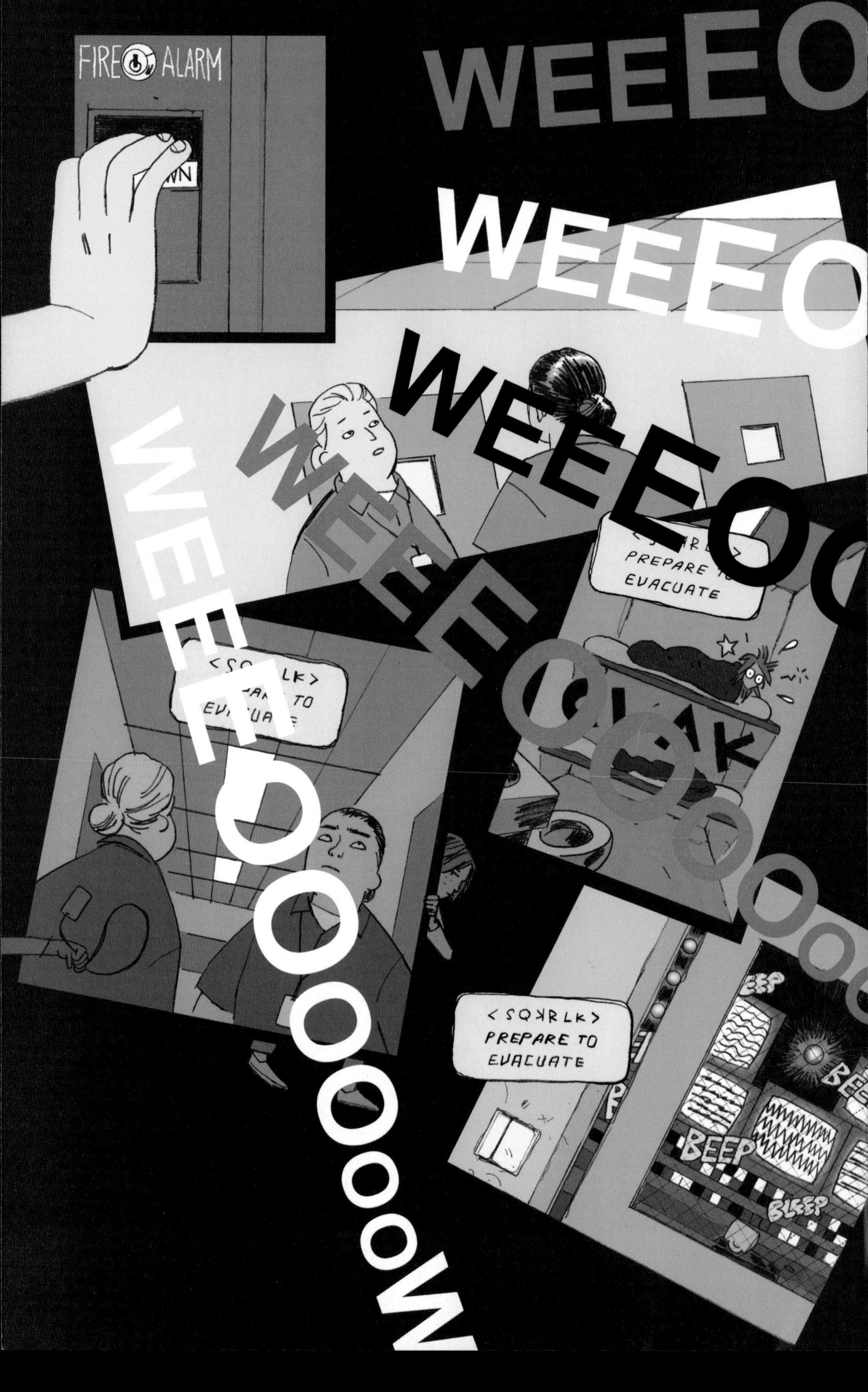
FIRE ALARM
WEEEO
WEEEO
WEEEO
WEEEOOOOO
WEEEOOOOOOOOOOW
<SQKRLK>
PREPARE TO
EVACUATE
<SQKRLK>
PREPARE TO
EVACUATE
BEEP
BEEP
BLEEP

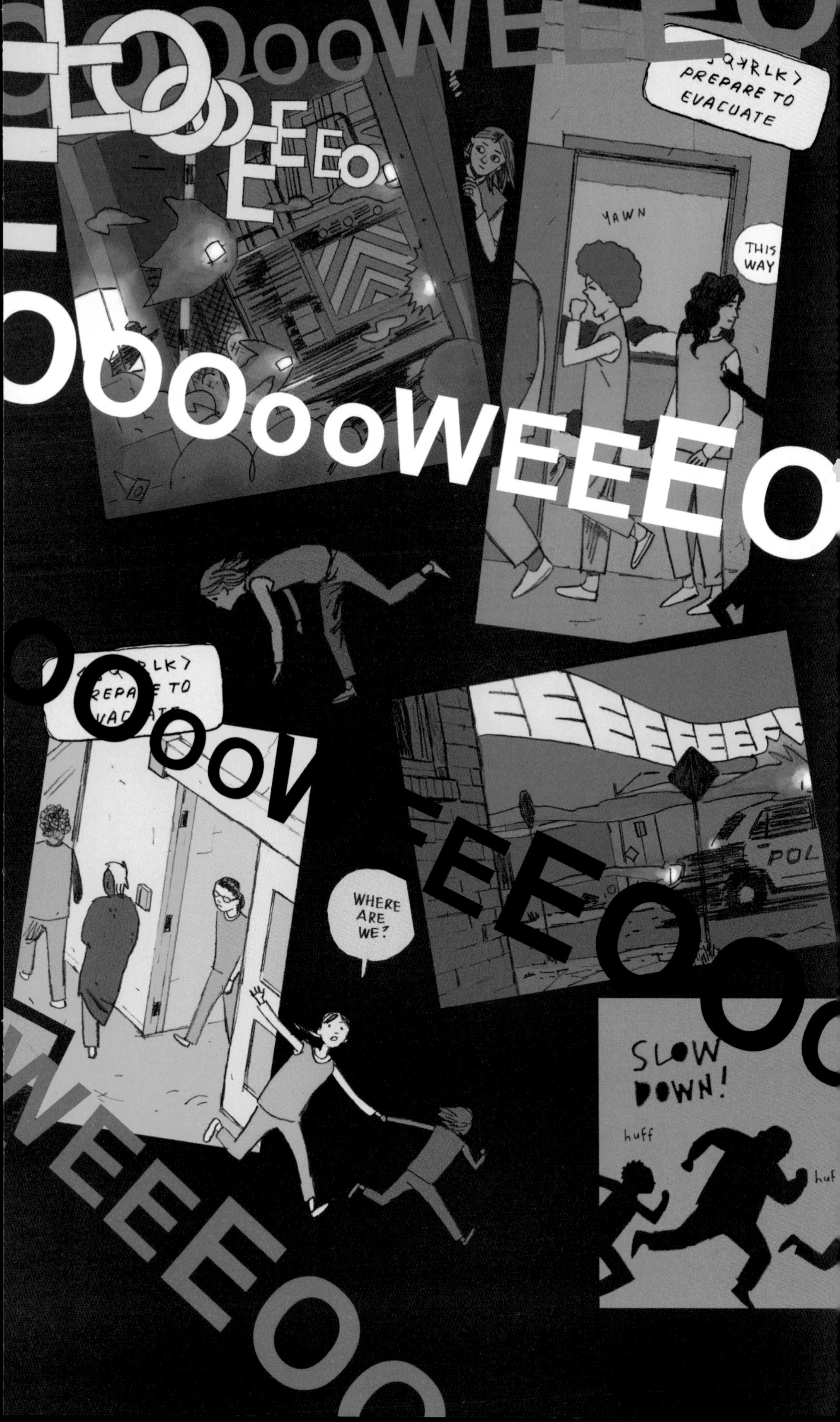
OOOOOWEEEEO
PREPARE TO EVACUATE
YAWN
THIS WAY
OOOOOWEEEEO
PREPARE TO EVACUATE
OOOOWEEEO
WHERE ARE WE?
SLOW DOWN!
huff
huff
WEEEEOO

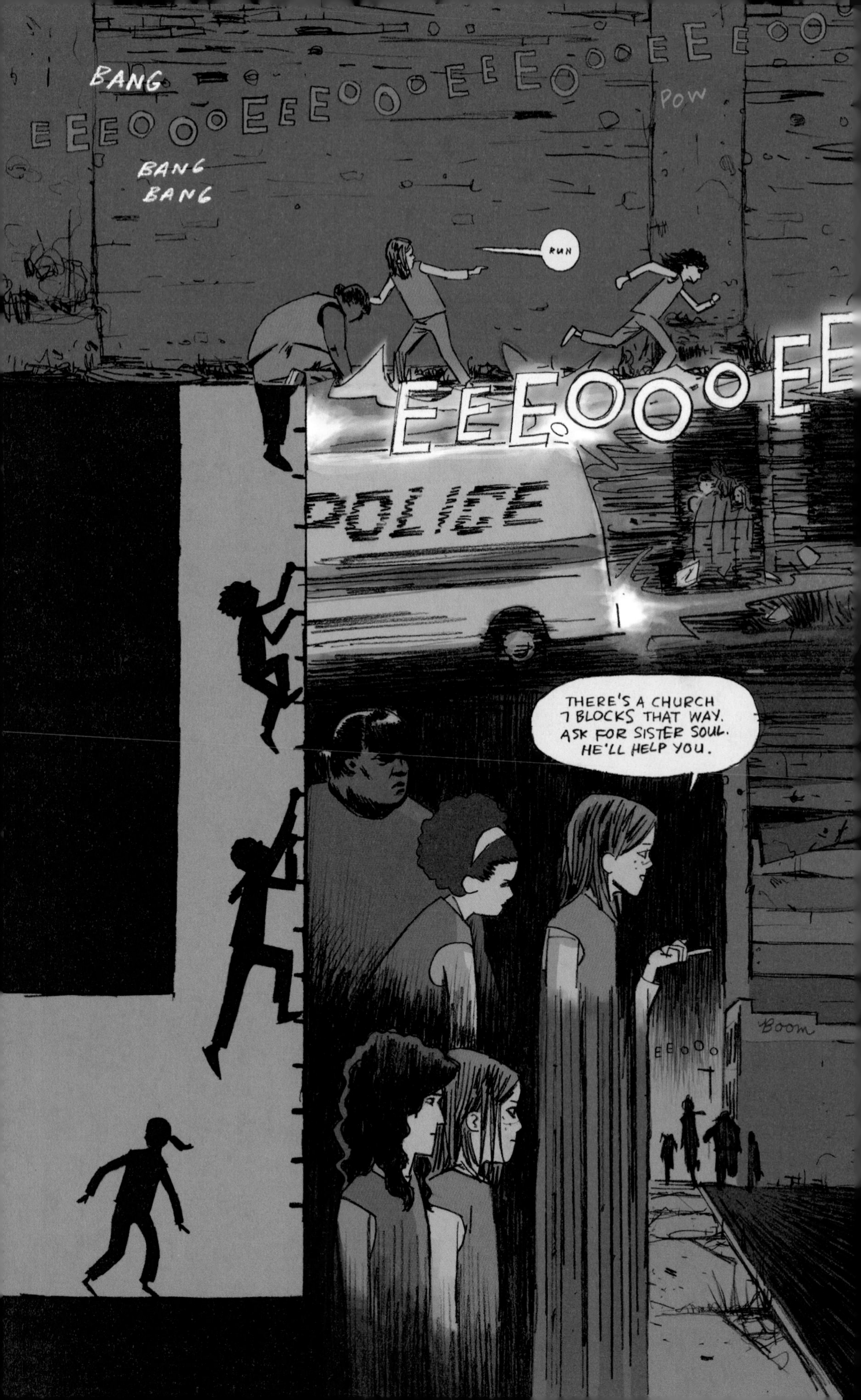
BANG
EEEOOOEEEOOOEEEOOOEEEOO
BANG BANG
POW
RUN
EEEOOOEE
POLICE
THERE'S A CHURCH 7 BLOCKS THAT WAY. ASK FOR SISTER SOUL. HE'LL HELP YOU.
Boom
EEOOO

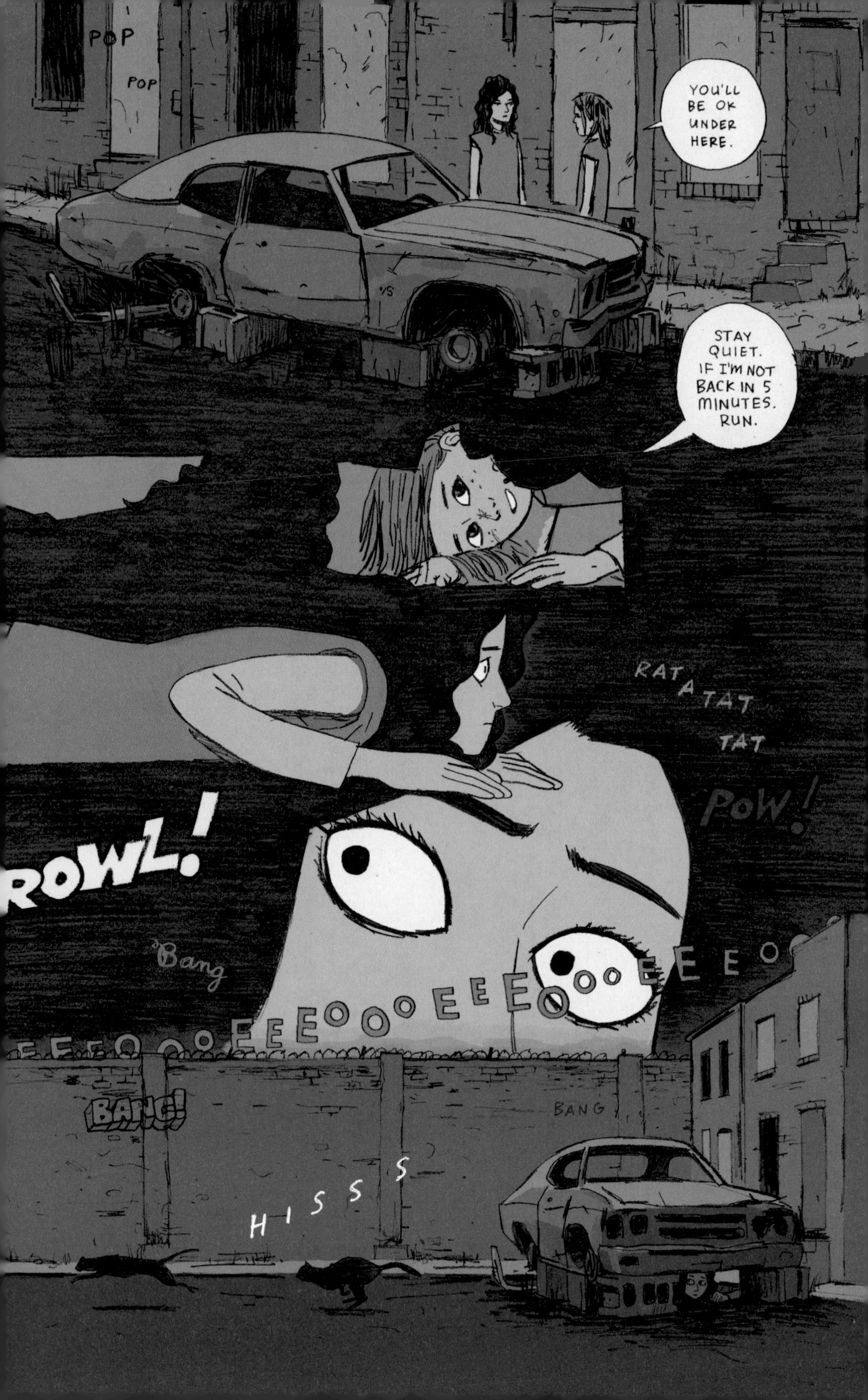
POP
POP
YOU'LL BE OK UNDER HERE.
STAY QUIET. IF I'M NOT BACK IN 5 MINUTES. RUN.
RAT A TAT TAT
POW!
ROWL!
Bang
EEEOOOEEEOOOEEEOOOEEEO
BANG!
BANG
HISSS

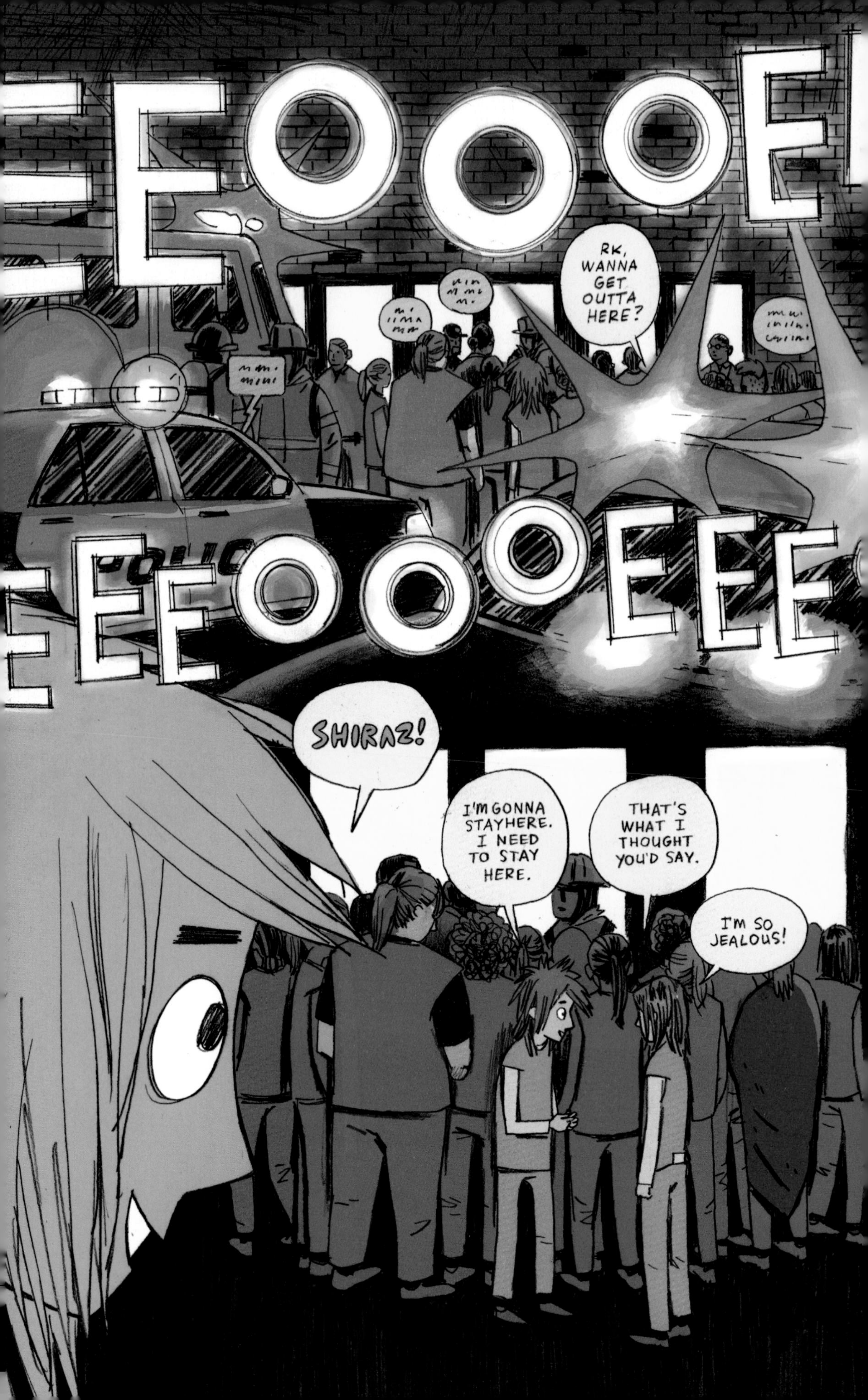
EEOOOEE
RK, WANNA GET OUTTA HERE?
EEOOOEEE
SHIRAZ!
I'M GONNA STAYHERE. I NEED TO STAY HERE.
THAT'S WHAT I THOUGHT YOU'D SAY.
I'M SO JEALOUS!

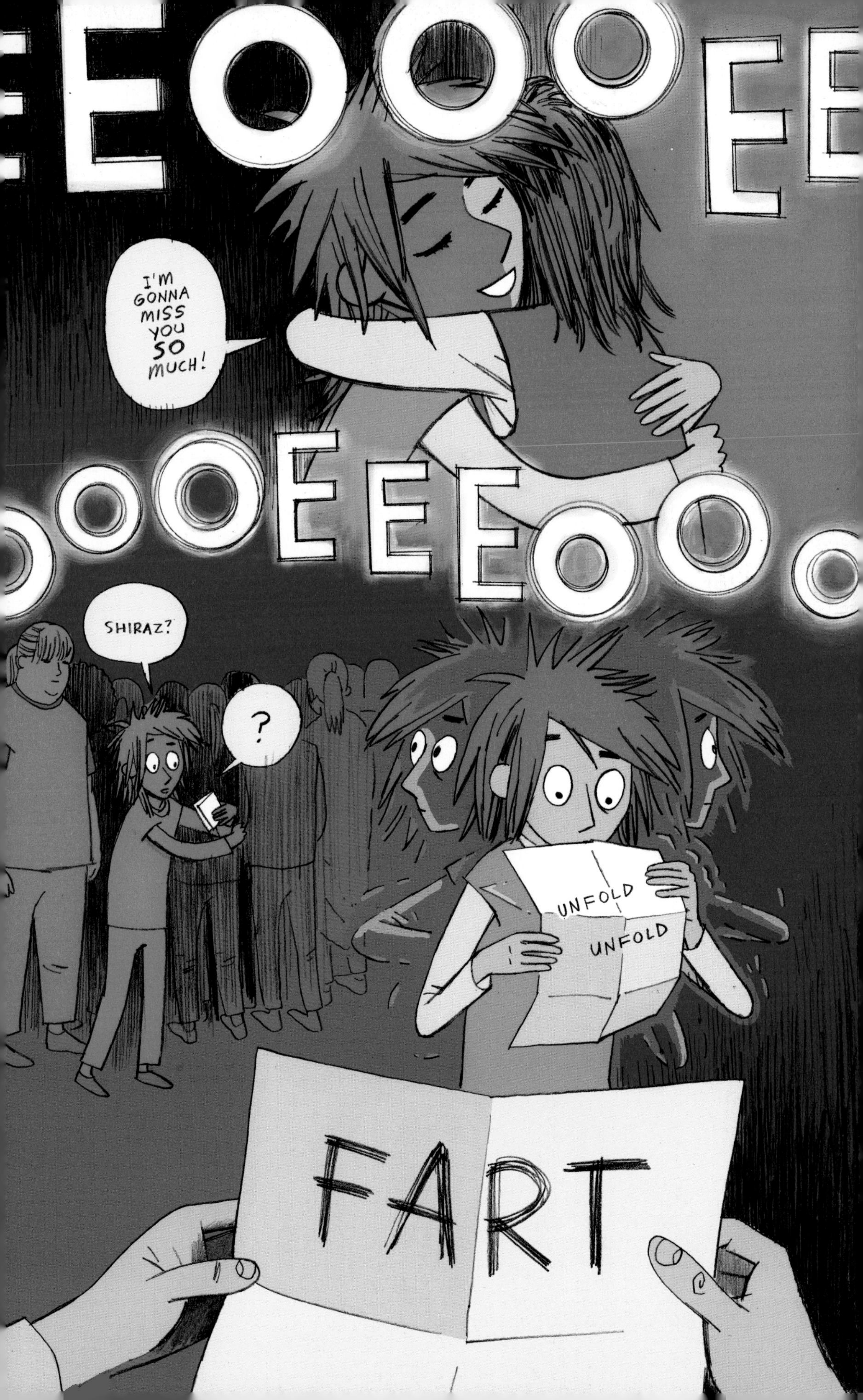
EEOOOOEE
I'M GONNA MISS YOU SO MUCH!
OOOEEEEOOO
SHIRAZ?
?
UNFOLD
UNFOLD
FART

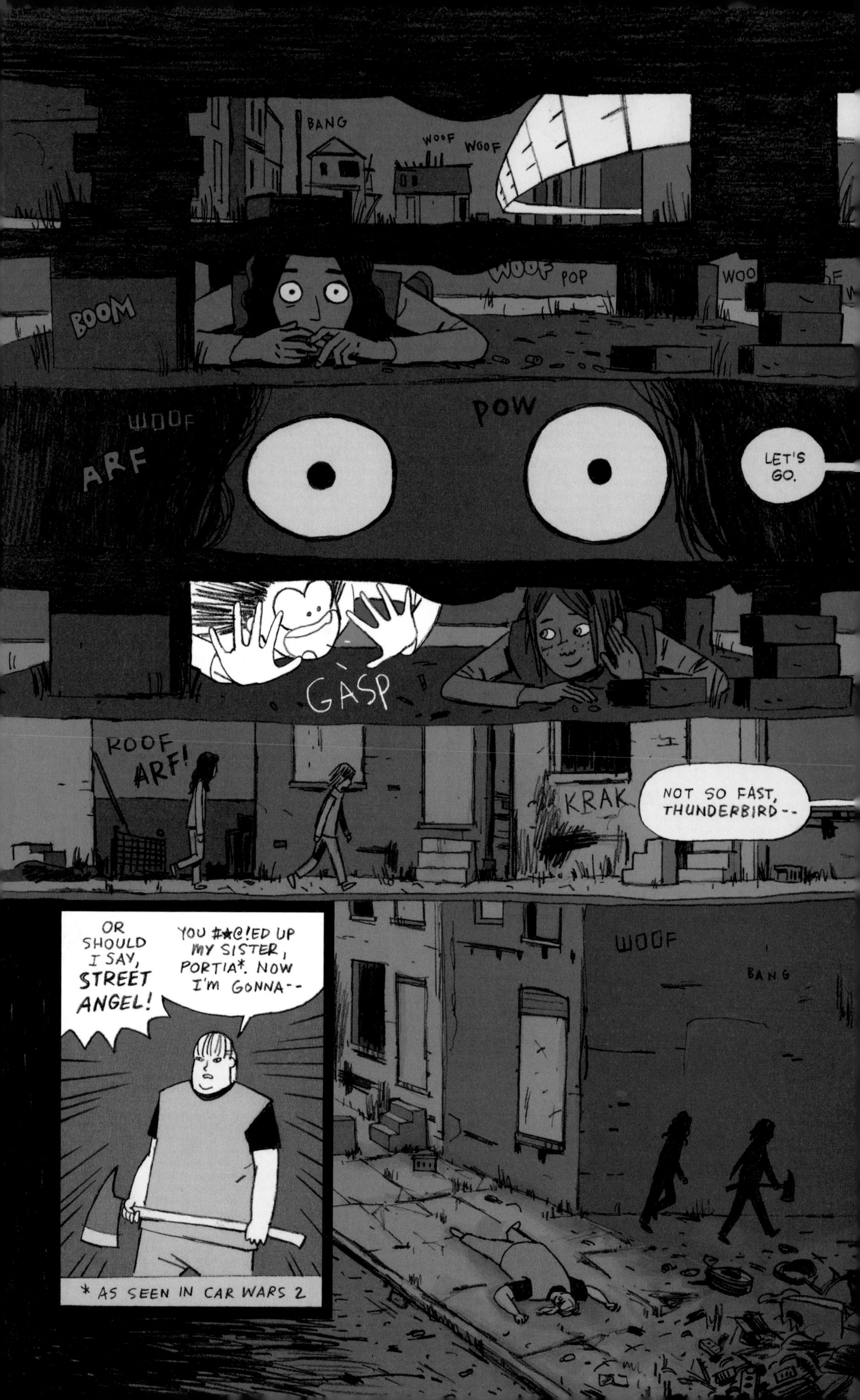

BANG
WOOF
WOOF
BOOM
WOOF
POP
WOO
WOOF
ARF
POW
LET'S GO.
GASP
ROOF
ARF!
KRAK
NOT SO FAST, THUNDERBIRD--
OR SHOULD I SAY, STREET ANGEL!
YOU #*@!ED UP MY SISTER, PORTIA*. NOW I'M GONNA--
* AS SEEN IN CAR WARS 2
WOOF
BANG

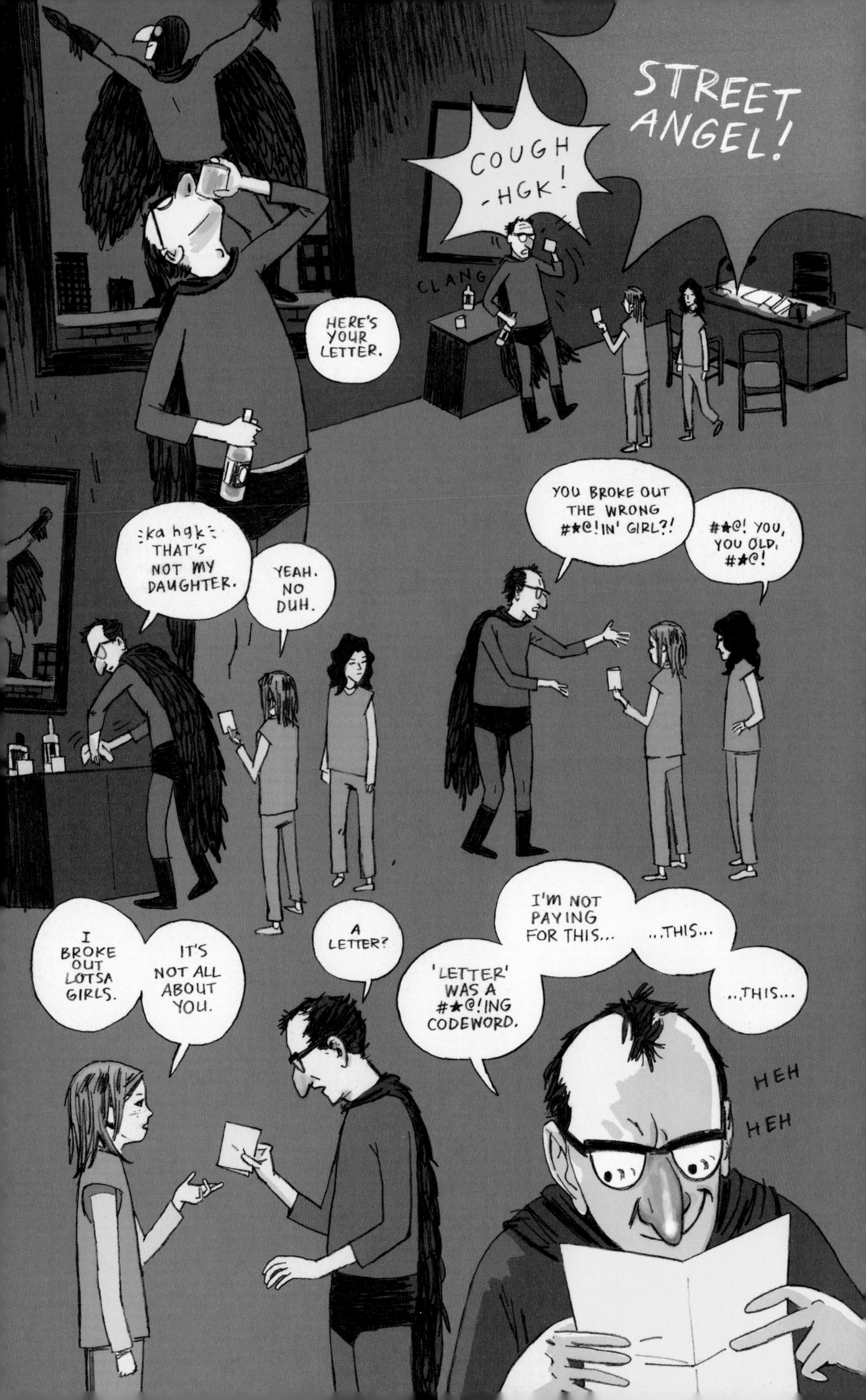
STREET ANGEL!
COUGH -HGK!
CLANG
HERE'S YOUR LETTER.
ka hgk THAT'S NOT MY DAUGHTER.
YEAH. NO DUH.
YOU BROKE OUT THE WRONG #★@!IN' GIRL?!
#★@! YOU, YOU OLD, #★@!
I BROKE OUT LOTSA GIRLS.
IT'S NOT ALL ABOUT YOU.
A LETTER?
'LETTER' WAS A #★@!ING CODEWORD.
I'M NOT PAYING FOR THIS...
...THIS...
...THIS...
HEH
HEH

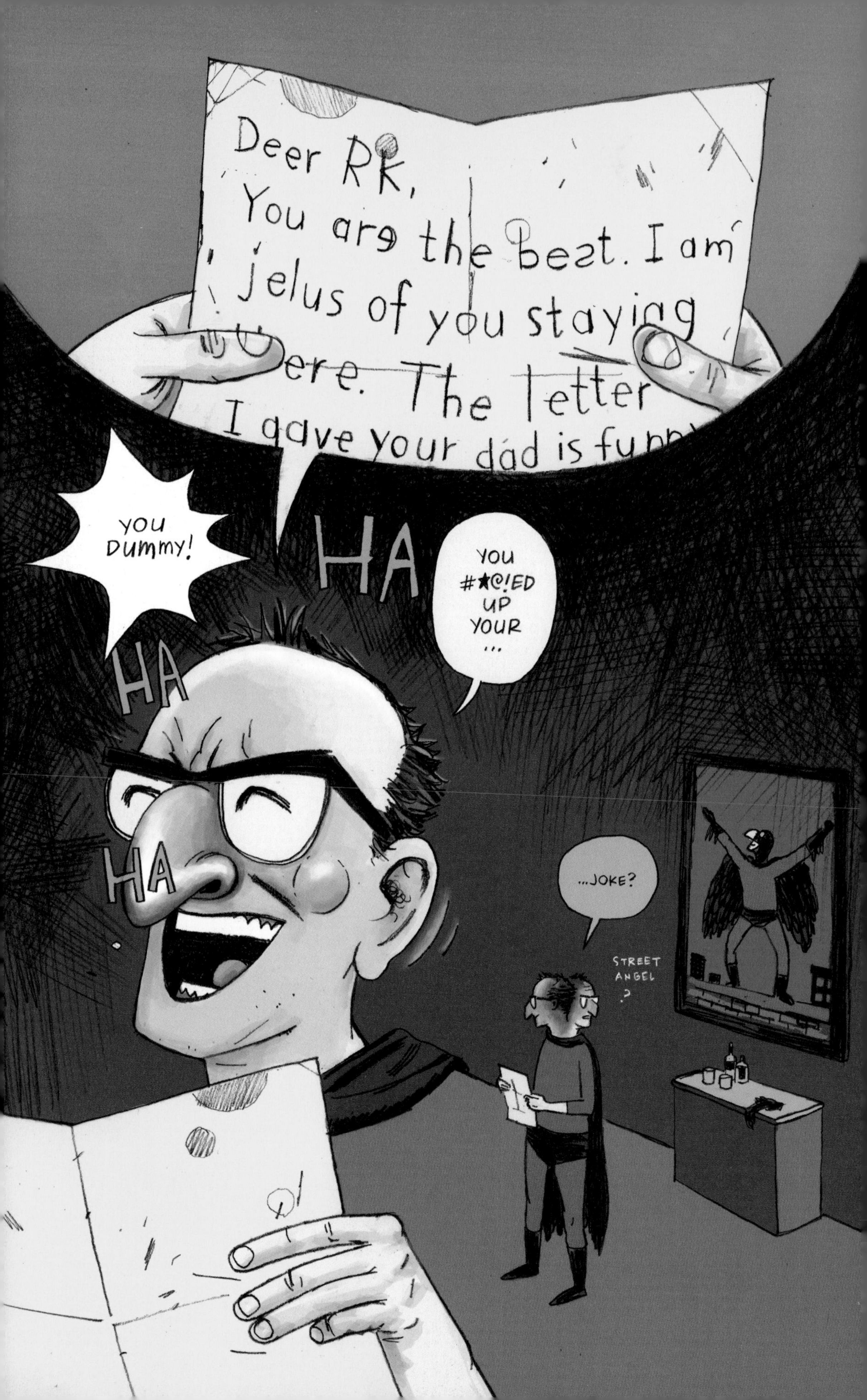

Deer RK,
You are the best. I am jelus of you staying
ere. The letter
I gave your dad is fu
YOU DUMMY!
HA
YOU #★@!ED UP YOUR ...
HA
HA
...JOKE?
STREET ANGEL ?

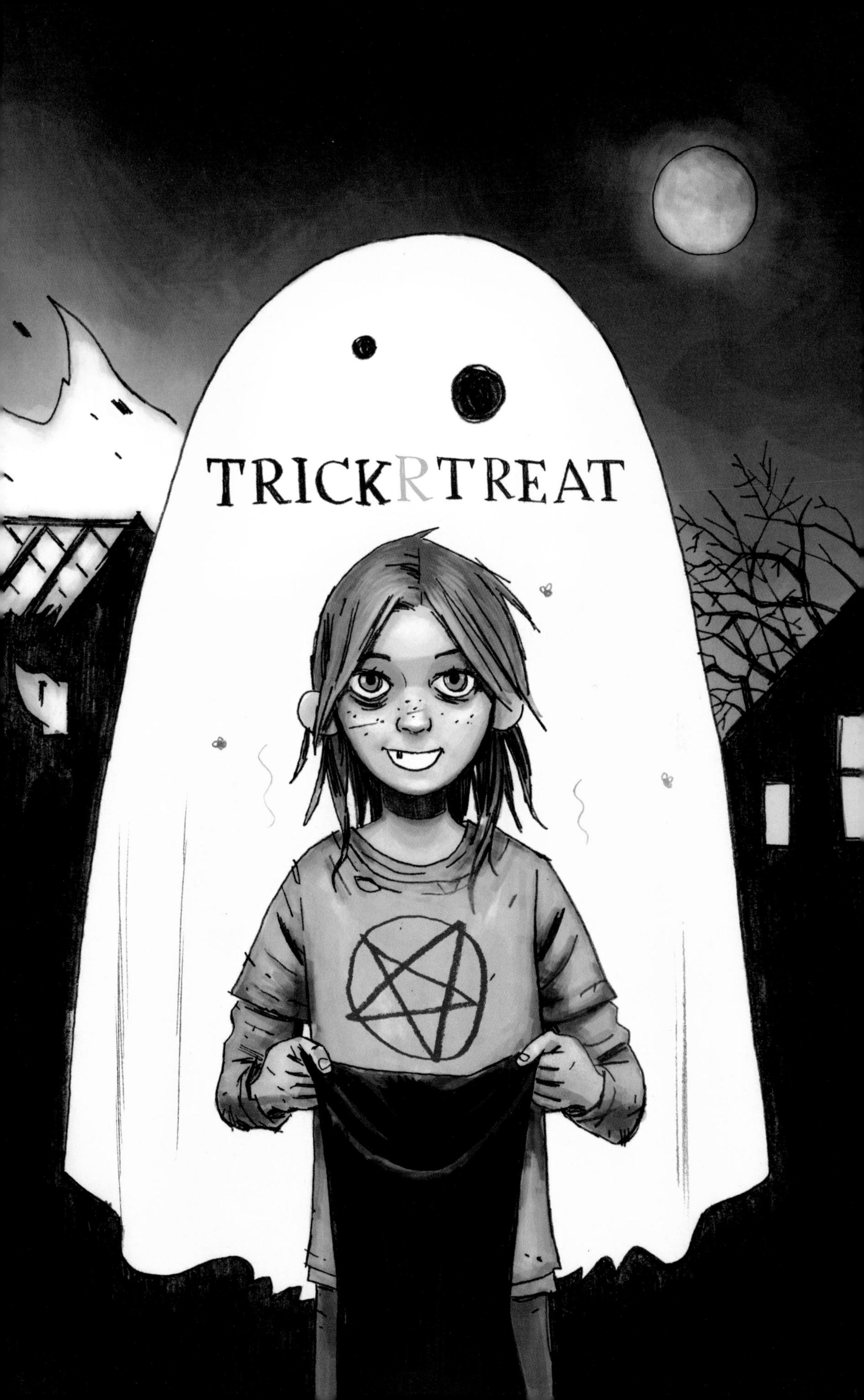
TRICKRTREAT

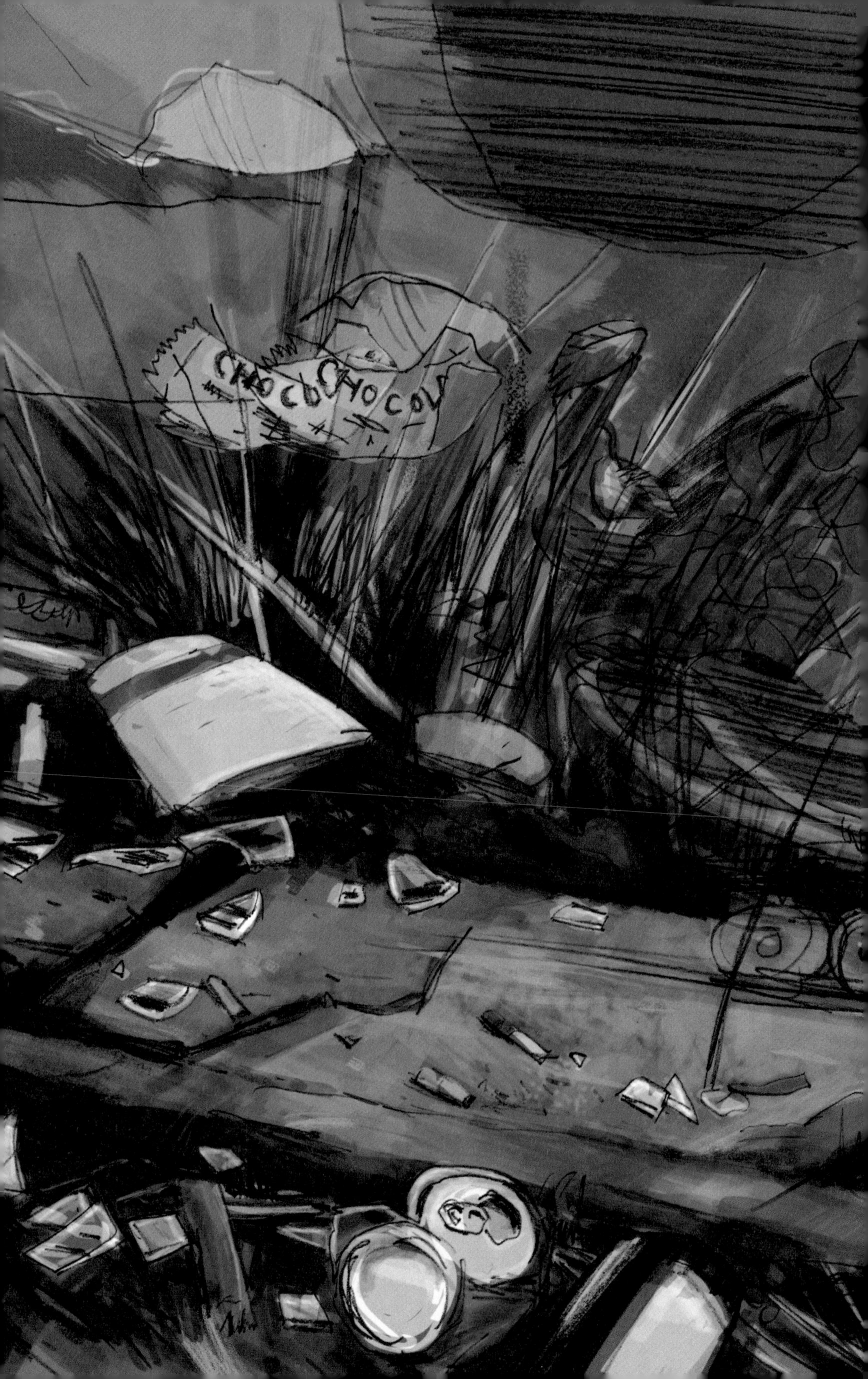
CHOCO
CHOCOLA

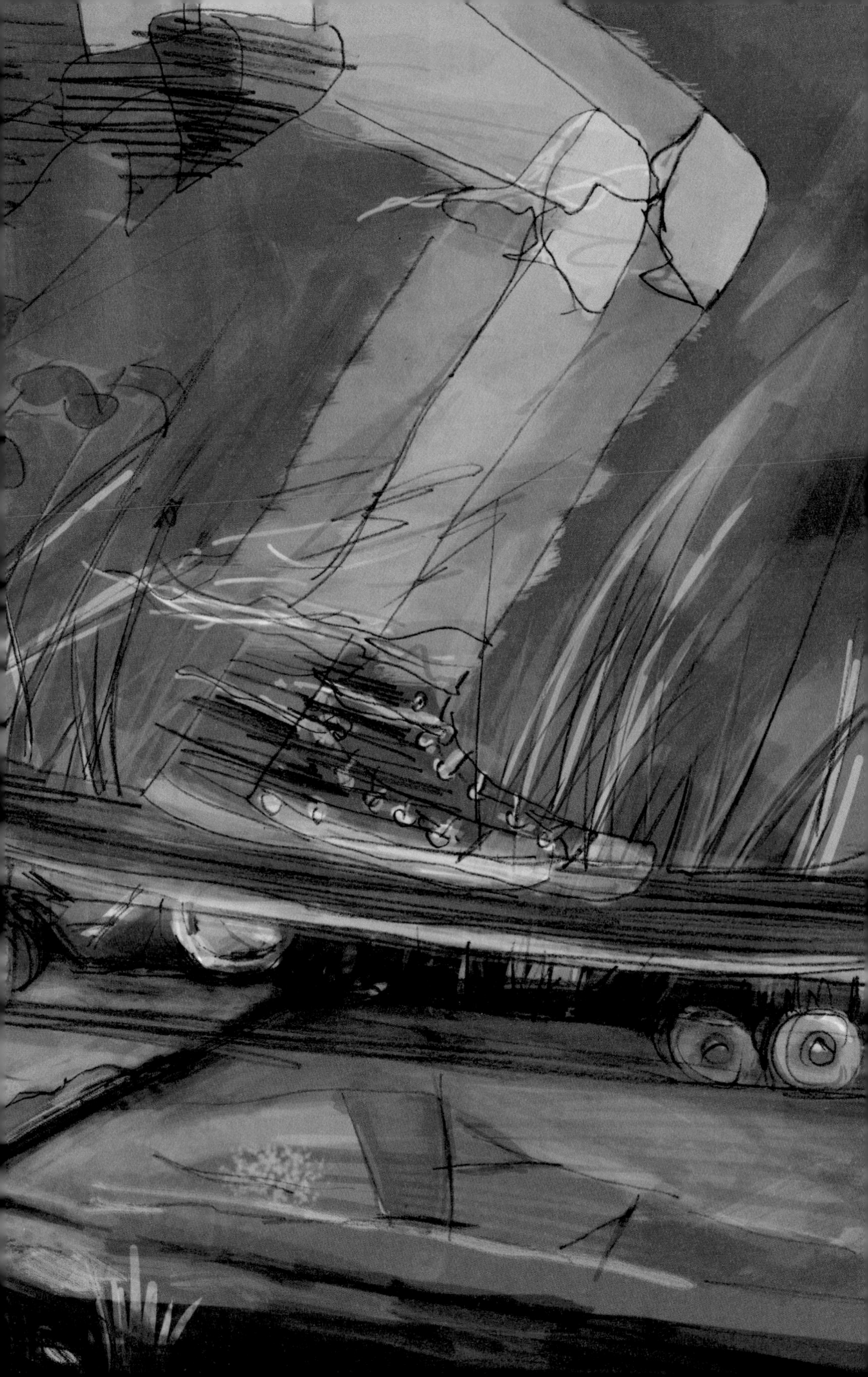

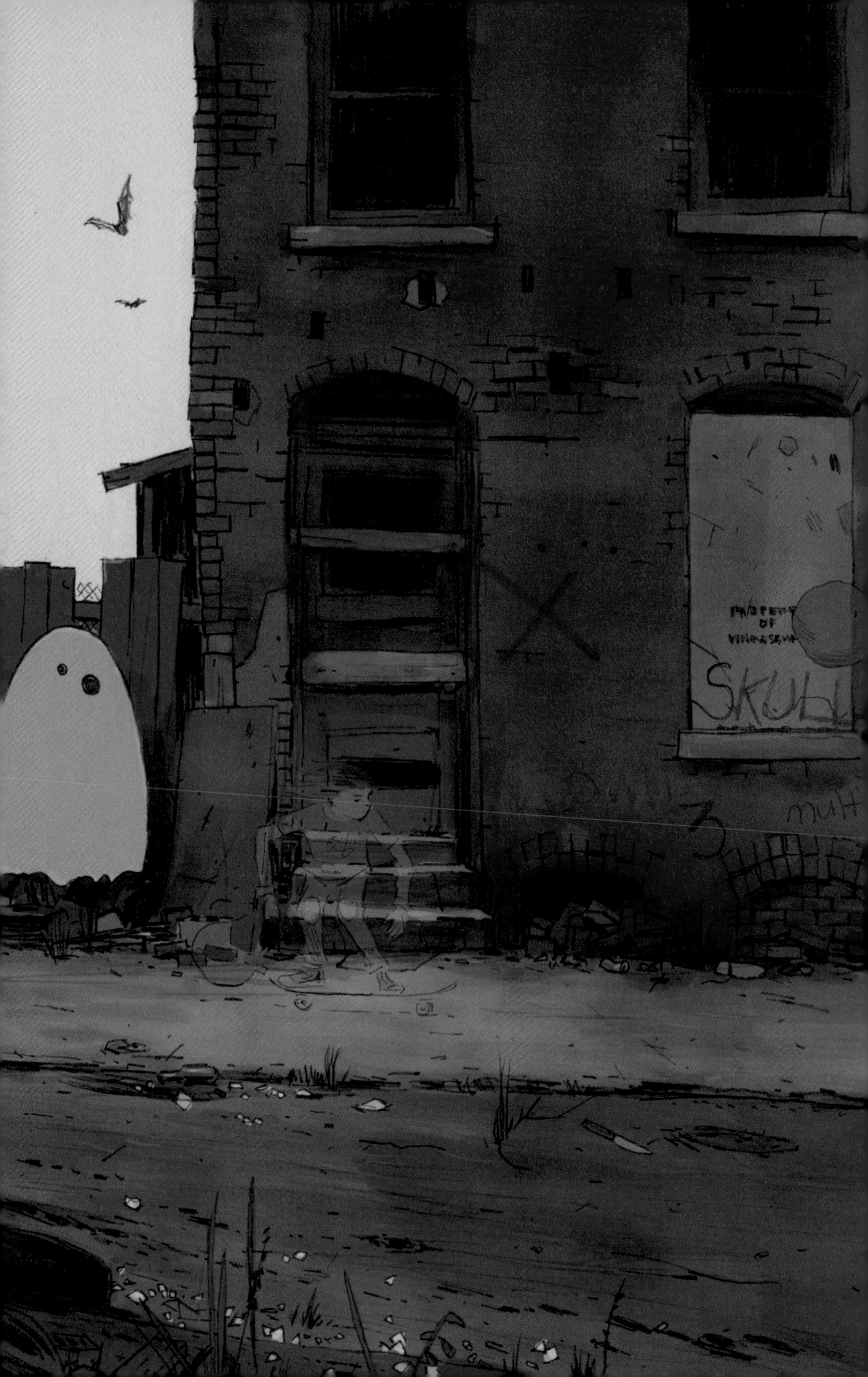
SKULL

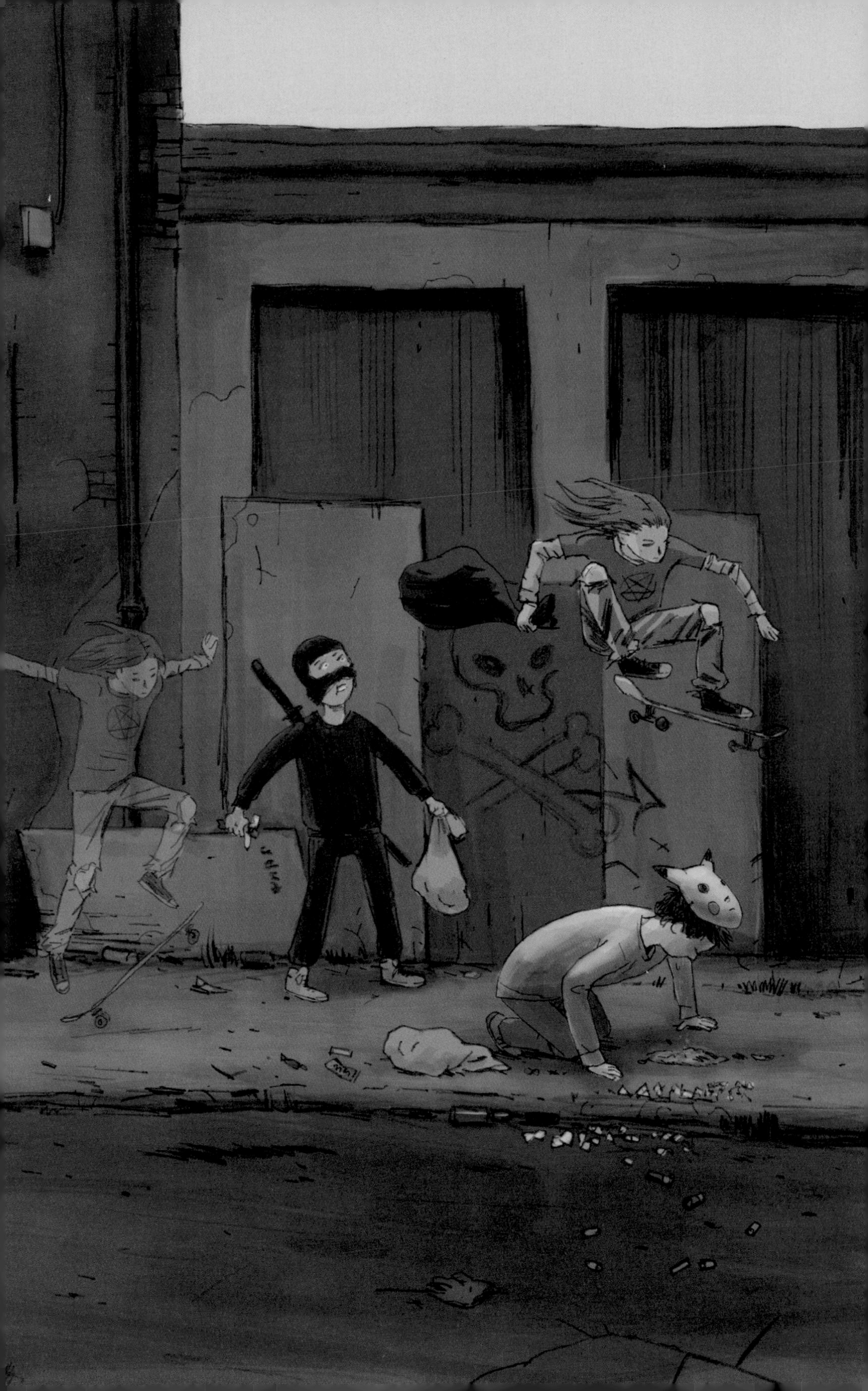

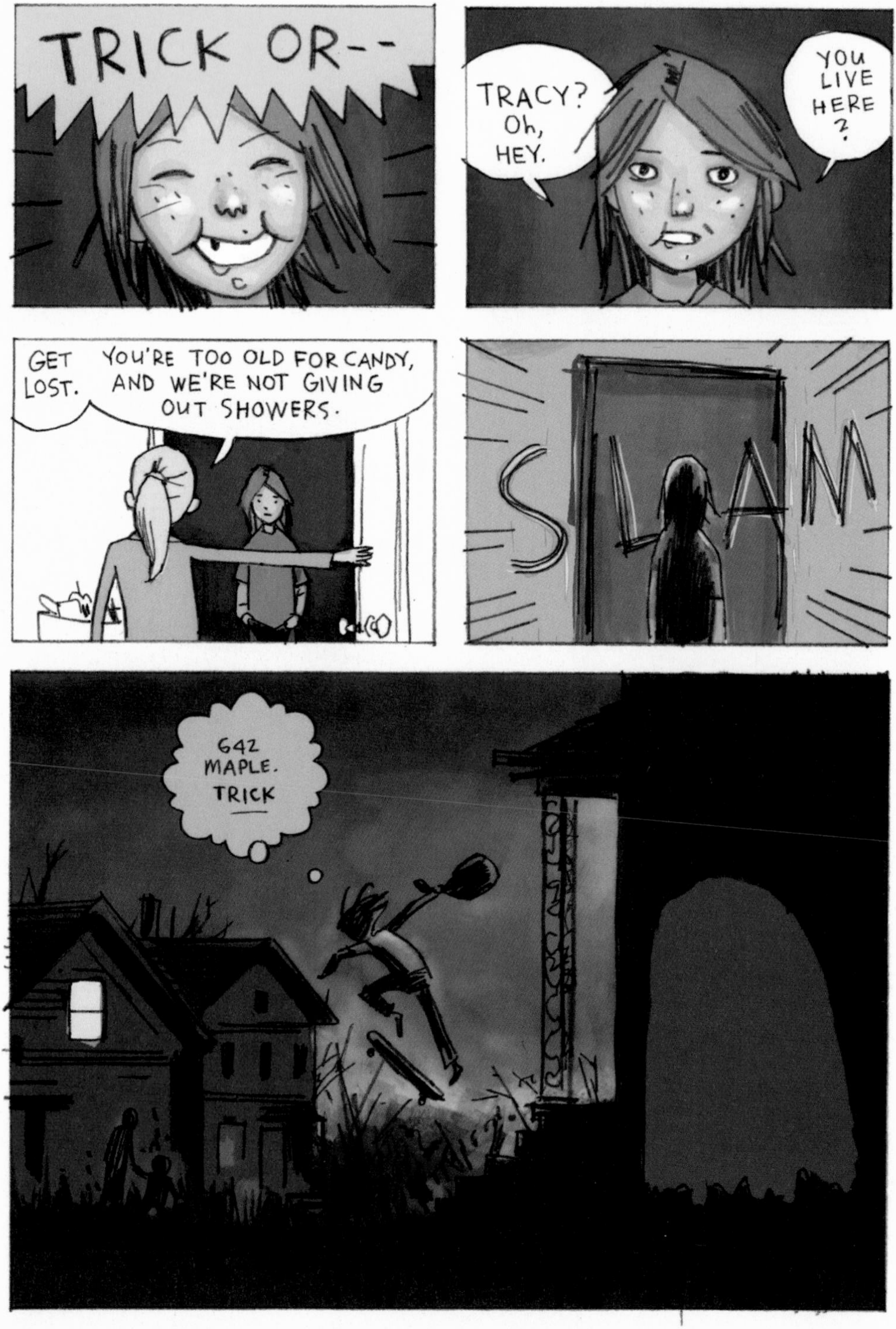
TRICK OR--
TRACY? Oh, HEY.
YOU LIVE HERE?
GET LOST.
YOU'RE TOO OLD FOR CANDY, AND WE'RE NOT GIVING OUT SHOWERS.
SLAM
642 MAPLE. TRICK

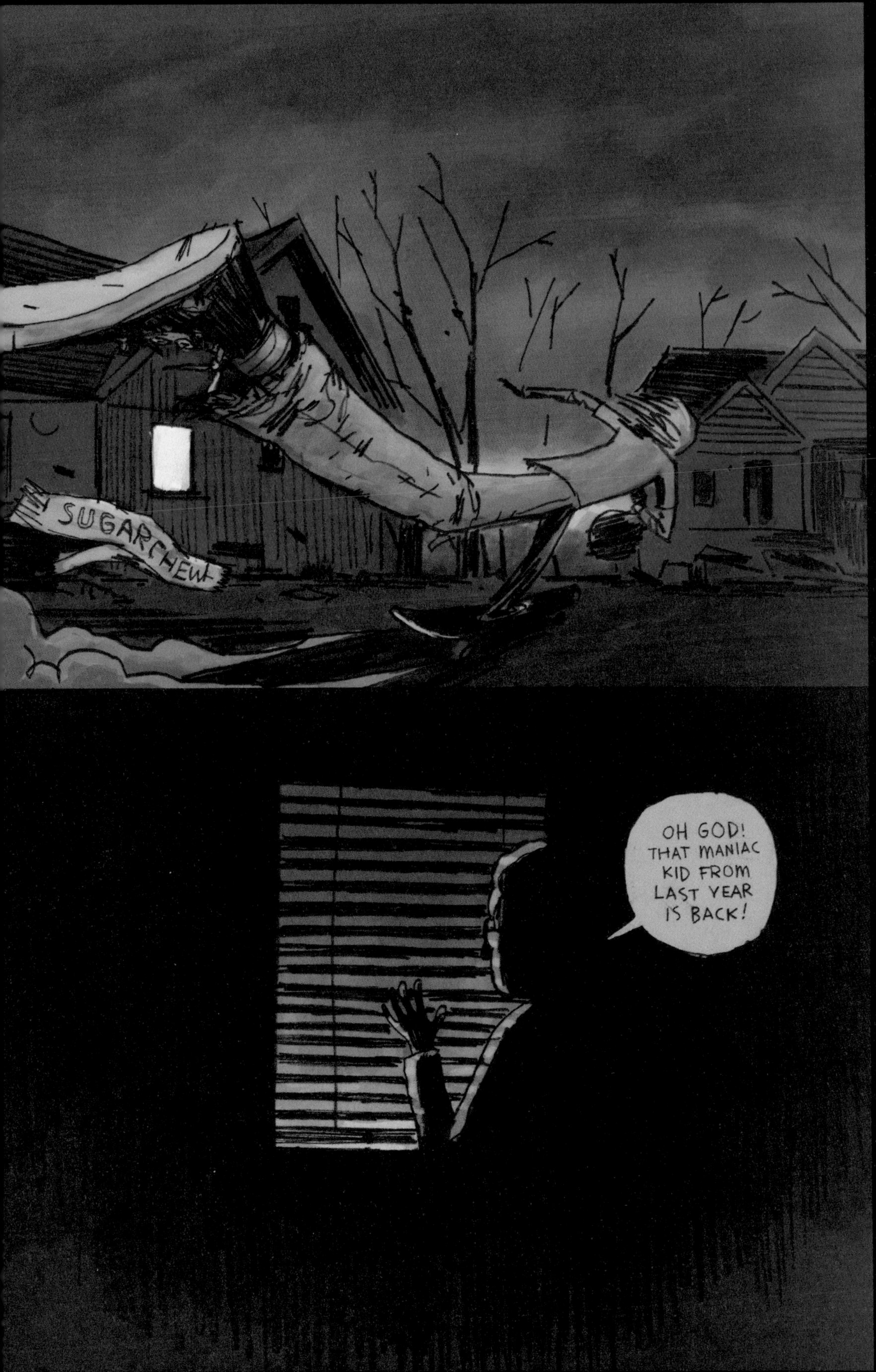
SUGARCHEW!
OH GOD! THAT MANIAC KID FROM LAST YEAR IS BACK!

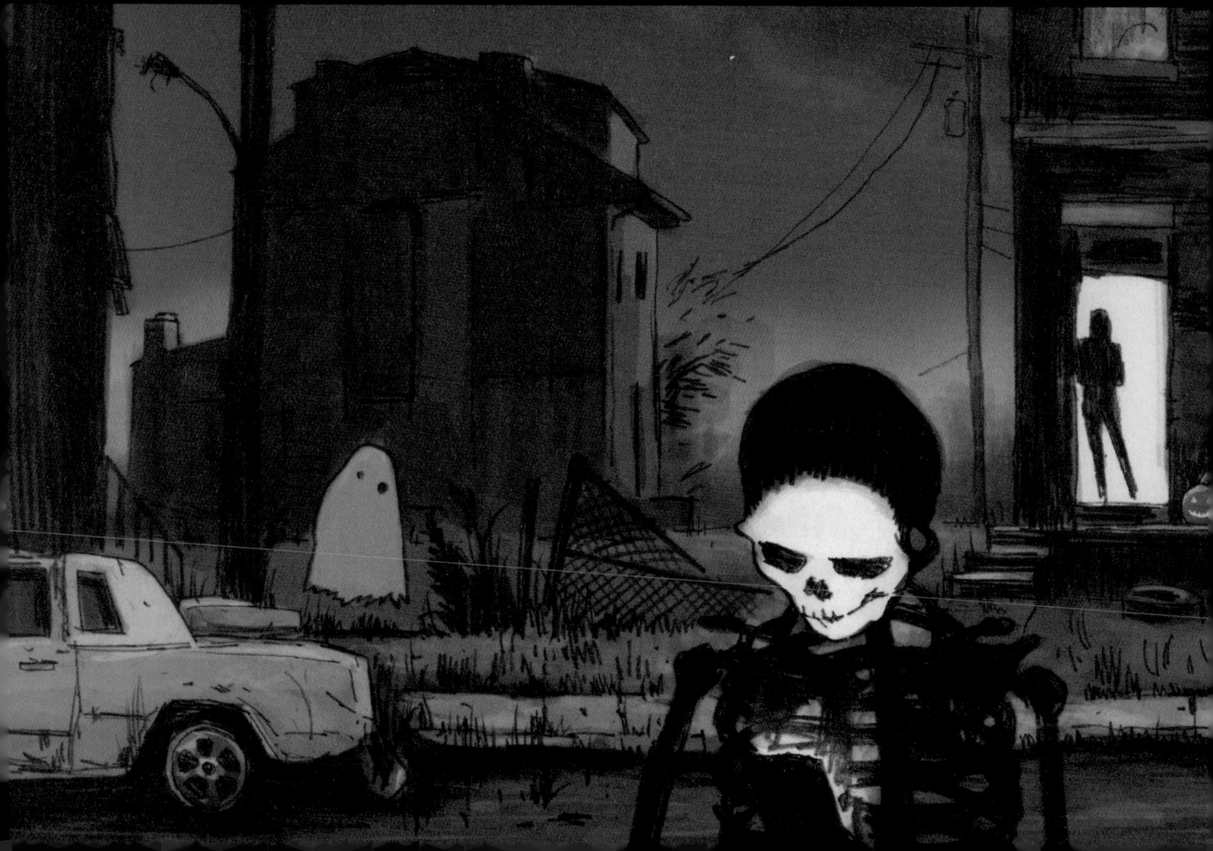

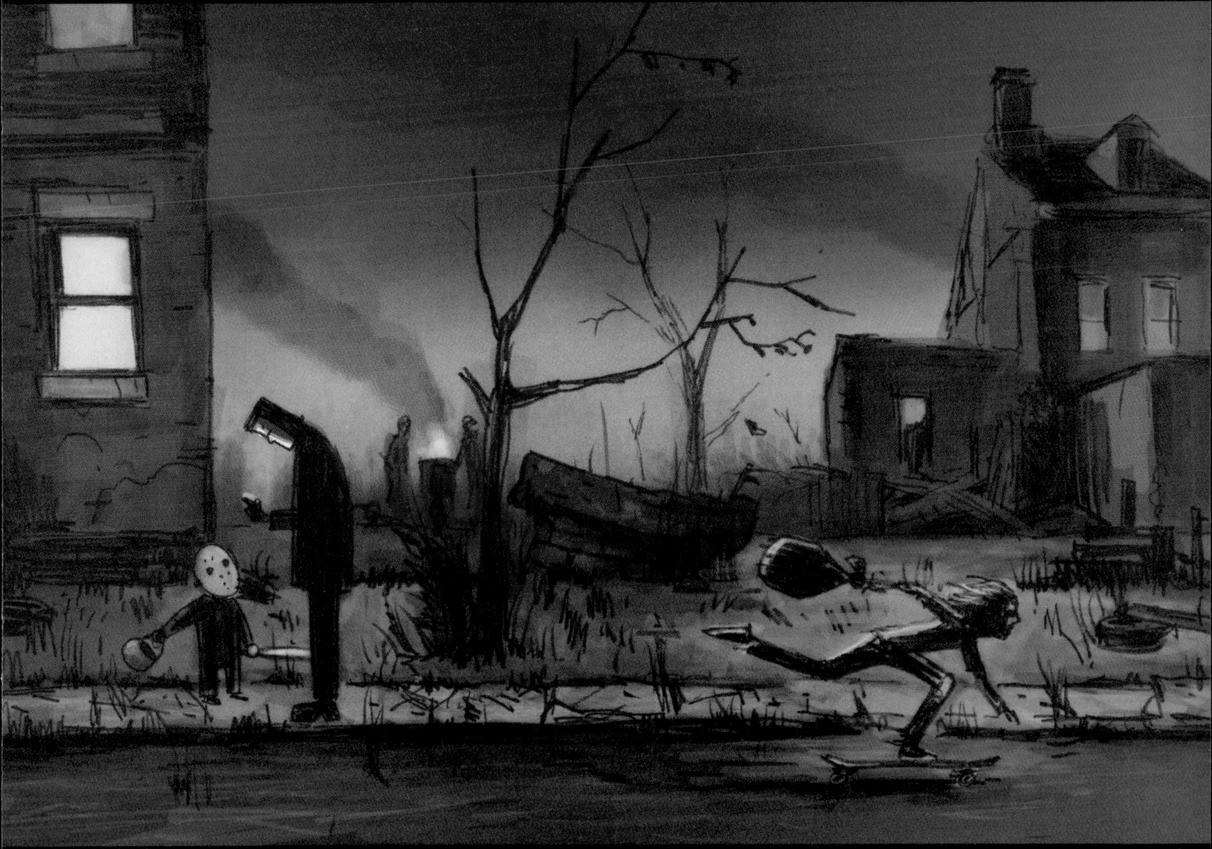

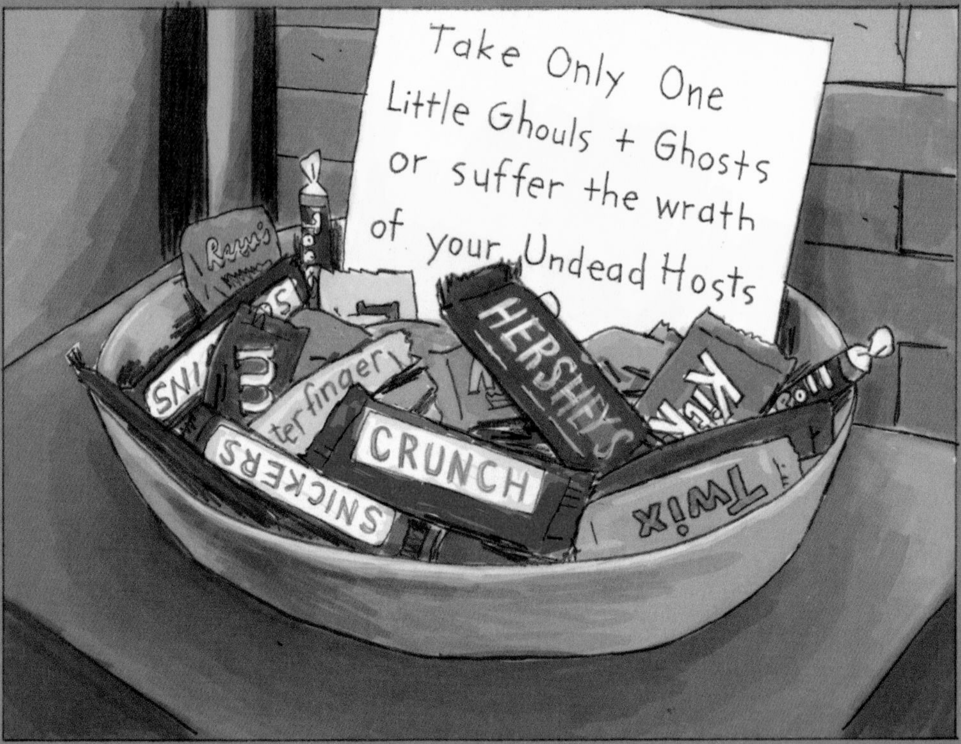
Take Only One
Little Ghouls + Ghosts
or suffer the wrath
of your Undead Hosts
HERSHEY'S
CRUNCH
SNICKERS
terfinger
SNI
Twix

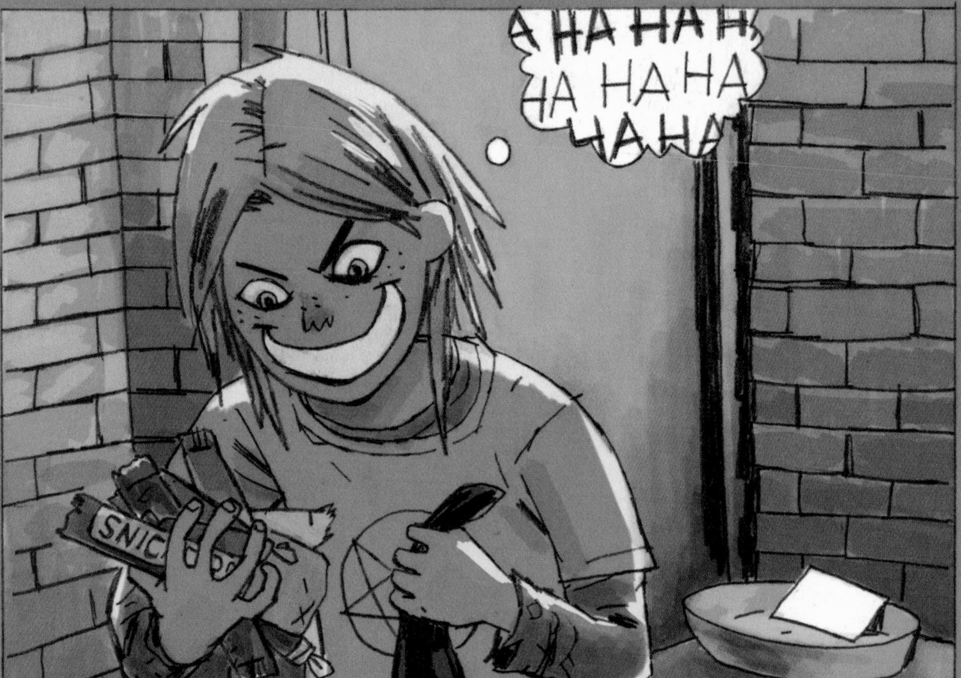
HA HA HA
HA HA HA
HA HA
SNIC

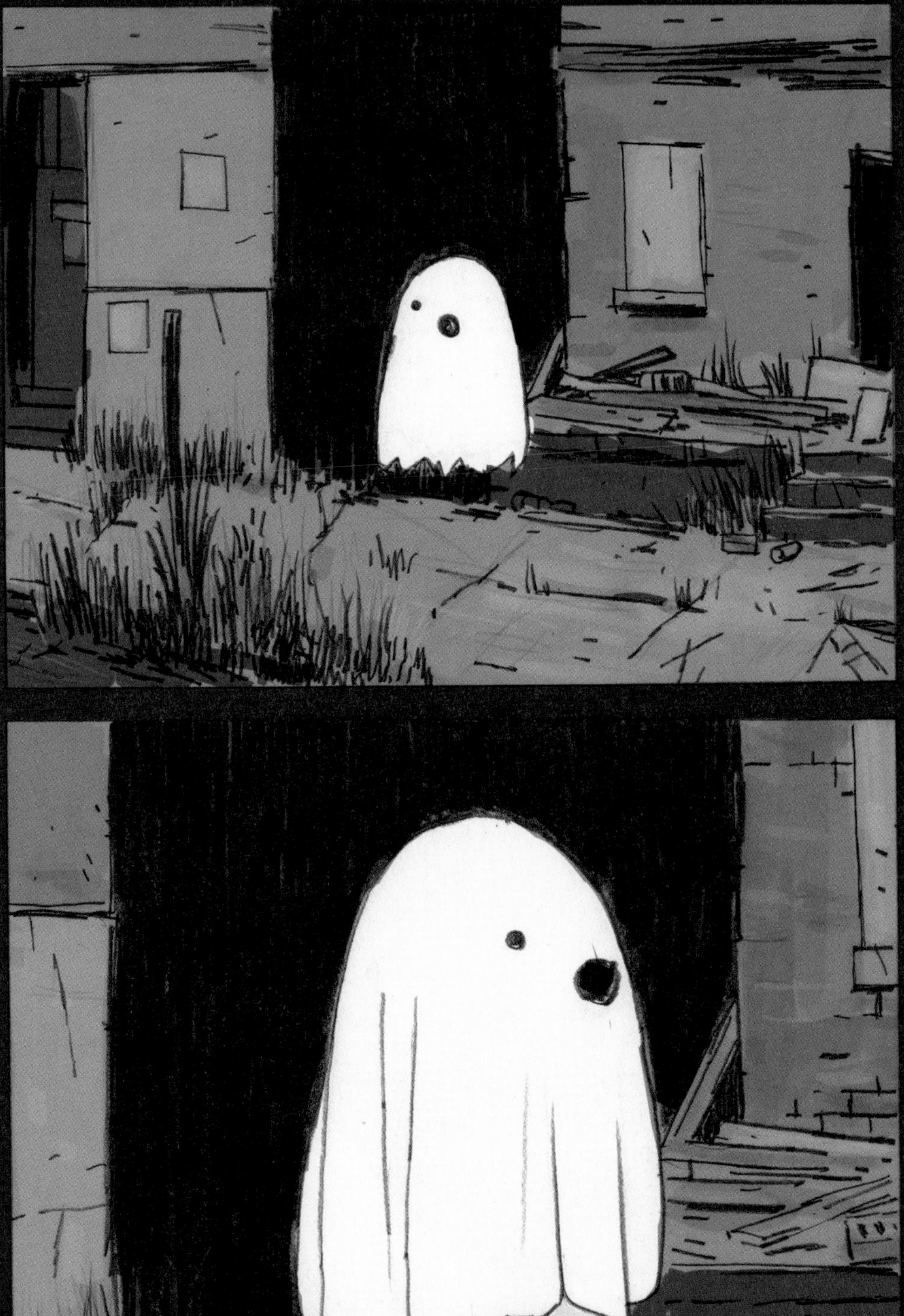

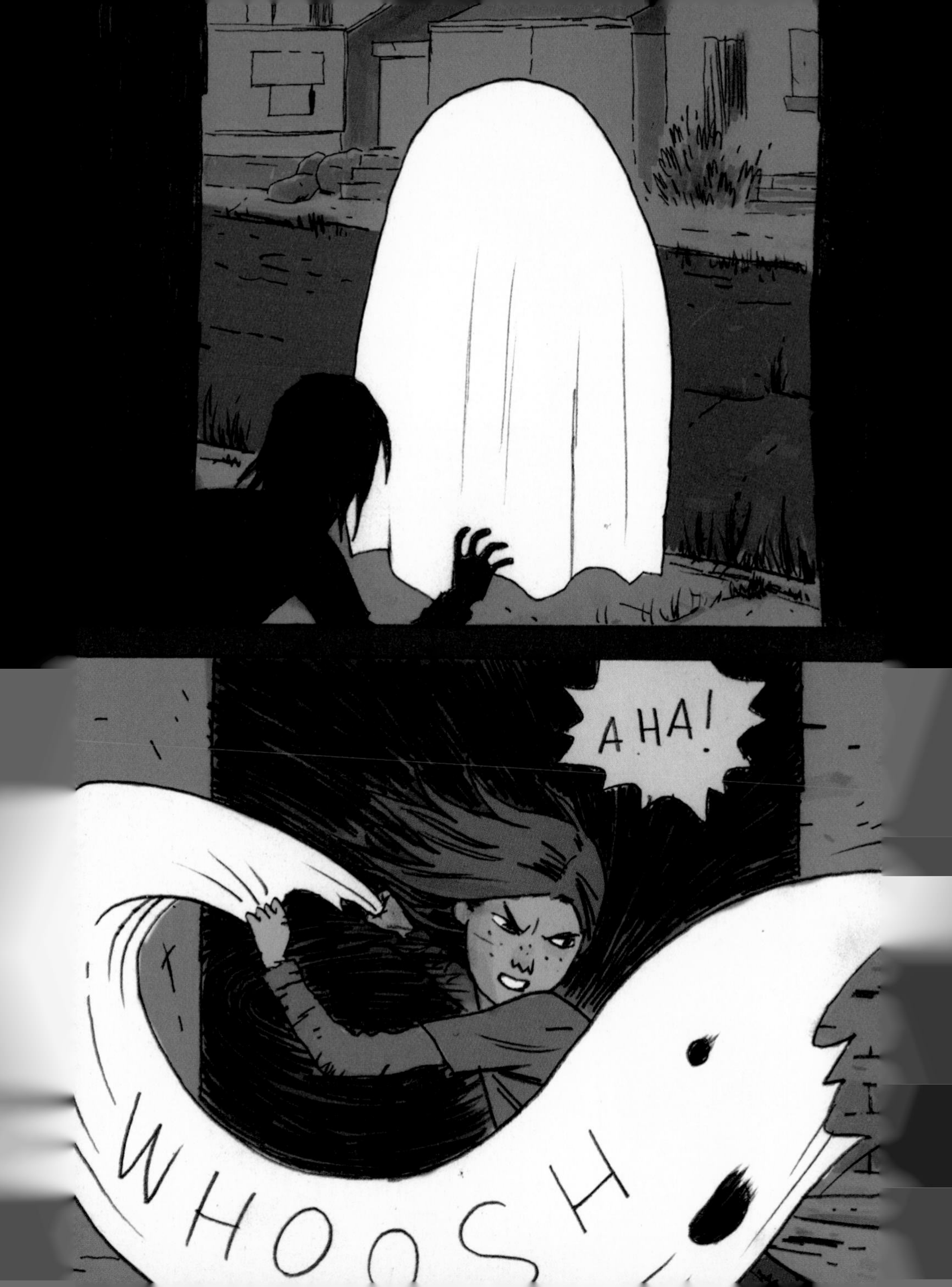
AHA!
WHOOSH

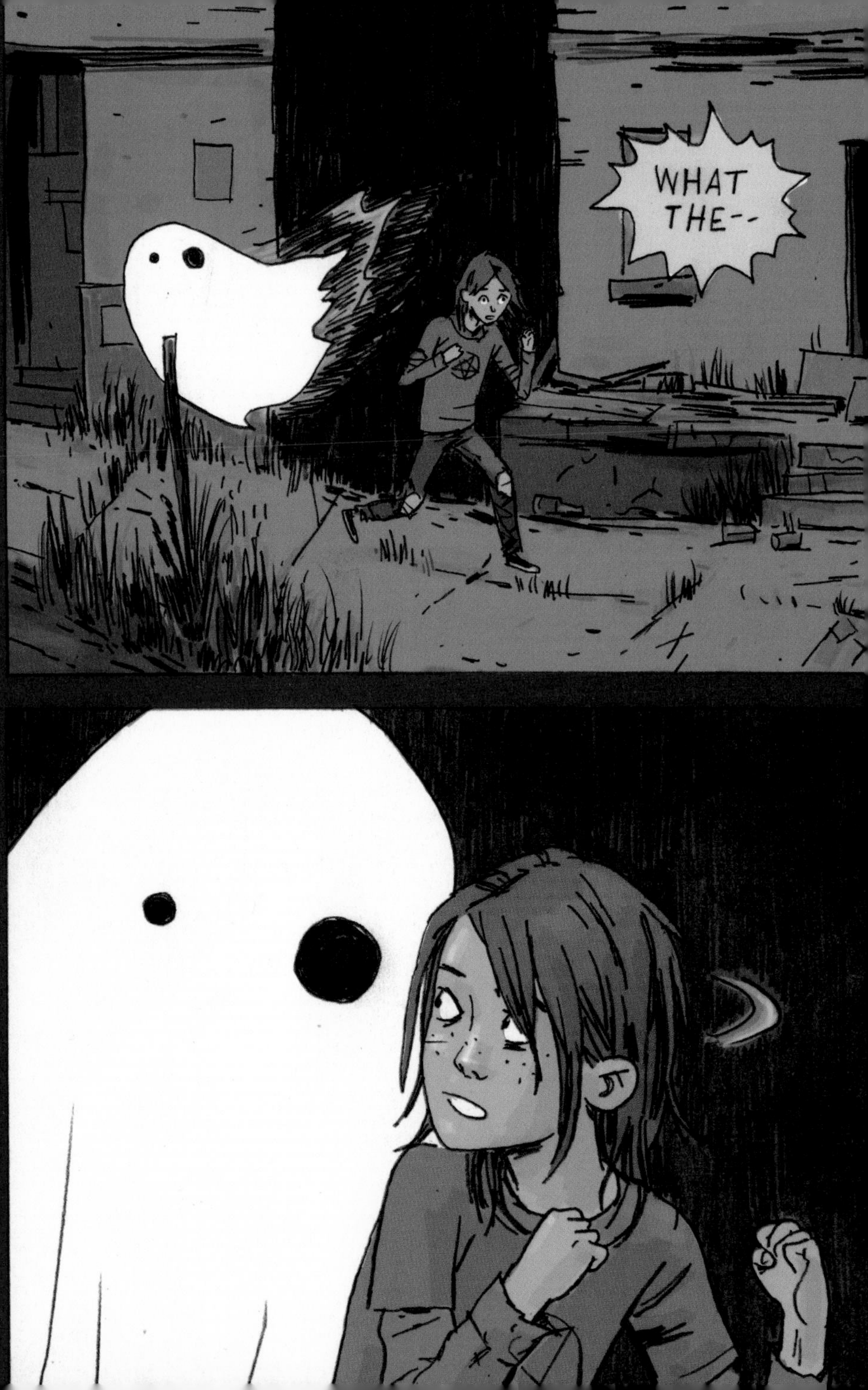
WHAT THE--

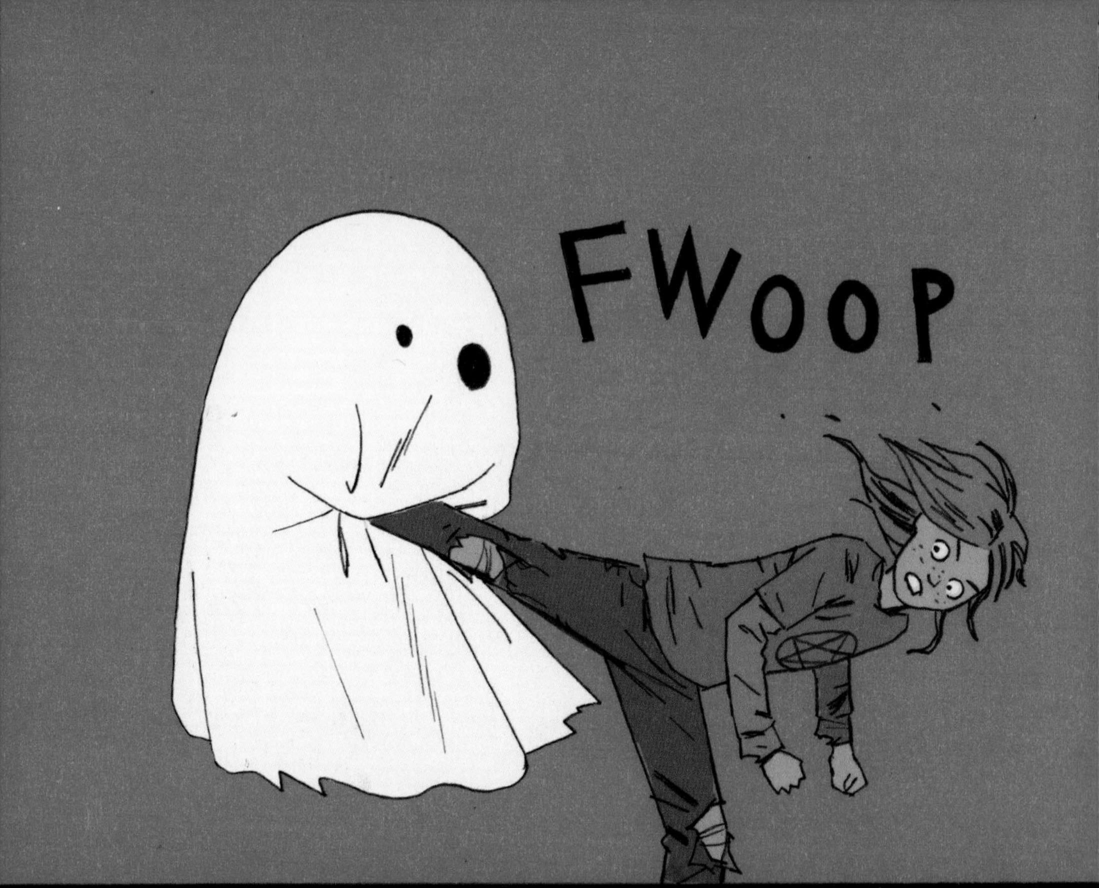
FWOOP

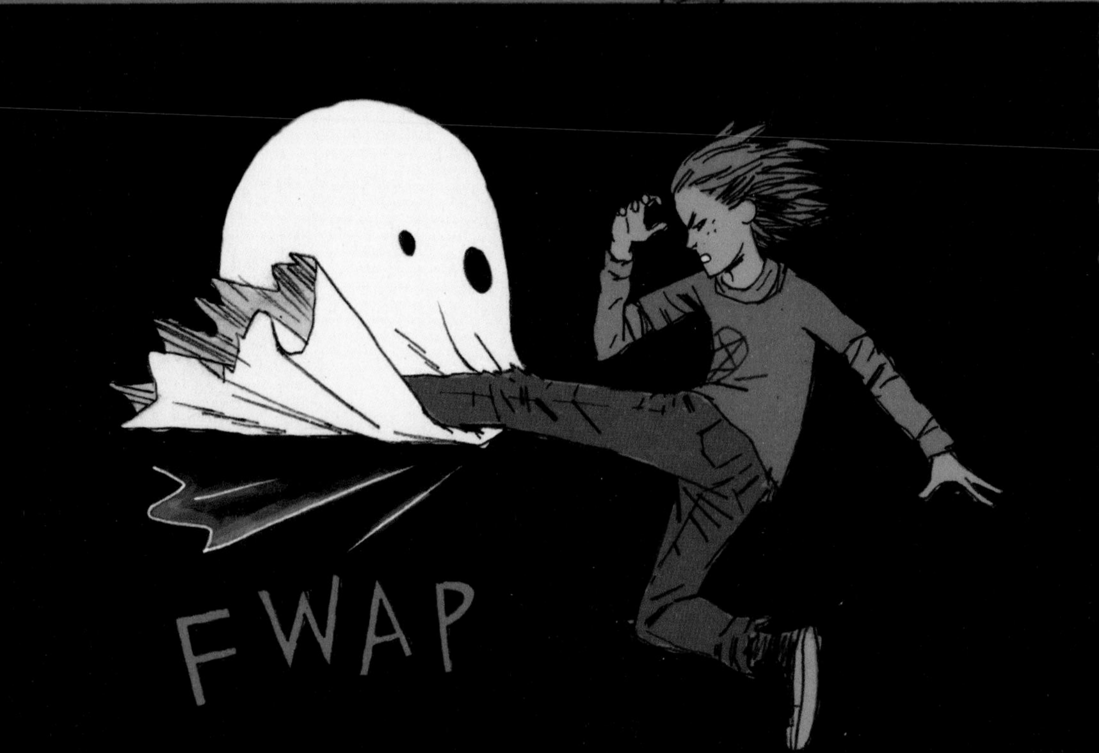
FWAP

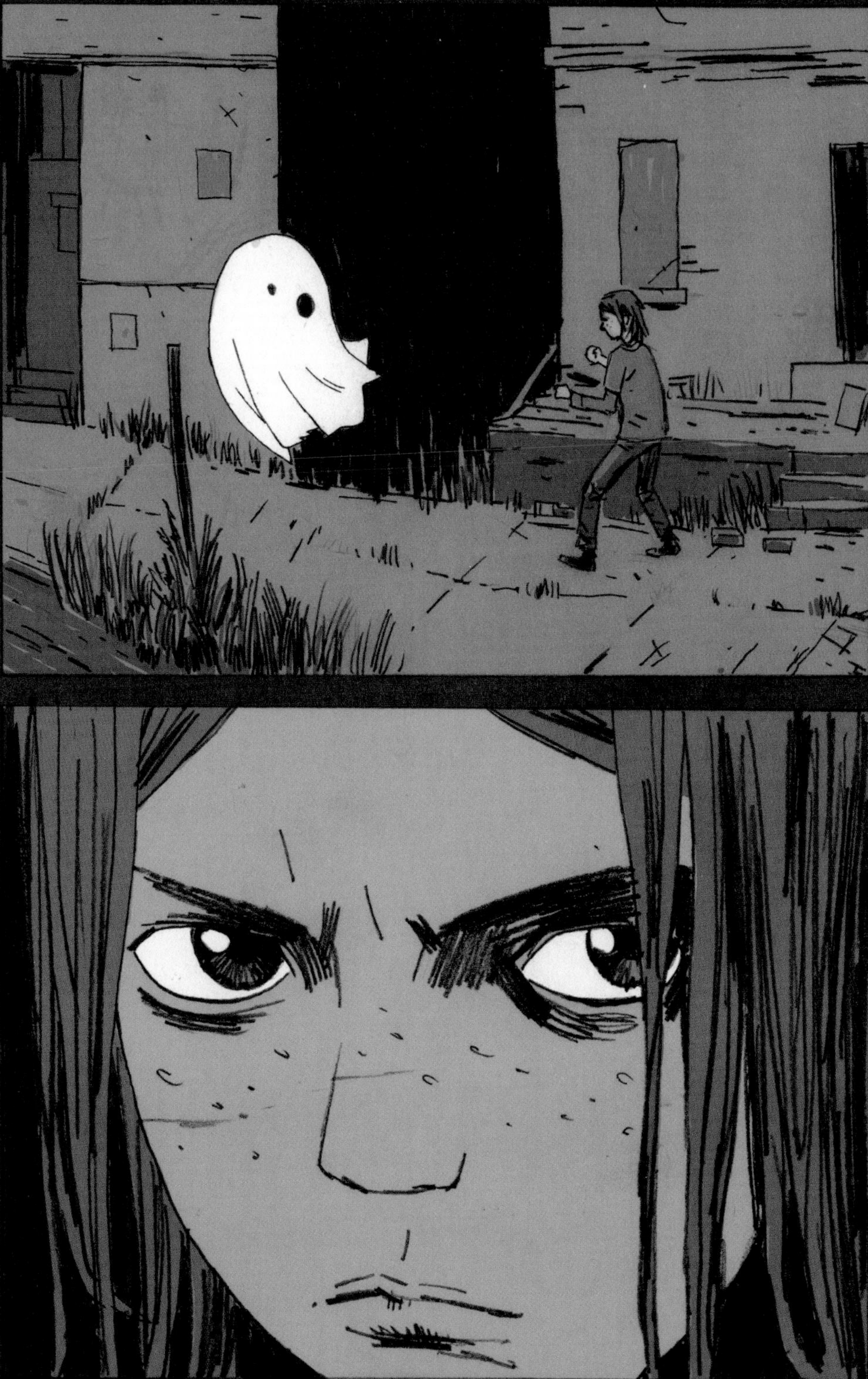

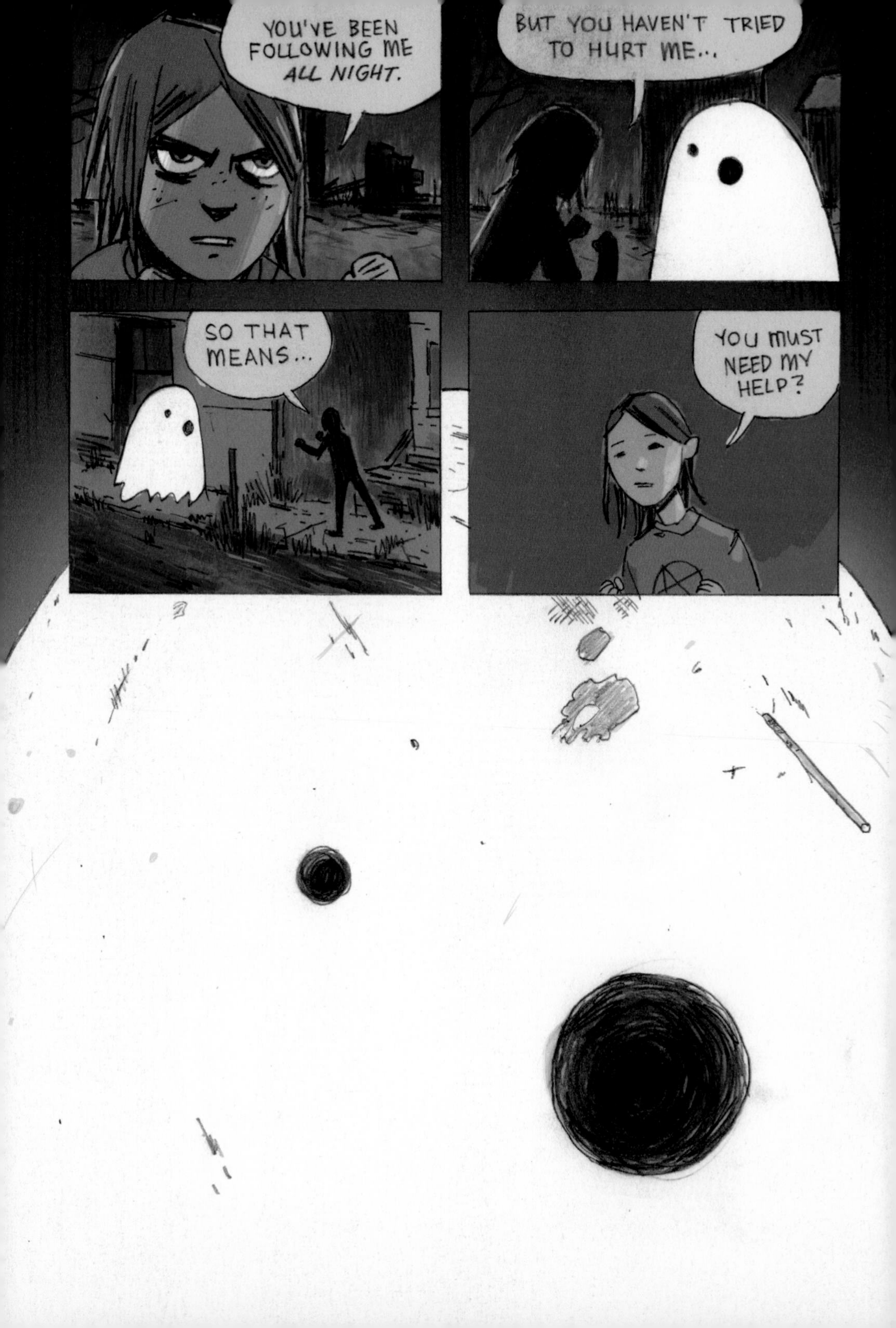
YOU'VE BEEN FOLLOWING ME ALL NIGHT.
BUT YOU HAVEN'T TRIED TO HURT ME...
SO THAT MEANS...
YOU MUST NEED MY HELP?

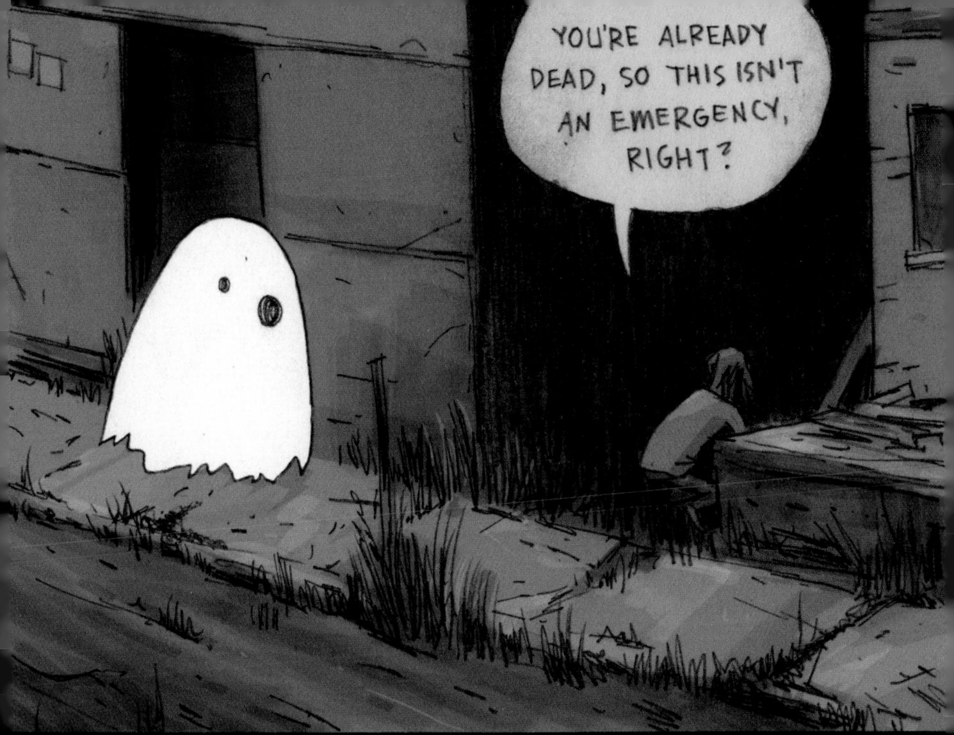
YOU'RE ALREADY DEAD, SO THIS ISN'T AN EMERGENCY, RIGHT?

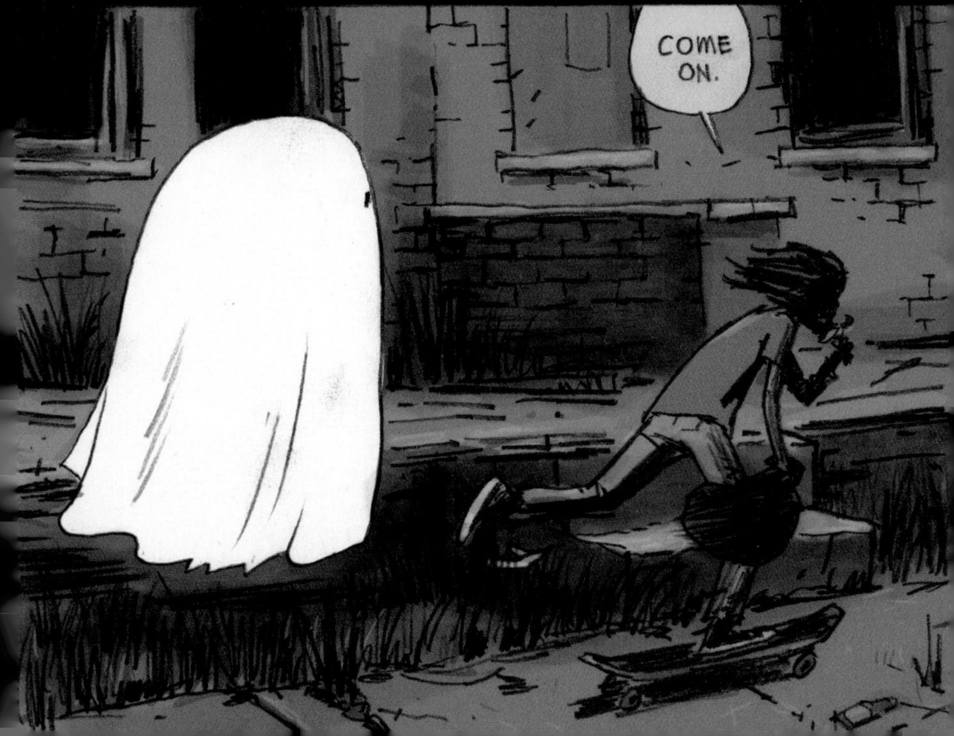
COME ON.

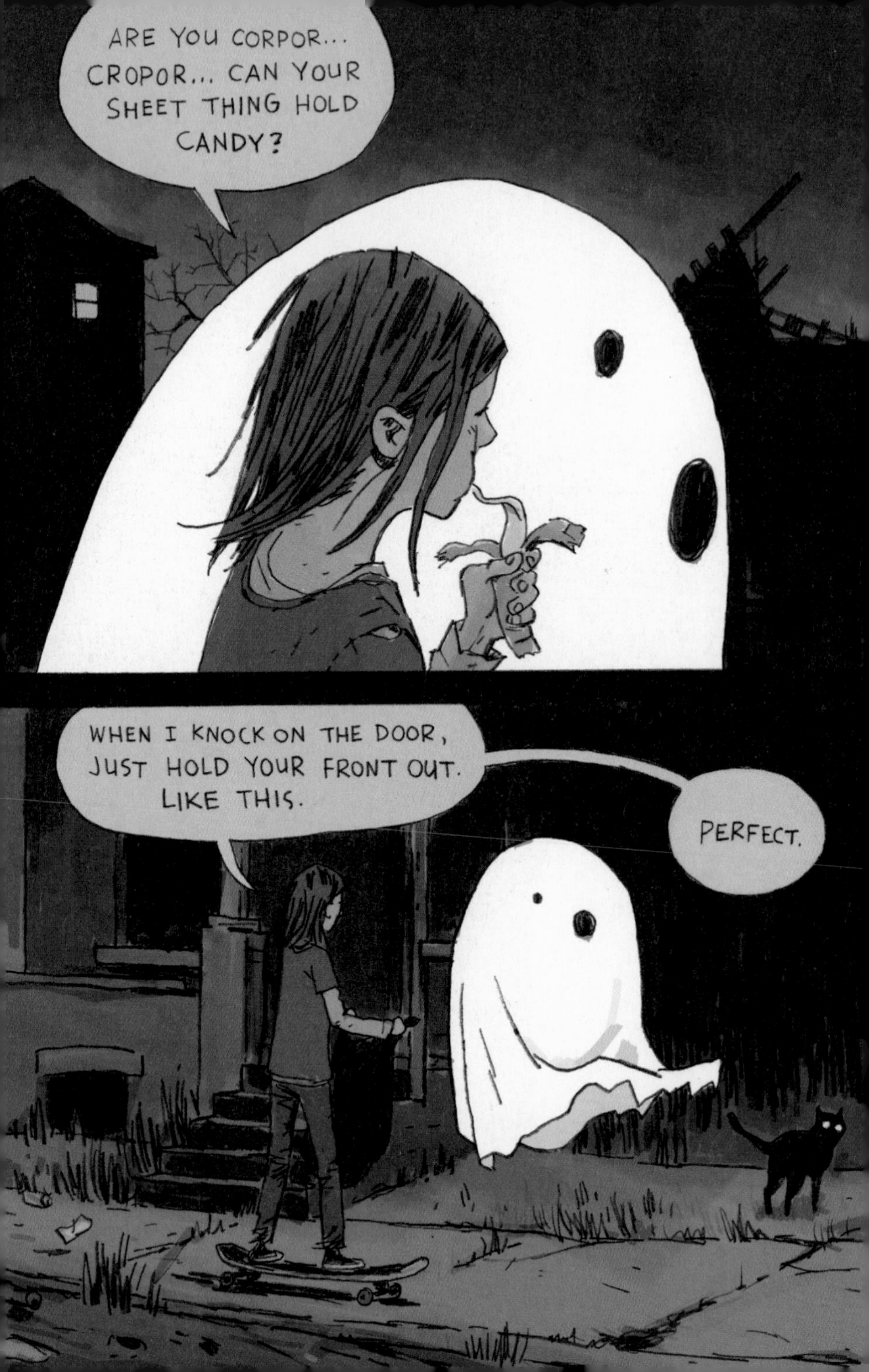
ARE YOU CORPOR... CROPOR... CAN YOUR SHEET THING HOLD CANDY?
WHEN I KNOCK ON THE DOOR, JUST HOLD YOUR FRONT OUT. LIKE THIS.
PERFECT.

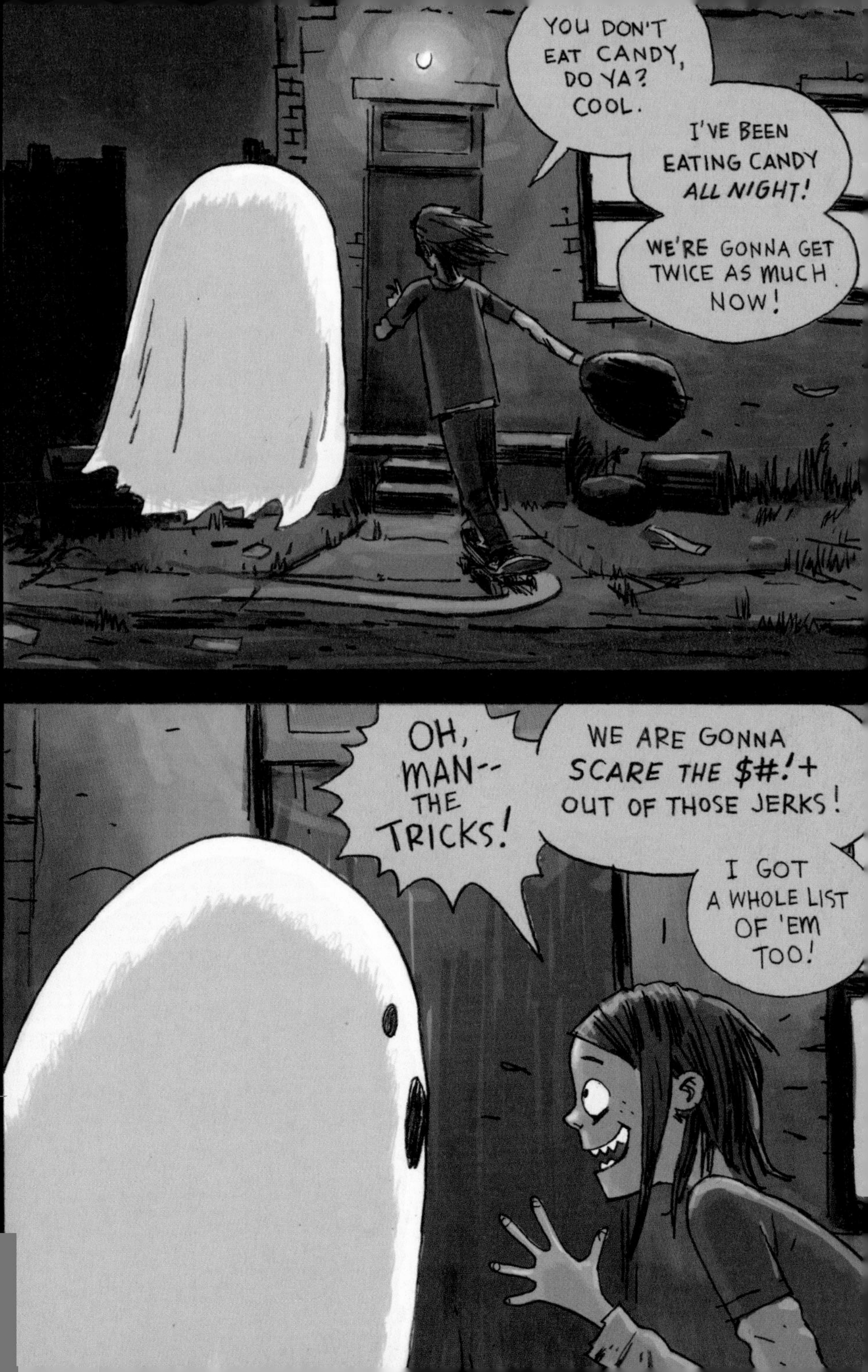
YOU DON'T EAT CANDY, DO YA? COOL.
I'VE BEEN EATING CANDY ALL NIGHT!
WE'RE GONNA GET TWICE AS MUCH NOW!
OH, MAN-- THE TRICKS!
WE ARE GONNA SCARE THE $#!+ OUT OF THOSE JERKS!
I GOT A WHOLE LIST OF 'EM TOO!

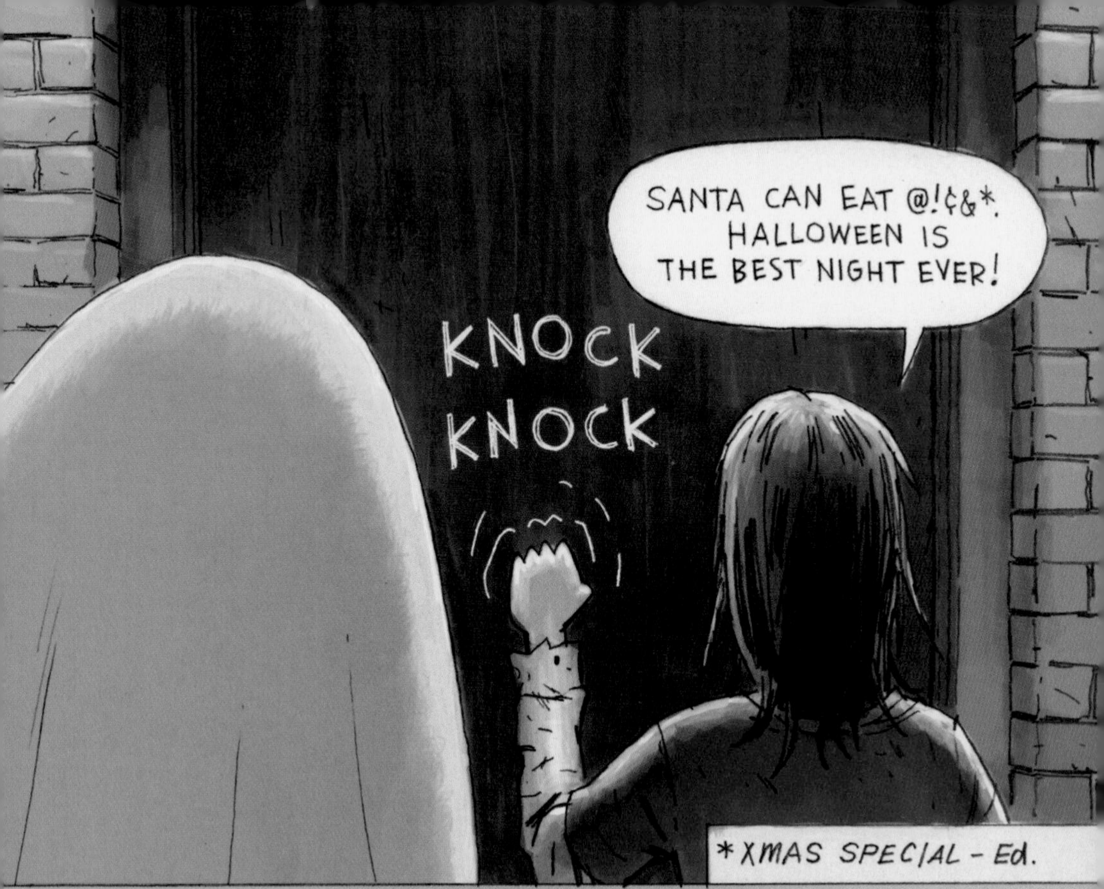
SANTA CAN EAT @!¢&*. HALLOWEEN IS THE BEST NIGHT EVER!
KNOCK KNOCK
*XMAS SPECIAL - Ed.

The End

JIM RUGG

Jim Rugg is an Eisner and Ignatz award WINNING **comic book** ARTIST, **illustrator**, DESIGNER, and cat dad.

His **books** INCLUDE *Street Angel*, *Afrodisiac*, the PLAIN Janes, NOTEBOOK DRAWINGS, RAMBO 3.5, and SUPERMAG. His YouTube channel — cartoonist KAYFABE WILL MAKE YOU ♥♡♥ COMBCS even MORE!!!

⊙ 🐦 @jimruggart
youtube.com/c/cartoonistkayfabe
jimrugg.com

BRIAN MARUCA

I hate doing a biography.
Every time Jim asks, the first thing he gets back is some kind of swear.
WHY DON'T I JUST HAVE A SET BLURB?
BECAUSE I LIKE TO COMPLAIN.
ALSO - anything I've worked on I've worked on through Jim and I assume he's got it covered in his bio.

So HERE'S A THING ABOUT ME THAT YOU WOULDN'T GET IN SOME CRUSTY 'OL BIO BLURB: I LIKE TO THINK THAT IF I WORRY ABOUT SOMETHING, IT WON'T HAPPEN (THAT SUPER VOLCANO UNDER YELLOWSTONE EXPLODING? YOU DON'T HAVE TO WORRY, BECAUSE I'M WORRYING ABOUT IT). **BUT**, AS I GET OLDER, I REALIZE THAT I'M FORGETTING ABOUT THINGS THAT USED TO WORRY ME AND NOW I HAVE TO WONDER IF SIMPLY WORRYING ABOUT "THE THINGS I'VE FORGOTTEN I WAS WORRYING ABOUT" GIVES ME ENOUGH WORRY - COVER. I'M NOT SAYING IF IT WORKS OR NOT, I'M JUST SAYING WE'RE ALL STILL HERE. SO IF VENICE WANTS TO IMPORT/EMPLOY ME TO WORRY ABOUT THEIR RISING WATER PROBLEMS, I'LL CONSIDER IT.

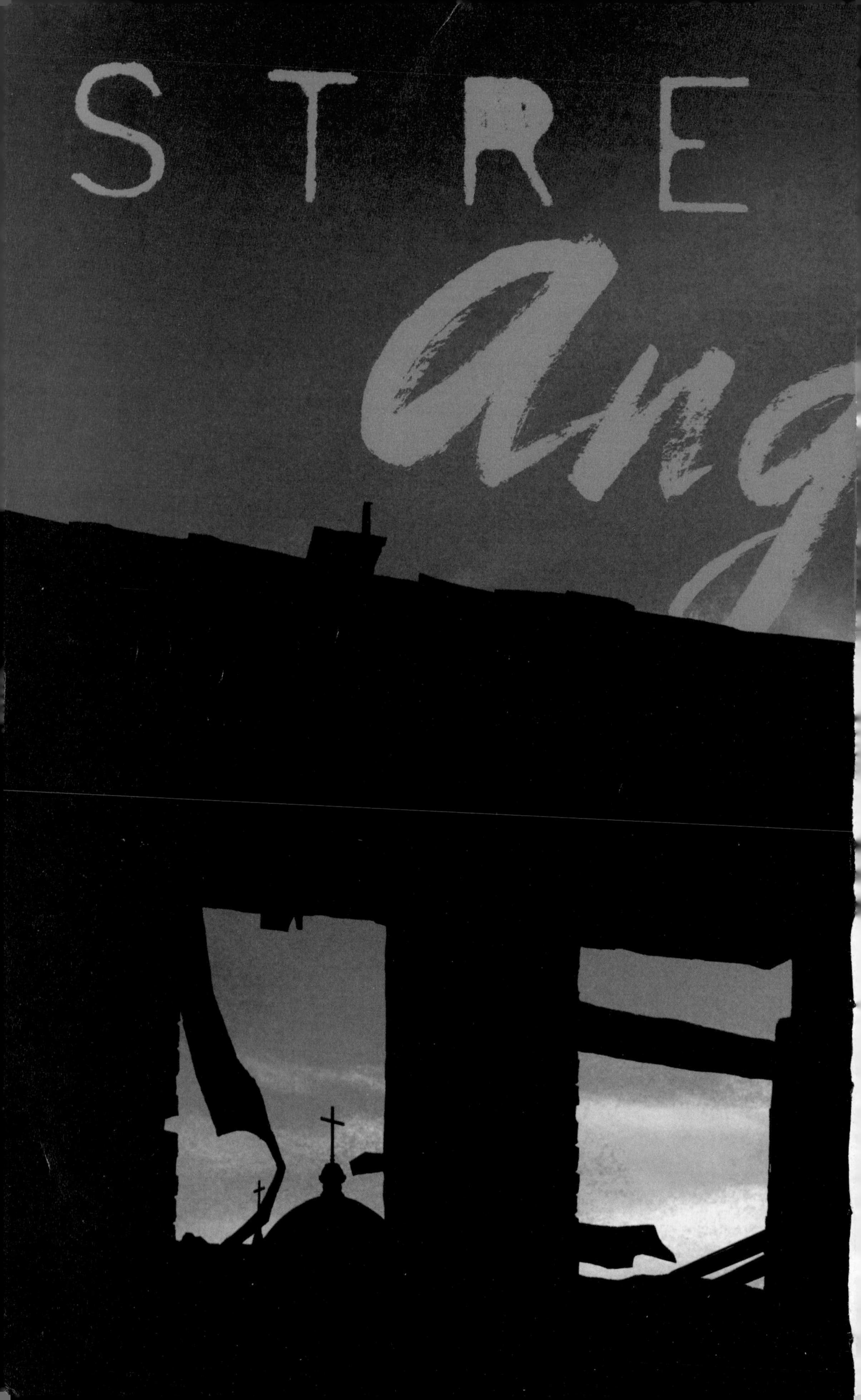
STRE
ang